Rave Reviews for Explore Puerto Rico!

♥ "In addition to the resorts and gourmet restaurants, the guide helps you find local eateries and inexpensive guesthouses." — *Caribbean Travel & Life*

♥ "Hands down the best guidebook to the island." — *Islands Magazine*

♥ "... a quality book that covers all aspects... it's all here and well done." — *San Diego Tribune*

♥ "These useful guides are highly recommended ..." — *Library Journal*

♥ "Pariser's guides are among my favorites, well researched and detailed. They always include helpful facts, the chapters on history and culture make excellent reading, and the practical details on each town and area are filled with insightful tips and tidbits." — *The Shoestring Traveler*

♥ "... a quality book that covers all aspects... it's all here and well done." — *The San Diego Tribune*

♥ "Crams lots of useful information into a portable, attractive book... both practical and user-friendly." — Amazon.com

♥ "One of the best writers about the Caribbean region."— *Travel Books Review*

♥ "I moved here last month, and I found your book invaluable." — Reader Wendy Formyn

♥ "Your book has been great help."— reader Jeffrey Burdick

♥ "If you are the sort of a traveler who doesn't like to be called a tourist, doesn't identify with the ugly American...and wants to understand the people you meet and the places you go — Harry's books are for you. Very informative...with a restrained and arid sense of humor." — *Culture Concrete*

Cover set in Sabon. Text set in Sabon and Avenir. Maps set in Avenir. Cover and text design by Harry S. Pariser. Cover photo by Harry S. Pariser. All other photos by Harry S. Pariser, except: ship in street (page 6, Roger Staiger), coqui (page 12, Hill and Knowlton), dinoflagellate (page 202, Joe Scott). Photos and maps by the author are available for license: contact the publisher. This guidebook was formerly published as *Adventure Guide to Puerto Rico*. Accept no substitutes.

Publishing History

First Edition: Guide to Puerto Rico and the Virgin Islands (Moon Publications, 1987)

Adventure Guide to Puerto Rico 1989
Second Edition: *Adventure Guide to Puerto Rico* 1992
Third Edition: *Adventure Guide to Puerto Rico* 1994
Fourth Edition: *Adventure Guide to Puerto Rico* 1997

Special Sales

Manatee Press titles are available at special discounts for bulk purchases for sales promotions or premiums. Special editions, including personalized covers, excerpts of existing guides, and business imprints may be printed upon demand. For more information contact Manatee Press at (415) 665-4829.

About the Cover

The cover photo (taken by Harry S. Pariser) is of a *vejigante* at Ponce's carnival.

Other Books by Harry S. Pariser

Explore Belize ISBN 1-55650-785-2
Explore the Dominican Republic ISBN 1-55650-814-X
Explore Costa Rica ISBN 1-893643-50-6
Explore the Virgin Islands ISBN 1-893643-53-0

Handheld computer versions (Palm OS and Windows CE) of Manatee Press guides are available at www.peanutpress.com.

Explore
Puerto Rico

Harry S. Pariser

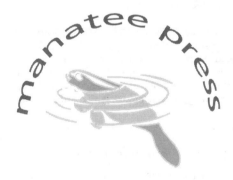

manatee press

San Francisco

This guide focuses on recreational activities. As all activities contain elements of risk, the publisher, author, affiliated individuals and companies disclaim any responsibility for any injury, harm, or illness that may occur to anyone through, or by use of, the information in this book. Every effort was made to ensure the accuracy of the information, but the publisher and author do not assume — and hereby disclaim — any liability for any loss or damage caused by errors, omissions, misleading information or potential travel problems caused by this guide, even if such errors or omissions result from negligence, accident, or any other cause.

Manatee Press
P. O. Box 225001
San Francisco, CA 94122-5001
(415) 665-4829
fax 810-314-0685

single-copy orders only: 800-729-6423

www.savethemanatee.com
www.SavorPuertoRico.com
editorial@savethemanatee.com

Distributed to the trade in the US and Canada by SCB (800-729-6423) and in the UK and Europe by Gazelle. Also available through Ingram, Baker and Taylor, Bookpeople, Quality, Unique, and Midwest Library Services. Copies are available through your local independent bookstore (www.booksense.org), Borders, Barnes and Noble, and Rand McNally. All books are for sale at www.savethemanatee.com, www.buy.com, www.amazon.com, www.powells.com, www.buy.com and through www.Caribbean-online.com.

Calling Puerto Rico

To call Puerto Rico from outside the island in the USA

Dial 1 + 787 + the number. Or 1 + 939 + the number for area code overlay calls.

From outside the US

Dial the international code + area code + the number

Note: All times, schedules, and prices are subject to change. Hotel prices are high season; discounts may be available. Hotel rates are before tax unless specified otherwise. Tax is 9% (11% if hotel has a casino), and there may also be a service charge.

Table of Contents

INTRODUCTION

Charts and Sidebars

free web updates

www.SavorPuertoRico.com

www.savethemanatee.com

Maps

Map English Equivalents

Alacadía	city hall	**Casa**	house	**Hacienda**	plantation	**Piscina**	pool
Arecife	reef	**Cayo**	small island	**Isla**	island	**Playa**	beach
Bahía	bay	**Cerro**	hill, peak	**Lago**	lake	**Puerto**	port
Balneario	public bch.	**Cueva**	cave	**Laguna**	lagoon	**Punta(Pta.)**	point
Barrio	neighborhood	**Ciudad**	city	**Mar**	sea	**Río**	river
Boca	river mouth	**Ensenada**	Inlet	**Parador**	country inn	**Ruta**	route
Bosque	forest	**Escuela**	school	**Parque**	park	**Sonda**	sound
Cabo	cape	**Estación**	station	**Pasaje**	passage		
Calle	street	**Estadio**	stadium	**Peaje**	toll		
Carretera	road	**Estatal**	state	**Pico**	peak		

Acknowledgements

Eric and Carolyn Egas for their hospitality and help on the Vieques section, Francia of the Lazy Parrot helped with Rincón. Many thanks to Deborah Berman Santana for her suggestions on parts of the introduction and other sections. Special thanks to Darril Tighe for her help with proofreading and her advice. Anna Conti helped with scanning. Lisa Maddocks (Oceans Unlimited) and Francia (Lazy Parrot) were of great assistance with the Rincón section. Special thanks go out to Frances Borden, for her help with arrangements, and Arnold Benus for his assistance and hospitality. Thanks to Ken Robertson for input on my Culebra chapter, and Jackie and Butch Pendergast for their help on the Culebra section and their hospitality. Thanks also go out to Roger Staiger, Beth Halpern, Nick Brokaw, Gordon Grimlund, Carl Kruse, Judith Amador, Carlos Padilla, Ricardo Betancourt, David A. Bailey (Whizzbang Designs), Nilda Cancel, and Aisha Langford and Joanna Allen from Hill and Knowlton. And thanks also to my mother who always worries about me.

Abbreviations

N	North	L	left
S	South	R	right
E	East	ft.	foot
W	West	km	kilometer(s)
pd	per day	mi.	mile(s)
ph	per hour	Bo.	*Barrio* (neighborhood)
pp	per person	C.	*Calle* (street)
pw	per week	Carr.	*Carretera* (road)
s	single	PO	Post Office
d	double	PST	Pacific Standard Time
t	triple	CST	Central Standard Time
add'l	additional	EST	Eastern Standard Time
OW	one way	GMT	Greenwich Mean Time
RT	round trip	DST	Daylight Savings Time
ha	hectare(s)		

About the Author

Mr. Pariser is a writer, artist, photographer, and graphic designer. Born and raised in southwestern Pennsylvania, he is a graduate of the College of Communications of Boston University. His first guide to the Virgin Islands, Guide to Puerto Rico and the Virgin Islands, was published in 1987. Mr. Pariser has lived in Japan: in Kyoto, in the historical city of Kanazawa (facing the Japan Sea), and in Kagoshima, a city at the southern tip of Kyushu across the bay from an active volcano. He has traveled extensively in Europe, Africa, Asia, Central America, and the Caribbean. His articles and photographs have appeared in *The Japan Times, Costa Rica Outlook, Belize First, Caribbean Travel & Life, the San Jose Mercury News, San Francisco Frontlines, Atevo.com*, and *Yack.com*, among others.

He lives in the Inner Sunset area of San Francisco. His favorite activities include hiking, backpacking, cooking, photography, art, and listening to music (especially African and jazz). Mr. Pariser received the Society of American Travel Writer's Lowell Thomas Award 1995 Best Guidebook Award (Silver) for his *Adventure Guide to Barbados*.

Reader's Response Form

Explore Puerto Rico

I found your book rewarding because _____
_____
_____

Your book could be improved by _____
_____

The best places I stayed in were (explain why) _____
_____
_____
_____

I found the best food at_____
_____

Some good and bad experiences I had were_____
_____

Will you return to the Virgin Islands?_____.

If not, why not? _____
_____
_____

If so, where do you plan to go? _____
_____
_____

I purchased this book at _____

I learned about this book from _____

Please include any other comments on a separate sheet and mail completed
form to Manatee Press or fax to 810-314-0685.
Or e-mail comments to editorial@savethemanatee.com.

About Manatee Press

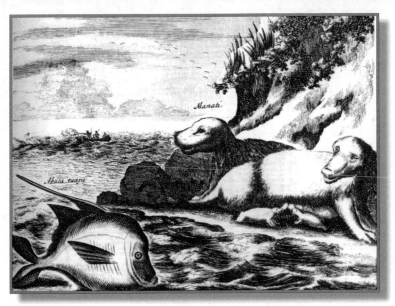

Manatees in old print. (© MAPEs MONDE).

Manatee Press was founded in San Francisco, California in order to provide travel guides which inform the reader about history, culture, and the environment of a destination. The manatee's only foe is man, and it has no natural predators. As such, its survival as a species depends upon the human species' willingness to change their interaction with nature as a whole.

Popularly known as the "sea cow," the manatee once ranged in habitat from Florida to Brazil. Europeans swiftly exterminated the creatures in the southern Caribbean. The last sighting in Trinidad was in 1910 when one was harpooned. Manatees move along the ocean floor (at a maximum pace of six mph) searching for food, surfacing every four or five minutes to breathe. Surprisingly, as the manatee's nearest living relative is the elephant, the creature was thought to be the model for the legend of the mermaid. Dwelling in lagoons and in brackish water, manatees may eat as much as 100 lbs. of aquatic vegetables per day. Strictly vegetarian, their only enemy, man, has hunted them for their hide, oil, and meat. Their numbers have dwindled dramatically. In other localities, their tough hides were used in machine belting and in high pressure hoses. Although community education may be the key to stopping hunting, propeller blades of motor boats continue to slaughter manatees accidentally, and the careless use of herbicides is also a threat.

Puerto Rico A to Z

Accommodation — Hotels in nearly every price range are available, including some bed and breakfasts. You'll also find some campgrounds. The nicest hotels tend to be small, intimate affairs, but there are a number of ultra-luxury hotels and resorts as well. *Paradors* are government-recognized small hotels which vary in quality and service. Rates listed in this book are representative, high-season rates which are double occupancy. They are subject to change, and expect low-season rates to be as much as 40% lower.

Airlines and airports — Puerto Rico's hub is the Luis Muñoz Marín International Airport which is near the Isla Verde area of San Juan. Domestic flights to Vieques, Culebra, Fajardo, Mayagüez, Ponce, and Aguadilla leave from here, as do connecting flights to destinations all over the Caribbean. The most prominent carrier is American, but many other major airlines fly here as well.

Area Code — To dial Puerto Rico from outside the US dial the country code and the number. It is necessary to dial calls with all ten digits (including the area code) when dialing within Puerto Rico.

Art and artists — There are a number of fine artists and craftspeople in Puerto Rico. The best art galleries are in San Juan, but craftspeople are found everywhere. Look for a sign saying "artesania."

Banking — Banks are open Mon. to Fri. from 8:30 AM–5 PM. Some banks have extended hours. ATM machines are widely available.

Buses — Outside San Juan, local bus service is very limited. Most transport is in *públicos*, privately-owned vans which run between cities and towns. Expect delays.

Business Hours — Generally 8 AM to 5 PM. Shops are usually open weekdays and Sat. from 9 or 10 AM to 5 or 6 PM. Banks are generally open 8 AM to 2:30 PM. and on Sat. from 9:45 AM to noon.

Camping —There are a number of campsites, but many require advance reservations.

Clothes —Informal is the rule. You won't need much if any in the way of warm clothing. However, if you are planning a night out on the town in San Juan, you should pack for this.

Car rental — Cars may be rented at the airports and at many hotels and even in smaller towns.

Credit Cards — All major credit cards are generally accepted.

Currency —The US Dollar.

Departure tax — Included in ticket cost.

Driving — Driving is on the same side as in the US. Valid drivers licenses are required. A credit card is required to rent a vehicle. Insurance is recommended.

Electricity —110 Volts AC

Gambling — Available in many large hotels. You must be 21 or over to gamble.

Internet —Public access is found in cybercafes, which are scattered throughout the island. Some libraries also offer access.

Language — Both Spanish and English are widely used. Most people can speak at least some English.

Laundry — Laundromats are found in towns. Most hotels will do laundry for a fee. Save by bringing some detergent and washing a few small items yourself.

Liquor Laws —Alcohol is available from any store. Bars are plentiful.

Mail — Expect it to take at least a week to the States. Rates are cheap.

Maps — Gas stations sell maps.

Marriage — Puerto Rico is a good place for a marriage and honeymoon.

Newspapers —The *Miami Herald* is available daily in tourist centers. The daily tabloid *The San Juan Star* is the only local English-language newspaper.

Population — The population of Puerto Rico is around 3.5 million. Some 1.4 million reside in the San Juan metropolitan area.

Pets —Leave them at home if at all possible.

Radio/TV — Many tourist hotels have satellite TV or cable. There are a number of AM and FM radio stations.

Restaurants — There are plenty of these. The *Mesones Gastronómicos* are government-recognized gourmet restaurants.

Ruins — There are a few places, including Tibes Ceremonial Center (near Ponce) and Caguana Ceremonial Center (near Utuado).

Shopping — There are plenty of places to shop. Some of the best include Old San Juan and the numerous malls and factory outlets.

Taxes — Government tax of 11% is added to rooms in hotels with casinos, 9% in hotels without casinos, and 7% on paradors. Some hotels add a 7–10% service charge to your bill.

Taxis — Metered. Shared taxis, called *publicos*, travel from place to place.

Telephones — Service is good. Internal calls are inexpensive. Phone cards are available and may be used.

Theft — Don't walk around San Juan at night with valuables. Never leave anything of value in an unprotected vehicle. Don't leave your things unattended on beaches.

Time — Puerto Rico operates on Atlantic Standard Time (three hours behind GMT, Greenwich mean time).

Tipping — Tipping as you would elsewhere in the United States.

Visas — Same as for the United States

Water — It is safe to drink tap water everywhere.

Weather — The average temperature runs around 82 degrees F (28 degrees C) from Nov. to May. Average beach temperatures are around 80 degrees F in the Summer and 76 degrees (28 degrees C) in the winter.

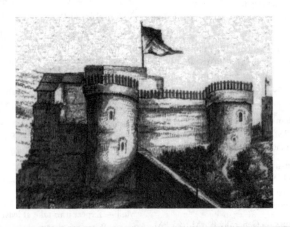

Introduction

Despite the fact that Puerto Rico has been part of the territorial United States since 1898, most Americans know little or nothing about the island. Yet Puerto Rico is one of the most exotic places in the nation — a miniature Latin America set in the Caribbean. And San Juan was a thriving town when Jamestown was still an undeveloped plot of land.

This very attractive island contains numerous forest reserves, beaches, ancient indigenous sites, an abundance of historical atmosphere, and the only tropical National Forest in the US.

Sadly, the vast majority of visitors get stuck in the tourist traps of Condado and never experience the island's charms.

The Land

The islands of the Caribbean stretch in a 2,800-mile (4,500-km) arc from the western tip of Cuba to the small Dutch island of Aruba. The region is sometimes extended to include the Central and South American countries of Belize (the former Colony of British Honduras), the Yucatán, Surinam, Guiana, and Guyana. The islands of Jamaica, Hispaniola, Puerto Rico, the US and British Virgin Islands, along with Cuba, the Caymans, and the Turks and Caicos islands form the Greater Antilles. Early geographers gave the name "Antilia" to hypothetical islands thought to lie beyond the equally imaginary "Antilades."

In general, the land is steep and volcanic in origin: chains of mountains run across Jamaica, Cuba, Hispaniola, and Puerto Rico, and hills rise abruptly from the sea along most of the Virgin Islands.

Geography

Smallest and most easterly of the Greater Antilles, Puerto Rico's 3,435 sq. miles (8,768 sq. km — roughly the size of Connecticut, Crete, or Corsica) serve as one of the barriers between the waters of the Caribbean and the Atlantic: the N coast faces the Atlantic while the E and S coasts face the Caribbean. The Virgin Islands lie to the E; to the W the 75-mile-wide (121-km) Mona Passage separates the island from neighboring Hispaniola.

The seas off the coast are peppered with numerous cays and some small islands. The small archipelago of Culebra and the island of Vieques lie off the E coast, while the even smaller Mona lies to the W. An irregular submarine shelf, seven miles at its widest, surrounds the island. Two miles off the N coast

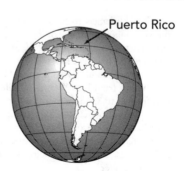

Puerto Rico

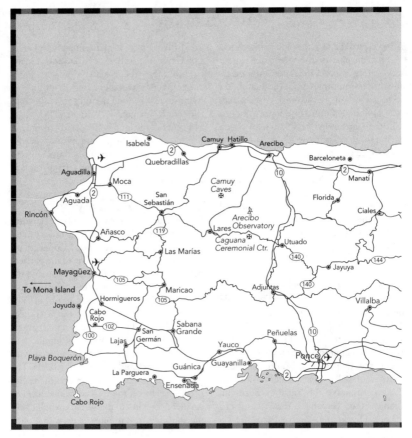

the sea floor plummets to 6,000 ft. (1,829 m); the Milwaukee Deep, one of the world's deepest underwater chasms at 28,000 ft. (8,534 m), lies 45 miles (72 km) to the N.

The nearly rectangular island runs 111 miles (179 km) from E to W and 36 miles (58 km) from N to S. Numerous headlands and indentations punctuate its coastline. Puerto Rico is the tip of a huge volcanic mass. The coastal plain, an elevated area of land that rings the island, encircles the mountainous center.

Two mountain ranges, the Luquillo and the Cordillera Central, cross the island from E to W. *The Sierra de Luquillo* in the E contains El Yunque ("The Anvil"), which reaches 3,843 ft. (1,171 m). A smaller range, the Sierra de Cayey, is in the SE.

The **Cordillera Central,** a broader *sierra* to the W, contains Cerro De Punta which, at 4,398 ft. (1,319 m), is the highest peak on the island.

Spectacular shapes along the NW of the island are the result of karstification — a process whereby, over a million-year period,

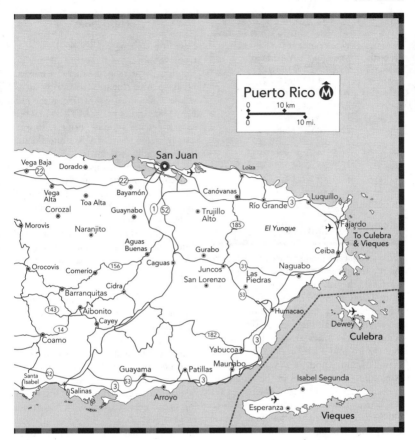

Puerto Rico Ⓜ

0 — 10 km
0 — 10 mi.

San Juan

Vega Baja · Dorado · Loiza
Vega Alta · Bayamón · Canóvanas · Luquillo
Corozal · Toa Alta · Guaynabo · Río Grande
Morovis · Naranjito · Trujillo Alto · El Yunque · Fajardo
Aguas Buenas · Gurabo · To Culebra & Vieques
Orocovis · Comerio · Caguas · Ceiba
Cidra · Juncos · Naguabo
Barranquitas · San Lorenzo · Las Piedras
Aibonito · Cayey · Humacao · Dewey
Coamo · Culebra
Santa Isabel · Yabucoa
Guayama · Maunabo · Isabel Segunda
Salinas · Patillas
Arroyo · Esperanza · Vieques

heavy rains seeping through the primary structural lines and joints of the porous limestone terrain carved huge caves, deep sinkholes, and long underground passages. As a result, the island is honeycombed with caves — one of the most extensive cave systems in the Western Hemisphere.

Of some 220 caves, only the Camuy caves have been commercially developed. There are a total of 57 rivers and 1,200 streams on the island. Commercially valuable minerals include iron, manganese, coal, marble, gypsum, clay, kaolin, phosphate, salt, and copper.

One final feature on the landscape that will not escape the notice of many visitors is the military presence. Some 13% of the land is occupied by the US military.

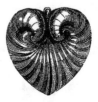

Climate

Month	Minimum	Maximum
Jan.	70 F 21 C	80 F 27 C
Feb.	70 F 21 C	80 F 27 C
Mar.	70 F 21 C	81 F 27 C
April	72 F 22 C	82 F 28 C
May	74 F 23 C	84 F 29 C
June	75 F 24 C	85 F 29 C
July	75 F 24 C	85 F 29 C
Aug.	76 F 24 C	85 F 29 C
Sept.	75 F 24 C	86 F 30 C
Oct.	75 F 24 C	85 F 29 C
Nov.	73 F 23 C	84 F 29 C
Dec.	72 F 22 C	81 F 27 C

Average daily temperatures in San Juan.

Climate

With an average temperature of 73°F during the coolest month and 79°F during the warmest, the island has a delightful climate. Located within the belt of the steady NE trade winds, its mild, subtropical climate varies little throughout the year.

Winter temperatures average 19° warmer than Cairo and Los Angeles, 7° warmer than Miami, and 4° warmer than Honolulu. Temperatures in the mountain areas average eight to 10° cooler than on the coast. Lowest recorded temperature (40°F) was measured at Aibonito in March 1911. Only five days per year are entirely without sunshine. Rain, which usually consists of short showers, is most likely to occur between June and October. The N coast gets much more rain than the S, with San Juan receiving 60 inches per year as compared with Ponce's 30 inches. Trade winds produce the greatest amount of rain in the mountain areas. El Yunque,for example, averages 183 in. (4,648 mm) per year, falling in some 1,600 showers.

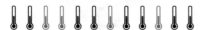

Hurricanes

Cast in a starring role as the bane of the tropics, hurricanes represent the one outstanding negative in an otherwise impeccably hospitable climate. The Caribbean as a whole ranks third worldwide in the number of hurricanes per year. These low-pressure zones are serious business. Property damage from them may run into the hundreds of millions of dollars.

A hurricane begins as a relatively small tropical storm, known as a cyclone when its winds reach a velocity of 39 mph (62 kph). At 74 mph (118 kph) it is upgraded to hurricane status, with winds of up to 200 mph (320 kph) and ranging from 60-1,000 miles (100-1,600 km) in diameter.

A small hurricane releases energy equivalent to the explosions of six atomic bombs per second. A hurricane may be compared to an enormous hovering engine that uses the moist air and water of the tropics as fuel, carried hither and thither by prevailing air currents — generally eastern trade winds which intensify as they move across warm ocean waters. When cooler, drier air infiltrates as it heads N, the hurricane begins to die, cut off from the life-sustaining ocean currents that have nourished it from infancy.

Routes and patterns are unpredictable. As for their frequency: "June — too soon; July — stand by; August — it must; September — remember." So goes the old rhyme. Unfortunately, hurricanes are not confined to July and August. Hurricanes forming in Aug. and Sept. typically last for two weeks, while those that form in June, July, Oct., and Nov. (many of which originate in the Caribbean and the Gulf of Mexico) generally last only seven days.

Approximately 70% of all hurricanes (known as Cabo Verde types) originate as embryonic storms coming from the W

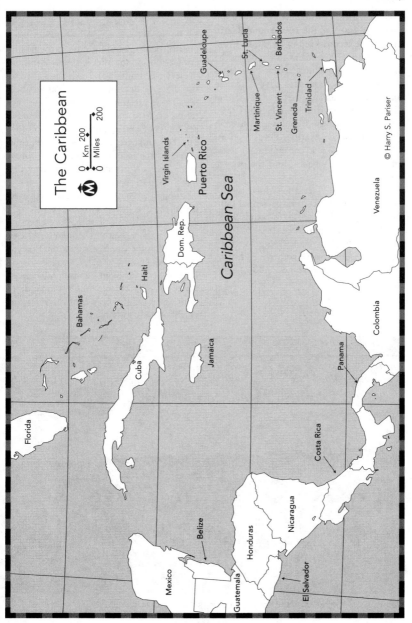

The Caribbean

0 Km 200
0 Miles 200

Guadeloupe
St. Lucia
Barbados
Martinique
St. Vincent
Grenada
Trinidad

Virgin Islands

Puerto Rico

Caribbean Sea

Dom. Rep.

Haiti

Bahamas

Cuba

Jamaica

Florida

Venezuela

Colombia

Panama

Costa Rica

Belize

Mexico

Honduras

Nicaragua

Guatemala

El Salvador

© Harry S. Pariser

coast of Africa. Fortunately, they are comparatively scarce in the area around Puerto Rico. Since record-keeping began in 1508, 76 hurricanes have wreaked havoc on the island. Four of the most recent hurricanes with serious consequences have been San Felipe (1928), San Ciprian (1932), Santa Clara (1956) and Hurricane Hugo (1989). The latter lashed the island with 140 mph winds. Hurricane Marilyn devastated St. Thomas in 1995, also causing major damage to Culebra, Vieques, and the eastern part of the island.

In Sept. 1996 Hurricane Hortense hit southwest Puerto Rico with torrential rains leaving 90% of Puerto Rico's people without electricity and potable water.

In Sept. 1998, Hurricane Georges crossed the island from E to W with winds hitting as high as 115 mph. Some 56,000 homes were destroyed.

Flora & Fauna

Puerto Rico's central location in the northern Caribbean, together with its variations in elevation, rainfall, and soil, has served to stimulate the development of a varied plant life. These variations account for five differing areas of natural vegetation: humid sea forest or marshland, humid wood forest, the humid tropical forest found in the center of the island, the subhumid forest along the NW coast, and the thorny dry forest on the S coast.

Although 75% of the island was covered by forest a century ago, today it's only 25%, with a bare 1% of the forest retaining its virginity. Natural ground cover can be found in the Caribbean National Forest (El Yunque) and the forest reserves of Puerto Rico. Although a considerable number of the 3,355 species of flora are indigenous, many have been introduced from neighboring islands.

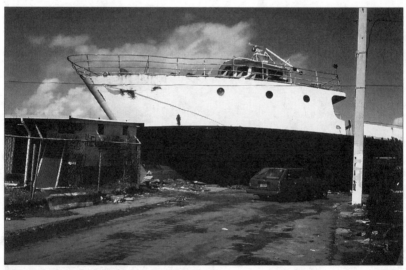

Hurricane Hugo grounded this ferry in Fajardo. (Courtesy of Roger Staiger).

Trees & Tropical Vegetation

TREES: Altogether, there are 547 native species of trees, with an additional 203 naturalized species — an incredible variety for such a small area.

The native **ceiba**, or silk cotton tree; famous for its enormous size, it may live 300 years or more.

Masks and eating utensils have traditionally been made from the gourd of the **higuero** or calabash tree.

Now rare, the **guayacán** (*lignum vitae*) has some of the densest wood in the world: it's so heavy that it sinks in water! It was once used interchangeably with money. Masts and prows in Spanish and Dutch ships were made from the wood; *guayacol*, an extract, was considered a remedy for cholera. As the trees take centuries to grow, supply could not keep up with demand. You can identify the tree by its compound dark green leaves, mottled peeling bark, and blue flowers.

Introduced more than two centuries ago, the Dominican **mahogany** has been used in furniture making and in carpentry work.

The **campeche** yields a red to black dye whose active ingredient, haematoxylin, can be used in treating dysentery; it was once exported to Europe. Its deciduous, compound leaves have small heart-shaped leaflets, and its gray fissured trunk is often fluted at its base. The fragrant yellow blooms produce oblong flat pods. The orange fissured bark of the **mabí** is fermented to make a form of root beer; its evergreen leaves are smooth on top but hairy underneath.

Distantly related to the coca, the **indio** produces blooming masses of small white flowers.

The unopened leaves of the Puerto Rican **hat palm** are still put to use in weaving fine hats and baskets, but the **ausobo,** a type of ironwood used for ceiling beams during the Colonial era, has virtually disappeared.

Having whorled leaves with spines at their base, yellow-brown bark, and white flowers, the **ucar** has been widely used for fenceposts; the yellow-shouldered blackbird commonly nests in its branches.

Easily recognized by its peeling red bark, the **almácigo** (gumbo-limbo) produces a latex that has been used for incense, glue, and medicine. Its cuttings have been planted in alignment to form living fences.

The graceful **alelí** produces a large white flower. Its long, thin evergreen leaves are popular with yellow-and-black caterpillars.

Imported trees include the Australian casuarina, the cassia, the Mexican *papayuelo*, the Indo-Malayan coconut palm, the mango, and the tamarind.

Ornamental vines and shrubs include bougainvillea, *carallita,* jasmine, hibiscus, shower of orchids, gardenia, thunbergia, poinsettia, and croton. Found along the coast, the sea grape has round, leathery leaves; it produces an edible, grape-like purple fruit.

CACTI: Any visitor to the island's drier areas will notice the proliferation of cacti and other scrub vegetation. Cacti were classified into a single genus comprising 24 species by Linnaeus in 1737. The name is Greek for "the bristly plant." The oldest

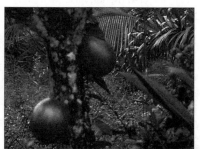

The calabash fruit is an example of "cauliflory" or flowering from the trunk.

INTRODUCTION

Heliconias

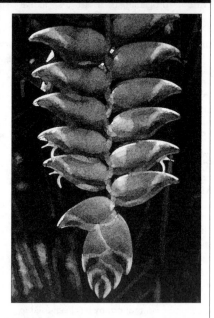

Famous worldwide as an ornamental, the heliconia lends an infusion of bizarre color and shape to the island's landscape. The name of these medium to large erect herbs comes from Helicon, a mountain in southern Greece believed to have been the home of the muses. There are thought to be around 200-250 species. Relatives within this category include the banana, the birds-of-paradise, the gingers, and the prayer plants.

The family name *Zingiberales* comes from the Sanskrit word *sringavera* which means "horn shaped" in reference to the rhizomes.

Each erect shoot has a stem and leaves which are frequently (although not always) topped by an inflorescence with yellow or red bracts. Each inflorescence may produce up to 50 hermaphroditic flowers. Leaves are composed of stalk and blade and resemble banana leaves. Flowers produce a blue colored fruit which has three seeds. Lured by the bright colored flowers and bracts, hummingbirds, arrive to pollinate the blooms. The birds spread pollen as they fly from flower to flower in search of nectar.

fossilized cactus remains are found in Colorado and Utah and date from the Eocene Era some 50 million years ago. Cacti have evolved to suit a hot, dry climate. Their need to reduce surface area — in order to deter evaporation and protect it from the sun's rays — have resulted in flattened, columnar, grooved, bumpy, globular, and barrel-shaped plants. Evolution has transformed their leaves into spines and their branches into areoles — localized regions that carry spines and/or bristles. The stems are responsible for photosynthesis. Shade and light diffusion is provided by bumps, warts, ribs, spines, and hairlike structures. These structures also serve to hinder evaporation and hold dew. Its thick, leathery flesh stores water effectively, is resistant to withering and can endure up to a 60% water loss without damage. Stomata (apertures) close during the day to prevent water loss, but reopen at night. Blossoms generally last for only one day, and nearly all depend upon animals for pollination.

Turk's Cap

VARIETIES: Named for its distinctive shape, the **pipe organ**

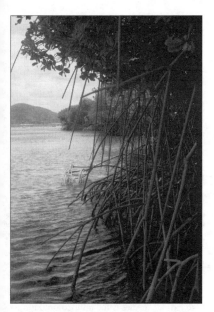

Mangroves are a vital link in the ecosystem.

or dildo cactus is generally found in the island's driest areas and has tall hollow stems that are used for food storage by birds.

The barrel-shaped **Turk's cap** is capped with red flowers, while the **prickly pear** is a small, rapidly spreading cactus that has innumerable spines and yellow flowers.

The squat **melon cactus** is pollinated by hummingbirds. It has pink flowers and fruit; its shallow spreading root system serves to capture water.

CACTUS-RELATED PLANTS: These plants have adapted to high temperatures and a lack of water by converting their leaves into spines. The large **century plant** has a rosette of thick spiked leaves at its base and sends up a 10-to 20-ft. stalk. It blooms after 20 years and then dies. The indigenous peoples of the Caribbean mixed its fiber with cotton and used the cord to weave hammocks.

The **aloe** is a single-stalked succulent renowned for its healing properties. It is native to Africa and the Mediterranean.

MANGROVES: Mangrove forests are found in greatly diminished numbers along the coasts. While the white mangrove is widely distributed on the island, the red mangrove is found only in Graeme Hall Swamp. These water-rooted trees serve as a marine habitat for sponges, corals, oysters, and other members of the marine community around its roots. Some species live out their entire lives here and many fish shelter or feed in and around them; lobsters use the mangrove environs as a nursery for their young. Above the water level, they shelter seabirds and offer important nesting sites. Their organic detritus, exported to the reef by the tides, is consumed by its inhabitants, providing the base of an extensive food web. Mangroves also dampen high waves and winds.

Red mangroves act as land builders by trapping silt in their roots and catching leaves and other detritus which decompose to form soil. Eventually, the red mangroves kill themselves off by building up enough soil to form dry land, cutting off their water supply. It is then that the black and white mangroves take over. Meanwhile, the red mangroves have sent out progeny in the form of floating seedlings — bottom-heavy youngsters that grow on the tree until reaching six in. to a foot in length. If they drop in shallow water, the seeds touch bottom and implant themselves, but in deeper water they stay afloat until dragging across a shoal and lodging.

Named after their light-colored bark, the **white mangroves** are highly salt-tolerant. If growing in a swampy area, they produce pneumatophores, root system extensions which grow vertically to a height that allows them to stay above the water during flooding or tides so they can carry on gaseous exchange.

The Paso Fino

Magnificent Paso Fino ("fine step") horses are national treasures. Their ancestors are the Arabian horses which arrived in Spain with the Moors.

Although the first horses were introduced in 1510, the Paso Fino is a 20th Century phenomenon. The first was Dulce Sueño, who was exhibited in 1935 at a Guayama fair. Dulce Sueño is considered the undisputed standard by which all other horses are measured, and mother of modern Paso Fino horses in Puerto Rico. Her sons, Guamani and Batalla, are the progenitors of the current stock of Paso Finos.

Darker-colored horses are preferred. A champion will have a medium, handsomely-muscled frame and fine long hair, and a strong skeleton. Although docile, it should carry itself with pride and elegance, walking with a short, rhythmic smooth, and elastic gate.

Today , there are some 8000 registered pure-bred Paso Fino horses. The four different organizations of breeders have united under the Alianza de Paso Fino de Puerto Rico.

The **black mangrove** also produces pneumatophores as well as a useful wood. The buttonwood is smaller than the others and is not a true mangrove. It is found on the coasts where no other varieties grow.

Three-quarters of the island's mangrove forests have been destroyed by development. And much of Puerto Rico's coral reefs have died as a result.

SEAGRASSES: Seagrasses (plants returned to live in the sea) are found in relatively shallow water in sandy and muddy bays and flats; they have roots and small flowers. The flat blades trap sediment, thus filtering the water.

One species, dubbed **"turtle grass,"** (*Thalassia testudinum*) provides food for turtles. Its ribbon-like leaves may reach more than a foot in length. The most common of the grasses, it has deeper root structures.

"Manatee grass" (*Syringodium filiforme*) may be recognized by its leaves which are round in cross section.

"Small turtle-grass" (*Halophila bailonis*) is characterized by small, rounded leaves which are generally paired. It is often found in deeper waters and appears delicate.

"Shoal grass" (*Halodule wrightii*) colonizes disturbed areas and can survive in water too shallow for the others.

Seagrasses help to stabilize the sea floor, maintain water clarity by trapping fine sediments from upland soil erosion, stave off beach erosion, and provide living space for numerous fish, crustaceans, and shellfish.

Animal Life

Except for bats, dolphins, and sea cows, Puerto Rico has no indigenous mammals. One extinct species is the multicolored mute dog, which the Native Americans liked to fatten up and roast. Cows, pigs, mongooses, and horses were all imported by the Spanish.

Although there was once a great demand in the Spanish Antilles for Puerto Rican horses and cattle, this industry has almost died out. **Paso Fino** and **anadura** horses are still held in high esteem; the former can walk at a pace that enables a rider to carry a full glass of water in his hand and not spill a drop. There are over 7,000 *Paso Fino* horses on the island. (See sidebar)

Mongoose, imported from India to combat rats and now-extinct poisonous reptiles, have propagated to the point where they have become an agricultural pest.

URL http://coralreef.gov
  Action plan on coral reefs
http://www.biogeo.nos.noaa.gov/ benthicmap/caribbean Download a map of coral reefs of the Caribbean

BIRDLIFE: Puerto Rico has approximately 200 species of birds, including the Puerto Rican grackle, the kingbird, the petchary, several species of owls, and the Puerto Rican sharp-shinned and West Indian red-tailed hawks.

Once a million strong, the colorful **Puerto Rican parrot** (see sidebar) now hovers near extinction, surviving only in the outback areas of El Yunque.

The endangered **Puerto Rican nightjar**, nearly invisible, its brown coloration disguising it in the brush, rests during the day.

The **pearly-eyed thrasher**, nesting in cliffsides and cave ceilings, is another species popular among birders.

The iridescent green **Puerto Rican mango hummingbird** lives in evergreen forests and feeds on nectar with its curved beak.

Among the smaller birds are the onomatopoetically named **pitirre** and the **reinita** ("little queen") which hangs out around kitchen windows and tables. The pitirre is small but fierce — it attacks much larger birds — and has been used as a symbol by the revolutionary group *Los macheteros*.

The **Puerto Rican whippoorwill** (*guaibaro pequeño*), **Puerto Rican tody** (San Pedrito, medio peso, papagallo), Puerto Rican woodpecker (**el carpintero**), the Puerto Rican grosbeak (**el comeñame**), and the Puerto Rican emerald hummingbird (**el zumbadorcito**) are other species of note.

REPTILES & AMPHIBIANS: If Puerto Rico can be said to have a national animal, it must be the diminutive *coquí*. This 1.5-inch (36 mm) streamlined treefrog has bulging eyes, webbed fingers and toes with 10 highly efficient suction discs, and smooth, nearly transparent beige skin. Its cry is enchanting, so sweet that it's sometimes mistaken by newcomers for that of a bird.

Once thought to be only a single species, the *coquí* actually comes in 16 varieties, but

The Endangered Puerto Rican Parrot

Known to the Tainos as the *iguaca*, the lovely Puerto Rican parrot (*Amazona vittata*) stands in danger of extinction. The smallest species found in the West Indies, the parrot seldom reaches more than a foot in length. Colored green with flashes of blue and red, this gregarious frugivore nests in four- to five- foot-deep cavities found in palo colorado trees in the cloud forest.

The Puerto Rican parrot mates for life. They breed during the dry season (Feb. to June). The parrots usually choose a large, deep tree cavity, generally in a Palo Colorado, to nest in. Females lay a clutch of three to four eggs, which hatch after 26 days, and the male brings food, which it regurgitates.

Fewer than 50 remain in El Yunque (the Caribbean National Forest) with another 72 held in captivity. The parrot numbers as one of the ten most critically endangered birds. Estimated to have numbered one million when Columbus invaded, their numbers plummeted to an all-time low of 13 wild specimens in 1975; half had disappeared with 1989's Hurricane Hugo.

Birds are being bred at an aviary in the forest, and parrots have successfully been transplanted to Río Abajo Forest. Unfortunately, the issue of the bird's survival has become a political football with the Fish and Wildlife Service, the US Forest Service, and the Puerto Rico Department of Natural Resources all attempting to assert control.

Currently, the birds are being bred for release. Although a thief broke into the aviary at the Caribbean National Forest in 2001, stealing an undisclosed number of birds, 16 captive-reared parrots were released that same year.

Keep the Beach Turtle Friendly

Here is a short list of things you may do. In addition, hotel owners may prohibit the use of pointed-end drink stands and minimize beachfront lighting.

 Leave native beach vegetation in place. Hawksbills hanker for beaches with green. Plants stave off erosion.

 Remove your garbage. Garbage will contaminate beach sand, and bacteria or fungus may infect sea turtle eggs. Garbage may also hinder hatchlings seeking to make their challenging waddle from egg to waves.

 Never, ever drive on a beach. Cars compact the sand which makes it harder for the sea turtles to dig out from or into sand. Vegetation is also destroyed.

 Make sure your beach chair is stacked in a pile, high and dry and as far from the edge of the beach as possible. Turtles, in order to safeguard their nests, lay eggs above the high water mark.

only two can sing. Its evening concert has won it a special place in the hearts of Puerto Ricans all across the island. In El Yunque, where they may be as thick as 10,000 per acre, studies have shown that the *coquís* climb trees nightly (where they find varied and more plentiful food sources) and then emerge at dawn, chirping *co-quí-quí* and *co-co-quí-quí* as they land. Scientists believe that their song is a claim of territorality. They are asserting their rights to the land as well as to the females within range.

Coquis have recently turned up in Hawaii. They have established themselves on Maui and the Big Island, and the state government is mounting an extermination campaign against them. The *coquí* most likely arrived here in plant potting material. The nonvoting Puerto Rican representative in Congress has asked Hawaii to halt the extermination campaign.

A rather different type of animal, the protected **giant tortoise** is closely related to its more famous cousins on the Galapagos.

SEA TURTLES: Culebra's population of giant **leatherback** turtles, which come ashore to lay their eggs, stand in danger of extinction. The leatherback, black with very narrow fins, gets its name from the black leathery hide which covers its back in lieu of a shell. Reaching up to six ft. (two m) in length and weighing as much as 1,600 lbs. (700 kg), its chief predator has been the poacher.

Another endangered species, the **green turtle,** has been plagued by mysterious tumors.

INSECTS AND SPIDERS: Some 15,000 species of insects include a vast variety ranging from the lowly cockroach to 216 species of butterflies and moths. **Mimes** are tiny, biting sand flies. The **guaba,** the local tarantula, is one of about 10 spiders on the island. Another is the **araña boba** or "silly spider."

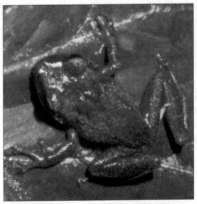

The coqui, the "national animal" of Puerto Rico, has managed to infiltrate Hawaii.

❧ Humpback Whales ❧

Migrating every fall from the polar waters through the passage between Puerto Rico and the Virgin Islands where they breed, these marine mammals may be sighted offshore from Dec. to May. One common place to see them is between outer Brass and Congo Cays. They travel in pods of three to 15. Humpbacks range in length from 30 to 40 ft. (12-15 m).

Acrobatically inclined, they leap belly-up from the water, turn a somersault, and arch backwards — plunging headfirst back into the watery depths with a loud snapping noise. When making deep dives, these whales hump their backs forward and bring their tail out of the water.

In addition to diving, male whales love vocalizing. Their moans, cries, groans, and snores are expressed in songs lasting up to 35 minutes. These go on for hours and may be heard by their comrades at distances of 20 miles. The probable reason for the tunes is to attract mates, but little is known about the songs. Up until the time of the first recording in 1952, stories of fishermen hearing eerie songs through their boat hulls were widely disbelieved. The whales have acute hearing so whaling boats have traditionally been sail-operated.

Humpbacks feed on small fish, plankton, and shrimp-like crustaceans — all of which they strain out of water with their baleen. They may devour as much as a ton per day during the feeding season (in the far N) in order to build up blubber for the long trip S to the Caribbean. Distinguished by their very long pectoral fins, scalloped on their forward edges, as well as by large knobs on their jaws and head, humpbacks are black-bodied with a white coloration on their underbelly. Humpbacks have managed to keep their boudoir practices out of the limelight, and no one has ever observed them mating.

One of a kind items, calves are light grey in color. Although they are virtually blubberless when expelled from the womb, they still weigh a ton. Mothers move in close to land for nursing. (Never disturb a mother and calf.) A calf feeds off of one or two teats, ordinarily lodged in slits, and down as much as 190 liters (50 gal.) of milk daily. The calf has a groove in his tongue and lower lip which enables him to funnel the milk. Whale milk has the consistency of yogurt and has a 40-50% fat content, in contrast to the 2% fat in human milk.

Calves become adults at between four and eight years of age. No one knows how long humpbacks live, and it will probably be the middle of the next century (when the first litter of monitored cows, born in 1975, dies out) that this may be determined. Overhunting during the early to mid-19th C has endangered these marine mammals; they have been internationally protected since the mid-1960s. If you see them, please do not approach too closely.

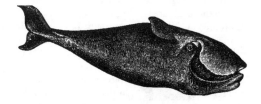

The bite of the **centipede**, which grows up to 15 inches (38 cm) long, will prove traumatic if not fatal.

Sealife

Other Marine Life

FISH: Species of fish include the leather jacket, sawfish, parrotfish, weakfish, lionfish, big-eye fish, bananafish, ladyfish, puffer, sea-bat, sardine, mullet, grouper, Spanish and frigate mackerels, red snapper, eel, barracuda, and a variety of sharks.

ECHINODERMATA: Combining the Greek words *echinos* (hedgehog) and *derma* (skin), this large division of the animal kingdom includes sea urchins, sea cucumbers, and starfish. All share the ability to propel themselves with the help of "tube feet" or spines. Known by the scientific name *astrospecten*, **estrella de mar** (starfish) are five-footed carnivorous inhabitants that use their modified "tube-feet" to burrow into the sea.

Sluggish **sea cucumbers** ingest large quantities of sand, extract the organic matter, and excrete the rest. Crustaceans and fish reside in the larger specimens.

Avoid trampling on that armed knight of the underwater sand dunes, the **sea urchin**. Consisting of a semi-circular calcareous (calcium carbonate) shell, the sea urchin is protected by its brown, pointed barbs. It uses its mouth, situated and protected on its underside, to graze by scraping algae from rocks. Surprisingly to those uninitiated in its lore, sea urchins are considered a gastronomic delicacy in many countries. The ancient Greeks believed they held aphrodisiacal and other properties beneficial to health. They are prized by the French and fetch four times the price of

The Conch

The Caribbean's most popularly edible mollusk, the conch (*Strombus gigas*), lives in one of the world's most popular seashells. Although humans have dined on conch for some 3,000 years, they are currently endangered by overfishing and are no longer found offshore near areas of high human density. Even on the small island of Anegada (in the British Virgin Islands) a perceptive visitor will note that the newer conch shell piles at the pier are composed of smaller and smaller conch. In fact these are not taken for consumption but to bait lobster traps — another species endangered by overfishing. Closed seasons are in effect in many Caribbean nations, but abuse is still rampant and the mollusk is clearly endangered.

Mother conches lay several spawn masses each season, and each may contain up to half a million eggs. More than 90% of these are eaten during their first three weeks when they swim freely in the ocean.

The Queen Conch's foremost reproductive realm is off the Turks and Caicos whose 99,974-sq.-mi. area (259,000 sq. km) exceeds the conch fishing grounds found in the remainder of the Caribbean.

oysters in Paris. The Spanish consume them raw, boiled, in *gratinés*, or in soups. In Barbados they are termed "sea eggs," and the Japanese eat their guts raw as sushi. Although a disease in recent years has devastated the sea urchin population, they are making a comeback.

CONTACT: If a sea urchin spine breaks off inside your finger or toe, don't try to remove it: you can't! You might try the cure people use in New Guinea. Take a blunt object to mash up the spine inside your skin so that it will be absorbed naturally. Then dip the wound in urine; the ammonia helps to trigger the process of disintegration. It's best to apply triple-antibiotic salve. Avoiding contact is best. Sea urchins hide underneath corals, and wounds are often contracted when you lose your footing and scrape against one.

SPONGES: Found in the ocean depths, reddish or brown sponges are among the simplest forms of multicellular life and have been around for more than a half-billion years. They pump large amounts of water between their internal filters and extract plankton. There are numerous sizes, shapes, and colors, but all can be recognized by their large, distinctive openings. Unlike other animals, they show no reaction when disturbed.

CNIDARIANS: The members of this group — anemones, corals, jellyfish, and hydroids — are distinguished by their simple structure: a cup-shaped body terminating in a combination mouth-anus which is encircled by tentacles. While hydroids and corals (covered later in this section) are colonial, jellyfish and anemones are individual.

The name of this group derives from the Greek word for another of its common characteristics: stinging capsules, or nematocysts, used for defense and for capturing prey. Hydroids spend their youth as solitary medusas, later settling down in colonies that look like ferns or feathers. Some will sting, and the best known hydroid is undoubtedly the Portuguese Man-of-War; its stinging tentacles can be extended or retracted. There have been reports of trailing tentacles reaching 50 feet. It belongs to the family of *siphonophores*, free-floating hydroid colonies that control their depth by means of a gas-filled float.

The true jellyfish are identifiable by their domes, which vary in shape. Nematocysts

are found in both the feeding tube and in their tentacles.

Also known as sea wasps, **box jellies** have a cube-shaped dome; a single tentacle extends from each corner. They have a fierce sting. If you should get stung by any of the above, get out of the water and peel off any tentacles. Avoid rubbing the injured area. Wash it with alcohol and apply meat tenderizer for five to 10 minutes. The jellyfish season runs from August to October.

Solitary bottom-dwellers, **sea anemones** are polyps with no skeleton. They use their tentacles to stun prey and force it to their mouths. Shrimp and crabs, immune to their sting, often find protection nearby. The tentacles may retract for protection when disturbed. One type of anemone lives in tubes buried in the muck or sand. Their tentacles emerge to play only at night.

CRUSTACEANS: A class of arthropods, crustaceans are distinguished by their jointed legs and complex skeleton. The **decapods** (named for their five pairs of legs) are the largest order of crustaceans. These include shrimp, lobsters, and crabs. The **ghost crab** *(ocypode)* abounds on the beaches, tunneling down beneath the sand and emerging to feed at night. Although it can survive for 48 hours without contacting water, it must return to the sea to moisten its gill chambers as well as to lay its eggs, which hatch into planktonic larvae. The **hermit crab** carries a

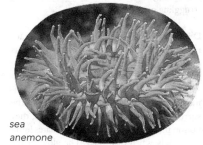

sea anemone

INTRODUCTION

Snorkeling Tips

◣ You can snorkel and swim for longer periods with confidence if you wear a tee-shirt while in the water.

◣ Be sure to make sure that your mask fits before snorkeling. Put the mask on your face, suck your breath in, and inhale through your nose. While you continue to inhale, the mask should stay on you. Try another shape if this does not work.

◣ Mustaches, a stand of hair, or suntan lotion may spoil your fit. Moustache wearers should use a bit of vaseline or lip balm to improve the seal.

◣ The strap is to prevent the mask from falling off, not to tighten the seal; it should be set up high for comfort.

◣ Before submerging, you should spit into your mask, coat the lens with your finger, and then rinse; this should have an anti fogging effect. Avoid exhaling through your nose: this may cause fog as well as release moisture.

◣ Snorkel only on the outer side of the reef on on low-wind or calm days, bring your own equipment or at least a mask you feel comfortable with (especially if you require a prescription mask).

◣ If you're using a kayak, it's a good idea to tie a line to it and carry it around when snorkeling.

discarded mollusk shell in order to protect its vulnerable abdomen. As it grows, it must find a larger home, and you may see two struggling over the same shell.

DINOFLAGELLATES: These microorganisms are a variety of protozoans known as "whippers" — single-celled animals with one or more tiny projecting flagella that function as lashes or whips. Because multibillion-member blooms of dinoflagellates drain the surrounding water of dissolved oxygen, they poison the water for fish. Dinoflagellates luminesce only when disturbed. The glow of the species *Noctiluca milaris* dims when they are anesthetized, and these microscopic unicellular creatures have been found to possess a time clock that limits the intensity of their flashes to the late-night hours. There are a few bioluminescent bays in Puerto Rico which are illuminated by dinoflagllates. The most famous of these are at La Parguera and on Vieques.

The Coral Reef Ecosystem

The coral reef is one of the least appreciated of the world's innumerable wonders. This is, in part, because little has been known about it until recent decades. A coral reef is the only geological feature fashioned by living creatures, and it is a delicate environment. Many of the world's reefs — which took millions of years to form — have already suffered adverse effects from human activities. One of the greatest opportunities the tropics offer is to explore this wondrous environment.

Corals produce the calcium carbonate (limestone) responsible for the build-up of offlying cays and islets as well as most sand on the beaches. Bearing the brunt of waves, they also conserve the shoreline. Although reefs began forming millenia ago, they are in a constant state of flux. They depend upon a delicate ecological balance to survive. Deforestation, dredging, temperature change, an increase or decrease in salinity, silt, or sewage discharge may kill them.

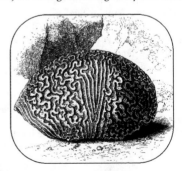

Don't Feed the Fish!

Despite the prevalence of the practice, there are a number of good reasons not to feed fish.

! Adding nutrients changes the reef's balance, causing a decline in water quality and clarity.

! Algae eating fish control algae growth, thus preventing them from overgrowing coral.

! Feeding night feeders (such as jacks and snappers) during the day interferes with the relationship between predator and prey and thus the natural balance.

! Human food is human food and may not meet their dietary requirements, thus making them more susceptible to illness.

! Fish fed by divers may become aggressive.

Because temperatures must remain between 68° and 95°F, they are only found in the tropics and, because they require light to grow, only in shallow water. They are also intolerant of freshwater, so reefs cannot survive where rivers empty into the sea.

THE CORAL POLYP: Although corals are actually animals, botanists view them as being mostly plant, and geologists dub them "honorary rocks." Acting more like plants than animals, corals survive through photosynthesis: the algae inside them do the work while the polyps themselves secrete calcium carbonate and stick together for protection from waves and boring sponges. Polyps bear a close structural resemblance to their relative the anemone, which feeds at night by using the ring or rings of tentacles surrounding its mouth to capture prey (such as plankton) with nematocysts, small stinging darts.

They are able to survive in limited space through their symbiotic relationship with the algae present in their tissues. Coral polyps exhale carbon dioxide and the algae

consume it, producing needed oxygen. Only half of the world's coral species have this special relationship and these, known as "hermatypic" corals, are the ones that build the reef. The nutritional benefits gained from this relationship enable them to grow a larger skeleton and to do so more rapidly than would otherwise be possible.

Polyps have the ability to regulate the density of these cells in their tissues and can expel some of them in a spew of mucus should they multiply too quickly. Looking at coral, the brownish algal cells show through transparent tissues. When you see a coral garden through your mask, you are actually viewing a field of captive single-celled algae.

A vital, though invisible, component of the reef ecosystem is bacteria, micro-organisms that decompose and recycle all matter on which everything from worms to coral polyps feed.

Inhabitants of the reef range from crabs to barnacles to sea squirts to multicolored tropical fish. Remarkably, the polyps themselves are consumed by only a small percentage of the reef's dwellers. They often contain high levels of toxic substances and are thought to sting fish and other animals that attempt to eat them. Corals retract their polyps during daylight hours when the fish can see them. Reefs originate as the polyps develop, and the calcium secretions form a base as they grow. One polyp can have a 1,000-year lifespan.

CORAL TYPES: Corals may be divided into three groups. The **hard** or **stony corals** (such as staghorn, brain, star, or rose) secrete a limey skeleton. The **horny corals** (sea plumes, sea whips, sea fans, and gorgonians) have a supporting skeleton-like structure known as a gorgonin (after the head of Medusa). The shapes of these corals result from the way the polyps and their connecting tissues excrete calcium carbonate; there are over 1,000 different patterns — one specific to each species. Each also has its own method of budding. Giant elk-horn corals may contain over a million polyps and live for several hundred years or longer.

The last category consists of the **soft corals**. While these too are colonies of polyps, their skeletons are composed of soft organic material, and their polyps always have eight tentacles instead of the six (or multiples of six) found in the stony corals. Unlike the hard corals, this group disintegrates after death and does not add to the reef's stony structure. Instead of depositing limestone crystals, they excrete a jelly-like matrix which is imbued with spicules (diminutive spikes) of stony material; the jelly substance gives flexibility. Sea fans and sea whips exhibit similar patterns.

The precious **black coral** is a type of soft coral and is prized by jewelers. Its branches may be cleaned and polished to high gloss ebony-black and, in this state, it resembles bushes of fine twigs.

COMPETITION: To the snorkeler, the reef appears to be a peaceful haven. The reality is that, because the reef is a comparatively benign environment, the fiercest competition has developed here. Some have developed sweeper tentacles that have an especially high concentration of stinging cells. Reaching out to a competing coral, they sting and execute it. Other species dispatch digestive filaments which eat their prey. Soft corals appear to leach out toxic chemicals (terpines) that kill nearby organisms. Because predation is such a problem, two-thirds of reef species are toxic. Others hide in stony outcrops or have formed protective relationships with other organisms. The banded clown fish, for example, lives among sea anemones whose stingers protect it.

The cleaner fish protect themselves from the larger fish by setting up stations at which they pick parasites off their carnivorous customers.

The sabre-toothed blenny is a false cleaner fish. It mimics the coloration and shape of the feeder fish, approaches, then takes a chunk out of the larger fish and runs off.

CORAL LOVE AFFAIRS: Coral polyps are not prone to celibacy or sexual prudery. They reproduce sexually and asexually through budding and join together with thousands and even millions of its neighbors to form a coral. (In a few cases, only one polyp forms a single coral.) During sexual reproduction polyps release millions of their spermatozoa into the water. Many species are dimorphic, with both male and female polyps. Some species have internal, others external, fertilization. As larvae develop, their "mother" expels them and they float off to form a new coral colony.

UNDERWATER FLORA: Most of the plants you see are algae, primitive plants that can survive only underwater. Lacking roots, **algae** draw their minerals and water directly from the sea.

One type of algae, **calcareous red algae**, are very important for reef formation. They resemble rounded stones and are 95% rock and only 5% living tissue.

PUERTO RICAN REEFS: Most common are fringing reefs, which occur close to shore, perhaps separated by a small lagoon. Elongated and narrow bank or ribbon reefs are offshore in deep water. Atolls and barrier reefs are absent. Fringing reefs exist at Seven Seas Beach in Las Croabas, Fajardo and along several other offshore cays in the NE corner of the island; at Guayama and Salinas; near Caja de Muertos Island off the coast from Ponce; at La Parguera; and off the coast of Mona Island. Bank reefs exist near Culebra and Vieques.

History

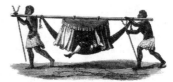

PRE-EUROPEAN HABITATION: Believed to have arrived 5,000-20,000 years ago on rafts from Florida via Cuba, the Arcaicos or Archaics — food gatherers and fishermen — were the first settlers. Little evidence of their habitation survives. The Igneri, a sub-group of Northern South America's Arawaks, are thought to have reached the island as early as 200 BC. They were agriculturists who brought tobacco and corn with them.

Last to appear and most culturally advanced, the Taínos arrived from the S between 1,000 and 1,500 AD. These copper-skinned, dark-haired people were expert carvers (in shell, gold, stone, wood, and clay) and skilled agriculturalists, cultivating cassava, corn, beans, and squash. They gave the island the name of Borinquen, "Land of the Noble Lord," after the creator Yukiyu who was believed to reside in the heart of the present-day Caribbean National Forest.

EUROPEAN DISCOVERY: During his second voyage in 1493, Columbus stopped off at the island of Santa Maria de Guadalupe. Here, he met 12 Taíno women and two young boys who said that they wished to return to their home on the island of Boriñquen (Puerto Rico). Columbus took them along with him as guides. On Nov. 19, the Taínos, spying their home island, leapt into the water and swam ashore. Columbus named the island San Juan Bautista ("Saint John the Baptist") after the Spanish Prince Don Juan. The island was colonized under the leadership of Juan Ponce de León in 1508, and he was appointed governor in 1509. Soon, Franciscan friars arrived with cattle and horses; a gold smelter was set up and production begun.

On Nov. 8, 1511, this first settlement was renamed Puerto Rico ("Rich Port") and a coat of arms was granted. King Ferdinand distributed the island's land and the 30,000 Taínos among the soldiers. Under the system of *repartimiento* ("distribution"), Native Americans were set to work in construction and in the mines or fields. Under a similar system, termed *encomienda* ("commandery"), they were forcibly extracted from villages and set to labor for a *patrón* on his estate.

Although, in return, the Taínos were supposed to receive protection and learn about the wonders of Catholicism, this system was a thinly disguised form of slavery. Ultimately, it led to the extinction of the native inhabitants as a distinct racial and cultural group.

The Taínos tragically assumed that these newcomers, owing to their remarkable appearance and superior technology, were immortal. A chieftain decided to put this theory to the test, and a young Spaniard,

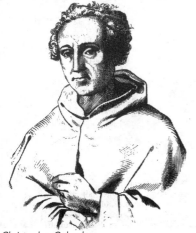

Christopher Columbus

Diego Salcedo, was experimentally drowned while being carried across the Río Grande de Añasco in the NW part of the island. When he did not revive after three days, the Taínos realized their mistake, at which point they killed nearly half the Spaniards on the island. The revolt was put down, however, and many Taínos fled to the mountains or neighboring islands. Most were freed by royal decrees in 1521, but it was too late: they'd already been absorbed into the racial fabric.

With the depletion of both Taínos and gold, a new profit-making scheme had to be found. That proved to be the new "gold" of the Caribbean: sugar. The first sugar mill was built in 1523 near Añasco, and the entire economy changed from mining to sugar over the next few decades. The first Portuguese slavers, filled to the brim with captive Africans intended to provide agricultural labor, arrived in 1518.

The city of Puerto Rico was moved to the site of present-day San Juan, whose name it

?!¿ US officials used the spelling "Porto Rico" to refer to the island from 1898-1932. General Nelson Miles, who headed the invading force, made the change. In 1932, Congress changed the name back in response to an April 1930 "unanimous request from the Porto Rico legislature."

took, and the entire island, in turn, was renamed Puerto Rico. Puerto Rico became one of Spain's strategic outposts in the Caribbean. Ignoring the economic potential of the island, hard-nosed military commanders appointed by Madrid treated the island as if it were one huge military installation.

An attack by Sir Francis Drake's fleet in 1595 was repelled, but the English Count of Cumberland launched a successful invasion in 1598. Harsh weather conditions, coupled with the effects of dysentery, caused him and his troops to exit shortly thereafter. The Dutch besieged San Juan in 1625; defeated, they did succeed in torching a

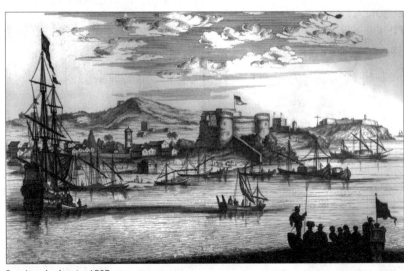

San Juan harbor in 1597

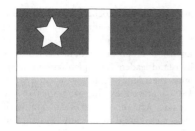

This Lares flag was intended to become the national flag of the Republic. It was designed by Dr. Ramon Emeterio Betances and embroidered by Mrs. Mariana "Golden Arm" Bracetti.

great deal of the city. With the island forbidden to trade except within the Spanish Empire, a brisk inter-island business in contraband goods (ginger, tobacco, and cattle hides) developed during the mid-16th century.

In April 1797, the British, under the command of Abercromby, led an unsuccessful attack against San Juan.

THE NINETEENTH CENTURY: The Puerto Rican political scene was divided into loyalists, liberals, and separatists. In March 1812, a new constitution, more liberal than the previous one, was approved, and Puerto Ricans became Spanish citizens. With the arrival of Canary Islanders, Haitians, Louisiana French, Venezuelans, and black slaves, Puerto Rico became a lively potpourri of cultures.

As the population grew, a new nationalism and a distinct sense of being Puerto Rican began to emerge. From 1825 to 1867, the island was governed by a series of ruthless, despotic military commanders known as the "Little Caesars." During the 1850s, Ramón Emeterio Betances became the leader of the separatist movement and founded the Puerto Rican Revolutionary Movement in Santo Domingo. (His ances-

tral home, at 155 C. Tetuán in Old San Juan) is now the headquarters for the Conservation Trust. At midnight on Sept. 23, 1868, several hundred rebels marched into and took over the town of Lares.

Hearing news of the revolt, the government placed reinforcements at nearby San Sebastian, and the rebels took to the hills. A guerilla war ensued and lasted a month. This was the famous *Grito de Lares* ("The Cry of Lares"). Even though this first (and only) attempt at rebellion failed, it is cited by *independentistas* as a major event in Puerto Rican history. In 1869, Puerto Rico sent its first representatives to the Cortes, the Spanish House of Representatives.

A law abolishing slavery became effective on March 22, 1873, though "freed" slaves had to continue toiling for their masters for another three years as indentured laborers; full civil rights were granted five years later. Led by Luis Muñoz Rivera, the Autonomous Party was formed in 1882.

On Nov. 28, 1897, Prime Minister Sagasta signed a royal decree establishing "autonomy" for Puerto Rico, though on paper only. A side effect of the pressure by the US on Spain to grant autonomy to Cuba and prevent a war, the charter actually made few fundamental changes in the island's status. Included in the package was voting representation in the two houses of the Spanish Cortes (legislature). However, it allowed the King of Spain to appoint the island's gover-

> "We say to the powers of the Old World. We will not allow you to acquire further possessions in the Western hemisphere. Yet we will take Porto Rico, and we reserve the right to take Haiti or Brazil or Cuba or any other part of the North or South Americas when we think proper to do so." — Senator Horace Chilton, *Congressional Record*, 1898.

nor, who in turn was authorized to suspend any constitutional guarantees, to control the legislature's output (and even suspend it if necessary), and to appoint seven of the 12 members of the Legislative Council (the Senate). The charter was never actually ratified by the Spanish parliament.

The Twentieth Century

AMERICAN INVASION: In the furor (spurred on by American newspaper barons Hearst and Pulitzer) over the explosion of the battleship *Maine* on February 15, 1898 in Cuba, President McKinley declared war with Spain. In July, just as the new government had begun to function, Gen. Nelson A. Miles landed on the island at Guánica with 16,000 US troops. The Puerto Rican campaign of the Spanish-American War lasted only 17 days and was described by one journalist as a "picnic." On Dec. 10, 1898, under the Treaty of Paris accords signed by the United States and Spain, Puerto Rico was delivered to the US as an "unincorporated territory," a status it retains to this day.

With no consultation whatsoever, the Puerto Ricans overnight found themselves under American rule after nearly 400 years of Spanish occupation. Intellectuals on the island had high expectations from the US government; after all, Gen. Miles had promised "to give the people of your beautiful island the largest measure of liberty (and) to bestow upon you... the liberal institutions of our government." Naturally, this meant attempting to make the Puerto Ricans as "American" as possible, up to and including changing the name to "Porto" Rico — in order to make it easy to spell.

Hopes for independence were dashed, however, as two years of military rule were followed by the Foraker Act. In effect from 1900 to 1916, the act placed Puerto Rico in an uncertain purgatory with the govern-ment a mix of autocracy and democracy. Americanization continued by importing teachers who taught classes entirely in English — an unsuccessful tactic. Requests by island leaders for a plebiscite to determine the island's status were ignored. In 1909, enraged by the provisions of the Foraker Act, the Puerto Rican House of Delegates refused to pass any legislation at all. This protest brought no change in status and, by the beginning of WWI, there was widespread talk of independence.

CITIZENSHIP: To secure the island as a strategic defense bastion and assure a ready supply of "raw materials" for the slaughter mills of Europe, Puerto Ricans were granted American citizenship by the Jones-Shafroth Act. Under this bill, which President Woodrow Wilson signed into law on March 2, 1917, Puerto Ricans automatically became US citizens unless they signed a statement rejecting it. If they refused, they stood to lose a number of civil rights, including the right to hold office, and would then be designated aliens. Naturally, only a few refused. Another request two years later for a plebiscite also failed.

In 1922, local politician Antonio Barceló tried a new approach: he proposed an association that would be modeled after the Irish Free State. The bill died in committee. The same year marked the formation of the Nationalist Party.

THE 1930s DEPRESSION: High unemployment, political anarchy, and near starvation reigned as the Depression years of the 1930s hit Puerto Rico even harder than the mainland. Pedro Albizu Campos, a Harvard Law School

Pedro Albizu Campos

graduate and former US Army officer, emerged as head of the new Nationalist Party. After members of the party turned to violence, followed in turn by police brutality and oppression, Campos and seven of his followers found themselves in jail in Atlanta, Georgia. On March 21, 1936, after a permit to hold a Palm Sunday parade was revoked by the government at the last moment, Nationalists went ahead with it anyway. As *La Bourinquena* played in the background, police opened fire on protestors, innocent bystanders, and fellow policemen. This event, known as *La Masacre de Ponce*, resulted in the deaths of more than 20 and the wounding of some 200 persons.

THE STERILIZATION CAMPAIGN: A little-known episode in Puerto Rican history is the sterilization campaign launched by the government. A 1937 law legalized contraception and sterilization (under the direction of a eugenics board). A mover and shaker behind the program was physician Clarence Gamble, a leader in the stateside eugenics movement and a heir to the Proctor and Gamble fortune.

An active campaign was launched during the mid-1940s as health department workers touted the benefits of *la operación* in rural areas. The operation (including its irreversibility) was often ill explained, and consent was obtained from women in labor or just after childbirth. A 1947 survey disclosed that more than 25% of the sterilized women regretted their decision. Catholics and *independentistas* teamed up in the 1950s to fight the campaign; the government, in turn, denied the existence of any organized effort to sterilize women.

The sterilization law was repealed in 1960. However, some 35% of Puerto Rican women of child bearing age had been sterilized by 1965; some two-thirds of this number were in their 20s. In 1989, more than 40% of the women between 15-49 had had their tubes tied.

LUIZ MUÑOZ MARÍN: Luiz Muñoz Marín, son of Luis Muñoz Rivera, and his Popular Democratic Party (PDP) came to power in 1940 with a 37% plurality. Perhaps the dominant figure in all of Puerto Rican history, Muñoz presided over the governmental, economic, and educational transformation of the island. He served for eight years as Senate majority leader before becoming the island's first elected governor in

Luiz Muñoz Marín

1948. After his election, he changed from being an ardent supporter of independence to being pro-commonwealth.

In 1946, Muñoz had kicked the *independentistas* out of his party, as he aligned himself with the Roosevelt administration.

The Puerto Rican legislature passed *la mordaza* (the "gag law") in May 1948. It imposed a fine of up to $10,000 and a maximum sentence of up to ten years in jail for anyone who "encouraged, pleaded, counseled, or preached the necessity, desirability or suitability of overthrowing, paralyzing or destroying the insular government, or any subdivision of it, by means of force or violence." The printing, publication, circulation, sale, or exhibition of literature which suggested the use of force against the Puerto Rican government was also made a felony. Modeled after the Smith Act in the US, it spurred a climate of fear. The reason for the act was to hamper support for independence. (The law was repealed in 1957).

On Oct. 30, 1950, there were *independentista* uprisings on the island. That same week, *independentistas* opened fire outside Blair House, President Truman's temporary abode in Washington, D.C. Resistance leader

INTRODUCTION

Pedro Albizu-Campos was charged with inciting armed insurrection and imprisoned.

COMMONWEALTH STATUS: On June 4, 1951, Puerto Ricans approved a referendum granting commonwealth status to the island. As the only alternative was continued colonial status, many Puerto Ricans failed to show up at the ballot box.

In a second referendum the new constitution was approved, and commonwealth status (*Estado Libre Asociado* or "free associated state") was inaugurated on July 25, 1952. (Ironically, this was the same month and day as the 1898 invasion). While the new status superficially resembled that of a state of the Union, Puerto Ricans still paid no income tax and were forbidden to vote in national elections or elect voting representatives to Congress. That same year the Independence Party came in second place in the elections, garnering 19.6% of the vote. This was an extraordinary achievement, given the fact that the gag law was still in effect.

In 1954, four Puerto Ricans (Puerto Rico natives but New York City residents) wounded five Congressmen when they opened fire in the House of Representatives in Washington.

In 1964, Muñoz stepped down, and Roberto Sánchez Vilella became the island's second elected governor. (Muñoz died in 1980).

A plebiscite sponsored by the *Populares* was held on July 23, 1967, although the statehooder Luis A. Ferré and *Independentista* Hector Alvarez Silver bolted to form their own parties. The buoyant economy, coupled with strong support for commonwealth status by the ever-influential Muñoz, caused a record turnout (with 65.9% of the eligible voters participating) in which 60% of the voters supported commonwealth status, 39% were for statehood, and .06% favored independence.

This plebiscite's results were tainted by US government interference — documented in a report during the Carter administration. The FBI's COINTELPRO program had deliberately set out to sow dissention among the ranks of the independence movement.

In 1968, Luis A. Ferré, head of the newly created New Progressive Party (NPP), was elected governor, and he began to push actively for statehood. Ferré's election was helped through a split in the PPD.

On Sept. 26, 1969, when an *independentista* was jailed for one year for draft evasion, college students set fire to the ROTC building at Río Piedras. In the aftermath, seven students were suspended, police shot at least one student, and subsequent marches and counter-marches degenerated into riots.

CERRO MARAVILLA: Carlos Romero Barceló of the New Progressive Party won the governorship over the Popular Democratic Party's Hernández Colón by 43,000 votes in 1976 and by a 3,000-vote margin in 1980. After the polls closed in 1980, Commandant Enrique Sanchez, security chief in charge of polling and a Romero henchman, refused for hours to turn over the ballots to the counting authorities. What happened to the ballots in that time remains a mystery.

On July 25, 1978 security forces shot and killed two *independentistas* atop Cerro Maravilla, one of Puerto Rico's highest peaks, which is topped with communications towers. Apparently, two youths, Arnaldo Dario Posado and Carlos Soto Arrivi, were lured by undercover agent Gonzalez Malave to the mountaintop to plant explosives. It is believed that the youths, one mentally disturbed and the other a teenager, were enticed there and then shot in order to discredit the independence movement.

Though no one will ever know the exact truth because there has been such an extensive cover up, the official government story has been thoroughly discredited. In addition, seven former police officers involved in the case have since been sentenced to 20-30 years each on charges of perjury and obstructing justice.

The FBI has admitted attempting to cover up the incident, and it is believed that the agency may have been in on the operation all along. Disclosure of possible involvement by members of his administration or by Romero himself in the entrapment at Cerro Maravilla was a major contributing factor in his 1984 defeat to the PDP's Rafael Hernández Colón. The first primary gubernatorial contest held in the island's history was held in June 1988. It pitted San Juan Mayor Balthasar Corrada del Río and Romero Barceló. Corrada won but went on to lose the November 1988 election to Hernández Colón.

In 1990, Hernández proposed selling the government-owned telephone company and using the proceeds (after paying off its $1 billion in debt) to create two "perpetual funds" of $1 billion each. One would have been used to improve public services (such as sewage and drinking water) and the other would have been earmarked for secondary education. Approval of the proposal would have required passage of a constitutional amendment. The sale never materialized. The offer was withdrawn in 1991 because there were no buyers at the price of $3 billion, which amounted to $3,000 a line!

THE 1992 ELECTIONS: In November Dr. Pedro Rosselló and the NPP won the elections by securing 49.9% of the vote in a three-way contest. The 47-year-old pediatrician faced the PDP's Senator Victoria "Melo" Muñoz, the daughter of former Gov. Luis Muñoz Marín, and Fernando Martín, who was the Puerto Rican Independence Party's (PIP) candidate. While Martín garnered just 79,000 votes (4.2%),

Muñoz gained 45% of the vote. Former governor Carlos Romero Barceló was elected Resident Commissioner.

THE ROSSELLÓ ADMINISTRATION: By the end of his first month in office, Rosselló had already signed into law a measure restoring English as an official language along with Spanish. This came despite a 100,000-strong rally held in Old San Juan protesting the measure. This repealed an earlier PDP statute that made Spanish the only official language. He also removed "Commonwealth of Puerto Rico" from the government stationery masthead and substituted "Government of Puerto Rico," following an NPP tradition. In 1993, he moved towards a controversial "community-school" concept which met strong protest from teachers who saw in it a move towards privatizing the educational system.

Also in 1993, a distressing new chapter was added to Puerto Rican history when National Guard troops began occupying public housing projects in Bayamón, Río Piedras, Hato Rey, Arecibo, Cayey, Humacao, Ponce, Mayagüez, and other municipalities where drugs were actively sold at *puntos* (drug distribution points).

After taking over the project, the guardsmen handed out pens, pencils, erasers, and other school equipment bearing the Guard's logo as well as the slogan "Say No To Drugs." Around 20 projects had been occupied by the end of Aug., and the government planned to occupy 10% of the island's 332 housing projects by the end of the year. Fences and access controls with bulletproof guardhouses have been constructed. Since the guards withdrawal, a permanent police presence has been maintained.

This policy, known as *mano dura* (hard hand), has come under sharp attack. Critics decry the militarization of the island as an unfortunate precedent and point out that the island-wide homicide rate has not decreased and that the dealers have been dispersed rather than stopped. While many housing project residents say they feel more secure, others worry about the future.

A wall has been erected around Lloréns Torres (a housing project completely occupied by the national guard and police in a March 1996 raid), which has effectively turned the project into a prison camp. One final criticism is that the people at the top of the drug pyramid, who apparently pose as respectable members of the Commonwealth's business community, are never apprehended; in a sense, the invasion of the housing projects is a war against the poor.

Another disturbing tendency was instituted that same year — controlled access to private urbanizations in which only those who lived there or had a valid reason for visiting were permitted entry. Residents collectively paid for the guards, although the Commonwealth Supreme Court ruled that residents opposing controlled access did not need to pay the monthly fees for the system.

Rosselló signed a controversial voucher initiative into law in Sept. 1993. It provided $1,500 in credits that would allow students to transfer to private schools with subsidies from the government. These funds may be used for books, uniforms, tuition, and/or tutoring.

The Puerto Rican Teachers Association filed a lawsuit in which they allege that the voucher program breaches the constitutional separation of church and state. The law was struck down by the Puerto Rican Supreme Court. (A similar 1999 plan was halted by an injunction.)

THE 1993 PLEBISCITE: In 1993 Puerto Ricans were given a chance to choose among three options: enhanced commonwealth backed by the PDP, statehood backed by the New Progressive Party, or independence backed by the Puerto Rican Independence Party. Each was identified by a simple geometrical symbol: a rectangle represented commonwealth, a circle stood for statehood, and a triangle represented independence. While Reagan and Bush appeared in TV commercials extolling the statehood option, commonwealth forces warned that the island would lose its language, culture, tax incentives, and — most distressingly — its Olympic team. One strong opponent of statehood was political right-wing pundit Pat Buchanan who argued that the two-language policy would set a precedent for "Balkanization."

Statehood advocates argued that entry into the US would decrease unemployment, thin the bloated bureaucracy (22% of total employment), and substitute two senators and six congressmen in place of the current non-voting Congressional representative.

The estimated 100,000 pro-independence voters were divided between the more radical faction favoring abstention and the rest who advocated participation. Congressional polls conducted in 1991 by the firm Analysis Inc. indicated that statehood lacked sufficient votes for passage. The enhanced commonwealth forces won the plebiscite by a margin of 48.4% to statehood's 46.2%.

After the Commonwealth "victory," the New Progressive Party announced that it would not provide public funds to the Popular Democratic Party to lobby Congress for changes in the Commonwealth status. While the government claimed that providing such funds would be unconstitutional, House Minority Leader José Enrique Arrarás alleged that Gov. Rosselló is "drunk with power" and that his "attitude is a cheap one that evokes the pampered child who, when he's not allowed to play, threatens to take away the bat and ball."

On the ballot, the PDP had promised to immediately propose to Congress the reformulation of Section 936 (see "Economy") to ensure the creation of more and superior jobs; protection for island agricultural products other than coffee (which is already protected); and extending Supplementary Security Income (SSI) to Puerto Rico and obtaining Nutritional Assistance Program funding equal to that received by the states. So far these proposals have not been submitted to Congress, probably because the Republican-controlled body would be unreceptive to these changes. Full food stamp funding along with SSI would cost an additional $1.5 billion annually.

The plebiscite was followed by years of stalling. In 1996 opportunistic Alaskan Republican Congressman Don Young introduced a bill promising to call for a plebiscite in 1998 which would force Puerto Ricans to choose between statehood or independence. After an outcry, it was decided to add commonwealth to the plebiscite, rendering it a rehash of the 1993 vote. No plebescite materialized.

THE OIL SPILL: On Jan. 7, 1994, the oil tank barge *Morris J. Berman* ran aground 16 miles from shore. While it was being towed a line broke (for the second time that morning) and the boat sank and settled on a reef. It spilled more than 26,000 of its 35,000-barrel contents onto the beaches. The oil spill cleanup cost the government around $65 million, a figure representing two-thirds of the entire amount set aside by Congress for such spills.

1996 EVENTS: At hearings for the Young bill (see above) in San Juan, rallies were mobilized by both parties; *popularistas* (PDP members) outnumbered NPP members by two-to-one. At a conference in 1996 in San Juan, Drug Enforcement Agency Chief Tom Constantine announced that he believes over 1,000 drug-trafficking and money-laundering groups operate in Puerto Rico and import 84 tons of cocaine per year which is valued at

more than $20 billion. Of this amount, 20% remains for sale on the island. According to Constantine, heroin is also now being smuggled through the island and 64% of all violent crimes on the island in 1995 have been linked to drug trafficking. He maintained that Puerto Rico is becoming a "bloody playground" and that the Columbia drug cartels make the American mafia families look like schoolchildren in comparison.

In a speech to the conference, *San Juan Star* reporter Manny Suárez pointed out that, while 10-20% of all shipments are interdicted, the profits are so enormous that "all a major importer has to do is to land about 5 to 10% of the shipments to have a money-making operation.... Interdiction is a failure.... (Great Britain) treat(s) addicts like sick people and we throw them in jail. Perhaps we should look at the British model to see what we could learn from it."

1998 EVENTS: First proposed by Gov. Hernández Colón in 1990, the Puerto Rico Telephone Company was sold in 1998 to a consortium led by GTE (now Verizon) for more than $2 billion.

In Sept. 1998, Hurricane Georges hit Puerto Rico. Some 56,000 homes were destroyed. Another plebiscite was held in December. "None of the above" won 50.3%!

1999 EVENTS: Sila Calderón won the Nov. elections, replacing Gov. Pedro Rosselló. Rosselló headed for Havard to teach a course on health reform at the John F. Kennedy school of business.

A new chapter in Puerto Rico's association with the US began on April 18,1999 when an F-18 fighter jet dropped a bomb which killed a civilian. (See Vieques chapter for details and late developments).

In Sept. 1999, President Clinton issued executive clemency for 16 members of the Armed Forces of National Liberation

❖ Important Dates in Puerto Rican History ❖

4–400 AD The Arcaico Indians settle on Puerto Rico.

120–400 AD The Igneri (or Saladoid) Indians arrive on the island from South America (possibly Venezuela) and settle on the north coast.

1000 AD The Taíno culture now dominates.

1493 Nov. 19. Columbus "discovers" the island of Puerto Rico on second voyage.

1508 Juan Ponce de León is appointed governor and founds Caparra, the first settlement.

1509 Government seat is moved and named Ciudad de Puerto Rico.

1513 The first royal proclamation authorizes the introduction of slaves.

1521 The capital is renamed San Juan while the entire island takes the name Puerto Rico.

1530 Having exhausted the gold supply, many colonists migrate to Peru in search of new plunder, while those remaining become farmers.

1595 Sir Francis Drake unsuccessfully attacks San Juan.

1598 The Count of Cumberland captures San Juan, holds it for seven months.

1625 An attack by the Dutch fleet is repelled but not before its troops sack the city.

1631 Construction begins on El Morro fortress in San Juan.

1680 Ponce is founded.

1760 Mayagüez is founded.

1775 Population reaches 70,000 including 6,467 slaves.

1778 Private ownership of land is granted by the Crown.

1797 British attack and pull out after a one-month siege.

1800 Island population reaches 155,406.

1812 Puerto Rico is declared a Spanish province under the new constitution and Puerto Rico is granted representation.

1814 Spanish constitution of 1812 is annulled.

1821 First of a series of 19th-century slave rebellions takes place in Bayamón.

1822–37 Tyrannical rule of Governor Miguel de la Torre, Spanish Commander defeated by Bolivar in Venezuela in 1821.

1833 Blacks forbidden to serve in the military.

1859 Patriot and leader Luis Muñoz Rivera born.

1860 Population reaches 583,308.

1868 The Grito de Lares revolt occurs.

1873 Abolition of slavery.

1891 *Independentista* leader Pedro Albizu Campos is born.

1897 Autonomy is granted by Spain.

1898 July 25. American troops land at Guánica and establish control.

1899 April 11. Spain cedes Puerto Rico to the US under the Treaty of Paris. Under the Foraker Act, Puerto Rico becomes a US territory; an American-led civil administration replaces the military.

1903 University of Puerto Rico established in Río Piedras.

1917 March 2. The Jones Act makes Puerto Ricans US citizens.

1937 March 12. "Ponce Massacre" occurs when police fire on an Independentista parade, killing 19 and injuring 100.

1938 The Popular Democratic Party is established. Attempted assassination of Governor Winship.

1942 Tugwell, last Puerto Rican governor, is appointed.

1946 Jesús Pínero becomes the first native appointed Puerto Rican governor.

1948 Luis Muñoz Marín becomes first elected governor of Puerto Rico. A speech by Pedro Albizu Campos at the University of Puerto Rico ends in violence. The Nationalists attempt to assassinate the governor. Four Nationalists are killed and one is seriously wounded. The Statehood Republican Party is founded.

1950 Public Law 600 permits Puerto Rico to draft constitution. Independentistas attack La Fortaleza; riots result. Nationalists attempt to assassinate President Truman in Washington (Nov. 1). One of the Nationalists and a guard die. An insurrection by Nationalists takes place in Jayuya and elsewhere.

1952 Puerto Ricans vote in a plebescite to reaffirm the commonwealth as their status.

1954 A group of Puerto Ricans stage an attack on the US Congress in the Capitol Building.

1965 Abolishment of literacy test under the Civil Rights Act.

1967 Commonwealth Status wins approval by 60.5% in a referendum.

1972 Roberto Clemente, Pittsburgh Pirate and island hero, dies in a plane crash while on an earthquake relief mission to Managua, Nicaragua.

1973 Bishop of San Juan, Luis Aponte Martinez, appointed Cardinal by Pope Paul VI.

1976 Carlos Romero Barcelo is elected governor of Puerto Rico under the New Progressive Party.

1978 Two pro-independence youth murdered by police in the Cerro Maravilla incident.

1980 Island population reaches three million.

1981 Los Macheteros attack a National Guard installation located at Muñoz Air Base in Isla Verde. Eight aircraft are destroyed.

1985 Miriam Naviera becomes the first woman appointed to the Puerto Rican Supreme Court. Seven members of Macheteros arrested in Connecticut.

1989 Hurricane Hugo hits the island and causes extensive damage.

1990 Antonia Novello is named US Surgeon General.

1992 Pedro Rosselló González is elected governor of Puerto Rico under the New Progressive Party.

1994 Puerto Ricans vote in a plebescite to reaffirm the commonwealth as their status.

1996 Pedro Rosselló González is reelected governor of Puerto Rico.

1997 The US Congress commences a public hearing process which will assess the island's status.

1998 Hurricane Georges causes $15 billion in damages. Another referendum on the status is held. The "none of the above" option wins by a margin of 48.8% to 45.6% for statehood.

2000 Sila María Calderón is elected the first female governor of Puerto Rico under the Popular Democratic Party.

(FALN). Although the intention was to booster wife Hilary's popularity with Puerto Rican voters, she had to distance herself from the controversial pardon.

2000 EVENTS: Despite the fact that Puerto Rico ranks second among all US states and territories in the number of HIV positive inhabitants, Roman Catholic lobbyists defeated legislation which would have authorized sex education in the public school system. "The bill proposed in Puerto Rico to make sex education a matter of law has been set aside," proclaimed Monsignor Matthew Habiger, president of the pro-life, pro-family group Human Life International. "Sex education is one of the foundation blocks of the culture of death," Monsignor Richard Welch cautioned. "The training of our children in sexual activity is a proven disaster. Children need to know and understand chastity."

2002 EVENTS: A former Puerto Rican education secretary, the Chamber of Commerce president and 15 others were charged in an alleged corruption scheme in early 2002.

Victor Fajardo, who served as the U.S. territory's education secretary from 1994 to 2000, and nine others, were arrested, including Richard D'Acosta, president of Puerto Rico's Chamber of Commerce, and Jose Omar Cruz, deputy education secretary under Fajardo. Warrants were issued for the arrest of six others. They were charged with stealing federal funds, extortion and money laundering.

The scheme is estimated to have involved $4.3 million in diverted federal funds and kickbacks. Some $1.5 million was diverted to political campaigns. Officials from both the pro-statehood New Progressive Party, in power at the time, and the anti-statehood Popular Democratic Party were involved. Much of the money was intended to fund computers and teacher computer training.

Angel Luis Ocasio Ramos, deputy chief of staff to then-Gov. Pedro Rosselló during the mid-1990s, was arrested in Dec. 2001 on two counts of conspiracy to interfere with commerce by extortion. (In 1999, high-ranking administration officials had been convicted of stealing $2.2 million meant for AIDS patients.)

Demonstrations, marking the nation's 50th anniversary of a commonwealth, were held on July 25th. While pro-commonwealth supporters gathered in San Juan, *independentistas* thronged to Guánica.

Government

There is possibly no other island of its size where politics is as hot an issue as it is in Puerto Rico. In spite of the fact that elections determine nothing save who will deliver what slice of the political patronage, Puerto Ricans eat, drink, sleep, and breathe politics. Some even consider politics to be Puerto Rico's national sport. In addition, Puerto Rico has one of the most curious political systems in the world. Although it's a colony of the US, the island has commonwealth rather than colonial status. Puerto Ricans have both US citizenship and freedom of travel to and from the States. Puerto Ricans may be drafted, yet they may not vote in US elections.

Administrative Organization

The Puerto Rican government is divided into executive, legislative, and judicial branches just as on the mainland. Governors are elected for a four-year term. The executive branch is extremely powerful and governors appoint more than 500 executive and judicial branch officials. The bicameral legislature consists of a 27-member *Senado* (Senate) and a 51-member *Camara de Representantes* (House of Representatives).

In order to prevent one party from dominating the legislature, both houses may be increased by additional minority party members when any one party gains more than two-thirds of the seats in an election. In this situation, the number of seats may be increased up to a maximum of nine in

the *Senado* and 17 in the *Camara*. These "at large" seats are apportioned among party members according to the electoral strength of each minority party. Contested decisions made by the Court may be reviewed by the US Supreme Court.

Puerto Rico is also part of the Federal District Court System. Instead of being divided into counties, Puerto Rico is sectioned into 78 *municipos* (municipalities) which each have a town or city; many of these are quite small. Each has a mayor and municipal assembly elected every four years. Education is left to the Commonwealth government. The municipalities also have their own coat of arms and flag, a tradition which dates back to Spanish rule.

Technically a congressman, Puerto Rico's non-voting Resident Commissioner sits in the US House of Representatives in Washington, D.C. Unlike other congressmen, he is elected only once every four years and represents a constituency seven times as large as the average.

The Question Of Status

The single most important and hotly debated issue in Puerto Rico centers on the issue of political status. There are three distinct possi-

Coat of Arms

Each municipality has its own flag and coat of arms. Each of the 78 coat of arms is topped by a crown which signifies if the municipality "belongs" to a bishop, marquee, or king. This crown also stands for the security and protection conferred by the muncipo on its residents. Each coat of arms is topped by three, four, or five castle-like towers. The number of towers shows whether it is a village, town, or city. These coats of arms are taken very seriously, and many Puerto Ricans owe allegiance to their municipo.

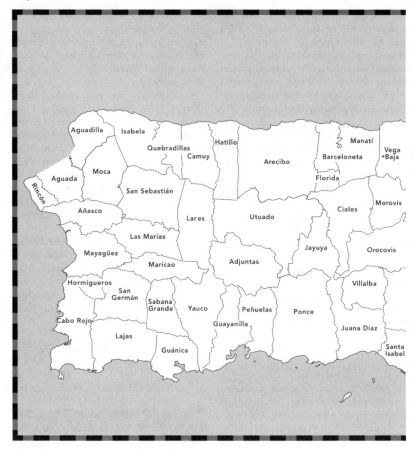

bilities for Puerto Rico's future status. One would be the continuation of the present commonwealth status in its current or modified form. The second is statehood. The third and least likely would be independence.

Modification of the commonwealth status would involve granting more autonomy to the island government while retaining ties with the US. Autonomy would be granted over trade tariffs, immigration, the minimum wage, and federal grants, and would be coupled with exemption from ICC and FCC regulations. Elevation to statehood, on the other hand, would require a severe economic transition. Chase Manhattan and Citibank, which provide most of the island's financing, would find themselves in violation of interstate banking regulations and would have to close their operations there. Income tax, now paid only to the local government, would have to be turned over to the federal government. Statehood would also mean forfeiture of tax-exempt status for Puerto Rico's industries.

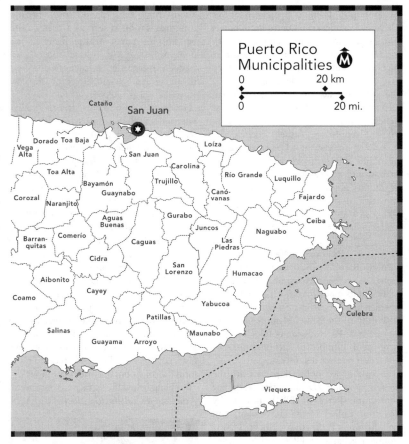

Puerto Rico
Municipalities
0   20 km
0   20 mi.

Support for statehood is becoming more generally accepted, not because the islanders have an explicit wish to enter the American mainstream, but because the politicians are selling the story that it will bring increased revenues and more money. And the idea is to become a state while retaining the benefits of being a commonwealth (such as the Olympic team).

The coconut palm is the symbol of the New Progressive Party, and its leaders assure followers that *los cocos* (dollars) will rain down on them after statehood is achieved.

However, there is little incentive for the US Congress to grant Puerto Rico statehood status. Statehood is controversial not only because most Puerto Ricans cannot speak English fluently, but also because Puerto Rico's large population and high birth rate would give it more congressional representatives than 20 other states.

Independence, the third and least likely alternative, is supported by a small but vocal minority. There has long been serious talk of independence in Puerto Rico, but as things stand now popular support is lacking. One reason is that Puerto Ricans fear the political and economic chaos that they have been told independence might bring. The independence movement in Puerto Rico has a long tradition of using terrorist tactics, which has resulted in official government repression. Attacks include the Nov. 1979 ambush of a US Army bus on the island in which two were killed and three wounded. The island is of such strategic military importance and is so economically tied to the US that a meaningful change in status is unlikely under the prevailing political and economic conditions.

Political Parties

If Puerto Rico's political status seems confusing, so are the vast number and varied politics of its many *partidos* (parties), some of which hardly engender enough support to be worthy of the name. There is no dominant party in Puerto Rican politics; instead, there are a number of factions, none of which ever receives majority support.

The two major political parties are the *Partido Popular Democratico* (Popular Democratic Party or PPD), headed by Governor Rafael Hernández Colón, and the *Partido* Progresivo Nuevo (New Progressive Party or PPN), led by Carlos Romero Barceló. Each has half a million hard-core supporters, out of a total two million registered voters.

The Popular Democratic Party supports continued maintenance of commonwealth status provided it is revised to allow more autonomy.

The PPN's Carlos Romero Barceló, nicknamed *El Caballo* ("the horse") by his detractors because he is allegedly stubborn, ruthless, and macho, served as governor from 1976-84. His party supports state-

hood for the island, but because Americanization is seen as a prerequisite, he and his party, whose members are dubbed *"estadistas"* ("statehooders") are frequently regarded as enemies of Puerto Rican culture. Current Governor Dr. Pedro Rosselló is also a PPN *estadista*.

Former San Juan Mayor Hernan Padilla's Puerto Rican Renewal Party is a PPN splinter party with 300,000 supporters. There are also two independence parties; the larger is the Puerto Rican Independence Party, formed in 1946 (after Muñoz Marín kicked out the *independentistas* from his party) and led by Rubén Berríos-Martinez.

The other is the Puerto Rican Socialist Party, which was established in 1971 as an outgrowth of the Pro Independence Movement that was founded in 1946. It was led by Juan Mari Bras and was superseded in Oct. 1993 by the New Independence Movement (NMI), headed by Rev. Eunice R. Santana. It advocated a boycott of the 1993 plebiscite and differs from the former organization in that it avoids Marxist-Leninist affiliation. It recognizes the importance of struggle by labor unions, feminists, environmentalists, and others to transform the conditions of life for these groups.

Bubbling below the surface are the *Fuerzas Armadas de Liberación Nacional* (FALN)

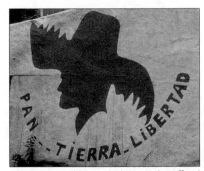

The jibaro and his straw hat are the official symbol of the Popular Democratic Party.

and the *Macheteros*. The FALN terrorizes targets on the mainland. The *Macheteros* go after such island targets as the San Juan Power Station and Fort Buchanan. They also claim responsibility for the Sept. 1983 robbery of the Wells Fargo terminal in West Hartford, Connecticut, which netted $7 million and is said to be the second largest heist in US history. Members of both groups were pardoned under the 1998 Clinton amnesty.

Economy

Background

Much is made of the economic "miracle" that is taking place in Puerto Rico. It's true that in 1999 Puerto Rico's GNP reached an estimated $29 billion; not only is this the Caribbean's highest, but it is billions above Cuba's, even though that country has a much larger area and three times the population. Per capita gross product (personal income) for 1995 was $7,296, and average family income in 1999 was $26,266 — the highest in the Caribbean after the US Virgin Islands but only 47% of Mississippi's, the nation's poorest state.

Yet, Puerto Rico's economy is troubled. Now economically interdependent with the US, the entire economic structure has undergone a thorough transformation since the US invasion in 1898. At that time Puerto Rico was a subsistence-level agricultural society largely dependent upon crops like sugar, coffee, and tobacco. While these are still of some importance to the economy, the overriding emphasis today is on manufacturing (which pays the highest wages: $10.48 ph on the average), with tourism coming second. In 1999, consumer debt was $15.8 billion.

AMERICAN INVOLVEMENT: The history of the Puerto Rican economy is the story of the US economic presence in Latin America rendered in microcosm. After cession by

Spain, the US financial barons deemed the Puerto Rican coffee crop, once the major generator of income, unprofitable. Devastated by the 1899 hurricane, coffee farmers were refused a loan by the Executive Council set up by the Americans to rule the island. As a consequence, the coffee economy was soon supplanted by sugar, and American companies were quick to establish themselves.

By 1930, 60% of the banking and 80% of the tobacco industry were under the control of American interests, and by 1935, nearly 50% of all lands operated by sugar companies were under the control of four big American concerns. Although a law had limited farms to 500 acres, these giants had an average of 40,000 acres each under their control! This trend has continued to the point where the small cane farmer has virtually disappeared, replaced by the large sugar corporations like those of the Serrallés family empire. The 1930's depression period hit Puerto Rico extremely hard and resulted in the decline of the sugar, needlework, and tobacco industries.

At the end of WWII, fewer than 10% of Puerto Rico's workers held industrial jobs. In order to modernize the island and spur the sluggish economy, Fomento, the Economic Development Administration, was set up to attract industry. The island's 1950 hourly wage of 40¢ was more attractive to employers than the $1.50 average wage stateside. A high rate of unemployment reduced the prospects for potential strikes.

Recent Events

OPERATION BOOTSTRAP: By offering 10-30 year tax exemptions and low wages, this program managed to lure 2,000 manufacturing plants to the island. Nearly 400 of these were operated by "Fortune 1,000" corporations. Needless to say, these companies are not here for altruistic reasons: they

INTRODUCTION

are here because, despite high power and shipping costs, tax incentives make the island a paradise for profitable investment.

Under Section 936 of the IRS Code (abolished in 1996), American companies paid no federal taxes on profits earned in Puerto Rico. After Congress acted in 1982 (and again in 1994) to slightly modify this section, US companies still earned billion-dollar profits.

The Treasury Department charged that the law has become a boondoggle, because it allows firms to reap huge profits while creating only a minimal amount of employment. Through a system known as "transfer pricing," corporations paid an inflated price for products purchased from their Puerto Rican subsidiary, thus reducing their US profits on paper and their taxable income along with it. The Treasury estimated that 50% of the tax-exempt income in Puerto Rico in 1980 was generated by this and other nefarious means such as transferring ownership of patents and trademarks to the island.

On August 20, 1996, the U.S. Congress repealed Section 936 of the U.S. Internal Revenue Code, with a clause that retains its benefit for ten years of existing corporations. Section 30A was created to substitute Section 936. Section 30A retains the essentials of the wage credit component of Section 936.

The current government is trying to revise other US tax sections (901, 956, etc.) to re-offer exemptions for Puerto Rico. in order to continue the Operation Bootstrap Model. Section 956 would be amended in order to exclude select "Qualified Corporations" out of 90% of US taxes. Companies might elect to deduct their dividends from their federal taxes. This is similar to the provisions currently made for Controlled Foreign Corporations.

THE CARIBBEAN BASIN INITIATIVE: Popularly known as CBI, this 1983 Reagan administration scheme allows any firm with a Puerto Rican plant to open a support facility in an eligible Caribbean nation and receive tax breaks. Because wages in these unionless countries are abysmally low and exploitive (50-70¢ ph), businesses can reap added profits.

Economic Sectors

MANUFACTURING: Tax exemptions and other advantages have lured 24 pharmaceutical companies to the island; Puerto Rico produces some 7% of the world's total supply of pharmaceuticals, and *all* of America's birth control pills. Tax incentives provided by Section 936 have lured these firms to the island. Although 936 has been phased out, proposed changes to Section 956 may reinstate these incentives in 2005. Besides savings on taxes, companies also avoid safety inspections: Puerto Rican men working in the birth control pill factories have begun to grow breasts after handling estrogen, some have had radical mastectomies, and others have become impotent. In the States, this would cause an outrage, but in Puerto Rico it has passed almost unnoticed.

At this point, the industry accounts for some 21,000 direct jobs or 14% of all employment in manufacturing. Its exports and imports exceeded $9.2 billion in fiscal 1992 or nearly a third of the total for trade. Manufacturing accounts for some 17% of total employment and generates 38.7% of the GNP and some $180 million in tax revenues, in addition to providing jobs in the construction, trade, and service industries. More than one-third of all manufacturing jobs are still in apparel and textiles. Many of these goods are destined for the US; the shoe industry ships 20 million pairs stateside each year.

The island is also the world's largest producer of rum. Excise taxes on each case of rum sold in the US are rebated to Puerto Rico's Treasury. However, more than half of the molasses used in its manufacture and most of the rum is exported in bulk and bottled on the mainland in order to keep down costs. To produce all of these goods, Puerto Rico uses incredible amounts of electricity, most of it generated by imported oil, making the island more dependent on foreign oil than any of the 50 states.

TOURISM: A growing sector, the tourism "industry" continues to increase its influence on the economy. Despite the tragic fire at the Dupont Plaza Hotel in Condado that claimed 96 lives on Dec. 31, 1986, hotel occupancy rates have continued to rise.

In fiscal 1991, tourism expenditures reached $1.4 billion, topping one billion for the third consecutive year. Tourism contributed approximately 6% of the gross domestic product and provided direct and indirect employment for some 60,000. Since 1985, more than $500 million has been invested, and total visitation has risen by more than 60%, with an 11.3% increase in cruise ship passengers and a 40% increase in daily flights. Hotel capacity has risen to more than 12,000 rooms. Wages in the hotel industry average around $7.50 ph.

MINING: Although the original impetus for Spanish conquest of the island was gold, mining is no longer a major industry. Even though rich copper deposits have been discovered in the Lares-Utuado-Adjuntas area in the heart of the Cordillera Central, a drop in the world copper price, coupled with the determined opposition of environmentalists and *independentistas*, kept the multinationals at bay. The area has been declared a community and environmental reserve.

Alexis Massol and Casa Pueblo

During the 1980s and 1990s, the Puerto Rican government granted mining permits for 37,000 acres of the Cordillera Central. In addition to destroying forests, the mining would have likely polluted the rivers (which supply drinking water to a million people).

In response to the proposed mining, Alexis Massol created Casa Pueblo, an organization which put on cultural events as a way to organize locals. Casa Pueblo was able to stave off mining in 1986 and 1983. Governor Pedro Rosselló signed legislation banning open-pit mining in 1995 and assigned control of the area's forests to Casa Pueblo in 1996, creating the first and only community-run reserve on the island. He is now pushing for it to become a UN-designated Biosphere Reserve. "A friend asked me if I live on another planet, but I seek all these things humbly," he says.

Prospects for the Future

It is unlikely that Puerto Rico's economy will improve in the near future. The sixth largest customer of US goods, Puerto Rico purchases some $4.5 billion annually in manufactured products from the States. This represents $3.5 billion in gross income for American business and workers, and employment for 200,000 Americans. This does not include, however, the profits stemming from transport of goods and people, from financial and banking transactions, and from insurance and advertising. Billions in federal funds are sent to Puerto Rico each year, in the form of personal transfers (such as food stamps and Medicare), and the rest for functions such as immigration, customs, and the military, the island's single largest employer.

Indeed, the relationship between Puerto Rico and the US resembles the proverbial one between the worker and the company store. Instead of company bills of promise, the Puerto Ricans shop with *cupones*. Some $100 million in food stamps (now distributed in the form of vouchers by the Nutrition Assistance Programs) reach around 53% of the populace and comprise some 10% of the total distributed nationwide. Although Puerto Ricans pay more for food and the cost of living in general is higher, federal subsidies make life comfortable. Rather than having the Puerto Ricans themselves pay for these subsidies or taxing the companies who reap immense profits, the American taxpayer is forced to foot the bill!

Currently, unemployment continues to rise. While the official figure hovers around 17%, unofficial estimates are higher. Teenage unemployment has soared to 60% (although a number are now employed in the crack trade). Including the men who have given up looking for work, the *ociosos voluntarios* (voluntary idle), there are more than 300,000 unemployed. As Puerto Rico cannot compete with Mexico or the Dominican Republic in terms of low wages, the island's future depends upon skilled labor.

Agriculture

Like the economy in general, the agricultural situation in Puerto Rico has been in constant flux since the US occupation in 1898. Sugarcane, once the backbone of the economy and still a major crop, has become an economic drain. The government buys most of the crop and operates its own sugar mills but, even with subsidies, the $5.15 minimum wage dictates that the cost cannot compete with neighboring nations like the Dominican Republic, where labor (imported from Haiti) is $2.50 pd. The government loses money on every pound of sugar, and this industry is little more than a costly, outmoded public employment program. Devastated by the 1899 and 1928 hurri-

canes, coffee production is now down to 30 million pounds per year and is raised by 13,000 farmers. Once another flourishing crop, tobacco's production levels continue to decline, and the largest processing plant shut its doors in 1977.

The government neglect of agriculture in favor of industry since WWII has served to guarantee that local products are ignored in favor of expensive imports from the States. The percentage of farmers in the workforce has plummeted from 35% to 5%, and 80% of all food is imported. Imported canned vegetables are favored over local produce, and citrus fruit is flown in from California and Florida while local fruit rots on the trees. Other imports include such staples as frozen meat, butter, eggs, and pinto beans

To its credit, the government is trying to reverse this trend by offering tax and other incentives to spur production. Locally grown rice is now being marketed by the government under the name *Arroz D'Aqui* ("rice from here"). In spite of these measures, it will be decades, if ever, before the island can feed itself.

Vanilla

Puerto Rico is the Caribbean's main producer and exporter of vanilla (*Vanilla plantifolia*). The vine grows in lowland tropical forests and, in the wild, grows up the trunk of trees up to a height of 30 ft. (9 m). The long, thin, pod-like fruit is picked unripe and then steamed or boiled and fermented for around a month. Vanilla was first processed by the indigenous peoples of the Caribbean and Mexico. The pods are put out in the sun to dry each day and then put in airtight containers at night, a process which renders them dark brown.

The People

Caribbean culture is truly creole culture. The word "creole" comes from *criar* (Spanish for "to bring up" or "rear"). In the New World, this term came to refer to children born in this hemisphere, implying that they were not quite authentic or pure. Later, creole came to connote "mixed blood," but not just blood has been mixed here — cultures have been jumbled as well. Because of this extreme mixture, the Caribbean is a cultural goldmine. The culture of a specific island or nation depends upon its racial mix and historical circumstances. Brought over on slave ships where differences of status were lost and cultural institutions shattered, the slaves had to begin entirely anew. In a similar fashion, but not nearly to so severe a degree, the European, indentured or otherwise, could not bring all of Europe with him. Beliefs were merged in a new synthesis born of the interaction between different cultures — African and European. Today, a new synthesis has arisen in language, society, crafts, and religion.

The Influence of Other Cultures

TAINO INFLUENCE: Once numbering some 30,000, the Taínos (the "good ones" in the Arawak language) have long vanished. Their spirit lives on in tradition, in the feeling of dramatic sunsets, and in the wafting of the cool breeze. Remaining cultural legacies include foods (*achiote*), place names (Mayagüez, Utuado, and Humacao, to name a few), words (such as "hammock" — an Indian invention), and native medicines still in use. Even the Indian name for the island, Borínquen, is still popular, and *La Borínqueña* is the national anthem. Many Spanish towns were built on old Indian sites; the *bateyes* of the Native Americans became the plazas of the Spanish. There are numerous archaeological sites, most notably those at Utuado and Tibes, and Old San Juan has a museum devoted to the island's Indians. Jayuya has an annual Indian Festival and an outlying museum.

AFRICAN INFLUENCE: This was the strongest of all outside influences on Caribbean islands with large black populations. Arriving slaves had been torn away from both tribe and culture, and this is reflected in everything from the primitive agricultural system to the African influence on religious sects and cults, mirroring the dynamic diversity of West African culture.

Puerto Rico was a special case in that there were never a large number of slaves imported, and all escaped slaves from other islands who landed on its shores were granted freedom. However, the island still reflects a strong African influence that shows up in religion, music, language, crafts, food, and other areas.

SPANISH INFLUENCE: Spain was the original intruder in the area. The Spaniards exited Puerto Rico in 1898, following 400 years of influence, and the island's culture is still predominantly Spanish, as are neighboring Cuba and the Dominican Republic. Most Caribbean islands, whether the Spaniards ever settled there or not, still bear the names Columbus bestowed on them 500 years ago. Although other European influences have had a powerful effect, Spanish continues to be the predominant language in the islands once controlled by Spain. Major Spanish architectural sites

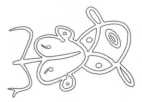

Taíno petroglyph depicting a river shrimp

remain in the old parts of San Juan and in Santo Domingo, the capital of the Dominican Republic.

AMERICAN INFLUENCE: The history of the US is inextricably linked with the Caribbean in general and Puerto Rico in particular. American influence in Puerto Rico predates American occupation. Television (especially cable), the proliferation of malls, and fast food continue to have their effect, as have the migration and return of Puerto Ricans to the mainland.

The Puerto Ricans

SOCIAL VALUES: No single description fits all Puerto Ricans; there are too many kinds of people for one mold to apply. And the impact of American colonialism, coupled as it has been with transmigration from the States, has had an immense effect. Social values are undergoing a rapid transformation as the economic base switches from agriculture to industry and manufacturing.

COMPADRAZGO: Literally "co-parentage," this important practice of social bonding resembles the system of godparents found in the States, but is much more solemn. Selected when a child is baptized, *compadres* and *comadres* can be counted on to help out financially in a pinch. A poor farmer may seek out a rich employer to be his child's *compadre.* The employer will assent because he knows that this will tighten the bonds between himself and his employee. Or such a relationship may be sought merely to cement a close friendship between males.

Like so many of the neighboring islands, Puerto Rico has forged a distinctive racial and cultural mix. The original inhabitants of the island, the Taíno, were forced into slavery. Some escaped into the mountains, where they intermarried with the local Spanish immigrant subsistence farmers as

Circular Migration

A major cultural influence on Puerto Rico has been the continual migration to, and return from, the mainland US. For more than four decades 1.5 million Puerto Ricans have migrated to the States annually and a similar number have returned.

The phenomenon began in 1900 when more than 5,300 Puerto Ricans emigrated to Hawaii between 1900 and 1901. They labored on the sugarcane plantations under horrific conditions. Although some migrated to the States during WWI to work, the numbers were comparatively small. Between 1947-1960, some 550,000 Puerto Ricans (or 25% of the population) migrated. There were a number of reasons for the migration. Operation Bootstrap resulted in farmers losing agricultural land. Puerto Ricans were actively recruited by US companies who sought out low-wage help. And the Puerto Rican government had required the FAA to set low airfares between the island and the mainland.

well as with the Africans. The offspring from those unions, the *jíbaro,* the barefoot-but-proud peasant, have come to be regarded as a symbol of the island. The name comes from the *Jivaro,* a fiercely independent tribe of Amazonian Indians whom the Spanish also called *Jíbaro.* And *jibaros* truly lived a highly individualistic and rugged existence. Residing in *bohíos* (thatch huts), they were virtually self-sufficient and skilled in the production of crafts. With the urbanization and industrialization, which have marked the 20th century, the *jíbaros* have dwindled in number, to emerge as a folk hero much like the American cowboys. Black slaves, although never arriving in the numbers that they did on surrounding islands, added another important ingredient to the racial-cultural stew. Today, some 60% of Puerto Ricans have some African blood.

But Puerto Rico's complex cultural blend doesn't stop there. French families arrived from Haiti and Louisiana in the late 18th and 19th centuries. Loyalist Spaniards and Venezuelans sought refuge here from newly independent Latin American republics. A flourishing sugar economy attracted Scottish and Irish farmers. After abolition, farmers and laborers emigrated from Spain's NW province of Galicia and the Canary Islands. Chinese coolies were imported in the 1840s to help build roads, and numbers of Italians, Corsicans, Germans, and Lebanese also arrived. American expatriates founded an Episcopal church in Ponce in 1873, and many more arrived after the American annexation in 1898. Cubans fleeing Castro arrived in the 1960s, as did Dominicans following the 1965 upheavals. Both of these have had a powerful influence: the Cubans on top of the social stratum, the Dominicans further down (with the most recently arrived Dominicans on the very bottom). All of the diverse ethnic groups, intermarrying and multiplying, have helped forge modern Puerto Rican culture.

Currently, some 9% of the population were not born on the island, and Dominicans continue to mount rickety *yolas* (small boats) and risk drowning and shark attacks to cross the dangerous Mona Passage. Paying up to $500 each, the smuggling has proved a popular and profitable business: there are an estimated 100,000-300,000 Dominicans on hand at any one time! Soon after arrival, they pick up a stolen or forged birth certificate and learn to talk like Puerto Ricans. Then, it's a simple matter to migrate to the States.

POPULATION: With 3.8 million people, Puerto Rico is one of the most crowded islands in the world. Its population density of over 1,110 persons per square mile is

---

All About Chupacabras

The chupacabra ("goat sucker") is a mythical beast which some believe to be systematically slaughtering animals in places such as Puerto Rico and Mexico. Its legend originated following the discovery of some dead goats in Puerto Rico which were alleged to have puncture wounds in their necks and their blood drained. *UFO Magazine,* in its March/April 1996 issue, claimed that there were more than 2,000 reported cases of animal mutilations in Puerto Rico, during the two previous years said to have been attributed to the chupacabra.

Hector Garcia, the director of Puerto Rico's Department of Agriculture Veterinary Services Division, maintains that the animals were killed by dogs.

The chupacabra is described as a bipedal creature, around four to five feet tall, which is a cross between a greyish humanoid alien (because the shape of its head and its bulging eyes) and some sort of dinosaur. The creature has two small arms, and three-fingered clawed hands and legs, Spinelike quills run down its back and are believed to enable it to fly. Needless to say, there are many other versions. Should you see one, let us know!

---

higher than in any of the 50 States. If the mainland United States were to be as densely populated, it would have some four billion people! And still another two million Puerto Ricans live within the continental United States. In fact, more Puerto Ricans reside in New York City than in San Juan. Most of them have been compelled to migrate by economic necessity; in recent years, however, declining economic opportunities in the States have reversed the trend and many have returned.

INTRODUCTION

Arturo Alfonso Schomburg

Arthur A. Schomburg was born in San Juan in 1874 as Arturo Alfonso Schomburg. Moving to NYC in 1891, he became involved in many Puerto Rican and Cuban nationalist and cultural organizations.

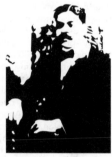

Schomburg's passion was to show the world how Africans and people of African descent had shaped world history. His mission was to make sure that it was known that the African descendants were capable people who had even surpassed Europeans achievements in some realms of endeavor. He also wished to infuse the Black community with racial pride.

Legend has it that this passion was aroused in a young Schomburg when a San Juan schoolteacher told him that Blacks had accomplished "nothing." The story is likely apocryphal, given that the few schools in San Juan at the time did not admit Blacks.

A prominent writer and educator founded the Negro Society for Historical Research in 1911, Schomburg was president of the American Negro Academy from 1920 to 1929, and he chronicled the Black history and culture of Harlem. In 1926, the New York Public Library purchased his collections of books and manuscripts, and he served as curator of the collection from 1932 until his death in 1938.

Today the Schomburg Center for Research in Black Culture, at 135th Street and Lenox Avenue in Harlem in New York City, houses more than 150,000 volumes of black history, and some five million artifacts, photographs, magazines, and manuscripts.

RACIAL ATTITUDES: As in all of the Caribbean islands, racial prejudice is part of a lingering colonial legacy. Although most Puerto Ricans have at least a pinch of *negrito* blood running through their veins, it is not socially desirable to admit it; the undesirability of being black stems from the fact that the blacks were once slaves. While the apartheid system of the American South never took root here, and Puerto Ricans do not believe in a biological inferiority of blacks, blacks are nevertheless stereotyped as being lower class and it is difficult for them to rise within the society.

Traditionally, upper and middle-class islanders have been the most concerned about *limpieza de sangre* (purity of blood). In the past, trials to prove purity of blood were conducted before an upper-class couple could marry. Today, although prejudice remains, it has been moderated over time: an upper-class man, for example, may marry a mulatto woman without much censure, but she may never be fully accepted by the wives of his associates. Factors such as economic position and social standing now tend to override racial considerations. Still, the darker child in a family may win less praise from his parents and be more likely to be teased by his brothers and sisters.

Interestingly enough, the term *negrito*, as used in society, is a term of endearment, implying a sense of community or communal belonging, while *blanquito* ("little white") usually implies the opposite. The latter term has historical roots: *Peninsulares*, islanders born in Spain, held a higher rank than *criollos*, Spaniards born on the island. Today, this term is still used in reference to the elite. The vast majority of Puerto Ricans today are neither black nor white, but *trigueno*, tan or swarthy in color.

 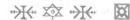

The **Global Campus Study Abroad Program** of the University of Minnesota (☎ 612-626-9000, ℮ 612-626-8009) offers Spanish-language study programs at Puerto Rican universities. (Other universities also offer such programs). **UMabroad@umn.edu**

Language

Spanish is the norm throughout the island. Although many Puerto Ricans can speak English, the more Spanish the visitor can speak, the better: outsiders who can speak Spanish are more readily accepted by locals.

Puerto Rico's Spanish is laden with borrowed English (*el coat* for example), local idioms, and numerous Taíno (yuca, iguana) and African words (*bembé, guarapo*).

An important element in Puerto Rican Spanish is the influence from the Jíbaro, farmers who were a mixture of Black, white, and mestizo. Their *criollo* (creole) speech has shaped Puerto Rican Spanish.

When speaking with Puerto Ricans, keep in mind that the "*tu*" form of address connotes a high degree of familiarity; don't jump from the more formal "*usted*" until the relationship warrants it. "S" sounds are muted and may even disappear at the end of syllables (as in *graciah* instead of *gracias* and *loh* instead of *los*). The "*ll*" and "*y*" sounds are pronounced like the English "js." Spanish words which end in *ado* (such as *pescado*) are generally pronounced as if the *d* is silent. And the terminal "e" sound is often truncated (as in *noch* instead of *noche*).

Puerto Rican Slang	
Abombao — bad smell	
Amogollao — poorly-cooked rice	
Afrentao — greedy	
Asopao — thick stew with chicken/rice	
Aguajero — person who only promises	
Averiguao — inquisitive person	
Bembe — party	
Bochinche — gossip	
Caserio — public housing project	
Chévere — cool, fantastic.	
Corillo — a group of friends	
Emborujo — a mess.	
Enfogonao — very angry	
Embrollao — deeply in debt	
Esmayao — extremely hungry	
Enchulao — blindly in love	
Janguear — to hang out with friends	
Jamona — spinster	
Jaleo — severe nausea	
Limber — a cube of solid flavored ice	
Monga — nasty flu or cold	
Pana — special friend, a buddy	
Pon — to hitchhike.	
Pata — lesbian	
Pato — male homosexual	
Revolú, Pujilato — a big mess, problem	
Tocallo — someone with same first name	
Tostao — crazy	
Uepa — celebration	
Vacilón — to have a good time	

Religion

Catholicism & Protestantism

CATHOLICISM: Although Puerto Rico is predominantly Catholic, its brand is a far cry from the dogmatic religion practiced in Italy. Distance, combined with the elitist attitudes of the all-Spanish clergy who chose to support slavery and exclude locals from the priesthood, have altered the religion here. Puerto Ricans have selected the rules and regulations they wish to follow while conveniently ignoring the rest. To them, being a good Catholic does not mean being dogmatic. Many strict Catholic couples, for example, have civil or consensual marriages and practice birth control.

PROTESTANTISM: Many other sects have proliferated here as well. Chief among these is Protestantism. Although the religion had reached the island prior to 1898, the US invasion spurred a rapid increase in its popularity. Facilitated by the separation of church and state decreed in the US Constitution, its emphasis on the importance of the individual, so much more in keeping with present-day society than the Catholic emphasis upon dogmatic ritual, won it many new converts. Also, because it provides the rural and urban poor a sense of emotional security in the face of a rapidly changing world, evangelical fundamentalism has gained in popularity. Presently, some 1,500 evangelical churches dot the island, and missionaries are sent to Europe and Africa to propagate the faith.

Spiritualism

As in other Latin areas, Catholicism has been lightly seasoned with a mixture of African and native Indian traditions. For example, the African influence on the costumes and statues in Loíza Aldea's patron saint festival is unmistakable, as is the dark-colored flesh of the Virgin of Monserrate. Some go so far as to claim that spiritualism (*espiritismo*) is the real religion of Puerto Rico. Illegal under Spanish rule, spiritualism surfaced only in this century. Some middle-class Catholics, while remaining formally within the confines of Catholicism, practice spiritualism at home. Few Protestants, on the other hand, are spiritualists because the stress on application of day-to-day ethical choices inherent in Protestantism runs counter to the spiritualist belief that one's fate is affected by

outside influences or by acts committed in a past existence.

Spiritualism is steeped in native Indian religion and folklore. The Taínos believed that *jipia* (spirits of the dead) slept by day and roamed the island by night, eating wild fruit and visiting relatives. Food was always left on the table because easily insulted *jipia* might haunt one's dreams at night if left unfed. Although many no longer know where the belief comes from, plastic fruit is still left atop refrigerators to appease hungry *jipia*.

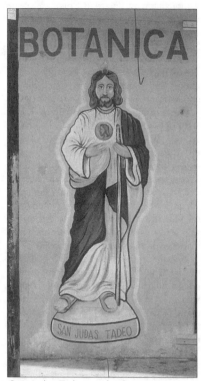

San Judas Tadeo marks the entrance to a botanica, a shop which sells items used in the practice of spiritualism.

Folk beliefs continue among some country folk. Some still believe in the **mal de ojo** or "evil eye." Although its possessor may be unaware of its power, one covetous glance upon a child, adult, or animal is believed to cause sickness or even death. Children have been traditionally protected by a bead-charm bracelet.

Spiritualism is also closely connected with folk medicine and healing. You should not mix "cold" things with "hot," or touch "cold" things when you are "hot." Otherwise you risk suffering *empache* or *espasmo*, stomach cramps or muscular disturbances. "Cold" food, banana or pork for example, must never be mixed with hot food like red meat or manioc. Never wash clothes in a "cold" area while you are "hot," and avoid taking a cold bath after getting heated up through physical exercise. *Botanicas*, the supermarkets of spiritualism, sell plants, herbs, oils, rubbing water, and spiritualist literature.

SANTOS CULTS: Another complement to Catholicism is the half-magical cult of the saints or *santos*. Most households have an image of one or two of these (see "Arts and Crafts"), usually St. Anthony and one of the Virgins. These are grouped together with the family crucifix and designated as the "Holy Family." Saints are selected in accordance with one's needs, and reciprocation is mandatory if devotions are to continue.

The relation between saint and worshipper is one of **promesa** (promise or obligation); promises are made by the devotee and carried out if wishes are granted by the saint. Certain goods are offered to the saint, who is expected to reciprocate by providing prosperity and good fortune. Gamblers and drinkers offer up dice, cards, pennies, small glasses of rum, lottery numbers, and pictures of beautiful women to their patron San Expedito. If the saint does not respond, the icon may be beaten and kicked out of the house.

Rituals of devotion, termed *rosarios*, are held to obtain relief from sickness or give thanks for recovery after an illness. Traditional events involving mass participation, such as the Rosario de la Cruz (see "events" under "Bayamón") and the **rogativa** or candlelight procession, are on the wane, as are *veladas*, or pre-funeral wakes in which neighbors gather at the home of a dying community member to render assistance in case of need.

Arts & Crafts

Puerto Rico's art reflects its cultural diversity. With a growing coterie of young, dynamic artists, the island also has an indigenous crafts tradition with roots in European, African, and Taíno traditions. The best places to see art (and antiques) are in San Juan's numerous art galleries.

The **Antiguo Convento del los Dominicanos,** C. Norzagaray 98 in Old San Juan on Plaza San José, houses **Libreria y Tienda de Artesanías** (☎ 787-721-6866), a superb craft and book shop (mostly Spanish-language title) which is open Mon. to Sat. 9 AM–5 PM. It's run by the Institute for Puerto Rican Culture.

Other shops are located inside Sixto Escobar Stadium near the Caribe Hilton and inside Plazoleta de la Puerta across from Terminal Turismo in Old San Juan.

Crafts are sold every weekend along Callejón de la Capilla in Old San Juan as well as in El Centro market inside Condado Convention Center. Annual crafts fairs are held on the grounds of the Bacardi Rum Plant, Cataño, San Juan, and in Barranquitas.

By far the best way to see local crafts, however, is by checking out the island craftspeople in their workshops. Hammock-making is centered in and

INTRODUCTION

around San Sebastian. Hats are made in Moca.

Other Puerto Rican crafts include ceramics, masks, musical instruments, wooden replicas of birds and flowers, and macramé. Two of the most important craft traditions, santos and mundillo, are described below.

SANTOS: Among the oldest and certainly the most impressive of Puerto Rican traditional crafts are **santos**, eight- to 20-inch-tall figurines representing saints, carved of capa or cedar wood, stone, clay, or gold. While the oldest date back to the 16th century, the santero's craft is a continuation of the indigenous Indian tradition in which small statues (cemi) were placed in every home and village as objects of veneration. Thus, the carving of santos seems to be linked to the pre-Columbian era. Just as every town had its patron saint, so every home had its santos who would offer protection. And just as some people substitute a TV service for a visit to church, so Puerto Ricans substitute santos worship for the traditional Mass.

Santeros, skilled carpenters using handmade tools, carved the statues out of wood, using natural dyes and sometimes even human hair to decorate them. Natural dyes were subsequently replaced by oils; the initial full-figure design was later joined by carvings of busts and group figures. Saints most commonly represented include the various Virgins (Pilar, Monserrate, Carmen, etc.) and the male saints (Jose, Rafael, Peter the Apostle, etc.).

Accompanying symbols render them easily identifiable. Just as Rafael carries his spear and fish trademark, so the Virgin of Monserrate holds the baby Jesus on her lap, and Saint Anthony is always shown with the infant Jesus and a book. Most

Santo statue in Porta Coeli in San German

popularly represented of the group figures are the Three Kings; others include the Nativity, the Trinity, and biblical scenes. Most remarkable of all the santos is the carving of the mano poderosa ("powerful hand"), a hand with five fingers terminating in intricately carved miniature images of various saints.

Although santos-making reached its artistic peak around the turn of the 20th century, santeros still practice their art at various locations all over the island. The best collections of antique santos may be seen in Old San Juan. The santos possess a singularly attractive and simple solemnity which remains as freshly inspiring today as the day they were carved. Unfortunately, it's difficult to find santos of similar quality being carved today and, new or antique, they are expensive.

MUNDILLO: A Spanish import, this type of lacemaking derives its name from the wooden box mundillo frame on which it is worked. It is also known as bobbin lace or pillow lace because its threads are wound on bobbins, and its patterns are anchored to pillows. Today, this technique of bobbin lacemaking, which has a 500-year tradition, can be found only in Spain and in Puerto Rico.

Torchon, or beggar's lace, was the technique first introduced and the one which still predominates today. Originally poorly made and of low quality, it has evolved into a highly intricate and delicate art form. The two traditional styles of lace bands are entredos, which have two straight borders, and puntilla. which have a straight and scalloped border. Although the craft once seemed destined to disappear from the island, today it is undergoing a revival.

One place to see mundillo is at the **Puerto Rico Weaving Festival** held annually at the

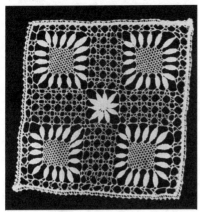

Mundillo lacemaking is a Spanish import.

end of April in Isabela (☎ 787-872-6400). Moca also has shops which sell *mundillo*.

ART AND ARTISTS: Expanding quickly after a belated start, Puerto Rican art has grown to include a wide range of artistic media, including mural art, innovative ceramics, and poster art. The story of Puerto Rican art begins with painter José Campeche (1751-1809); indeed, painting on the island can hardly be said to have existed before him. His works, which deal exclusively with religious themes, are easily identified through their characteristic style. A self-trained artist who mixed his own pigments, Campeche is today recognized as one of the great artists of the Americas.

The next painter to hit the big time was **Francesco Oller** (1833-1917). Studying art in France and Spain, he returned to the island to create many masterpieces. Known as the first Latin American impressionist, this contemporary of Pissarro and Cézanne was commissioned by King Alfonso of Spain to be Court Painter for six years. A museum in Bayamón now shows his work.

An artistic renaissance took place during the 1950s when many artists returned to the island after studying in the States. During this period, poster art emerged as an important medium of artistic expression. Another art form which has gained popularity in recent years is the mural. Mural art, which draws on everything from complex Taíno symbology to religious themes, decorates the sides of buildings of all sizes and shapes. Modern Puerto Rican artists of note include Francisco Rodón, Carlos Irizarry, Carlos Osorio, Rafael Turfino, Lorenzo Homar, Carlos Raquel Riviera, and Julio Rosado del Valle.

Music & Dance

Although many legacies of European, African, and Taíno traditions survive in Puerto Rico, none are as expressive of cultural feeling or as illustrative of intercultural blending as music and dance. The story of Puerto Rican music begins with the Taínos. At least one instrument, the *guiro* or *guicharo*, a hollow, notched, bottle-shaped gourd played with a wire fork, has been handed down by the Taínos; musicologists speculate that the *areytos* (Indian dance tunes) have also influenced the development of Puerto Rican music. Spanish influence is also evident in the design of musical instruments. Puerto Ricans have transformed the six-string Spanish guitar into four different instruments: the *tiple*, *cuatro*, *bordonua*, and *requinto*, which differ in shape, pitch, and number of strings.

> **Nóches de Galerías** are held in Old San Juan from 6–9 PM during the first Tues. of the month from Feb. to May and from Sept. to Dec. This is a great chance to mingle with locals and check out the art world.

The 10-string *cuatro*, so named because it is tuned in fourths, is the most popular instrument today. Other instruments include the *maracas*, round gourds filled with small beans or pebbles, and the *tambor*, a hollowed tree trunk with an animal skin stretched on top. Bands of troubadours once traveled from town to town like European wandering minstrels.

cuatro

FOLK MUSIC: Varied and multifarious. The *seis* is probably the liveliest and most popular of all Puerto Rican music. Originally limited to six couplets, its more than 40 versions, composed of eight-syllable lines, range from contemporary to century-old standards. While some are representative of particular areas (*seis Bayamones* from Bayamón, for example), others are representative of the way the music is danced. Their names may derive from the area or region where the dance originated, the style of dance, or the composers or most famous performers. A story set to song, the *decima* may carry a deep message. *Decimas* are strictly metered into 10-line stanzas controlled by eight-syllable lines and alternating rhyme structure.

Another of the more popular forms of Puerto Rican music is the *danza*. Created in the 1850s, its refined, classical score resembles a minuet; the *danza* is a uniquely Puerto Rican musical interpretation of this Spanish Caribbean form. Juan-Morel Campos, known as the father of the *danza*, is the best-known early composer. Unlike the Cuban *contradanzas* (the model for the Puerto Rican danzas), his compositions have a Chopinesque feel to them.

The most famous composer of popular music is Rafael Hernández, who died in 1966. Known for such hits as "El

---

Lamento Borincano

*L*amentos have been called the protest songs of the Spanish colonial era. But they are not angry but sad, addressing their sorrows to God or some listener. The Spanish expression *llori-cantar* ("to sob and sing") is illustrative of this type of ballad which expresses the woes of oppression, discrimination and slavery.

Lamento Borincano is perhaps the most famous lamento of all. It was penned by Rafael Hernández, born in 1891 to a poor Black family in Aguadilla. He wrote the tune while living in NYC's Spanish Harlem in 1929, and it was first recorded by Canario (sung by Davilita) in 1930. Hernández encapsulated his childhood experiences through the life of a *jibaro* who sets out with his mare to sell his produce in the market. Thwarted from selling his wares because no one can afford them, he returns home. "What will become of Borinquen. my dear God? What will happen to my children and my home?," he sings.

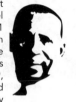

The best introduction to *Lamento Borincano* is the superb two-CD set **Lamento Borincano**, offered by Arhoolie. It's an excellent production which includes a 55-page booklet with photos, lyrics, and notes.

Cumbanchero" and "Lamento Borincano," Hernández is idolized on the island.

BOMBA Y PLENA: These two most famous types of music coupled with dance are usually grouped together, although in reality they are totally different forms. While the *plena* possesses the elegance and coquetry of the Spanish tradition, the *bomba* has the beat of Africa. Though the origin of both the *bomba* and the *plena* is uncertain, some maintain that their

Puerto Rico is a good place to stock up on CDs — especially if your taste runs towards Latin music. In addition to local stores, Spec's, a Miami-based chain, has opened up in a number of locations islandwide. Cuban salsa bands, whose releases may be hard to find elsewhere, are well represented. While you won't find CDs or cassettes any cheaper (and used CD stores are scarce), you will save because there is no sales tax.

arrangements were influenced by the Taíno *areytos* (epic songs danced to by the Native Americans); certainly both are a mixture of European and African influences — although African elements predominate in the *bomba*. Some say that the *plena* was brought to the island by a couple from St. Kitts. Historians do agree, however, that the *plena* first emerged in Ponce.

Once an important social event, the *bomba* provided the working people the only available relief from the monotonous drudgery of everyday life. Usually on Saturday or Sunday nights or on special occasions and festivities, the dance was performed in a circle. The soloist stood next to the drums, and the chorus stood behind the singer. While the soloist sang, the chorus provided the harmonies. The dancer, entering in front of the drums, performed the *piquete* (coquettish dance) before saluting the drums and exiting. The *bomba* is really a dialogue between drummer and dancer. The first drummer (*repicador*) challenges the dancer to a duel while the second drummer maintains the basic rhythmic pattern. The dance lasts as long as the dancer can successfully challenge the drummer. Unlike similar dances found elsewhere, the drummer follows the dancer rather than vice-versa.

The different rhythms of the *bomba* (the *Cunya, Yuba, Cuende, Sica, Cocobale, Danua, Holande*, etc.) represent the diverse ethnic roots of the dance. While the first five are African names, the latter two represent adaptations of Danish and Dutch styles learned from arriving immigrants. Another style, *Lero*, is an adaptation of the French circle dance, *le rose*. Today, the bomba is performed only in lower-class black communities, and most Puerto Ricans have no contact with it.

CLASSICAL MUSIC: Interest in classical music has grown over the years in Puerto Rico, and the island has its own symphony orchestra and conservatory. A great inspiration was cellist and conductor **Pablo Casals**, who retired at age 81 to the island, his mother's birthplace, to spend his last years there. Each year, generally in June, the month-long **Casals Festival** draws artists from all over the world to perform his music. Be sure to visit the museum in Old San Juan which highlights his life.

The most notable native classical musician was master pianist **Jesus Maria Sanroma** (1902-1984), who toured and recorded

Merengue and Murder

The Commonwealth's police chief Pedro Toledo alleged that the NYC-produced "El Venao," a merengue tune about an unfaithful wife shot by her husband, is responsible for a rash of shootings on the island. Composer Ramon Orlando, a fervent evangelical Christian who answers his phone with the phrase "Christ Loves You," insists that the lyrics are simply a complaint about infidelity. The word *venao* is a contraction of *venado* ("deer" or "venison") and is a label used to describe naive adulterers. Although the song became one of the island's top hits for 1995, members of the religious right asked stations to remove it from their playlist. Thankfully, most stations refused to heed the call.

Puerto Rican Festivals and Events

Jan. 1	New Year's Day
Jan. 6	Epiphany or Three Kings Day; traditional day of gift-giving
Jan. 11	Birthday of Eugenio De Hostos, Puerto Rican educator, writer, and patriot (half-day)
Jan. 15	Martin Luther King Day (half day)
Jan.	San Sebastian Street Fiesta in Old San Juan. Crafts, shows, arts, games, processions,dancing, and *paso fino* horses on display.
Feb.	Washington's Birthday (half-day, movable)
March 22	Emancipation Day
April	Good Friday (movable)
April 16	José de Diego's Birthday
May	Memorial Day (movable)
June 24	St. John the Baptist Day
July 4	Independence Day
July 17	Luiz Muñoz Rivera's Birthday
July 25	Commonwealth Constitution Day
July 27	Dr. José Celso Barbosa's Birth
Sept.	Labor Day (movable)
Oct.	Columbus Day (movable)
Nov. 11	Veteran's Day
Nov. 19	Puerto Rico Discovery Day
Nov.	Thanksgiving (movable)
Dec. 25	Christmas Day

 Putumayo Records has an excellent series of world music compilations. Their **Puerto Rico** disk contains tunes by major salsa artists.

title of Court Singer. After earning and spending an estimated $2 million, Paoli returned home to the island in 1922, where he taught music to the island's youth. Other famous Puerto Rican opera singers include Pablo Elvira and Justino Diaz.

MODERN MUSIC: Although born and bred in New York's Caribbean melting pot, **salsa** (Spanish for "sauce") and the Dominican-originated **merengue** blare from every car stereo and boom box on the island. El Gran Combo, comprised of 13 or so members and led by pianist Rafael Ithier, who is the band's only remaining original member, is one of Puerto Rico's contributions to the *salsa* scene. They have recorded more than 60 albums. Major *salsa* figures of Puerto Rican extraction include pianists (and brothers) the late Charlie and (still alive and kicking) Eddie Palmieri, trombonist Willie Colón, percussionist Ray Barretto, and the late, great timbale wizard Tito Puente. Born in Ponce, José "Cheo" Feliciano was one of the most famous island-born *salsa* singers. Ismael Rivera is another famous Puerto Rican bandleader, composer, and percussionist. Vocalist Gilberto Santa Rosa is another homeboy made good.

Of late, upstart Neoricans such as Marc Anthony and Ricky Martin have garnered wide acclaim by mixing salsa with pop in a very successful effort to reach a wider audience. Pop singer Chayanne (the stage name of Puerto Rico-born Elmer Figueroa Maple) has recently joined their ranks. While good for the financial well being of the artists concerned, this does not mean that there has

internationally. A friend and collaborator of Casals, he promoted both symphonic music on the island and the *danza,* recording, editing, and performing the latter.

OPERA: Puerto Rico is also the birthplace of famed operatic tenor **Antonio Paoli** (1872-1946), who performed for Czar Nicholas II of Russia, Kaiser Wilhelm of Germany, and the Emperor Franz Joseph of Austria. The latter bestowed upon him the

been a growing appreciation of either the roots of salsa or the best modern performers.

Sonora Ponceña, one of Puerto Rico's oldest salsa bands, released a live album commemorating its 45th anniversary in 2000. Founded by pianist Enrique "Quique" Lucca in Ponce in the mid-1950s, the band was influenced by Cuban bands Sonora Matancera and Arsenio Rodriguez. They were one of the first bands to produce the music which has become known as "salsa."

Despite ambivalence regarding its Dominican roots, *merengue* also has quite an audience. Although there have not been any homegrown *merengue* stars in the past, this has changed and Los Sabrosos Del Merengue, Prime Tono Rosario, Elvis Creapo, and Olga Tañon are Puerto Rican merengue stars. Unfortunately, rap music is also popular here; rap singer Fransheska, the "Queen of Rap," is one of the most popular stars. Her music is styled "meren-rap," and she has recorded four albums that have stormed the charts throughout Latin America. The most popular Puerto Rican male rap star is probably Vico-C. Pop.

Festivals & Events

The Latin nature of the island really comes to the fore in its celebration of festivals and holidays. Puerto Ricans know how to relax and have a good time. Although the centuries-old custom of midday siesta is in danger of extinction, **Viernes social** or "social Friday" is still popular. Every Friday men gather to eat *lechon asado* (roast pig) and gossip and gamble at local roadside stands.

Most other celebrations, however, are in a religious vein. Many of these are famous, including those at Hormigueros and Loíza. The Festival of St. John the Baptist in San Juan on June 24 is one long night of partying. Every town on the island has its *fiestas patronales* or patron saint festival. They always begin on a Friday, approximately ten days before the date prescribed. Although services are held twice a day, the atmosphere is anything but religious. Music, gambling, and dancing take place on the town plaza, and food stalls sell local specialties. On the Sunday nearest the main date, *imagenes* or wooden images of the patron saint are carried around the town by four men or (sometimes) women. Flowers conceal supporting wires and the base is tied to the platform to prevent it from falling.

A generally somber atmosphere prevails during **Holy Week** (**Semana Santa**), the week surrounding Easter, when processions and pageants are held island-wide. **Las Navidades** or the Christmas season, which stretches from Dec. 15 to Jan. 6, is the liveliest time of the year. Marked by parties and prayers, it's a time to get together with friends. Everyone heads for **el campo** ("the country") to join in celebrating the occasion with friends and loved ones. Out in the countryside, groups of local musicians known as **trulla** roam from house to house singing **aguinaldos,** or Christmas carols.

Nacimientos (nativity scenes) are set up in homes and public places, the most famous being the one near San Cristóbal fortress in Old San Juan. Some are traditional and attractive. Others are plastic and gauche.

On **Nochebuena** (Christmas Eve) most people attend **Misa del Gallo** (Midnight Mass) before returning home to feast on the traditional large supper known as **cena**. On Jan. 6. **Epiphany** or Three Kings Day is celebrated. The night before, children traditionally place boxes of grass under their beds to await the arrival of the Three Kings, Gaspar, Melchor, and Baltazar. After the camels have eaten all the grass, the kings leave presents in the now empty boxes. On the day itself, the Three Kings are put up in front of the Capitol, and candy and toys are

Puerto Rican Festivals by Month 🎻

JANUARY

Aguada	Velorio de Reyes
Añasco	Festival Mayuco
Bayamón	Fiesta de Reyes
Cagua	Fiesta de Reyes
Camuy	Velorio de Reyes
Cidra	Cabalgata de Reyes Magos
Coamo	Actividad Día de Reyes
Dorado	Festival de Reyes
Florida	Festival de Reyes
Guánica	Verbena San Antonio Abad
Mayagüez	Festival de Reyes
Mayagüez	Festival del Blanco y Negro
Mayagüez	Nuestras Fiestas Patronales
Sabana Grande	Festival de Reyes
San Juan	Festival de la Calle San Sebastián
San Juan	Festival de Teatro de Muñecos
San Juan	Festival de Teatro Títere
San Juan	Festival Folklórico International
San Lorenzo	Trulla de Reyes
San Sebastián	Festival de la Novilla
San Sebastián	Nuestras Fiestas Patronales
Toa Baja	Fiesta de Reyes

FEBRUARY

Arecibo	Carnaval Arecibeño
Arroyo	Carnaval de Cristobal Sanchez
Camuy	Carnaval Río Camuy
Cidra	Festival Teatro Myrna Vazquez
Coamo	Nuestras Fiestas Patronales
Dorado	Carnaval del Plata
Guayama	Festival de la Candelaría
Humacao	Festival de la Pana
Jayuya	Festival Jíbaro del Tomate
Lajas	Festival Internacional Chiringa
Lajas	Nuestras Fiestas Patronales
Loíza	Festival del Burén
Loíza	Nuestras Fiestas Patronales
Manatí	Nuestras Fiestas Patronales
Mayagüez	Festival Nacional de la Danza
Ponce	Festival de Carnaval Ponce de León
Quebradillas	Festival de la Chiringa
Sabana Grande	Gran Verbena Petatera
Salinas	Carnaval Abey
San Juan	Festival de Carnaval
San Juan	Festival de Claridad

Vega Alta	Carnaval Vegalteño
Vieques	Festival Cultural
Yauco	Festival del Café

MARCH

Cabo Rojo	Festival de los Cuarentes
Cabo Rojo	Festival del Pescao
Coamo	Semana Santa
Guánica	Festival de la Independencia
Gurabo	Nuestras Fiestas Patronales
Juana Díaz	Carnaval del Maví
Lajas	Fería Agropecuaria
Las Marías	Festival Fundación Pueblo
Maricao	Fiesta de Acabe del Café
Quebradillas	Nuestras Fiestas Patronales
San Juan	Festival de Teatro Puertorriqueña
San Lore.	Festival La Chiringa
Vega Alta	Festival de la Caña
Guayanabo	St. Patrick's Day Parade

APRIL

Adjuntas	Festival del Gigante
Aguadilla	Fiestas San Antonio
Arroyo	Festival Negra
Cayey	Fería Regional de Artesanias
Cidra	Festival de la Educacion
Comerio	Carnaval de Primavera
Dorado	Festival de Teatro Infantil
Guánica	Festival del Pescao
Guayama	Festival Pionero Artesana
Guayanil	Festival La Chiringa
Guaynabo	Nuestras Fiestas Patronales
Humacao	Fiesta de Bomba y Música
Juana Díaz	Festival Sapo Toro
Luquillo	Festival de Playa
Rosario	Festival Añasco's Anón
Sabana Grande	Festival del Soberao
San Juan	Fería de Artesanía Femenina
San Juan	Orchid Show
Vieques	Festival Plenero

MAY

Adjuntas	Festival de la Cidra
Aguadilla	Verbena de Corrales
Añasco	Festival de Teatro
Arecibo	Nuestras Fiestas Patronales

Bayamón	Nuestras Fiestas Patronales
Cabo Rojo	Festival del Ostión
Cabo Rojo	Festival del Tejido de Sombrero
Caguas	Festival del Coquí
Camuy	Nuestras Fiestas Patronales
Carolina	Nuestras Fiestas Patronales
Coamo	Actividad Madre Ejemplar
Coamo	Tradicionales Rosarios de Cruz
Dorado	Festival de Cruz
Fajardo	Festival de Bomba y Plena
Guayama	Carnaval Deportivo
Guayama	Festival de Primavera
Guayama	Rosario de la Cruz
Guayanilla	Festival de la Cruz
Guayanilla	Festival de Playa
Hormigueros	Fiesta de la Dulce Caña
Hormigueros	Semana de Segundo Ruiz
Isabela	Festival del Tejido
Juana Díaz	Semana Lloreniana
Lajas	Festival Piña Cabezona
Mayagüez	Carnaval Mayagüezano
Moca	Festival del Camarón
Morovis	Festival del Camarón
Peñuelas	Nuestras Fiestas Patronales
Ponce	Festival de Cruz
Ponce	Festival Playa de Ponce
Rincón	Festival del Coco
Sabana Grande	Nuestras Fiestas Patronales
San Germán	Festival de la Caña
San Juan	Concurso Nacional de Trovadores
San Juan	Concurso Nacional del Cuatro
San Juan	Concurso Nacional del Guiro
San Juan	Festival de Cruz
San Juan	Fest. de la Música Puertorriqueña
San Juan	Semana de la Danza
Santa Isabela	Festival del Mangó
Toa Alta	Nuestras Fiestas Patronales
Toa Baja	Festival Arte y Cultura
Utuado	Fería de Artesanía

JUNE

Aguada	Festival de Playa Noche San Juan
Aguadilla	Festival Playero
Aguas Buenas	Festival de la Rosa
Añasco	Festival del Merengue
Barceloneta	Festival de Verano
Barranquitas	Nuestras Fiestas Patronales
Caguas	Noche de San Juan
Camuy	Día de San Juan

Cataño	Noche de San Juan
Ceiba	Nuestras Fiestas Patronales
Coamo	Actividad Padre Ejemplar
Coamo	Festival de la Juventud
Comerío	Festival Jibaro
Corozal	Carnaval San Juan Bautista
Corozal	El Carnaval de Corozal
Culebra	Nuestras Fiestas Patronales
Dorado	Nuestras Fiestas Patronales
Guánica	Festival Jueyero
Guayama	Festival Populares
Guyama	Nuestras Fiestas Patronales
Guayanilla	Festival del Marisco
Guayanilla	Festival Virgen del Carmen
Guaynabo	Día Nacional de la Salsa
Isabela	Nuestras Fiestas Patronales
Lajas	Festival de Chiringa y Tiguero
Lajas	Festival de la Chiringa
Loíza	Festival Bomba y Plena
Maricao	Nuestras Fiestas Patronales
Maunabo	Nuestras Fiestas Patronales
Naguabo	Festival Diplo
Narajito	Festival Artes y Cultura
Narajito	Festival San Antonio
Orocovis	Nuestra Fiestas Patronales
Salinas	Festival del Pescao
San Juan	Festival Casals
San Juan	Festival de Verano
San Juan	Nuestras Fiestas Patronales
Santa Isabela	Carnaval del Juey
Toa Baja	Nuestras Fiestas Patronales
Vega Alta	Festival del Panapen

JULY

Adjuntas	Nuestras Fiestas Patronales
Aguadilla	Festival del Atun
Aguadilla	Festival del Pescao
Aguadilla	Festival Música de Verano
Aguadilla	Verbenas
Aibonito	Festival de Flores
Aibonito	Nuestras Fiestas Patronales
Arecibo	Festival Playero
Arroyo	Nuestras Fiestas Patronales
Barceloneta	Nuestras Fiestas Patronales
Barranquitas	Fería Nacional de Artesanias
Bayamón	Ann. José Celso Barbosa
Bayamón	Festival de Artesanías
Bayamón	Festival del Chicharrón
Cabo Rojo	Cruce de Bahía de Boqueron
Cabo Rojo	Festival del Melón

INTRODUCTION

Cabo Rojo	Nuestras Fiestas Patronales
Cabo Rojo	Retorno a la Arena
Camuy	Festival Playero Penon Brusi
Carolina	Festival de la Caña
Cataño	Nuestras Fiestas Patronales
Cidra	Festival Tradicionales
Cidra	Nuestras Fiestas Patronales
Coamo	Aniversario de Coamo
Coamo	Festival Deportivo y Musical
Comerio	Festival El Jobo
Comerio	Festival La Paila
Culebra	Nuestras Fiestas Patronales
Fajardo	Nuestras Fiestas Patronales
Guánica	Desfile 25 de Julio
Guánica	Nuestras Fiestas Patronales
Guayanilla	Carnaval del Pueblo
Hatillo	Nuestras Fiestas Patronales
Lajas	Festival del Pescao
Loíza	Festival de Santiago Apostol
Manatí	Festival de Los Manatí
Mayagüez	Festival del Seco
Morovis	Nuestras Fiestas Patronales
Orocovis	Festival del Camaron
Patillas	Festival Monte y Mar
Ponce	Festival de Bomba y Plena
Río Grande	Nuestras Fiestas Patronales
Sta. Isabela	Nuestras Fiestas Patronales
Toa Baja	Festival Playero
Vega Alta	Festa de la Piña
Vega Alta	Paseo de la Virgen
Vieques	Nuestras Fiestas Patronales
Villalba	Nuestras Fiestas Patronales

AUGUST

Añasco	Festival Sta. Rosa de Lima
Barranquitas	Festival Viva Mi Calle
Cayey	Nuestras Fiestas Patronales
Cayey	Reconocimiento al Jíbaro P.R.
Coamo	Festival La Flor
Coamo	Festival Macuya
Coamo	Semana Nacional Afuera
Comerío	Nuestras Fiestas Patronales
Culebra	Carnaval Deportivo
Dorado	Festival de la Cocolía
Fajardo	Festival de Piel de Seda
Juncos	Carnaval Valenciano
Juncos	Ferias Junqueñas
Mayagüez	Carnaval
Mayagüez	Festival del Mangó
Patillas	Nuestras Fiestas Patronales

Ponce	Festival de la Quenepa
Rincón	Nuestras Fiestas Patronales
Salinas	Nuestras Fiestas Patronales
San Juan	Aniversario del Mercado de Ar.
San Juan	Festival de Cerámica
Toa Baja	Festival Banda de Música

SEPTEMBER

Aguas Buenas	Nuestras Fiestas Patronales
Añasco	Festival del Chipe
Arecibo	Festival Folklorico Arecibeño
Camuy	Fería de Artesano
Coamo	Festival Jardines de Santa Ana
Coamo	Festival Madrileño
Fajardo	Fiesta Típica El Paraíso
Florida	Nuestras Fiestas Patronales
Hormigueros	Nuestras Fiestas Patronales
Jayuya	Nuestras Fiestas Patronales
Juana Díaz	Nuestras Fiestas Patronales
Juncos	Nuestras Fiestas Patronales
Lares	Festival de Lares
Moca	Festival del Cuatro
Moca	Nuestras Fiestas Patronales
Naranjito	Nuestras Fiestas Patronales
Orocovis	Fería Artesanía
San Germán	Festival del Anón
San Juan	Festival Cultural del Niño
San Juan	Festival de Bomba
San Juan	Festival of Inter-American Arts
San Juan	Sinfónica de Puerto Rico
San Lorenzo	Festival Bordado y Tejido
San Lorenzo	Nuestras Fiestas Patronales
Toa Baja	Aniversario de Levittown
Trujillo	Nuestras Fiestas Patronales
Utuado	Nuestras Fiestas Patronales
Vega Baja	Nuestras Fiestas Patronales
Vieques	Festival Casabe
Yauco	Nuestras Fiestas Patronales

OCTOBER

Aguada	Festival del Juey
Aguada	Nuestras Fiestas Patronales
Aguadilla	Nuestras Fiestas Patronales
Aibonito	Festival de la Montaña
Añasco	Festival del Chipé
Arroyo	Festival del Pescao
Caguas	Nuestras Fiestas Patronales
Canóvan	Nuestras Fiestas Patronales
Ceiba	Festival de la Raza

FESTIVALS

Ciales	Nuestras Fiestas Patronales
Cidra	Festival Desc. de P.R.
Cidra	Festival Talento Pitri
Coamo	Festival de Bomba y Plena
Corozal	Festival del Platano
Corozal	Nuestras Fiestas Patronales
Florida	Festival Cultural Río Encantado
Guánica	Festival Cultura
Guayama	Fería Artesania y Música
Guayama	Festival Cultural Luis Palés Matos
Guaynabo	Carnaval Mabo
Jayuya	Festival Indígena
Lajas	Festival Gallístico
Lares	Festival Almojábana
Lares	Festival Hacienda Rabano
Luquillo	Festival de Platos Típicos
Luquillo	Nuestras Fiestas Patronales
Naguabo	Nuestras Fiestas Patronales
Río Piedras	Nuestras Fiestas Patronales
San Germán	Nuestras Fiestas Patronales
San Juan	Festival de la Música
San Juan	Festival de Teatro Internacional
San Juan	Garden of PR Opening
Toa Baja	Festival de la Zafra
Yabucoa	Nuestras Fiestas Patronales

NOVEMBER

Aguada	Fería de Artesanías
Aguada	Festival Desc. de P.R.
Aibonito	Festival de la Montaña
Barceloneta	Festival Folklórico
Cayey	Festival Tierra Adentro
Cidra	Festival Paloma Sabanera
Coamo	Festival la Yuca
Coamo	Festival Músical y Deportivo
Culebra	Festival de Artesanía
Dorado	Acción de Gracias
Dorado	Festival de P.R.
Fajardo	Festival de Chiringa
Humacao	Festival de Santa Cecilia
Isabela	Festival de Gallo
Las Marías	Nuestras Fiestas Patronales
Maunabo	Festival Platano
Mayagüez	Fería Regional De Artesanias
San Sebastián	Expo Arte
Santa Isabela	Carnaval del Pavo
Villalba	Festival Areyto

DECEMBER

Adjuntas	Festival Navideño
Añasco	Festival de la Bellas Artes
Arroyo	Festival Música Puertorriqueña
Cabo Rojo	Festival de la Paleta
Coamo	Parrandas Navideñas
Dorado	Festival de Navidad
Guánica	Festival Navidad
Guayama	Verbenas
Guayanil	Nuestras Fiestas Patronales
Hatillo	Festival de las Mascaras
Humacao	Nuestras Fiestas Patronales
Juana Díaz	Festival Puertorriqueñas
Juana Díaz	Festival Santos Reyes
Lares	Nuestras Fiestas Patronales
Las Piedras	Nuestras Fiestas Patronales
Manatí	Festival Navideño
Maunabo	Festival de Navidad
Mayagüez	Apertura Epoca de Navidad
Mayagüez	Festival de Navidad
Orocovis	Encuentro Nacional Santeros
Ponce	Nuestras Fiestas Patronales
Sabana Grande	Festival de Trovadores
Sabana Grande	Festival del Burén
Sabana Grande	Festival del Petate
San Germán	Festival de Navidad
San Juan	Criollisimo Ballet
San Juan	Festival Infantil Arlequín
San Juan	Festival Old San Juan Christmas
San Juan	Iluminación de Belen
San Juan	Navidades (Christmas Events)
Toa Baja	Fiesta de Navidad
Utuado	Fiesta de Navidad
Vega Alta	Nuestras Fiestas Patronales

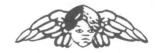

INTRODUCTION

given away on the grounds of El Morro fortress in Old San Juan by the governor.

Transport

Arrival
By Air

Although the days of bargain basement flights are over, it's still possible to visit Puerto Rico relatively cheaply. And though the only really cheap way to get here is to swim, you can still save money by shopping around. A good travel agent should find the lowest fare for you; if he or she doesn't, find another agent, or try doing it yourself. In these days of airline deregulation, fares change quickly so it's best to check the prices well before departure and then again before you go to buy the ticket. Advance purchase excursion fares, weekday and night flights, and one-way fares are among the options that may save you money. The more flexible you can be about when you wish to depart and return, the easier it will be to find a bargain.

Whether dealing with a travel agent or with the airlines themselves make sure that you let them know clearly what it is you want. Don't assume that because you live in Los Angeles, for example, it's cheapest to fly from there. It may be better to find an ultrasaver flight to gateway cities like New York or Miami and then change planes. Fares tend to be cheaper on weekdays and during low season (mid-April to mid-December). You must now pay $13.20 additional in tax to fly in or out of San Juan airport, which works out to an extortionate $26.40 RT added to your ticket. Expect to pay around $350 RT from JFK, $400 RT from Chicago, and $620 RT from Los Angeles.

INTERNET BUYING: Online, you can try priceline.com, orbitz.com, and hotwire.com in search of Internet-only bargains. Be sure to compare, and type in a range of dates because the fares can vary dramatically.

FOR SAN JUAN: Flying to San Juan from Charlotte, Philadelphia, and (seasonally) from Orlando, USAir (☎ 800-842-5374) is one of the most important carriers serving the Commonwealth. (It is still operating while in Chapter 11). Delta flies directly from Atlanta. American Airlines also flies nonstop from NY, Boston, Bradley Field (CT), BWI and Dulles (Washington), Chicago, Tampa, Orlando and Miami to San Juan. Jetblue (☎ 800-JETBLUE) flies from NYC to San Juan. Spirit Airlines (☎ 800-772-7117) flies from Denver, Chicago, La Guardia, Atlantic City, Orlando and Fort Lauderdale to San Juan.

FOR PONCE: American Eagle flies to Ponce from San Juan.

FOR MAYAGÜEZ: American Eagle flies to Mayagüez from San Juan.

FOR CULEBRA AND VIEQUES: Isla Nena (☎ 877-812-5144) is the only airline flying from the international airport to Vieques and Culebra. Vieques Air Link (☎ 787-722-3736, 787-723-9882 in San Juan) flies to Culebra and Vieques from Isla Grande and Fajardo.

FROM CANADA: There are no direct flights. Air Canada (☎ 800-776-3000) will connect you to Continental and American flights from Montreal, Ottawa, and Toronto.

FROM THE UK: British Airways offers service to San Juan through its code sharing with American Airlines.

Departure and Excursions

EXCURSIONS FROM PUERTO RICO: As the island is a Caribbean hub, you might wish to combine your visit with trips to other islands. LIAT (☎ 888-791-0800) flies to many of them.

✈ Airlines Serving Puerto Rico ✈

ACES
☎ 800-846-2237.
http://www.aces.com.co

Aeromar
☎ 877-237-6627
http://www.aeromarairlines.com

Air Caraibes
☎ 877-772-1005.
http://www.aircaraibes.com

Air Plus Charter
☎ 787-791-8181

Air Santo Domingo
☎ 866-288-3939.
http://www.airsantodomingo.com

Air St. Thomas
☎ 800-522-3084.
http://www.airstthomas.com

ALM
☎ 800-327-7230
http://www.airalm.com

American Airlines
☎ 800-433-7300
http://www.aa.com

American Eagle
☎ 800-433-7300
http://www.aa.com

American Trans Air
☎ 800-225-2995.
http://www.ata.com

Avianca
☎ 800-284-2622.
http://www.avianca.com

BWIA International
☎ 800-538-2942
http://www.bwia.com

Cape Air
☎ 800-352-0714
http://www.flycapeair.com

Condor
☎ 800-524-6975
http://www.condoramericas.com

Continental Airlines
☎ 800-231-0856.
http://www.continental.com

COPA Airlines ☎
800-359-2672
http://www.copaair.com

Delta Airlines
☎ 800-221-1212
http://www.delta.com

Iberia
☎ 800-772-4642
http://www.iberia.com

Isla Nena Air Service
☎ 877-812-5144
http://www.islanena.8m.com

Jet Blue
☎ 800-JETBLUE
http://www.jetblue.com

KLM (Northwest)
☎ 800-374-7747
http://www.nwa.com

LACSA-Grupo TACA
☎ 800-225-2272.
http://www.grupotaca.com

LIAT
787-791-0800.
☎ http://www.liat.com

Martin Air
☎ 800-366-3734.
http://www.martinairusa.com

North American Airlines
☎ 787-643-3455,
718-656-2650
http://www.northamair.com

Northwest Airlines
☎ 800-374-7747
http://www.nwa.com

Seaborne Airlines
☎ 888-359-8687
http://www.seaborneair-
lines.com

Spirit Airlines
☎ 800-772-7117
http://www.spiritair.com

United Airlines
☎ 800-241-6522
http://www.ual.com

US Air
☎ 800-428-4322
http://www.usairways.com

Vieques Air-Link
☎ 888-901-9247
http://www.vieques-island.com

FOR THE VIRGIN ISLANDS: A number of small airlines fly to the American and British Virgin Islands.

BY SEA: **Transportation Services** (☎ 340-776-6282) runs from St. John to Fajardo a few times per month ($80 RT).

FOR THE DOMINICAN REPUBLIC: American and Air Santo Domingo fly from San Juan to Santo Domingo and return.

BY BOAT: Ferries del Caribe (☎ 787-622-4800, 787-832-4800) runs the *Millennium Express* from Mayagüez to Santo Domingo, the Dominican Republic's capital. The large ferry, which holds some 250 cars and more than 500 passengers, has a video casino, restaurant, bar, cafeteria, and a theater that shows action thrillers. RT tickets are $150 summer and $170 winter. Cabins for two are $50 each. Bringing a vehicle adds $60 each way to the total.
http://www.ferriesdelcaribe.com

AIR CHARTERS: There are a number of small airlines which run flights by demand. **Charter Flights Caribbean, Inc.** (☎ 787-791-1240, 810-1362, 398-3181) fly to St. Thomas and St. Croix in the USVI and Beef Island (Tortola's airport) and Virgin Gorda in the BVI.
http://www.guiapr.com/charter

Inter Island Express (☎ 888-253-4556) flies to St. Barths, Nevis, and other islands.
http://www.interisland.express.com

Caribbean Helicorp (☎ 787-722-1984) offer Caribbean-wide helicopter and plane charters.
http://www.caribhelicorp.com
info@caribhelicorp.com

CULEBRA AND VIEQUES: call **Air Culebra** (☎ 787-742-0446). **Flamenco** (☎ 787-742-1040) also offers charters.

Tours

PACKAGE TOURS: As they say, all that glitters is not gold. This cliché may be old but it is certainly pertinent when it comes to package tours! If you want to have everything taken care of, then package tours are the way to go. But they do have at least two distinct disadvantages: almost everything has already been decided for you, which takes much of the thrill out of traveling, and you are more likely to be put up in a large characterless hotel (where the tour operators can get quantity discounts), rather than in a small inn (where you can get quality treatment). So think twice before you sign up. Also, if you should want to sign up, read the fine print and see what's *really* included and what's not. Don't be taken in by useless freebies that gloss over the lack of paid meals, for example.

BIRDING TOURS: Field Guides (☎ 512-327-4953,✆ 512-327-9231; Box 160723, Austin, TX 78716-0723) offers worldwide tours. Their Puerto Rican tour (which also includes Jamaica) generally leaves in the Spring and focuses on El Yunque, Guánica, and Maricao. On the trip you may see such species as scaly-naped woodpeckers, pearly-eyed thrashers, elfin woods warblers, Puerto Rican todies, Puerto Rican lizard cuckoos, green mangos, or Puerto Rican nightjars.
http://www.fieldguides.com

Getting Around

Unless you are driving yourself, you'll need to have patience! Always allow plenty of time to get to any island destination. City bus service in San Juan is cheap but painfully inefficient and slow.

Around the island, there is no longer any regular passenger bus service. Unscheduled but cheap rural services run all over the island, including along the mountain road from Arecibo (Carr. 10) down to Ponce.

> ⚠ A number of highways are highly congested and should be avoided. Among these are Highway 2 on the N Coast, Hwy. 3 on the E Coast, anywhere around Bayamón, and other areas. Don't underestimate the amount of time it may take to get somewhere. Many of the roads are curvy, and the coastal roads can be packed with cars.

Públicos are Ford vans with seats which serve as shared taxis. They hold from 12-15. A cheap and convenient form of transportation, they can be picked up or left at any point. Identifiable by the letter "P" on the license plate, their route is listed on the windshield. Unfortunately, except for the San Juan-Ponce and other runs originating from San Juan, they cover only short hops between towns. This may mean changing vehicles innumerable times before reaching your final destination. Hitchhiking is slow but very possible and a good way to pass the time while waiting for buses.

HELICOPTER: Coptco (☎ 787-729-000) offers charters and tours.
http://www.coptco-pr.com

Hiking

An alternative to local transport or renting a car is the **Fondo de Mejoramiento** (☎ 787-759-8366), a local travel organization that conducts tours to various spots of scenic, historical, and cultural interest. Participants are asked to refrain from gathering plants or littering. It sponsors an annual hike which traverses the entire 165-mile Panoramic Route from Maunabo to Mayagüez over the course of 16 weekend days. It has some 1,300 family members.

In Aibonito, the **Piedra Restaurant** (☎ 787-735-1034) is the meeting place for hikes through the Cristóbal Canyon. Call for information.

Renting A Car / Driving

The island's poor internal transportation system makes this an option you'll want to consider. If you don't have insurance, however, make sure you purchase coverage for the rental vehicle. Car theft is a problem here! All too often roads are poorly marked, so getting anywhere can be an adventure in itself.

Be aware of **Transit Law #126**, requiring that every child under age four must be strapped into a protective seat. Puerto Rican law also prohibits the rental of scooters and motorbikes. Cars can be rented at the airport; a valid US driver's license is required. Expect to pay at least $25 per day, but weekend specials and a weekly rate may be available. Insurance is additional. Smaller companies frequently offer better deals.

As you should do everywhere, read the contract thoroughly, especially the fine print. Ask about unlimited mileage, free gas, late return penalties, and drop-off fees. In general, it's preferable to avoid driving in San Juan. Not only is it congested, it has the highest rate of carjacking in the US.

TIMES AND DISTANCES: From San Juan it takes around 45 minutes to drive to **Fajardo** (34 miles) or to **El Yunque**, 40 minutes to drive to **Humacao** (34 miles), 1.5 hours to **Guayama** (44 miles), 1.5 hours to **Coamo** (49 miles), 1.5 hours to **Camuy Caves** (60 miles), 1.5 hours to **Ponce** (70 miles), 2.5 hours to **San Germán** (76 miles), 2 hours to **Mayagüez** (98 miles), 2 hours to **Aguadilla** (81 miles), 2.5 hours to **Utuado**, one hour to **Arecibo** (48 miles), and 30 minutes to **Dorado** (19 miles).

SUGGESTED ROUTES: One advantage of renting a car is that you can explore remote routes which are poorly served by public transportation. We highly recommend that you tour all or part of the *Ruta Panorámica* (see sidebar). Although improvements are being made, roads remain inadequately signed;

Ruta Panorámica

The Ruta Panorámica. is not one route, but a collection of forty-plus scenic roads which traverse the island's heartland. As they are not always well marked, and because they have a lot of twists and turns, this route can be challenging.

However, you are well rewarded by the panoramic views as well as the opportunity to see parts of Puerto Rico which few visitors frequent.

A good road map is highly recommended. Even then you may get lost at times.

The total route is 165 mi. (264 km) long, but you'll drive much more if you wish to visit sites and attractions enroute. If your time is limited, the best alternative would be to pick a section of the route and stick to that. Otherwise, take three days or more to make this trip, and remember to allow plenty of flex time.

Some major attractions may be visited by taking only a minor detour. These include the Arecibo observatory, the Río Camuy Cave Park, Hacienda Buena Vista, and the Caguana Indian Ceremonial Center.

Spanish for Drivers

Adelante Ahead

Calle sin Salida Dead end

Peligro Danger

Desvio Detour

Salida Exit

Neblina Fog

Lomo Hill or Bump

Desprendimiento Landslide

A la izquierda To the left

Puente Estrecho Narrow bridge

Transito One way traffic

No Estacione No parking

Cruce de Peatones Pedestrian crossing

A la Derecha To the right

Carretera Cerada Road closed

Zona Escolar School zone

Semaforo Signal light

Resbala Mojado Slippery when wet

Baden Speed bump

Pare Stop

Peaje Toll station

No Vire No turn

Ceda Yield

driving can be confusing. Roads will flood easily in the back country during heavy rainstorms. Driving at night along mountain roads can be stressful. You may encounter traffic jams in small towns such as Yauco. It helps to know some Spanish for obtaining directions, but people are very helpful. Gas starts at around $1.50/gallon and is cheapest in towns. (It is sold by the liter). A good map is a necessity. You'll have the best time if you don't set a rigid schedule for yourself and just play it by ear.

HIGHWAYS: Considering its size, Puerto Rico has an astounding number of major arteries to accommodate its million-plus vehicles. During the past 25 years, some 85 miles of new roads have been constructed and another 140 miles are planned.

Toll roads charge 35-70 cents per booth. Keep change handy. If you don't have change, head for a booth marked "C."
http://www.dtop.prstar.net

Internal Air Transport

Small airlines fly to the outlying islands of Vieques and Culebra (see sections for details); American Eagle flies daily from San Juan's

 The best **maps** of Puerto Rico are by ITMB and by Berndtson. You can also buy a good map at any gas station.

international airport to Ponce and Mayagüez. (Also see "charters" which was previously mentioned.)

Ferries

Passenger ferries leave daily from Fajardo to Culebra and Vieques. Another ferry route of note is the **Aquaexpress** service running from Old San Juan to Cataño and Hato Rey. Intended largely for local residents, a passenger boat service (free) is available on Dos Bocas Lake.

Accommodations

Accommodations on the island are not cheap in general but, if you hunt around, you may find some bargains. Expect to spend around US$45 d and up for simple rooms. Quality establishments (such as small hotels) will be much more, say $100 and up. Large resorts start offering rooms in the hundreds of dollars. Camping is possible, and campsites are listed, but the island is not well set up for camping, and security may be a problem. Rates in this book generally do not include the government tax on rooms: *paradores* 9%, hotels 9%, and hotels with casinos 11%. Some hotels may add 10-15% service charge.

CENTROS VACACIONALES: Clusters of rental cottages situated at Boquerón, Cabo Rojo, Humacao, Maricao, and Arroyo. These are available to "bona fide family groups" for $65 per night with a minimum stay of two and a maximum stay of seven nights. Units sleep six. Bring your own sheets or rent them. Villas are $109.

Payment must be with a credit card. For more information and a reservation form (apply 120 days in advance) contact Oficina de Reservaciones, **Compania de Fomento Recreativo, (☎ 787-722-1771/1551, 787-721-2800 ext. 225, 275). For more infor-

mation and a reservation form (apply 120 days in advance) write to Oficina de Reservaciones, Compania de Fomento Recreativo, Apdo. 9022089, San Juan PR 00904-2089.

PARADORES: Attractive buildings set in lush surroundings, the government-endorsed **paradores** were planned to be inexpensive inns originally. Now, they're moderately priced and normally empty during the week. (See chart). Many inns calling themselves "parador" are not part of the system, and some establishments that call themselves "hotel" are part of the system. Reserve from the States by dialing 800-443-0226. You can also reserve in Old San Juan at 301 San Justo (☎ 787-721-2400, 787-721-2884). Call toll-free within the island at 800-462-7575.
http://www.travelandsports.com/pa.htm

APARTMENT AND CONDOMINIUM RENTALS: These are best reserved in advance. You can now find a wide variety on the internet.

Run by the affable Michael Giessler, **La Caleta** (☎ 787-725-5347) offers short- and long-term rentals in Old San Juan. They are reliable and recommended.
http://www.thecaleta.com
questions@thecaleta.com

Beachview Apartments (☎ 877-812-1067) have rentals in the San Juan area.
http://www.beachviewapartments.com
info@beachviewapartments.com

In Luquillo, to the E of San Juan, **Playa Azul Realty** (Box 386, Luquillo, PR 00673, ☎ 787-889-3425, 787-889-3939) rents studio, one- , two- , and three-bedroom apartments. Most are air conditioned; all come with fully equipped kitchens, have guard service, face the ocean, and have beach and pool facilities.

BV Real Estate (☎ 787-863-3687, ☏ 787-860-4565; Box 1327 Fajardo, PR 00738) also offers short- and long-term rentals in the Fajardo and Luquillo areas. Vieques and Culebra rentals are listed under their specific sections.

http://www.bvrealty.com

Food & Drink

You'll find plenty of places to eat. Cafeterias serve everything from grilled cheese sandwiches to rice and beans. Simple local restaurants, and their more expensive cousins, serve the most elaborate combinations of Spanish and other cuisines imaginable. In addition, there are the fast-food joints and a proliferation of pizzerias.

Combining African, Indian, and Spanish cuisine into something new and refreshingly different, food on the island provides a unique culinary experience. Although similar to Dominican, Cuban, and other Caribbean cuisines, it has its own distinct flavor. Seasonings used include pepper, cinnamon, fresh ginger, cilantro, lime rind, *naranja agria* (sour orange), and cloves. **Sofrito**, a sauce used to flavor many dishes, combines **achiote** (annato seeds fried in lard and strained) with ham and other seasonings. Many dishes are cooked in a **caldero**, a cast-iron kettle with a rounded bottom.

SNACKS: Street vendors and *cafeterias* sell a wide variety of tasty, deep-fried snacks. **Alcapurrias** contain ground plantain and pork, or (less commonly) fish or crab fried in batter.

Amarillos en dulce are yellow plantains fried in a sauce of cinnamon, sugar, and red wine.

Bacalaítos fritos are fried codfish fritters made with the dried, salted cod imported from New England.

Selecting a Room

These days you can preview a wide variety of rooms on the internet. You can also make reservations ahead of time. The website www.WhereToStay.com posts hotel reviews which can give you a good idea. If you definitely need a reservation, a wise precaution is to call ahead. If you're driving, you can always cruise around in the early afternoon and seek out a place to stay. This may not work on weekends and during holidays. If you're traveling in a group, you should be aware that some places charge by the room rather than the number of people, so this might be one way to keep costs down. Remember that the lower priced hotels offer better values, much more charm, and have a more interesting clientele. As one reader put it, "the travelers one encounters ... tend to be more interesting than the people in the Condado area or resorts like El Conquistador. The people who go to the traditional resort locales don't seem to have much interest in knowing anything about the landscape outside of the pool, the beach, the bar, and the casino."

Finally, if you are planning on making a number of long distance calls from your hotel room, be sure to check out phone prices (including connection charges) before booking.

Empanadas are made with yucca or plantain dough stuffed with meat and wrapped in plantain leaves.

Pastelillos are fried dough containing meat and cheese. They are sometimes made using fruit and jam. **Empanadillas** ("little pies") are larger versions available on some parts of the island. **Pasteles** are made from plantain or *yautia* dough which has been stuffed with ground pork, garbanzo beans, and raisins, then wrapped in plantain leaves.

Piononos are a mixture of ground beef and ripe plantains dipped in a beaten egg batter and then fried. **Surullitos** or **sorullos** are deep-fried corn meal fritters. **Rellenos de papa** are meat-stuffed potato balls fried in egg batter. **Mofongo** is mashed and roasted plantain balls made with spices and **chicharron** (crisp pork cracklings).

SOUPS AND SPECIALTIES: Not particularly a vegetable-producing island, Puerto Rico nevertheless has its own unique **verduras** (vegetables), including **chayote** and **calabaza** (varieties of West Indian squash), **yuca** (cassava), **yautia** (tanier), **batata** (a type of sweet potato), and **ñame** (African yam). All are frequently served in local stews.

Asopao is a soup made with rice and meat or seafood.

Lechón asado or roast pig is an island specialty. Served in local **lechoneras**, it's tastiest when the pig's skin is truly crisp and golden.

Chicharrón, chunks of crispy pork skin, are sold alongside. Other pork dishes include **cuchifrito**, pork innards stew, **mondongo** (an African stew of chopped tripe), and **gandinga** (liver, heart, and kidneys cooked with spices).

Carne mechada is a beef roast garnished with ham, onion, and spices. Goat is also quite popular and **cabro** (young or kid goat) is considered a delicacy.

Fricasé, a dish made with stewed chicken, rabbit, or goat, is usually accompanied by **tostones**, plantains that have been fried twice.

Sopa de habichuelas negras (black bean soup), is a popular dish, as are the standards **arroz con habichuelas** (rice and beans), and **arroz con pollo** (rice and chicken).

SEAFOOD: One of the most popular seafood items is actually imported from New England. **Bacalao** (dried, salted codfish) is cooked in several ways. **Bacalao a la Viscaina** is codfish stewed in rich tomato sauce. **Serenata** is flaked **bacalao** served cold

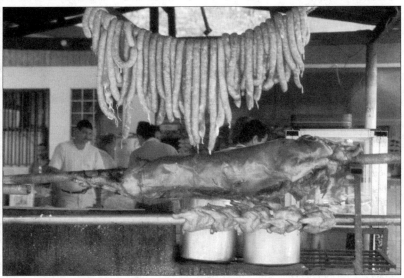

Lechon Asado, *roast pig, is a Puerto Rican specialty..*

🍴 Puerto Rican Food A to Z 🍴

Aguacate — avocado

Alcapurrias — ground plantain and pork or fish or crab fried in batter

Amarillos en dulce — yellow plantains fried in a sauce of cinnamon, sugar, and red wine

Arroz con dulce — sweet rice pudding

Arroz con habichuelas — rice and beans)

Arroz con pollo — rice and chicken

Asopao — soup made with rice and meat or seafood

Bacalao a la Viscaino — codfish stewed in rich tomato sauce

Bacalaítos fritos — fried codfish fritters

Bien-me-sabe — sponge cake with coconut sauce

Carne mechada — beef roast garnished with ham, onion, and spices

Cazuela — rich pumpkin and coconut pudding

Chapín — trunkfish

Chicharron — chunks of crispy skin

Chillo — red snapper

China — orange

Coco frío — chilled drinking coconuts

Corazón — custard apple, Jamaica apple, bullock's heart

Cubano — sandwich containing ham, chicken, and cheese inside a long, crusty white bread

Cuchifrito — pork innards stew

Empanadas — yuca or plantain dough stuffed with meat and wrapped in plantain leaves

Empanadillas — larger versions of *pastelilloss* (available on some parts of the island)

En escabeche — pickled Spanish-style

Ensalada de pulpo — a tasty salad centering on octopus.

Flan — caramel custard

Fricase — a dish made with stewed chicken, rabbit, or goat

Gandinga — liver, heart, and kidneys cooked with spices

Guanábana — soursop

Guineo — bananas

Jobo — hogplum

Jueyes — land crab

Langosta — local lobster

Lechón asado — roast pig

Lechosa — papaya

Malta — unique-tasting, non-alcoholic malt beverage made with barley, malt, cane sugar, corn grits, and hops

Mamey — mammee apple; a brown, nearly round fruit

Maví — local root beer made from tree bark

Medíanoche — a "midnight" sandwich which contains pork, ham, and cheese.

Mero — sea bass

Mofongo — mashed and roasted plantain balls made with spices

Mojo isleño — an elaborate sauce which includes olives, onions, tomatoes, capers, vinegar garlic, and pimentos

Mondongo — an African stew of chopped tripe

Naranja — the sour orange

Níspero — sapodilla

Panapen — breadfruit; roasted or boiled as a vegetable

Parcha — passion fruit

Pasta de guayaba — guava paste

Pasteles — made from plantain or yautia dough which has been stuffed with ground pork, garbanzo beans, and raisins and wrapped in plantain leaves

Piononos — mixture of ground beef and ripe plantains dipped in a beaten egg batter and fried

Pastelillos — fried dough containing meat and cheese; sometimes made using fruit and jam

Piña — pineapple

Piragua — shaved ice covered with tamarind or guava syrup served in a paper cup

Plátano — plantain

Pulpo — octopus

Quenepa — "Spanish lime" a Portuguese delicacy about the size of a large walnut

Queso de hoja — mild-flavored, local soft cheese

Rellenos de papa — meat-stuffed potato balls fried in egg batter.

Serenata — flaked bacalao served cold with an oil and vinegar dressing and toppings like raw onions, avocados, and tomatoes.

Sopa de habichuelas negros — black bean soup

Surullitos (sorullos) — deep-fried corn meal fritters

Tamarindo — tamarind

Tembleque — coconut pudding

Tostones — plantains that have been fried twice

with an oil and vinegar dressing and toppings like raw onions, avocados, and tomatoes. Although some seafood like shrimp must be imported, many others like **chillo** (red snapper), **mero** (sea bass), **pulpo** (octopus), and **chapín** (trunkfish) are available locally.

Fish dishes served **en escabeche** have been pickled Spanish-style. **Ensalada de pulpo** is a tasty salad based on octopus. **Mojo isleño** is an elaborate sauce made of olives, onions, tomatoes, capers, vinegar, garlic, and pimentos. The most famous dishes are **langosta** (local lobster), **jueyes** (land crabs), and **ostiones** (miniature oysters that cling to the roots of mangrove trees). The damming of the island's rivers has brought about a decline of another indigenous delicacy, **camarones de río** (river shrimp).

CHEESE AND SANDWICHES: Queso de hoja is the very milky, mild-flavored, local soft cheese. It must be eaten fresh. It is often combined with the local marmalade, **pasta de guayaba** (guava paste).

INTRODUCTION

Many types of sandwiches are also available. A **cubano** contains ham, chicken, and cheese inside a long, crusty white bread. A **medianoche** ("midnight") contains pork, ham, and cheese.

DESSERTS: Puerto Rican desserts are simple but tasty. They include **arroz con dulce** (sweet rice pudding), **cazuela** (rich pumpkin and coconut pudding), and **bien-me-sabe** (sponge cake with coconut sauce), **tembleque** (coconut pudding), and **flan** (caramel custard). The last is an egg custard baked in a *baño de maría,* a set of two interlocking pans, one of which is filled with hot water. French in origin, *flan* is now widespread in the Spanish-speaking world.

Ice cream is found islandwide. You can patronize Baskin Robbins or try the local ice cream, which often comes in fruit flavors and tends to be more like sherbet than true ice cream. (Lares has a great local place).

FRUIT: Although many fruits are imported from the US, Puerto Rico also grows a large variety of its own. Brought by the Spaniards in the 16th century, the sweet orange is known as **china** because the first seeds came from there. Vendors will peel off the skin with a knife to make a **chupon**, which you can pop into your mouth piece by piece.

Naranja is the sour orange.

Guineos or bananas, imported by the Spanish from Africa, come in all sizes, from the five-inch **niños** on up. Brought from southern Asia, the **plátano** or plantain is inedible until cooked. Puerto Rican **piñas** (pineapples) are much sweeter than their exported counterparts because they are left on the stem to ripen.

The white interior of the **panapen** or breadfruit is roasted or boiled as a vegetable. Some bear small brown seeds, **panas de pepita**, that are boiled or roasted.

Dining and Hotels

It's always a good idea to consider your eating habits when booking accommodations. For example, if you eat breakfast, you should think about what you may need or want to eat and when. Check to see when breakfast (or even coffee) will be available. Many hotels serve a complimentary breakfast, which is often continental. Consider whether this will satisfy you or not. Find out what other meals are available and how far it is to other restaurants. Vegetarians or those who simply shun meat and fowl will want to know if the restaurant will have anything for them to eat. Remember, it always pays to inquire before rather than after!

Another fruit indigenous to the West Indies, **lechosa** or **papaya** is available much of the year.

The oval **parcha** (passion fruit) with its bright orange pulp was given its name by arriving Spaniards who saw its white and purple flowers as a representation of the Crucifixion in botanical form. It is high in vitamins A and C as well as iron.

Coconut palms arrived in 1549 from Cape Verde, Africa via Dutch Guiana. Their nuts are chilled and served as **coco frio** (see below). You drink the water straight from the shell.

The sour-tasting, green-skinned **guanábana** (soursop) can be used to make a delicious fruit drink; it is a native fruit, and can weigh as much as 10 lbs.

A regional native, the **mamey** (mammee apple), is a brown, nearly round fruit which is high in pectin.

The **níspero** (sapodilla) is a fruit originally from the Yucatán.

The **quenepa** or "Spanish lime" is a Portuguese delicacy about the size of a large walnut; its brittle green skin cracks open to reveal a white pit surrounded by pinkish pulp. It is related to the litchi nut, which is a prized Chinese fruit.

The **corazón** (custard apple, Jamaica apple, bullock's heart) is a small, heart-shaped fruit that grows mostly in the wild.

When cross-sectioned, the **caimito** (star apple), an Antilles native, has a star-shaped outline; its sweet pulp has a custard-like consistency.

Island **aguacates** (avocados) are renowned for their thick pulp and small seeds.

Acerola, the wild W Indian cherry, has from 20-50 times the vitamin C of orange juice.

The little-known **jagua** (genipap or marmalade box) has a strong scent; many find it repugnant. Its dye was used by S American natives to tattoo their flesh and scientists have found it has antibiotic properties.

The **tamarindo** (tamarind) is the fruit pod of a tree native to Africa and the Middle East; the tree is known for its long life — sometimes spanning two centuries. Its sticky pods are used to make a popular fruit drink.

Known as the golden apple or Jew's plum, the **jobo de la India** has a delicious fruit used in marmalade and in juices.

The related but smaller **ciruelo** (*jobito* or Spanish plum) is a Mexican native whose wood is often used for fenceposts.

Enjoyed for its aromatic fruit more than its nut, the **pajuil** (cashew) grows wild. Its shell is poisonous.

DRINKS: Delicious fruit drinks are made from passion fruit and others. These are usually found at roadside stands in the countryside. **Lotus** is the government brand canned pineapple juice. (Some Puerto Ricans maintain it's the best thing the government does!)

> 🛈 ＼⏐／ Drinking on the streets of Old San
> ／⏐＼ Juan is punishable by a $500 fine!

Limber (or *piragua*) is shaved ice covered with tamarind or guava syrup served in a paper cup; it's named after Charles Lindbergh, the famous pilot.

Cool **cocos frios** or green drinking coconuts are available just about anywhere for around 75¢. Malta is a unique-tasting, non-alcoholic malt beverage made with barley, malt, cane sugar, corn grits, and hops. **Mavi** is a local root beer made from tree bark.

ALCOHOL: Blue laws are nonexistent in Puerto Rico; alcohol may be purchased anytime, anywhere.

BEER: Locally brewed India and Medalla beers are available in seven- and 12-oz. bottles or in cans at every *colmado* or bar.

Because brews were required to be sold in either 10 oz. cans or specially designed amber 12-oz. bottles, other brands were not readily available until recently. This law (designed to discourage imports) was repealed in 1992 after Heineken and Miller joined with a local distiller to challenge the law, and a beer war has resulted. Now also available are the extremely popular Miller Genuine Draft, Corona, Coors, Heineken, Bud, Michelob Golden Draft, Rolling Rock, Schlitz, Schaefer, and other brands. Premium beers such as Samuel Adams are also competing for market share.

RUM: Puerto Rico is the world's largest rum producer and accounts for 83% of US sales. Rum production began in the 16th century with production of *pintriche* or *cañita* (bootleg rum), a spirit that is still popular today.

Under the Mature Spirits Act, white rum must be distilled for at least one year at a minimum of 180 proof and gold label (amber colored rum) for three years at 175 proof. Añejo, a special blend, requires six years.

Although all of the 26 brands are roughly equivalent, Bacardi is the largest distiller on the island. (See "San Juan Bay and Cataño" under "Old San Juan" for tour information). Serralles

🍺 Who are the Coors? 🍺

Coors Beer is one of the most popular brands of beer in Puerto Rico. Yet, it has a surprising history which few know about. During the 1970s, it was accused of spying on its workers, discriminating against minorities (including gays, blacks and Latinos) and even forcing employees to take polygraph tests to question them regarding their sexual orientation. Coors Brewing Company had also refused to negotiate a collective bargaining agreement with its workers. The outspoken and conservative management at Coors fired workers when they went out on strike. In 1977, workers launched a boycott against Coors. This boycott was confined to the South and West, as Coors was a regional product at this time.

Coors has worked aggressively to change its policies and image since the late 1970s. Indeed, Coors' former Chairman Bill Coors' son, Scott Coors, is openly homosexual. And Coors now regularly runs ad campaigns, offers domestic partner benefits to its gay workers, and supports projects ranging from a Black Heritage festival to a resource center for Latinas.

Questions, however, still remain. William Coors, a brother employed by the company, made a racially-charged speech in 1984. William Coors told a minority business group in Denver that if they thought it was "unfair" that their "ancestors were dragged here in chains against their will... I would urge those of you who feel that way to go back to where your ancestors come from, and you will find out that probably the greatest favor that anybody ever did you, was to drag your ancestors over here in chains, and I mean it." Later in the same speech Coors said, "... they (Blacks) lack the intellectual capacity to succeed."

The Coors family has supported far-right, anti-gay groups such as Free Congress and the Heritage Foundation via the Coors family's Castle Rock Foundation. Heritage fellows are serving in the G. W. Bush administration. Labor Secretary Elaine Chao, is a Heritage "Distinguished Fellow." Chao opposes gays and lesbians serving in the military, has attacked the US Supreme Court for ruling against a Colorado voter initiative which would have repealed State lesbian and gay civil rights laws, and has demanded to end funding for a legal aid group because of its "actions [that] advance the goals of homosexual activists." The Castle Rock Foundation has also supported far-right demagogue David Horowitz and his Center for the Study of Popular Culture. Horowitz commanded headlines in 2001 after he ran campus newspaper ads which suggested that Black Americans benefited from slavery. Horowitz also decries the "destructive agenda" of "gay and lesbian liberationists." To be fair, the Coors Brewing Company, and the foundation and family are separate entities. However, there is a close association between the two. Coors drinkers beware!

(known for its Captain Morgan Spiced Rum and Don Q Rum) is the second largest.

All other brands (such as the distinctive Barrilito) take raw rum from these two distillers and fabricate their own unique brands.

Drinks such as *piña coladas* and banana daiquiris were developed especially for the tourist trade. **Piña coladas** are made by combining cream of coconut with pineapple juice, rum, and crushed ice.

URL http://www.gicco.com
Purveyors of Puerto Rican coffee

Aside from alcohol, the most popular drink in Puerto Rico must be coffee. It is served either as *café* or *café con leche* (coffee essence with steamed milk) along with generous quantities of sugar. *Pocillo* or *café negro* is a demitasse cup of strong coffee served after dinner.

TIPS FOR VEGETARIANS: Puerto Rico is most definitely a carnivorous island, so the more you are able to bend or compromise your principles, the easier time you'll have. If you're a vegan (non-dairy-product user), unless you're cooking all of your own food, you will find it even more difficult, but fruits may be your salvation. The local rice and beans is a good staple, but it can get monotonous after a while, and the beans are often cooked with pork. Salads are also widely available, and there are Chinese restaurants as well.

If you do eat fish, you should be aware that locals eat it fried and that it (along with dishes such as *tostones*, green fried plantains), may have been fried in lard or in the same oil as chicken or pork. If you eat a lot of nuts, plan on bringing your own because those available locally are expensive. The same goes for dried fruits such as raisins.

> "A note about food. Neither of us eat pork or shellfish and I pity any vegetarian who visits PR. I had brought with me health food-type snack bars which came in handy. At times I felt the whole country was bathed in a cloud of pork-aroma. You warn about that, but perhaps you should be even more direct."
> — comment from reader

As a final note, if preparing pasta dishes, you should note that tomato sauce sold in supermarkets frequently includes beef powder for flavor, so check the label carefully before purchasing.

NOTE: Places serving vegetarian food are listed frequently in the dining recommendations.

Sports & Sporting Events

Water Sports
Swimming

All the island's beaches must have unrestricted access by law. The island's *balnearios* provide lockers, showers, and parking. They are open Tues. to Sun., 9 AM–5 PM, summer, and 8 AM–5 PM, winter. Admission is free, but parking is $2. *Expect beaches to be packed on weekends.*

A list of the major ones follows: **Playa Escambron**, Ave. Muñoz Rivera, Puerto de Tierra; **Playa Isla Verde**, Carr. 187, Km 3.9 (both accessible by city bus); **Playa Punta Salinas**, Carr. 868, Km 1.2, Cataño; **Playa Sardinera**, Carr. 698, Dorado; **Playa Cerro Gordo**, Carr. 690, Vega Alta; **Playa Luquillo**, Carr. 3, Km 35.4; **Playa Seven Seas**, Carr. 987, Fajardo; **Playa Sombe**, Carr. 997, Vieques; **Playa Punta Santiago**, Carr. 3, Km 77, Humacao; **Playa Punta Guilarte**, Carr. 3, Km 128.5, Arroyo; **Playa Cana Gordo**, Carr. 333, Km 5.9, Guánica; **Playa Boquerón**, Carr. 101, Cabo Rojo; **Playa Añasco**, Carr. 401, Km 1, Añasco.

Scuba Diving & Snorkeling

Puerto Rico is an exceptionally fine place to dive or snorkel. A large number of operations, many of which are Puerto Rican owned and managed, offer instruction and rentals. Operators from San Juan to Humacao can dive both their areas and more remote locations such as Culebra and Vieques. With an average underwater temperature of 80°, the visibility in many places is well over 100 ft., with 70 ft. being an average. Owing to the frequent rainfall and freshwater runoff, Puerto Rican waters have a lower visibility than elsewhere in the Caribbean, but the runoff does attract a large number of fish, and it may be possible to see a manatee. Sharks are not a problem. Besides San Juan, scuba operations are also found in Isabela, Fajardo, at La Parguera, and on Culebra and Vieques.

DIVE SPOTS: Here, we give a summary of dive spots. More details are under the specific locations. Popular locations off the coast of **San Juan** include Figure Eight Reef, the Molar, and Horseshoe Reef. Here you can find tunnels, overhangs, small caves (ranging down to 30 ft.), and a number of lava rock formations housing everything from seahorses to banded coral shrimp.

The many small islets off the coast of **Fajardo,** along with coral formations, underwater caves, and sunken sailboats, provide an excellent variety of dive spots. Names of sites here include Becerra Reef, Corona, Superhero, the North Shore, and the Slope. Cayo Diablo, to the E, offers a great collection of sealife. In addition, dives off of Culebra, Vieques, Icacos, Palominos, and Palomonitos are available. In this area you might spot everything from French angelfish to hairy hermit crabs to an octopus.

Off of **Culebra,** there's a tugboat wreck and a coral zone called the "Impact Area." The latter is known for its arch formations.

Offshore from **Humacao,** there are a number of sites, including Basslet Reef (35-60 ft. in depth), and the Drift and the Canyon.

 Obtain a copy of the **Puerto Rico Scuba Guide** from the Puerto Rico Tourist Board.

Approximately five to seven miles offshore from **La Parguera** is an outer shelf where the sea bottom contours slope outward to form vertical walls. Here you can find a great variety of marine life from gorgonian corals to moray eels to dolphins and wall-lined sand trenches. Stingrays and eels are common at the Playground, the Trenches, and the Ninth Floor here. Phosphoresence occurs at Enrique Reef, which is just a few minutes offshore. Other opportunities lie near the pinnacle reefs and islets which are closer to land.

A seawall dropoff is around 20 min. offshore from **Guánica,** on the S coast and to the W of Ponce. The canyons here are lined with coral, and stingrays, moray eels, and sea turtles may be seen.

Closer to Ponce, **Caja de Muertos** has diving offshore as does Cayo Berberia and Cayo Derrumbadero.

In the NW, Crash Boat in **Aguadilla** is a popular dive site; Bajura in Isabela is known for its ring of coral caverns surrounding the 30-ft.-deep Blue Hole. Reefs are also found off **Mayagüez** and off the beach next to Rincón's lighthouse.

Isla Desecheo, a 260-acre uninhabited island about 15 miles from **Rincón,** offers clear water, reefs and caverns, and multitudes of fish. **Mona** and **Monito** also have great diving, but require a multi-day trip.

DIVING AND INSTRUCTION: There are numerous charter companies. located in most tourist areas, which offer PADI certification and other instruction. These are all listed in the text.

SNORKELING AND REEFS: Good snorkeling spots are in Vieques, Culebra, off of Fajardo, and along the S coast. Ponce offers good diving in the horseshoe-shaped barrier reef (15-40 ft. out from the offshore islands of Caja de Muertos, Cayo Cardona, Cayo Ratones, and Cayo Caribe), which stretches W from Ponce to Tallaboa.

Puerto Rico's most unusual spot is an anchorage off Cayo Santiago (Monkey Island), from which you can snorkel in six-ft.-deep water and watch macaque and rhesus monkeys.

Coral reefs are found near La Parguera in the SW and off Caja de Muertos. Puerto Rico's best coral reefs are off Mona Island, a six-hour boat ride from the E coast.

Surfing , Windsurfing, and Hang Gliding

SURFING: If you don't bring your own board, rentals are widely available. The most popular location is **Rincón** on the NW coast; the world championship was held here in 1968.

Playa María, nearby, is the first of a series of surfing beaches that stretch around to Aguadilla and over to Isabela. Owing to the submerged rocks and high waves, this area is best left to the experienced.

Others include **Pine Grove** in Isla Verde; **Los Aviónes** and **La Concha** in Piñones (E of Isla Verde); **Los Tubos** next to Tortuguero Lagoon in Vega Baja (only during the winter); **Jobos** (near Isabela); and **La Pared** (to the E of Luquillo). Culebra's **Ensenada Honda** is another popular spot.

Boards may be rented (around $25/day) from **Wave Rider** (☎ 787-722-7103), which is next to the Caribe Hilton in Puerto De Tierra.
http://www.waveriderpr.com

Cool Runnings, 2412 C. Laurel in Punta Las Marias, also rents boards.

Playero Surfing (☎ 787-722-4384) is a good place to learn about breaks. It is at 64 Ave. Condado, next to Walgreens.

http://www.playero.com

WINDSURFING: Different areas have different conditions. While ocean swells are found on the N shore, flat water sailing is available along the E and SW coasts. Long board and slalom conditions are found year round. Aficionados will prefer visiting in the winter when Atlantic storms cause swells.

The most popular locations include **Condado Lagoon** (calm water, steady winds), the **Ocean Park beaches**, the area SE of Playa Luquillo on the NE shore, **Boquerón** (in the SW), and in **Ensenada Honda** on Culebra. Most major hotels rent equipment.

The E end of Isla Verde is popular with advanced boardsailors. Contact **Lisa Penfield Windsurfing** (☎ 787-796-1234) here. La Parguera Bay has good slalom conditions. Nearby Cayo Enrique, while protected from the waves, is wide open to the winds.

In Punta Las Marias at the shopping center, **Velauno** (☎ 787-727-0883, 728-8716), 2434 C. Loíza, offers rentals, lessons, and information.
http://www.velauno.com

On the **NW shore**, experts-only beaches include Jobos, Wilderness, and Surfers' beaches. **Other good windsurfing spots** in this area include Añasco, Boquerón, Crash Boat (Aguadilla), and the Shacks (Isabela). Windsurfing rentals are also available in **Palmas del Mar** (☎ 787-852-8114) in the SE.
http://www.www.windsurfingpr.com

The **PBA World Cup Tour** is held annually in **Isabela**.

HANG GLIDING: Team Spirit Hang Gliding (☎ 787-850-0508) offers glides in the El Yunque area.

http://www.mailways.net/teamspirit

Deep Sea Fishing

Thirty world records have been broken with fish caught from the island's seas. Half- and full-day charters are available. You can expect tuna, mackerel, yellow and blackfin tuna, bonefish, yellowfish, blue marlin, wahoo, and tarpon.

While marlin are best caught from late Jan. through May, sailfish and wahoo can be caught in the fall, dorado (dolphinfish) from Nov. through early April, and yellow tuna, blackfin tuna, and skipjack (oceanic bonito) are caught year round.

San Juan charters include **San Juan Fishing Charters** (☎ 787-723-0415, 781-7001, evenings); **Southern Witch Charters** (☎ 747-9247), **Marina Services of the**

Deep Sea Fishing	
Fish	**Location**
Season	
Blue marlin	*100 fathom edge*
All year. July-Oct. best.	
White marlin	*100 fathom edge*
All year. May-June best.	
Sailfish	*Offshore* Oct. to April;
Oct. to Feb. best.	
Wahoo	*Offshore*
All year. Oct. to Dec. best.	
Allison tuna	*Offshore*
All year. Nov. to April best.	
Dolphin (fish)	*Offshore*
Spring, Fall, and Winter; Spring is best	
Kingfish	*Reef-banks*
All year; Spring is best.	
Tarpon	*Inshore*
All year. Nov. to May best.	

Caribbean (☻ 787-723-2409), **Maragata Yacht Charters** (☎ 787-850-7548), **Castillo Watersports** (☎ 787-791-6195, 726-5752, evenings); and **Benítez Deep Sea Fishing** (☎ 787-723-2292, 724-6265).

Also try finding a charter at **La Parguera** in the SW and at **Puerto Real** near Mayagüez. The **Club Náutico International Billfish Tournament** is held here in Sept. In its fourth decade, it is the longest running tournament of its kind in the world.

The **Cangrejos Yacht Club Blue Marlin Tournament** takes place in Aug.

Tourmarine Adventures (☎ 787-851-9259), in Joyuda on the W coast, offer charters for around $350 per half day, $500 per full day.

http://www.fishinginpuertorico.com

LAKE FISHING: Rental equipment is not yet available, so bring your own. Try Lago Dos Bocas near Utuado, Lago Cidra, Lago Patillas, Lago Toa Vaca (in Villalba), Lago Yauco, and Lago Guajataca (in Quebradillas). Fish you might catch include catfish, peacock bass, largemouth bass, tilapia, and sunfish.

Sailing & Boating

Chartering a boat is another popular activity. Be prepared for a few discomforts: handheld showers situated right next to the toilets are standard fare. Plan your itinerary at least six months in advance if you're interested in peak times like February, March, Easter, Thanksgiving, and Christmas. The poorest conditions for sailing run from the end of August through the middle of October. Bring dramamine if you get seasick.

Boats can be rented at **La Playita Boat Rental,** 1010 Ave, Ashford, Condado (☎ 787-722-1607) and the **Condado Plaza Hotel Watersports Center** (☎ 787-721-1000, ext. 1361). Fajardo is now the major charter center. Boats can also be rented at

The most useful book for yachting is **Yachtsman's Guide to the Virgin Islands and Puerto Rico**, published by Tropic Island Publishers (PO Box 611141, North Miami, FL 33161) which gives you in-depth sailing information. You can expect to spend $1,000-$2,000 pp for an eight-day/seven-night cruise with all meals, alcohol, and use of sports equipment included.

Dorado, at Palmas del Mar near Humacao and at Puerto Real near Mayagüez. From La Parguera, you can charter a motorboat to explore the offshore cays.

MARINAS: The **San Juan Bay Marina** (☎ 787-721-8062) is at Stop 10, Ave. Fernández Juncos in Miramar.

Set on Demajagua Bay on the E shore at Carr. 3 at Km 51.2, the **Puerto del Rey Marina** (☎ 787-860-1000) has slips for 700 boats and can accommodate vessels up to 200 ft. Also in Fajardo are the **Villa Marina** (☎ 787-728-2450, 787-863-5131) and **Puerto Chico Marina** (☎ 787-863-0834; Carr. 987). **Isleta Marina (Club Náutico de Puerto Rico)** (☎ 787-863-0370) is off the coast from Fajardo.

The **Marina de Salinas** (☎ 787-752-8484) is on Carr. 52 in Salinas.

The **Marina de Palmas** (☎ 787-852-6000, ext. 2551) is in Palmas del Mar, Humacao.

REGATTAS: Initiated in 1981, the **Discover the Caribbean Series** is a major event for mono-hull sailing aficionados in Puerto Rico and throughout the Caribbean; it follows International Yacht Racing Union Rules.

The three-day **Velasco Cup Regatta** and the **Las Américas Regatta**, held in Fajardo in March, mark the start of the Caribbean Ocean Racing Circuit.

In July is the **Budweiser Around Puerto Rico Race,** which begins at El Morro in Old San Juan.

On Labor Day is the **Copa de Palmas** held at the Palmas del Mar Resort.

In October Fajardo hosts the three-day **Kelly Cup Regatta**.

POWER BOAT RACING: Offshore power boat racing is quite popular, especially on the W coast from Mayagüez S to Boqueron Bay. While local races are held throughout the year, the biggest event is the Caribbean Offshore Race, an international event which often attracts celebrities. Contact **Offshore Power Boats** (☎ 787-787-6161) for information.

KAYAKING: There are some organized trips, including one out of San Juan. These are listed in the text. Rentals are widely available at public beaches and from surf shops. Expect to pay around $10 ph, $40 pd for one- and two-person kayaks. Kayaking is growing in popularity, and kayak rentals may now be found in many places.

Land Sports
Tennis

The island boasts more than 100 courts and most of the large hotels provide pros. Court fees can be as high as $15 or more.

An abundance of courts are found around San Juan. **San Juan Central Park**, Calle Cerra, has 17 lighted courts (☎ 787-722-1646).

Hotels with courts include Caribe Hilton, Carib Inn, Condado Beach, Condado Plaza, and El San Juan. Out on the island there are courts at the Dorado hotels and at Palmas del Mar Resort; Club Riomar in Río Grande; Hotel Copamarina (Guánica); at Punta Borínquen (Aguadilla); and at other locations.

Sights and Activities Key

🔺 Archaeological site

⊕ Forest reserve, natural attraction

✠ Historical site, cave, other attraction

🌴 Lighthouse

🏄 Surfing

🌀 Bioluminescent Bay

⛳ Golf course

🏖 Beach

🤿 Dive site

🚲 Bicycle path

🐋 Whale watching

260
(263) Page *(map)*

Isabela
Camuy Hatillo
306 Arecibo
306 Cueva del Indio

Barceloneta

296 Desecheo
Aguadilla
298
Quebradillas
Guajataca
303
Camuy Caves
311
310 Río Abajo
Dos Bocas
Guajataca
Manatí

Moca
San Sebastián
111

Aguada
281
Rincón
289

Añasco
119
309
Lares
Arecibo Observatory
Río Abajo
308
Florida
Ciales

315

279 Mayagüez
Caguana Ceremonial Center
313
Utuado
140
316
Jayuya
Toro Negro
144

To Mona Island
285, 286
Joyuda
279 Hormigueros
283 Fish Hatchery
Maricao
Adjuntas
140
320, 321
Villalba

Cabo Rojo
267
105
San Germán
Susúa
260
Sabana Grande
Luchetti
260
Guilarte
320
Peñuelas
253
254 Tibes

Lajas
100
102
Yauco
Buena Vista
256 Ponce

Playa Boquerón
270
261
Guánica
Guayanilla
2

La Parguera
Ensenada
Guánica
260, 263
Caja de Muertos
252

Cabo Rojo
278
Bioluminescent Bay **270**

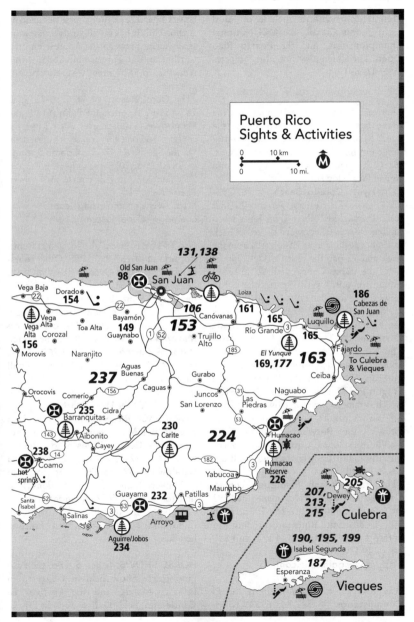

**Puerto Rico
Sights & Activities**

0   10 km
0   10 mi.

131, 138

Old San Juan
98 San Juan

Vega Baja   Dorado
154

106
Canóvanas   **161**

Loiza

186
Cabezas de
San Juan

Vega
Alta Alta Corozal
149
Bayamón
Guaynabo

153

Río Grande   **165**
Luquillo

156
Morovis

Toa Alta

Naranjito

Trujillo
Alto

El Yunque
169, 177   **163**

165

Fajardo
To Culebra
& Vieques

Ceiba

237

Aguas
Buenas
Caguas

Gurabo

Juncos

Naguabo

Orocovis   Comerío
235 Cidra
Barranquitas

San Lorenzo

Las
Piedras

238
Coamo
hot
springs

Aibonito
Cayey

230
Carite

224

Humacao

232
Guayama   Patillas

Yabucoa

Humacao
Reserve
226

Santa
Isabel

Salinas

Arroyo

Maunabo

**207,
213,
215**

Dewey

205

Culebra

Aguirre/Jobos
234

190, 195, 199
Isabel Segunda

187
Esperanza

Vieques

75

Tennis tournaments include the **Bud Light Tennis Classic**, the **MCI National Championships,** and the **Puerto Rico Open**. The Commonwealth also competes in the Davis Cup.

Golf

There are so many places to play that the island has been dubbed "Scotland in the Sun." Resort green fees are in the $65-100 range but may be lower if you are a guest. (Fees at places such as Aguirre and Aguadilla are lower.)

The **Hyatt Dorado Beach** (☎ 787-796-1234, ext. 3710) offers two courses that were designed by Robert Trent Jones when Laurence Rockefeller owned the resort back in 1958. Clocking in at 7,500 yards from the back and 72 par, the East Course is longer than the West Course, whose fairways extend for 6,913 yards Spectacular ocean views can be found at holes 10 and 18.

Other, less difficult Trent Jones courses are built on coastal plains at the **Hyatt Cerromar** (☎ 787-796-1234, ext. 3210). The North Course is 6,841yds. and the South Course extends for 7,047 yards.

In Río Grande on the E coast is the **Westin Río Mar** (☎ 787-888-8815/8816), which is famous for its narrow, challenging 6,845-yd., par-72 course. Also in Río Grande, the **Berwind Country Club** (☎ 787-876-3056), a private club, opens for visitors on Tues., Thurs., and Fri. It has a 6,991-yard layout.

The **Bahía Beach Plantation** course, Carr. 187 in Río Grande, opened in 1992 (☎ 787-256-5600, ✆ 787-256-1035). Each hole is different. Rates are around $75 before 1 PM, $50 from 1–4 PM, and $30 after 3 PM. Cart is included.
http://www.golfbahia.com

Way over on the eastern tip is the **El Conquistador** (☎ 787-863-6784) which

boasts a par-72, 18-hole course designed by Arthur Hill. It has 6,700 yards of fairways sandwiched between the Atlantic and the Caribbean. Rates are around $185, with a reduction to $115 after 2 PM. Hotel guests pay less.

The **Doral Resort** (☎ 787-285-2256, ✆ 787-852-6273) offers the **Palm** ($110) and **Flamboyán** ($100) courses. After 2 PM, the charge is $65 on either course. It's open daily In the SE, the 6,647-yard **Coamo Springs** (☎ 787-825-1370) is the only 18-hole, par-72 championship golf course in southern Puerto Rico.
http://www.coamosprings.com
coamogolf@coamosprings.com

An 18-hole course is also located at **Punta Borínquen** (☎ 787-890-2987) Other courses include the **Luis Ortis** (☎ 787-786-3859, 787-787-7252) in the metropolitan area, the 18-hole **Punta Borinquen** in Aguadilla, the 9-hole **Aguirre Golf Course** on the S coast, and the **Club Deportivo de Mayagüez** (☎ 787-851-8880). The **Ponce Hilton & Casino** (☎ 787-259-7676/7777, ✆ 787-259-7674, 800-HILTONS) will have a new 18-hole golf course in 2003.

Other Land Sports

HORSEBACK RIDING: This is available at **Palmas del Mar Resort** near Humacao, **Santurce's Centro Ecuestre de Puerto Rico** (☎ 787-728-4530), at **Hacienda Carabali** (☎ 787-795-6351; Carr. 992, Km 4, Mameyes), and at other locations. Post time for racing at **El Commandate** (☎ 787-724-6060), to the E of San Juan in Canóvanas, is 2:30 on Sun., Wed., Fri., and holidays.

HORSE SHOWS: *Dulce Sueño*, the Paso Fino Horse Show held in Guayama in February-March, and the *Festival La Candelaria*, held the first week in Feb. in

🌐 Puerto Rico Eco/Adventure Tours 🌐

AdvenTours
Luquillo
Specializes in NE and SW. Bird-watching, hiking, kayaking, biking, backpacking, private tours, coffee plantations, Culebra, and Mona, pre/post cruise tours. Daily, reservations required.
☎ 787-530-8311
http://www.angelfire.com/fl2/adventours

Aventuras Tierra Adentro
268 A Piñero Ave., Univ. Gardens. San Juan
Rappelling, rock climbing, canyoning, caving
☎ 787-766-0470
http://www.aventurastierraadentro.com

Copladet Nature & Adventure
Soller St. 528, Matienzo Center, San Juan
Nature and adventure tours.
☎ 787-765-8595
copladet@coqui.net

EcoXcursion Aquatica
Carr. 191, Km 1.7 Río Grande
Kayak day tours and bioluminescent bay kayak tour, rainforest hikes and mountain bike tours.
☎ 787-888-2887

Encantos Ecotours
San Juan and other locations.
Group tours. Historical, cultural, and nature tours. Eco-sensitive. Personal service.
☎ 787-272-0005.
http://www.ecotourspr.com

Island Adventures
Rt 996 Km 4.5, Puerto Real. Vieques
Bioluminescent Bay Tour
☎ 787-741-0720
http://www.biobay.com

Piñones Ecotours
Carr. 187, Boca Congrejos Bridge
Biking, hiking, kayaking, gear rentals.
☎ 787-253-0005
http://www.ecotourspr.com

Tropical Beaches Tours
Aguadilla
Guided tour packages.
☎ 787-895-7736.
http://home.coqui.net/tours

the town of Manatí, are two of the best Paso Fino events. Other competitions include Bayamón's three-day **Equi-Expo** in Jan. and the **Copa Dorado** in April.

POLO: Set on 25 acres bordering the Río Loíza, the **Ingenio Polo Club** (☎ 787-752-8181) hosts the Rolex Polo Cup in March.

BOWLING: There are a number of lanes scattered across the island. **Tower Lane Bowling** (40 lanes!) is in the San Juan suburb of Levitown, **Paradise Bowling** is in Hato Rey, **Ponce Bowling** is in Ponce, **Cupey Bowling** is in Trujillo, and **Western**

Bowling is in Mayagüez. The week-long **Tirolcocos International Bowling Tournament** is held in June at Tower Lane Bowling.

CYCLING: The **International Cycling Competition** is held in Sabana Grande annually during the second week in May. The **Tour Gigante de Puerto Rico** is another major event. Contact the **Cycling Federation** (☎ 787-721-8755) for details.

MOUNTAIN BIKING: Cycling on roads can be dangerous. **Bike Stop** (☎ 787-782-2282), **Condado Bicycle** (☎ 787-722-

INTRODUCTION

6288), and **Isabela Mountain Bike Tours** offer mountain bike excursions. Some of these also rent bikes out.
isabelabiketours@yahoo.com

MARATHONS: In its third decade and leading the pack, the 20-km **San Blas Marathon** (☎ 787-825-1094) takes place in Coamo in Feb.

The 42-km **Enríque Ramirez Marathon** (☎ 787-899-1081) takes place in Lajas during April and qualifies runners wishing to compete in the Olympics and in the Central American Games.

The 12-km **Women's Marathon** (☎ 787-892-3500) is an international race held in Guayanilla in Dec.

The **Modesto Carrión** (☎ 787-734-2928) is in Juncos in Nov. Held in March, the **Diet Pepsi Five Mile** (☎ 787-734-2928) starts in San Juan's Central Park and finishes in Santurce. The 40-mile **La Guadalupe Marathon** (☎ 787-840-4141) is run in November in Ponce.

BASEBALL: The **Caribbean League** includes five teams; their season stretches from Oct. to March. In San Juan, you can see games by the **San Juan Metros** and the **Santurce Crabbers** at Hato Rey's Hiram Bithorn Stadium.

BASKETBALL: There's a six-team **professional league** as well as a 16-team **amateur league**. Obtain a current schedule from the Federación de Baloncesto.

VOLLEYBALL: Held during the last weekend in May, the **National Beach Volleyball Tournament 2-on-2** is followed by the final event during the last weekend in June. This features the top 16 teams; it's followed in turn by the **Caribbean Beach Tournament** in Aug.

Dayhiking Checklist

✔ Water (two quarts)

✔ Binoculars

✔ Windsurfing sandals

✔ Food/snacks

✔ umbrella

✔ swim trunks

✔ small towel

✔ camera

HIKING: The island is an excellent place to hike. Major locales include the Caribbean National Forest (El Yunque), Culebra, Carite Forest Reserve, Gúanica Forest Reserve, and Toro Negro Forest Reserve. The Caribbean National Forest provides the most extensive trails, with Guánica's dry forest reserve coming in second. Hiking trails are detailed throughout the text of the travel section.

Birdwatching

Despite the island's small size, there are 273 species of birds, 12 of them endemic. Good birding spots include the forest reserves, especially Guánica where you might see the Puerto Rican tody, the Puerto Rican tanager, the Puerto Rican lizard cuckoo, or the elusive and nocturnal Puerto Rican nightjar.

The Maricao Forest Reserve is home to the Puerto Rican vireo and to scaly-naped pigeons. Puerto Rican parrots can be spotted only in the Luquillo Mountains and in the Caribbean National Forest. For more information, see the "Hiking" section, as well as specific entries in the travel section.

Cockfighting

Popular long before the construction of the first Puerto Rican court in 1764, this "sport" flourished until banned after the American occupation in 1898. It was prohibited on the grounds that it led to animal mistreatment and gambling. Naturally, cockfighting did not disappear — it went underground. Giving in to the inevitable, Gov. Robert Gore legalized the sport in 1933. He signed the "Rooster Law" with a feather from Justicia, a famous fighting cock.

There are some 134 *galleras* (cockfighting arenas) which have attracted more than a million spectators annually. In rural areas, men and women are seated separately, with women high up in the back. The roosters are specially bred and pampered, and a *gallero* may spend 15 years refining his line. A champion bird can fight on for a few years. Roosters are entered according to weight, size and type of spurs used, and the starting bet may range from $100 to $5,000 and upwards.

The rooster's natural spurs are generally cut off and a standard-length spur is attached with tape, thread, and wax. Although natural spurs that have been polished by an artisan can run as much as $300 per pair or more, plastic spurs (around $20) are the most popular ones used today. A fight is timed at 20 mins., and feathers fly frenetically for the duration. If you wonder who is winning, it's the one with the bloodiest spurs.

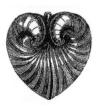

Coral Bleaching

Coral Bleaching occurs when the anthrozoans, which form the coral, expel their algae, thus declaring a divorce from their symbiotic relationship. These algae, which provide the mascara for the otherwise vanilla coral, provide 90% of the coral's protein.

When coral is heated, their algae lose their abilities to photosynthesize. They take it out on their housemates, the coral, with an assault of free radicals (toxic oxygen-containing molecules). These are created because the algae have no place to put their absorbed light energy.

The coral kick the algae out and then turn white. While they can survive for a while, waiting for more benign conditions to return, they will die if things don't improve.

Ensuing global warming has the coral worried, along with the divers and snorkelers who come to visit them in their subterranean kingdoms. If ocean temperatures continue to rise, many of our coral reefs will die.

MONITORING OTHER DISEASES : Professor Raymond L. Hayes Jr. has put together a six-page spiral bound set of laminated photo ID cards which illustrate 15 common reef diseases. Each picture is captioned in English and Spanish. The idea is that recreational divers can help document the spread of coral diseases. The set fits right in your BC pocket on your vest. Information about reporting data is included on the back of the card. A set is $10. Send a check to Dr. Raymond Hayes, Office of Medical Education, Howard University College of Medicine, 520 W St., NW, Washington, DC 20059. Proceeds go to the Association of Marine Laboratories of the Caribbean (AMLC) and to the Global Coral Reef Alliance (GCRA), both of which are non-profit NGOs.

rhayes@Howard.edu

𝕶𝖓𝖔𝖜 𝕿𝖍𝖞 𝕻𝖆𝖗𝖙𝖓𝖊𝖗!

Vacation Planning Checklist

Instructions: Photocopy an enlarged version of this sheet (available in pdf format at our website: **www.savethemanatee.com**) and distribute to each person planning the trip and have them fill it in. Check all that apply to each question.

I'm traveling for ❏ business ❏ pleasure ❏ adventure ❏ other_____
_____

I expect to spend $ for a room or other_____

I prefer ❏ resorts ❏ camping ❏ rental ❏ B&B ❏ small hotel ❏ other_____
_____

My interests are ❏ historical sites ❏ museums ❏ galleries ❏ beaches ❏ water sports (specify_____ ❏ snorkeling ❏ diving ❏ hiking ❏ birdwatching ❏ other _____

I plan to get around by (check all that apply) ❏ rental car (type) _____ ❏ local bus ❏ charter bus ❏ taxi ❏ foot ❏ tour ❏ other (describe)_____

I like to travel (check all that apply) ❏ alone ❏ sometimes in a group ❏ leisurely ❏ moderate ❏ fast ❏ breezing through

I expect to spend $__ daily including $__ on lodging. $__ on food $__ on transportation, and $__ on other activities.

I am most interested in visiting/doing (describe in depth): _____
_____
_____
_____
_____
_____
_____
_____
_____
_____
_____

Practicalities

Basics

VISAS: All visitors from abroad (except Canadians) require a US visa. It's better to obtain a multiple entry visa and, if possible, to do so in your own country. Fill out forms perfectly; consular officials tend to be aggravatingly picayune.

CONDUCT: The more Spanish you speak the better. Keep in mind that, while Puerto Rico is part of the United States, Latin cultural mores prevail here. Men and women alike tend to dress conservatively. If you want to be accepted and respected, dress respectably. Bathing attire is unsuitable on main streets. Nearly a century of US colonial rule has had an effect here and you can expect some acrimony along with the hospitality. But, once people come to know you, they will accept you.

HEALTH: Medical care is usually on a first-come, first-served basis. Although the quality of medical and dental services is reasonably high, it's not quite up to mainland standards. Most physicians are centered in San Juan, Ponce, and Mayagüez.

Hospital costs are slightly lower than in the States, and Medicare and all other Stateside hospitalization policies are honored. Equipped with 24-hour emergency service, the **Ashford Memorial Hospital**, 1451 Ashford Ave. in Santurce, has many English-speaking staff members.

San Juan's **Hyperbaric Medical Facility** (☎ 787-281-2794, 787-281-2797) has a decompression chamber for divers with the bends.

For help in obtaining a physician, call the **Medical Association** (☎ 787-725-6969) or check the Yellow Pages of the telephone directory under *Médicos Especialistas*.

Either arrive with an adequate supply of any medications you may require, or bring your doctor's prescription with you.

Although diseases like malaria that had been a problem in the past have been eliminated, bilharzia, a disease spread by snails carrying the larvae of the parasite *schistosoma*, is something to watch out for. The chancs of infection are remote, but it's best to be circumspect when bathing in freshwater pools near human habitation.

DRUGSTORES: There are more than 40 Walgreens on the island, as well as a large number of local pharmacies.

- painkillers
- antihistamine tablets
- hydrocortisone cream (1%)
- sunscreen
- insect repellent
- band-aids
- antiseptic
- water purification tablets
- prescription medicines

WHAT TO TAKE: Bring as little as possible, i.e., bring only what you need. It's easy just to wash clothes in the sink and thus save lugging around a week's laundry. Remember, simple is best. Set your priorities according to your needs. If you're planning on doing an exceptional amount of hiking, for example, hiking boots are a good idea. Otherwise, they're an encumbrance. With a light pack or bag, you can breeze through from one town to another easily. Confining yourself to carry-on luggage also saves waiting at the airport. See the chart below for suggestions and eliminate unnecessary items.

THEFT: Theft should not be a problem if you're careful. By all means avoid the slum areas of San Juan, don't flash money or possessions around and, in general, keep a low profile.

■ Beaches can be dangerous at night, and don't leave anything in a tent.

■ Keep copies of your credit card numbers and passport or other ID separately

TRAVELING WITH CHILDREN: Puerto Rico is as safe as anywhere for children. Be sure to inquire at your hotel as to extra charges for children and if they'll even be accepted. You can save money by dining at local restau-

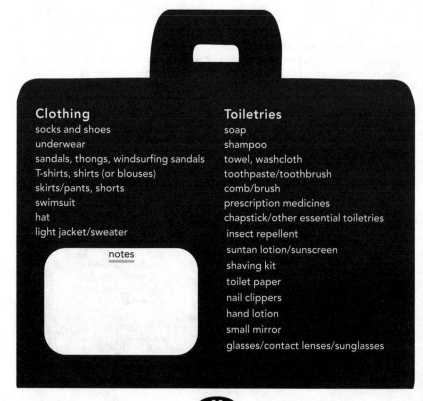

Clothing
socks and shoes
underwear
sandals, thongs, windsurfing sandals
T-shirts, shirts (or blouses)
skirts/pants, shorts
swimsuit
hat
light jacket/sweater

notes

Toiletries
soap
shampoo
towel, washcloth
toothpaste/toothbrush
comb/brush
prescription medicines
chapstick/other essential toiletries
insect repellent
suntan lotion/sunscreen
shaving kit
toilet paper
nail clippers
hand lotion
small mirror
glasses/contact lenses/sunglasses

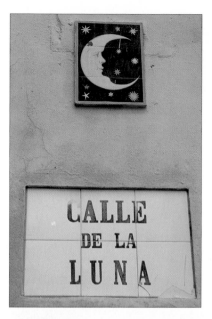

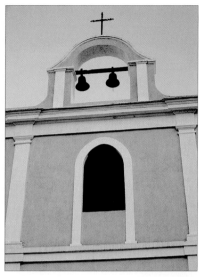

Top: Old San Juan street; Loiza church (1646)
Bottom: Music lessons in Old San Juan

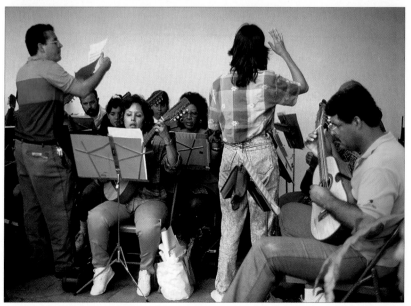

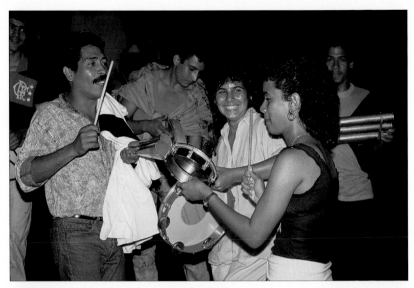

Above: Music making, Old San Juan. Below: Folkloric dancing, Ponce

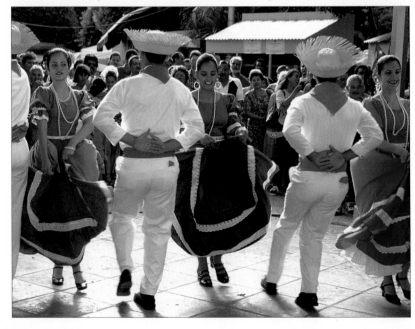

Travel Tips: Single-Parent Families

🐾 Involve your children in your research and decisions. Talk to them about what you are planning to do.

🐾 Try to spend a third of the time on a trip doing things you like, a third on activities you and your child or children like and a third doing things you both enjoy.

🐾 Plan on visiting places that each child is interested in. A school is always a good choice.

🐾 Plan your trip in detail in writing. Save a copy afterwards for future reference.

🐾 Record any driving or travel directions. Have a child read them to you while driving.

🐾 Make a packing list and give a copy to adolescents so they can be in charge of their preparations.

🐾 Nutritious snacks and water come in handy whether on a plane or a bus.

🐾 Have your children assist with baggage and other tasks such as map reading.

🐾 Be sure to thank your children for their help.
— Brenda Elwell, publisher, *Single Parent Travel Newsletter* and author of *The Single Parent Travel Handbook*
http://www.SingleParentTravel.net
globalbrenda@yahoo.com

Facts About Jet Skis

▼Jet skis account for 40% of all boating injuries.

▼Jet skis traverse shallow and sensitive inshore waters, areas where ordinary water craft can not go.

▼Jet skis have caused injury and/or death to manatees, seal pups, nesting loons and other species.

▼Jet skis discharge as much as a third of their raw gas and oil mixture into the water. Each year jet skis spill the equivalent of four Exxon *Valdez* tankers full of raw petrochemicals into US waters. A two-hr. ride may emit enough to cover an eight acre pond. The oil byproducts also damage the environment.

▼Jet skis have been banned from Canada to the Florida Keys. They are banned in the VI National Park.

http://www.earthisland.org/bw

rants. Keep an eye on the kids while they're in the water. There are no lifeguards. Also, make sure that they apply sun protection, are not overexposed to sun, and get sufficient liquids. Remember to bring whatever special equipment you'll need. Disposable diapers and baby food are available but expensive. Be sure to inquire at your hotel as to extra charges for children and if they'll even be accepted.

During the summer, you can take your children to **Cascadas Water Park** (☎ 787-891-1005) near Aguadilla.

In San Juan, don't miss the **Museo del Niño** (described under Old San Juan), and Bayamón has the Luis A. Ferré Science Park (described under Bayamón).

NOTE: Child- and family-friendly attractions are noted with a 🏃 symbol throughout the text.

♿ Federal law commands that all public buildings have wheelchair access, and the larger hotels are built to suit the needs of the disabled.
Wheelchair Getaway (☎ 800-868-8028, cell 787-378-9192) offers tours for the disabled.

GAY AND LESBIAN TRAVEL: The San Juan area has many guesthouses and small hotels which cater to gay and lesbian travelers. Hotels and bars are listed throughout the text. There are a number of resource guides to Puerto Rico on the internet.

While on the island, you may contact the **Gay Pride Coalition** (☎ 787-261-2590).

College students may connect through the **College Community Pro Gay Equality Group** (☎ 787-764-0000, ext. 6389) at the University of Puerto Rico in Río Piedras and at the **Gay and Lesbian Support Group** (☎ 787-764-0000, ext. 5683, 5684) which is also in Río Piedras.

The staff of **Scriptum Books** (☎ 787-724-1123) Ave. Ashford 1129, and the Atlantic Beach Hotel (☎ 787-721-690, may also be of help.

GETTING MARRIED: You must bring your driver's license or passport (mandatory for non US citizens). A blood test (☎ 787-767-9120) must be taken within ten days prior to the ceremony. If appropriate, a divorce or death certificate must be presented. You must obtain forms from the **Dept. of Health** (☎ 787-728-7980) in San Juan. They are available by mail (allow two months) from the Demographic Registry, Apdo. Box 11854, Fernandez Juncos Station, San Juan, PR 00910

ENVIRONMENTAL CONDUCT: Dispose of plastics properly. Remember that six-pack rings, plastic bags, and fishing lines can cause injury or prove fatal to sea turtles, fish, birds, and other marine life. Unable to regurgitate anything they swallow, turtles and other sea creatures may mistake plastic bags for jellyfish or choke on fishing lines. Birds may starve to death after becoming entangled in lines, nets, and plastic rings. All of these items take hundreds of years to decompose and can do a lot of damage in the interim.

 Daytrippin'
What to take on a day trip? Water, money, swim suit, towel, sunscreen, reading material, camera and film, snorkeling gear (if not provided), shoes if hiking), snack food.

☺ Puerto Rico Dos and Don'ts ☺

➡ ***Do*** try local food and try to patronize local restaurants as well as gourmet bistros.

➡ ***Don't*** just stay lounging around your hotel. *Do* get around and explore, but don't over-extend yourself and try to do too much; There's always the next visit.

➡ ***Do*** try to conserve energy by switching off lights and a/c when you leave your hotel room. *Don't* dump your garbage at sea or litter in town.

➡ ***Don't*** remove or injure any coral, spear fish, remove tropical fish, or annoy turtles or touch their eggs. *Do* not feed fish. *Don't* wear jewelry while swimming or diving. *Don't* stand on anything other than sand. *Do* show respect for the underwater environment. *Don't* swim in rough surf.

➡ ***Do*** try to get out of the San Juan metropolitan area and explore some of the smaller towns as well as the natural areas.

Doing It Differently

Many visitors to Puerto Rico miss out on a lot. Here are some suggestions to get more out of your trip.

❧ Plan in advance to visit either or both of the National Trust properties, Hacienda Buena Vista or Los Cabezas de San Juan.

❧ Spend a day exploring Old San Juan. Don't make plans, just roam around and see what places you come across.

❧ Spend three or more nights in a place. Try to get to know the area. You can't see the entire island unless you have months available.

❧ Plan a picnic and have fun shopping at a local market. Check out small local bars and restaurants, many of which have great atmosphere.

❧ Don't try to go too far in a single day. Puerto Rico may not be large, but it takes a long time to get to places, and the fun is being out of the car and not behind the wheel.

Puerto Rico Itineraries

If you have 3 days: Spend one day at the Condado, Isla Verde, or Luquillo beaches; one day in Old San Juan; and one day in El Yunque, Loíza, or exploring.

If you have 5 days: Spend one day at the beach, one day in Old San Juan, one day in El Yunque or on a day trip, and spend two nights out on the island.

If you have one week: Spend one day at the beach, a day in Old San Juan, one day in El Yunque or on a day trip, and spend some nights out on the island or on Vieques or Culebra.

Places not to be missed if you have time: See the museums in Old San Juan and visit El Yunque, Vieques, Culebra, Coamo (hot springs); walk around and explore small towns like Aibonito, Barranquitas, or Jayuya; hike in one of the nature preserves such as Guánica; visit a National Trust site like Hacienda Buena Vista or El Faro; see the restored section of Ponce and the outlying archeological site at Tibes; visit Utuado's Caguana ceremonial ball court; and travel to coastal sites like Cabo Rojo.

Remember that the Caribbean National Forests and the Commonwealth's reserves were created to help preserve the environment and refrain from carrying off plants, rocks, animals, or other materials. Buying black coral jewelry also serves to support reef destruction, and turtle shell items come from an endangered species. On St. John remember not to feed the donkeys or to leave food within their reach. Environmental organizations are listed in the text.

UNDERSEA CONDUCT: Respect the natural environment. Take nothing and remember that corals are easily broken. Much damage has already been done to the reef through snorkelers either standing on coral or hanging onto outcroppings.

As stony corals grow at the rate of less than half an inch per year, it can take decades to repair the desecration caused by a few min-

utes carelessness. It's wise to keep well away just for your own protection: many corals will retaliate with stings and the sharp ridges can cause cuts that are slow to heal.

In order to control yourself, make sure that you are properly weighted prior to your dive. Swim calmly and fluidly through the water and avoid dragging your console and/or octopus (secondary breathing device) behind you. While diving or snorkeling resist the temptation to touch fish. Many fish (such as the porcupine) secrete a mucous coating which protects them from bacterial infection. Touching them removes the coating and may result in infection and death for the fish. Also avoid feeding fish, which can disrupt the natural ecosystem. In short, look, listen, enjoy, but leave only bubbles.

PRACTICALITIES

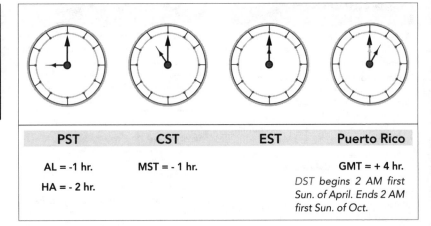

PST	CST	EST	Puerto Rico

AL = -1 hr.   MST = - 1 hr.   GMT = + 4 hr.

HA = - 2 hr.   *DST begins 2 AM first*
                                                                     Sun. of April. Ends 2 AM
                                                                     first Sun. of Oct.

BOATING CONDUCT: In addition to the behavior patterns detailed above, always exercise caution while anchoring a boat. Improperly anchoring in seagrass beds can destroy wide swatches of seagrass, which take a long time to recover. If there's no buoy available, the best place to anchor is a sandy spot which causes relatively little environmental impact. Tying your boat to mangroves can kill the trees, so it is acceptable to do so *only* during a storm.

In order to help eliminate the unnecessary discharge of oil, maintain the engine and keep the bilge clean. If you notice oil in your bilge, use oil-absorbent pads to soak it up. Be careful not to overfill the boat when fueling. Emulsions from petrochemical products stick to fishes' gills and suffocate them, and deposits in sediment impede the development of marine life. Detergents affect plankton and other organisms, which throws off the food chain.

When you approach seagrass beds, slow down because your propeller could strike a sea turtle. Avoid maneuvering your boat too close to coral reefs. Striking the reef can damage both your boat and the reef. Avoid stirring up sand in shallow coral areas. The sand can be deposited in the coral and cause polyps to suffocate and die. If your boat has a sewage holding tank, empty it only at properly equipped marinas. Avoid using harsh chemicals such as ammonia and bleach while cleaning your boat; they pollute the water and kill marine life. Use environmentally safe cleaning products whenever possible.

Boat owners should avoid paint containing lead, copper (which can make mollusks poisonous), mercury (highly toxic to fish and algae), or TBT. Finally, remember that a diver-down flag should be displayed while diving or snorkeling.

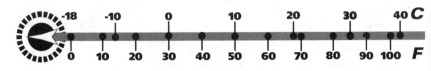

e Puerto Rican Environmental Organizations e

Campers Association of Puerto Rico ☎ 787-760-4122

Caribbean Environmental Information ☎ 787-751-0239

Caribbean Standing Network ☎ 787899-2048, ext. 800; ☎ 787-462-8124

Citizens for the Conservation of the Environment of Aguada ☎ 787-868-4656

Commission of Justice and Peace ☎ 787-765-0606

Committee of Guayanabo Neighbors for the Well-being of the Environment
☎ 787-731-7225

Committee of Yabucoa Citizens for Quality of Life, Inc. ☎ 787-893-1567

Committee to Save Guánica, Inc. ☎ 787-821-2302

Committee to Save the Environment of Guayanilla ☎ 787-835-2341

Committee to Save the Environment of Juncos ☎ 787-734-4491

Conservation Trust of Puerto Rico ☎ 787-722-5834

Ecological League of Rincón Carlos Gastón (☎ 787-823-5646),
Sandra Ríos Miranda (☎ 787-823-3663)

Environmental Coalition of Puerto Rico ☎ 787-765-4303, ☎ 787-767-0820

Environmental Organization of Yuquiyú (Mary Casillas) ☎ 787-889-6212

Highland Friends of the Environment ☎ 787-828-1449.

Mayagüez Citizens for Health and Environment ☎ 787-265-6266

Missión Industrial of Puerto Rico ☎ 787-765-4303

Natural History Society of Puerto Rico ☎ 787-726-5488, ☎ 787-728-1515, ext. 283

Neighbors United for a Better Environment: (Angel G. Quiles) ☎ 787-743-2413
 or (George Flores) ☎ 787-744-6250.

Organization of the Environmental Communities of the East ☎ 787-893-7803.

Puerto Rican Association of Water Resources ☎ 787-729-6951

Puerto Rican Conservation Foundation ☎ 787-763-9875

Scientific and Technical Services, Inc. ☎ 787-759-8787/8675

Speleological Society of Puerto Rico ☎ 787-767-0687, 783-7688

Vieques Conservation and Historical Trust ☎ 787-741-8850

PRACTICALITIES

Metric Conversion Chart
1 inch = 2.54 centimeters
1 foot = .3048 meters
1 mile= 1.6093 km
1 km = .6214 miles
1 acre = .4047 hectares (ha)
1 sq. km = 100 ha
1 sq. mi. = 2.59 sq. km
1 ounce = 28.35 grams
1 pound = .4536 kilograms
1 quart = .94635 liters
1 US gallon = 3.7854 liters
1 imperial gallon = 4.5459 liters

Money & Measurements

The monetary unit is the US dollar (called "*dolar*" or "*peso*") which is divided into 100¢ (referred to as "*centavos*"or "*chavitos*"). Nickels (5¢) are referred to as "*vellons*" or "*ficha.*" Quarters (25¢) are called "*pesetas.*" If coming from abroad, it's better to change your money in a major US city or carry traveler's checks. Banks are open from 9 AM–2:30 PM, and ATMs (called ATH, "at any hour," here) are readily available; use the ones with private glass door entrances for security at night. Major credit cards are accepted virtually anywhere.

If you would like to bring back a souvenir for your coffee-drinking friends, consider buying an eight oz. package of ground Puerto Rican coffee. Two brands with attractive labels (and taste to match) are Rioja and Adjuntas. These, along with others, should be obtainable in large and small food stores islandwide.

Measurements are a confusing mixture of American and metric. Gasoline and milk are both sold by the liter (*litro*). While road distances are given in kilometers, road speed signs and car speedometers use miles per hour. Land elevations are expressed in meters, but land is sold in units called *cuerdas*, equal to .97 acre. Weights are measured in pounds (*libras*) and ounces (*onzas*); a *tonelada* is a ton. *Pulgadas* are inches, and *pies* are feet. The Commonwealth operates on Atlantic Standard (Eastern Standard + one hour) time. When the Eastern US is operating on daylight savings, both are on the same time.

Shopping & Customs

SHOPPING: Opening hours vary but stores are generally open from Mon. through Sat., with some stores closing for an hour in the afternoon. Aside from local handicrafts, there isn't much to buy that can't be found cheaper (or at the same price) somewhere else. Some of the better buys are at the factory outlets (Farah, Hathaway, etc.) in Old San Juan. Jewelry is also a popular item in stores here, but know your prices at home. There's an import tax on photographic equipment and accessories, so bring your own. T-shirts make good souvenirs as do local coffee beans (about $4/lb. at Pueblo in Old San Juan). Rum is cheap and no import duties are charged if bringing it to the States, but other imported hard liquor is expensive and not worth bringing back.

Ron de Barrilito, Bourget, Creme de Cacao Liqueur, Coquito Trigo Coconut Creme Liqueur, and Bacardi Añejo are all examples of Puerto Rican liquors you can bring back. Rum is generally cheaper in town at the market than in the duty-free shops at the airport.

Although heavy to carry, Lotus pineapple juice makes a unique gift.

Shopping Tips

● *Know your prices.* Do research on the local prices for the goods you wish to buy.

● *Buy what you need.* Don't feel compelled to buy because you are here.

● *Know the differences.* Gold that is 24 karats in the US and Canada is marked 999 in items of European manufacture; 18 k gold is 750, and 14 k gold is 585.

● *Shipping is available.* But make sure you understand the liability coverage and costs involved.

Parcha-flavored Tang is sold only on the island, as are traditional syrups made from tamarind, coconut, and guanábana, which are used to top shaved ice.

Poultry and mangoes and most other citrus fruits are among the agricultural products prohibited from export to the States.

You can bring breadnuts, avocados, plantains, quenapas, pineapples, and papayas. Citrus fruits must be inspected.

You may also bring back dried or cured herbs, dried and preserved insects, cocoa beans, banana leaves, tamarind bean pods, dried and cleaned snail shells and seashells, and fresh cut or dried medicinal plants, and other such esoteric items.

For details, call the quarantine division of the US Department of Agriculture in San Juan at 787-253-4505 or call your local customs office prior to departure.

CANADIAN CUSTOMS: Canadian citizens may make an oral declaration four times per year to claim C$100 worth of exemptions which may include 200 cigarettes and 40 ounces of alcohol. In order to claim the exemption, Canadians must have been out of the country for at least 48 hours. A Canadian who's been away for at least seven days may make a written declaration once a year and claim C$300 worth of exemptions. After a trip of 48 hours or longer, Canadians receive a special duty rate of 20% on the value of goods up to C$300 in excess of the C$100 or C$300 exemption they claim. This excess cannot be applied to liquor or cigarettes. Goods claimed under the C$300 exemption may follow but merchandise claimed under all other exemptions must be accompanied.

GERMAN CUSTOMS: Residents may bring back 200 cigarettes, 50 cigars, 100 cigarillos, or 250 grams of tobacco; two liters of alcoholic beverages not exceeding 44 proof or one liter of 44 proof-plus alcohol; two liters of wine; and up to DM300 (or Euro equivalent) of other items.

Broadcasting & Media

TELEVISION, NEWSPAPERS, PERIODICALS: TV serves up a combination of the worst American programming rendered into Spanish and bad local imitations of the worst American programming. As is the case with radio and the press, it dishes up AP and UPI stories as news. There are a number of daily papers: The English-language tabloid the **San Juan Star** is the least partisan. Superficial and bland, its magazine format provides little investigative reporting. Even its editorials are borrowed.

El Nuevo Dia is the personal property of Luis A. Ferré Enterprises. The most important contemporary newspaper, it was founded in Ponce in 1909. Businessman and (later) governor Luis A. Ferré purchased the paper in the 1950s. It has a daily circulation of some 230,000. It controls around 70% of the island's advertising market. Despite its links with Ferré, it has tried to maintain an independent stance.

The almost comically grotesque **El Vocero**, the tabloid newspaper of the mass-

PRACTICALITIES

⊂ Puerto Rico on the Internet ⊃

The numbers of Puerto Rican websites have grown in recent years. Many are listed elsewhere in this book. Others can be found through search engines. Here is a list of just some of the more interesting and useful ones.

General Information

http://www.SavorPuertoRico.com Information, photos, updates, mailing list

http://www.travelandsports.com Good information on Puerto Rico

http://www.caribbean-on-line.com Information including travel forums

http://www.puertoricoisfun.com Governmental travel booking site

http://www.gotopuertorico.com Government tourism site

http://www.escapetopuertorico.com Useful information

http://welcome.topuertorico.org Great web site

http://www.prol.com General website for the island

http://www.puertoricowow.com General information site

http://home.coqui.net/ciales15 Great links page

http://www.lib.utexas.edu/maps/puerto_rico.html Online map collection

http://www.puertorico-herald.org *Puerto Rico Herald*, news and information

http://www.primerahora.com News in Spanish.

http://www.estrelladepr.com News in Spanish

http://www.vocero.com Ghoulish news in Spanish

http://www.superpagespr.com Information and Yellow Pages

Specialized Information

http://www.srh.noaa.gov/sju Current weather

http://www.letsdine.com Restaurants

http://www.tablespr.com Puerto Rican restaurants

http://www.where2stay.com Hotel reviews

http://www.prhta.org Puerto Rico Hotel & Tourism Association

http://www.woofbyte.com/puertorico Gay and lesbian info

http://memory.loc.gov/ammem/prhtml/prhome.html Library of Congress history

http://www.avesdepuertorico.org Puerto Rican birdwatching site

http://www.elboricua.com Puerto Rico cultural site

http://www.boricua.com Puerto Ricans on the internet

Regional Websites

http://www.ponceweb.org Official Ponce site

http://www.rinconpr.com Rincón information

http://www.rainforestsafari.com Northeastern Puerto Rico information

http://www.enchanted-isle.com Useful Vieques and Culebra site

es, is full of really gory, bloody murders, many of which are featured on the cover which has gory photos and red-ink headlines. Locals joke that, if you squeeze a copy, blood will ooze out. It has a circulation of around 259,000.

There are also a number of free publications, including the monthly *Tropic Times*, which caters to nautical types in the Fajardo area.

San Juan is a "city magazine" published once every six weeks by the *San Juan Star*. It has good political coverage and some amusing articles.

La Era de Ahora is a Spanish-language new-age monthly which features ads for "professional rebirthers," overpriced yoga workshops, the latest idiotic James Redfield tome, and the like.

Tu Salud is a natural foods advertising tabloid.

Puerto Rico Breeze is the island's bilingual gay advertising tabloid.

PUERTO RICO ON THE INTERNET: Although the World Wide Web is still developing, there are a number of places you can access information on Puerto Rico. Many are listed in the chart, and others are in the text. You should search for others on Google.

Caribbean Internet Service, located in San Juan, is an Internet provider. You can contact them at ☎ 787-728-3992 or 1-800-59-CISCO, or visit them on the Internet at **http://www.Caribe.net** Datacom Caribe,

Inc. also offers Internet services; visit them at **http://www.coqui.net** for more information.

Entertainment

The liveliest nightlife is found in Old San Juan. The Puerto Rico Tourism Company's **LeLoLai VIP card** may be purchased for around $10 at authorized travel agencies and hotels (Condado Plaza, Condado Beach, Caribe Hilton Regency, and La Concha). It gives access to a different tour or musical event daily.

Outside of the metropolitan area, things tend to be quieter, but Ponce has some relatively good nightlife.

There are a number of annual **music festivals** such as the **Heineken Jazzfest** (☎ 787-277-9200) held each May (generally over Memorial Day Weekend) and the Michelob **Dry Jazz and Latin Music Festival** at Bellas Artes in June. During the fall months, the **Noches Borinqueñas** offers a series of island-wide open-air free concerts by such artists as Roy Brown.

Movie theaters are found all over the island. A current listing is at:
http://www.caribbeancinemas.com

Puerto Rican raves are also a feature on the cultural landscape.
http://www.tsunami-trance.com

GAMBLING: Casinos are found in San Juan, Ponce, and Mayagüez; they are most-

?!¿ In recent decades, Puerto Rico has become a center for film-making. Movies shot here (or partially shot here) include *Frogmen, Contact, Heartbreak, Captain Ron, Swiss Family Robinson, Amistad* (which used El Morro and San Cristobal forts), *Executive Decision,* and *Golden Eye.*

ly in large hotels. The Puerto Rican Tourism Company has been operating slot machines since 1974; machines in the 20-odd casinos rake in some $900 million each year. You'll find blackjack, roulette, craps, and baccarat here. The island's lottery, which was first held in 1814, is a venerable way to throw some hard-earned cash down the drain. Approximately 300,000 tickets are sold weekly by some 15,000 licensed agents and 3,000 vendors. They receive some $70 million annually in commission

Calculating Gambling Odds

To calculate odds in a slot machine multiply the number of stops exponentially by the number of reels. For example, a machine with 22 stops (pictures of cherries and the like) should be multiplied four times (22 x 22 x 22 x 22) to produce odds to win the top prize at 1:234,256. Most machines have 22, 32, 64, or 72 stops. Odds are much better on a three-reel, 22-stop machine (1:10,648) than on a four-reel, 72-stop machine (1:26,873,856). A machine with a top prize of $10,000 delivers that in coins, not dollars! If you hit the jackpot, you will be paid by check and the money will be reported to the government. All of the "Progressive Jackpot" machines are identically programmed and have the same chance of winning. If you're playing these, put down the total number of coins allowable for the maximum jackpot return.

Enjoying Your Honeymoon

Honeymoons are a very special trip, and honeymooners feel a lot of pressure to have a perfect experience. Andrea Rotondo Hospidor, destination wedding expert and editor of **www.GetawayWeddings.com** *offers some tips to maximize your experience:*

- Check all your travel reservations a week before departure.

- If possible, don't leave the same day as your wedding reception. Enjoy your wedding day. It's very special.

- Don't overschedule your honeymoon with tours and other activities. Relax the first day. Schedule a spa treatment, hit the beach, and explore the local area. Have a leisurely meal, get to know some of the locals, and dance under the stars.

- Don't expect everything to be perfect or everything to go perfectly all of the time. Take a deep breath and enjoy the time together. This is an opportunity to spend quiet time together, reflect on your past, and begin planning your future together.

- Keep a honeymoon journal. This will become a keepsake that you'll treasure forever. Write down your thoughts and feelings about your wedding day, your arrival, the people that you meet, and other adventures. When you return home, paste a few photographs and postcards in your journal. This is a memento you'll fondly return to and, perhaps someday, share with your children.

for their efforts. Each of the 49 weekly drawings offers a $150,000 prize; $1 million is dispensed thrice annually. There are thousands of computerized lottery terminals islandwide, dispensing Loto and *Pega Tres* ("Pick Three") tickets. With the latter, you select a three- or six-digit number with a $1 minimum which has a 1:1,000 chance of winning a $500 prize.

PRACTICALITIES

i Puerto Rico Tourism Offices **i**

UNITED STATES

PUERTO RICO
Box 4435/#2 La Princesa Drive
Old San Juan Station, PR 00902
☎ 800-866-7827
☎ 809-721-2400/2483
✆ 787 725-4417

NEW YORK
666 Fifth Avenue, 15th Floor
New York, NY 10103
☎ 212-586-6262
☎ 800-223-6530
✆ 212-586-1212

CORAL GABLES, FLORIDA
901 Ponce de Leon Blvd., Suite 101
Miami, FL 33181
☎ 305- 445-9112
☎ 800-815-7391

LOS ANGELES, CALIFORNIA
3575 Cahuenga Blvd. # 560
Los Angeles, CA 90068
☎ 213-874-5991
☎ 800-874-7257
✆ 213-874-7247

ELSEWHERE

CANADA
41-43 Colbourne Street, Suite 301
Toronto, Ontario M5E 1E3
☎ (416) 368-2680
☎ (800) 667-0394 (Canada only)
✆ 416-368-5350

GREAT BRITAIN/SPAIN
Calle Serrano 1-2 Izq., 28001, Madrid
34-91-431.2128
✆ 34-91-577 5260
☎ 800-898920 (toll free from UK)

GERMANY
FVA Puerto Rico
c/o Discover The World Marketing
Eifelstrasse 14a, 60529 Frankfurt
☎ (49) 69-350047
✆ (49) 69-350040

SPAIN
Calle Capitan Haya, 23, 1-7-4 28020
Madrid, Spain
☎ 011-341-5556851
✆ 011-341-5567286

ITALY
Piazza Caiazzo, 3
20124 Milano
☎ (39) 02-667-14403
✆ (39) 0 2-669-2648

FRANCE
5 bis, rue de Louvre
75001 Paris
☎ 33-1-44-778800
✆ 33-1-42-600545

ARGENTINA
Piso 9, Oficina D Calle Santa Fe 882
Buenos Aires 1059
☎ (54-11-4) 314-4525
✆ (54-11-4) 313-3173

BRAZIL
Rua Rodolpho Troppmayer, 33
Ciudad de Sao Paulo
Estado de Sao Paulo 04001-010
☎ (55-11) 3051-7541
✆ (55-11) 3887-8719

MEXICO
Vicente Suárez # 64-A
Col. Condesa
Mexico, D.F. 06140
☎ (52) 5553-2730, ext. 13/14
✆ (52) 5211-9583

Because of the extortionate cost of intra-island calls, the most economical thing to do is to buy a prepaid phone card (sold in drugstores and convenience stores) either before or after your arrival. This can allow you to call anywhere, anytime for 25¢/minute or less. Rates are lower after 5 PM and on weekends.

Useful Puerto Rican Phone Numbers

Bus Information ☎ 787-250-6064
Conservation Trust ☎ 787-722-5882
Convention Bureau ☎ 787-725-2110
Emergency ☎ 911
Golf Association ☎ 787-721-7742
Hotel and Tourism Assn. ☎ 787-725-2901
Information 411
Le Lo Lai schedule ☎ 787-723-3135
Paradors ☎ 787-800-366-7827
Puerto Rico Tourism Co. ☎ 787-721-2400
Police ☎ 787-793-1234
Traveler's Aid ☎ 787-791-1054/1034
Weather ☎ 787-253-4588
Wheelchair Getaway ☎ 800-868-8028

The system is designed to tap on the *bolita*, the underground lottery. Some $136 million was garnered by this government-perpetuated scam in fiscal 1994-1995. With less favorable odds, Loto is not as popular. Income tax is withheld and prizes are dispensed over a number of years as opposed to all at once. Puerto Ricans also bet some $300 million on horses per year. You can buy a ticket for as little as 35¢. Pools allow you to select three two-race combinations or a six-race combo.

BETTING: Thoroughbreds race at the **El Comandante** racetrack on Sun., Wed., and Fri.
http://www.comandantepr.com

Services & Organizations

PHONE SERVICE: Phone service is run by the Puerto Rico Telephone Authority, which was created in 1974 to own and run the Puerto Rico Telephone Company (PRTC). With more than a million access lines, Puerto Rico has one phone for every three persons. Cellular service is available through the PRTC and Cellular One Puerto Rico. The pay phone is 25¢, but service is deplorable and it can cost as much to call from one side of the island to the other as it does to call the States. To use a pay phone, wait for a dial tone *before* inserting money.

The number for local information (if it's not busy!) is **411**.

For intra-island calls — more expensive than calling the same number from the States — dial the number; to call outside Puerto Rico, dial **1** plus the area code and number; for credit card or third-party calls, dial **0**.

800 and **888** numbers may be reached by dialing **1** first. For information in English, see the Blue Pages in the center of the telephone directory.

Available in some hotels and other locations, **Go/Fax** telephone stations provide ⊖ service; you need to use a credit card. The island's area codes are **787** and **939** The **939** area code is an overlay, so you must now dial the area code with all ten numbers for both 787 and 936.

MAIL: Rates are the same as in the US proper. Postal service is reliable. Have mail sent c/o General Delivery, San Juan, PR 00936; this is the General Post Office on Ave. Roosevelt in Hato Rey.

TOURIST INFORMATION: Tourist information centers are in Old San Juan at La Casita (Pier 1), Condado (next to the Condado Plaza Hotel), in Ponce at Plaza Las Delicias, and at the San Juan and

Sea Turtle Facts

 Sea turtles return to the beach where they were hatched to nest.

 A turtle's sex is largely determined by the the ocean temperature. Eggs raised in warmer waters turn female. Not suprisingly, cooler temperatures bring males.

 Sea turtles may take 20-30 years to grow up. Only one of every thousand eggs will result in a turtle which will reach sexual maturity and reproduce.

Aguadilla international airports. Be sure to pick up a copy of *Que Pasa,* the free quarterly guide to Puerto Rico.

ORGANIZATIONS: The island's oldest and best known nonprofit organization is the **Conservation Trust** (☎ 787-722-5882; Box 4747, San Juan, PR 00902-4747), which has been responsible for the preservation of forests, beachfronts, marshes, a canyon, and a coffee plantation over the past two decades.

Originally funded by contributions from a petroleum refinery and the petrochemical industry channeled through Fomento, funding now comes via the profits of US manufacturing subsidiaries that operate under section 936 of the IRS code. Over 14,000 acres have been preserved so far, and millions have been invested.

The Trust's latest victory has been the acquisition of 164 acres fronting the Bahía Ballena on the S coast, which had been slated for a Club Med. It was acquired in 1992 after a 20-year battle.

Individual memberships are $30 per year and include a newsletter subscription, a free pass to one of the two Trust sites, and a discount at the gift shops on purchases over $20.

Earthwatch (☎ 800-776-0188) is an organization that allows you to visit Puerto Rico and to participate actively in valuable research. Volunteers contribute financially and receive an unusual experience at the same time.

http://www.earthwatch.org

The **PEN Club** (☎ 787-724-0859/4669), which hosts an annual literary competition, can be reached at Apt. 11 N, C. Hernández 721, Miramar, PR 00907.

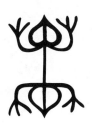

San Juan & Environs

The City of San Juan

As the second oldest city in the Americas (after Santo Domingo) and oldest city in the territorial United States, San Juan presents two distinct faces to the world. One is a vast, sprawling collection of towering concrete monoliths, freeways with crazy drivers, and bleak but functional housing projects with attractive murals painted on their sides. If it appears to have grown too fast, it has.

Its other face is that of Old San Juan, which retains the original flavor of the city — what the rest of the city must have been like before the svelte skyscrapers arrived. This is the preferred area to stay in, if architecture, history, culture, and (to some extent) nightlife are your chief concerns.

The metropolitan area of San Juan is divided and subdivided into a number of districts, many of which overlap, and it's nearly impossible to say where one stops and another begins. Sprawling Metropolitan San Juan (pop. 1.6 million) reaches out to touch the municipalities of Bayamón, Canovanas, Carolina, Cataño, Guaynabo, Loíza, Toa Baja, and Trujillo Alto. More than one-third of all Puerto Ricans live in this concentrated 300-sq.-mile area, the island's economic, political, social, and cultural capital.

ARRIVING BY AIR: All international flights (and some domestic) arrive at **Luis Muñoz Marín International Airport** which is located on the easternmost side of town. Moneychangers, banks, coin lockers, bookstores, and other facilities are at the refurbished airport. In a separate building are a rum-tasting bar and the government-operated tourist information service. The girls here are content to sit and gaze off into the distance, read newspapers, or sample scratch-and-sniff ads in fashion magazines, but they will help if cornered. Be sure to pick up a copy of *Que Pasa* and any other material they may have.

If you don't have too much luggage, you may take local buses to Old San Juan and Condado (see chart). Be prepared for a **long** wait and make sure that you have the right stop: one each on the same side goes towards Old San Juan (and Isla Verde and Condado) and towards Carolina. You should be at the stop marked "San Juan" on the upper level. Otherwise, there are always plenty of taxis (see the box on the next page). Be **sure** that they put the meter on! Displaying a sentry box logo, white **Taxi Turisticos** charge set rates by the destination zone. Metered cabs start at $1 (with a $3 minimum) and charge ten cents for each additional ⅓ mi. and ten cents for each 45 seconds of wait time.

Limousines also run from out front. Service is very irregular so it's best to call the **Airport Limousine Service** (☎ 787-791-4745) to find out when the next one is leaving.

SAN JUAN

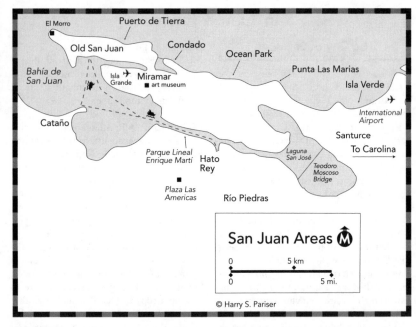

Completed in mid-1994, the **Teodoro Moscoso Bridge**, a toll road and bridge crossing San José, connects the airport with Hato Rey by linking up Ave. Iturregui with Ave. Baldorioty de Castro.

GETTING AROUND: San Juan was originally served by streetcar lines. Although these have disappeared, streetcar stops are still used to identify locations. Watch for yellow obelisk posts or the upright metal signs (reading **Parada** or *Parada de Guaguas*) that identify bus stops. For reference purposes, Stop 8 is near Parque Muñoz Rivera in Puerto de Tierra; Stop 10 is in Miramar; Stop 18 is near Ave. Roberto H. Todd; Stop 30 is the Fomento Building in Hato Rey; and Stop 40 is the University of Puerto Rico at Río Piedras.

The best thing that can be said about the bus system is that the buses are a/c. There

are bus kiosks with ads that protect you from rain, but they offer no route map or other information. Although buses have digital readouts indicating their destinations, these may not be accurate so be sure to ask. Stops identify a specific area rather than a location.

In an attempt to improve service, the bus service was split into two systems in 1990. The regular city buses are 25¢ (no transfers).

Metrobus runs service (65¢) to Río Piedras every 5-15 minutes from 6 AM to midnight. Otherwise, service is irregular and ends early in the evening. You can expect to wait. A bus terminal is in in the dock area of Old San Juan. Other terminals are at Río Piedras, Country Club, Cataño, and Bayamón. The most frequented route is outbound on Ave. Ponce de León and inbound (towards Old San Juan) on Ave. Fernandez Juncos.

San Juan Car Rental Firms

AAA
☎ 787-791-2609
www.aaacarrentalpr.com

Afro
☎ 787-724-3720

Airport Rent A Car
☎787-791-0069

Avis
☎ 800-874-3556
http://www.avis.com

Budget
San Juan Metro
☎ 800-527-0700
http://www.budget.com

Charlie
☎ 800-289-1227
http://www.charliecars.com

Hertz
☎ 800-654-3131
http://www.hertz.com

L & M Car Rental
☎ 800-666-0807
http://www.lmcarrental.com

Leaseway of Puerto Rico
☎ 800-468-2647
http://www.leasewaypr.com

National Car Rental
☎ 800-227-7368
http://www.nationalcar.com

Popular Auto
☎ 787-257-4848
http://www.popularautopr.com

Target Car Rental
☎ 787-728-1447
http://www.targetrentacar.com

Thrifty
☎ 800-367-2277
http://www.thrifty.com

Tropical Car Rental
☎ 787-791-2820
http://www.tropicalcarrental.com

For specific information phone the **Metropolitan Bus Authority** (☎ 787-767-7979) or **Metrobus,** (☎ 787-763-4141).

NOTE: An 11.8-mile, 16-station light rail system, the Tren Urbano, is under construction. Costs have skyrocketed to $2 billion, and the project is running well behind schedule. Look for it in 2004 at the earliest.

Another alternative is to ask around about *públicos,* which run from Old San Juan through several metropolitan area destinations including Río Piedras and Bayamón.

Metered taxis charge $1 initially with 10¢ for each additional 1 ⅓ mile. Be sure they

put down the meter; San Juan taxi drivers are, according to no less an authority than the former Tourism Company Executive Director Miguel Domenech, *estafadores* or "thieves." You should note that it may be difficult to get a taxi out of Old San Juan on Sat. night. The Taxis Turisticos (see sidebar) are a good alternative.

A series of free open-air wheeled trains, manufactured by a California specialty vehicle company, traverse some of the streets of Old San Juan. These are useful for a rest or for getting your orientation, but their tortoise-like pace makes them an inef-

🚌 San Juan Bus Routes 🚌

Here are the major routes as provided by **AMA** (☎ 787-767-7979). All information is subject to change. Buses are best avoided during Sundays and holidays, when runs are severely curtailed. Keep in mind that most stop running around 8 PM. Allow plenty of time to get to your destination. Buses take the longest route between two points, and traffic can be very congested. Departure frequency is listed for weekday daytime only.

A-3 Runs from Río Piedras to Hato Rey, along Ave. Roosevelt, to San Patricio and Cataño This bus runs every 15 min. weekdays.

A-5 Runs from Old San Juan to Stop 18 to Calle Loíza to Isla Verde to Los Angeles to Iturregui. Leaves weekdays every ten min.

A-6 Runs from Río Piedras to PR-3 to Ave. Campo Rico to Iturregui to Plaza Carolina to Carolina. Leaves weekdays every 15 min.

A-9 Runs from Río Piedras to Ave. Barbosa to Ave. Borínquen to Stop 18 to Old San Juan. Leaves weekdays every 20 min.

B-4 Runs from Río Piedras to Centro Médico to Ave. San Patricio to San Patricio. Leaves weekdays every 20 min.

B-8 Runs from Old San Juan to Stop 18 to Ave. Kennedy to San Patricio. Leaves weekdays every 20 min.

B-15 Runs from Río Piedras to San José to Hato Rey to Acuaexpreso. Leaves weekdays every 20 min.

B-16 Runs from Acuaexpreso to Hato Rey to Eduardo Conde to Stop 18. Leaves weekdays every 20 min.

B--21 Runs from Old San Juan to Condado to Stop 18 to Fernández Juncos to Plaza Las Américas. Leaves weekdays every 20 min.

B-28 Runs from Río Piedras to Ave. Piñero to Ave. San Patricio to San Patricio. Leaves weekdays every 20 min.

B-40 Runs from Río Piedras to Puente Moscoso Moscoso Bridge) to International Airport to Isla Verde to Piñones. Leaves weekdays every 20 min.

B-52 Runs from Río Piedras to Villa Nevárez to Centro Médico to Santiago Iglesias to Ave. Los Filtros to Bayamón. Leaves weekdays every 20 min.

C-10 Runs from Acuaexpreso to Hato Rey to Ave. Borínquen to Eduardo Conde to C. Loíza to Condado to Isla Verde to Stop 18. Leaves weekdays every 30 min.

C-11 Runs from Acuaexpreso to Hato Rey to to Ave. Borínquen to Eduardo Conde to Llorens Torres (housing project). Leaves weekdays every 30 min.

C-18 Runs from Río Piedras to El Señorial to Cupey Gardens. Leaves weekdays every 30 min.

C-26 Runs from Río Piedras to Venus Gardens. Leaves weekdays every 30 min.

C-27 Runs from San Patricio to Calle Escorial to Santiago Iglesias to Ave. Muñoz Rivera to Guaynabo. Leaves weekdays every 30 min.

C-29 Runs from Río Piedras to San Francisco to College Park to Ave. Muñoz Rivera to Guaynabo. Leaves weekdays every 30 min.

C-31 Runs from Río Piedras to Calle Paraña to Carr. #1 to Ave. Los Cumbres to Ave. Emilio Pol. Leaves weekdays every 30 min.

C-41 Runs from Acuaexpreso to Hato Rey to Río Piedras to Villa Prades to Campo Rico to Iturregui. Leaves weekdays every 30 min.

C-42 Runs from Iturregui to Ramal Estate to Sabana Abajo to Plaza Carolina to Villa Carolina to Carolina. Leaves weekdays every 30 min.

C-43 Runs from Iturregui to Vistamar to Sánchez Osorio to Plaza Carolina to PR-887 to Carolina. Leaves weekdays every 30 min.

C-44 Runs from Iturregui to Campo Rico to Ave. Roberto Clemente to Plaza Carolina to Carolina. Leaves weekdays every 30 min.

C-45 Runs from Iturregui to Los Angeles to International Airport to Isla Verde. Leaves weekdays every 30 min.

E-91 Runs from Santa Juanita to PR2 to San Patricio.

E-92 Runs from Magnolia Gardens to PR-2 to San Patricio.

ME Runs from Río Piedras to Hato Rey to Old San Juan. Leaves weekdays every 10–12 min.

M-I Runs from Río Piedras to Hato Rey to Santurce to Old San Juan. Leaves weekdays every 6-7 min.

M-II Runs from Stop 18 to Hato Rey to Ave. Roosevelt to San Patricio to PR-2 to Bayamón. Leaves weekdays every ten min.

---

ficient and cumbersome way to get around. A better idea is to use your feet. Assuming you are in halfway decent physical condition, no place in Old San Juan is beyond walking distance. Walking is definitely the best way to savor the atmosphere of the place, and you'd miss many things by getting around any other way. (The Condado area is similarly compact and may also be covered on foot). The section on sights which follows is arranged sequentially from El Morro to San Cristóbal, allowing the entire old town to be systematically and thoroughly explored.

CAR RENTAL: There are numerous agencies; many of the larger ones are listed in the chart. Gasoline is sold by the liter, and a gallon runs around US$1.40. Most service stations are open daily from early in the morning until 10 PM or so at night.

Speed limits are set at 55 mph on the highways. Civic congestion limits urban speeds. Driving is on the right.

If traveling with young children, don't forget to ask for a car seat.

SCOOTERS AND BICYCLES: Wheels for Fun (☎ 787-725-2780, 204 C. O'Donnel (near Plaza de Colón in Old San Juan) rents out scooters and bicycles on an hourly or daily basis.

Bicycle Rental & Sales (☎ 787-722-6288), 1122 Ave. Ashford (across from Wendy's) offers bike rentals.

Adrenalina (☎ 787-727-1233), 4770 Ave. Isla Verde (near Andy's Cafe), has a variety of bikes including tandems and baby trailers. Reserve in advance.

TRAILS: Areas to bike in include the perimeters of **Old San Juan**, the **Parque Lineal Martí Colli** (avoid rush hour), and the **Pasa Tablado** in Piñones.

Old San Juan

For the amount of history, culture, and atmosphere that is packed into its seven-

Taxis Turisticos

Taxis Turisticos have been designed to cope with complaints from tourists concerning San Juan's taxis. Drivers must take a course in road safety and English before they receive their public driver's licenses. These taxis are painted white and have an official logo on their doors. For trips leaving from the airport and the Tourism Piers in Old San Juan, a set flat-rate tariff applies. Others are metered. Rates are $1 plus 10¢ for each ⅓ of a mile. Each piece of additional luggage: 50¢. The charge for waiting time is 10¢ per 45 seconds. From 10 PM–6 AM, there is a $1 surcharge. The minimum charge is $3, and tips are not included.

For more information, call the **Public Service Commission** (☎ 787-756-1919).

Zone One International Airport to Isla Verde (including Punta las Marias. $8
Zone Two Airport to Condado $12 (includes Ocean Park, Miramar)
Zone Three Airport to Old San Juan and Cruise Piers (including Puerto de Tierra) $16.
Zone Four Piers to Old San Juan $6
Zone Six Piers to Condado (including Ocean Park, Miramar) $10
Zone Seven Piers to Isla Verde $16

 The best days to plan a visit to **Old San Juan** are from Wed. to Fri. Many museums are closed on Monday and Tuesday, and numerous cruise ships dock on these two days as well. On weekends the town tends to jam up as SanJuaneros come in for R & R. A great walk is from San Juan Gate at Paseo de Princesa to El Morro.

square-block area, no place in the territorial US can begin to touch Old San Juan. Perched on the western end of an islet bordered on the N by the Atlantic and on the S and W by a vast bay, the town is connected to the mainland by the historic San Antonio Bridge. When seen from the harbor, the town takes on the appearance of a gigantic amphitheater with its ramparts and castles forming the outer walls. Colonial Spain is alive and well here. The brilliantly restored architecture complements what was well-preserved to begin with.

Old San Juan is not a place to hurry through. It cannot be seen in a day and can barely be appreciated in a week. Like a cup of the finest Puerto Rican coffee, it must be savored and sipped slowly.

Stroll through the streets and take in the local color. See men playing dominoes, girls hanging out on the street corners waiting for marriage, groceries being hauled up to a second floor balcony with basket and rope. Get acquainted with the local characters: watch the crippled man on crutches who suddenly begins to move at top speed as soon as he is out of the sight of tourists. Or, if you're lucky, you might see the man who occasionally brings his pet snake out for a walk, holding it coiled in his hand and startling his unaware friend seated in a café. Or you might see the drunk singing a soliloquy on a streetcorner.

With some 5,000 residents, the panorama of people and events is constantly changing. Feed the pigeons in Parque de las Palomas or take in the view from the top of El Morro or San Cristóbal. With the exception of the obnoxious police, and some antipathy towards visiting marines, nobody hassles anybody in Old San Juan. Enjoy.

HISTORY: Founded as a military stronghold in 1510, San Juan Bautista became a flourishing and attractive settlement by the end of the 19th century. It was originally called Puerto Rico and the island was called San Juan. On the way back to Spain, a cartographer mixed up the map labels.

Although the town lacks an historic hospital, university, or any of the other significant architectural structures found in Santo Domingo, its buildings nonetheless have a distinctive charm and appeal of their own.

After the American invasion in 1898, Old San Juan deteriorated. Most of it became a red-light district until 1949, when the seven-block downtown was declared a historical zone. Beginning in 1955, the Institute of Puerto Rican Culture, under the highly imaginative and insightful leadership of Ricardo Alegría, began the tremendous task of restoring the old buildings and homes in this historical area. Restoration of private residences was encouraged by legislation, which granted five- to ten-year tax exemptions to owners of buildings that had been partially or fully restored, and offered bank loans with liberal terms for performing restorative work.

Rather than becoming a pretentious museum piece, Old San Juan is a living historical monument where the past and present intermingle freely. The area has been designated as a United Nations World Heritage Site, and an additional $100 million has been pumped into the historic zone in the past few years.

One new development is the widening of C. Marina, which has been paved with cobblestones. Created from a former parking lot, the $16 million Quincentennial Plaza commemorates Columbus' "discovery." Two needle-shaped columns on its highest spot point to the North Star. It also has a fountain with 100 streams; three flights of stairs symbolize the next 300 years.

GETTING HERE: To get to Old San Juan from Isla Verde or the airport follow Carr. 26 to the W; this road merges into Carr. 25 at the San Antonio Bridge. Watch for signs reading "San Juan" or "Old San Juan" along the road. Continue along Carr. 25; the Capitol will be on your L; Fort San Cristóbal will be on your R. Note that public parking is extremely limited.

The best place to park is the public parking lot at **La Puntilla**. If traveling here from the Condado or other city areas, it's better to take a bus or a taxi.

Transport and Tours

GETTING AROUND: At the bus station, you can take a trolley-shaped bus. There are at least three routes. The trolleys are very slow, so the best thing is just to walk. No place is that far from the terminal, and it is much less frustrating.

The *Acuaexpreso*, a ferry (75 cents) departs from Hato Rey and arrives near the Wyndham Hotel. It's a nice way to get a tour of the harbor.

TOURS: All tours require advance booking. Gary Horne's **Tortugas Kayak** (☎ 787-725-5169) offers kayaking tours of the waters surrounding the old city as well as out at Piñones. On the Piñones trip ($45 pp), you'll ply through mangroves, see tree iguanas, and go snorkeling (equipment provided). These trips are popular, and Gary has a good reputation.
http://www.kayak-pr.com
kayakpr@hotmail.com

Colonial Adventures (☎ 787-729-0114) offers a variety of walking tours around Old San Juan.

Legends of Puerto Rico (☎ 787-531-9060) offer tours which range from a nightlife tour to a ghost story tour.

Gonzalo de León (☎ 787-253-2571) also offers tours.

A **free walking tour** is offered at the city hall (*municipio*, ☎ 787-721-6363, ext. 279). It takes a bit over an hour, and you should reserve the day before.

Caribbean Carriage Company (☎ 787-797-8063) offer tours of the town in horse-drawn carriages. Tours start at Plaza Dársenas near Pier 1 in Old San Juan. Prices range from $30-$60 per couple.

Old San Juan Sights

El Morro
Fuerte San Felipe Del Morro

A walkway leads up to this dramatic structure, the most impressive legacy of the Spanish empire in Puerto Rico. If you're here on a weekend, you'll find Puerto Ricans relaxing: babies in strollers, tots pedaling tricycle-like machines, a zillion colorful kites flying, the works.

Along with its sister structure in Havana, Brimstone Hill on St. Kitts (British), and Haiti's La Citadelle, El Morro is one of the premier forts in the Caribbean. Invincible from attack by sea during its time, it is now administered by the National Park Service. It's open daily from 9-5 and there is no admission charge; call for information on free guided tours (☎ 787-729-6960).

Enter the small but cool museum and see the exhibits. The rooms on the fifth level were used as living quarters. The doors were made of ultrahard *ausobo* wood, which is now a protected species. See the carefully labeled spots where *The Forge*, *The Kitchen*, and *The Latrine* once were. The steep and dark triangular staircase, once an emergency passage, leads to the gun emplacements. Be sure to watch your step on the way down. The cannons on the Santa Barbara Bastion, also on the upper level, were found in the sea.

THE FORT'S HISTORY: Built to protect San Juan Harbor, gateway for supply ships headed to Spain's many colonies to the W and S, construction (in 1539) was spurred after recurring attacks by royally commissioned pirates and Carib Indian raids. The site of the fort was moved several times before the present outer fortification was completed in 1584. It was not completed in today's form until 1783, 199 years later, through the efforts of two Irishmen (O'Reilly and O'Daly), by which time about 40,000 man-years had been spent building the fortifications and city walls. Sir Francis Drake, pursuing a cargo of gold pesos being temporarily stored in the fortress vaults, struck on Nov. 22, 1584, and was repulsed.

In 1598 the Earl of Cumberland attacked the Santurce area of San Juan with his 20 ships. Fighting tooth and nail, the Spanish, weakened by dysentery, held out for two weeks before surrendering. Cumberland and his forces were delirious with pleasure until they too succumbed to dysentery, followed by an epidemic of yellow fever. After just four months of control, the English sailed away, leaving 400 of their comrades buried. In 1625, the fortress was attacked by the Dutch, but this time the Spanish survived the attack and began work on San

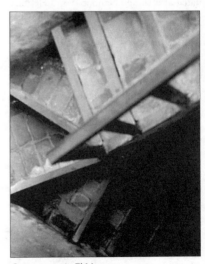

Steep steps in El Morro

Most Romantic Places to Kiss

San Juan has a lot of great places.

➤ On a San Juan balcony

➤ Along the waterfront at sunset

➤ On the grounds of San Cristobal or El Morro

➤ In the botanical gardens at the university in Río Piedras

Fun Facts about San Juan's Forts

▶ While El Morro was built to stave off sea attacks, San Cristóbal was designed to stave off land invasions.

▶ The white flag with the jagged red cross you see flying is the Cross of Burgundy, a Spanish military flag used during the 16th-18th centuries to identify forces loyal to the Spanish crown.

▶ English troops occupied El Morro for six weeks in 1598.

▶ Although the forts were modified constantly, it took an estimated half century to complete El Morro and around 25 years for San Cristóbal.

▶ San Cristóbal is much larger than El Morro. It covers 27 acres and is the largest Spanish-constructed New World fortification.

▶ There are no secret tunnels connecting the fortresses with other edifices.

▶ The forts' moats never held water. Their purpose was to protect the bottom of the walls from enemy cannon fire.

Cristóbal on the other side of town, to provide further defense. An attack by British Lt. General Abercromby in 1797 failed (see "Plazuleta de la Rogativa"), and the last attack came during the Spanish-American

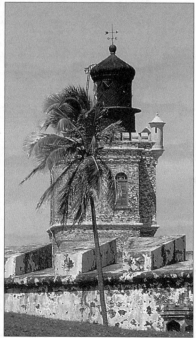

El Morro

War, when El Morro's batteries returned fire on US Admiral Sampson's fleet. El Cañuelo, which can be seen across the bay, was constructed to ward off hostile landings on the W side. The present structure was rebuilt in stone in the 1660s.

Since 1977, $33 million has been spent on repairs to the fortress, including filling in cavities gouged by the sea under the Santa Elena bastion and under the N wall. A 750-ft.-long breakwater, constructed by Pennsylvania's Maitland Construction Company at a cost of $7.88 million, was completed in October 1990. About 176,060 tons of stone were used in its construction.

Admission is $2 for adults; $1 for senior citizens and children. The same ticket gets you into San Cristóbal and vice versa.

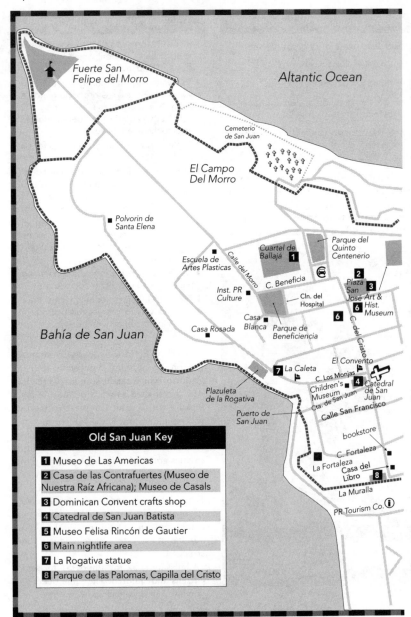

Fuerte San
Felipe del Morro

Altantic Ocean

Cemeterio
de San Juan

El Campo
Del Morro

Polvorin de
Santa Elena

Escuela de
Artes Plasticas

Calle del Morro

Cuartel de
Ballajá **1**

Parque del
Quinto
Centenario

C. Beneficia

Inst. PR
Culture

Cln. del
Hospital

Casa
Blanca

2
Plaza
San
José
3
Art &
6
Hist.
Museum

6

Casa Rosada

Parque de
Beneficiencia

Bahía de San Juan

C. del Cristo

El Convento

7 La Caleta

C. Los Monjas

Children's
Museum
Cta. de San Juan

4
Catedral
de San
Juan

Plazuleta
de la Rogativa

Puerto de
San Juan

Calle San Francisco

bookstore

C. Fortaleza

La Fortaleza

Casa del
Libro
8

La Muralla

PR Tourism Co. ⓘ

Old San Juan Key

1 Museo de Las Americas

2 Casa de las Contrafuertes (Museo de
Nuestra Raíz Africana); Museo de Casals

3 Dominican Convent crafts shop

4 Catedral de San Juan Batista

5 Museo Felisa Rincón de Gautier

6 Main nightlife area

7 La Rogativa statue

8 Parque de las Palomas, Capilla del Cristo

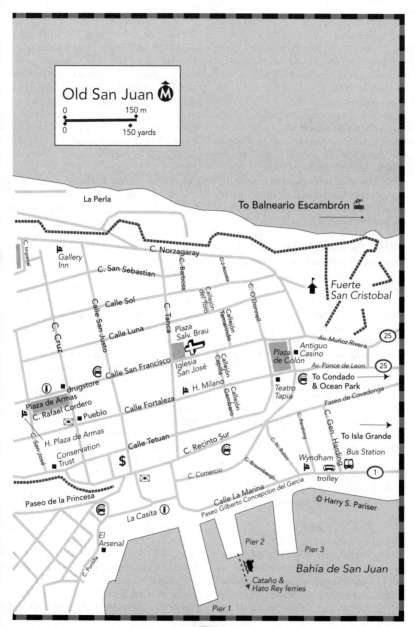

Old San Juan

0 — 150 m
0 — 150 yards

La Perla

To Balneario Escambrón

C. Imperial

Gallery Inn

C. Norzagaray

C. San Sebastian

C. Barbosa

Callejón del Toro

C. O'Donnell

C. Acosta

Calle Sol

C. Tanca

Calle San Justo

Calle Luna

C. Cruz

Plaza Salv. Brau

Callejón Tamarindo

Fuerte San Cristobal

Av. Muñoz Rivera

25

Calle San Francisco

Iglesia San José

Callejón Capilla

Callejón Gambaro

Plaza de Colón

Antiguo Casino

Av. Ponce de Leon

25

drugstore

H. Milano

Teatro Tapia

To Condado & Ocean Park

Plaza de Armas

C. Rafael Cordero

Calle Fortaleza

Paseo de Covadonga

Pueblo

C. San José

H. Plaza de Armas

Conservation Trust

$

Calle Tetuan

C. Recinto Sur

C. Pershing

C. N. Rubio

To Isla Grande

Wyndham

C. Gen. Harding

Bus Station

C. Comercio

C. Braumbaugh

trolley

1

Paseo de la Princesa

Calle La Marina

Paseo Gilberto Concepcion del Garcia

© Harry S. Pariser

La Casita

El Arsenal

C. Puntilla

Pier 2

Pier 3

Bahía de San Juan

Cataño & Hato Rey ferries

Pier 1

NEAR EL MORRO: The **Polvorín de Santa Elena** (Santa Elena Gunpowder Magazine), is a chimney-topped structure to the L of the entrance. The **Escuela de Artes Plásticas** (School of Fine Arts) is an interesting place to walk by. It has a small restaurant which serves inexpensive lunches.

Containing two attractive patios, the former **Asilo de Beneficiencia** (Home for the Poor) dates from the 1840s. It now houses the headquarters of the **Institute for Puerto Rican Culture** (☎ 787-724-0700), which has some small galleries with changing exhibits that are well worth a visit. It's open daily 9AM–5 PM. The new **Parque de Beneficiencia** is in the background.

Cemeterio de San Juan

Dramatically situated below towering El Morro, this cemetery contains the graves of such prominent Puerto Ricans as Pedro Albizu Campos and José de Diego. The circular neoclassic chapel, dedicated in 1863, is a most unusual architectural edifice. Note its eerie stained-glass reflection. Full-size weeping widows, realistically cut from marble, stand and kneel over graves. Long rows of tombs are set into the wall Etruscan-style, while faded and frayed Puerto Rican flags fly over graves. As space is at a premium, the grave of a less distinguished relative may be dug up and the bones transferred in order to make way for a new arrival. Legendary *independentista* Pedro Albizu Campos is interred here. It's worth a visit, but stay clear at night or risk finding a knife at your throat.

La Perla

Elegant by comparison to the slums which line the banks of the Martín Peña Channel, this slum, situated along the Atlantic to one side of Cemeterio de San Juan, is a crowded group of houses that stretch from just below the remains of the colonial wall down a steep slope to the filthy beach below. Most houses have TVs (even satellite dishes) and other conveniences, while the better part of the slum is served by electricity, water and sanitation service. The area is a center for drug trade and other activities; it is recommended that you not come here unless it's with a local you trust. Bring nothing of value. La Perla is the place where Oscar Lewis penned *La Vida,* his classic study of prostitution.

Casa Blanca

One of the gems of Old San Juan. Entering through the gates at 1 San Sebastián, a cool courtyard with a garden and beautiful chain of fountains is to the left. (You may also enter via the doorway across from Casa Rosada on the city wall side). Straight ahead is a house which has been restored to resemble a 17th-century nobleman's home, with simple but beautifully designed antique furniture and attractive white rooms. It also contains a small ethnographic museum which features a miniature replica of a Taíno village. Even older than La Fortaleza, this house was designed to be given to Ponce de León as a reward for his services. Ponce, however, went off to search for the fountain of youth in Florida and, meeting his end from an Indian's poisoned arrow, never returned.

A hurricane destroyed the original structure and it was replaced by another in 1523. It still stands today and has been incorporated into the original. In 1779, after more than 250 years residence, Ponce de León's descendants sold it to the government, which expanded the structure for use as housing for military troops and engineers. Taken over by the US military in 1898, it was vacated in 1967 and declared a National Historical Monument the following year. Its library has a superb collection of Caribbean literature in Spanish and

English. The complex (☎ 787-724-4102) is open Tues. to Sat., 9–noon, 1–4:30 PM; $2 admission to the museum ($1 for children). Guided tours are available.

Museo de San Juan

The **San Juan Museum** (☎ 787-724-1875), a former marketplace located on C. Norzagaray (corner MacArthur) was first restored by the City of San Juan in 1979. It is a historical museum and art gallery which has both permanent and changing exhibits. Its 128-seat theater shows a historical video and hosts performances. It is open Tues. to Fri., 9 AM–4 PM, and is open on Sat. and Sun. from 10 AM–4 PM.

Museo de las Américas
Cuartel De Ballajá

This building once housed the Spanish troops and their families. Recently restored, the imposing structure still is largely empty. Most of it is a museum awaiting exhibits to fill it. There are a number of beautiful brass water fountains, which don't function owing to a lack of pressure.

Set on the second floor, the **Museo de Las Américas** (open Mon. to Fri, 10 AM–4 PM, Sat. and Sun. 11 AM–5 PM; ☎ 787-723-8772) is intended eventually to cover the hemisphere's cultural development. Inaugurated in 1992, its **Artes Populares de Las Américas** contains an extensive folk art collection representing the full range of the Americas — from Paraguay to Cuba, Brazil to Haiti and Bolivia. There are old pictures of Puerto Rican villages, a phenomenal carved gourd from Peru, folk art from the US including carved whirligig dancers and a rooster weathervane, indigenous clothing from S America, musical instruments, including a harp from Venezuela, a Puerto Rican *cuatro* or 10-stringed guitar, a rustic tin banjo from Haiti, and a collection of masks from all over. Naturally enough,

many of the exhibits relate to religion, some of them dealing with the influences of African religions on the New World. There are offerings to the dead from Mexico, an *abakua* (devil) costume from Cuba, a model *capilla campesina* (countryside chapel), and *manos poderosas* (powerful hands) from Puerto Rico — one of them topped by a group of women. Another room shows the artifacts found in Barrio Bállaja. There are several other rooms on this floor housing special exhibits. It is often open for the *Noches de Galerías*, the art gallery openings held the last Tues. of each month.

Across the street, the offices of the **Institute for Puerto Rican Culture** have displays, including pictures of petroglyphs. Its E door opens onto the **Plaza del Quinto Centenario.** Raised, and reached by a series of steps on each side, this plaza has a fountain with 100 jets and a large pillar reaching to the stars. As previously mentioned, the $16 million Quincentennial Plaza commemorates Columbus' "discovery."

Iglesia de San José

Oldest church still in use in the Americas, **San José Church** was built by Dominican friars as a monastery chapel. Originally dedicated to St. Thomas Aquinas, it was renamed by Jesuits who took it over in 1865. The Gothic ceilings are unequaled in this hemisphere. The church is most famous for what is missing or moved; most of the items currently on display have been donated. Ponce de León's tomb, after a 350-year rest, was moved to the cathedral. His coat of arms can still be seen to the left of the main altar. The famous Flemish masterpiece, The Virgin of Bethlehem, brought to the island in 1511, was stolen (and presumably deflowered) in 1972. During the 1898 US Navy bombardment, a cannonball crashed into one window and mysteriously disappeared; the chapel, crypt, and convent remained untouched. The church is right on Plaza San José. It's usually open Mon. to Fri. 8-3 and Sat. 8-noon, but may sometimes be be closed during these times. Mass is celebrated Sun. at noon.

Antiguo Convento del los Dominicanos

At C. Norzagaray 98, dominating Plaza San José, this former convent houses the *Libreria y Tienda de Artesanías* (☎ 787-721-6866), a superb craft and book shop (mostly Spanish-language title) which is open Mon. to Sat. 9 AM–5 PM. It's run by the Institute for Puerto Rican Culture.

Built in 1523 on land donated by Ponce de León, it's one of the major historical buildings in the city. After the closure of all convents in 1838, it was converted to a barracks. Following the American occupation in 1898, this was the center of the US Antilles Command until its termination in 1966. Carefully restored, it is now a showcase for cultural events. Concerts are held on occasion in the huge paved courtyard that lies below the beautiful arcaded galleries lined with carved wooden railings. You can see music lessons being given here on Sat. mornings.

Museo de Casals

This collection of memorabilia includes cellist Pablo Casals' medals, sweater, cello, domino set, a yellow plaster of Paris cast of his hands, and even his pipes — including one carved in the shape of Wagner! It also holds manuscripts, photographs, and an extensive videotape library upstairs consisting of tapes from the Casals Festival; they are played on request. At 81, the famous cellist chose to spend the last years of his life here, the birthplace of both his wife and his mother, and he established the Casals Music Festival. Open Tues. to Sat., 9:30AM–5:30 PM; ☎ 787-723-9185. Admission is $1 adults, 50 cents children.

Casa de los Contrafuertes

Directly on Plaza San José at C. San Sebastián, next-door to the Museo de Casals, the Casa de los Contrafuertes may be the oldest private residence remaining in Old San Juan. The house was constructed in the early 18th century, and its name means "heavily buttressed."

It now houses the **Museo de Nuestra Raíz Africana** (☎ 787-724-0700, ext. 4239) which has a set of remarkable exhibits. Downstairs you'll find masks and musical instruments and the horrors of the slave trade. Another area tells the stories of important Black Puerto Ricans. One other room holds a collection of paintings. Upstairs, you'll find masks, maps, musical instruments, and an exhibit on the Orisha cult. It's open Tues. to Sat., 9:30 AM–5 PM and on Sun. from 11 AM–5 PM.

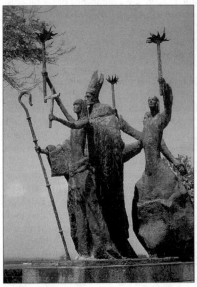

La Rogativa

The **Casals Festival** draws performing artists from all over the world. It generally takes place in June. Contact the tourist board for more information.

midnight, despite the steady barrage from his ships.

Concluding that the town was being supplied by troops from the countryside, he ordered the fleet to sail, giving rise to the legend that the city had been saved by Ursula and her cohorts.

Plaza de San José

Restored to its original condition by the Institute for Puerto Rican Culture and reconditioned during 1988, the Plaza is quiet and peaceful during the daytime. It was the liveliest place in town at night, until the Cardinal (who doesn't even live here) complained about the noise! The statue of Ponce de León, first governor of Puerto Rico, was cast using melted bronze cannons captured in the 1797 British attack.

Plazuleta de la Rogativa

Designed and built by an Australian residing in Puerto Rico, this remarkable statue — which has a touching spiritual character to it — is located in a small plaza next to the sea wall near Caleta Las Monjas. It was donated by a citizens' group to mark San Juan's 450th birthday in 1971.

The statue commemorates a legend concerning the siege of San Juan in 1797. After taking Trinidad on Feb. 17 of that year, Lt. General Abercromby proceeded to San Juan with 60 ships containing nearly 8,000 troops. With the British apparently preparing to close in for the kill, the governor, weakened by dysentery, asked the head bishop to arrange a *rogativa* (procession) through the streets. The bishop, in turn, asked that it be held in honor of Santa Catalina (St. Catherine) and Ursula. The evening candle and torch procession moved from Catedral de San Juan Bautista through the streets. Abercromby became alarmed when he saw the huge masses of torchlights and heard the frenzied continual ring of church bells increasing in tempo until

La Fortaleza

At the end of C. Fortaleza stands the oldest executive mansion in the Western Hemisphere. La Fortaleza was in operation three centuries before the Washington White House had even been designed. Its name, meaning "The Fortress," derives from its original use. Though replaced by El Morro, it continued to serve as part of the city's defense system. The $2 million in gold and silver that Sir Francis Drake sought during his 1595 attack was kept here. Occupied twice (by the Dutch in 1625 and the British in 1898), it had to be rebuilt in 1640 after the Dutch left. Usage as a governor's mansion dates from 1639 and continues today. It was completely remodeled in 1846.

Pass by the security guards to join a guided tour of the downstairs area. You must be dressed properly. It's open weekdays except holidays; call 787-721-7000, ext. 2211, 2323, and 2358 for the tour times. Inside, visit Santa Catalina's chapel, descend into the dungeon, and note the Moorish garden with its 19th-century parish tiles. If you stick your hand in the water, you will surely be granted any wish you request.

http://www. fortaleza.gobierno.pr

Catedral de San Juan Batista

San Juan's cathedral is set on C. Cristo across from Plazuleta de las Monjas and El Convento Hotel. Once a small, thatched-roof structure when built in 1521, the cathedral was completed in its present state in 1852. The only holdovers from

Pillar in Plaza del Quinto Centenario

the earlier structure are the partially restored Gothic ceiling and the circular staircase. See the remains of that ardent Catholic Ponce de León, who rests in a marble tomb. The wax-covered mummy of St. Pio, a Roman martyr killed for his belief in Christianity, is encased in a glass box. He has been here since 1862. To his right is a wooden replica of Mary with four swords stuck in her bosom. There are many, many beautiful stained glass windows. Curiously, electric lights have replaced votive candles. Pay $1 to have them switched on. It's open Mon-Sat from 8 AM–4 PM and Sun. from 8 AM–1 PM.
http://www.catedralsanjuan.com

Museo Felisa Rincón De Gautier

At Caleta de San Juan 51 nearby stands a memorial to a living saint: Felisa Rincón de Gautier, once Mayor of San Juan (1946–68). The former home of this pompadoured dynamo has been turned into a small museum. Well worth a visit but notable more for its architecture than its contents, the attractive house contains displays of the keys to cities offered her, along with various medals. Altogether she received 131 decorations and was named Woman of the Americas in 1954 by the Union of the American Women of New York. It's open Mon. to Fri. from 9 AM–4 PM.

The Children's Museum (El Museo del Niño)

🎠 The Children's Museum (☎ 787-722-3791) is one of the most unusual places in Old San Juan, and it is an example of a positive American influence. Founder Carmen Vega visited similar museums in the States and based her museum on them. Devastated by a fire in 1995, it had to be completely rebuilt. The ground floor is designed with tiny tots in mind. There are mirrors your kids can write on, and you can watch little bundles of joy gleefully descending the fabric slide. You can put on your own puppet show. On the second floor is a dentist's office ("Visitemos al Dentista") where it's explained what a visit is all about. Various art projects are pursued in the art room, there's a miniature *colmado* where food is purchased with play money, a barbershop, shortwave station, and T-shirts for sale on the first floor. Admission is $2.50 for all ages and sizes of children.
http://www.museodelninopr.org
info@museodelninopr.org

Casa Rosada

Near the Rogativa statue, this attractive "pink house" was built in 1812 to serve as a barracks; it later became an officers' quarters. Although closed at present, it has been remodeled with the intent that it may perhaps someday serve as a museum for Puerto Rican crafts.

Provincial Deputation Building

This restored building's cloister-like design is done up in late neoclassical style. Puerto Rico's first representative body, the **Antigua Diputacíon (Provincial Deputation)** was housed here. It seems appropriate that the building's current occupant is the US Department of State (☎ 787-722-2121). It's right at Plaza de Armas (on C. San Francisco at C. San José) and is open Mon. to Fri. 8–noon and 1–4:30 PM.

The **Intendancy Building**, located on the corner of San José and San Francisco, was once the office of the royal Spanish Exchequer. It now houses Puerto Rico's State Department (787-722-2121). The building (see above) once housed the island's first representative body. They began doing business on July 17, 1898, after Puerto Rico was granted autonomy by Spain. The US invaded only two weeks later. Both are open Mon. to Fri. 8-noon, 1–4:30 PM.

Plaza de Armas

This relaxed square has pay telephones, supermarkets, small cafeterias, a fruit vendor, and a shaved ice cart. Representing the four seasons, the four statues presiding over the oblong plaza are more than a century old. Originally a marketplace (Plaza de las Verduras or Plaza of the Vegetables), it was designed to be the main plaza before Ponce de León moved the capital from Caparra. Used during the 16th century for military drills by local militia, it was also the center of local nightlife. Bands played and singles walked around the square or sat in rented chairs. When the locals were replaced by Spanish garrisons, their cry of "Present arms!" resulted in a name change to Plaza de Armas.

Remodeled in 1988 under the administration of San Juan Mayor Baltasar Corrada, it is now so spanking new that it has lost much of its ambiance. The shade trees which once graced the plaza were felled in a misguided attempt by the architect to restore the plaza to what it was in the beginning of this century.

Also on the plaza is a small **Pueblo** supermarket. **Kiosko 4 Estaciones** has *piña coladas*, tuna sandwiches, coffee, and other fare. It's a great place to relax and let local life go by. **El Mesón Sandwiches** offers pizza and baked potatoes, among other dishes.

Alcaldía

The San Juan City Hall is right on Plaza de Armas. Construction of this building, designed along the lines of its counterpart in Madrid, began in 1602. It was finally completed, after many delays, in 1799. During the years when it functioned as a city hall, numerous important events took place here, including the inauguration of the first Puerto Rican legislature and the signing and ratification of the decree abolishing slavery. The last restoration was in 1975. A tourist information center is on the ground floor (formerly a jail) next to a small gallery with frequent exhibitions. Open Mon. to Fri., 8 AM–4 PM; ☎ 787-724-7171, ext. 2391.

La Casa del Libro

This museum of rare books and illuminated manuscripts, housed in a beautifully restored 18th-century townhouse, opened in 1958. Its 5,000-book collection, said to be the best of its kind in Latin America, includes over 200 books that date back to the 16th century and manuscripts dating back 2,000 years. Other books are reference works on the graphic arts. Conveniently located at C. Cristo 255, it's open Tues. to Sat. (except holidays), 11 AM–4:30 PM.
http://www.lacasadellibro.org

La Capilla del Cristo

At the foot of C. Cristo stands what must be the smallest chapel in the Caribbean. It is dedicated to the Christ of Miracles, and there are at least two stories explaining its origin. One claims that it was originally just an altar that prevented people from accidentally falling over the wall into the sea. The other story is more involved. On June 24, 1753, a rider, participating in the annual patron saint festival, missed the turn at the end of C. Cristo and plunged into the sea. Miraculously, he was not injured, and the chapel was constructed to commemorate the event. In 1925 the city government planned to demolish the chapel, but after vehement public protest, the idea was abandoned. On Aug. 6 every year, the chapel's feast day, the Cardinal of Puerto Rico officiates at a High Mass. The chapel is open Tues. from 10 AM–3:30 PM.

Parque de las Palomas

At the end of Cristo St., next to Cristo Chapel, is this small gem of a park, perched at the top of the city wall — a nice place to sit early in the morning. Hundreds of pigeons circulate between the trees and the fountain. Feathers fly about everywhere. Caution is advised because they are not toilet trained. A man sells snacks and birdseed at the entrance.

Bastion del Las Palmas

Originally constructed in 1678 as a gun emplacement, Bastion del Las Palmas once served as an integral part of the city's defense system. Now it's a small park overlooking San Juan Bay. Grab some morning caffeine at the coffee shop on San José and come here for the view. The statue off to the side is of Venezuelan patriot Gen. Miranda, a comrade in arms of Bolivar against the Spanish whose liberal views led to his internment here.

Plaza de Colón

Once much larger, this square was formerly named Plaza de Santiago after the gate of the same name. In 1893, to mark the 400th anniversary of Columbus' discovery of Puerto Rico, the plaza was renamed and a statue of the explorer unveiled. Ponce de León's statue was then moved to Plaza San José. The plaza was renovated in 1988. Nowadays, it's chiefly of interest for the nearby Tapia Theater.

Fuerte San Cristóbal

A strategic masterpiece, this imposing fortress still dominates the E side of town. In its prime, it covered 27 acres and contained seven independent but interlocking units. Although much smaller now than its more famous cousin El Morro, it has a slightly less touristy atmosphere. It's nice to spend the morning sitting and relaxing on the upper level fortifications, taking in the view and getting some sun. Enter the fortress and find the visitor center, a former guardhouse, on the left. The small museum, located across from the administrative offices on the ground floor, has illustrations detailing how the fort was constructed, a scale model of the original fortification, and other exhibits.

A separate room, opened for groups or for individuals with the assistance of a ranger, displays a wonderful reproduction of a soldiers' barracks. The uniforms, muskets, and tableware are all made by craftsmen from models, and the twin facing rows of borderless bunk beds were still in use in Europe as recently as 50 years ago.

There's also a good gift shop on this level, and you can buy this book here. A Military Archives serves as a repository of information on Spanish Caribbean military history; it may be visited for research Mon. to

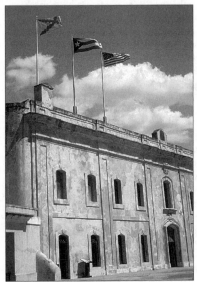

San Cristobal, one of two amazing forts

Thurs., from 10AM–3 PM. On the second floor is a series of low, concave arches and barren rooms. Downstairs, the bronze cannon on an artillery mount was brought down from Delaware, while the iron cannons, which deteriorate faster in the salt breeze, were taken from the ocean.

Five 150,000-gallon cisterns are on the lower level, and another is on the uppermost level. Water was obtained by rope and bucket, and animals were prohibited inside the fort to prevent contamination. Now, the water is emptied into the sea. The statue of Santa Barbara, patron saint of the fort, also on the ground level, was venerated by the soldiers. The red-and-white flag flying from the upper level is the red cross of St. Andrew. In use from the 16th to 18th century, it symbolizes 400 years of Spanish culture in Puerto Rico. Check out the view of the Devil's Sentry Box, built during the 17th century at ocean level. A sentry posted here disappeared one night, leaving no trace save his armor, weapons, and clothes. He was thought to have been possessed by the devil. In actuality, he had run off with his girlfriend from La Perla, and they were found to be happily settled on a farm near Caguas years later. From this viewpoint it's possible to see whales migrating from November to January.

THE FORT'S HISTORY: After El Morro proved unable to defend the city, construction began on San Cristóbal in 1634 and continued for the next 150 years. The basic structure, however, had been completed and joined to the city walls by 1678. Like El Morro, it was built entirely with materials gathered from the shoreline. Irishmen O'Reilly and O'Day enlisted in the Spanish army and developed ideas for its construction.

Incorporating the most advanced ideas of the time, the complex contained six small forts supporting a central core. These were interconnected via an amazingly complex arrangement of passageways, moats, tunnels, bridges, roads, ramps, and dungeons. To storm the central fortress, the enemy would have to take over the six outer forts under continuous fire. Explosives placed under the moats could be ignited if the enemy gained control. In 1898, San Cristóbal aimed its guns at an American Naval force, firing the first round in the Spanish-American War. After the American occupation, the US Army moved into the fort. In 1949, it was placed under the National Park Service and opened to the public in 1961.

Open daily, 9 AM–5 PM; call 787-729-6920 for information on guided tours. Admission is $2 for adults; $1 for senior citizens and children. The same ticket gets you into El Morro and vice versa.

Plaza Salvador Brau

This small plaza, also known as La Baradilla, was once the haunt of local politicians. Set next to the **Iglesia San Francisco** here, the Catholic Academy opened in 1920 and was condemned in 1964. It has been scheduled for condo conversion since the 1970s, but nothing has happened. If it is torn down, the plaza may be extended to cover it.

> "You are transformed as soon as you touch the cobblestones. It doesn't matter if you walk from Tapia to El Morro 300 times a year, you are always astonished and overwhelmed. And your state of mind changes."
>
> — Margarita Gandia B., Old San Juan realtor and local preservationist

Paseo de la Princesa is an ideal place for a romantic sunset stroll. The **La Princesa** (☎ 787-724-2930) here serves inexpensive local dishes.

Terminal Turismo

See tour boats come in at Old San Juan's Terminal Turismo. Take a stroll at night while the ships are in and watch the tourists. The cruise ship terminal offers free rum punches when the tourists arrive. Chauffeured by guayabera-sporting drivers holding walkie-talkies, the taxis outside whisk them off to Condado, depriving them of the opportunity to sample Old San Juan's wonderful nightlife.

Across the street is **Intermodal**, a commercialized and expensive municipal crafts center. It replaced the former Plazoleta del Puerto in 1994.

Casa de Ramón Power y Giralt

The 250-year-old home of the island's first representative to the Spanish parliament has been purchased (and has been beautifully restored) by the **Conservation Trust** (☎ 787-722-5834). At C. Tetúan 155, it's open Tues. to Sat., 10 AM–4 PM. It has a small but great gift shop and exhibits ranging from Taíno artifacts to stuffed cased birds with soundphones that allow you to hear their calls. Offices are in the back, and they should be able to help you with reservations at Hacienda Buena Vista or at Cabezas de San Juan. A stop won't take much time and is highly recommended.
http://www.fideicomiso.org

El Arsenal

Built in 1800, El Arsenal, a former naval station, was the last place in Puerto Rico to be handed over after the 1898 US takeover. This is where the Spanish general waited for the ship which would return him and his men to Spain. Exhibitions are held here. Open Wed. to Sun., 9–noon and from 1–4 PM; ☎ 787-724-5949.

La Casita

Built in 1937 for the Dept. of Agriculture and Commerce, La Casita ("little house") serves as a branch of the tourist board. From outside the Casita you can see San Juan Bay, the Caribbean's busiest container and cruise ship terminal. The pink **Aduana** (Customs House) is to your R. From here you can continue down the Paseo de la Princesa, which has been attractively landscaped; the fountain with its bronze sculptures affirms the island's cultural roots. It is a favored makeout spot for couples at night.

La Princesa

A former jail, La Princesa serves as headquarters of the tourism institute and as a fine art gallery; it's open Mon. to Sat. from 9 AM–5 PM. It has the island's most ornate toilets. If you go through the rear doors and out to the R you can see the remains of prison cells. To the R from the entrance you can continue on to the restored *muralla* (city wall). Dating from the 1700s, it is made of sandstone blocks which may be up to 20 ft. thick. It terminates at **La Puerta de San Juan** (San Juan Gate), which is the first of the three city gates built and the sole one remaining. Once the main gate for dignitaries and cargo entering the city, it now serves only to ornament the roadway which passes through it.

During the 17th century, sloops anchored in the small cove just N of La Fortaleza. New bishops and governors, entering the city through this gate, would be escorted under a canopy to the cathedral where a *Te Deum* Mass would be offered in thanksgiving for the safely completed voyage.

San Juan Bay & Cataño

Acuaexpreso, the new Cataño ferry (☎ 787-788-1155), runs across San Juan Bay to the suburb of Cataño. En route it offers great views of El Morro and other historic buildings. You can pay the 50¢ fare with tokens or with two quarters. Board at Pier #2 next to Terminal Turismo in Old San Juan. Ferries leave every half-hour from 6 AM–9 PM. Another ferry, whose entrance is to the L (75¢) runs to the financial district of Hato Rey in 20 minutes; it has frequent problems despite the fact that each boat cost more than a million dollars to purchase. There's an ice cream shop and magazine store in the terminal building. The Cataño area has been plagued by government-imposed pollution problems, The Commonwealth operates the Palo Seco power plant, which spews out a fine precipitate matter blamed for environmental problems, These range from asthma to having furniture covered with a fine black soot.

Cataño has a great environmental website: http://home.coqui.net/rosah

Bacardi Rum Factory

The **Bacardi Rum Factory** (☎ 787-788-1500), on the outskirts of Cataño, offers free daily tours of its facilities and drinks on the house served under a huge yellow, bat-shaped canopy. (Bacardi's first distillery housed a colony of fruit bats, thus the logo). It's a long walk (45 minutes) to the entrance so it's better to take the minibus. While the minibus is a bit pricey ($1.25) for the distance concerned, you do arrive right in time for the start of the tour. If arriving on foot, a guard will open the gate; walk straight and then turn right. Orange and yellow train-buses carry visitors around the grounds. Although there are regular times posted, tours leave whenever there are sufficient passengers. Each section of the distillery has its own guide. You'll visit the distillery, the ersatz museum, and other sites. It'll seem more interesting if you take advantage of the free drinks *beforehand*.

It's open Mon. through Sat. (excluding holidays) from 9–10:30 AM and noon–4 PM. Tours leave on the half-hour. A crafts fair here, held on the first and second Sundays in Dec., features exhibits and sales by over 200 craftsmen on the grounds.

Also in the vicinity of Cataño is **Cabras Island**. Formerly two separate islands, Cabras and Canuelo, they have been connected by a causeway. Here are the ruins of 17th-century **Fort Canuelo** and the remains of a leper colony. Great place for a picnic. Seafood restaurants are at Palo Seco nearby. **Punta Salinas Public Beach** is alongside Boca Vieja Bay near Levittown.

Old San Juan Practicalities

ACCOMMODATIONS: Although Old San Juan is the best place to base yourself for exploring the metropolitan area, there's a dearth of hotels. **The Galeria** (☎ 787-722-1808, ✆ 787-724-7360), C. Norzagaray 204, is a small guesthouse run by a sculptress. Her work is on display, and the place has a charming medieval feel to it. Rates run around $150 d to $350 d including breakfast.

http://www.thegalleryinn.com
reservations@thegalleryinn.com

Set on the borders of town right across from the cruise ship terminal, the 242-room **Wyndham Old San Juan Hotel and Casino** (☎ 787-721-5100, ✆ 787-289-1910; 800-468-2779), 100 Brumbaugh at Portuario, opened in late 1996. It charges from around $225-$575 d. Facilities include restaurant health club, casino, and rooftop pool.

Rooms have phone, cable TV, coffee maker, and hair dryer. Suites are more luxurious.
http://www.wyndham.com

The 58-rm. **Gran Hotel El Convento** (☎ 787-723-9020, ☏ 787-721-2877; Box 1048, San Juan 00902), a restored 300-year-old Carmelite Convent is situated in the heart of the old town at C. Cristo 100, on the corner of Caleta de San Juan and across from the Catedral de San Juan. First opened as a hotel in 1962, it was completely renovated at a cost of $15 million in 1996. It's worth a visit even if you aren't staying here. Facilities include a restaurant, casino, small pool, sundecks, meeting facilities, and Jacuzzi.

Guests use a card in the elevator to take them to the hotel's floors. There is a breakfast lounge (breakfast is included) which has newspapers and serves wine and *hors d'ouevres* in the late afternoon.

Rooms have TV/VCR, phone, hair dryer, CD player and tape deck, and other amenities, including a perhaps unwelcome bathroom scale. Much more expensive suites are also available. It's come a long way from a nunnery. Rates run around $200-375 d.
http://www.elconvento.com
elconvento@aol.com

The 30-room **Hotel Milano** (☎ 787-729-9050, 877-729-9050, ☏ 787-722-3379), C. Fortaleza 307, is a great new addition to the limited number of hotels here. It has a bar and good restaurant on its roof. Rates are $80-$135 which includes continental breakfast. Rooms have cable TV, phone, a/c, and small refrigerator.
http://www.hotelmilanopr.com
hmilano@coqui.net

Formerly the Hotel Central, the 51-rm. **Hotel Plaza de Armas** (☎ 787-722-2751, 888-300-8008), C. San José, charges around $105 s, $115 d plus tax. It has some handicapped-accessible rooms and continental breakfast is included in the rates.
http://www.ihppr.com

LOW BUDGET: There's not much to offer in this area. The old town could really use a youth hostel! One alternative, recommended by readers, is the **Enrique Castro Guest House** (☎ 787-722-5436; Box 947, Old San Juan PR 00902), C. Tanca 205, which offers rooms for around $20 d and $80 pw (a/c rooms are $120 pw). Don't expect much in terms of facilities here.

LONGER TERM: If staying for an extended period, ask around about renting a room or an apartment. One of the most pleasant places to stay is **The Caleta** (☎ 787-725-5347; San Juan, PR 00901), Caleta de las Monjas 11, which offers modest but fully furnished studio apartments (phone optional) right in the heart of town near the Rogativa statue. Above a coin laundry, it's quiet, friendly, safe, and secure, and manager Michael is friendly and hospitable. He also has a wide variety of rentals at other locations available. Expect to pay from around $400/mo. He also offers daily and weekly rates at this and other locations.
http://www.thecaleta.com
reservations@thecaleta.com

FOOD: The streets are lined with various eating houses and restaurants ranging from the comparatively plush ones lining C. Cristo to budget eateries on the other side of the town.

Highly recommended and reasonable is **Gopal** (☎ 787-724-0229), a *restaurante vegetariano* run by a Hare Krishna-ized Puerto Rican family. Natural food dishes like *sopa de vegetales*, tortillas, spinach, broccoli, lasagna, and a variety of fresh fruit drinks (rather sugary) are lovingly dished out by Jayapatni and her family. Try the combination plate ($4.25 for a "small" plate). It's at C. Tetuan 201 B and is open from 7-3, Mon. to Friday. The spacious, elongated room features some great Indian miniature paintings that are well worth checking out. Saturdays at 4:30 PM you'll find free food, *Bhagavad-Gita* reading, and bhakti yoga practice.

For honest Puerto Rican home cooking try **El Jibarito**, Mr. and Mrs. Ruiz's place, at C. Sol 276.

Tasa de Oro, corner of C. Tanca and C. San Justo, serves up rice and beans and other traditional foods.

At C. San Justo 207, **La Mallorquina** (☎ 787-722-3261) serves traditional Puerto Rican cuisine including *asopao*, the house specialty.

Cafeteria Manolin, C. San Justo 258 in back of the Banco Popular, serves reasonably priced food.

Higher but still not unreasonably priced is **La Bombanera**, at C. San Francisco 259; it is well known for its coffee and sweets. A sign here proclaims *"Vendemos Café Expresso Solamente"* ("We only serve expresso.") It also serves seafood dishes.

Arepas y Mucho Mas (☎ 787-724-7776), C. San Francisco 366, serves Venezuelan fare at reasonable prices.

Siglo XX, C. Fortaleza 355, is a coffee shop-style restaurant serving dishes such as paella. Catering to a Puerto Rican crowd, it has counter service, breakfast specials, and both inexpensive and moderate prices.

Café La Mallorca, at C. San Francisco 300, bordering Plaza de Jíbaro, serves good food at reasonable prices.

Butterfly People, C. Fortaleza 152, serves lunch, offering quiche, sandwiches, and the like. It is furnished with batik and butterfly murals and has a shop. It may be moving to a new location.
http://www.butterflypeople.com

Cafe Zaguán, C Tetuán 359, offers reasonably priced entrees including soups and ceviches. Vegetarian dishes are available by request. It is located opposite the Teatro Tapia. Sit at the tables outside and savor the streetlife. Dinner is served Tues. to Sat.

from six to midnight.

Next door to Zaguán, **Il Grottino** (☎ 787-723-8653), C. Tetuan 361, serves gourmet pizza as well as other Italian dishes. Expect to spend around $30 pp.

The very expensive, **La Bella Piazza** (☎ 787-728-8203) serves Italian food in a friendly yet upscale environment.

SNACKS, SANDWICHES, AND DRINKS: Just around the corner from C. Tetuán on C. San José, **Cafeteria Los Amigos** has the cheapest morning coffee in town along with inexpensive sandwiches made on Puerto Rican-style bread. It is one of the most atmospheric of all the local eateries: you might be in a small town in the hills. It's closed on Sun.

Another local, inexpensive **sandwich shop** is at C. Mendez Vigo and Luna.

El Mesón is at Plaza de Armas.

At C. Fortaleza 364, **Cafeteria Safari** has daily specials.

Las Tertulias, C. Cristo 105, has a pleasant atmosphere and offers sandwiches, shakes, and expresso.

Maria's, C. Cristo 204, is famous for its delicious but pricey fresh frozen fruit drinks.

Located on Plaza Colón and moderately priced, **Café Berlin** (☎ 787-722-5205; C. San Francisco 407) serves drinks and innovative food (including vegetarian dishes) and has art exhibits. It generally has a good collection of newspapers to read.

A *heladeria* (ice cream parlor) on Plaza San José has inexpensive *batidas* (shakes) and cones. **Pueblo** has a branch on Plaza de Armas with whole coffee beans, cold beer, and everything else you might want. There's also an expresso and ice cream joint or two out on the plaza itself.

TOURISTY EATERIES: One local landmark is the busy **Hard Rock Cafe**, Recinto Sur

253. A visit here is like being instantaneously transported back to the US mainland. The restaurant is a modern-day shrine to rock stars (some of them little known), and is more worth a visit to look at its walls rather than to "Save the Planet." Artifacts here include one of The Band's gold records, Guns and Roses memorabilia, Quicksilver Messenger Service posters, John Hartford's guitar, John and Yoko's *Wedding Album*, a Phil Collins gold record and autographed drum sticks. Prices are high and entrées are largely for committed carnivores, but there's a vegetarian burger for $7.50; coffee is $1.50. It's open daily, and there's a souvenir shop where you can add to your collection of Hard Rock Cafe T-shirts.

There are also a number of fast food restaurants. We advise you to stick to local food.

FORMAL FOOD: There are a large number of gourmet eateries here. Expect to spend $30 pp on up.

Set in a 200-year-old building, **Il Perugino** (☎ 787-722-5481), C. Cristo 105, serves gourmet Italian dishes. It has unusual homemade pastas, good desserts, and an extensive wine list.

La Otra Cosa (☎ 787-722-2672) offers gourmet indoor and outdoor dining Its specialty is the prawns served with garlic butter.

Gourmet Carli Café Concierto (☎ 787-725-4927) is a very expensive restaurant with indoor and outdoor dining., The owner plays his Steinway grand piano most evenings. It is at Plazoleta Rafael Carríon, C. Recinto Sur at San Justo in the Banco Popular building.

At C. Recinto Sur 306, **Al Dente** (☎ 787-723-7303) serves Sicilian food and fresh fruit drinks. Dishes include pasta alla pescatore and salmon served in garlic with roasted red pepper sauce. An appetizer cart is wheeled right up to your table. In addition to mannequins, it has abstract paintings, a large aquarium, and an antique Italian flag.

Gourmet **Yukiyu** (☎ 787-721-0653, 787-722-1423), C. Recinto Sur 311, serves fresh sushi as well as seafood and meat. Expect to spend at least $30 pp.

The **Royal Thai** (☎ 787-725-8424), C. Recinto Sur 315, offers curried lobster tail, red curry clam soup, and scallops served with tamarind sauce over cellophane noodles. It's owned and operated by a Thai woman. Expect to spend around $20 pp for a meal.

The **Vietnam Palace Seafood Restaurant** (☎ 787-723-7539), Recinto Sur, offers entrees for around $10.

Marisoll (☎ 787-725-7454), C. Cristo 202, is set in the patio of an old building and serves entrées like fresh salmon in a polenta crust with *champagne buerre blanc*.

Located right on Plaza San José, **Patio de Sam** (☎ 787-723-1149), C. San Sebastián 102, serves a variety of local specialties including seafood crepes.

Bohemia, C. San Sebastián 103, serves German dishes and has a beer garden.

At C. San Sebastián 106, **Amadeus** (☎ 787-722-8635) serves traditional Puerto Rican cuisine as well as seafood and even rabbit.

Baru (☎ 787-977-7107), C. San Sebastián 150, offers a mix of Caribbean & Mediterranean dishes in an elegant atmosphere.

At C. Cristo 202, **Il Perugino** (☎ 787-722-5481) is a very expensive, intimate eight-room Italian bistro.

Specializing in oysters, **La Ostra Cosa**, C. Cristo 154, serves gourmet food outdoors. Expect to spend around $30 pp.

At C. Cristo 250, **Ambrosia** (☎ 787-722-5206) features Italian daily specials. It offers $9-$12 entrées. It has tables outside as well as in.

At Callejón de la Capilla 312 (corner C. San Francisco), **El Mesón La Gran Tasca**

(☎ 787-722-5322) offers Spanish tapas and other entrées.

At C. Tetuán 367 behind the Teatro Tapia, **La Chaumiére** (☎ 787-722-3330) is a very popular, very expensive ($21 and up for entrées) gourmet French restaurant. A two-story restaurant, this long-running success resembles a French inn.

Chamo's, C. Tanca 259, serves expensive seafood paella as well as lunchtime specials.

Also on C. Tanca, the **Caribbean Deli** (☎ 787-725-6696) serves up a good mix of sandwiches and local specials.

At C. Norzagaray 424, **Amanda's** (☎ 787-722-1682) serves fish, vegetable dishes, and fruit frappés. It is noted for its French and Mexican fare, as well as its cocktails. Expect to spend around $30 pp.

At C. Fortaleza 317, **Tasca del Callejón** (☎ 787-721-1689) serves seafood, paella, and meat dishes.

The **Parrot Club**, C. Fortaleza 363, serves ultra-gourmet "Nuevo Latin" dishes and is popular with the elite. It has live jazz. Its sister restaurant, **Dragonfly** (☎ 787-977-3961), across the street at C. Fortaleza 364, serves Asian-Caribbean fusion cuisine. Expect to spend $30 pp at either. **http://www.parrotclub.com**

El Pictoteo (☎ 787-723-9621), is a tapas bar set inside the El Convento, C. Cristo 100. It is a good place to fill up with appetizers if you want good food yet are not particularly hungry.

Rick's American Café (☎ 787-723-3982), C. Tetúan 364, serves an international menu that includes seafood.

Pito's Seafood (☎ 787-724-4515), C. San José 56 serves every manner of seafood in gourmet fashion.

Don Corleone (☎ 787-723-0408), C. Fortaleza 206, offers gourmet Sicilian cuisine.

Set in the Hotel Milano, **Panorama** (☎ 787-729-9050), C. San Justo 307, serves gourmet Puerto Rican cuisine.

Trois Cent Onze (☎ 787-725-7959, C. Fortaleza 311, serves French cuisine in a top-notch romantic atmosphere. Expect to spend around $30 pp.

At C. Fortaleza 320, **Bistro Gámbaro** (☎ 787-724-4592) serves elaborate gourmet *prix fixe* cuisine in an intimate, elegant atmosphere.

Tantra (☎ 787-977-8141), C. Fortaleza 356, is an expensive gourmet Indian restaurant with ambience appropriate to the name. Expect to spend around $30 pp.

Café San Juan Bistro, C. Cruz 152, serves sandwiches, Puerto Rican dishes, and vegetarian food — all in an art gallery setting.

Café de Puerto (only open to non-members for lunch) is near the cruise ship terminals, as is **La Isla Bonita**.

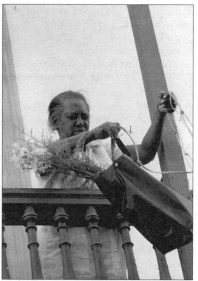

Lowering and raising baskets are a well established part of Old San Juan streetlife.

ENTERTAINMENT: For its size, Old San Juan has a greater concentration and more variety of nightlife than any city in the United States. Cobblestone-lined streets are packed wall to wall with nightspots ranging from sleaze bars to elite discos. Its dynamic and unmistakably Latin environment gets wild at night — especially on weekends when cars pour in. Everyone is desperate to see and be seen in this modern version of the *paseo*, the traditional evening stroll along the plaza. Well-heeled couples promenade up and down C. Cristo. Fashionable clothes and tons of makeup are everywhere in evidence — with everyone heading up to the bar-lined streets surrounding the Plaza San José.

On the Plaza, in addition to the young middle-class bar scene, there are sometimes jams with conga bands or folk musicians. It has gotten so wild up here at times that the police have come and fired shots into the air. Plenty of action and atmosphere in the surrounding streets as well. Innumerable bars, scattered throughout the town, have pool tables, TVs, and pinball machines. Here you can drink a beer for as little as $1 or so.

Yet another alternative is watching cruise ship passengers, especially in the evenings when you'll see women who look as if they are decked out for a cocktail party come to shop. You might see a guy with "Video Fun Day" written on his t-shirt taping teenyboppers from a ship who are doing their rendition of Arrow's "Hot, Hot, Hot."

INFORMATION: Check the "Performance" section of the Thursday *San Juan Star*'s "Entertainment Guide" to find out what's going on. *Que Pasa* also has listings. Another way is to check for posters.

MUSIC AND THEATER: El Quinqué (☎ 787-722-5378) has jazz on Thurs. evenings at 9. **Café La Violeta**, C. Fortaleza 56, features a dark, romantic environment that seems expressly designed for romantic tête-à-têtes. A pianist plays Thurs. to Sat. from 9-2 AM. **Tetuán 20**, C. Tetuán 255, features live guitar music Thurs. and Fri. evenings.

Pianists perform nightly (10-3 AM) at **Café Alejandro**, on O'Donnel between Fortaleza and Tetuán.

For formal theater, try the **Tapia**. It is named after the writer Alejandro Tapia y Rivera (1826-1882), a major figure in 19th C. Puerto Rican literature and drama.

CLUBS: Things aren't what they used to be; the yuppification of the old town has clearly had an impact and there are few good clubs with live music.

La Rumba (☎ 787-725-4407), C. San Sebastian 152, features live music (rock and salsa) from Thurs. through Sat. nights. Its stage is defaced with Coors Light and Bud banners. The crowd is very much Generation X, and things start hopping only from 10 PM.

Cafe ?, C. San José 157, attracts a youthful crowd and has live music.

Lupi's Mexican Grill, C. Recinto Sur 313, also attracts a youthful crowd and has live music.

The **Parrot Club**, C. Fortaleza 363, has Latin jazz most nights from 8 PM.

Cafe Tabac, C. Fortaleza, features live jazz Thurs. to Sun. from Oct. to March.

Lazer, C. Cruz 251, is a hiphop-oriented disco. It caters to a very decked-out, youthful crowd, including cruise ship passengers with vouchers.

The Steam Works (☎ 787-725-4993), C. Luna 205, is a gay bath.

BARS: There are a number of watering holes scattered around the old town. Up C. San José is **El Batey**, an *Americano* hangout which is open until the last cat goes home.

Don Pablo is a colorful bar at C. Cristo 103 that has unusual artwork. The decor includes sexist Bud and Finlandia posters, a moose head covered with cobwebs, and video game machines. An attached laundry offers to wash your clothes as you booze and schmooze it up.

In the El Convento, **El Bohemio** is a pick-up scene for the cell phone set.

Nono's, corner of Cristo and San Sebastián, is a popular see-and-be-seen bar for young Sanjuaneros.

Out at Fernandez Juncos 521, **St. Tropez Pub** provides scantily clad diversions for well-heeled Puerto Rican males.

EVENTS AND FESTIVALS: Most of the island-wide festivities find their fullest expression here. A **Puppet Theater Festival** is held in Jan., as is an **international folklore festival** and the **San Sebastián Street Fiesta** is a famous event. This popular street fair has everything from processions and dancing in the plaza to displays of Paso Fino horses. The streets are absolutely packed. The festivities commence with the parade of *Cabezudos*, men and women wearing colorful masks which depict characters from Puerto Rican folklore such as Juan Bobo, La Loca, and La Jibara.

The **Festival de Claridad** (Festival of Clarity) takes place in Feb.

The **Festival de Teatro Puertorriqueño** (Festival of the Puerto Rican Theater) is held at the Tapia Theater in March.

The **Fiesta de la Musical Puertorriqueña** is held inside the Dominican Convent in May.

The **Heineken Jazzfest** is held in May. http://www.prheinekenjazz.com

The **Festival de Verano** (the Summer Festival) is in June, as are the **Michelob Dry Jazz** and **Latin Music Festival**s (held at Bellas Artes), and the **Casals Festival** (which attracts the top names in classical music).

Centering on around June 26, San Juan's most famous fiesta, the **Fiesta de San Juan Batista**, is dedicated to San Juan Bautista. Inhabitants (including the mayor) flock to the sea for the traditional midnight dip, which is believed to wash away sin.

A **ceramics fair** takes place in August.

The **Fiesta de los Artes Interamericanos** (☎ 787-725-7334) offers ballet, theater, and music. It is generally held in late Sept.

The **Fiesta de Pelicula** takes place each Oct.

These events are subject to change, so check the latest issue of *Que Pasa* to find out what, indeed, is happening.

The **Fiesta Artisanos de Bacardi** (☎ 787-788-1500, ext. 5240) is held on the first two Sun. of Dec. brings together craftsmen and women from all over the island.

Every Sun all-year from 4 PM (6 PM on Sats.), **La Casita** provides a backdrop for free performances. You might see puppets, music, or dance.

CRAFTS: The **Antiguo Convento del los Dominicanos,** C. Norzagaray 98 in Old San Juan on Plaza San José, houses *Libreria y Tienda de Artesanías* (☎ 787-721-6866), a superb craft and book shop (mostly Spanish-language title) which is open Mon. to Sat. 9 Am–5 PM. It's run by the Institute for Puerto Rican Culture.

Pacopepe, corner of C. Recinto Sur and C. Tanca, sells t-shirts and other fashionware made with handpicked Peruvian cotton.

For a selection of *mundillo* lace from all over the island, visit **Aguadilla en San Juan** (☎ 787-722-0578), C. San Francisco 352.

Imported Mayan-woven handicrafts are sold at **Tata,** C. Cristo 202. You can also find crafts and craft-like items (spray can stencil art for example) at the night market near the Banco Popular.

For information on visiting crafts shops all around the island contact the **Puerto Rico Cultural Affairs Office** (☎ 787-723-0692).

ANTIQUES: El Alcazar (☎ 787-723-1229), C. San José 103, has two annexes and claims to be the largest antique shop in the Caribbean. It has a wonderful collection of antiques from all over the world.

Not quite antique but certainty old, and within anyone's budget, **Downtown Records**, C. San Francisco 363, has a highly eclectic collection of bricabrac.

FACTORY OUTLETS: Clothing is one of the best buys in Old San Juan. Several factory outlets sell discounted clothes made on the island. **Valu** is at C. San Francisco 208. **London Fog Factory Outlet Store** is at C. Cristo 156. **Pfaltzgraff**, a factory store with "bridal and gift registry," is at C. Cristo 205.

OTHER CLOTHING: Specializing in swimwear, **Wet** is at C. Cristo 252. For motorcycle gear try **Storm Riders** at C. Cruz 252.

SOUVENIRS: There are a number of unusual stores here. **Bovedá**, C. Cristo 209, has a unique collection of items.

Señor Frog's Official Store, C. San Francisco 265, offers wonderfully inventive T-shirts as well as other souvenirs.

Barrachina, C. Fortaleza 104, has free rum samples but higher prices than the supermarkets.

Hecho a Mano, C. San Francisco 260, offers a fine selection of crafts.

At C. Cristo 154, **Spicy Caribbee** offers a wide variety of sauces and other food items.

For a most unusual selection of products, try **Condom Mania** at C. San Francisco 353.

DMR, C. Luna 204, offers a beautiful collection of antique furniture reproductions.

An **Artisan Fair** is held on Plaza Hostos on Sat. and Sun.

On Old San Juan's **"Nóches de Galerías"** (☎ 787-723-6286), held the first Tuesday of the month from Feb. to May and from Nov., Some 15 Old San Juan galleries open their doors on the first Tues. from 6–9 PM. This is a great introduction to Old San Juan. Be sure to check it out if you're in town. It's one of those see-and-be-seen affairs.

JEWELRY STORES: These include **London House** at C. San José 206; the **Silver Gallery** inside the Arcade Mall at C. Cristo 206; **Joseph Machina,** C. Fortaleza 101; **Leather & Pearls**, C. Cristo 202; **Barrachina's**, C. Fortaleza 104; **Rainbow Jewelery** at C. Fortaleza 105; **Maximo**, C. San Francisco 250; **Faro**, C. Fortaleza 357; **Gitana**, C. Fortaleza 304; **Catala** at Plaza de Armas; **Corsalina**, C. San Francisco 350; **Ramon Lopez**, C. Fortaleza 256; **One Stop Shopping**, C. San Francisco 302; **Nayor**, C. San Francisco 250; **Yas Mar**, C. Fortaleza 205; **Boveda**, C. Cristo 209; and **Joyeria Demel**, C. Fortaleza 261. For reproductions, try **Impostors**, C. Tetuán 200 (at C. Cruz).

ART GALLERIES: Puerto Rican artists are well represented in Old San Juan's many galleries. In addition to the exhibits held inside Casablanca, the Balaja, La Arsenal, the Alcaldía, and the Museo de Arte y Historia, there are a number of private galleries.

Galeria Fosil Arte (☎ 787-725-4252), C. Cristo 200, sells paintings as well as artistic creations made from coral and limestone fossils.

Atlas Art, C. Cristo 208, displays the work of Spanish artist Botello (who once worked here) and other artists.

Galeria W. Labiosa (☎ 787-721-2848) sells the work of painter Wilfredo Labiosa as well as others.

The **Frank Meisler Gallery** (☎ 787-722-7698), C. Fortaleza 101, displays the artist's humorous sculptures.

Sala de Arte, an unusual gallery with great recorded music, is at C. San José 101.

Galería Luigi Marrozzini is at C. Cristo 156. **Galería M.S.A.** is at C. San Francisco 266. **Galería San Juan** is on C. Norzagaray at the corner of San C. Justo. **Fenn Studio/Gallery**, San José 58, represents local artists.

DMR Gallery (☎ 787-722-4181), C. Luna 204, sells hand-crafted furniture.

Galería Santa Bárbara, C. Luna 277, houses a selection of old maps and illustrations. **Roberto Parrilla** (☎ 787-722-2732) exhibits his paintings at C. Luna 360.

Over in Santurce, the **Galería Raices** (☎ 787-723-8909, 787-754-6271), 316 de Diego, is another fine gallery.

For a complete list of galleries and openings, check the *San Juan Star*'s Weekend section's "What's Happening" feature.

CIGARS: The **Club Jibarito** (☎ 787-724-7797), C. Cristo, is a luxury cigar store.

HATS: Olé (☎ 787-724-2445) will hand-tailor a hat for you.

BOOKS AND MUSIC: The **Cronopios** (☎ 787-724-1815) bookstore, which is excellent, is located near the corner of San José and Tetuán.

Saravá, C. Tetuán 207, is one of the world's most attractively designed music stores. Set in a lovely old building, it has two stories with extensive CD collections — salsa, merengue, African, even New Age.

INFORMATION: Minimal tourist information is provided in offices in the **Alcaldía** (City Hall, ☎ 787-724-7171) on Plaza de Armas, at the main offices in La Princesa (which is on the *paseo* of the same name),

and at **La Casita**, a small renovated building near the end of C. Tanca at the waterfront. Don't expect to be helped unless you ask them.

SERVICES: The **post office** is located at C. Fortaleza 153. An **ATH terminal** is at the Roig Bank at C. Cruz and C. Tetuán.

An a/c library is located inside Casa Blanca. Another is in the **Seminario** at C. Cristo 52.

The Calling Station (☎ 787-724-1124, ✆ 724-7072) is across from the Teatro Tapia at C. Tetuán 357. It does not have a minimum charge for calls, and it has copy, video telephone, video rental, and fax services. You can call the UK here for $1/min.

The **Mailing Station,** which offers mailboxes, money orders, packing, and access to a full range of shipping services. A message board holds notes for cruise ship arrives, and the cruise ship schedule is posted.

Another similar operation, **Phone Home** (☎ 787-721-5431, ✆ 787-721-5497) is at C. Recinto Sur 257D and across from the PO. Lamour Video, C. San Justo 254, offers video rentals.

Laundromats are located at corner of C. Cruz and C. Sol, as well as next to La Caleta Apartments near the Rogativa statue. There's also one on C. O'Donnell near Plaza de Colón.

INTERNET ACCESS: Set in the Wyndham on C. La Marina, **Soapy's Station** is open daily from 10AM–10 PM. It charges $6/hr.

The **Cybernet Café** (☎ 787-791-3138), 5575 Isla Verde is open daily from 10-10. It charges around $8/hr.
http://www.cybernetcafepr.com

If you wish to buy flowers for that hot date (or to soothe that angry wife, mistress, or girlfriend), **Anflora flower shop** is located at Calles Cruz and Sol.

BANKS: For changing money, using ATH (instant teller) machines, and cashing traveler's checks, the **Banco Bilbao-Vizcaya**, C. Tetuán 251, and the **Royal Bank of Canada**, C. Tetuán 204, are open Mon. to Fri. from 9 AM–2:30 PM. The **Caribbean Foreign Exchange** (☎ 787-722-8222) is at C. Tetúan 201 B.

PHARMACIES: At Plaza de Armas, **Puerto Rico Drug Company** (☎ 787-725-2201), C. San Francisco, has Spanish-speaking computerized pulse machines, vitamins, postcards, music, magazines, and schlock to bring back to tasteless relatives. **Luma** (☎ 787-722-0334) is also on C. San Francisco. **Walgreens** is at the corner of corner of C. Cruz and C. San Francisco, and a 24-hr. **Walgreens** (☎ 787-725-1510) is at at Ave. Ashford 1130 in Condado.

Newspapers (including The New York Times) are found at the drugstores as well as near the post office.

Metropolitan San Juan

Puerta de Tierra

Literally named "Land at the Door," this compact area, once right outside the old city walls, was originally settled by freed black slaves. Nowadays, Puerta de Tierra contains US Naval Reserves, the Capitol and other governmental buildings. Avenida Ponce de León runs right through its center.

SIGHTS: Seat of the Puerto Rican bicameral legislature, the **Capitol** was constructed during the 1920s. Its magnificent dome, with its coat of arms, hangs over an urn displaying the 1952 constitution. It's open Mon. to Fri., 8:30 AM– 5 PM. For guided tours, call 787-721-6040, ext. 253.

The once-exclusive Casino de San Juan, constructed in 1917 for the Casino de Puerto Rico social club, has since been renamed the **Manuel Pavia Fernandez Reception Center** and converted to use by the State Department. It has recently been restored with marble floors and walls and a 12-foot chandelier (open Mon. to Fri., 8 AM–4:30 PM; ☎ 787-722-2121).

A statue of patron saint **San Juan Bautista**, across from the Capitol and overlooking the small beach below, bears an uncanny resemblance to Mr. Natural of underground comic book fame.

Constructed at a cost of $22 million, the **Parque de Tercer Milenio** contains **Balneario Escambrón**, a stretch of beach, which offers lifeguards, showers and bathrooms and restaurants. It is open 7 AM–7 PM daily.

Gracefully landscaped **Muñoz Rivera Park** contains a statue of its namesake which stands near **El Polvorín**, an ammunition depot and small museum. The park, which first opened in 1983, now has a tram car which runs one km and takes 6½ minutes. Muñoz Rivera is open from 9 AM–5 PM, Tues. to Sun.

Eighteenth-century **Fort San Jerónimo**, entered from the rear of the Caribe Hilton, once housed a museum featuring dummies wearing military uniforms of different eras, ship models, and other war material. It now stands empty.

ACCOMMODATIONS: The least expensive is **Hotel Ocean Side** (☎ 787-722-2410), Ave. Muñoz Rivera 54.

Considered to be one of the outstanding examples of art-deco architecture to be found in the Caribbean, the **Radisson**

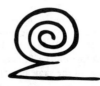

Taíno petroglyph of a snail

Normandie Hotel (☎ 787-729-2929/3083,☞ 787-729-1923), Ave Muñoz Rivera at C. Rosales, was restored in 1988. Originally constructed in 1939 by a prominent local engineer in honor of his French wife, it was intended to mimic the famous French ocean liner the *Normandie*. Facilities include a beachside pool with terrace, two restaurants, ballrooms, and a corporate floor and business center. There are 180 a/c guest rooms (including 115 suites); each has cable TV, minibar, coffeemaker, phones, and hair dryers. Some have sitting rooms. Specially designed rooms for the disabled are also available. The hotel is set on Ave. Muñoz Rivera at the corner of C. Rosales. Winter rates for rooms run from around $200 s and $210 d. A full American breakfast is included.
http://www.normandiepr.com

The 646-rm. **Caribe Hilton** (☎ 787-721-0303; ☞ 787-725-8849, 800-468-8585; Box 1872, San Juan, PR 00902) is set on 17 acres. The island's oldest resort hotel, its earliest building dates from 1849. At one time visitors to the island came here directly from the airport and (aside from time spent shopping in Old San Juan), the hotel environs were as much of the island as they saw. The hotel's most recent renovation, to the tune of $50 million, came in 1999. Its open-air lobby, graced with beige marble and regal columns, has a sunken bar which overlooks the pool. It has 602 rooms and suites with balcony, mini-bar, and TV. Its facilities include a casino, three-level pool and wading pools, six tennis courts, squash and racquetball courts, car rental and airline reservation services, an oceanfront spa, two non-smoking floors, and three restaurants and two bars. There is also an executive floor with top-flight services.
Rates run from $295 s, $320 d up to $1,200 for the most expensive suite. For more information, call 1-800-HILTONS in the US, (800) 268-9275 in Canada, 0800-289-303 in the UK.
http:// www.caribehilton.com

FOOD: A preeminent place (and one you won't want to miss) is **El Roble**. With a deli out front and a large restaurant in the back, here you can find an assortment of everything from beer and cheese to Cuban cigars from Miami. El Almendro nougats from Spain are a delicacy as are *turrones*, the locally produced Christmas candies. Try to grab a slice of cheesecake after it comes out fresh from the oven. For $9 an entire can of peaches imported from Spain can be yours. Try *quesito*, a tasty cheese pastry. Pancho Romano and the *empanadas* (meat pies) are also recommended.

Other restaurants include **Ponce de León Pizza Parlor**, **Restaurant La Imperial** (another deli), **Hao Hao** (Chinese fast food and ice cream), and the **Cathay**; all are along Ave. Ponce de León. The **Delibank**, set inside the Citibank Tower at Ponce de León 2521, offers more than 40 sandwiches on your choice of bread.

DINING: The **Tasca** is at Ave. Muñoz Rivera 54.
At Ponce de León 307, **La Bota** serves light dishes, including Puerto Rican food.
At Ave. Fernández Juncos 521, the **Latin American Café** has casual Cuban food.
At Parada 7.5 on Ave. Muñoz Rivera, the cliffside **Dumas** (☎ 787-721-3550) serves up Spanish-influenced international cuisine. **Marisqueria Atlántica** (☎ 787-722-0890), Lugo Viña 7 (also in Isla Verde), specializes in seafood, including paella and Maine lobster.
The **Escambrón Beach Club** (☎ 787-724-3344), behind the Normandie, is an inexpensive Puerto Rican restaurant and popular night spot.

HOTEL DINING: The Radisson Normandie has the **Normandie Restaurant** (☎ 787-729-2929) which features dishes ranging from Chinese to Italian. In the Caribe Hilton, **El Batey del Pescador** (☎ 787-721-0303) has a variety of dishes; the seafood menu is expanded on Fri. evenings. In the same hotel and overlooking the sea, the very expensive **Peacock Paradise** serves Chinese and other cuisine. Also here, the **Rotisserie Il Giardino** serves N Italian and international dishes.

SHOPPING: Buy handicrafts at **Mercado de Artesanía Puertorriqueña** inside Parque Muñoz Rivera and at **Mercado Artesanía Carabalí**, Parque Sixto Escobar. The former is open only on Sunday. A number of small shops line Ave. Ponce de León.

CIGARS: **EMV International House of Cigars** (☎ 787-782-6871), 1203 Ave. American Miranda, Perparto Metropolitano makes and sells some of the island's finest cigars.

SIGHTS AND SERVICES: A postal station is located along Ave. Ponce de León. The **Archives and General Library**, at Ave. Ponce de León 500, has served as a library, cigar factory, and rum plant. It displays books and archives from the collection of the Institute of Puerto Rican Culture. Its small chapel might seem to be an unusual feature, but keep in mind that it was originally designed as a hospital. It's open Mon. to Fri. from 8 AM–5PM and is a great place to read otherwise expensive imported newspapers.

Also try the small library inside the ornate **Biblioteca Atenea Puertorriqueña**, Ave. Ponce de León.

Opened on July 1, 2000, the **Museo de Arte de Puerto Rico** (☎ 787-977-6277, ext. 2245), De Diego 300, is a welcome addition to the San Juan scene. It's W wing is housed in a neo-classical building (once part of the municipal hospital) which was built in 1920. It houses the 18-gallery permanent collection. The newly built E wing is a five-story structure which has a three-story atrium, computer learning center, interactive family gallery, conservation laboratory, studios and workshops, and a gourmet restaurant and café. Admission is $5 adults, $3 children, senior citizens, and disabled. Tour packages for groups 20 or more are offered. It is open Tues. to Sun. from 10 AM–5 PM and Wed. from 10 AM–8 PM. It is closed on Mon.
http://www.mapr.org
info@mapr.org

TOURS: Sunshine Tours (☎ 800-955-6689) in the Radisson Normandie offers tours to El Yunque, the old town, Ponce, Camuy Caves, and a Shopper's Special to St. Thomas.

Miramar

This high-class residential area is just across the bridge from Puerta de Tierra. The many beautiful homes in Miramar include several by architect **Antonin Nechodoma**, whose work shows the marked influence of Frank Lloyd Wright. Yachts shelter at Club Naútico on the bay side of the bridge.

Isla Grande is just beside Miramar to the W. Formerly a US Naval base, it is now the site of Isla Grande Airport (domestic) which has flights to Culebra and Vieques. The airport's future may be in doubt; it sits on some valuable real estate. A large number of birds can be seen in this area.

Set on 110 acres, the controversial new $143-million **Puerto Rican Convention Center** will open in 2004. It will have a hotel, casino, shops, and trade center.
http://www.prconvention.com

ACCOMMODATIONS: Located at Ave. Ponce De León 801, **Hotel Excelsior** (☎ 787-721-7400, 800-289-4274, ✆ 787-723-0068; San Juan, PR 00907) has catered to the business crowd for more than three decades now. It has a pool, bar, two restaurants, sports complex, and tennis courts. The 140 a/c rooms and suites offer refrigerator, cable TV, and balcony; rooms with kitchenettes and two-room suites with kitchenettes are also available. Guests are offered complimentary coffee, shoe shine, and newspaper. It charges from around $160 d.

The 48-room **Miramar** (☎ 787-722-6239, ✆ 787-723-1180; Santurce, PR 00907), Ave. Ponce de León 606, is geared towards visiting businessmen; rooms are around $100 d and include tax.

http://www.miramarhotelpr.com
jsanchez@miramarhotelpr.com

The 45-room **Olimpo Court** (☎ 787-724-0600, ✆ 787-723-0068), Miramar 603, offers a/c rooms; studios have kitchenettes. Rates start from $50 d.

Next door at Ave. Miramar 605, 50-room **Hotel Toro** (☎ 787-725-5150/2647) is geared to business travelers. Rates range from around $30 s, $42 d.

FOOD: Open until 9, the **Pueblo Supermarket** in the Miramar Caribbean Tower has the usual stuff, including bulk coffee beans. Ave. Ponce de León and surrounding side streets are literally lined with places to eat.

The **Museo de Arte** features gourmet **Pikayo** (☎ 787-721-6194), Ave. de Diego 300. It combines Puerto Rican, French, and California nouvelle cuisine. It is expensive, and entrees start at around $20.

For sandwiches and expresso try the **Panadería y Repostería** at the corner of Ave. Miramar and Ave. Ponce de León.

At Ponce de León 604, **Café Fornos** (☎ 787-722-3120) serves Puerto Rican, Spanish, and other dishes including *paella valenciana*.

HOTEL DINING: D'Arco is at the base of Hotel Toro, Ave. Miramar 605.

In the Excelsior Hotel at Ave. Ponce de León 801, award winning, very expensive **Augusto's** (☎ 787-725-7700) serves distinct dishes such as lobster ravioli along with a wide variety of wines.

Café Miramar here is an expensive but informal coffee shop serving three meals daily and a Sun. brunch.

The Olimpo Court has **Chayote** (☎ 787-722-9385), a gourmet c*omida criollo* restaurant. This restaurant is the second founded by restaurateur Alfredo Ayala, a former industrial engineer who returned to Puerto Rico to start a gourmet restaurant which would feature Puerto Rican food. His first was Ali-Oli. The first of its kind, it has spawned innumerable imitations.

The **Bistro de Paris** (☎ 787-721-6194), in the Hotel Excelsior at 801 Ave. Ponce de Leon, serves gourmet French food inside and on the poolside terrace. Entrees run around $20.

ENTERTAINMENT: The **Fine Arts Cinema** (☎ 787-721-4288), Ave. Ponce De León 654, has high quality first run films. Other theaters are farther down the road in Santurce.

The **Black Angus** is one of the local meat markets. The "hoofers" here have a lower incidence of AIDS than the street hookers nearby (because they insist that their customers use condoms). Other such clubs are in the vicinity.

A seamy gay dance club, **Eros** (☎ 787-722-1131), Ave. Ponce de León 1257, stands next to the Teatro Metro.

Plaza Mercado, C. Canals, has frequent outdoor live music shows on weekend evenings.

SERVICES: The **Calling Station** (☎ 787-722-8085, ✆ 787-722-8066) is across from the Pueblo and next to the Banco Popular at Ave. Ponce de León 655. It has copy, video telephone, and ✆ services, with no minimum charge. Many airline offices are based here, including Iberia, Viasa, Lufthansa, and Dominicana.

ISLA GRANDE AIRPORT: Situated at the end of a long stretch of road near the tractor trailer "Sea Train" terminal sits small and funky Isla Grande, which served as the island's first international airport. Inside are a *cafeteria* and several airlines, including Flamingo (a charter airline which flies to Culebra), and Vieques Air Link (which flies to Vieques and on to St. Croix).

Hill Aviation (☎ 787-723-3385) offers helicopter tours of Old San Juan and beyond.

Isla Grande Flying School (☎ 787-722-1160, 787-725-5760) rents small planes for solo and dual flying with a three-hour minimum. Fuel, oil, and liability insurance are included. Unfortunately, the only way to get to this airport is via a long, hot walk, your own wheels, or by taxi.

Santurce-Condado

Once the most exclusive area in the city, Santurce has changed as businesses move over to the neighboring financial district of Hato Rey. Condado, the tourist strip on the main bus route between Old San Juan and the rest of the city, is as near to a perfect replica of Miami Beach as you'll find in the Caribbean.

HISTORY: Founded as Cangrejos (later San Mateo de Cangrejos), the area was the

---

Condado Snorkeling

The best places to snorkel are at Dog Rock, the jetty at the public beach near the Condado Plaza Hotel in Condado. This shallow site (under 10 ft.) provides the opportunity to get an idea of what you may find underwater in the Caribbean.

Another alternative is in Isla Verde, off a jetty set between the Holiday Inn and the El San Juan.

---

main agricultural and meat supplier to Old San Juan from the 17th century onwards. Inhabited mostly by freed slaves and Maroons (refugees from slavery on other islands), its name changed to Santurce.

The bridge linking Condado with Puerto de Tierra was constructed originally in 1910 by two brothers (the Behns) who were early 20th-century immigrants from St. Thomas. The name (*Dos Hermanos,* "Two Brothers") of the current rebuilt and enlarged structure still refers to Hernand and Sosthenes who, after acquiring the Puerto Rican Telephone Company, went on to found ITT! C. Luchetti is named after their mother, Madame Luchetti.

Ave. Ashford's namesake is Dr. Bailey K. Ashford, who came to the island with the occupying American troops. He discovered that hookworms are the root cause of anemia.

During the turbulent late 1950s in Cuba and after the revolution which followed, Condado was quick to soak up the tourists (and many Cubans) who fled, seeking a more hospitable environment.

SIGHTS: The area's most unusual "sight" must surely be the Tunel Minillas in Santurce. It's nicknamed the "carwash" because of its leaky roof.

The **Museo de Arte Contemporáneo Puertorriqueño** (Museum of Contemporary Puerto Rican Art, ☎ 787-268-0049) is inside

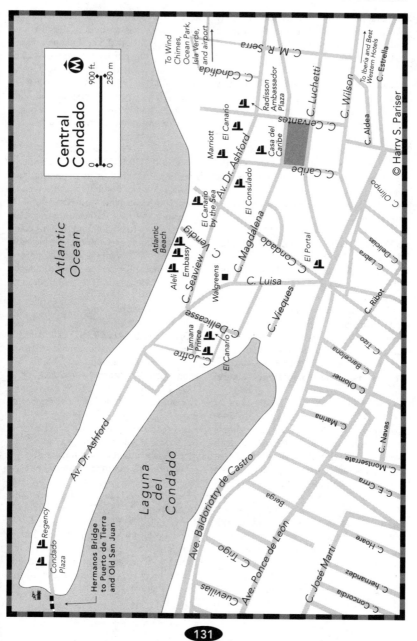

Central Condado

900 ft.
250 m

Atlantic Ocean

Atlantic Beach

To Wind Chimes, Ocean Park, Isla Verde, and airport

C. Cándida

C. M. R. Serra

C. Wilson

To Iberia and Best Western Hotels

C. Estrella

Radisson Ambassador Plaza

Marriott

El Canario

Av. Dr. Ashford

Cervantes

C. Luchetti

C. Aldea

Casa del Caribe

C. Caribe

El Canario by the Sea

Av. Dr. Ashford

El Consulado

C. Magdalena

C. Olimpo

Aleli

C. Seaview

Venidig

C.

C. Condado

El Portal

El Canario

C. Labra

C. Delicias

Walgreens

C. Luisa

C. Vieques

C. Ribot

Delilcasse

C. Tizo

Tamana Prince

C. Barcelona

Joffre

El Canario

C. Olomer

C. Marina

Regency

Condado Plaza

Av. Dr. Ashford

Hermanos Bridge to Puerto de Tierra and Old San Juan

Laguna del Condado

Ave. Baldoriotry de Castro

Berga

C. E. Crta

C. Montserrate

C. Navas

C. Hoare

Cuevillas

Ave. Ponce de León

C. Trigo

C. José Martí

C. hernandez

C. Concordia

© Harry S. Pariser

131

the Barat Bldg. in the Sacred Heart University which is off of Ave. Ponce de León in Santurce; it's open Mon. to Fri. from 9 AM–5 PM. Exhibits rotate.

BEACHES: The small Condado Beach may be reached by streets (C. Vendin, C. Earle, and C. court) from Ave. Ashford.

To reach a better one, head towards Santurce (in the direction of Isla Verde) and make a L on C. King's Court. Heading past the stoplight, you'll run right into the beach. This clean white sand beach is long and wide with palm trees.

Ocean Park also has a nice beach as does **Isla Verde**.

CONDADO GUESTHOUSE ACCOMMO-DATIONS: Embassy Guest House (☎ 787-725-8284/2400, ℱ 787-725-2400, 800- 468-0615; Condado PR 00907), is at C. Seaview 1126, a street off of Vendig leading from Ave. Ashford. It features rooms with a/c, fans, and cable TV starting at around $70 d; more expensive rooms have kitchenettes, and a restaurant is just across the street. It is gay friendly.
http://home.att.net/~embassyguesthouse

At Sea View 1125, **Alelí by the Sea** (☎ 787-725-5313/3895, ℱ 7877-721-4744; Condado PR 00907) offers nine simple rooms running around $65-100 d with semi-private bath and a/c. Use of the shared kitchen and living room is included, as is a sundeck on the beach. One guest recommends the oceanfront room.

The **Arcade Inn Guest House** (☎ 787-725-0668, 787-728-7524; Condado, PR 00901), C. Taft 8, has personal service. Breakfast is served on the patio. Rates start from around $65–85 d.

Down the street at C. Taft 53, the **Wind Chimes Guest House** (☎/ℱ 787-727-4153, ℱ 787-728-0671, 800-946-3244) is

a restored Spanish-style villa. It has 12 rooms with a/c or fans. Cable TV and breakfast is included. Local phone calls are free. Rates range from around $80–125 d. The same owners run the **Casa del Caribe** (☎ 787-722-7139), 57 C. Caribe, which is a slightly less expensive version. The hotel has an outstanding website.
http://www.atwindchimesinn.com

The 29-room **El Consulado** (☎ 787-289-9191, 888-300-8002, ℱ 787-723-8665), Ave. Ashford. 1110, is set in an attractive Spanish colonial building which served as the Spanish consulate from 1957-1974. It is geared towards business travelers, so frills are kept to a minimum. Rooms come with a/c, phone, queen or two double beds, and cable TV. Some have refrigerators. Continental breakfast is served on the patio, and Hermes is next door. Rates run around $85–115 d.
http://www.ihppr.com

CONDADO SMALLER HOTELS: A member of the International Gay Travel Association and right on the beach, the 37-room **Atlantic Beach** (☎ 787-721-6900, 787-722-3089, ℱ 787-721-6917; C.Vendig 1, Condado PR 00907), has a restaurant. Rates run around $100–$150 d. Reportedly, the rooms are small, and it is hard to get a "guest" in to your room.
http://www.atlanticbeachhotel.net
reservations@atlanticbeachhotel.net

The 22-room **El Prado Inn and Apartments** (☎ 787-728-5925, 787-468-4521; 800-728-5925; ℱ 787-725-6978; Condado PR 00908), C. Luchetti 1350, is centrally located and offers a/c or fan rooms with private baths; poolside continental breakfast is included. Rates run from around $90–$140 d.

The 48-room a/c **El Portal del Condado** (☎ 787-721-9010, ☏ 787-724-3714; Box 10133, San Juan, PR 00908), C. Condado 76, offers rooms with cable TV, radio, phone, and refrigerator; it's walking distance from the beach. Rates range around $95–$115 d.
http://www.hotelelportal.com

At Ashford, 1317 the **El Canario Inn** (☎ 787-724-2793/3861, ☏ 787-722-0391, 800-533-2649; Condado PR 00907) has 25 rooms from $85 d. Rooms are a/c with phone and cable TV and rates include breakfast.

The 40-room **El Canario By the Lagoon Hotel** (☎ 722-5058, 742-4276, ☏ 787-723-8590, 800-533-2649; Condado PR 00907), C. Clemenceau 4, charges from around $105-$155 d. All rooms are a/c and have cable TV, phone, and balcony. Breakfast is complimentary.

Completing the trio, the **El Canario By the Sea** (☎ 787-722-8640, ☏ 787-725-4921, 800-533-2649; Condado PR 00907), C. Condado 4, offers 25 a/c rooms with radio and cable TV. This three-story green building is just 50 ft. from the beach. A continental breakfast is served to guests. Rates run from around $115–$130 d.
http://www.canariohotels.com

The **Iberia Hotel** (☎ 787-723-0200, 787-722-5380, ☏ 787-724-2892), Wilson 1464, charges from $90 d. and is located in an exclusive residential area Rooms have with a/c, cable TV, phone and bath. It has the **La Fonda de Cervantes Restaurant.**

CONDADO LARGE HOTELS: At Ave. Ashford 999, the **Condado Plaza Hotel & Casino** (☎ 787-721-1000, ☏ 787-722-7955, 800-624-0420; Box 1270, San Juan PR 00902) has a casino, fitness center, water sports center, nightclub, and piano bars. Most of its 550 a/c rooms have king-size beds, phones, individual climate controls, remote control cable TVs (equipped with "Spectravision"), and private terraces. More expensive rooms have Jacuzzis. Its Plaza Club is a "hotel within a hotel" and offers special services. There are a total of seven restaurants, ranging from Chinese to Italian to NY-style pizza. A very small beach adjoins the property.

Rates start from around $185 s, $205 d during the off-season and range up to a top of $1,100 s or d for the Plaza Club Suite during the peak season.
http://www.condadoplaza.com

The **Regency Hotel** (☎ 800-468-2823, 787-721-0505, ☏ 787-722-2909; Box 364484, San Juan, PR 00936-4484), Ave. Ashford 1005, has 127 a/c rooms have cable TV, refrigerator, and private balcony. Other facilities include pool, restaurant and banquet facilities, piano bar, and secretarial service. A private boardwalk connects with the Condado Plaza Hotel and its casino. (Facilities are shared between the two hotels) A complimentary continental breakfast is served daily from 7–9 AM. Rates run around $185-$280 d. Superior rooms, studios, and one-bedroom suites are more expensive.
http://www.hotelbook.com

The beachfront **Ramada San Juan Hotel** (☎ 787-723-8000, ☏ 787-722-8230, 800-854-7854, ☏ 602-443-6543) is a 95-room a/c, recently-remodeled "boutique-style" hotel located at Ave. Ashford 1045. Facilities include a pool, restaurant, banquet facilities, and a Corporate Lounge. Rates range from around $135-230 d.
http://www.ramadasanjuan.com

The $131 million **San Juan Marriott Hotel & Casino** (☎ 787-722-7000, 800-

228-9290, ☎ 787-289-6182) opened in 1995 at Ave. Ashford 1309, the site of the Dupont Plaza, which burned to the ground on New Year's Eve 1986. It has 512 rooms, 17 suites, thee restaurants, casino, business services, conference areas, beauty salon, pool, spa, Jacuzzi, tennis courts, and a parking garage. Rates run from around $270-$350 d.
http://www.marriottpr.com

With a choice of 233 rooms including 87 suites, the **Radisson Ambassador Plaza Hotel & Casino** (☎ 787-721-7300, ☎ 787-723-6151, US/worldwide 800-333-3333; Ave. Ashford 1369, San Juan, PR 00907-9955) offers deluxe rooms complete with balconies, cable TV, radio, refrigerator, and sitting room. Its nine-floor suite tower has 87 two-room suites; each has a living room and bedroom as well as two TVs, three phones (one with fax), and personal computer modems. Facilities include four restaurants and lounges, casino, health spa, game room, and roof-top swimming pool. It was recently renovated and expanded at a cost of more than $45 million. Rates start at $210 s and $220 d.
http://www.radisson.com/sanjuanpr_ambassador

The 146-rm. **Diamond Palace Hotel & Casino** (☎ 787-721-0810, ☎:787-725-7895, 800-468-2014, Ave. Condado 55, is right by the beach. Rooms and suites are equipped with cable TV, small fridge, and microwave. It has two restaurants. It charges around $145-195 d.
http://www.diamondpalacehotel.net

Overlooking the lagoon at C. Joffre 1, the 95-room a/c **Tamaná Princess Comfort Inn** (☎ 787-724-4160, 787-721-6072, ☎ 787-723-2282; Box 19355, San Juan, PR 00910) has a pool and rooms with cable TV. Other facilities are nearby. Rates run from around $100–$120 d.
http://www.choicecaribbean.com

SANTURCE HOTELS: Hotels in Santurce include the **Hotel Capri**, Fernandez Juncos 902 (☎ 787-722-5663); **Hotel Colonial, Inc.**, Fernandez Juncos 1902 (☎ 787-727-1440); **Hotel Dos Hermanos**, Duffaut 263 (☎ 787-725-4349); **Hotel Metropol**, Ponce de León 1661; and the **Hotel San Jorge**, Ave. Ponce de León 1700.

SANTURCE LARGE HOTELS: The184-rm **Hotel Pierre/Best Western** (☎ 787-721-1200, ☎ 787-721-311, 800-528-1238; Box 12038, San Juan, PR 00914), is at De Diego 105 in Santurce, It has deluxe a/c rooms with TV and phone and charges around $150$165 d. It is near a beach, tennis courts, and shopping.
http://www.hotelpierresanjuan.com
reservations@hotelpierresanjuan.com

At C. Clemenceau 6, the 48-room **Days Inn Condado Lagoon** (☎ 787-721-0170, ☎ 787-724-4356; Box 13145, Santurce PR 00908) has five-star rooms priced from around $120–$230 d.
http://www.daysinn.com

CONDADO FOOD: The casual **Cadillac Café**, Ave. Ashford 1021, serves deli sandwiches and Italian and meatball subs; it has work on the walls by local artists.

Hacienda Don José (☎ 787-722-5880), Ave. Ashford 1025, is a "Mexican" restaurant which has reasonable prices. A Chili's is across the street, and **Santelmo**, a 24-hr. cafe with reasonable prices, is across the street.

Gourmet **Hermes** (☎ 787-723-5151), Ave. Ashford 1108, serves seafood and other dishes.

?!¿ Puerto Rico has around 12,000 hotel rooms. Hawaii, a place of similar size, has 80,000.

Salud (☎ 787-722-0911), Ave. Ashford 1350, a natural health food restaurant and store, serves great food. It's open from Mon. to Sat., 9 AM–8 PM.

Danny's International Pizzeria y Cafeteria (☎ 787-724-0501), Ave. Ashford 1352, is a popular pizza place.

Via Appia, Ave. Ashford 1350 (next door to Salud), serves pizza and pasta in a more upscale atmosphere.

Zabór, C. Candida, is also nearby. Set in a refurbished mansion, this expensive gourmet restaurant offers Caribbean, Italian, and Asian fusion dishes. It is open only for dinner.

At Ave. Ashford 1372, **Il Grotino** is an Italian "wine bar" and restaurant with ('natch) an extensive wine list.

The **Pattiserie Delicatessen**, Ave. Ashford 1504, serves light dishes for lunch or dinner.

Bordering the Plaza de la Libertad, **C'est La Vie!**, Ashford and Magdalena, serves a variety of tapas and other light fare.

Another **Salud Juice Bar** is at Ave. Magdalena 1400.

Ramiro's (☎ 787-721-9049), Magdalena 1106, offers expensive gourmet Spanish *haute cuisine*. Castilian dishes are given an artistic flourish.

At Magdalena 1108, **Cielito Lindo** serves innovative and inexpensive Mexican dishes such as chicken with mole sauce.

In the Centro Europa Bldg. on Ave. Ponce de León, **Pizzeria Uno** serves deep-dish Chicago-style pizza as well as pasta and other dishes.

CONDADO DINING: Honoring famous entertainers in a multilevel club, the inexpensive **Hall of Fame** (☎ 787-721-5570), Ave. Ashford 1020, serves tapas and dishes ranging from simple to elaborate.

Offering innovative Italian cuisine, **Caruso** (☎ 787-723-6876), Ave. Ashford 1104, is open daily.

Marisquería La Dorada (☎ 787-722-9583), Ave. Magdalena 1104 at Ashford, serves gourmet Puerto Rican-style seafood and other dishes.

Antonio's, in a converted mansion at C. Magdalena 1406 (☎ 787-723-7567), offers Spanish and other international specialties.

At C. Magdalena 1108, the very expensive **Los Faisanes** (☎ 787-725-9076) serves a variety of international gourmet dishes.

Expensive, gourmet **Urdin** (☎ 787-724-0420), Ave. Magdalena 1105, serves Spanish-influenced Caribbean cuisine. Its name comes from the Basque word for "blue," the motif of the dining room.

Don Pepe at C. Condado 72 offers dishes ranging from paella to eel; it is also expensive.

Zabó (☎ 787-725-9494) at C. Candida 14 specializes in New England clam chowder as well as a host of other dishes.

At Ave. Condado 74, the **Marisquería Miró** (☎ 787-723-9593) is a famous gourmet restaurant which serves lunches and dinners. Named after the famous Spanish painter, it cooks the dishes of his Catalan homeland, and his prints hang on the wall.

Popular **Ajili-Mójili** (☎ 787-725-9195), Ave. Ashford 1052, features Puerto Rican cuisine and serves dishes such as *arroz con pollo*. It features dishes from all over the island and is considered to be one of the island's finest *criollo* restaurants.

At Ave. Condado 106, **Compostela** (☎ 787-724-6088) serves great gourmet, expensive Spanish food. Specialties include salmon tartare with caviar and salmon with mustard seed sauce. It has an extensive wine list.

CONDADO HOTEL DINING: Lotus Flower (☎ 787-722-0940) inside the Condado Plaza, serves Dim Sum lunches as well as Szechwan and Hunan entrées. The Condado Plaza also has **La Posada** which provides 24-hr. service, informal dining, and a salad bar. Also in the Condado Plaza, **Tony Roma's** (☎ 787-722-0322) specializes in ribs. Another Condado Plaza restaurant, **Capriccio** (☎ 787-725-9236) serves a good selection of seafood, pasta, and other dishes. Informal **La Posada** is also here. Its offerings include a salad bar and a buffet breakfast.

In La Concha Hotel, **Sirenas** (☎ 787-721-0690) serves California and Caribbean-style seafood.

In the Regency Hotel, the **St. Moritz** (☎ 787-721-0999) serves fish and veal topped with exotic sauces.

Open 24 hrs., the **Café del Arte** (in the Condado Beach Hotel) serves a variety of tapas, sandwiches, and salads. Also in the Condado Beach Hotel, **Vivas Restaurant** (☎ 787-721-6090) serves very expensive "New World" cuisine.

The informal **Adagio** (☎ 787-721-6090, ext. 1745) here offers N Italian cuisine.

In the Ambassador Plaza, the very expensive and gourmet **Giuseppe Ristorante** (☎ 787-721-7300) serves N Italian cuisine.

Set in the Ramada Hotel, the **Ocean View** (☎ 787-723-8000) serves a variety of local specialties.

In the Hotel Tamaná Princess, the **Pikayo** (☎ 787-721-6194), C. Joffre 1, serves international dishes ranging from Cajun to Puerto Rican.

Atop the Black Diamond Hotel, **Martino** (☎ 787-722-5356) serves authentic and delicious northern Italian dishes.

The Marriott has **La Vistas** (☎ 787-722-7000), which (of course) commands an ocean view and offers nightly cultural specials. One night may be Mexican, another Argentinian.

SANTURCE FOOD: There are innumerable places to eat, and the usual fast-food chains are everywhere in evidence. For Puerto Rican food try any *cafeteria,* or **Criollisimo,** 2059 Ave. Edo Conde, Santurce; **Restaurant La Borincana,** 1401 Fernandez Juncos; **Delin's Café,** C. Antonsanti 1502; and **Restaurante El Ateneo,** Figueroa 610.

Inexpensive and intimate, **La Buena Mesa,** Ponce de León 606, offers Puerto Rican food.

How Kow, Magdalena 1408, features Cantonese and Szechuan dishes.

For inexpensive Chinese dining you can also try **Honolulu,** Del Parque 413.

With a 1950s Cuban feel to it, **Havana's Café** (☎ 787-725-0888), Del Parque 409, serves Cuban food which is quite popular. No credit cards.

Set across from the market, **Tasca El Pescador** (☎ 787-721-0995), C. Dos Hermanos 178, serves moderately-priced Puerto Rican lunches and dinners.

On Carr. 26 next door to Target Car Rental, **Pomarrosas** (☎ 787-268-6270) serves Puerto Rican fare in a room crowded with knicknacks and antiques.

The **Pabellón de las Artes** is on Plaza Juan Morel Campos at the Centro de Bellas Artes; it is aimed at pre- or post-concert diners.

SANTURCE DINING: Specializing in Cuban cuisine, renowned **Metropol** is at De Diego 105. **Aurorita** (☎ 787-783-2899), De Diego 303, is an ultra-popular Mexican restaurant; mariachi bands serenade on weekends. **Mangére** (☎ 787-792-6748), De Diego 311, is one of the best Italian restaurants. At De Diego 316, **El Palacio de las Pastas** offers lunch specials as well as moderate-priced dinners. **El Paso,** De Diego 405, is an inexpensive Puerto Rican restaurant.

At C. San Jorge 609, very expensive and gourmet **La Casona** (☎ 787-727-2717) is all mahogany and stained glass; its Spanish-based creative dishes include lobster salad. It is set in an old home,

A popular seafood restaurant, **Fish & Crab** (☎ 787-781-6570) is at Matadero Rd. 301.

La Buona Lasagna (☎ 787-721-2488), Diez de Andino 104, serves a wide variety of Italian dishes as well as organic Italian wines.

The **Fleria** (☎ 787-268-0010), C. Loíza 1754, serves moderately-priced Greek fare.

HOTEL DINING: In the Hotel Best Western Pierre, the **Petit Pierre** (☎ 787-721-2100) serves French-style seafood in an intimate setting. Also in the Best Western, the **Village Bake Shop** serves baked goods along with sandwiches and other light fare.

SUPERMARKETS: A large **Pueblo** is at 114 De Diego and is open 24 hrs. daily. Sample prices: bass filets $7.89/lb., potatoes 5 lbs./$2.79, onions 2 lb. bag/$1.49, apples 3 lbs./$2.99, cauliflower $2.99/each, broccoli $1.99/each, carrots 5 lbs./$2.99, red bell pepper $2.99/lb., French bread $1.29/lb, apple cider $4.49/64 oz, carrot juice 32 fl oz/$3.69, papaya $1.19/lb, watermelon 89¢/lb., avocados 99¢/each, sugar $2.49/5 lbs., Yauco select coffee $10.99/10 oz, Mazola corn oil $2.49/48 oz., rice 3 lbs/85¢, lge. eggs/doz. $1.45, milk $1.54/half gallon, Minute Maid orange juice $3.99/64 oz, Häagen-Dazs ice cream $3.69/pint. It also has a deli and stand-up café with cut rate food.

Vega's Supermarket is at **Hotel Condado Lagoon**, 6 Clemenceau, Condado. **Santurce Market** is on C. Canals.

A **Walgreens** (☎ 787-725-1510), Ave. Ashford 1130, is open 24 hrs. daily, and it has an ATM machine.

ENTERTAINMENT: Stargate (☎ 787-725-4664), Ave. RH Todd 1, is a disco designed to resemble an Egyptian temple. It plays no Latin music, has a minimum age for admission of 23, and caters to yuppies. It has a cigar bar, appropriate furnishings and decor, and two multi-level dance floors. Admission ranges from $10-20, and a yearly pass is $750.

An underground scene is found at **Asylum** (☎ 787-723-3258), Ave. Ponce de Leon 1320, which has everything from comedians to cabaret acts.

Amadeus is a disco inside the El San Juan.

The **Luis A. Ferré Centro des Bellas Artes** (Performing Arts Center, ☎ 787-724-4747, tickets ☎ 787-620-444), largest and best of its kind in the Caribbean, is also the most attractive building in the entire area. Since it opened in 1981, the Center has featured internationally acclaimed musicians, ballet stars, opera and experimental dance performances, lectures, drama festivals, jazz concerts, and musical comedies. Student discounts are available. Be sure to get there early or buy tickets in advance if you want the cheaper seats You may dine before or after events at the restaurant on the premises.

Nuestro Teatro presents plays dealing with Puerto Rican life and social realities.

The Greenhouse, Ashford Ave. 1200, has live entertainment from 11 on Wed., Sat., and Sun. nights.

Flamingo Road Bar & Restaurant (☎ 787-723-0013), Ave. Ashford 1313, has live bands on weekends. Touristic shows are put on regularly at the major hotels in the area; check *Que Pasa* for listings.

Divas (☎ 787-721-8270), 1104 Ashford Ave., is a "gentleman's club," code words for an upscale strip joint with trimmings.

LESBIAN AND GAY: Condado is also a center for gay nightlife. **Vibration** bills itself as the "best men's cruising bar." It's at 51 Barranquitas in Condado.

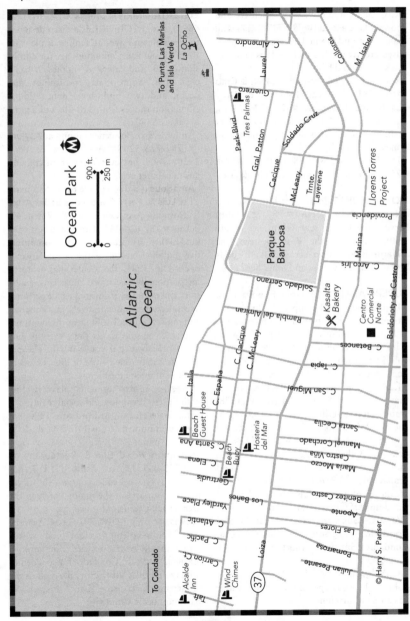

Ocean Park

Atlantic Ocean

900 ft.
250 m

To Punta Las Marias
and Isla Verde

La Ocho

Parque Barbosa

Llorens Torres Project

Kasalta Bakery

Centro Comercial Norte

To Condado

© Harry S. Pariser

The **New Bachelor** (☎ 787-721-3945), Ave. Condado 112, is a disco.

Bars include **Downstairs Bar** at the Condado Inn, Condado 6; Junior's (☎ 787-723-9477), C. Condado 602; **La Laguna** (☎ 787-723-7386), Barranquitas 53; and **Cups** (☎ 787-268-3570), a lesbian hangout at San Marcos 1708.

CINEMA: In Santurce, the three-cinema **Metro** (☎ 721-4288) is at Ponce de León 1255, and the three-cinema **UA Paramount** (☎ 725-1103) is at Ave. Ponce de León 1313.

SERVICES AND INFORMATION: Bell, Book, and Candle, Condado's leading bookstore, is at De Diego 102. They have a fine selection of books.

(Other bookstores, including **Borders Books and Music,** are out at Plaza Las Américas).

Alianza Francesa (Alliance Francaise) is at Rosario 206, Santurce. They have a library and present films and other cultural events. The **Dutch Consulate** is at First Federal Savings, Stop #23, Ave. Ponce de León.

The unisex **Muscle Factory** (☎ 787-721-0717), a gym, is at Ave. Ashford 1302.

YOGA: The **Shanti and Yakeen Relaxation Response Center** (☎ 787-725-5888r, Ave. Ashford 884-B, offers yoga classes.

TRAVEL AGENCIES: Contact **Travel Network** (☎ 787-725-0960), 1035 Ashford; **Turismo Internacional** (☎ 787-721-1347), 1045 Ashford; or **Prime Market Travel** (☎ 787-791-3602/5151) in ESJ Towers over in Ocean Park.

Out in Dorado, **Rico Suntours** (☎ 787-722-/2080) offers a wide variety of trips including ones to St. Thomas, to the racetrack, to the observatory, El Yunque, and Ponce.

CAR RENTAL: Charlie's (☎ 787-728-6525) is at Ave. Ashford 890. Others are in the vicinity.

CYCLING: Bicycle Rental & Sales (☎ 787-722-6288), 1122 Ave. Ashford (across from Wendy's) offers rentals.

Ocean Park

This area, sandwiched between Santurce and Isla Verde, has a number of small hotels. It also has an attractive beach which is popular both with gays and college students (on weekends).

The 11-room, two-apartment **Numero Uno** (☎/✉ 787-726-5010, 787-727-5482; Ocean Park, PR 00911), C. Santa Ana 1, is set in a quiet residential area. It offers great restaurant (see below), two sundecks, a patio, and a pool with bar. Functional rooms command ocean views, and two apartments come with kitchenettes. Guests are loaned beach towels and chairs. Rates run around $135-265 d.

The 17-room **Tres Palmas Guest House** (☎ 727-4617, ✉ 727-5434, 888-290-2076, Isla Verde, PR 00913), Park Blvd. 2212, offers attractive a/c bedrooms with separate entrances. There's a sundeck, Jacuzzi, pool, and shared cable TV. Food is served, breakfast is included, and major holidays see free feeds. Rates run around $80-130 d. **http://www.trespalmasinn.com**

At Ave. McLeary 1853, the 15-room **Beach Buoy Inn** (☎ 787-728-8119, 800-221-8119, ✉ 268-0037; Ocean Park, PR 00911) has a sunroof and garden patio. Rooms have color TV, a/c and fans, and a refrigerator. Rates run from around $60 d.

The 19-unit **Hostería del Mar** (☎ 787-727-3302/0631, ✉ 787-268-0772; Ocean Park, PR 00911), C. Tapia 1, faces the beach and has rooms run around $75-240 d. Glistening white, it is an oasis away from the hustle and bustle. The attractive rooms have rattan furniture, and many command ocean views. The four apartments have kitchenettes. Its restaurant has many vegetarian dishes as well as standard fare. **hosteria@caribe.net.**

The **Ocean Park Beach Inn** (☎/✆ 728-7418, 800-292-9208), C. Elena 3, is gay friendly. Rates run from $110 d. **http://home.coqui.net/opbi**

The ten-room **L'Habitation Beach Guest House** (☎ 787-727-2499), C. Italia 1957, is French-owned and gay friendly. The simple yet comfy rooms have a/c and fans. It has a bar and snack bar, and beach towels and chairs are loaned.

OCEAN PARK FOOD: At Tapia 1, **Hosteria del Mar** serves a variety of vegetarian dishes and offers a Sun. brunch.

At María Moczó 57, **Mona's** serves Mexican food.

Set in Numero Uno Guest House, gourmet **Pamela's** (☎ 787-726-5010) offers up gourmet Caribbean fusion cuisine including lunchtime specials.

Pepin's, Ave. Isla Verde 2479, has great tapas.

The **Antique Café Museum** (☎ 787-727-6620), Loíza 2473, serves US and Argentine dishes. It has more than a thousand antiques on display.

Mango's Café (☎ 787-727-9328), Laurel 2421, is inexpensive (less than $10 for entrées) and serves Caribbean cuisine from both the English and Spanish speaking islands. They serve a mean veggie Rasta Burger. It doubles as a hangout at night.

At C. Caoba 35 and open daily, **Che's** (☎ 787-726-7202) serves both Argentinian and Italian dishes.

At C. Laurel 2413, the **Golden Unicorn** (☎ 787-728-4066) specializes in Szechuan dishes.

Dining is also available in nearby Punta Las Marias, an area to the E of Ocean Park.

Isla Verde

Located to the W of the airport, Isla Verde is one of San Juan's main hotel areas. The area's development commenced with the opening of the San Juan Intercontinental in 1958. The hotel was managed by a subsidiary of now-defunct Pan Am, which influenced its location. After it was sold in 1961, five acres were promptly sold to the Loews Corp., which built the neighboring Americana (It was then renamed the Sands and later demolished. The San Juan Grand now stands in its place.) Development has taken off from there. Isla Verde is convenient in terms of arriving and departing but does not offer much in terms of authentic Puerto Rican flavor.

It does have a very popular beach with good snorkeling. To get here, enter C. Tartak from Ave. Isla Verde. Valet parking is available at the Hotel Colonial for $5 for the first two hrs.

ISLA VERDE SMALLER HOTELS AND GUESTHOUSES: Near the beach along Isla Verde's main drag, the **Borínquen Beach Inn** (☎ 787-728-8400, 866-728-8400, ✆ 787-268-2411; Box 6241, Isla Verde, PR 00914) offers 12 a/c rooms with cable TV and phone for around $65-100 d. **http://www.borinquenbeachinn.com**

At C. Rosa 4, the **Don Pedro Hotel** (☎ 787-791-2838; Isla Verde, PR 00979) has 17 rooms, a pool, bar, and restaurant. Rates run from around $65–$85 d. At C. Amapola 6, **La Playa** (☎ 787-791-1115, 800-791-9626, ✆ 787-791-4650; Isla Verde, PR 00979) is on the ocean and offers 15 a/c rooms with cable TV and phone. It has a popular bar and restaurant, the **La Playita** which serves food on a deck above the

water. Rates run around $90-115 d.
http://www.hotellaplaya.com
manager@.hotellaplaya.com

The 15-room **El Patio** (☎ 787-726-6298/6953; Isla Verde, PR 00979) offers a/c rooms and a communal kitchen, pool, and laundromat. Rates range around $60-90 d.
http://home.coqui.net/jaimegon

The 46-unit **Casa Mathiesen Inn** (☎ 787-726-8662, 787-667-8860, ☻ 268-2415, 800-677-8860; San Juan, PR 00979), C. Uno 14, offers free transport to and from the airport. Rooms have a/c and fans, cable TV, and radio. The inn has a pool, restaurant, and bar. More expensive rooms have kitchenettes. Rates range from $58-84 d.

The **Hotel Casa de Playa** (☎ 787-728-9779, ☻ 727-1334, 800-829-3636; Isla Verde, PR 00979) has 20 units. Rooms with a/c and fan, cable TV, and phone start at $80; rates include breakfast.
The Empress Oceanfront (☎ 787-791-3083, 800-678-0757, ☻ 787-791-1423; Isla Verde, PR 00913), Amapola 2, has a seafood restaurant. Rates range around $128-188 d.
http://www.empresshotelpr.com

Blue-and-white 63-room **Mario's Hotel and Restaurant** (☎ 787-791-3748/6868, ☻ 787-791-1672; Box 12366, Isla Verde, PR 00979), C. Rosa 2, offers free satellite TV in its rooms. Rates range around $70-90 d.
Located on the third floor of the airport, the 57-room **International Airport Hotel** (☎787-791-1700, ☻ 787-791-4050; Box 38087, San Juan, PR 00937) offers soundproof a/c rooms with TV and radio. Rates range from around $85-$100 d.

IN VILLAMAR: The **Green Isle Inn** (☎ 787-726-4330, 800-677-8860, ☻ 787-268-2415; San Juan, PR 00979), C. Uno 36, offers 21 rooms with a/c, TV, and phone, as well as free airport pickup. Rates start from around $58-84 d.
http://www.greenisleinn.com

ISLA VERDE LARGE HOTELS: There are a number of these from which to choose.
The 332-room, 57-suite, a/c **Wyndham El San Juan Hotel & Casino** (☎ 787-791-1000, ☻ 787-791-6985; Box 2872, San Juan, PR 00902), Ave. Isla Verde, is San Juan's premier luxury hotel. It offers a "Cigar Bar" (with an attached cigar and pipe shop), 11-hole miniature rooftop golf course, jazz bar, French bistro, a conference center with meeting and banquet rooms, botanical garden, two pools, five Jacuzzis,three tennis courts, children's program, and a health club/spa. The antique chandelier-illuminated 13,000-sq.-ft. lobby features 250-year-old French tapestries.

Originally built by Pan Am as the San Juan Intercontinental, it was sold to a group of private investors in 1961, and they renamed it the El San Juan. This hotel then reigned supreme as the Caribbean's shining star from the mid-1960s through the mid-1970s. The oil embargo damaged tourism, and they hotel was eventually offered up for sale in 1984. Williams Hospitality purchased it for $7.5 million, and they spent $50 million on renovations. Wyndham purchased Williams, and the hotel is now one of their standouts.

The main tower suite features a whirlpool bath and wet bar; the garden room has a patio and Jacuzzi and wet bar, and the *casita* offers a sunken Roman bath.

The hotel is famed for its nightlife and entertainment. Mon. and Wed. see folkloric performances; Tues. is classical and jazz piano night. Thurs. and Fri. attracts all of

San Juan's cognoscenti for salsa. Guests at the hotel have included the likes of Rod Stewart, Jimmy Carter, Isabel Allende, O. J. Simpson, Celia Cruz, Henry Kissinger, and Jennifer Lopez.

For dining and snacks, there are numerous places to try: the rooftop **Margarita Bar** and the **Ranch**, a country and western bar and restaurant has a mechanical bull, Others include **Yamato** (Japanese) restaurant nightclub/casino, **Scoops** ice cream parlor, **Back Street at Hong Kong** restaurant, and **Piccola Fontana**, an Italian restaurant.

Entertainment venues include **Club Tropicoro** (an elegant 1930s dinner-style club with a flamenco show) and **Belle Epoque** salon (dancing and cabaret shows). There is 24-hour room service, a beach, and three tennis courts, as well as water sports such as windsurfing, scuba diving, snorkeling, and sailing. Rooms have individually controlled a/c as well as fans, TV/VCR, radio, stereo tape deck/CD, bathroom TV, three telephones, and in-room bar. (One-story beachfront *casitas* are also planned). It charges from $295 s and $325 d during the high season. Renovated for $30 million in 1995, the hotel is under the management of the San Juan-based Williams Hospitality Group. For information and to book, call Leading Hotels of the World at ☎ 800-223-6800 or the hotel directly at 800-468-2818.

Rates start at around $395 standard (plus tax) and range upward to around $3,000 pn for the Monarch Suite.
http://www.wyndham.com/Resorts/SJUES

Set across from the El San Juan and Ritz Carlton hotels at Isla Verde 6530, the 200-room **Hampton Inn and Suites** (☎ 787-791-8777, 800-HAMPTON, ✆ 787-791-8757) offers suites, business center, meeting rooms, health spa, concierge floor, and pool. compli-mentary local phone calls and Continental breakfast are included in the rates. Rooms range around $179-219 d.
http://www.hamptoninn.com

The 414-rm. **Ritz-Carlton San Juan Hotel and Casino** (☎ 787-253-1700), Ave. Los Gobernadores 6961, opened in late 1997. It has the room amenities one associates with the chain, including cable TV, and phones with data ports. It also has a great restaurant, spa, business center, children's room, tennis, water sports, and a large pool. Rates run around $265-2,000 d.
http://www.ritzcarlton.com

The 16-story **San Juan Grand Beach Resort and Casino** (☎ 787-791-6100, ✆ 787-253-2510, 800-544-3008, 800-443-2009), Ave. Isla Verde 187, opened on the site of the Sands Hotel in late 1998. It borders a popular beach, has six restaurants, casino, three bars, pool, Jacuzzi, spa, nightclub, business services, meeting rooms, children's room, and a concierge service at the Plaza Club all-suite floor. It has 381 rooms and 19 suites.

Opened in 2000, the 84-room **Water Club** (☎ 787-728-3666, 888-265-6699), C. Tartak 2, is a boutique hotel. Each and every room has ocean views, and beds are poised to take in the views. A "wet bar" is on the 11th floor, and the next level has a pool. Other characteristics include waterfalls behind glass, including the elevators, theatrical lighting, floor to ceiling windows, and stained glass doors. It also has a gourmet restaurant. Rates start at around $200 s or d. It was peviously known as the Colony San Juan Beach Hotel.
http://www.waterclubsanjuan.com

The 400-rm. **Inter-Continental San Juan Hotel and Casino** (☎ 787-253-1700, 800-468-9076, ✆ 787-253-2510) Ave. Los

Gobernadores, has private concierge floors, six restaurants, disco, and attractive decor. Rates run from around $239-749 d. It is set amidst tropical gardens.
http://www.intercontisj.com

With 450 a/c rooms and studio apartments, the 17-story 450-unit **ESJ Towers** (☎ 787-791-5151, ℻ 787-791-4241; 800-468-2026; Box 2200, Carolina, PR 00979) is directly on the beach next to El San Juan at Ave Isla Verde 6165. Its attractively furnished condo apartments have fully equipped kitchens. Facilities include a restaurant/lounge, pool, fitness club, tennis courts, golf course, and watersports. Rates run from around $145-$460 d.
http://www.esjtowers.com

The 300-room **Embassy Suites Hotel & Casino** (☎ 787-791-0505, 888-791-0505, ℻ 787-791-0555), C. Tartak 8000, includes a casino, a fitness center, pool and restaurant. Its spacious one-bedroom suites have a separate living and working area, wet-bar, and microwave. Rates run around $265-350 d.
http://www.embassysuitessanjuan.com

The 96-room **Travelodge of Puerto Rico** (☎ 787-728-1300, ℻ 787-727-7150; information 800-468-2028; Box 6007, San Juan, PR 00914) charges from around $90 s to $140 d in season. Deluxe executive-floor rooms have Jacuzzis. All rooms have a/c and cable TV.

Set one block from the ocean and a 10-minute ride from the airport, the **Carib-Inn Tennis Club and Hotel** (☎ 787-791-3535, ℻ 787-791-0104, 718-235-9841, ℻ 718-235-0997; Box 12112, Loíza St. Station, San Juan, PR 00914) offers 225 a/c rooms with color cable TVs, phones, and balconies/porches. Facilities include eight tennis courts, adult and children's pools, spa, restaurant, convention facilities, and gam-

bling arcade. Rates start at $70 s and $75 d for standard rooms and rise to $105 s and $110 d during the winter season. More expensive superior, deluxe, jr. suites, and regular suites are available. It was refurbished during 2002.

In Isla Verde on the beach, the **Holiday Inn Crowne Plaza** (☎ 787-253-2929, ℻ 787-253-2081, ☎ 800-468-4578; Box 38079, San Juan, PR 00937) offers standard rooms from around $185 s and $205 d. Its 254 a/c rooms and suites have cable TV. Facilities include two restaurants, theme casino, fitness center, nightclub, babysitting, pool, watersports, and nearby golf and tennis. It has been refurbished in 2002.

The 115-rm. **Howard Johnson** (☎ 787-728-1300, ℻ 787-268-0637), Ave. Isla Verde 4820, has rooms, suites, and an executive floor. Rates run around $125-195 d. Rooms and suites include cable TV, coffee maker, microwave and refrigerators. Rates run around $125-$195 d.

ISLA VERDE FOOD: Mi Casita, at the Plazoleta de Isla Verde, serves inexpensive breakfasts as well as Puerto Rican dishes.

At McLeary 1954, lively **Dunbar's** (☎ 787-728-2920) serves BBQ dishes and desserts.

Borínquen Grill and Brewing (☎ 787-268-1900), Ave. de Isla Verde 4800, serves microbrews and complimentary repasts.

Tiramisu (☎ 787-726-3162), Marginal Villamar at C-19, serves good moderately-priced Italian dishes.

Kasalta's, C. McLeary 1999, is a bakery that opens at 6 AM. It serves breakfast and other dishes.

La Casita Blanca (☎ 787-726-7340), C. McLeary 1999, is a popular local spot for lunch and dinner. Politicians sometimes dine here.

At Ave. de Isla Verde 6070, **Bagelfields** (☎ 787-253-3633) serves bagels and lox.

On Carr. 187, the informal **Oyster Bar** sells clams, oysters, and seafood salad.

Open 24 hrs., **Duffy's**, Isla Verde 9, serves steaks and seafood dishes as well as all-you-can-eat spaghetti on Wed. evenings.

Chanteclair, a small coffee shop on the Plazoleta, has innovative dishes and $8 lunch specials.

At the Condado Racquet Club on C. Tartak, the **Hungry Sailor Restaurant** serves meat dishes.

At Km. 1.3 on Carr. 187, **Lupi's** is a Mexican restaurant that doubles as a sports bar.

ISLA VERDE DINING: Marisqueria Atlántica (☎ 787-726-6654), C. Loíza 81 (also in Puerto de Tierra) specializes in seafood including paella and Maine lobster.

In Isla Verde Mall, **Los Chiles** (☎ 787-253-3551) serves Mexican dishes.

At the Ritz, **The Vineyard** (☎ 787-253-1700) serves very expensive gourmet cuisine. It has an excellent wine list.

Inside Mario's Hotel, casual **Plaka** (☎ 787-791-3470) offers Greek food.

With both outdoor and indoor dining, **Puerta al Sol** (☎ 787-268-7475), Loíza 2446, has Puerto Rican gourmet cuisine.

In the Tropimar Beach Club, the gourmet **Casa del Mar** (☎ 787-791-0035) is a famed, very expensive restaurant which has a popular Sun. brunch.

Offering Italian dishes and open daily, inexpensive **Freddo** is inside the Hotel Casa de Playa (☎ 787-728-9779).

Pizzaiolo, a Brazilian-style pizzeria, is at Isla Verde 47.

On Carr. 187 at Km.1.5, **Metropol** (☎ 787-791-4046) specializes in Cuban cuisine and is part of a chain of three.

Expensive **La Scala** (☎ 787-791-3740), C. Rosa 2, has fine Italian cuisine.

Casa Dante (☎ 787-726-7310), Isla Verde 39, serves its special version of *mofongo*.

In Villamar at 35-A Marginal, **Pizzarella** (☎ 787-268-2433) serves a variety of imaginative gourmet pizzas from $10-21, depending upon size.

An intimate family-style restaurant, **Marina** (☎ 787-728-3628), C. Marginal, specializes in Puerto Rican and other gourmet cuisine.

ISLA VERDE HOTEL DINING: Set in the Holiday Inn Crown Plaza, beachfront **Holly's Café** serves pasta, sandwiches, seafood, and other dishes.

Back Street Hong Kong (☎ 787-791-1224) is located in El San Juan, in a pagoda that once formed part of the Hong Kong Pavilion at the 1962 World's Fair. It serves Chinese regional (Szechuan, Hunan, and Mandarin) cuisine.

At El San Juan, **Piccola Fontana** (☎ 787-791-0966) serves N Italian cuisine and has wonderful seafood, and the highly regarded and very expensive. **Dar Tiffany** (☎ 787-791-7272) serves seafood dishes (Maine lobster) as well as meat.

In the Sands are **Café Tropical**, an open-air poolside restaurant and **Don Juan**, an intimate and very expensive bistro that serves dishes such as salmon over pineapple. Also in the Sands, the very expensive and intimate **Dumpling House** has a wide range of Chinese regional cuisines, and the very expensive **Valentino** (☎ 787-791-6100) serves N Italian dishes. Yet another Sands bistro is the very expensive **Reino del Mar,** offering seafood and meat entrées daily. With a special late-night menu in addition to salads, sandwiches, seafood, and steaks, **Tucano Restaurant** is the least expensive restaurant found in the Sands.

Inside the Empress Hotel, C. Amapola 2, the inexpensive **Sunny's Ocean View Terrace** serves BBQ dishes, crab and shrimp balls, and other seafood.

ISLA VERDE SHOPPING: At the corner of Los Gobernadores, the **Isla Verde Mall** has a wide variety of shops ranging from jewelers to optometrists to hair stylists.

Cool Runnings here sells reggae discs and related items.

ISLA VERDE SERVICES: Friendly **Charlie Car Rental** (☎ 787-728-2418/2420, 787-791-1101) has its offices facing the Marbella del Caribe.

INTERNET ACCESS: The **Cybernet Café** (☎ 787-791-3138), 5575 Isla Verde is open daily from 10-10. It charges around $8/hr. **http://www.cybernetcafepr.com**

Many hotels also offer internet access.

ISLA VERDE NIGHTLIFE: The place to go is **Babylon** (☎ 787-722-1900) in the El San Juan. Bring your tux if you have one. The **Chico Bar** here specializes in salsa.

Martini's (☎ 787-791-6100), Ave. Isla Verde 187, attracts the young and gentrified set each weekend.

Hato Rey

Sometimes called the Golden Mile or the Wall Street of the Caribbean, Hato Rey is notable mainly for its skyscrapers, those lyrical concrete-and-steel paeans to the wonders of capitalist endeavor. The huge federal complex, the offices of Fomento, as is the gigantic Bancos de Santander and its fiduciary compatriots. Without these, Hato Rey would be nothing more than a desolate, land-filled marsh.

GETTING HERE: Buses run from Old San Juan, and *Acuaexpreso* also has a ferry (75¢).

SIGHTS: Managed by the Puerto Rican Park Trust, the **Enrique Martí Colli Lineal Park** is named after a Puerto Rican environ-mentalist and businessman who passed on in 1992. When complete, it will extend for 11 miles and include biking, jogging, and hiking trails extending from Río Piedras to Old San Juan. You may access it via the 1.5-mile elevated pedestrian walkway that extends around the perimeter of the Martín Peña Channel.

ACCOMMODATIONS: Hotel Europa (☎ 787-763-1524) is at C. Navarro 64.

HATO REY FOOD: Naturalista y Vegetariano (☎ 787-758-6405) is at C. Duarte 205. At C. César González 553, **Booby's** is an inexpensive family-run restaurant serving Puerto Rican food.

For buffet dining, **Gourmet To Go** (☎ 787-766-4079), Tnte. César González 437, serves innovative Puerto Rican dishes. At C. Barbosa 597, **La Guitarra** serves a variety of tapas and other Spanish dishes.

For Puerto Rican food, **Metropolitan Restaurant and Coffee Shop** is at the Metropolitan Shopping Center.

At Ave. Ponce de León 507, **La Cueva del Chicken Inn** sells cock-a-doodle-doo in all formats.

BAKERIES: **La Ceiba**, Ave. Roosevelt, is one of the best bakeries around.

HATO REY DINING: In the Royal Bank Center Lobby, **Yuan** (☎ 787-766-0666), appropriately named after the Chinese currency, offers very expensive Szechuan dishes for lunch and dinner daily.

Specializing in Cuban cuisine, **Metropol** (☎ 787-751-4022) is at FD Roosevelt 124.

Hunan House (☎ 787-252-8039), FD Roosevelt 141, also serves Szechuan dishes and offers inexpensive lunchtime specials.

The **Yum Yum Tree** (☎ 787-753-7743), FD Roosevelt 131, serves Mandarin Chinese fare.

At FD Roosevelt 164, **El Caney** (☎ 787-764-7559) has Puerto Rican dishes such as *mofongo relleno de mariscos* (stuffed mofongo).

La Trattoria (☎ 787-764-4801) at FD Roosevelt 231 serves fresh pasta, seafood, and other dishes as well as "gourmet" pizza.

The **Deli Restaurant Argentino**, FD Roosevelt 235, serves Italian, Puerto Rican, and Argentinian fare daily.

El Paseo, FD Roosevelt 244, serves fine, inexpensive Puerto Rican dishes.

At FD Roosevelt 254, **Los Chiles** (☎ 787-751-1747) has Mexican cuisine; *fajitas*, the house specialty, are prepared tableside.

At FD Roosevelt 284, **Maxim de Puerto Rico** (☎ 787-796-1234) serves French and other international dishes.

A deli restaurant, **La Canasta**, FD Roosevelt 313, serves a variety of salads and sandwiches.

On the second floor at FD Roosevelt 315, **Don Andrés** (☎ 787-754-0232) offers Mexican food; the owner is a mariachi singer who entertains nightly.

La Trattoria, FD Roosevelt 321, has homemade pasta, fresh "gourmet pizza" and seafood dishes.

At FD Roosevelt 352, the gourmet and very expensive **Zipperle** (☎ 787-763-1636) has German, Puerto Rican, and Spanish dishes.

Margarita (☎ 781-8452), FD Roosevelt 1013, serves Mexican dishes and has live music.

Porto Bello (☎ 787-277-0911), FD Roosevelt 1144, serves gourmet Italian dishes.

At FD Roosevelt 1247, **Mesón Gallego** (☎ 787-783-5866) serves paella and other Spanish fare.

Casa María (☎ 787-793-8890), FD Roosevelt 1344, offers gourmet Mexican dishes.

Inexpensive **Viva Brazil** (☎ 787-758-5659), Quisqueya 13, serves up Brazilian fare with a flair.

El Cairo (☎ 787-273-7140), Ensenada 352 at FD Roosevelt, is an inexpensive Lebanese/Middle Eastern restaurant; stuffed cabbage is its house specialty. http://www.elcairopr.com

Tierra Santa (☎ 787-754-6865), FD Roosevelt 284, serves Middle Eastern dishes and offers belly dancers. Prices are moderate.

At América B-20, corner FD Roosevelt, **Restaurant y Marisquería Fruit de Mer** (☎ 787-764-5509) specializes in seafood.

Booby's (☎ 787-753-8181), Tnte. César González 553, is an intimate, inexpensive Puerto Rican restaurant.

Moderate **Jerusalem Restaurant** (☎ 787-764-3265), O'Neill 1-6, serves Arab dishes, including vegetarian entrées. It is known for its belly dancers as well as its food.

El Chotis Taberna Española (☎ 758-3086), O'Neill 187, offers a variety of tapas and other dishes.

At Bolivia 52, the **Coachman Steakhouse** (☎ 787-753-8838) is a favorite with businessmen.

Casa Italia (☎ 787-250-7388), at C. Domenech 275, serves a variety of Italian dishes.

Offering Cantonese and Szechuan specialties, **Kimpo Garden** (☎ 787-767-0810), C. Jesús Piñero 264, serves lobster, chicken and other dishes.

Tokyo Grill (☎ 787-754-7646), Muñoz Rivera 504, has *teppanyaki* tables and serves sushi.

Tapatío (☎ 787-781-2006), at C. Jesús T. Piñero 1025, serves Mexican food.

At C O'Neill 177, **Muelle 13** (☎ 787-767-7825) serves beef and seafood dishes.

Tango's (☎ 787-759-8190), C. O'Neill 179, specializes in meat dishes.

Romantic **Johnny's Restaurant** (☎ 787-763-2793), C. Domenech 208, has Puerto Rican-style seafood and other dishes.

At Bolívar 59, **El Mesón de Porrón** (☎ 787-250-8156) is a Spanish-style restaurant with international and Puerto Rican dishes.

El Chotis Taberna Espanola, C. 187 O'Neill, features Spanish cuisine.

El Belén (☎ 787-282-6332) is a Middle Eastern restaurant that provides vegetarians with a wide selection; it's at Piñero 312A.

Bogart's Pub and Grill (☎ 754-6878), C. Hostos 352, serves pub-type fare and has Bogart memorabilia galore.

Mesón Tropical (☎ 787-751-7669), E Roosevelt 111, serves Spanish and international dishes and is known for its singing waiters.

SERVICES: The **General Post Office** is on Ave. Roosevelt. Take a Hato Rey-bound bus from the terminal in Old San Juan. **Plaza Las Américas**, a gigantic shopping mall with some 200 stores, is a playground for the affluent. Branches of **Galería Botello** and **{Paréntesis}** are located upstairs, while **Thekes Bookstore** is on the first floor. And a **Borders** has opened as well. All have good selections.

Some 25 restaurants are also located at the remodeled La Terraza here on the third level. There's a **Sears,** and **Toys R' Us** is across the road.

Since it opened in 1968, the mall has been graced with two historical events. Luís Muñoz Marín spoke here in 1972, and Pope John Paul discoursed in 1984.

At C. Federico Costa and C. Chardón, the **Plaza Acuática** (☎ 787-754-9500) offers water sports, a playground, and a miniature golf course; it's open weekends.

Río Piedras

Río Piedras, the student area of the city, has the University of Puerto Rico, the attractive Paseo de Diego (cheaper than the shopping malls), and a great market near the bus terminal. At the center of the campus stands the Roosevelt bell tower. Done up in a gaudy pink, it is Spanish-influenced but bears a passing resemblance to a South Indian Tamil Nadu Hindu temple. Theodore Roosevelt donated the money and so received the dubious distinction of having it named for him. See the three sculptured heads set in front of the bell tower. The campus has a laid-back atmosphere with students playing guitars and petting in the José M. Lazaro Library. Largest general library on the island, it contains the Juan Jiminéz Room, which displays memorabilia belonging to the famous Spanish expatriate poet.

The small but intriguing **Museo Historia, Antropología y Arte** (Museum of Anthropology, History, and Art, ☎ 787-763-3939) next to the library, features archaeological artifacts as well as special art exhibitions. It's open Mon. and Tues. and Fri and Sat. from 9 AM–4:30 PM, and on Wed. and Thurs. from 9 AM–8:45 PM, and on Sun. from 1:30–4:30 PM.

Located on C. De Diego, the **Río Piedras Market** has fairly wide aisles numbered with signs showing the produce being sold. It is packed with fruits (pineapples, papaya, golden-skinned oranges), common and more exotic vegetables (*yuca, yautia*), and island spices (ginger, mint, cilantro). An arcade section sells clothes. The best time to visit is early morning when merchants and farmers unload trucks and pack booths. Savor the atmosphere.

Set between Río Piedras and Trujillo Alto on the C. Marginal off the expressway, the **Casa-finca de Don Luis Muñoz Marín** (constructed circa 1930) has been restored and now functions as a small museum. It's

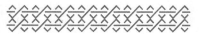

at Km 181 on Carr. 181 and is open Wed. to Sun. from 9-3. It's run by the **Fundación Luis Muñoz Marín** (☎ 787-755-7979). http://www.munoz-marin.org

ACCOMMODATIONS: Gay friendly **Glorimar Guest House** (☎ 787-759-7304, 724-7440, ☻ 787-725-2400) is at 111 University Ave., three blocks from the university. It has daily, weekly, and monthly rates.

Set in the heart of Río Piedras, the 29-rm. **El Centro Hotel** (☎ 787-751-1335, ☻ 787-751-0930) has a/c rooms with color TV. Conference rooms and business center are available. It charges around $100 d.

FOOD: Many cheap places to eat. **Esquina Universidad**, on the corner of Ponce de León and Gandara, is a popular student hangout. There's also the usual assortment of fast food places, including a Taco Maker at Ponce De León 1000.

Energy, a health food store and restaurant, is at Diego 2 (open Mon. to Sat., 9-3; ☎ 787-764-2623).

El Romano, Diego 8, is a local restaurant which also offers pizza slices.

Restaurante Vegetariano Mary's, C. Robles 53, is inexpensive and good!

Los Mexicanos, Ave. Universidad, is inexpensive, and accordingly popular with students.

Sun y Cream, at Ponce de León 1004, is a cheap Chinese restaurant which also serves ice cream.

Tomas Ice Cream, across the street, is an attractive student meeting place.

El Buen Gusto, 1117 C. William Jones, is a local restaurant with cheap prices.

El Isleño (☎ 787-250-8046), at Lomas Verdes 1790 in Plaza Olmedo, is a good Puerto Rican restaurant.

Middle East is at Padre Colón 207.

El Pacifico (☎ 787-274-5756), C. 43 SE #893 at America Mirando, is a high quality, expensive seafood restaurant.

El Lucero de Salud (☎ 787-273-1313), Ave. Américo Miranda 1160, offers courses in living foods in Spanish and serves vegetarian breakfasts and lunches.

A NY-style deli, **Howard's Deli and Pub** is set in the Caribe Shopping Center.

At Muñoz Rivera 1000, **Café Valencia Restaurant** (☎ 787-764-3790) offers dishes such as paella.

On Carr. 1 at Km 25.1, **Félix** (☎ 787-720-1626) is a family-run restaurant specializing in Puerto Rican home cooking, including seafood dishes.

Tacolandia is at Las Vistas Shopping Center and offers a wide range of tacos, including vegetarian items.

ENTERTAINMENT: The **Casals Festival** takes place on the University of Puerto Rico campus during May. The University also offers a cultural activities series featuring ballet and classical music performances and avant-garde films. For information, contact **Actividades Culturales** (☎ 787-764-0000, ext. 2563/2567).

The **El Señorial** (☎ 787-741-2387) offers a choice of four films daily.

SHOPPING: There are two shopping malls here — the Reparto Metropolitano and the 65 De Infanteria.

BOOKSTORES: Librería La Tertulia (☎ 787-765-1148) corner of Amalia Marín and Gonzales, and **Libreria Hispanoamericano**, 1013 Ponce de León, are open Mon. to Saturday. Other bookstores are in Plaza Las Américas, Hato Rey.

AGRICULTURAL EXPERIMENTAL STATION: Operated by the University of Puerto Rico, this facility is still in Río Piedras but way off in the boonies near the intersection of Carr. 1 and Carr. 847. Pack a picnic lunch.

The 140-acre **Jardín Botanica** or **Botanical Garden** here is open Tues. to Sun. 9-5 (☎ 787-763-4408). There's no admission charge to visit this enchanting area, which includes an orchid garden with exotics like dendrobiums, epidendrums, vandas; a heliconia garden; a bamboo "chapel,"a "Monet Garden," and a palm garden with 125 species.

Broad paths traverse an incredible range of vegetation, from a flaming African tulip tree and croton bushes to endless varieties of palms and ferns. Woody lianas hang from trees. Cool off in one of several libraries and check in the Forest Service office for detailed info about El Yunque's rainforest.

It's open from 6 AM-6 PM daily. Guided tours are available by reservation. **http://www.upr.clu.edu**

Bayamón

A suburban municipality of San Juan, Bayamón has shifted from being an agricultural to an industrial community. It's still growing rapidly. More than 230,000 people and some 170 factories make their home here.

The city is renowned for its *chicharrón*, a local delicacy (from the Spanish verb *achicharrar* ("to crisp"), which originated when slaves, given the skin torn from pigs by the Spaniards, hung them over the coals to dry. The grease dripped into the fire and the result was a crisp and curly morsel that is now one of the most popular Latin snacks.

GETTING HERE: Take a bus from San Juan or find one of the buses that occasionally run from Old San Juan. Yet another alternative is to take the Cataño ferry (50¢) and then a *público*.

SIGHTS: Just before Bayamón on Carr. 2, Km 6.4 at Guaynabo, are the ruins of **Caparra**, the first colonial settlement on the island. Established by Ponce de León in 1508, it was abandoned for the Old San Juan site 12 years later. Only the masonry foundations, uncovered in 1936, remain. To the rear, a small museum contains Taíno artifacts and tools, weapons, and tiles found at the site (☎ 787-781-4795; open Tues. to Sat., 8:30 AM–4:30 PM).

Inside the municipality itself, directly across from the City Hall, the immaculately landscaped grounds of **Central Park** contain a country house, which functions as a small museum, and the only locomotive train remaining in Puerto Rico, which runs through the grounds. This museum also displays artifacts excavated during archaeological digs at the site.

Junghanns Park, several blocks to the W, features trees from all over the world which were planted by the local botanist of the same name.

Adjacent to Bayamón's plaza and in the heart of the historical zone, the former city hall contains the **Museo de Oller**, named after the famous local resident realist-impressionist painter (open daily from 8 AM–4:30 PM; ☎ 787-787-8620). This recently restored neoclassic building (dating from 1907) is painted in shades of blue, pink, and yellow — evocative of a San Francisco gingerbread house.

Inside, the first level has one room dedicated to Francois Oller's portraits of local notables, with another room containing indigenous artifacts and a collection of Taíno skulls. The remaining rooms are largely devoted to the remarkable artwork of the local artist Tomas Batista. His work includes bronze and fiberglass busts and fossilized stones carved into the shape of gigantic seashells.

The top floor contains gubernatorial and mayoral portraits by local artist Tulio Ojedo and a genuine mayoral desk belonging to the current mayor. It's obvious who was backing the museum.

Another room illustrates the history of Bayamón complete with the making of *chicharrones* and the daily life of the *jíbaro*. There's even a shovel from the 1977 groundbreaking of a Union Carbide plant. The museum is completed with yet another room of Indian artifacts.

From the museum, enter the placid and tranquil **Paseo Barbosa**. Here, you might see a young girl standing and combing her boyfriend's hair as he sits on a bench. Or a mother sitting with her children, taking a break from shopping. Or pretty schoolgirls, with plaid vests and white blouses, parading through on their way to and from school.

Continue along to the **Barbosa House**. The interior of the house contains antique furniture, small library, and memorabilia relating to José Celso Barbosa, journalist, physician, and political head of the pro-statehood Republican Party. It may or may not be open to the public.

The **Luis A. Ferré Parque de las Ciencias** (☎ 787-740-6868) a science park, is near downtown on Carr. 167 to the S of De Diego. It includes the Dr. Ventura Barnes Natural Science Museum, an amphitheater, the Space Rockets Plaza, the Planetarium, a native archeological museum, health pavilion, artificial lake, and a small zoo. Not a bad place to take children. It's open Wed. to Fri. from 9-4; Sat., Sun., and holidays from 10-6. Admission is $5, discounts for children and seniors.

Escape Town (☎ 787-795-5722) is an amusement park on the second floor of the Cinema Río Hondo in the Plaza Río Hondo. It's open Thurs. and Fri. from 2-9 PM and on Sat. and Sun. from 11 AM-9 PM.

EVENTS AND FESTIVALS: The traditional *fiestas patronales*, titled *Fiestas de Cruz,* are held in early May. Although this event has its origin in the 18th century, many of the original traditions connected with it have been lost. Once held in a local house, the main event (carrying the cross up the nine steps) now takes place along the Paseo Barbosa. Traditionally, a nine-step altar is prepared and lavishly adorned with flowers and royal palm leaves; candles are placed on each step. After the recitation of *El Rosario Cantado de la Santa Cruz* each night, the cross is moved up one step higher until, on the ninth night, it reaches the top. Traditional refreshments like *guarapo de caña* (sugarcane juice) and *maví* are served at the end of each night's service.

Artisans' festivals are held throughout the year.

Large concerts take place at the 23,000-seat Juan Ramón Loubriel Stadium here. Madonna's "The Girlie Show," which was performed here in 1993, aroused great controversy. Charging that it would corrupt the young and promote pornography, Cardinal Luis Aponte Martinez wrote the Governor a letter asking him to speak out publicly against Madonna. He refused. Her appearance was marked by demonstrations. Madonna raised further ire by caressing a Puerto Rican flag during her performance. In retaliation, local clerics launched a campaign to hang black ribbons on trees in protest. Puerto Ricans paid close attention: The show sold out immediately, despite ticket prices as high as $125.

PRACTICALITIES: For information visit the **Bayamón Tourism Office** (☎ 787-780-3056, ext. 280-281). in their offices on the first floor of the surrealistically modern *Alcaldía*.

Morgan's is an a/c pub on the Malecón. It offers seafood dishes.

SHOPPING AND CRAFTS: Local *crafts-people* sell in Central Park each Sunday.

A feminist-run handicraft center, **El Centro Feminista**, is located at C. F No. 8 Hnas., Davilas, Bayamón.

Anchored by a 40-lane bowling alley, the $6 million **Tower Lanes** shopping center affords you the chance to shop in the former property of drug dealers: It was confiscated from Jorge and Victor Torres who were convicted of drug trafficking and money laundering charges.

Vicinity of San Juan

San Juan can serve as an excellent base for becoming acquainted with the island, especially if you are renting (or have) your own vehicle. A good portion of the island may be comfortably explored in a day's excursion. Destinations like El Yunque, Loíza Aldea, and Humacao make good daytrips. Many snorkeling and diving trips leave from Fajardo.

There are also many small towns like **Gurabo** (small art museum, Museo de Arte e Historia de Gurabo C. Santiago 2), Guaynabo, and **Cidra** (stay at Hotel Flora del Valle, Carr. 172, Km 7.4;☎ 787-739-8864), which offer the visitor with limited time an inside look at Puerto Rican life.

TOURS, EXCURSIONS, AND CHARTERS: **Blackbeard West Indies Charters** (☎ 787-887-4818) runs snorkeling trips from Villa Marina in Fajardo to Icacos, Palaminos, or Palominitos Island.

Operating out of Isla Verde's Laguna Gardens Shopping Center, **Mundo Submarino** (☎/✆ 787-791-5764; Isla Verde, PR 00979) operates a full-service dive shop and has a variety of trips as well as scuba instruction.
http://www.mundosubmarino.net
mundo@mundosubmarino.net

A 53-ft. sailing catamaran, the **Traveler** (☎ 787-863-2821/4267; Box 664, Puerto Real, PR 00740) charges $55 pp ($10 add'l for RT transportation from San Juan) for trips from Fajardo's Villa Marina to an unnamed "tropical island." Lunch, snorkel gear, and some drinks are included.

Scuba Centro (☎ 787-781-8086), 1156 Ave. F. D. Roosevelt in Hato Rey, offers offshore dives, in locales ranging from Vieques to Culebra to the SE.
http://www.scubacentro.com
info@scubacentro.com

La Casa del Buzo (☎/✆ 787-753-3528) runs scuba trips all over, has classes, and offers rentals and repairs.
buzo3@tld.net

A 40-ft. sailing catamaran, the **Spread Eagle** (☎ 787-863-1905/5875, ✆ 852-2443; Box 1740, Luquillo, PR 00773) also leaves from Villa Marina.

Captain Jack Becker (☎ 787-860-0861) offers trips which take from two to seven passengers; snorkel gear is provided and "attorneys and kids tolerated." Scandinavian stewardesses are taken free of charge.

Operating out of C. Amapola 1 in Isla Verde but departing from Fajardo, **Captain Jayne Sailing** (☎ 787-774-1748; Isla Verde, PR 00979) runs a fleet of charter boats; skippers are also available.

Caribbean Divers: Fun Boats (☎/✆ 787-722-7393; Box 5041, San Juan, PR 00936) is at Fajardo's Villa Marina. They operate a 53-ft. catamaran.

Castillo Watersports (☎ 787-791-6195/6100 ext. 344; eve. 726-5752, ✆ 726-6998; Doncella 27, Punta las Marias, Santurce, PR 00913) offers deep sea and light tackle fishing. Their 46-ft. catamaran, *Barefoot III,* has sailing, snorkeling, and a picnic for around $45 pp.

Set next to Club Náutico at the San Juan Marina, **Caribe Aquatic Adventures** (☎ 787-724-1882, ☏ 787-723-6770; Box 2470, San Juan, PR 00902-2470) offers scuba instruction, wind surfing, and fishing, as well as a variety of cruises and trips. They also make a trip to a (not-quite) "deserted island."
http://www.caribeaquaticadventure.com

The **Makaira Hunter** (☎ 787-397-8028, 250-0140, ext. 18744, ☏ 787-768-2828, ; PMC Box 402, San Patricio Plaza, San Juan, PR 00920) is available for charter.

Departing from Fajardo, **Erin Go Bragh** (☎ 787-860-4401, ☏ 787-863-5253, cell 787-409-2511) is a 50-ft. sailing ketch that offers both short and long trips. They will take up to six and offer personalized service.
http://www.egbc.com
egbc@coqui.net

In Puerto Del Rey Marina on Carr. 3, **Club Náutico Powerboats** (☎ 787-860-2400, ☏ 787-860-2401, 787-863-5253; Box Q, Fajardo, PR 00740) offers fishing, diving, and snorkeling trips.

San Juan Water Fun (☎ 787-643-4510, 787-931-4510) has parasailing, sailing, and banana boat rides.

Southern Witch/Fishing (☎ 787-721-7335, 787-731-9252; HC-01, Box 20484, Caguas, PR 00625) operates a 22-ft. boat with tarpon and reef fishing for one to four persons. at Dorado.

For **diving** at Dorado, contact **Adventure by the Sea** (☎ 787-251-4923, ☏ 787-261-0946), C. 2J2, Santa Maria, Toa Baja, PR 00949 or the **Dorado Marine Center** (☎ 787-796-4645, 787-250-0140, ext. 2226, ☏ 796-7323; 271 Méndez Vigo, Dorado, PR 00646).

CAVE EXPLORATION: For the truly adventurous, contact **Aventuras Tierra**

Adentro (☎ 787-766-0470, ☏ 787-754-7543) takes groups of eight to 12 hikers through the Río Tamana's underground canyons. You float and walk through caves on your way to the campsite which is just below the Arecibo Observatory which you visit at sunset. On the second day, you must jump 25 ft. into a pool and then descend another series of caves where you'll encounter bats and petroglyphs. Participants must supply wetsuits and snacks; everything else is provided. This trip costs $130.

Other trips available include a visit to the Cueva Yuyú ($55) and descending by rope in the Cueva Resurgencia ($60).
http://www.aventurastierraadentro.com

Caguas and Vicinity

Caguas (pop. 173,961) is the largest inland town on the island.
http://www.www.caguas.gov.pr

Caguas has the **Antigua Alcaldía de Caguas** (dating from 1856) on C. Muñoz Rivera and the **Catedral Dulce Nombre de Jesús de Caguas** (1928) on C. Conchado; both are in front of Plaza Palmer. In the same area, the **Plaza de Recreo** (1950) is one of the best examples of Art Deco found in Puerto Rico.

Doubling as the Museo Histórico de Caguas, the **Antigua Carnicería de Caguas** (☎ 787-746-0669; open from Mon. to Fri., 8:30-noon, 1–3:30 PM) dates from 1871 and is one of the best examples of this type of building found on the islands.

An attractive **private residence** is the La Casita Verde on C. Monseñor Berríos at C. Acosta.

The **Museo de Arte de Caguas** (☎ 787-743-3400) is on C. Ruiz Belvis at C. Padial. It's open Tues. to Fri. from 9AM–noon and

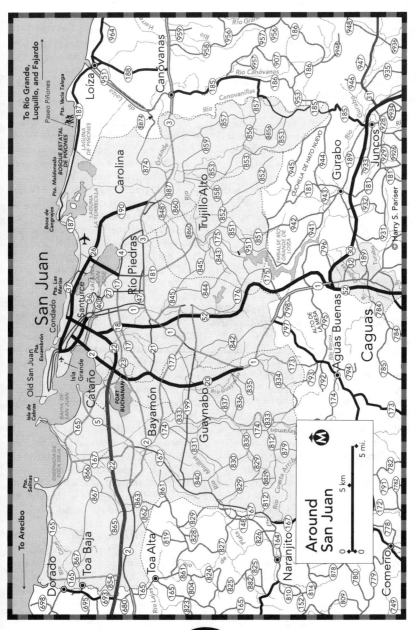

Around San Juan

from 1 PM–4:30 PM, and on Sat. from 8:30AM-noon and 1-3:30 PM.

The **Museo del Tabaco Herminio Torres** (☎ 787-744-2960). C. Betauces at C. Padial St.. It has exhibits which show the art of creating handmade cigars, It's open from Tues.-Fri. from 8:30 AM–4 PM and on Sat. from 8:30 AM–4 PM.

Aguas Buenas to the S is noted for its caves along Carr. 794. However, they have been found to be a source of histoplasmosis, a respiratory disease, and a visit is not advised.

San Lorenzo, to the SE of Caguas, has the Sanctuario de La Virgen del Carmen, on Carr. 181 at Carr. 7740, a religious site which includes a chapel, the "Holy Hill" and the "Three Crosses."

ACCOMMODATIONS: A 125-rm. **Hampton Inn** is scheduled to open in Caguas in 2002 or so.

For a tryst, you can try the **Hotel OK Executive** (☎ 787-789-9696), which offers a private disco and heart-shaped Jacuzzi in its suites; it's at Km 26 on Carr. 1 in front of Avon.

Hotel Villa Arco Iris (☎ 787-741-9492), is on Carr. 698, Barrio Río Cañas.

Hotel The Rose (☎ 787-747-1314) is on Carr. 175 at Km 1.3 in Barrio San Antonio.

The Bambu Motel (☎ 787-747-9491) is on Carr. 796 at Km 27.2 in Río Cañas.

At **Gurabo** to the NE, **Hacienda Mirador** (☎ 787-737-3747, ☏ 787-737-4060), Carr. 942 in Jaguas Lomas, has 36 rooms, a restaurant, a swimming pool, and tennis courts.

DINING: You can dine near Caguas on Carr. 1 at **El Paraíso** (☎ 787-747-2012; Km 29.1), which offers Puerto Rican and international dishes, or at **Alameda** (☎ 787-743-9698), which has steak and seafood.

Around 40 minutes by car from San Juan, **Papa Juan's Restaurant** (☎ 787-737-2227/4020) is a romantic dining getaway in Gurabo's Barrio Jaguas Lomas at the end of Carr. 942. Set dinners are around $20. There's a happy hour, and live music is featured on weekends.

Dorado

Reachable either by car, limousine, or small plane, **Dorado** is the island's oldest resort town. Its two large hotels, Hyatt Dorado Beach and Hyatt Regency Cerromar Beach, are famed for their pools, golf courses, and casinos. A free shuttle bus runs between the two resorts on the half-hour. These are guest-only facilities, but there is a beach, **La Playa del Dorado**, to the W of town along Carr. 693; make a R at the Gulf station. Parking is $2. Dorado is 27 km (17 mi.) W of San Juan and is reached via Hwy. 22 and Carr. 165.

SIGHTS: On the town plaza, the **Museo y Escuela de Arte Marcos Juan Alegría** (☎ 787-746-1433) shows the work of local artists.

Set in the plaza's SE corner, the **Galería Doctor Marcelino Canino** shows the skeleton of a Taíno woman as well as other archaeological artifacts.

Museo y Centro Cultural Casa del Rey (☎ 787-796-1230), by the main plaza on C. Méndez Vigo, exhibits antique furniture.

The **Sanctuario del Cristo de la Recón**, Paseo del Cristo, is reputed to contain "the world's largest indoor image of Jesus Christ."

OUTLYING ATTRACTIONS: 🏛 To the S, Corozal has the **Centro Historico y Turistico del Cibuco** (☎ 787-859-3060), a recreational complex which includes exhibits by artisans, a lake with paddleboats, restaurant, small museum, and a

walkway leading into **Cueva de Los Quintero**, a cave with Taíno petroglyphs. It also has the **Barbería Histórica**, a traditional barber shop, which is the only one of its kind which remains. Its **Area Recreativa El Rancho** (☎ 787- 859-3060) has meeting facilities and a pool. Corozal also hosts the **Festival Nacional del Plátano** during the last weekend in Sept.
http://www.corozalpr.org

EVENTS: Events taking place in Dorado include the **Dorado Del Plata Carnival** in early Feb., the *fiestas patronales* and the **Junior Island Amateur Golf Championship** in mid-June, and the **Honda Classic** in mid-July.

ACCOMMODATIONS: The a/c **Hyatt Regency Cerromar Beach** (☎ 787-796-1234, ☒ 787-796-4647, 800-233-1234; Cerromar Beach, Dorado, PR 00646), with 506 rooms and suites, offers scuba and snorkeling, tennis, bike rentals, a pool with three-story water slide, separate river pool, 21 tennis courts, jogging track, health club, a variety of restaurants, and a complimentary continental breakfast. Rates run from around $385-485 d.

The 298-room, two-story **Hyatt Dorado Beach Resort and Country Club** (☎ 787-796-1234, ☒ 787-796-2022, 800-233-1234; Dorado, PR 00646), which was originally designed to meet the specifications of Laurance Rockefeller, shares facilities with the Hyatt Cerromar Beach and has a windsurfing school. Rates run from around $175-2000 d. Free blue-and-white trolleys run between the two resorts. Food is expensive; drinks cost around $7 each.
http://www.www.hyatt.com

At 201 Dorado Del Mar Blvd., **Embassy Suites Beach & Golf Resort** (☎ 787-796-6125, ☒ 787-796-6145) is a beautiful 174-suite hotel which also offers 55 two-room apartments. Breakfast and evening cocktail reception are included. Rates run around $245-620 d.
http://www.embassysuitesdorado.com

The **Hyatt Hacienda del Mar Resort** (☎ 787-796-3000, ☒ 787-796-3610, 787-796-1266) is a timeshare located on the grounds of the Hyatt Cerromar Beach Resort & Casino. It has studio, and one- and two-bedroom units available Rates range from $225-1000 d. It is near the casino, and all facilities are available.
http://www.hyattvacationclub.com

DINING: El Ladrillo (☎ 787-796-2120), in town at C. Mendez 224, serves *paella* and other gourmet dishes. This is the best restaurant in town and is noted for its seafood.

Virtually across the street, The **Country Cheese Sports and Oyster Bar** (☎ 787-278-2015) serves your sports crowd-type fare and offers live music on weekends. **El Navigante** is in the same area.

On C. Marginal parallel to Carr. 693 at Carr. 697 (Costa de Oro), **La Terraza** (☎ 787-796-1242) has a variety of inexpensive seafood dishes.

On Carr. 693 at Costa de Oro, **El Malecón** (☎ 787-796-1645) serves seafood, including lobster with creole sauce and parmesan.

Set at Km 8.1 on Carr. 693 near the Hyatts, the expensive **Jewel of China** (☎ 787-796-4644) provides a feast of regional entrées. **Mangére**, which also has a branch in San Juan, serves Italian food.

Others are **Los Naborias**, Carr. 690, and **La Familia**, Carr. 690 on the way to Playa Cerro Gordo.

Finally, **food stands** line Carr. 165.

HOTEL DINING: In the Hyatt Regency Cerromar Beach, set against a backdrop of gardens and waterfalls, expensive **Medici's** (☎ 787-796-1234) serves N Italian cuisine. In the same hotel are **Sushi Wong**, with Chinese and sushi dishes, and **Swan Café**, serving light meals.

In the Hyatt Dorado Beach, expensive **Su Casa Restaurant** (☎ 787-796-1234) offers strolling musicians and a romantic atmosphere. The **Ocean Terrace**, also here, serves lighter food.

SERVICES AND SHOPPING: For car rental in Dorado try **Vias Dorado** (☎ 787-796-6404), Carr. 693 Marginal, Costa de Oro, and **Avis** (☎ 787-796-7243) is the Hyatt Cerromar.

Jorge Cancio Arte y Artesanias is at the Hyatt Regency Cerromar Beach.

A **Walgreens** is at C. Méndez Vigo in Dorado.

Prime Outlets Puerto Rico, the island's first outlet mall, operates on Carr. 2 at Km 54.8 in Barceloneta.

Dorado Outdoor Adventures

FISHING: The **Dorado Marine Center** (☎ 787-796-4645) has packages and equipment for both fly and deep sea fishing.

GOLF: This is what Dorado is perhaps best known for. The 6937-yd. **Dorado del Mar Golf Course** (☎ 787-796-3065), 200 Del Mar, is a Chi Chi Rodriguez design and opened in 1998. Its signature hole is the 10th, which runs along the cliffs overlooking the water. It is open daily from 6 AM-6 PM.

The 6841-yd. **Hyatt Cerromar North Course** (☎ 787-796-8915), Carr. 693, is a. Robert Trent Jones designed course which opened in 1970. It's open daily from 7AM-5:30 PM.

The 7047-yd. **Hyatt Cerromar South Course** (☎ 787-796-8915), opened in 1970. It has lagoons; breezes may pose a challenge. It's open daily from 7AM-5:30 PM.

Another Robert Trent Jones-designed course, the 6980-yd. **Hyatt Dorado East Course** (☎ 787-796-8961), Carr. Rt. 693 opened in 1958. It was renovated in 1999 at a cost of $7 million. It's open daily from 7AM-5:30 PM.

Also designed by Robert Trent Jones, the 6858-yd. **Hyatt Dorado West Course** (☎ 787-796-8961), Carr. 693, opened in 1960. It is buffeted by gusts from the Atlantic, which may make it a challenge. It's open daily from 7AM-5:30 PM.

HORSEBACK RIDING: **Tropical Horseback Riding** (☎ 787-720-5454), C. Carazo 2, Suite 201 in Dorado, offers horseback riding, kayaking and biking. **http://www.homestead.com/horserides /index.html**

Farther West

Reserva Forestal de Vega Alta is past Vega Alta on Carr. 2. Hotel Cerro Gordo (☎ 883-4370) here is on Carr. 690 at Km 4. You can camp at the *balneario* (☎ 787-883-2730) at Cerro Gordo at Carr. 690 in Vega Alta. It costs around $13 per tent, and there are a huge number of spaces.

Vega Alta hosts the **Piña festival** (☎ 787-883-5900) every July;.

Vega Alta's claim to fame came some years back when residents went on a spending binge after digging up steel drums — presumably buried by drug traffickers — which contained millions of dollars! Residents are believed to have made off with $11 million, which they used to buy everything from VCRs to new homes. In 1990, the FBI arrested 30 in the drug ring; they had been smuggling cocaine from Colombia via the Dominican Republic since 1985.

Farther on is the town of **Manatí,** which was founded in 1738 and now produces the entire US supply of Valium and

Librium. Here, the restored 2,265-acre **Hacienda La Esperanza** was once one of the largest sugar plantations on the island. It will be transformed into a living historical farm by the Conservation Trust of Puerto Rico and may be visited with their permission. It was one of the largest and most advanced of the island's sugar plantations during its years of operation (1804-1888). In addition to the colonial plantation house (listed as a historical monument in the National Register of Historic Places), the 19th-century sugar mill machinery is also being restored. Part of an alluvial plain (the Río Grande of Manatí), the estate has coves and dunes along its five miles of coastline, along with steep, conical karst formations.

Sixto Escobar Cultural Center (☎ 787-846-4199), C. Gerogetti 57 near Plaza Halcón, is a museum featuring archeological artifacts. It's open from Mon. to Fri. from 8 AM–4 PM.

The **Sixto Escobar Electronic Library** (☎ 787-846-70560 is a museum which exhibits memorabilia relating to famous boxer Sixto Escobar, who was inducted into the Hall of Fame in 1950. It's open from Mon. to Thurs. from 10 AM-9 PM, and from Fri. to Sat. from 8 AM–4:30 PM.

Leaving from Sector La Boca in Barceloneta, **Paseadora de la Boca** (☎ 787-858-4178) runs guided 20-minute boat trips on the rivers on weekends and holidays from 10 AM; group trips are available by reservation on Mon., Tues., and Wed.

Six beaches — **Playa Mar Chiquita**, **Playa Tortuguero** (which has a hideous *balneario*), **Playa Chivato**, **Playa de Vega Baja**, **Playa Cerro Gordo**, (nice beach, camping, surfing, beach rentals, see below), **Playa de Dorado** — and **Laguna Tortuguero** (a freshwater lagoon: see following) lie along a series of winding roads running up the coast to the N. Find them using a good road map.

Laguna Tortuguero has some 2,000 *caimanes* (caymans), a type of alligator indigenous to Central and S America. Disastrous to the ecosystem, their presence has proved a boon to nearby **Vega Baja** (pop. 30,000). The town's souvenir shops sell stuffed caymans and restaurants serve their meat as a delicacy. Prepared in stews, fried and put in salads, or deep fried in batter, the cayman reportedly tastes like rabbit or lobster. Released into the lagoon after a short-lived pet craze came to an end some three decades ago, the caymans have become pests, consuming dogs, cats, small pigs, yearlings, and the lagoon's wildlife (affecting its ecological balance).

The caymans can grow up to six or seven ft. and can live up to 20 yrs. Although generally timid, the females are the more violent of the two sexes and can be dangerous during egg-laying, which lasts from June to Sept.

They grunt like dogs when disturbed or when fighting with each other. Hunting at night, locals trap the caymans in snares and then wrap their snouts with electrical tape.

Meanwhile, Russian scientist Sergei Sktachkov, a researcher at Puerto Rico's Institute of Neurobiology, has been using cayman eyes to study their cells in an effort to better understand retina functioning.

Morovis , to the S of Vega Baja, is famous for its many artisans including **Julio Negrón Riviera** (☎ 787-862-0342) and **Aurelio Cruz Pagán** (☎ 787-862-4583). Believe it or not, the town Burger King, Carr. 115, shows traditional wooden toys made by local artisan Francisco Aponte Cabrera. Be sure to check out **Panaderia La Patria**, on Carr. 115, which has the oldest still-functioning bread oven in Puerto Rico (1862).

ACCOMMODATIONS: Playa de Cerro Gordo (☎ 787-883-2730) offers camping for around $15. Beach houses are also for rent by **Blankimar** (☎ 787-855-3412) and

Roberto Clemente

Roberto Clemente Walker , one of the most famous baseball players of all time, was born in Barrio San Anton in Carolina, Puerto Rico on Aug. 18, 1934. Clemente played amateur baseball before joining the Santurce Crabbers. He then signed with the Brooklyn Dodgers, who sent them to play with their top affiliate, the Montreal Royals.

In 1954, the Pittsburgh Pirates drafted Clemente, and he played his the whole of his eighteen -year major league baseball career (1955 to 1972) Playing in two World Series, he clocked up record scores, twelve Gold Glove awards, and fathered three sons with his Puerto Rican wife Vera.

"Our people have lost one of their great glories, " Gov. Rafael Hernández Colón, declared at Roberto's funeral. Soon afterward, the five-yr. waiting period was waived for Clemente, and he was inducted into the Baseball Hall of Fame.

http://www.robertoclemente21.com

Beach House Rentals (☎ 787-883-0356, 883-8251)

Off Carr. 687, the desperate or horny can find accommodations at the **Hotel El Molino Rojo** or the **Hotel El Molino Azul**. These "love hotels" charge around $25 per eight hours.

In the town of Ciales to the S, **La Estancia Restaurant and Inn** (☎ 787-871-0518), is on Carr. 615 at Km 4.5 in Bo. Pozas and is right by the Río Toro Negro.. It has four furnished apartment suites which sleep six. This is a great getaway. Rates are $65 d including tax. Children under 12 are free, but others are $11 pp.

http://www.atenas.com/laestancia/
estancia@atenas.com

DINING: There are a number of local restaurants, including seaside dives. Be sure to explore.

In Carr. 690, **Naborias** (☎ 787-883-4885) specializes in dishes such as *langosta rellena*.

Gourmet dining is available at **Su Casa** (☎ 787-884-0047), Carr. 670, Km 1.0, and at **Manatubón** (☎ 787-854-8639) which is on Carr. 149 at Km 7.5. **Festival Playero Los Tubos** (☎ 787-786-0062) is, a beach festival with music and water sport events, takes place in early July.

On Carr. 149 at Km 7.5, **Manatuabón** (☎ 787-854-8639) serves gourmet specialties such as *berenjenas a la martebello* (eggplant with cheese).

Casa Bavaria (☎ 787-862-7818) is a beer garden set between Moravia and Orocovis. Owned by a German-raised Puerto Rican and his German wife, it's the closest thing to Germany you will find in Puerto Rico. It is open Thurs. to Sun. for lunch and dinner.

SERVICES: José Colón (☎ 787-871-2948) is reputedly one of the the best guides for birders in Puerto Rico.

Heading East

On the eastern outskirts of San Juan are the **Club Gallístico** (☎ 787-791-1557; open 2-9 PM on Sat; Carr. 888, Km 2.6), a cockfighting pit and public beach at Isla Verde and, farther on, the **Roberto Clemente Sports City**. Dedicated to the memory of the Pittsburgh Pirates baseball demigod who died in a 1972 aircrash (see sidebar), *Ciudad Deportiva* has facilities for teaching sports to deprived children. Open daily from 9 AM–noon and 2 PM-7 PM, it's located on C. Icurregui off the Los Angeles Marginal Rd. in Carolina.

Carolina is also noted for **Plaza Carolina**, a large shopping mall. Here, you can imagine yourself back home as you visit Sears, J.C. Penney, and The Gap. *La Plazoleta* here offers a wide variety of food shops.

Paso del Indio

U nearthed during the construction of the expressway between Vega Baja and Vega Alta, the archaeological site of Paso del Indio contains traces of three cultures (Igneri, Pre-Taíno, and Taíno) which span 1,100 years. As three settlements were buried under floods, they are relatively well preserved and thus easily studied. Researchers are studying tool use, age, and diet. Many of the dead are under 12 and died from malnutrition.

Also located in Carolina are the **Antigua Alcaldía de Carolina** (1872), C. José de Diego at Plaza de Recreo; the *second* **Antigua Alcaldía de Carolina** (dating from 1927), C. Arsuaga at De Diego; and the **Iglesia de San Fernando** (1860) on C. Muñoz Rivera.

A bit farther near Piñones along Carr. 187 lies **Boca de Cangrejos** ("Point of the Crabs"), a fishing village. Birdwatchers here may see the common tern, the little blue, tricolored and green-backed heron, the black-necked stilt, and the spotted sandpiper.

BY PÚBLICO: *Públicos* leave from Old San Juan, Stop 18 in Santurce, and from Río Piedras. In general, it is easiest to head W towards Arecibo from Bayamón (Old San Juan), or Sto 18, and head S from Río Piedras or Caguas. To go E from Río Piedras is easiest. A bus leaves at uncertain intervals from the bus terminal in Old San Juan for Barranquitas. Expect to pay around $16 to Mayagüez and $10 to Ponce.

Hitchers (keeping in mind that Puerto Ricans may be reluctant to pick them up, and it may be dangerous) will do well to take transport out of the urban congestion to a place where a thumb has room to breathe.

INTERNAL FLIGHTS: American Eagle flies to Ponce and Mayagüez daily. **Vieques Air Link** flies from San Juan's Isla Grande to Vieques and Culebra, and **Isla Nena** flies to Culebra and Vieques from the international airport.

FOR THE VIRGIN ISLANDS: Airlines flying back and forth change frequently. Be sure to bring along a copy of *Explore the Virgin Islands* by Harry S. Pariser (Manatee Press, 5th edition 2002).

FOR ST. THOMAS: American Eagle flies as does **Cape Air** (☎ 800-352-0714).

FOR ST. JOHN: Once in St. Thomas, take a ferry to St. John from Charlotte Amalie ($7) or Red Hook ($4).

FOR ST. CROIX: Cape Air (☎ 800-352-0714) and **American Eagle** fly, but you will likely have to stop and/or change planes in St. Thomas. **Vieques Air Link** flies from Vieques.

FOR THE BRITISH VIRGIN ISLANDS: American Eagle, and LIAT fly to Tortola daily.

FOR THE DOMINICAN REPUBLIC: The most reliable airline is American. Bring a copy of *Explore the Dominican Republic*, third edition, by Harry S. Pariser (Hunter Publishing).

FOR THE CONTINENTAL UNITED STATES: Most cities are readily accessible through direct or interconnecting flights. See "Arrival" in the Introduction. If traveling to the airport during rush hour, be sure to allow plenty of time.

FOR COSTA RICA: LACSA flies. See *Explore Costa Rica* by Harry S. Pariser (Manatee Press 4th edition, 2000).

⚓ The Columbus Statue Controversy ⚓

After years of searching for a home, "Birth of the New World," a giant statue of Columbus appears to have found some sort of a home in the San Juan suburb of Cataño. Russian sculptor Zurab K. Tsereteli attempted to donate the 600-ton colossus to many US cities during the 1990s, but none wanted it. It was rejected by NYC, Baltimore, Columbus, Miami, and Ft. Lauderdale.

Theriginal plans called for the 295-ft.-high statue to form the centerpiece of a tourism complex á la Epcot Center.

The municipal authorities planned to cover the $30 million cost through a bond issue. Because some neighborhoods lack sewage facilities, the streets flood when it rains, and unemployment is around 13%, some local malcontents voiced their disapproval to this act of urban edification. The fact that the mayor had ordered construction of a nine-story, $7-million City Hall had already irritated more than a few. The Federal Aviation Agency ordered the height of the statue lowered. The government decided to move the statue, and those locals whose homes were to be razed for the project raised their voices in opposition.

An all-around *simpatico* kind of guy, sculptor Tsereteli told the homeowners that he too had lost his home in Georgia (USSR) because it had had to make way for civic "improvements."

Although still more than twice the height of the Statue of Liberty without her pedestal, Chris had been cut down 51 ft. owing to fears that he might interfere with airport operations. Environmentalists pointed out that because Esperanza Park is on a spit of sand created by landfill, the statue would sink in the event of an earthquake.

Sculptor Tsereteli is no stranger to controversy. His 310-ft. statue of Peter the Great towers over the Moscow River. Protestors wired it with explosives during construction in 1997 but then decided that detonation might hurt passersby. His 400-ft.-high War Memorial Obelisk, also in Moscow, is popularly called "the roach on a pin" because its Goddess of Victory statue on top is too small to be recognizable.

Although Columbus' ship was most likely steered by a bar directly connected to the rudder, the statue shows him steering with a wheel. Critics charge that the arms are too long and the head too small. Columbus has one hand raised in greeting, a pose which makes him seem a bit absurd.

The parts arrived for the statue in Oct. 1997 in some 2,500 pieces. The head arrived from Miami and the rest from St. Petersburg, Russia.

After an opposition member of the Town Assembly moved to block the project, Judge Juan Maldonado Torres ruled that the town needed to renew the contract with developer VCF. The original contract had given rent to the developer for $1 per year. In return, VCF would provide $92 million in funding for construction of the statue and waterfront restoration. VFC would have been granted the right to charge admission for the next 30 years!

At present, the parts of the statue are gathering grass in Cataño.

So close to San Juan yet a world apart, this area includes the African influenced municipality of Loíza, the beach town of Luquillo and the port town of Fajardo. El Yunque, the island's most extensive tract of remaining rainforest rounds out the picture. While the main highway is both congested and defaced by modern sprawl, the towns preserve more of a traditional flavor.

Although this area has already seen substantial tourist development, more is planned. If you would like to see the remaining nature preserved, contact the Caribbean Action Network.
http://actionnetwork.org/PRAN/home.html
enlacepr@caribe.net

Loíza Aldea & Environs

Named after the Indian princess Luisa who died fighting beside her lover, the Spaniard Mejia, this area is the sole remaining center of Afro-Hispanic culture on the island.

The *municipo* itself is divided into four parts — Piñones, Plaza, Mediana Baja, Mediana Alta. Its history dates back to the 16th century when African slaves were brought in to work the sugarcane fields and pan for gold in the river. They were supplemented by escaped and recaptured slaves from other islands.

Today, the majority of its population of approximately 30,000 are freed descendants of these Yoruba slaves. The local leadership is trying to deny the presence of African influence in the area, attempting to substitute Indian instead, because there is no political capital to be gained from being black in Puerto Rico.

The town of Loíza Aldea was founded in 1719, and its **Iglesia del Espíritu Santo y San Patricio** (begun 1646) in the Plaza de Recreo is the island's oldest active parish church. Its *fiestas patronales* of San Patricio take place around Mar. 17, and the **Festival de Burén** (named for a flat cooking stone) is held in Feb. Loíza is one of the three poorest municipalities in Puerto Rico. It is the birthplace of famous Puerto Rican bandleader, vocalist, percussionist, and composer Ismael Rivera (1931-1987).

GETTING HERE: Possibly the most exciting part of the trip. Take a bus from Old San Juan's bus station to the end of the line in **Piñones** (Carr. 187) where many stalls serve traditional, African-influenced foods.

The action here is at the **Reef Bar and Grill**, which offers a variety of American fare, often accompanied by live reggae or calypso music. Food here is fried fish fritters and the like. This is a great place to catch a sunset.

Also in this area (Carr. 187, Km 5.4) is **Hemingway's Place** (☎ 787-791-4212), which serves a popular Sun. brunch. From Piñones onward the feel of Africa is in the air.

The **Soleil Beach Club and Bistro** (☎ 787-253-1033) offers up blues, salsa, and jazz with their food in the evenings.

El Pulpo Loco is a colorful seafood restaurant.

Pasa Tablado

This bike path begins just before crossing the bridge which enters into Piñones from San Juan. It heads through mangroves along the coast and intersects with Carr. 187, off and on. You may follow the path further into Loiza or begin at Condado and ride along past Ocean Park and Isla Verde to the start of the path.

Eastern Puerto Rico

1. Caribbean National Forest (El Yunque)
2. Luquillo Beach
3. Cabezas de San Juan
4. Humacao Reserve
5. Húcares Beach
6. Palmas Del Mar resort

If you have a vehicle or don't mind hitching you can continue on the road, which runs six miles along unspoiled white sand beaches (nicknamed the lovers' lane of Puerto Rico). Then cross the Espíritu Santo River bridge which spans the Río Grande de Loíza, the island's roughest and only navigable river. An alternate but less spectacular route is to take a *público* from Río Piedras plaza.

ENVIRONMENTAL THREATS: The area's distinctly laid-back and near-deserted ambiance has been continually threatened by plans to build condominiums, hotels and high-cost housing developments in its Vacia Talega sector. The latest version of a three-decade old project proposed by P.F.Z. Properties Inc. would be known as "Costa Serena." The developers claim that the $223.5 million development of 1,290 condo units would benefit the local economy, but the community and many Puerto Ricans feel that the development will negatively affect

> ☀ Avoid the Piñones area at night. Also, be sure to leave your car near a vendor's booth (give them a couple of dollars if necessary to watch the car) or have a member of your group stay with the car. This area may look like El Campo, smell like El Campo, but it is very close to highly urbanized San Juan.

the largest stretch of mangroves on the island. The Piñones Forest was designated as a critical coastal wildlife habitat by the Department of Natural and Environmental resources in 1972. The community also fears that the 51-acre project is just the first phase of P.F.Z. Properties' development, and will open the door to more urbanizing and megatourism projects, eventually displacing the traditional Afro-Caribbean community.

PRACTICALITIES: The only accommodations option is **Centro Vacacional UIA** (☎ 787-876-1446).

FOOD: Restaurants include **El Parilla** (☎ 787-876-3191), which serves seafood, Carr. 187 at Km 6.2 and **Doña Hilda**, at the corner of Carr. 188 and Carr. 951.

Downscale eateries called **buréns** (after the long, flat skillets used) are at the end of the beach at Las Carreras. They serve serving authentic local dishes at low prices.

Fiestas Patronales de Loíza

Loíza's three-day tribute to Santiago (St. James) is the most famous fiesta on the island. St. James, first of Christ's disciples to be martyred, made a comeback during the Middle Ages when, descending from the skies on horseback, he slaughtered many Moors, thus ensuring a Spanish victory. His popularity with the *conquistadore* crowd confirmed by this action, he became their patron saint in the Old World as well as the New. Yoruba slaves were forbidden

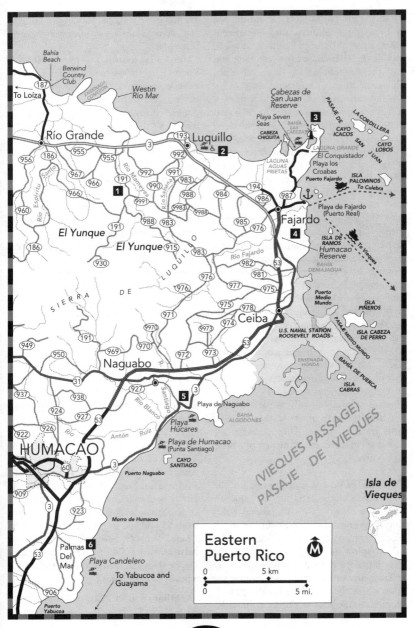

Eastern
Puerto Rico

0   5 km
0   5 mi.

by their Catholic masters to worship the god of their choice, the omnipotent Shango, god of thunder, lightning, and war. Noting the resemblance between their god and the Catholic saint, they worshiped Shango disguised as Santiago.

In the early part of the 17th century, a fisherman on his way to work found a statuette of a mounted Spanish knight hidden in a cork tree, and he took it home. When he came back later, the statue was nowhere in sight. Returning to the tree he again found it secreted, and brought it back home only to have the same thing happen once more. After the third occurrence, he took the statue to the local priest who, identifying it as Santiago, blessed it. The statue ceased wandering, and the local patron saint festivities commenced.

Today, there are three images, the latter two brought from 19th-century Spain. Homage is paid to each image on separate days. The original, primitively carved statue, known as *Santiaguito* or "Little James," has been dedicated to children. The others are dedicated to men and women respectively. *Mantenedoras* ("caretakers") take care of each of the three statues; they organize raffles and collect donations.

Strings of *promesas* (silver charms) hanging from the base of the statues are gifts from grateful devotees. These *promesas* are fashioned in the shape of the part of a body to be cured.

THE FESTIVAL: For nine days before the fiesta begins on the 26th July, the *mantenedora* of Santiago de los Caballeros holds prayer sessions at her house during which elderly women and children chant rosaries and couplets honoring the saint. On the first day of the festival, a procession led by a flag bearer proceeds to Las Carreras, the spot where the original statue appeared. Stopping at the houses of other *mantenedo-*

ras along the way, the statues are brought out and both carriers and flag bearers kneel three times.

The Loíza festival is famous all over Puerto Rico for the beauty and uniqueness of its costumes: *Vejigantes,* who represent devils, wear intricately crafted, colorfully painted coconut masks adorned with horns along the tops and sides. *Locas*, female impersonators with blackened faces and exaggerated bosoms, wearing clothes that don't match, pretend to sweep the streets and porches along the way.

Caballeros, who represent Santiago, wear brightly colored clothes, ribbons and bells, and a soft wire mask painted with the features of a Spanish knight.

Viejos wear shabby clothes and masks made from shoe boxes or pasteboard.

Recently, the festival has been modified; outsiders, who know little of the traditions involved, now make up the majority of the participants. Consequently, the festival has become something of a carnival with salsa music replacing the indigenous *bomba y plena*. The festival is also becoming confused with Halloween; in 1982, E.T. won the prize for best costume.

The **Centro Cultural** has a small collection of relics. It is to the E of the town plaza.

CRAFTS: The **Ayala family** (☎ 787-76-1130), on Carr. 187 at Km 6.6 in Mediana Alta, make and sell the best festival *vejigante* masks. Before his death in 1980, the family patriarch Castor Ayala was the pre-eminent mask maker in Loíza. Prices range from $50 on up. To get here, turn L at the Chique alcoholic beverage store and enter between two buildings. Then turn L at a bicycle shop and then turn R and watch for a peach-colored home.

Another shop (☎ 787-876-7006) is on C. 5 off Carr.187. Near the Ayala's, **Estúdio**

> **Friquitines** (seafood kiosks) are on Hwy. 3, just W of the turnoff for Playa Luquillo. Here, you can dine on whole fried fish, conch salad, and codfish fritters amidst funky ambience.

de Arte Samuel Lind, (☎ 787-876-1494) shows the artist's paintings, sculptures, and silkscreens.

FROM LOIZA: Return to the plaza to catch a *público* back to San Juan, or cross the bridge to return via Piñones.

The Río Grande & Luquillo Areas

The main way out of San Juan to the east is by a highway (Carr. 3) with highly unpastoral surroundings: pharmaceutical plants and shopping malls galore. A new highway has been proposed (Carr. 66 which would have connected Río Piedras to Canóvanas and Loíza), but the Supreme Court blocked the project, owing to environmental concerns, in 2000.

Near Fajardo and within easy reach of the side road to El Yunque, **Playa Luquillo** is the most famous beach in Puerto Rico. It is, however, frequently crowded and not always clean. (Definitely avoid coming here on weekends). At the end of each day (5 PM) a white ambulance with screaming siren runs along the beach. Admission is free, but parking costs $2. The Balneario also offers showers (25¢).

Its **Mar Sin Barreras** (Sea Without Barriers) facility allows the disabled to take a dip by using a ramp.

> **URL** Luquillo's web site
> **http://www.luquillopr.com**

There are no facilities on the beach but everything is a block away on the road paralleling Carr. 3.

Further E near the Plaza you can find **La Pared** (The Wall), a surfing beach, although serious surfers will go to **La Selva**. **Playas San Miguel** and **Convento** stretch on to the E.

In town, at the traffic light where the banks are, you can head to the coast to find **Playa Azul**, another white sand beach. It is flanked by ugly development, and it offers no facilities, but it is good for swimming.

If you clamber over a jetty of rocks here, you will find some six mi. of sand. This area is known as La Selva and El Convento (which is the easternmost portion). It terminates at Playa Seven Seas.

FESTIVALS AND EVENTS: Río Grande has a carnival celebration in mid-July that includes a traditional coastal burial of a sardine; events usually take place on weekday evenings and throughout the day and night on weekends.

SIGHTS: Luquillo has the **Alcaldía de Luquillo** (1925), C. 14 de Julio at C. Jesús T. Piñero on the Plaza de Recreo; it shows both neoclassic and neo-Spanish influences. In front of the Plaza, the Iglesia de San José dates from 1932. The abandoned 19th-century ruins of the **Panadería García** are in back of C. Fernando García 308, which is off of Carr. 3. In Río Grande is the **Iglesia de la Virgen del Carmen** (approx. 1880), C. del Carmen 55 at the Plaza de Recreo.

Río Grande/Luquillo Practicalities
ACCOMMODATIONS: The Sol Melia-owned **Paradisus** resort is scheduled to open in 2003 or 2004. This 500 rm. hotel will have a golf course, and, eventually, a sister hotel which will be all-inclusive.

Another, more staid alternative is the 11-room **Trinidad Guest House**, 6A Ocean Drive in Luquillo (☎ 787-889-2710, ⊜ 787-889-0640). Rooms rent from around $60 s, $75 d. Some rooms share a bath. This hotel was formerly the Parador Martorell.
http://www.trinidadguesthouse.com
trinidad51@aol.com

Le Petit Chalet (☎ 887-5802/5807; Box 182, Río Grande, 00745) offers a tranquil atmosphere that is ideal for birdwatchers.

The **Luquillo Beach Inn** (☎ 787-889-1063, 787-889-3333, ⊜ 787-889-1966), Ocean Drive 701, is set a block from Playa Azul and has one and two-bedroom villas, Rates run from $125 for a one-bedroom to $150 for a two-bedroom apartment. Ask about weekday rates.
http://www.home.coqui.net/jcdiaz
jcdiaz@coqui.net

The 15-unit **Río Grande Plantation Resort** (☎ 787-887-2779, ⊜ 787-888-3239), a "Conference and Learning Center," has a pool, convention center, rooms, and a set of villas. Each two-story villa has TV/VCR, refrigerator, microwave, and Jacuzzi. It provides personal attention, and is on the grounds of an 18th-C sugarcane plantation. It's on Rt 956 at Km 4.2. Rates run from around $125-300 d.
http://www.riograndeplantation.com
rgplantation@riograndeplantation.com

Other alternatives include the **Berwind Recreational Facilities** (☎ 787-256-3010; Carr. 187, Km 4.7) and **Motel Patria** (☎ 787-887-7763; Carr. 967, Km 1.1) in Río Grande.

Camping is available at Luquillo's *balneario* at Km 35.4 on Carr. 3.

SPAS: The **La Casa Day Spa** (☎ 787-887-4359, 212-260-5823; Box 1916, Río Grande, PR 00745) is a spa which was founded by entrepreneurial therapist and talk show guest Jane Goldberg. A variety of massages are offered, as are body wraps (mud, herbal), facial regeneration, and colon therapy. Treatments run around $50-$70, with one as low as $20 and another as high as $135. Tai Chi, dance, and other classes are available, as are custom-designed tours and hikes. The hotel is off of Carr. 186 at Ramal 9960, Km 0.9.
http://www.lacasaspa.com
lacasa@lacasaspa.com

IN PALMER: Set on 481 acres and reminiscent of a Caribbean great house, the 600-room **Westin Río Mar Beach Resort & Country Club** (☎ 787-888-6000, ⊜ 787-888-6204, 800-4-RIOMAR) is a $178.5 million project that opened in 1996. It features a ballroom, casino, country club, business center, health club, beach club, sailing, boating, diving, surfing, windsurfing, horseback riding, hiking, two championship golf courses, and a mile-long beach. It now has the Ocean Villas, a set of Caribbean-style villas with full kitchen, and balconies set in two, five-story buildings. The villas have their own small conference room. Rates run from $195 d for standard rooms to $3,950 for the best suite.

Dining is at your choice of a total of seven restaurants or lounges, which include an international café and bistro, **Palio** (N Italian dinners), the **Grille Room**, **La Estancia** (Spanish), a tapas bar, a beachfront grill and bar, and the **Players' Lobby Bar**.
http://www.westinriomar.com

At the Westin Río Mar, **Ocean Villas** (☎ 787-888-6000, 800-WESTIN-1, ⊜:787-888-6235), 6100 Río Mar Blvd. on Carr. 968 at. Km 1.4, is a set of 58 premier luxu-

ry beachfront villas They offer one-, two- and three-bedroom oceanfront units which have kitchens, living and dining areas and balconies which overlook the ocean. They share the Westin's facilities. Rates range from around $675-$1075 d.
http://www.theoceanvillas.com

The seven-unit **Caribe Mountain Villas** (☎ 787-769-0860, 787-863-5296, ☏ 787-769-0860) Carr. 857, Km 6 in Carolina, is a nature hideaway set in the foothills of El Yunque, just a half-hr. from the airport. It has a pool, tennis courts, gardens and a great view. Rates round from around $100-140 d.
http://www.caribevillas.com
Kerstin@caribe.net

CASA CUBUY ECOLODGE: On El Yunque's S side, this intimate guesthouse (☎ 787-874-6221; Box 721, Río Blanco, Puerto Rico 00744) is at Km 22 on C. 191. It provides an ideal atmosphere for sunbathing, hiking, and relaxing. Some trails on the luxuriantly verdant property lead to pre-Columbian petroglyphs. Rates start at $80 s or d. Both regular and vegetarian meals are available. Massages are $50. Visitors should note that there are no trails directly into the main part of El Yunque from this area so you will have to drive around to get into the park and access trails. The owners, Marianne and her son Matt, relate that "There are some hiking trails on this side of El Yunque. We are within the boundaries of the forest so our guests step off the terrace and onto the paths that lead into the forest and to rivers and waterfalls. Rental cars are the best means of getting here." This guesthouse has a good reputation with visitors.
http://www.casacubuy.com
info@casacubuy.com

NEARBY: Cabañas de Yunque (☎ 787-874-2138; HC1 Box 4449 Naguabo, Puerto Rico

00718-9716) has budget rooms off of Carr. 191. Owner Robin Phillips leads hikes. His wooden cabins are surrounded by fruit trees and afford awesome views. Cabins have one full-size bed and two fold-up cots. Cabins rent for $35 d. a night ($25 d each add'l night. Camping available by request.
http://www.rainforestsafari.com/Phillips.htm
phillips@east-net.net

FOOD: Sandy's Sea Food Restaurant & Steak House (☎ 787-889-5765), C. Fernández Garcia 276 in Luquillo, offers fare ranging from a number of *asopaos* to *mondongo*, from lobster and shrimp dishes to poultry and meat.

Lolita's (☎ 787-889-5770) is on Carr. 3 at Km 41.8 in Luquillo; it serves some mean nachos and offers tasty margaritas.

The Greek Garden (☎ 787-889-0530) offers Greek dishes such as stuffed grape leaves with rice and mousaka. To get here turn R at the first traffic light in Luquillo near the twin condo towers. Then make the first L and them a quick R into the parking lot.

Back to Nature (☎ 787-889-5560) is a health food restaurant and natural foods store. It's in Barrio Fortuna, Sector Villa Solís.

At Jesús T. Piñero 2 and housed in a small blue building on the main plaza in Luquillo, **Victor's Place** (☎ 787-889-5705), Jesús T. Piñero, specializes in seafood. It has been here for more than 60 years, and is a local mainstay.

Blue Jeans Bar & Grill, next to the church and above the bakery in Luquillo, offers daily specials as well as Mexican, American, and traditional dishes.

The **Brass Cactus** (☎ 787-889-5735) serves American food and has a great many TVs, usually tuned into sporting events.

El Flamboyán, next door, serves local food.

Chianti Grill offers Italian dishes.

El Rancho, in Luquillo on Carr. 3 at Km 32, offers food ranging from fried rabbits to shrimp nuggets. They also have pony rides.

On Carr. 191 at Km 1.3, **Las Vegas** (☎ 787-887-2526) serves Puerto Rican cuisine, including seafood dishes such as *salmorejo marino* (seafood stew).

Offering a great view but slow service, **Restaurante Montemar,** on Carr. 969 off of Carr. 191, serves Puerto Rican dishes.

On Carr. 877 at Km 6.6 and overlooking the Río Espíritu Santo, **Villa Pesquera** (☎ 787-887-0140) specializes in seafood. Check out the catch of the day. Good place for a sunset drink.

Don Pepe is located on Carr. 3 at Km 31.3 which is between Carr. 191 and 968 (near the entrance to El Yunque). It serves Tex-Mex dishes as well as international cuisine and has live music from Thurs. to Sun. nights.

Mirabueno (☎ 787-809-5809), on Carr 3 near Río Grande, serves gourmet dinners which are created by an award-winning Spanish cook.

Chef Wayne (☎ 787-889-1962, 889-2911) presides over his skilled staff of cooks in a white house on an unmarked road off of Carr. 922. Grilled Caribbean lobster and other gourmet delights are available. A Sunday buffet is priced at less than $20 pp. Call for reservations and directions.

HOTEL DINING: At the Westin Río Mar, **Cactus Jack's** offers award-winning Tex-Mex dishes, and **Shima's** has good (if expensive) sushi.

SHOPPING: **Cerámicas Los Bohio** (☎ 787-887-2620) sells pottery, some of which employs Taíno motifs. It's on 65th Industry at Km 21.7.

The **Treehouse Studio** (☎ 787-888-8062), on an unmarked road off of Carr. 3, sells colorful watercolors. Call ahead.

Río Grande/Luquillo Outdoor Adventures

SURFING AND INFORMATION: La Selva **Surf Shop** (☎ 787-889-6205) is a block away from the beach near the plaza at C. Fernández García 250; you can find good surfing information here.

KAYAKING AND WINDSURFING: Kayaks may be rented at **Playa Luquillo.**

At Playa Azul, **Playa Azul Lagoon & Sea** (☎ 787-776-0483) rents kayaks for around $10/hr., $30/day.

At the Westin, **Iguana Water Sports** (☎ 787-888-6000, ☎ 787-888-6204, 800-4-RIOMAR) rent out windsurfing equipment and sea kayaks.

DIVING: **Divers' Outlet** (☎ 787-889-5721, 888-476-3483), C. Fernández García 39, Luquillo, offers courses and certification, rentals, and diving trips.

Alpha Scuba (☎ 787-327-5108, 787-327-3990), C. Fernandez Garcia in Luquillo, runs a variety of snorkeling and diving trips, including trips to locales as far away as Mona.
http://alphascuba.tripod.com/alphascuba
alphascuba@caribe.net

GOLF: At Km 4.2 on Carr. 187, **Bahía Beach Plantation** (☎ 787-256-5600, ☎ 256-1035) operates an 18-hole course and offers rental clubs and lessons. Each hole is different. Rates are around $75 before 1 PM, $50 from 1–4 PM, and $30 after 3 PM. Cart is included.
http://www.golfbahia.com

Berwind Country Club (☎ 787-876-3056) has an 18-hole course in Río Grande. It has tight fairways and challenging greens. It is open to guests on weekdays.

Westin Río Mar Country Club (☎ 787-888-401) operates two courses, both of which are flanked by El Yunque on one side and the Atlantic on the other. Designed by pro Greg Norman, its River Course offers challenging fairways and bunkers. Renovated in 1996, the Ocean Course has slightly larger fairways.

The **Inter-Continental Cayo Largo Resort** (☎ 787-801-5000) will have a golf course when it opens in 2003.i

TENNIS: The **Westin Río Mar Beach Resort & Country Club** (☎ 787-888-6000, ✆ 787-888-6204, 800-4-RIOMAR) has 13 courts; four are lighted.

HORSEBACK RIDING: El Rancho (☎ 787-889-6160, 787-860-7858; see above) has ponies and **Hacienda Carabalí** (☎ 787-889-5820, 787-889-4954; Carr. 992, Km 4, at the bridge) offers both trail and beach rides by reservation only from $20 on up. **hcarabal@coqui.net**

SWIMMING: In addition to the famous Luquillo and the others already mentioned, **Playa Las Picúas**, NE of Río Grande at Carr. 187, Km 2, borders the Berwind Country Club. It is in a bay near the mouth of the Río Espíritu Santo. It has no facilities, and is popular with locals on weekends.

KAYAKING AND OTHER TOURS: EcoXcursion Aquatica (☎ 787-888-2887), on Carr. 191 at. Km 1.7 in Río Grande, offers kayak day tours as well as bioluminescent bay Kayak trips, rainforest hikes, and mountain bike tours

---

URL Official El Yunque website:
http://www.southernregion.fs fed.us/caribbean
Useful site for the area:
http://www.elyunque.com

El Yunque (The Caribbean National Forest)

Forty km SE of San Juan, the Luquillo Mountains rise abruptly from the coastal plain. Although 3,526-ft. (1,075-m) El Toro is actually the highest, the area is called El Yunque after the 3,493-ft. (1,065-m) peak. The Taíno name *yuque* (white land) was transformed by the Spanish into *yunque* (anvil), which the peak does resemble when viewed from the N. Luquillo is a corruption of *Yukiyu* (the god of happiness and well being), who the Taíno believed lived amid the mountainous summits.

The only tropical forest in the US National Forest system, its 27,846 acres contain 75% of the virgin forest remaining in Puerto Rico, the headwaters of eight major rivers, four distinct types of forest, and a wealth of animal and plant life.

Admission is $3; the park is open from 9 AM–5 PM. It is closed only on Christmas Day.

GETTING HERE: Easily accessible by car, it's less than an hour drive from San Juan. Follow Carr. 3, from which Carr. 186 and Carr. 191 branch off. While 186 traverses the W boundary of the forest, 191 cuts through its heart. Hiking trails branch off this road. A landslide has closed 191 to traffic at Km 13.5 so it's no longer possible to pass through to the S.

Hitching along 186 and 191 can be slow (and possibly dangerous), and there's no public transportation through the forest. Sadly, the only practical way to visit is to have your own wheels or someone who will drop you off and then pick you up again.

TOURS: A large number of companies offer tours, but unfortunately do not do any serious hiking.

HISTORY: First protected under the Spanish Crown, the 12,400 acres of Crown Forest were proclaimed the Luquillo Forest Reserve by President Theodore Roosevelt in 1903. Since the creation of the first Forest Service office in the area in 1917, the reserve area has continued to grow; the name was changed to Caribbean National Forest in 1935. It is now also known as the Luquillo Experimental Forest and Biosphere Reserve.

Rainforest Ecosystems

Rainforests contain the planet's most complex ecosystem, and rainforests have a richer animal and plant life than any other type of forest. Unlike other areas in which living organisms face conflicts in the face of a hostile climate, in the rainforest organisms struggle for survival primarily against each other. Each being — whether plant, animal, insect, or microbe— has been able to develop its niche. and because there are so many species, numerous examples of specialized niches can be found.

Rainforests occur in regions without major seasonal variation (although rainfall does vary during the year) and where more than 70 in. (1,800 mm) of rain fall annually. When seen from the air, the canopy appears uneven because there are trees of varied species and stages of development.

VARIETIES: There is no single "true rainforest," and forest botanists have varying definitions of the term. It may be argued that there are some 30 types including such categories as semi-deciduous forests, tropical evergreen alluvial forests, and evergreen lowland forests — each of which can be further subdivided into three or four more categories. Equatorial evergreen rainforests comprise two thirds of the total. As one moves away from the equator on either side the forests develop marked wet and dry seasons.

CLOUD FORESTS: Cloud forest is another name for montane rainforest which is characterized by heavy rainfall and persistent condensation due to the upward deflection of moisture-laden air currents by mountains. Trees here are typically short and gnarled. Puerto Rico's most famous rainforest area is El Yunque. The so-called elfin woodland or forest is so named because of its stunted, moss-covered trees.

TROPICAL DRY FORESTS: Rainforests without as much rain, the tropical dry forests, once covered Pacific coastal lowlands stretching from Panama to Mexico, covering an area the size of France. Today, they have shrunk to a mere two percent of the total area and only part of this is under protection; the Guánica Reserve in Puerto Rico is one protected area.

LAYERS: Life in the rainforest is stratified in vertical layers. The **upper canopy** contains animals which are mainly herbivorous and, in Central America, have prehensile tails. They rarely descend to earth. Typically more than a hundred feet (30 m) in height, these canopy trees generally lack the girth associated with tall trees of the temperate forest, perhaps because there are fewer strong winds to combat and each tree must compete with the others for sunlight.

The **next lower layer** is filled with small trees, lianas, and epiphytes. Some of the plants are parasitic, others use trees solely for support purposes.

The **ground surface layer** is littered with branches, twigs, and foliage. Most animals here live on insects and fruit; others are carnivorous. Contrary to popular opinion the ground cover is thick only where sunlight filters through sufficiently to allow such vegetation; secondary forest growth is generally much more impenetrable than old growth forest.

The extensive root system of the trees and associated fungi (*mycorrhizae*) form a thick mat which holds thin topsoils in place when it rains. If these are cut, the soil will wash away; the steeper the slope, the faster the rate of runoff. As most of the nutrients are regenerated via the ecosystem, the land soon deteriorates after cutting. As the sun beats down on the soil, sometimes baking it hard as a sidewalk, the crucial fungal mat and other organic life die off. It may take hundreds — if not thousands — of years to replace important nutrients through weathering, rainfall, or volcanic eruption, and such forests may never recover.

INTERACTIONS: As the name implies, rainforests receive ample rain, which promotes a rich variety of vegetation. Animals and insects, in turn, must adapt to that variety. Lowland rainforests receive at least 100 in. (2,540 mm) of rain. Although some rainforests receive almost no rain during certain parts of the year, they are generally cloaked in clouds from which they draw moisture. The high level of plant-animal interaction—taking forms such as predation, parasitism, hyperparasitism, symbiosis, and mutualism—is believed by many biologists to be one major factor promoting diversity. The interactions are innumerable and highly complex: strangler figs steal sunlight from canopy trees; wasps may pollinate figs; bats and birds transport seeds and pollinate flowers. When a species of bird, for example, becomes rare or extinct, it may have an effect on a tree which depends heavily upon it to distribute its seeds. There is no such thing as self-sufficiency in a rainforest; all life is interdependent.

BIODIVERSITY: Those who are unfamiliar with the rainforest tend to undervalue it. Tropical deforestation is one of the great tragedies of our time. We are far from cataloging all the species inhabiting the rainforests, and when the forests are cut down, many species can be lost forever.

More than 70% of the plants known to produce compounds with anticancerous properties are tropical, and there may be many cures waiting to be found. Cures for malaria and dysentery have been found in the forests. Louis XIV was cured of amoebic dysentery by ipecac, a South American plant that remains the most effective cure. Cortisone and diosgenin, the active agents in birth control pills, were developed from Guatemalan and Mexican wild yams.

These are some of the 3,000 plants that tribal peoples use worldwide as contraceptives. Continued research could yield yet other methods of birth control. Not all rainforest products are medicinal. Rice, corn, and most spices — including vanilla, the unripe fermented stick-like fruits of the Central American Orchid, *vanilla fragrans*—are also medicinal. Other products native people have extracted from the rainforest include latex, resins, starch, sugar, thatch, dyes, and fatty oils. The rainforest also acts as a genetic pool, and when disease strikes a monoculture such as bananas, it's possible to hybridize it with rainforest varieties to see if this produces an immunity to pests or fungus.

GREENERY AND GREENHOUSE: Biodiversity is only one of many reasons to preserve the forest. They also act as watersheds, and cutting can result in flooding and erosion as well as increased aridity. Much rain is produced through the transpiration of trees, which helps keep the air saturated with moisture.

Although it is commonly believed that rainforests produce much of the earth's oxygen, in fact there is an equilibrium between the amount mature forests consume through the decay of organic matter and the amount they produce via photosynthesis. However, many scientists believe that widespread burning of tropical forests releases large amounts of carbon dioxide into the atmosphere.

The amount of carbon dioxide in the atmosphere has risen by 15% in the past century (with about half of this occurring since 1958), and forest clearance may account for half of that gain. As carbon dioxide, along with other atmospheric elements, traps heat that would otherwise escape into space, temperatures may rise. Rainfall patterns would change and ocean levels would rise as the polar ice packs melt. In many areas, deforestation has already had an adverse effect on the environment. Although many uncertainties remain about the "greenhouse effect," one certainty is that by the time the effects are apparent they will be irreversible.

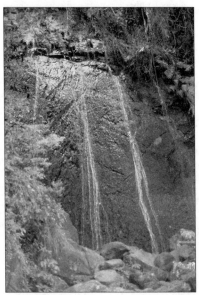

Waterfall at El Yunque.

FATE OF THE FORESTS: Just a few thousand years ago, a belt of rainforests, covering some five billion acres (14% of the planet's surface) stretched around the equator. Wherever there was sufficient rainfall and high enough temperatures there was rainforest. Over half the total area has now been destroyed, much of it in the past few hundred years with the rate accelerating after the end of WWII. Squatters and logging continue to cause deforestation throughout the region. At current rates, much of the remaining forest will vanish by the end of the century. One reason for the expansion into the forests is the need for arable land in areas where land ownership is concentrated in a few hands and most peasants are landless. For example, in El Salvador fewer than 2,000 families control 40% of the land. Cattle ranching, logging, mining, and industry are other reasons to cut the forests. Forests do not recover easily.

El Yunque Flora and Fauna

FLORA: Encouraged by the more than 100 billion gallons of water that fall on the forest each year, the vegetation is prolifically verdant. There are four different types of forest, which support 250 tree species — more than in any other National Forest. Only six of these 250 can be found in the continental United States. *For more information about rainforests read the preceding section.*

ENVIRONMENTAL PROBLEMS: As any visitor to the island will realize, the area surrounding San Juan has become increasingly urbanized. Some 600,000 people now reside in the surrounding area. Although the US Forest Service had been authorized to create a buffer zone around the national forest; the funds were never allocated. Farmlands and forests — where El Yunque's creatures could forage for dietary supplements — have vanished in the wake of development, and the streams are drying up as well.

FOREST ECOSYSTEMS: On the lower slopes is the forest. Nearly 200 species of trees can be found in this forest environment (with some 33 different kinds appearing within a single acre!) along with numerous small but lovely orchids. The dominant tree which gives this forest its name, the *tabonuco* can be recognized by its whitish bark which peels off in flakes. Contrary to what one might expect, these trees grow slowly: the circumference of their stems may increase only an eighth of an inch per year. Growing in valleys and along slopes above 2,000 ft. is the **colorado forest**, called humid montane or montane rainforest elsewhere. The short, gnarled trees often have hollow trunks. Many are 1,000 years old or more.

In one difficult-to-reach area is a 2,500-year-old *colorado* tree with a circumference of 23 ft., 10 inches. These aged trees house the nests of the Puerto Rican parrot. Curiously, these *palo colorado* trees are related to the titi bush, a shrub which thrives in coastal plain swamp from Florida to Virginia.

The **palm forest**, at the next level, is composed almost completely of *sierra* palms (also known as cabbage or mountain palms) complemented by a few *yagrumos*. Masses of ferns and mosses grow underneath as well as on the trees. Limited to the highest peaks and ridges, the dwarf forest is composed of trees 12 ft. high or less. Mosses and liverworts grow on the ground, on tree trunks, and even on leaves.

Also known as elfin forest, **dwarf forest** is the result of a number of factors. The trees are continually buffeted by 32-mph trade winds and face a nearly permanent overcast sky, which hinders photosynthesis and other biochemical reactions. In better con-

ditions (i.e., sun and shelter) at the same altitude elsewhere in the forest, normal tropical forest (montane thicket) containing many sierra palms replaces dwarf forest. Also, the soil — the result of weathering by rain on volcanic rock — is both boggy and highly acidic. The trees act as a filter to trap rainwater. Dwarf or elfin forest is found above 2,000 ft. on Pico del Este, Pico del Oeste, Mt. Britton, and on El Yunque. The forest has 46 species of trees and shrubs.

EPIPHYTES: Taken from the Greek words meaning "upon plants," El Yunque's luxuriant verdancy commonly associated with rainforests depends upon these hangers on. Although they can be found in other forests on the island, the combination of rain and warmth unique to this rainforest help them

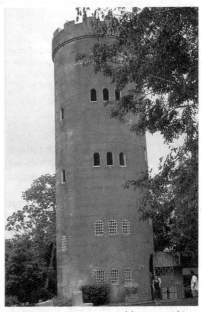

Mt. Britton tower resembles something straight out of Monty Python

How Old Are the Rainforests?

The rainforests were once believed to have been stable environments for 60 million years or more. However, thinking on this point has shifted owing to research conducted from the 1970s onward.

As the northern temperate zone underwent radical shifts in temperature during glacial and interglacial periods (with a resulting movement of ice sheets and shifts in vegetation and fauna), the tropics also underwent equally radical alterations known as pluvials (wet, warm periods) and interpluvials (dry, cold periods). As the glaciers would descend, the tropics would enter an interpluvial. Much of the Amazon had dry, scrub vegetation as recently as 6,000 years ago.

How old are the Americas' tropical ecosystems? *Quite young!* The land mass was not even in place in Central America—along with the connections to Columbia and Mexico—until about three million years ago. This region is believed to have had its origins in the "Galapagos Hot Spot," an active area of sea-floor spreading which drifted slowly until reaching its present position. This same process had happened previously, and the mass continued on through the Caribbean—forming Cuba and the Antilles as it went.

The rainforests, therefore, should not be viewed as timeless, stable relics but rather as dynamic, changing ecosystems whose vegetation shifts as climates change and new species colonize new areas as they become available and accessible to seeds. Rainforests are diverse because most times of the year are reasonably suitable for plant growth and animal activity.

In contrast, the temperate zone not only has a winter—which weeds out species through the environmental stresses it poses—but the northern hemisphere was also largely covered with glaciers (or affected by ice sheets) until relatively recently. Consequently vegetation is still recolonizing habitats there; recent studies of fossil pollen indicate that forest composition has undergone striking changes in the past 5,000 years. This is another reason why the tropics boast more species. Also, as many species have had their origins here, the number of species dwindles as you leave the area.

— from information supplied by Costa Rican resident biologists Drs. Díana and Milton Lieberman

flourish here. Approximately 10% of the world's 250,000 kinds of vascular plants are epiphytes. Most tropical orchids are epiphytes. Don't make the mistake of thinking that these plants are parasitic. Although they are unwelcome guests, most do not feed on their hosts (as do the dodder and mistletoe). Generally, they arrive in the form of tiny dustlike seeds and establish themselves on moss or lichen, which serves as a starter. Unlike epiphytes, vines and lianas remain rooted in the soil.

BIRDS: Many rare species are found here, including the green, blue, and red Puerto Rican parrot (*Amazona uttata*), a protected species (see the box below). Once common throughout the island, fewer than 50 now survive within the forest confines. It may be possible to spot one from either the patio next to the restaurant or in the picnic area behind the visitors' center. Other birds — like the Puerto Rican tanager, the bare-legged owl, broad-winged hawk, the quail-dove, and the scaled pigeon — are common here, although rare elsewhere. You may be able to spot a green mango hummingbird near La Coca Falls or an elfin woods warbler along El Toro Trail and in the dwarf forest. Still other species include the Puerto Rican screech-owl, the Puerto Rican woodpecker, the Puerto Rican tanager, the

What You Can Do to Save the Forests

- *Start at home* Much of North America's old growth forest is under threat from the timber industry. It is unrealistic to expect nations like Indonesia, Brazil, and Costa Rica to save their forests if the US and Canada cut theirs down. In particular, the government-subsidized rape of the US National Forests and the destruction of British Columbia's old growth must be halted.

- *Visit the rainforests* Showing an interest in the rainforest reinforces pride in the forests and instills a sense of value in local people. When you return, tell your friends and relatives about what you've seen.

- *Boycott tropical products* Don't purchase imported tropical birds, snakes, or animal hides. Avoid buying products made of teak, mahogany, or other tropical woods unless you are positive that the furniture comes from tree farms and not from virgin rainforest. Encourage retailers to question the source of their products.

- *Organize* If you live in a major city such as New York, there is likely to be an environmental organization for whom you can volunteer. If there is not, start your own! For maximum effectiveness, coordinate your efforts with groups operating in tropical nations.

- *Educate yourself* The most important hope for the human race is education. Read as much as you can, see as much as you can, and write to your political leaders and to newspapers to inform people what you have seen.

Puerto Rican lizard-cuckoo, and the Puerto Rican bullfinch.

OTHER ANIMALS: Snakes are scarce, poisonous ones nonexistent. There's the Puerto Rican boa, which may grow up to 13 ft., but you are unlikely to see one. *Coquí* frogs croak from every corner, and small fish, shrimp, and crayfish live in the streams. There are also tales of small green men living in the forest, undoubtedly an endangered species these days. You'll have to be either extremely lucky or have a hyperactive imagination if you expect to have an encounter.

ENVIRONMENTAL PROBLEMS: Ironically, the very means that gives visitors access to the forest has had detrimental effects. Cutting roads through steep terrain causes landslides. Accordingly, much controversy surrounds the possibility of reopening Carr.

191, which has been closed since Hugo. Perhaps not coincidentally, the parrot population, which had fallen from around 200 in the 1950s to 50, began to recover after the road's closing. Still, some people are pushing for the road's reopening.

As any visitor to the island will realize, the area surrounding San Juan has become increasingly urbanized. Some 600,000 people now reside in the surrounding area. Although the US Forest Service had been authorized to create a buffer zone around the national forest; the funds were never allocated. Farmlands and forests — where El Yunque's creatures could forage for dietary supplements — have vanished in the wake of development, and the streams are drying up as well.

El Yunque Hiking and Practicalities
RANGER STATIONS: Yohaku lookout tower is the best destination for nonhikers.

♣♣ Common Misperceptions About Rainforests ♣♣

☞ Rainforests are not "the lungs of the planet." Mature trees produce as much oxygen as they consume. The danger in destroying rainforests lies with the effects on rainfall, flooding, and global warming resulting from increasing amounts of carbon dioxide being released into the atmosphere.

☞ Rainforests are not bursting at the seams with colorful plants, wild orchids, andanimals. The overwhelming color is green; flowers are few; and the animal you're most likely to see is the ant.

☞ Rainforests are not a renewable resource. It is impossible to cut trees without destroying other plants and affecting the environment.

☞ Rainforests are not merely a source of wood. There are other values associated with them which must be considered.

☞ Once damaged, rainforest does not simply grow back as it once was. It may take centuries for the complex ecosystem to regenerate. Reforestation cannot restore the environment.

☞ Despite its rich appearance, rainforest soil may not be fertile. Most of the nutrients are contained in the biomass.

☞ There is no need to "manage" a rainforest. They've been doing just fine for eons on their own. Everything in the rainforest is recycled, and anything removed has an effect.

☞ "Selective" cutting has detrimental consequences because it affects the surrounding soil quality and weakens the forest as the strongest specimens are removed. No way has yet been found to exploit a rainforest so that all species may be preserved.

☞ One "endangered" species cannot be effectively protected without safeguarding its ecosystem as well. Botanical gardens or seed banks cannot save important species. These are too numerous in quantity, seeds have too short a lifespan, and the species depend upon animals for their lifecycle equilibrium.

☞ Any reduction in consumption of tropical hardwoods will not preserve rainforests. The only effective method is to protect the forests in reserves and parks. The forests are falling at too fast a rate for any other methods to be effective.

It commands great views from its top, and it doubles as a small bookstore. Restrooms are available in its parking lot. It's on Carr. 191, Km 8.9.

Centro de Información Sierra Palm is a small ranger office with rest rooms and a small office. Leave your car here and hike or picnic.

Centro de Información Palo Colorado is at the entrance to the Mt. Britton and other trails.

An easy trail from here is the **Baño del Oro** (Bath of Gold). It begins at a defunct swimming pool, the Civilian Conservation Corps-constructed Baño Grande, which dates from the 1930s and loops a mi. (1.5 km) through the "Palm Forest."

The **El Caimitillo** shares its trailhead and runs a half-mi. (one km). Palo Colorado, a red-barked tree, is dominant in this area. This short trail (0.2 mi., .6 km) rises from 2,067 ft. (630 m) to 2,427 ft. (740 m). It takes around 15-20 min OW. It has interpretative displays about the Puerto Rican parrots, including samples of nests.

HIKING: Among the 50 km of hiking trails, the principal ones include El Yunque, Mt.

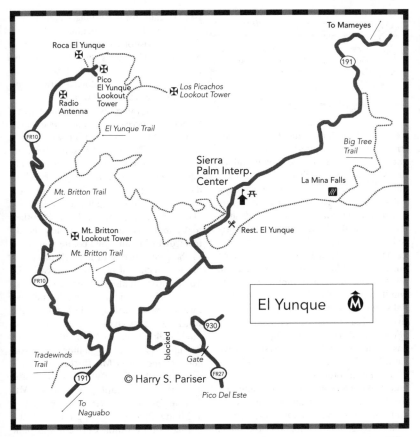

To Mameyes

191

Roca El Yunque ✠

✠ Pico
El Yunque
Lookout
Tower

✠ Los Picachos
Lookout Tower

✠ Radio
Antenna

El Yunque Trail

*Big Tree
Trail*

FR10

Sierra
Palm Interp.
Center

La Mina Falls

Mt. Britton Trail

✠ Mt. Britton
Lookout Tower

Rest. El Yunque

Mt. Britton Trail

FR10

El Yunque Ⓜ

930

*Tradewinds
Trail*

blocked

Gate

191

© Harry S. Pariser

FR27

*To
Naguabo*

Pico Del Este

Britton, Big Tree, and El Toro/Tradewinds, which rises to the top of El Toro peak (3,533 ft.).

Trailheads are located on Carr. 186 at Km 10.6 and on Carr. 191 at Km 13.5. While La Coca Falls and Yohaku Lookout Tower are on or near Carr. 191, you must hike to reach La Mina Falls or Pico El Yunque and Los Picachos Lookout Towers.

HIKING PRACTICALITIES: The trails are well maintained, but no fresh drinking water or toilet facilities are available.

Although locals drink out of the mountain streams, it's not advisable unless the water has been treated first. Bring food, waterproof clothing, hiking boots, and a compass. Long-sleeved clothing is advisable because there are some poisonous plants (and razor grass) along the trails. Although there are a number of food stands on the way up, **Mameyes**, along Carr. 3, is the last place to buy food.

TRAIL DETAILS: Commencing just below the Yohaku lookout tower on Carr. 191, *La*

If you want to get away from the crowds but don't have a lot of time, try visiting the attractive falls at **Juan Diego** (at Km 9.8 on the R). You can easily hike in to two levels of falls; the third is a stiff hike up. It's truly an idyllic spot.

Coca Trail is damp and leads through streams and near waterfalls. It's a rough and muddy trail; you need your hiking boots. A walking stick is recommended. Take the trail located between La Coca Falls and the Yohaku Lookout center downhill from Carr. 191; it descends until it crosses the Río La Coca twice and is preceded by a stream each time it crosses. Río La Mina is next. It has a nice swimming hole. If you follow this trail (.7 mi., 1.2 km, 30–45 min.) uphill past another waterfall, you'll come to the 35-ft. high **La Mina Falls**. It's marked by a footpath over the river and is a popular bathing spot.

From La Mina Falls, the **Big Tree Trail** passes through *tabonuco* forest to reach Carr. 191. This paved trail (.7 mi. .4 km) is located on the other side of the river. If you take it to the R, you will be on an interpretive trail, which has signs in both Spanish and English telling you about forest fires. Allow around 40 min. for the hike. Although asphalt paved, it can be steep in some places. If you listen you may hear the buzzing whistle of the bananaquit, a black and yellow native bird. This road will take you out to Carr. 191 at Km 10.4. Head downhill to return to your car.

El Yunque Trail (2.4 mi, 4.4 km, 4–5 hrs. RT) begins in the Caimtillo Picnic Area and ascends via sierra palm and *palo colorado* forests to the dwarf and cloud forests of Mt. Britton and El Yunque as well as to the top of Los Pichacos, Roca Maracas, and Yunque Rock. One way to hike it is to start from El

Baño Grande, the upper ranger station, take El Yunque Trail (originating at the Palo Colorado Visitor's Center) to the R and head uphill. The trail is challenging and can be steep and muddy. At the halfway mark, it changes from gravel-reinforced native sandstone to a steep and narrow trail.

Passing several trails, you come to **Los Picachos**. Proceeding less than five minutes you come to a steep set of trails which leads to the top. The summit is some 20 ft. in diameter and has a four-ft. wall surrounding it. From the top of El Yunque on a clear day it's possible to see St. Thomas or even as far as the British Virgin Islands.

Heading down, backtrack to the other fork you passed earlier which heads towards El Yunque. Just before you come to the peak, there's an unmarked trail to the R, which will take you to nearby El Yunque Rock. It also has some great views.

Backtracking, continue along the trail and then follow the road up to El Yunque Peak, which has high tech installations (antennas, satellite dishes and the like). Take the road downhill for about 15 minutes until you come to the paved **Mt. Britton Trail** (1.3 km, .8 mi., 40 min. OW) on your L, which you take uphill until you come to **Mt. Britton Tower** — something straight out of a Monty Python set. A product of the Civilian Conservation Corps, it was built between 1930 and 1935 and is named after a famous botanist from the NY Botanical Garden who studied here. You can find this book in the gift shop along with a beautiful selection of postcards.

Return on the same trail to the loop road. Either direction goes back to Carr. 191. If you started by the ranger station, take the loop road down to your L; make another L to get to your car. If you go to your R, it leads to Carr. 191 further uphill where the gate closes the road to vehicular traffic. Taking that road on foot, you can head S to

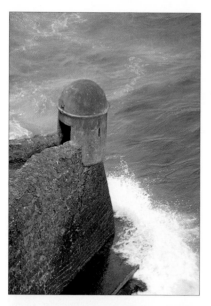

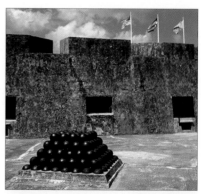

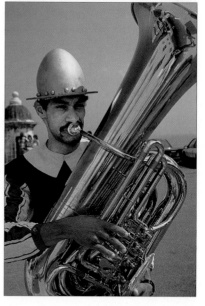

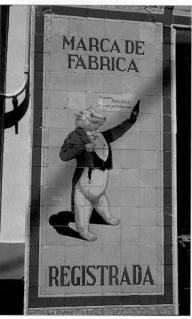

Some of the delights of Old San Juan, a place you might spend days exploring. From clockwise at top: Devil's Sentry Box, flags and musician at San Cristobel Fort in Old San Juan; El Morro; and colorful sign in Old San Juan.

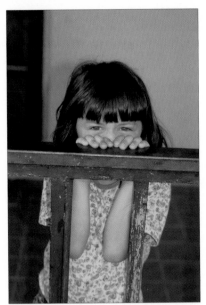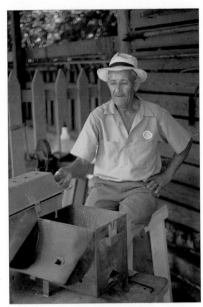

Top: Culebran girl (left); coffee grinding at Hacienda Buena Vista near Ponce (right)
Bottom: dentistry exhibit at Children's Museum in Old San Juan (left); girl in Ponce (right)

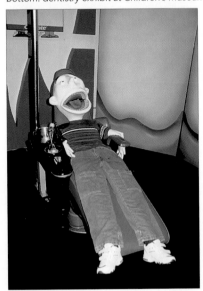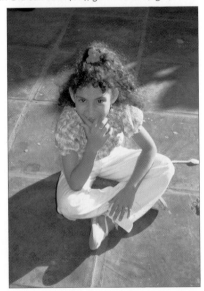

the landslide, where you'll come to the six-mile, 9.6-km *Tradewinds/El Toro Trail.* From this trail, which begins near the aviary and workers' housing area along Carr. 191 at Km 13.5, you can reach El Toro (392 ft., 1074 m), one of the most remote peaks in the area. At this starting point you will find yourself between two radio transmission towers.

Follow the ridge W to the summit before descending to Cienaga Alta, a forest ranger station located along Carr. 186. Unpaved and beautiful, it's about seven or eight miles, and you need seven to 10 hrs. Start hiking from Carr. 186, which is the road that leads from Carr. 3 up through El Verde and heads towards Cotui.

It's advisable to start from this western-most side of the trail because the first thing you'll do is climb El Toro Trail. As it's a steep ascent, you should not do it at the end of your hike. When you descend from the top, put on long pants and a long-sleeved shirt because you'll come across razor grass. As you proceed down the trail, you will traverse a number of hills. There's no dependable supply of running water so bring your own water with you.

The trail ends again on Carr. 191; if you took it from El Verde side once you reach Carr. 191, you would make a L to the gate which closes it off; you would need two cars (one dropping you off and one picking you up) for this hike; it is very enjoyable, however, simply walking in for an hour or so from Carr. 191, then backtracking.

An alternative is to begin hiking at Km 20, five or six km from Florida.

NOTE: El Yunque area has a bad reputation regarding theft so leave *nothing* of value in your car, and exercise like caution while hiking in the area.

BICYCLING: The closed portion of Carr. 191 is the best bicycle path. Along the path you see hibiscus, coleus, and wandering Jew.

OTHER PRACTICALITIES: Best place to orient yourself is at **El Portal** (The Gateway, ☎ 787-888-1880), a visitor's center that opened in 1996. The 12,000-sq.-ft. center contains interactive displays as well as a video theater. It's just a few km in from the entrance road. Obtain additional information from Caribbean National Forest, Box B, Palmer, PR 00721; ☎ 787-888-5656. Topographical maps are available in the field office (open weekdays) at the base of the forest.

Buy Puerto Rican snacks at stands along Carr. 191. The first kiosk to your L as you approach (at Km 7.8) is **El Bosque,** which has vegetable (and sometimes lobster, shrimp, or crab) tacos and soy or chicken *piñonos.* Camping is permitted in most areas of the forest; permits are available at the Service Center. Accommodations are listed under "Río Grande and Luquillo" above.

Wyndham El Conquistador Resort

Set on a bluff commanding a spectacular view of offshore islands, the $225 million **Wyndham El Conquistador** (☎ 787-863-1000, 800-468-5228, ✆ 787-791-7640) resort is the largest self-contained "total escape" tourist resort readily available to upscale US travel groups. It opened in late 1993 with an initial 935 rooms; a total of 1,300 rooms are projected. Currently, there are 918 rooms and suites. The project was financed by the Kumagai Construction Company and Williams Hospitality. Promoting "instant gratification," an 18-hole golf course, gambling, horseback riding, discos, health clubs and other facilities and activities are available. There's a 55-slip marina, five swimming pools, and 16 restaurants, as well as shops, a large casino, an 18-hole golf course, and four different "villages," including an old colonial village.

Curiously, the hotel's site has functioned in its past lives as a Maharishi Mahesh Yogi meditation institute and as an evangelical Christian mission.

Offlying **Isla de Palominos**, under lease from its owners, serves as a "fantasy island" which offers water sports from jet skiing to wind surfing. Transportation (bus, limo, or helicopter) is provided from a special reception lounge in San Juan's airport.

Restaurants here include Blossoms, which has both Chinese and Japanese dishes (including sushi). Rates start at $300 d and range up to $2290. If you are not staying at the hotel, a $4 parking fee is commanded.

GOLF: The resort's **golf course** (☎ 787-863-6784) which boasts a par-72, 18-hole course designed by Arthur Hill. It has 6,700 yds. of fairways sandwiched between the Atlantic and the Caribbean. Rates are around $185, with a reduction to $115 after 2 PM. Hotel guests pay less.

LAS CASITAS: On the same property, at 1000 El Conquistador Ave, 162-unit **Las Casitas** (787-863-1000, ✆ 787-863-6758, 800-468-8365) is a set of one-, two-, and three-bedroom suites set on a 30-ft. cliff. All of the Conquistador's facilities are available for the use of Las Casitas guests, and the **Golden Door Spa** (which got rave reviews from a *Conde Nast Traveler* writer) is on its grounds. It offers a gamut treatments including herbal wraps and facials. The **Le Bistro** restaurant serves gourmet food, and there is poolside cafe as well. Rates run from $695-1675 d.
http://www.wyndham.com

Fajardo

Often seen by visitors as a small, sleepy town, Fajardo only comes alive during its **patron saint festival** (Santiago Apóstol) every July 25. It once served to supply pirates, and today it serves as a yachting haven. Offlying cays include Icacos, Palominos, Palominitos, Diablo, and Cayos Lobos.

Públicos run to the outlying areas of Las Croabas and La Playa-Puerto Real from the plaza. There's nothing much in Las Croabas either except Seven Seas Beach and a few restaurants.

Puerto Real has the **Casa de Aduanas** on C. Union, which dates from 1930. **La Playa** has a customs house, post office, and ferry terminal.

To avoid the downtown area if you are heading for Las Croabas (El Conquistador), take the "Avenida Conquistador" exit to the N on Hwy. 3. Continue to the second traffic light, turn R, and keep going for around a mi. until the junction with Carr. 987 which is on your L.
www.municipiodefajardo.org

Fajardo Practicalities

GETTING HERE: Públicos run from Río Piedras in San Juan. If you're planning to take a ferry, be sure to get one headed to La Playa, or you may end up having to take another *público* from town. You may also charter a taxi from San Juan for around $50.

ACCOMMODATIONS: Set on the waterfront, the 20-room **Delicias Hotel** (☎ 787-863-1818/1577; Box 514, Fajardo, PR 00740), Carr. 195 at La Playa, features a/c rooms from around $60. It is sometimes closed.

A comfortable and hospitable bed-and-breakfast, **Parador Fajardo Inn** (☎ 787-860-6000, ✆ 787-860-5063; Box 4309, Puerto Real, PR 00740) offers a/c rooms with phones and cable TV; rates start from around $90 d. Its **Scenic Inn** has rooms at lower rates. They have meeting rooms which hold up to 120, and two restaurants: the **Starfish** and the **Blue Iguana Mexican Restaurant and Bar**. Other dining is nearby. It's been recommended by a reader.

Fajardo Beaches

The best beach in Fajardo is at Seven Seas along Carr. 987. This horse-shoe-shaped, palm lined beach is crowded on weekends and during the summer months. Follow the beach E to **Playa Escondido** where you will find off-shore reefs. This beach is generally deserted. If you follow a trail through the bush at the NW end of the beach, you will reach an area known as **El Convento.** From here, a deserted stretch runs all the way to Luquillo, a distance of around six mi.

Playa Demajagua, S of Fajardo, is a nice, quiet, and generally calm, beach. If there is no breeze, there may be sand flies.

While swimming be sure to be aware of the moderate to strong currents found along the E coast. There are often no life-guards.

To get here turn off Carr. 3 at the Esso station and head past the Amigo store before turning R at the pharmacy, (Farmacia Monte Brisa) and just follow the signs that say "Inn." Or you can go straight at this intersection and follow the signs to the "Family Hotel-Parador."Or you may urn left at the flashing red light; turn R at the boat shops; turn R at the "T" in the road, and turn left at the next "T" in the road. Then take the next left into the Fajardo Inn, which is on Carr. 195. It is within walking distance of the ferry terminal, and you can find even lower-budget hotels in the vicinity.
http://www.fajardoinn.com
info@fajardoinn.com

In Las Croabas and also known as *La Familia*, the **Family Hotel-Parador** (☎ 787-863-1193, 787-863-1140, ℮ 787-860-5345; HC 00867, Box 21399, Fajardo, PR 00648), Carr. 987, offers 28 a/c rooms with TV and refrigerators. There's a dive school as well as children's and adult pools. It has a fine

restaurant and continental breakfast is served to guests. Rates are around $80 d. For more information/reservations, call 800-443-0266 in the US or 800-981-7575 (or 787-721-2884 in San Juan) in Puerto Rico.
http://www.hotellafamilia.com

On Carr. 987 and at Km 2.7 in Villa Las Croabas, the 14-rm. **Anchor's Inn** (☎ 787-863-7200, 787-863-3363, ℮ 787-860-6934) has attractive, modern rooms, as well as nine units with kitchen, cable TV, and parking. The hotel has a pool and a good restaurant.It is set on a seaside bluff. It has a good restaurant (see below). It is within walking distance of beach, marinas, fishing boats and catamarans. Rates run from around $60-71 d
http://www.anchorsinn.homestead.com
/anchorsinn.html

CONDOS: **B. V. Real Estate** (☎ 787-863-3687) offers a wide variety.
http://www.bvrealty.com

IN CAYO LARGO: Opened in 2003, the 314-rm. **Inter-Continental Cayo Largo Resort** (☎ 787-801-5000, ℮ 787-801-5001), No. 1 Great House Road in Cayo Largo, is set on 883 oceanfront acres. It offers a 7,000-yard, 18-hole golf course, a 12,000 sq. ft. European Spa, 1,100 slip marina, beautiful beaches, five restaurants, four lounges, a health spa, eco-tours, a heliport and private airport, tennis, sports instruction and an airport shuttle service. Rates run around $300-600 d.
http://www.intercontinental.com

IN CEIBA: In Ceiba along Carr. 977, the nine-room **Ceiba Country Inn** (☎/℮ 787-885-0471; Box 1067, Ceiba, PR 00735) is a relaxed and personalized bed-and-breakfast set in the country amidst breezy rolling hills. There's a large Spanish-style veranda which has a BBQ which guests may use.

Rooms have small refrigerators. One family room has two queen-size beds. Rates run around $60 s and $75 d.
http://www.geocities.com/countryinn00735
prinn@juno.com

Casa Marshall (☎ 787-885-4474, ☻ 787-885-0482; APDO. 402, Ceiba 00735), is run by Dennis and Beverly Marshall.This four-bedroom hillside property rents from $100 d plus tax. Children under 12 stay free.
casamar@puerto-rico.net

CAMPING: Pitch a tent within the confines of **Playa Seven Seas**, Carr. 987, Km 5, for around $12 per tent.

FOOD: There are a number of inexpensive places to eat downtown including some pizza joints. **Willam's Pizza**, next to the Colegio Interamericano, is a good bet. The **Centro Naturismo Moderno**, C. Barceló 4, sells health food products. On C. Las Croabas, expensive **La Fontanella** (☎ 787-860-2480) serves gourmet Sicilian dishes.

Also expensive, **Restaurant Du Port** (☎ 787-860-4260) is inside the Puerto del Rey Marina and offers seafood, French, and international food.

Sardinera (☎ 787-863-0320), C. Croabas at Km. 5.5, stands amidst a group of seafood kiosks, and, as its name implies serves seafood—ranging from pastelitos (seafood-stuffed turnovers) to crab stew. It closes at 7 PM daily.

On Carr. 987 and at Km 2.7 in Villa Las Croabas, **Anchor's Inn** (☎ 787-863-7200) serves gourmet seafood dishes such as *filete de chillo tropical* (snapper filet).

In Puerto Real, **Rosa's Seafood** (☎ 787-863-0213), Tablazo 56, is a simple family-style restaurant; dishes here include lobster salad and other seafood dishes as well as seafood-stuffed *mofongo*. Two *arepas* (john-nycakes) are served with each meal. It is more expensive than other, similar restaurants.

Offering free delivery within Fajardo, Luquillo and Ceiba, **Antonino's Pizza** is in town. **Pizza Hut** (☎ 787-860-0070/0090) is set inside the Villa Marina Shopping Center.

La Banda (☎ 787-860-9162) is a pierside restaurant at Puerto Del Rey Marina, Carr. 3, Km 51.2.

Nuevo Velero, next to Skipper Marine, offers great value in local and Cuban dishes. Although not much in appearance, it is a friendly bar where you can get a good inexpensive meal.Locals dining here like to discuss politics.

SHOPPING AND SERVICES: Walgreens, Walmart, and the other usual suspects are in or near town. At the Villa Marina, a shopping center, **Ricky's Cyber Pizza** (☎ 787-860-4230) offers internet connections for around $5 ph. **Peek-a-Boo** at the El Conquistador charges around $16 ph.

CAR RENTAL: A one-day car rental is a good way to make a day trip to Luquillo or El Yunque. **Avis** (☎ 787-863-2735) is on Carr. 987 at the Wyndham El Conquistador; **L & M Car Rental** (☎ 787-860-6868), Hwy. 3 at Km 43.8; **Leaseway of Puerto Rico** (☎ 787-860-5000, Hwy. 3 at Km 44.4. **Popular Auto** (☎ 787-863-4848), Hwy. 3 in the Fajardo Shopping Mall. Fajardo (airport and hotel shuttle offered), **Thrifty** (☎ 787-860-2030), Hwy. 3 at Km 51.4 in Marina Puerto del Rey, and **World Car Rental** (☎ 787-860-4808) C. 26 in Fajardo.

SHOPPING: The Paradise Store (☎ 787-863-8182), Carr. 194, Km 0.4, sells chocolates and other gift items.

The **El Conquistador** also has a few stores around it.

NIGHTLIFE: Set on C. Marginal at the Puerto del Rey exit off of Carr. 53, **Caribbean Blues** (☎ 787-860-0060, 860-1222), is the E coast's best live music venue. Jazz, rock, and blues are on the audio menu, and a modest cover is charged. Be warned that it is popular with military men from Roosevelt Roads, so, as Shrub mouthpiece Ari Fleischer advises, you may wish to 'watch what you say.'

MARINAS: Set on Demajagua Bay on the E shore on Carr. 3 at Km 51.4, **Puerto del Rey Marina** (☎ 787-860-1000) has slips for 750 boats and can accommodate vessels up to 200 ft. It has a dive center, sailing school, haul-out facility, French restaurant, condos, and the Plaza del Puerto shopping plaza. Trips to Vieques's bioluminescent bay and elsewhere may be arranged here.
http://www.marinapuertodelrey.com

The **Villa Marina Yacht Harbour** (☎ 787-728-4250), is at Carr. 98 at Km 1.3.
http://www.villamarinapr.com

Marina Puerto Chico (☎ 787-863-0834) is at Carr. 987, Km 2.4
Marina Puerto Real (☎ 787-863-2188) is at Playa Puerto Real.
The Sea Lovers Marina (☎ 787-863-3762), Carr. 987 at Km 2.3, Playa Sardinera, is a simple family-run marina which caters to local residents.They have a restaurant and rent slips to guests.
The **Wyndham El Conquistador Marina** (☎ 787-863-6594) is at Ave. El Conquistador 1000.

Fajardo Outdoor Adventures

DIVING: Offering scuba and snorkeling trips, **Sea Ventures Pro Dive Center** (☎ 787-863-34830, 800-739-3483) has been around for a long time. They offer PADI certification as well as excursions to some 20 different dive spots.They are located at Hwy. 3, Km 51.2, in Puerto del Rey Marina.
http://www.divepuertorico.com

The **Caribbean School of Aquatics** (☎787-728-6606). C. Taft 1, Apt 10F. Fajardo, in operation since 1963, is a NAUI and PADI scuba operation which also offers snorkeling and sailing trips.
Scuba Centro (☎ 787-781-8086) operates a catamaran from Villa Marina in Fajardo.
http://www.scubacentro.com

Palomino Divers (☎ 787-863-1077), at the El Conquistador, offers scuba and snorkeling trips.
Also at El Conquistador, **La Casa del Mar Dive Shop** (☎ 787-863-1000, ext. 7917, ☏ 788-860-1604) offers snorkeling and diving trips (around $70 for a one-tank, and $85 for a night dive) and offer a variety of programs, including ones for children.
http://www.lacasadelmar.net

The *Fun Cat* (☎ 787-728-6606), a catamaran, also offers diving and snorkeling trips.
NOTE: For other information on dive operations, charters, and excursions from Fajardo, see the "Vicinity of San Juan" section.

DIVE SITES: There are many fine sites near Fajardo. Here are a few.

Just W of the island of the same name, **Cayo Lobos** is a novice 3–30-ft. dive (1–9 m). Archways, tunnels, and caves galore are present here. Watch for blue tan. parrotfish, and star coral. Night diving here is good, and it is a popular snorkeling spot as well.

Set off the NW edge of Isla Palaminos, **Ralph Point** is a good novice dive that commences 10 ft. (3 m) below the surface and descends to 60 ft. (18 m). This is a great place to see many common reef fish, including trumpetfish, blenny species, and sergeant majors. If you look carefully, you may sport some mantis shrimp.

Big Rock, Little Rock is a novice site set to the NW of Palamino. It is part of a fringing reef with bits of patch reef. As it is a leeward site, it is protected, and you will see more delicate coral than here than at the windward sites. The depth is from 30 to 60 ft. (9-18 m).

Popular **Diablo**, set off of **Cayo Diablo** which is four mi. (6.4 km) E of Cabezas de San Juan, is part of a chain and has an attractive beach. The hard coral here plays host to barracuda, blue chromis, yellow-and-white goatfish, and other species. This is a novice dive with a depth of from 15–50 ft. (4.5–15 m). Unfortunately, Hurricane Georges (1998) dumped a ton of sand on the reef.

SAILING: The area has four marinas (as listed previously), and **Puerto Del Rey** is the largest. **Learn to Sail** (☎ 787-863-7703), Puerto Del Rey Marina, offers sailing lessons and kayak rentals. Sea Ventures (above) also organizes boating and sailing trips.

Erin Go Bragh (☎ 787-860-4401, ✆ 787-863-5253, cell 787-409-2511), a 50-ft. sailing ketch, offers crewed charters for trips. They're based at Puerto Del Rey Marina. They will take up to six and offer personalized service.
http://www.egbc.com
egbc@coqui.net

The 43-ft. **Ventajero 3** (☎ 787-645-9129) can also be chartered.
http://www.sailpuertorico.com

The **Fun Cat** (☎ 787-728-6606), is a catamaran which may also be chartered.

Tropic Key Charters (Box 1186,Fajardo, PR 00738; ☎ 787-860-6100, ✆ 787-860-7592; 800-888-5186) are another alternative.

Captain Mingo (☎ 787-860-7327, 787-383-6509) has trips which leave from the Villa Marina Yacht Club.

Acsent Charters (☎ 787-647-5795), Carr. 987 at Km 1.3, offers sailing trips.

Castillo Tours and Watersports (☎ 787-791-6195, 787-725-7970, 787-726-5752, ✆ 787-268-0740), operate the **Barefoot III** and **Stampede** catamarans.
http://www.castillotours.com

Chamonix Catamaran (☎ 787-885-1880) run snorkel trips, and sunset and dinner cruises. They work with family reunions, weddings, and corporate events. They also have a double-decker party boat.
http://www.snorkelparty.com

East Wind Catamaran (☎ 877-937-4386) is a spacious 62-ft. catamaran which features glass-bottom windows and waterslide. It's based at Puerto Del Rey Marina.
http://www.eastwindcats.com

Fajardo Tours-Traveler Catamaran (☎ 787-863-2821), Sta. Isidra III, E-41 Street 3, Fajardo, operate a Traveler 50-ft. sailing catamaran and a 58-ft. fishing boat. They offer sunset and other excursions as well as charters.

Ventajero Sailing Charters (☎ 787-645-9129), Marina Puerto del Rey, offer day sails and overnight charters aboard a six-person, 43-ft. sailboat.
http://www.sailpuertorico.com

OTHER WATER EXCURSIONS: Palaminos Water Taxi, at the Conquistador, takes hotel guests across daily between 9 AM–4 PM. If they have booked an activity on the island, they will take non-guests across as well. It is possible to swim to the deserted islet of Palominitos here. However, jet skis may spoil your enjoyment. On Palaminos, Hidden Cove is a nude beach.

At the fishing marina at **Bahía Las Croabas**, near the end of Carr. 9987, you may negotiate a charter a boat to Icacos.

Expect to pay around $10-20 pp for them to drop you off and pick you up. Spanish may be necessary for the negotiation. **Raymundo Hernández and family** (☎ 787-863-2471, cell 787-642-3116) operate several fishing sailboats and are available for charters for around $150 pd for groups of up to six.

Experienced souls with credential may rent a motorboat from **Club Nautico International** (☎ 787-863-5131, 800-NAUTICO and 800-BOAT RENT in FL).

Excursions on catamarans and sailboats *East Wind* (☎ 787-860-3434, cell 787-409-2485), and *Spread Eagle II* (☎ 787-887-8821).

PARASAILING: The **El Conquistador** and **Westin Río Mar** both operate services.

KAYAKING: In Las Croabas, **Caribe Kayak** (☎ 787-889-7734) run night trips to the great bioluminescent **Laguna Grande** as well as day trips around the mangroves.

FISHING: Tropical Fishing & Tournaments (☎ 787-266-4524) operates from the **El Conquistador**.
http://www.tropicalfishingcharters.com

You may also try **Roulette Charters** (☎ 787-850-7442) in Humacao.

Light Tackle Paradise (☎ 787-874-2294, 787-646-2585), at Villa Marina runs fishing trips and fly-fishing classes.

Shiraz Fishing Charters (☎ 787-285-5718; Villa Station, Suite #164, Fajardo) operate deep sea fishing trips as well as snorkeling by request. They also run out of Palmas del Mar.
http://www. www.charternet.com/fishers/shiraz

HANG GLIDING: Team Spirit (☎ 787-850-0508) offer courses as well as trips for qual-

ified individuals.The glides take place around El Yunque.
http://www.mailways.net/teamspirit
tshg@coqui.net

HORSEBACK RIDING: Palaminos Ranch (☎ 787-760-8585) will take you riding on this Conquistador-controlled island. Rates are around $55 pp for the hour ride which offers great views.

FROM FAJARDO: For information about excursions by boat, see the "Vicinity of San Juan" section. *Públicos* for Luquillo, Río Piedras, Juncos, Humacao, etc. leave from the *publicó* station which is within walking distance of the town plaza. **note:** Ferry departures may have increased by the time of your arrival. For information/reservations, call 863-0705/0852 or 800-981-2005. In case you wish to bring a car across, ferries also take cargo. Buy your ticket at the window to the R. Go around through the gate and to your L.

Culebra y Vieques Restaurant is near the loading dock. Other places to eat are nearby, along with a PO and pay phones. If you need to park a car, secure parking is around $3 pd.

FOR CULEBRA: The passenger ferry departs Mon. to Fri. at 930 AM and at 3 PM. ($2.25, 1.5 hrs.). Sat., Sun., and holidays, departures are at 7 AM, 2 PM, and 5:30 PM, and ferries leave at 8 AM and 2:30. PM. A cargo ferry also runs. **Vieques Air Link** (☎ 787-863-3366) flies to Culebra.
http://www.vieques-island.com

FOR VIEQUES: Ferries ($2, take 1 h. for cargo ferry; 1.5 hr. for cargo ferry.) leave Mon. to Fri. at 7 and on Sat. and Sun. at 9, 3, and 6. A cargo ferry also runs. **Vieques Air Link** (☎ 787-863-3366) also flies daily.
http://www.vieques-island.com

FOR ICACOS: Rent a sailboat or sail your own to this deserted island. Camping permitted.

Cabezas de San Juan Nature Reserve
(Reserva Natural de las Cabezas de San Juan)

Purchased in 1975 by the Conservation Trust for $5.7 million, the 316-acre *Las Cabezas de San Juan* Nature Reserve lies on the island's NE tip. It comprises a number of different ecological communities including mangroves, coral reefs, a dry forest and a series of lagoons; the largest lagoon (Laguna Grande) is seasonally phosphorescent. This wide variety of ecosystems in such a small area is part of what makes the reserve so special. It is the only place on the island where all but one of Puerto Rico's natural communities (the rainforest) can be viewed in a single area. The neoclassical restored lighthouse, El Faro, was constructed at the end of the 19th century. Formerly operated and still owned by the US Coast Guard, it now serves as a visitor's center and educational museum. It houses a nature exhibit, a small aquarium, and an observation deck with views of El Yunque and the USVI. It has been restored using 19th-century techniques. http://www.fideicomiso.org

VISITING THE RESERVE: Reservations (☎ 787-722-5882, 787-860-2560 on weekends) are required. Admission is $5 for adults and $2 for children under 12. Wheelchair access is limited. Guided tours are offered daily at several times, but tours in English are available only at 2. A trolley takes you through the reserve, thus limiting environmental impact. There's a gift shop. To get here take Carr. 26 from San Juan to Carr. 3. where you head E towards Carolina and take the first Fajardo exit. Make a L from Carr. 3 onto Carr. 194. Turn L at the traffic light on the corner of the Monte Brisas Shopping Center and then turn R at the next traffic light. Continue until you hit Carr. 987 where you turn L and head straight until you reach the reserve.

Getting to Vieques and Culebra

You may fly from San Juan Isla Grande, San Juan International, Fajardo, or St. Croix (Vieques only). Flights from International cost more than flights from Isla Grande. Charter flights are also available from San Juan to Culebra or Vieques. It costs about $20 for a taxi between the two airports. Check specific "getting here" sections for information.

A taxi (metered) to Fajardo will probably run you about $70. The maximum number of passengers is five. It may also be possible to reserve a taxi in advance for around $50.

If you have more than two people, you might find it economical to charter a van to the Fajardo airport or ferry. Leaseway (787- 860-5000, 1-800-468-2647) rents a one-way vehicle from $25 to $60 (minivan), plus insurance ($14-$22) and a drop charge of $25-$60. The will take you to the ferry or airport from their Fajardo office. You may do this in reverse. Other companies also offer this service.

Finally, if you are a bit adventurous, the públicos (shared taxis) are a great way to get from San Juan to Fajardo and onward to Vieques and Culebra via ferry. You need to take a taxi or bus to the Río Piedras terminal. Try to get one which runs to the "playa," so you will not have to transfer in town. Allow a few hours in order to make sure that you arrive in time.

Set seven miles off the eastern coast of Puerto Rico, Vieques, a very special island possesses its own distinct magic. Its name comes from the Taíno word *bieques* ("small island"). Its nickname, La Isla Neña (Daughter Island), refers to its relationship with the main island. Horses roam freely all over the island, which once hosted pineapple and sugar plantations and more than 50 magnificent beaches. Its rainy season runs from August. to Nov., and you can expect storms from June to Nov.

Undoubtedly, Vieques would have become one of the major tourist destinations in the Caribbean were it not for the fact that over 70% of its 26,000 acres was arbitrarily confiscated by the US military in 1948 (see "history.").

Regrettably, the guise of National Security prevents the Navy from announcing when it is they will bomb. Pro- and anti-Navy elements are both present, and you'll note that *fuera la marina* is frequently stenciled on buildings.

Although General Electric ("War is our most important product") has established a plant here, the promises remain largely unfulfilled. The government remains the largest employer. Today, aside from tourism, there is little employment here, and welfare continues to be a major source of income.

The military occupation continues to thwart development as well as the full utilization of the island's many resources. The military claims that the bombing is still needed and that the idea of troops landing as an amphibious force under air cover (something that has not happened since the Korean War) is a probability. Retired Admiral Eugene Carroll, Vice President of the Center for Defense Information, disputes this claim. He says that it would be too costly in lives.

FESTIVALS AND EVENTS: A **cultural festival** is held in the Fortín in Isabel Segunda (☎ 787-741-1717 for information) every March or April. It features music, theater, and a book and craft fair.

Paired with the local carnival, the *fiestas patronales* are celebrated in mid-July.

Taking place on Isabel Segunda's plaza in Nov., **El Festival de las Arepas** glorifies the local johnnycakes.

HISTORY: The island was originally known as Bieques by its aboriginal inhabitants, but the first Spanish referred to it and neighboring islands as "Las Islas Inutiles" (The Useless Isles). The presence of land crabs caused the island to be dubbed Crab Island by the buccaneers. The Taínos here led revolts against the Spanish, but were even-

URL Vieques Web Sites
http://www.vieques-island.com
http://www.enchantedisles.com
http://www.elenas-vieques.com
http://www.islavieques.com
http://www.viequeslibre.org

tually subdued, and captives were shipped to Puerto Rico.

First explored in 1524 by Capt. Cristóbal de Mendoza, former governor of Puerto Rico, Vieques was occupied at various times by the British and French. It was established as a municipality in 1843, and construction of a fort began built that same year. It was formally annexed by Puerto Rico in 1854. Sugarcane became the major crop and, at its peak, the island had four *centrales*, large sugar mills that processed 20,000 tons of sugar annually.

In 1898, the gunboat *Yale* arrived, and Lt. Cont and his detachment landed. Tensions eased after it was realized that Cont and his men had no intention of eating babies as had been rumored and greatly feared. After the colonel commanding the Fortín explained that he could not surrender without firing a shot, Cont gracefully allowed him to fire off a volley.

As sugarcane continued to rise in price, the population grew — rising to 11,651 in 1920. Working conditions began to improve after a 1915 general strike. And Vieques became known as "sugar island." The sugar economy began to decline during the 1930s. One project brought work for a brief period during the 1940s. The US government expropriated 70% of the island in 1940, and Roosevelt set out to make Vieques the "Pearl Harbor of the Caribbean." The Navy promised to return the land as soon as the war was over.

Although Pearl Harbor would later serve to discredit the concept, a sea wall was planned which would stretch from Culebra on the N to Vieques on the SE to Roosevelt Roads on the main island. Fleets would be concentrated here. Work on a breakwater that would have harbored the British fleet (should the Germans have taken the UK) proceeded day and night. The Navy abruptly stopped work after it became strategically unnecessary.

Over the decades, locals have suffered much at the hands of the Navy. Noise from air and sea target bombardment, annoying in itself, was devastating when coupled with the structural damage to buildings and the dramatic decrease in the fishing catch caused by sea pollution.

In 1948 the US Navy, acting on a 1942 authorization, took control of two-thirds of the island. An average of $47 per acre was paid out to eight owners for 21,000 acres where subtenants were living. Of the tenant farmers, 3,000 out of the 9,000 either left the island on their own initiative or were resettled on St. Croix. Some 4,000 were relocated elsewhere on Vieques. Population plummeted from 14,000 in 1941 to the present 9,000. Many left to find work in San Juan, St. Croix, or elsewhere.

At the end of the 1940s, 4,000 acres were put under the control of the Puerto Rican Agricultural Development Company (PRACO), which began cattle and dairy farming, egg production, and coconut and pineapple plantations. Employment rose, but PRACO was replaced by the Land Authority of Puerto Rico in 1955, an agency which leases excess land to be used by a few landowners who have herds of Brahman cattle.

US President John F. Kennedy proposed to take over the entire island in 1961. Locals were to leave. Their ancestors were to leave with them. The cemeteries were to be emp-

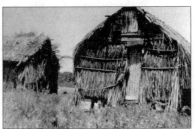

Vieques homes during the turn of the century

tied because there would be no grave visitations allowed. Gov. Luis Muñoz pointed out that the cemetery disinterments would provide Fidel with great propaganda, and the plan was dropped. However, the bombing continued, with an average of 3,400 bombs exploding each month for decades.

In 1971, Puerto Rican Independence Party leader Rubén Martinez Berriós helped organize a "beach-in." Berriós and supporters were arrested for their nonviolent protest, and he spent three months in jail.

On Feb. 6, 1978, 30 fishing boats protested joint exercises held between Brazil and the US, halting them for some hours. In 1975, Gov. Hernández Colón sought an injunction against the Navy's use of the Vieques Weapons Range. Millions of dollars in legal fees later, the Vieques Accord was reached on Oct. 12, 1983. The Navy promised to create more jobs by attracting defense contractors, to reduce the size of its firing range, and to allow part of its land to be used for a forestry project that would grow 100 acres of mahogany trees. (These were later cut for a radar installation). Vieques was the site of a rehearsal for the 1983 Grenada invasion.

Decade after decade, the protest movement has gained support. One single event finally catalyzed the government into active opposition. Protest was mobilized by the April 19, 1999 death of David Sanes Rodríguez, an employee who was killed by two wayward 500-ton bomb dropped from an F-18 fighter jet. The Catholic Church joined activists to mobilize against continuing the bombings, causing politicians to line up behind them. A huge demonstration was mounted on Feb. 21, 2000. Even Gov. Pedro Rosselló began mouthing the slogan "Not one more bomb!"

A police riot squad peacefully evicted the protestors from the Camp Garcia grounds on May 4, 2000. Those arrested included US Rep. Nydia Velásquez (D-New York), New York Sate Assemblyman Roberto Ramirez, and NYC Councilman Juan Rivera. Famous

for her role in the 1954 armed protest at the US House of Representatives, Lolita Lebrón, 80, was also arrested.

After the rabid Republicans began attacking the protest movement, Rosselló was summoned to the Clinton White House. An agreement emerged in which the US would pay $40 million in compensation to the island's inhabitants for a further three more years of bombing using so-called "inert" ammunition. A planned referendum will allow the Navy to once again use live bombs. If this live ammo use is restored, the Navy would pay another $50 million in "benefits." The move did not win clerical support. Even right-wing evangelist Jorge Raske called the deal "an immoral act of abuse of power."

Protests escalated in 2001. Vocalist Ricky Martin, Miss Universe Denise Quiñones August, actor Benecio del Toro, and boxer Felix Trinidad joined the opposition. Robert F. Kennedy was imprisoned for participating in protests as was the Rev. Al Sharpton, who embarked on a badly needed hunger strike. Kennedy's sixth child was born while he was in jail, and was christened Aidan Caohman Vieques Kennedy. In June, Jesse Jackson met with Gov. Sila Calderón after his wife was arrested in a demonstration.

In early August 2001, 53 people were arrested for trespassing on Navy land.These included independence leader 73-year-old Juan Mari Bras, his son and his grandson were arrested Monday several hours after they entered Navy land.

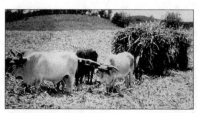

Harvesting sugarcane in Vieques in the 1950s

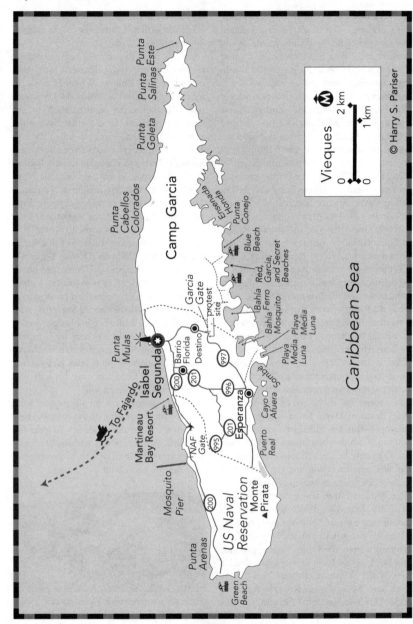

© Harry S. Pariser

Unfortunately, the Sept. 11, 2001 attack on the World Trade Center in New York City dealt a setback to the drive to remove the Navy.

Congress passed legislation in Dec. 2001 which would stop the Navy secretary from leaving Vieques until a site was secured which would provide "equivalent or superior" levels of training.

In early Jan. 2002, a federal judge dismissed Puerto Rico's lawsuit to stop the federal government from resuming Navy bombing exercises. Judge Kessler dismissed the case "for lack of subject matter jurisdiction." She said the federal Noise Control Act "does not provide plaintiff a cause of action to sue in federal district court for the violations alleged."

In April 2002, U.S. Magistrate Gustavo Gelpi sentenced anti-U.S. Navy activist Robert Rabin to six months in prison for trespassing on Navy land in Vieques. Gelpi maintained that his decision rested on the national state of emergency declared by the U.S. government after the Sept. 11 terrorist attacks. Rabin replied that, although federal authorities "want to apply the antiterrorism law...they have the dilemma of facing a peaceful force. Each bomb will be answered by civil disobedience," he said.

FLORA AND FAUNA: Brown pelicans, other birds, and leatherback and hawksbill turtles are found on the island.

GETTING HERE: It's a bumpy but beautiful hour-long trip by launch from Fajardo. Pass by Isleta Marina, Palaminos, Lobos, Isla de Ramos, and other small islands. Ferries ($2, take 1.5 hrs) leave Mon. to Fri. at 9:30 AM, 1, 3, and 4:30 PM and on Sat. and Sun. at 9 AM, 3, and 6 PM. A cargo ferry also runs. To get to Fajardo, you can either take a *público* (around $10) or charter a taxi (about $50).

BY AIR: Vieques Air Link (☎ 787-722-3736, 787-723-9882) flies from San Juan's Isla Grande daily, as well as from Fajardo and St. Croix.
http://www.vieques-island.com

Isla Nena (☎ 888-263-6213) flies from the International airport.
http:/www.islanena.8m.com

GETTING AROUND: There is limited *público* service from Isabel Segunda to Esperanza. Rates are $2 pp, and you can also arrange with drivers to pick you up at a specified time and to give you a tour. Hitchiking is possible.

CAR RENTALS: Contact **Dreda & Fonsin's Rent-a-Car** (☎ 787-741-8397/8163; Box 243, Vieques, PR 00765), C. AG Mellado 333; **Steve's Car Rentals** (☎ 787-741-8135, cell 787-593-9618); **Island Car Rentals** (☎ 787-741-1666; Box 423, Vieques, PR 00765) on Carr. 201 next to Crow's Nest; **Vieques Car Rental** (☎ 787-741-8691) and **Marcos' Car Rentals** (Bo. Montesantos, ☎ 787-741-1388), **Mario Acabá Car Rental** (Bo. Montesantos, ☎787-741-2394) **Diaz Car Rentals** (☎ 787-741-8163), **Maritza Car Rental** (Carr. 201 Bo. Florida, ☎ 787-741-0078), and **Vieques Car & Jeep Rental** (☎ 787-741-1037).
http://www.viequescarrental.com

Isabel Segunda

Founded in 1843, Isabel Segunda is named after Spain's Isabel II, who ruled from 1833-68. This small town has the feel of a village. Locals ride horses through the main streets while dogs sleep placidly under cars. Although none too attractive, the town does have a number of flamboyant trees which bloom in season. The town plaza has a bust of Simon Bolivar, who paid a visit to Vieques in 1816, a 19th-century city hall, and a antique church.

ISABEL SEGUNDA SIGHTS: There's not much to see in the town itself. The major thing to see is undoubtedly **Fortín Conde de Mirasol**, which dominates the town. The last Spanish bastion (1843) undertaken in the Caribbean, this fort was never finished. To get here turn R at the Muñoz Rivera Plaza and follow the hill up.

Under the leadership of curator Robert Rabin, the fort has been meticulously restored with beautifully finished wooden staircases, cannon, etc., and now serves as a small museum. It's open Wed. to Sun. from 10 AM–4 PM($2 admission).

The stunning panoramic views from the fortress windows and terraces would alone be reason enough to visit. Puerto Rico and Culebra are visible as are vistas of the lush surroundings around Isabel Segunda.

Inside are exhibits relating to the indigenous peoples and archaeological digs on the island, agricultural tools, old maps, and the effects of the US military occupation and bombing on the island. There is also a splendid collection of artwork relating to the Vieques Libre struggle. Their gift shop is also well worth checking out.

OTHERS: On the main square is the **Casa Alcaldía de Vieques** (C. Carlos Le Brun at C. Benítez Guzmán), which dates from around 1845 and is still in use.

El Faro de Punta Mulas (☎ 787-741-0060) is right in town. Built in 1896, this white-painted stone lighthouse has a reflector (built in Paris in 1895) whose beam may be seen from as far as 16 miles away. It has a small museum.

Casa Delerme is an old house at C. Muñoz Rivera and C. A Mellado, built in the 1850s. The second house of the owner, **Casa de Augusto Delerme**, is at C. Benítez Guzmán 7 and dates from the same era. Both are private residences.

Davies Base is just outside town.

OUTLYING SIGHTS: Camp García Base was once the place to go for beaches. At the entrance you would obtain permission to visit the beautiful and isolated Red, Yellow and Blue beaches, imaginatively named by the Navy (and described below in case you visit when entry has been cleared).

Meanwhile, you may visit the protest encampment at the Camp Garcia Gate which is your opportunity to participate in history (Robert Rabin, one of the movement leaders, dubs it "antimilitourism." Before the military drove off the protesters, he maintains, "local businesses never had it so good.")

Red Beach is near **García Beach,** which has a cave and and has popular with nudists. Never officially named, **Secret Beach** lies off a road between Red and Blue. It has great snorkeling. At the E end of the road, **Blue Beach** is popular with Puerto Ricans during the Easter vacation. **Purple Beach** is on the NE coast and is accessed by the same road.

Spectacular **Green Beach** is in the former Naval Reservation to the NW; sand gnats here can be a pain. It has great snorkeling at the S tip of the beach, about 20 ft. offshore. Be sure to snorkel off the pier as well. It is like a miniature aquarium. You'll find plenty of starfish, bristleworms, sea urchins, and a multitude of fish. It's superb for beginners because the area right by the pier is relatively shallow. Beaches also stretch along the road between town and the airport to the W. **Gringo Beach** (good snorkeling offshore) is now graced with the **Martineau Bay Resort**.

According to legend, a 16th-century island chief hid the sacred treasures of his tribe from the *conquistadores* in a large cave at the top of **Mt. Pirata**, highest point on the island. The roar you hear inside the cave is his ghost. The peak is in the island's W, in land relinquished by the Navy. It's a steep drive straight up to near the summit where you will find a locked gate.

From Vieques, you can continue on to St. Croix with Vieques Air Link (☎ 787-863-3020).

Archaeological digs are being conducted at **La Hueca**.

Mosquito, the long pier on the isolated NW coast, was built to shelter the British fleet in the event England fell to Germany in WWII. Once used to load sugar cane for transport to Puerto Rico, it is now used to bring supplies from Roosevelt Roads.

The **Vieques Conservation and Historical Trust** (Box 1472, Vieques, PR 00765), a local conservation group, is endeavoring to preserve **Puerto Mosquito**, one of the world's last phosphorescent (bioluminscent) bays. See "Excursions" in the Esperanza section for information.

Isabel Segunda Practicalities

ACCOMMODATIONS: There are a few small but not especially cheap hotels in town.

Set on the N Shore Rd. past the ferry landing and the lighthouse, **Water's Edge** (☎ 787-741-1128, ☐ 787-741-0690; Box 1374, Vieques, PR 00765) is the top in-town pick. It is comfortable yet laid back. The oceanfront location means that you can open your window and let the tradewinds cool you or use the fan or a/c. The (unswimmable but most attractive) beach is just a few steps from the pool.

Rooms have fans and a/c, cable TV, balconies, and (mostly superfluous) mosquito nets. Rates run from around $76.30 d to $150 d (includes tax). The villa is $300 pn or $1800 for the week.

Its gourmet **Oasis Restaurant** is one of the best in town. There's also a two-bedroom luxury villa ($1,800 and $2,500 pw) for rent. It has a private pool, sun deck, and laundry facilities.
http://www.watersedgeguesthouse.com
h2oedge@coqui.net

Near the entrance to town from Esperanza and the Airport, the **Tropical Guesthouse** (☎ 787-741-2449) offers clean but simple rooms for $50 s, $75 d.

The 35-room a/c **Ocean View** (☎ 787-741-3696/2175, ☐ 787-741-0545; Box 124, Vieques, PR 00765) is on Plinio Peterson just minutes on foot from the ferry terminal. Rates start from $65 d. Two-rm. suites (hold four) are $75. It has a Chinese restaurant.

NEAR TOWN: Set on a hilltop in Barricada Fuerte and commanding a spectacular view, the 16-room **Sea Gate** (☎ 787-741-4661, ☐ 787-741-2978; Box 747, Vieques, PR 00765) is run by the Miller family. They offer free transport to and from the airport and ferry, to and from Sun Bay, or to and from Red Beach. Rates run from $45 to $60 per room. They also have a cottage ($80) which can sleep four. It is, however, not for caninephobes: the Millers have a number of dogs.
http://www.seagatehotel.com
seagate@coqui.net

Offering 16 large a/c rooms with kitchenettes and patios or balconies, the **Crow's Nest** (☎ 787-741-0033, 877-276-9763, ☐ 787-741-1294), Carr. 201 at Km 1.6, has a swimming pool, gazebo, bar and restaurant. A rec room has TV/VCR, games, and a library. Complimentary continental breakfast served daily. Rates run around $90-$360 d plus 9% tax.
http://www.crowsnestvieques.com
thenest@coqui.net

Owned by the same people who run Casa Cubuy near El Yunque, **Adventures Inn** (☎

787-741-1564), Monte Santo, is a five min. drive from Isabel Segunda and a ten min. walk to the beach. Rates are around $70 d; $15 a'ddl. A one-bedroom unit (sleeps four) rents for around $100 pn. All are a/c with bath and quite comfortable.

http://www.east-net.net/cubuy/vieques.html
adventuresinn@casacubuy.com

LA FINCA CARIBE: A spacious, fully furnished six-bedroom guesthouse set on five acres of land in the Pilón area, **La Finca Caribe** (☎ 787-741-0495, ✆ 787-741-3584; Apdo 1332, Vieques, PR 00765) is set on a hillside three miles from the nearest beach. It began life as a women's retreat and is now run by expatriate Alaskans.. Simple and very practical in its construction, one of the nicest things about the house is its integration with nature. Small lizards come right in to visit you and birds nest by the porch. At night you have the 360° orchestral symphony of nature surrounding you. The first floor consists of a kitchen, dining, and patio/living area. There's a comfortable hammock and chairs and tables on the porch, a completely equipped large kitchen (refrigerators, microwave, range, oven, spices), washing machine, pool, a library, stereo, and large bulletin boards. Each of the six rooms has a loft and queensized bed. There is also a *casita* and a *cabaña*. You may rent the entire house ($3,200 pw) and external buildings, just the house, or stay in a guest room (around $65 pn).

http://www.lafinca.com
info@lafinca.com

MARTINEAU BAY: The **Martineau Bay** (☎ 787-741-4100) resort is at Gringo Beach. It has two restaurants, the Paso Fino and the poolside Isla Neña. Originally planned to be a Rosewood Resort, it is now independent. Opening is expected in 2003. The adjacent 32-rm. **Hacienda Trópico** is expected to open in 2003.

RENTALS: Connections (☎ 787-741-0023, 800-772-3050; ✆ 787-741-1228; Box 358, Vieques, PR 00765) is one major agency; it is located next to the Crow's Nest in Barrio Florida. They have an extensive list of rentals.

Also contact **Island Vacations Rentals** (☎ 741-1666; Box 1508, Vieques, PR 00765) and **Villa Estrella** (☎ 787-741-1228).

Mango Vieques (☎ 787-741-0292) is set at Monte Santo near the center of the island. It is a second-floor two-bedroom apartment with kitchen, dining room, and great views.

http://www.mangovieques.com
mangoInfo@mangovieques.com

Two-bedroom **Villa Vista Bella** (☎ 800-346-4205, 603-745-3365) sits atop a hill overlooking Isabel Segunda, with a panoramic view .The villa is completely furnished and has a pool. Write Tony McCann at the Kancamagus Motor Lodge, Pollard Road, Lincoln, New Hampshire 03251. *Other listings are found under Esperanza.*

HIX ISLAND HOUSE: Also in Barrio Pilón, **Hix Island House** (☎ 787-741-2302) is on Carr. 995 near the junction with Carr. 201. This attractive guesthouse has rooms with kitchens and yoga classes.

http://www.hixislandhouse.com
hixisle@coqui.net

FOOD: One of the chief gourmet restaurants in town, **Café Media Luna** (☎ 787-741-2594, ✆ 787-741-3068) is set in an attractive old building at 351 AG Mellado in town. It is run by the amiable Ricardo and Monica. Its menu combines Latin, French, Indian and Asian cuisines.

Wai Nam Restaurant is in the **Ocean View**; it has lunch specials and is open daily, serving Chinese fast food, beer, and ice cream to the tune of salsa.

Vieques

VIEQUES

© Harry S. Pariser

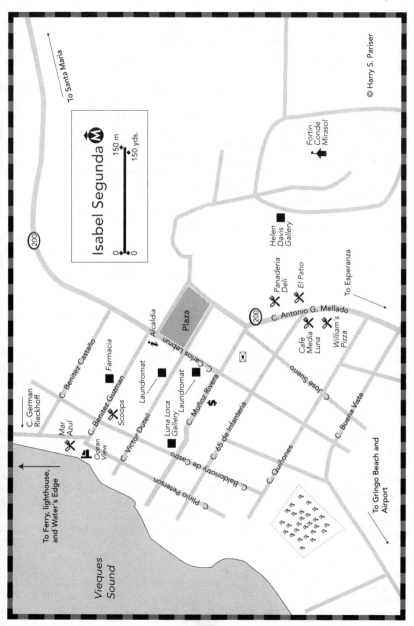

195

Near the plaza, **Taverna Española** serves dishes such as *cazuela de mariscos* (seafood stew) and paella. Service can be slow.

Right near the ferry, **Café Mar Azul** is a popular *gringo* hangout which has good inexpensive food.

Also near the ferry, **Cafeteria El Serrucho** sells cheap sandwiches. It is open before ferry departure in the morning.

El Puerto serves local food.

Located above the fish shop, **Johan's Bar & Restaurant** offers fresh fish, conch, and lobster.

The Green Palace (seafood and daily specials) and **Willam's Pizza**, both on C. AG Mellado, serve pizza.

In the Centro Commercial, **Nelson's Café** has burritos and tacos.

Near the road to the airport, the a/c **Richard's Café** serves a variety of seafood dishes.

Tradewinds has the **Oasis**, a gourmet restaurant with a popular Sunday brunch.

NEAR TOWN: On the ocean at Playa Monte Santo to the W, the **Vieques Country Club** (☎ 787-741-1863) serves meat and seafood lunches and dinners in the open air.

In Barrio Florida, the **Crow's Nest** has the **Island Cafe** (☎ 787-741-0033). It's on Carr. 201 at Km 1.6.

Nearby, **The Galley** serves lunches daily; they specialize in pizza.

BAKERIES AND SNACKS: Panadería y Repostería Candy, C. AG Mellado 352, has breakfasts and sandwiches in addition to baked goods. Open daily from 5, **Panadería y Repostería Lydia**, C. Benitez Guzmán, also has sandwiches.

The largest supermarket in town is **Supermercado Portela**, C. Baldorioty 15. **Supermercado Morales** is just outside town in Barrio Monte Santo.

It's a good idea to reserve a rental car before arriving on Vieques or Culebra.

SERVICES: Right inside the *Alcaldía* (City Hall) on the main square, the tourism department (☎ 787-741-5000) has some information. Be sure to try and find a copy of **The Vieques Times** — a valuable resource.

http://www.viequestimes.com
vqsstimes@coqui.net

You might also try to find a copy of the **Vieques Visitors Guide**, which has some useful information. And the Vieques Map, a free map published annually by Whizzbang Designs, is also quite useful.

http://www.capecodislandhouse.com/Map2001.html

For taxis and tours contact **Vieques Tours** (☎ 787-741-8640). **Vieques Laundromat & Dry Cleaner** is on C. Victor Duteil.

The **Banco Popular**, C. Muñoz Rivera, has an ATM. The **post office** is nearby.

For your health care needs, **Grupo Médico Familiar del Este** (☎ 787-741-8569) is at C. Muñoz Rivera 112. Centro de Salud de la Familia (☎ 787-741-2151) is just S of Isabel Segunda along Carr. 997, and **Farmacia Libertad** and **Farmacia San Antonio** are on C. AG Mellado.

SHOPPING: Open from 9:30 AM–1 PM from Mon. to Sat., **Galería Isabela** is a small craft shop behind the PO.

The **Second Time Around**, a thrift shop at 558 Plinio Peterson, sells a lot of intriguing items. Their motto is "If we don't have it today, try tomorrow."

Zona Tropical sells reggae T-shirts.

A shop across from the post office sells **tee shirts**.

LOCAL SPECIALTIES: The **Miel Isla Niña** ($7 for 2.5 lbs.) produced by the **Vieques Bee Farm** (☎ 787-741-2132 for tours).

ENTERTAINMENT: A popular watering hole, **Café Mar Azul** is set right on the ocean in town. For those craving a bit of blood and gore, **cockfighting** takes place at a mid-island arena, on Sun. afternoons during the winter months.

Outside of town on Carr. 995, **Chez Shack** (☎ 787-741-2175) serves good food and has live music.

EXCURSIONS: In addition to the activities listed under Esperanza, **Water's Edge Guest House** (☎ 787-741-1128, ☻ 787-741-3918) will hook you up with activities. **rehillism@aol.com**

Esperanza

This is the island's second largest community. Taxis (around $3) meet arriving ferries. In addition to beaches, there're also dive shops and night excursions to the phosphorescent bay. It is quite easy to spend a few days or more here and still find things to do.

SIGHTS AND BEACHES: The 1963 film *Lord of the Flies* was filmed here; you can still see the hangar-like structure now incorporated into the grounds of a folded government-sponsored parador that remains. There's a *balneario* at Sunbe (Sun Bay) beach, a long, gorgeous stretch of palm trees and placid ocean.

Hike to **Navio** and **Media Luna** beaches nearby. While Playa Media Luna has little surf and resembles a giant swimming pool, Playa Navio is a bit more turbulent. Although conditions here can be ideal for body surfing, the undertow is vicious so take care. One trail off of Media Luna goes to a cove with coral formations and a salt-water pond popular with seabirds.

Crossing a promontory between Media Luna and Navio, another trail terminates at a boulder-strewn cliff with a great lookout point. Be sure to wear long pants on this trail or face the consequences.

The **Vieques Historical and Conservation Trust** (☎ 787-741-8850) operates the **Museo de Esperanza** here. Open Tues. through Sun. from 11-3, it features an archaeological exhibit as well as two aquariums. There's a gift shop, and their reforestation program distributes free trees.

The **Indian Burial Site** is off Carr. 997 to the E. The site is fenced off.

Carr. 997 has "cow" warning signs which advise drivers to watch for cows or horses.

Esperanza Practicalities

ACCOMMODATIONS: It's possible to camp at the *balneario* at Sun Bay ($4 per tent). Note, however, that this beach is notorious for thieves — *never* leave anything unattended.

Posada Vistamar (☎ 787-741-8716; Box 495, Vieques, PR 00765) has small rooms with private baths for around $65 d. It is one block from the water, atop a hill at the W end of C. Almendro. It has great *criollo* food.

Banana's (☎ 787-741-8700, ☻ 787-741-0790; Box 1300, Vieques, PR 00765) is another small guesthouse with an attached restaurant. Simple rooms have a/c or fans. **Rates** run from around $50-$60 d pd.

Amapola Inn and Tavern (☎ 787-741-1382, ☻:787-741-3704), is on the main stretch at C. Flamboyan 144, and charges around $65-$75 d for a/c rooms. **http://www.enchanted-isle.com/amapola**

The **Trade Winds Guesthouse** (☎ 787-741-8666; Box 1012, Vieques, PR 00765) has rooms for around $60-75 d on up and offers great breakfasts. It has been recommended by readers. **tradewns@coqui.net**

Good snorkeling is found off of Cayo Afuera, across the way from Esperanza.

Casa Cielo (☎ 787-741-2403) is a six-acre retreat with great views, pool, and gazebo bar. It charges from $175–$225 d, and the entire house may be rented. It is currently for sale, so it may or may not be available as a guesthouse for long!
http://www.enchanted-isle.com/casacielo
cielo@coqui.net

Set in an old plantation house which is a historical monument, **La Casa del Frances** (☎ 787-741-3751/0717, ☻ 787-741-2330; Box 458, Vieques, PR 00765), on Carr. 996, has 18 rooms, a private pool, and restaurant. Room rates start at around $155 s or $180 d including tax and service. Some rooms will hold up to six.
http://www.enchanted-isle.com/lacasa

La Piña Vacation Apartments (☎/☻ 787-741-2953; C. Acacia 222, Vieques, PR 00765) is another alternative. Rates run around $60 and up.

Inexpensive but spartan **Betty's Guest House** is behind Bananas.

The **Chateau Esperanza Guest House and Cafeteria** (☎ 787-741-8722/2294; Box 204, Vieques, PR 00765) has three rooms (holding up to three persons each) for around $30.

The spartan **Guest House Ruiz** (☎ 787-741-3296) charges around $30 s and $55 for four in a room.

Nicknamed the **Chateau Relaxo**, a house at the corner of C. Magnolia and C. Robles offers rooms for around $50/wk. The owners also sell fish downstairs and cut hair.

The 16-unit **Hacienda Tamarindo** (☎ 787-741-8525, ☻ 787-741-3215; Apdo. 1569, Vieques, PR 00765), Carr. 996 at Km. 4.5 on Vieques, may be distinguished by the large tamarind tree, which rises through its center atrium. Rooms and common area are imaginatively designed with collected art and antiques. Rooms have either a/c or fan. Children should be over 12. The hotel commands great views. Rates are from around $155–$225 d; a full breakfast is included. Service (10%) and room tax (9%) is added.
http://www.enchantedisle.com/tamarindo

Sandwiched between La Hueca and Esperanza, the **Inn on the Blue Horizon** (☎ 787-741-3318, ☻ 787-741-0522; Box 1556, Vieques, PR 00765) has four villas set on 20 acres. Only two rooms have a/c, there are no TVs or phones in the rooms, and breakfast is included The atmosphere is one of casual elegance, and a lot of thought has gone into the rooms. It charges around $150–300 d.
http://www.innonthebluehorizon.com

RENTALS: Contact **Vieques Villa Rentals** (☎ 787-741-8888; C. Gladiolas 494). The latter has a wide variety of rentals ranging from coastal homes to ones commanding views from the inland heights.

The **Acacia Apartments** (☎ 787-741-1856), C. Acacia, has four apartments.
http://www.enchanted-isle.com/
ByOwner/acacia.htm
AcaciaApts@aol.com

FOOD: The **Villa Posada Parador** has delicious, authentic Puerto Rican dishes (like fish *asopao*). Fresh, piping-hot traditional Puerto Rican bread is available early mornings at **Gerena Bakery**. **Colmado Lydia**, next door, is well stocked with provisions. There are a number of **food trucks** here with local dishes. **La Tienda Verde**, C. Robles, also sells groceries.

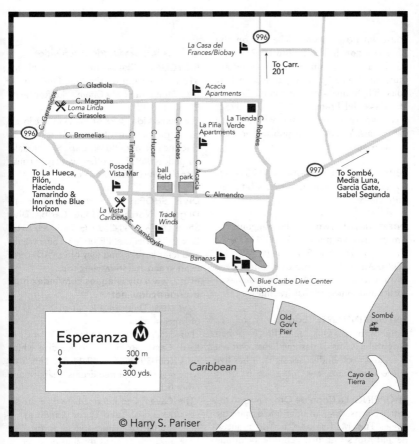

The scale bar reads:

Esperanza ☉

0 ——— 300 m
0 ——— 300 yds.

Caribbean

© Harry S. Pariser

The Esperanza (☎ 787-741-8675) serves three meals daily and offers special activities such as a Wed. cookout and a Thurs. hermit crab race.

Kathleen's serves dishes such as falafel, *quesadillas*, and conch fritters daily from noon–5 PM.

El Quenepo (☎ 787-741-8541) serves seafood and Puerto Rican dishes.

The **Trade Winds** has a restaurant that offers seafood dishes and fresh fruit.

Bananas has good food, including pizza, in a terrace atmosphere.

Comidas China, a greasy spoon on the main drag, has dishes like Chicken Cordon Bleu. Here, you can eat in the "dinning hall" and have ice cream in flavors such as "chery-vainilla."

Other places to eat include **La Concha** and **El Gringo Viejo.**

Set on the hillside of La Huce, two miles W of Esperanza, **La Campesina** (☎ 787-741-1239) is open 6:30–9:30 PM from

Wed. to Sun. It serves grilled items.

OUTLYING HOTEL DINING: The **Inn on the Blue Horizon** has **Café Blu** (☎ 787-741-3318), a locally-famous gourmet restaurant, which also has a "Cigar Tree" where you can light up a stinky and imbibe Port.

La Casa del Frances (☎ 787-741-3751) serves gourmet food made with tropical ingredients. You may dine poolside or in the dining room.

SERVICES: Zoraida Morales (☎ 787-741-6031), C. Magnolias 425, offers **babysitting** services.

ENTERTAINMENT: Two popular hangouts are **Amapola Tavern** (☎ 787-741-1382), C. Flamboyan 144, and **Bananas** (☎ 787-741-8700). Amapola is more of a sports scene (with a wide-screen TV) while Bananas is livelier and sometimes has live music.

ENTERTAINMENT: Eddie's is on C. Flamboyan at Orquidea. **El Trapezon Oriental** has lots of flashing lights, chicken wire, and neon Budweiser signs. It has live music which starts late.

SHOPPING: **La Copa de Oro** is next to the tennis courts. A small boutique despite the name, **The Mall** is at Casa de Frances. Behind **Kim's Cabin** which offers clothing and other items, **Peppers** has spicy condiments as well as crafts.

Bali Llama is a boutique which sells clothing from Bali for men, women, and children.

Casa Vieja Gallery is out at Inn on the Blue Horizon.

Near Esperanza across from the pineapple factory, **Taller de Arte Taína** (☎ 787-741-0848) is a women's pottery workshop that recreates indigenous-style pieces. Constructing handmade works using the

tried-and-true coil method, it has operated since 1991.

Esperanza Outdoor Activities

BICYCLING: **Bike rentals** are available for $10 pd from Inn on the Blue Horizon, or from **Don't Yank My Chain Bike Rental** (☎ 787-741-3042).

La Dulce Vida (☎ 787-617-2453) are located at the bottom of the road leading to Hacienda Tamarindo on Carr. 996 at Calle Orquideas #69. They offer a variety of trips. http://www.bikevieques.com

DIVE SHOPS: Dive shops include **18 Degrees North** and **Blue Caribe Dive Shop** (☎ 787-741-2522 ☻ 787-741-1313; Box 1574, Vieques, PR 00765). Blue Caribe also rents kayaks, and they offer PADI certification and and snorkeling trips.
http://www.divevieques.com/index.htm
bcaribe@coqui.net

DIVE SITES: There are a lot of good spots off of Esperanza.

Directly S of the pier and to the W of Cayo Real, **Castle Reef** is a novice dive which runs from 30 to 35 ft. (9-11 m). This low-lying reef hosts spotted drums, snapper, and other fish.

The Caves is an intermediate dive site set near the end of Cayo Tierra (Land Cay), a long and narrow sandy spit set to the E of Esperanza which gives the illusion of being an island. This intermediate dive ranges from 25-35 ft. (7.5-11 m). Visibility is not the best, the current can be rough, and it has been damaged by storms. However, the caves host nurse sharks, croakers, and other species.

Just 15 min. by boat and 1.5 mi. (2.4 mi.) from shore, **Anchor Reef** is a novice dive named after its hallmark Spanish anchor. This ia low-lying reef, at a depth of 50 to 60 ft. (15-18 m), which has two bowl-like depressions filled with soft coral. Watch for barracuda, spider crabs, rays, and creole jacks.

Doughnut Reef is a shallow patch which is around a half-hr. and three mi. (4.8 km) to the W of Esperanza. It's a novice dive and is covered with soft coral. Watch for sailfish blenny, moray eels, and lobster.

Set two mi. (3.2 km) SW of Esperanza, **Angel Reef** is a novice dive which ranges from 40-60 ft. (12-18 m). Spur and groove formations are found here, as are two Spanish anchors which are deeply embedded in coral. Watch for grey angelfish, yellow wrasse, and fantastic soft coral including lavender sea fans.

Set 1.5 mi. (2.4 km) to the SW of Esperanza, **Patti's Reef** has a set of sand channels lined with giant elkhorn and boulder star coral. Search the holes and crevices for doctorfish, mackerels, hawkfish, and other species. This novice dive runs from 20 to 40 ft. (six to 12 m).

Set two mi. (3.2 km) to the SW of Esperanza, **Patti's Reef II** is slightly farther away from the shore. It has a pair of sandy holes which are encircled by high-rise hard coral outcrops. Watch for boulder star or mountainous star coral, soft corals such as sea fans and sea rods, and sergeant majors, butterflyfish, parrotfish, stingrays, sea cucumbers, and others.

The most distant site, **Blue Reef** is six mi. E of Esperanza and two mi. (3.2 km) S of Blue Beach. At a depth of 60-80 ft. (18-24 m), this reef has great visibility (60-100 ft) and is generally done as a drift dive. Watch for sponges and a variety of fish here.

FISHING: Lowell's Bait and Tackle (☎ 787-741-1344) rents rods and other gear and have guided trips.

The Caribbean Fly Fishing Company (☎ 787-741-1337) offers charters. They will take you fly fishing for bonefish or deep sea excursions.

El Malacrio (☎ 787-741-5012, cell 787-510-0430) also runs charters and conducts diving and snorkeling trips.

VISITING THE BIOLUMINESCENT BAY: Island Adventures (☎ 787-741-0720) offers 1.5-hr. trips ($20 pp) to the bioluminescent bay on its *La Luminosa*, an electric launch. The Feb. 2001 issue of *Travel and Leisure* listed this bay as one of the 50 "most romantic places on earth."

Just getting to the departure point is an adventure. You travel on unpaved roads, through the bush and past beaches. The bus pulls over as you rendesvous with your launch. You might feel as if you are smugglers meeting an illicit cargo or illegal immigrants meeting a departure boat.

The launch pulls off, and you head into the bay. Its narrow entrance, flanked by a coral head, helps it maintain its dinoflagellate population. There are not a lot of bays like this in the world. Two in Jamaica and one in the Bahamas were devastated by bad environmental decisionmaking. As is commonplace, the underlying interactions within the ecosystem failed to be understood. One of Jamaica's phosphorescent bay's mangroves were defoliated in order to make it more accessible; a second then had the mangroves cut. It is now realized that it *is* the mangroves which sustain the bay, because their leaves provide the nutrients which the dinoflagellates require in order to flourish. Ironically, the mangroves, through fulfilling their role as land builders, will one day doom the dinoflagellages as the lagoon turns to soil.

Worries about the current lagoon include lighting on the shore (which might cause the microorganisms to photosynthesize at night as well as day) and development. However, a growing recognition of the bay's importance, is having its effect.

Once anchored in the bay, you have the choice of either dipping your hand in a bucket and swirling it about to see the effects or donning a flotation belt and entering the water. The choice is clear.

Once in the water, swooshing with your arms and kicking with your legs produces swirls of neonlike blue color, rather like those sparklers you may have waved on a July 4th night as a child. A slimy, glowing lump may startle you and interrupt your reverie. This is a comb jelly, a harmless bioluminescent jellyfish. Catch one if you can! The coolest thing to do is to take some water in your mouth and let it trickle out.

Moonless nights are the best. For dramatic and demonic effect, ingest a bit of water and let it trickle out.

http://www.biobay.com

A very different trip is offered by **Blue Lagoon Kayaks** (Caribbean Expeditions, ☎ 787-741-0025, 787-383-8129) which offers trips to the lagoon by kayak as well as instruction and half- and full-day trips and rentals.

bluelagoonkayaks@aol.com

Agua Frenzy Kayaks (☎ 787-741-0913) offers tours of Mosquito Bay as well as kayak rentals.

Another trips is offered by **Craig** (☎ 787-741-8675). Moonless nights are best.

OTHER TRIPS: Offering day sails and moonlight cruises, the **_Arawak_** (☎ 787-741-8675) is based in Esperanza.

FROM VIEQUES: There is no service to Culebra; you must return to Fajardo first. Ferries to Fajardo run from Mon. to Fri. at 7, 11, and 3 and on Sat. and Sun. at 7, 1, and 4:30. For information call 787-741-4761.

BY AIR: **Vieques Air Link** (☎ 787-741-8331/8211) flies to Fajardo, St. Croix, and to San Juan. **_Isla Nena_** (☎ 800-981-9355) and **_CaribAir_** (☎ 800-981-0212) also fly.

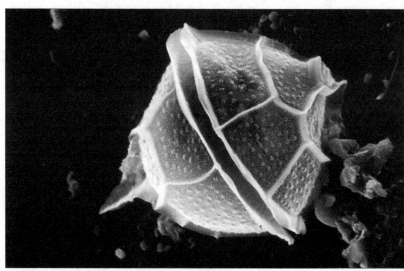

A dinoflagellate as seen under an electron microscope.

Notes

Notes

Culebra

Set 22 miles to the E of Fajardo across a blue expanse of sea, the miniature archipelago which is Culebra consists of the seven-by-four-mile island of Culebra in the company of 23 other islands, cays, and rocks. This area still remains relatively unspoiled and set apart from the world. Much of its land, which includes dry scrub and mangrove swamps, has been designated a National Wildlife Refuge.

The lack of rainfall not only ensures good weather but has the secondary effect of causing low sedimentation — thus producing healthy coral reefs and remarkably clear water.

Today, Culebra largely remains a neglected and forgotten backwater, to the point where it is sometimes maintained that the island is Puerto Rico's stepchild. Aside from tourism, the only business here is the R.D. Medical plant, which makes medical tubing for blood transfusions and injections. It employs 75.

There's not much for a visitor to do except ponder what to eat next, which beach to go to, and which video to rent. These are likely the biggest decisions you'll have to make during the day. There is little crime and people are quite friendly towards visitors.

The climate and easygoing atmosphere have attracted a large number of mainlanders, some of whom appear to be apt candidates for leading characters in a future Ann Tyler novel. Despite their seeming prevalence, many are snowbirds. Because the tourism industry is largely immigran run, their apparent strength in numbers is actually illusory; locals far outnumber them.

Perspectives on life held by residents are best represented by their cars' bumper stickers, which run the gamut from "Support the Marines" to "I get my energy from the sun." Culebrans also express their sentiments by writing on boulders such sentiments as "CRISTO VIENE PRONTO. REPIENTENTE!"(This boulder has been dynamited, presumably sending its divine sentiments out to permeate the moral ethos of the cosmos.) You may still see a home painted with anti-military slogans which stands on the way to the airport.

The one thing that definitely binds both local and indigenous *culebrense* alike is that many smoke like chimneys from the time they are teenagers. The island is getting to be a busier place. However, you will still find a deserted Flamenco Beach on a weekday during the slow season.

Things are changing however. A number of larger developments are opening up, and these threaten the island's easygoing ways and pose serious challenges to its infrastructure. We encourage you to patronize the smaller hotels.

?!¢ The US Navy still owns land in Culebra. It has the Flamenco and Zoni lagoons as well as other land. at the Observation Post (which overlooks Flamenco).

While many Culebrans can speak English, they will appreciate it if you try to speak Spanish with them. Remember that the island is no place for yuppies or those looking for nightlife and resort-style accommodation.

Web sites about Culebra
URL http://www.islaculebra.com
http://www.culebra.org
http://www.culebra-island.com
http://www.emeraldisles.com

GETTING HERE: The cheapest (and most scenic and culturally enlivening method) is to take a *público* from the terminal in Río Piedras to the dock at Fajardo (You may have to change in the town to a car marked *playa*). Then board the ferry, which takes a scenic two hours to Dewey on Culebra. On the way, you pass Isla Marina to your R and Palomino and Icacos to your L; you can also see Cayo Bola de Funcé (Corn Flour Bowl) off in the distance.

The **ferry** runs from Fajardo from Mon. to Fri. at 9:30 AM and 3 PM and on Sat., Sun., and holidays at 9 AM, 2:30 PM, and at 6:30 PM. The **cargo ferry** (for you and your car) runs from Mon. to Fri. at 3:30 AM and 4 PM. On Wed. there is an add'l ferry at 10 AM. Fare is $2.25 each way.

If you wish to bring your car on the **car ferry**, note that it does not run on weekends, and *reservations are advisable* so make plans accordingly. If the weather is good, the trip is remarkably beautiful. However, if seas are rough, it's soaking salt spray and barf bags galore. If the ocean appears to be rough, grab a seat downstairs, unless you relish getting soaked to your skin by salt spray. To check ferry times, call 787-742-3161 in Culebra and 787-863-0705 in Fajardo.

You may also charter a vehicle and take the ferry. Another alternative is to rent a car in San Juan and drop it off at the Fajardo office; they will generally give you a lift to the ferry terminal.

BY AIR: *Be aware that inclement weather conditions may prevent you from flying.* **Vieques Air Link** (in San Juan, ☎ 787-863-3020 in Fajardo, 787-742-0254) flies from Fajardo as well as from San Juan's Isla Grande Airpor(tel. *Isla Nena* (☎ 800-981-9355) flies from the International Airport in San Juan. It costs around $75 to fly ($45 from Isla Grande). You are permitted 25 lbs. of luggage on a scheduled flight. After this limit, it costs $1/lb.

For chartered flights call **Air Culebra** (☎ 787-742-0446) costs around $200 for up to five people.
http://www.airculebra.com

Flamenco (☎ 787-742-1040) also offers charters.

WHO SHOULD COME: Snorkelers and divers will find great opportunities in the Culebran mini-archipelago, as will bird-watchers and hikers. The island not a place to come to if you're in a rush. Nor is there much here to entertain children in the usual sense. But, while they may not be able to shake hands with Mickey Mouse, they will encounter a natural wonderland which they will always remember.

It is hilly, so if you are disabled, access may be a problem. While the streets of Dewey have curved corners for wheelchair access, the telephone poles stand roundly in the face of access. At least the thought was there.

Culebra is not inexpensive, and there are no truly low budget accommodations (save camping), but the island provides value for money in terms of overall low-key ambiance. It isn't for people who wish to be catered to or who need all of the conveniences. Most of the hotels are fairly basic.

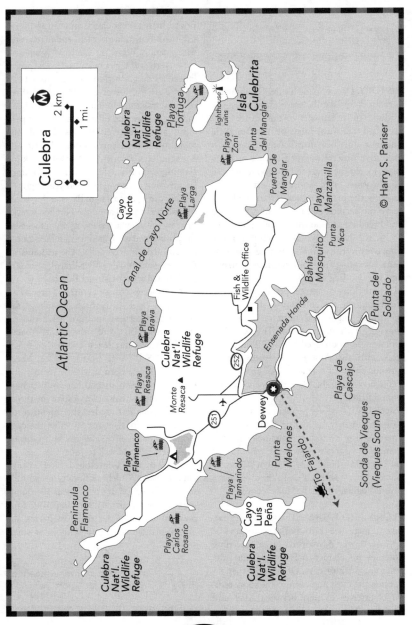

© Harry S. Pariser

Culebra

0   1 mi.

0   2 km

Atlantic Ocean

Peninsula Flamenco

Culebra Nat'l. Wildlife Refuge

Playa Flamenco

Playa Resaca

Playa Carlos Rosario

Monte Resaca ▲

Culebra Nat'l. Wildlife Refuge

Playa Brava

Playa Larga

Cayo Norte

Canal de Cayo Norte

Culebra Nat'l. Wildlife Refuge

Playa Tortuga

Isla Culebrita

lighthouse ruins

Playa Zoni

Punta del Manglar

Puerto de Manglar

Playa Manzanilla

Punta Vaca

Fish & Wildlife Office

Bahía Mosquito

Punta del Soldado

252

251

Playa Tamarindo

Dewey

Punta Melones

Cayo Luis Peña

Culebra Nat'l. Wildlife Refuge

Ensenada Honda

Playa de Cascajo

To Fajardo

Sonda de Vieques (Vieques Sound)

Fishing bats may be seen at the Dinghy Dock at dusk.

HISTORY: Under Spanish rule, Culebra and surrounding islands were designated as Crown lands. Transfer to the US in 1898 specified that these lands be used for their "highest and best use." Accordingly, an executive order Roosevelt signed in 1903 surrendered the lands to Navy control.

Eight years later, Roosevelt, after reconsidering the matter, ordered that the lands serve the secondary purpose of a preserve and breeding ground for native seabirds. In 1936, the Navy (perhaps assuming noise improves fertility among nesting seabirds) began strafing and bombarding Culebra and surrounding islands.

Despite long years of protest, both by locals *and* by the commonwealth government, the pigheaded military continued playing with their toys. The Culebra Committee, sponsored by the PIP in coalition with the American Friends Action Group, had constructed a chapel on Flamenco Beach. In 1975, the Navy discontinued firing.

Since 1975, the local population has swelled to approximately 2,500. The island is gaining attention for its tourist potential, and the number of visitors is growing. The island was hit by 1996's Hurricane Marilyn (some 50 homes were destroyed and 200 more were severely damaged) but has fully recovered.

FLORA AND FAUNA: The Culebra group has a huge sea bird population; several species have developed large breeding colonies on Flamenco Peninsula and surrounding offshore cays. Of the more than 85 species, the most numerous is the sooty tern, which arrives to nest between May and October. The sooty tern's eggs are highly prized by local poachers, and rat and feral cat predation add to their endangerment. They mainly breed on Cayo de Agua and Cayo Yerba off Culebra's W side. The population has diminished to around 160,000.

There are four other species of terns, three of boobies, the laughing gull, Caribbean martin, osprey, and other birds. Brown pelicans, an endangered species, live in the mangrove trees surrounding Puerto de Manglar on Culebra's E side. Don't look for flamingos on Playa Flamenco: the military bombardment drove them out years ago!

A few cattle, remnants of the roaming herds of yesteryear, stroll amid the bombed wrecks of army tanks, which stand as monuments to the absurd and demented wastefulness of the military-industrial complex. The seldom-seen Culebra giant anole (a huge lizard), resides in the forested areas of Mount Resaca.

Four species of sea turtles breed on Culebra's and Culebrita's beaches: the Atlantic loggerhead and green sea turtles, the hawksbill, and the leatherback. Leatherbacks may reach a length of 6.5 ft .(two m) and weigh up to 500 kg. These turtles have been exiled from one Caribbean beach to another by poachers and developers. Here too, despite the threat of stiff penalties under the Endangered Species Act, local poachers value the eggs as a protein source and an aphrodisiac. They nest from March to June.

As part of a well-developed, interdependent ecosystem, Culebra's flora is inseparable from its fauna. Mangrove forests surrounding the coasts provide a roosting ground for birds above the water while sheltering sea anemones, sponges, and schools of small

?!¿ White-tailed deer were imported by the Navy for "sport" hunting.

fish among the tangle of stiltlike roots in the shallow water. Nearly 80% of Culebra's coastline is bordered by young and old coral reefs. Multicolored miniature mountain ranges of brain, finger, elkhorn, and fire corals shelter equally colorful and numerous schools of tropical fish.

ENVIRONMENTAL PROBLEMS: Increased touristic interest in Culebra is having deleterious effects. The island is battling to maintain its ambiance in the face of Mammon and his money. Enforcement of zoning regulations has been lax. One example is the Culebra Beach Resort, which has built a fourth floor, one floor higher than is permitted by rural building codes. In addition, houses have been constructed illegally by squatters along Ensenada Honda, the island's principal bay.

Another problem is the Costa Bonita project, a major development in progress which is reached by taking the road after the Fish and Wildlife turnoff on the Main Rd. Environmental impacts have apparently not entered into the discussion, and the development is being foisted on the island. In 2002, the municipality refused a request to construct a 160-boat pier on the bay. Another large hotel, Vista Bonita, is under construction along the Playa Resaca Rd. A 32-unit hotel, Bahía Marina, opened and then closed.

The last land survey was done by the Spaniards in 1887 and is very inaccurate, which makes prosecution difficult. As there is no municipal sewage system, much of it goes into the water. Two federal agencies have agreed to pay 75% of the $9 million cost of constructing a sewer system; the remaining funds will be loaned by the Aqueduct and Sewer Authority. Beach sand has been removed and roads illegally constructed. Turtles have vanished from Playa Tortuga on Isla Culebrita, victims of the dearth of sea grass, which has been killed off by boat propellers and anchors. In addition, fishermen have been net fishing in turtle nesting grounds (which is not illegal!).

The endangered West Indies whistling duck has disappeared from Laguna Flamenco.

One bright spot has been the establishment of a no-take zone at Cayo Luis Peña.

BEACHES: The island's most famous beach is **Playa Flamenco**, a long stretch of beautiful sand which has only two hotels along its shores. On a low-season weekday this beach is wonderfully peaceful. As it's somewhat isolated, be sure to bring everything you need. Changing rooms are provided.

Two wrecked tanks serve as reminders of the military occupation, as do a hilltop observation post and a set of shark pens (the remains of a US Navy experiment) on the E end. The calmest areas are to the L, and it's rather like being in a gargantuan shallow saltwater swimming pool.

This long and lovely beach was temporarily closed to camping in 1993 because too many main islanders were coming here, drinking and using drugs, and getting bombed out of their skulls. The rumor mill had it that the last straw came when a prominent judge's 14-year old daughter was raped.

Currently, you may camp on the beach but fees are $10 per tent, per day. It's a long walk from town, but there's irregular *público* service ($3) available. Expect crowds of Puerto Ricans from the main island during the summer and holidays.

From the beach, you may head to the L on foot to reach **Negro** and **Blanco** beaches or head up the trail in back of the parking lot to reach several rough beaches with good snorkeling.

Snorkeling on Flamenco is not the best. The best locations are up the beach as far as you can comfortably walk or off the edges of the former shark pens.

Visitors on Culebra may help out with nightly turtle watches from late Feb. until late July by calling the Deparment of Natural Resources and the Environment in San Juan. (☎ 787-724-3724, 787- 724-3647). Most of the nesting turtles are leatherbacks, but hawksbills also nest here. In order to avoid harming turtle hatching, do not drive on the beaches or visit them during May, June, and July. Walking at the water's edge or near the trees will also help prevent any potential damage.

Sea turtle Egglaying

The first recorded observation of egglaying was by the Dutch in 1592. Turtles lay eggs at night. after searching for a spot which the high tide will not reach, the mother turtle becomes totally involved in digging the nest, shoveling out the round nest with her paddle-shaped hind legs. Crouching over the nest, which may reach 164 in. (50 cm) in depth, she expels an average of 100 eggs together with a lubricating fluid. After covering the nest with sand, she returns to the sea. During the two hour or so procedure, she heaves constant sighs and her eyes tear, presumably to clear her eyes of sand. Facing the world's greatest obstacle course, the hatchlings race to the sea two months later. Very few survive to breeding age some 30 years later. Those females that do will return to nest on the same beach. No turtle, tagged on one Costa Rican nesting beach, has been found nesting on any other beach, and genetic tests suggest that green turtles only nest on the beach where they were born.

To get to Flamenco from town you must turn L at the airport; you will pass the Ferreteria González hardware store en route. Allow an hour on foot. If you wish to take a taxi back, there is a pay phone which you can use to call one. The ranger will also call one for you.

HELI PAD: To get to the **heli pad**, take the first road past the airport and and to the R. Follow this dirt road until you come to a fork which is next to an abandoned Navy lookout post. From here take a concrete road to the R, turning L at the next fork and continuing up the hill until you arrive at an old yellow and red Navy post. Park here and hike 15 min. up a steep hill to the lookout point. From here you can see Playa Resaca.

PLAYA RESACA: Visiting **Playa Resaca** ("undertow") is a true adventure. To get here you must hike a long way down through thorny brush. It can be difficult to find your way toward the end. After emerging in a mangrove forest, a path leads down to the magnificent beach, which is generally deserted and without shade but has heavy surf. It's like a tourist brochure, but without the hotel. Along the way you might see a hermit crab, a snake slither by, or a land crab.

Be sure to bring a good supply of water, as none is available. Good shoes and long pants are strongly recommended. Allow

about an hour to hike up the road to the starting point and about half an hour down. **note:** You aren't supposed to visit during turtle nesting season.

PLAYA BRAVA: **Playa Brava** (meaning "rough") is called that because of its continual heavy surf. To get here head out of town on Carr. 250; watch for the Km 4 marker and then turn L after you pass the "1908 building." Park near the gate (around a mile further) and then begin walking. The first part of the hike is along a road which climbs up; you then head down and along a flat trail graced with trees and butterflies. Take the first R off this road and head for the beach. Be sure to see the well just before it. Some 30 ft. deep, it is made of hand-fit stone. The water is brackish, so your cow can drink but not you.

You'll probably have it all to yourself. There is a vicious undertow so be careful!

Both Brava and Resaca are leatherback turtle nesting beaches, and development on either would spell the end of the species on Culebra; even a small light can confuse hatchlings, who head into it instead of towards the sea. They may stumble into one of your footprints in the sand and become trapped.

PLAYA TAMARINDO: To get to **Playa Tamarindo**, take Carr. 251 towards Flamenco but turn Lonto the first dirt road to the L past the end of the airport runway. You'll come to a private house, and you'll see a parallel road to the R. Eventually, you'll see the tamarind tree that gives the area its name. This calm beach offers fair snorkeling. The Tamarindo Estates have a bar and grill.

PLAYA CARLOS ROSARIO: From Tamarindo you may walk to **Playa Carlos Rosario**. Head NW and climb over boulders. (Or you may head along the path which begins to the L of the parking lot at Flamenco. Head up a hill and then wind your way down to a beach). The path from Tamarindo arrives at this first beach as well. From here you must take a R along the peninsula to Carlos Rosario which is around 100 yds. farther on. An alternative is to take a water taxi or rent a motorboat. The sandy beach is flanked by coral outcrops. To snorkel, find the channel to the R where you'll find a coral wall. Look for a white plastic bottle which marks the channel and continue around it to the R where you'll find the best place for snorkeling. Another area is to the L of the beach where you'll find a large rock formation which juts into the sea. Patch coral graces the face of the bottom of the cliff here.

"The Wall" is a great **snorkeling area** which is .25 mi. past Carlos Rosario in the direction of Punta Flamenco. It is best visited by water taxi.

PLAYA ZONI: The main road on the island terminates near **Playa Zoni**, at the E side of the island, which is an important turtle nesting beach. This is a spectacular drive along a great road. Park right before the unpaved part at the end and then walk. From the road's end (some 20 min. from town) you can see St. Thomas. Offshore, there's fair snorkeling, and you may hike up the N coast from this point as well. The beach offers decent snorkeling but is best suited to R&R. It is named after an Englishman who once lived here.

PUNTA MELONES: Melones, a point rather than a beach, is well suited for snorkeling and sunset photography. To get here take the road towards the hospital from town, pass the **Felipa Serrano Center**, and park before the hill leading to a private development. There are two good snorkeling spots here. Snorkel from the rough coral beach (to the L) to the point (marked by a Coast Guard navigation light). A second spot is superior. Head up the beach to a group of rocks and snorkel offshore. The tip of the point is quite deep so beware. Either return here later or stay for the sunset.

PUNTA SOLDADO: Soldado, a coral beach best suited for snorkeling, is on the S side. Cross the bridge in town and head L until the end of the road, where you must hike in. Head to the R down the hill; the best snorkeling is to the SE (to your left, around 50 yds. offshore); the majority of the reef is under 10-30 ft. of water. The area is quite rocky. Watch for the occasional prize shell among the broken ones.

Other beaches are on Luis Peña and Culebrita (see below under "Culebrita").

OTHER SIGHTS: Right in town is a **drawbridge**. Constructed by English engineers, it was designed to allow passage for two fishing boats. These boats have disappeared from the area, as the water is so shallow it

Culebra Snorkeling Sites

A number of sites are described in the text. Here are the best:

Carlos Rosario *A beach to the NW*
Playa Tamarindo *A beach to the NE*
The Wall *Near Carlos Rosario*
Punta Melones *A spot to the W of town*
Playa Soldado *A beach to the SW*
Luis Peña *An offshore island*
Culebrita *An offshore island*

only allows the passage of small motorboats. The bridge is useless and remains undrawn; indeed, it should never have been built.

Another fiasco is **Cayo Pirata**, so named because it provided shelter to pirate ships, which was supposed to have been turned into a museum. The local government managed to run out of money before the project was completed, and it currently has some overgrown picnic tables that are accessible only if you have your own boat. It is used once or twice a year for a government party. The rest of the year it is left to its rabbits; rabbits now live here in *Watership Down*-dwarfing multitudes because someone is breeding them! As any visitor will soon learn, both God and the Puerto Rican government work in mysterious ways.

A couple of miles out of town you come to the closed desalinization plant to the R. The "1908 Building" here has become the **San Ildefonso Museum**. It currently exhibits a number of Spanish, Taíno, and pre-Taíno artifacts, which were found by diver Gene Thomas, and photographs and masks.

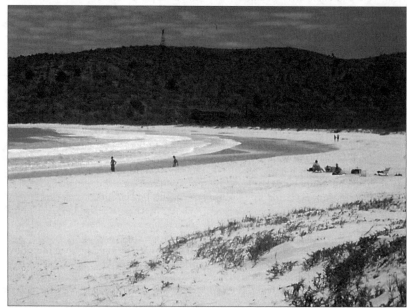

Culebra's Playa Flamenco is about as close to perfection as you can find in a beach.

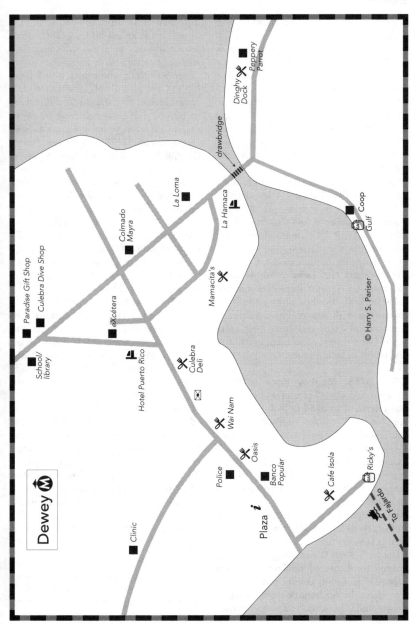

Dewey Ⓜ

Peppery Parrot

Dinghy Dock

drawbridge

La Loma

Colmado Mayra

Paradise Gift Shop

Culebra Dive Shop

eXcétera

School/ library

Hotel Puerto Rico

La Hamaca

Mamacita's

Culebra Deli

Wai Nam

Oasis

Police

Banco Popular

Plaza *i*

Clinic

Cafe Isola

Ricky's

Coop

Gulf

© Harry S. Pariser

to Fajardo

Another collection is from archaeologist Norma Medina who conducted a dig in NE Culebra. Some of the items date as far back as 700 BC. The museum is looking for patrons, so visiting millionaires please take note! It plans one day to be open Mon. to Fri. from 8 AM to noon. Weekday afternoons are planned to be devoted to cultural events for children. Meanwhile, times are irregular, so call ahead. For information contact curator **Dolly Camareno** (☎ 787-405-3768).

Outside of town and back on the main road to the E at Barrio Frailes, the sole remaining structure from the **Antiguo Pueblo de Culebra** (old Culebra village) dates from 1889. It's currently closed and is not particularly impressive.

Continuing on the same road you come to the **Recursos Naturales y Ambientales** (Ministry of Natural Resources and the Environment). Further down, you pass mangroves with lots of birds. Epiphytes grow out of cacti, and you'll pass rusty barbed wire fences, dildo cacti, and a very few Brahman bulls grazing.

DIVE SITES: Monkey Rock is W of Culebra past Cayo Yerba. This novice site has a depth of 15 to 55 ft. (4.5–17 m). It is suitable for divers and snorkelers. Watch for schools of bigeye, reef butterflyfish, lobster, moray eels, and schools of fish.

Cayo Ratón, due N of the island of the same name, is a great place to see colorful schools of fish. Visibility can be up to 100 ft. on clear days.

At a depth of 14-45 ft., the reef called the **Impact Area** has a wide variety of fish as well as large sea fans.

The 50-ft. **Arch Dive** visits gigantic arch-shaped coral-covered boulders that host schools of gloriously colored fish.

At 65 ft., the **Amberjack Hole**, to the W Dewey and Cayo Luis Peña, is an interme-

diate dive with a depth of 50 to 60 ft. (15-18 m). It has an enormous boulder often saturated with colorful fish, including schools of amberjack, its namesake.

Cayo Ballena or **Whale Rock** is set **1/2** mi. NE of Cayo Norte. This intermediate dive centers around the gorgeous coral that flank its periphery. The depth is from 30–90 ft. (9–27 m). It is best visited from May to Nov.

Set just .8 mi. (1.3 km) E of Cayo Norte, **Genquí** has well-defined tunnels, caves, and canyons. The caves are some of Puerto Rico's largest found underwater, and they host hordes of nocturnal fish. Conditions can be variable here, and this intermediate dive is 20-50 ft. (6-15 m) in depth.

An open water dive ranging from 50-75 ft., **Anchor Reef** was once used by the Navy as an anchorage. Artifacts to be found here range from an anchor and chain to a number of old bottles.

The **Tug Boat** features a tugboat sunk in 40 ft. of water. This ten to 30 ft. (3-9 m) intermediate dive site is .8 mi. (1.3 km) to the SE of Punta Vaca, which, in turn, is off of Culebra's SE. This site is best visited from May to Oct. Coral are just beginning to swallow the craft, but it is easy to visit the wheelhouse. Staghorn coral proliferate in this area.

Sail Rock is a great intermediate dive site where you may swim with turtles and witness great coral formations. It is an intermediate dive, set 5.3 mi. (8.5 km) E of Punta Vaca. The depth is from 30 to 90 ft. (9–27 m), and although part of the Virgin Islands, it is popular with local divers.

> The Navy subjected Culebra and its cays and reefs to intensive bombing for decades. Unexploded ordinance is a fact of life. As Recursos Naturales y Ambientales advises, "Please do not go near any visible bomb."

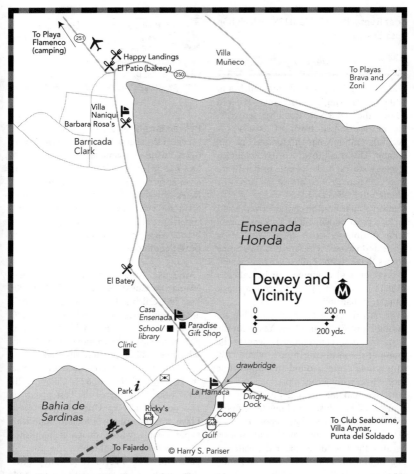

To Playa Flamenco (camping)

251

Happy Landings
El Patio (bakery)
250

Villa Muñeco

To Playas Brava and Zoni

Villa Naniqui
Barbara Rosa's

Barricada Clark

Ensenada Honda

El Batey

Casa Ensenada

Dewey and Vicinity

0   200 m
0   200 yds.

School/ library

Paradise Gift Shop

Clinic

drawbridge

Park

La Hamaca

Dinghy Dock

Bahia de Sardinas

Ricky's
GAS

Coop

To Club Seabourne, Villa Arynar, Punta del Soldado

Gulf

To Fajardo

© Harry S. Pariser

Expect to see barracuda, parrotfish, and grouper. Three pinnacles nearby teem with life. There can be surge and heavy surf in this area.

GETTING AROUND: In town, no spot is too far to walk. If you're staying outside of town, you may want to have a car ($50 pd) to get around. (You may ask your hotel to arrange a rental in advance). However, your feet or a bicycle($13 pd) can still take you to a lot of places. A *público* ($2) runs between the town, the airport, and Playa Flamingo. If you don't hitch or bike, you'll want to rent a vehicle for at least one day during your stay. To get to Culebrita or Luis Peña you'll need to charter a water taxi, which will run about $40 pp RT to Culebrita and $20 pp RT to Luis Peña. You may also rent a motorboat from **Culebra**

Boat Rental (☎ 787-742-0278), which is in Casa Ensenada.

Dewey

When the US Navy moved onto Culebra in 1903, locals living in settlements scattered all over the island were forcibly resettled in the newly created town of Dewey (or Pueblo), built on what had formerly been a swamp. This small town has five *colmados* (grocery stores) and a couple of hardware stores. There're no movie theaters or (thankfully) video arcades.

Dewey might best be characterized as an architectural hodgepodge. A clean, cutesy little Caribbean town filled with frilly white and pastel Victorians it is not. Some homes have been built over the water. Everything and anything can be called a "Villa" (or even a "Villa"!), from a shack on up to a mansion.

The only times the town comes to life are during Holy Week, and New Year's. In the past, the best entertainment was to be found at the local courthouse, where lawsuits would center around an inopportune sneeze by a visiting roof repairman or a dispute over moving a rock. But, sadly, the courthouse has closed, and one less opportunity for fun has been lost to posterity.

Definitely bring your mask and snorkel because the *real* life is under the water. A pair of binoculars will also come in handy for viewing bird life.

ACCOMMODATIONS: All hotels generally offer free airport pickup and delivery. There are no large hotels here as of yet, but none of the hotels are particularly cheap for what you get.

If you're planning on staying a week or more, you should consider renting a vacation home. Contact **Vacation Planners** (☎ 787-742-311, ☏ 787-742-1060) and

 Police are also fond of giving tickets for not wearing seatbelts or driving bare chested. (Women may not be ticketed for this). Also, be careful where you park. Ticketing is enforced!

Pelican Enterprises (☎ 787-742-0052).

Set next to the drawbridge and convenient to town, **Posada la Hamaca**, C. Castelar 68 (☎ 787-742-3516; Box 338, Culebra, PR 00775) is an attractive Spanish-style nine-room inn. Rates run about $65–75 d for rooms and $85d for efficiencies plus tax; weekly discounts are available. Rooms are small.
http://www.posada.com
pat@ticnet.com

Attractive and a/c with balconies, **Mamacitas Guest House** (☎ 787-742-0090; Box 790, Culebra, PR 00775) has five small apartments. Rates are around $60 d and $70 for a room with a kitchen (holds three); if you pay for six nights, the seventh is on the house. It has one handicapped-accessible room.

Set off of C. Escudero, **Casa Ensenada** (☎ 787-742-3559; Box 611, Culebra, PR 00775-0061) is one of the best places to base yourself in town. Once known as Casa Llave, it is now run by a friendly American expat couple whose daughter publishes *Travelmaps*, one of the best free tourist guide maps to Puerto Rico. They offer three units: a bedroom with Queen bed, studio with twin beds and a three-room apartment with king bed. All have a/c, fans,

 Culebran beaches often offer little shade, so be sure to bring some cover-up clothes with you. Although the island is small, it can take a while to get places so allow at least a day to tour the island.

kitchen or partial kitchen, private bath, satellite TV/VCR and free kayak use. Prices range from $50-$130; one day complimentary rent with weekly rental. Each has an independent entrance, and there's a terrace and private dock in back
http://culebrarentals.com
casaensenda@aol.com

Also relatively near the pier and just off C. Tacita, the **Hotel Puerto Rico** (☎ 787-742-3372) is a true Caribbean classic; rooms rent for around $30 s and $40 d. This is for budget travelers who relish an island feel. However, it is very basic.

The **Villa Nueva Guesthouse** (☎ 787-742-0257; Apdo. 303, Culebra 00775) is economical; rooms have shared baths.

Overlooking the Bahía de Sardinas, **Harbour View Villas** (☎ 787-742-3855/3171, 800-440-0070; Box 216, Culebra, PR 00775) are completely furnished. There's a kitchen in each of the truncated A-frame-style units. Individual rooms may also be available. Rates are around $95 d; the "suite" (a unit with mini-kitchen and balcony) is $75. Extra adults are $15 each.

Villa Boheme (Ensenada Honda, ☎ 787-742-3508) charges around $75. Facilities include use of kitchen.

Renting efficiency apartments for a couple or a family of four, tranquil **Villa Fulladoza** (☎/☖ 787-742-3576; Box 162, Culebra, PR 00775-0162) charges from $55–$75 per room. A phone and washing machine are available for use.

Tamarindo Estates (☎ 787-742-3342/3343; Box 313, Culebra, PR 00775), with fully equipped a/c apartments way out at Playa Tamarindo off the road to Playa Flamingo, is another alternative. They have a pool. You'll need a jeep if staying here.

BARRICADA CLARK ACCOMMODATIONS: Villas Naniqui (☎ 787-742-3271; Box 606, Culebra, PR 00775) offers completely equipped cottages priced at around $55 pn.

TOWARD PUNTA SOLDADO: Club Seabourne (☎ 787-742-3169, ☖ 787-742-3176; Box 357, Culebra, PR 00775, 866-CULEBRA) is the island's most deluxe accommodation. The new owners, who took possession in 2002, have invested more than $400,000 in renovations. There are now 24 rooms, as well as small villas, a "Crow's Nest," and two cottages (around $200-250 d). The last can house up to four for an additional surcharge above the double occupancy rate. Rooms have neither phone nor TV, and the honeymoon suite provides a nice getaway. The "club" also has a screened dining room, a pool, and a lounge/library with TV. Rental yacht moorings are also available. Rates include airport pickup/drop-off and a continental breakfast; tax is additional. Its restaurant, the **White Sands**, has wicker furniture and offers gourmet international and Caribbean fare.
http://www.culebra-island.com
vplanns@coqui.net

PUNTA ALOE ACCOMMODATIONS: This area is also to the S of town. **Bayview Villas** (☎ 787-742-3392, 787-765-5711; Box 674, Culebra, PR 07775), a set of two

1,500-sq.-ft. villas, rent for $1,300–$1,400 each out of season and for $1,400–$1,500 each in season. The very attractive villas come fully equipped and sleep up to six. They each have a living/dining/sleeping area, phone, washing machine, and ceiling fans; attention is personal. They overlook the bay.

Villa Arynar (☎ 787-742-3145; Box 744, Culebra, PR 00775-0744) is run by a friendly retired Naval commander and his wife. Overlooking the water, one of the two attractive bedrooms available has a balcony. There's a common room with refrigerator, books, and games. This is for people who want to kick back and relax and (preferably) stay a while. It is as if you were visiting friends with a great house as paying guests. In fact, the surroundings are so pleasant you may have a hard time leaving their front deck! Rates start from $90 d daily; reduced weekly rate is available. http://www.enchanted-isle.com/villaarynar

AT PLAYA FLAMENCO: Culebra Beach Villas (☎ 787-755-2930, 787-760-2930) has 33 units with kitchens. Facilities range from efficiencies to beachfront penthouse suites. Rates run $125-$275 pn plus tax. http://www.culebrabeachrental.com

Next door, the **Villa Flamenco Beach** (☎ 787-742-0023) is less expensive and has studios upstairs and a family-sized apartment downstairs with a kitchen. It rents for around $600-$720 pw. esmer@coqui.net

CAMPING: Camping is now available at Playa Flamingo for a charge of $10 pd, per tent. Keep in mind that the beach is remote from town, so you should try to bring as much as possible of what you need. Also, it is flooded with Puerto Ricans escaping the mainland on holidays and summer weekends.

FOOD: You'll pretty much find serviceable but not much ultra-gourmet food is available. Prices are high relative to local restaurants in Fajardo.

Right near the ferry, **Café Isola** is the only place around to grab a sandwich for a late (post 3 PM) lunch. It's open daily (except Tues. and Wed.) to 5 PM.

Serving both breakfast and lunch, **Mamacitas** offers Puerto Rican and other Caribbean cuisine including fish steaks and pasta dishes. Vegetarian burritos are $3.

A popular hangout for expats, **Oasis** has Italian food including whole pizza pies ($6) and slices ($1.25), and eggplant parmesan.

Near the canal, The **Dinghy Dock** offers three meals daily (as well as daily specials) in an attractive setting. It has a profane happy hour which attracts many locals.

Hidden away next to the **Fisherman's Cooperative, Restaurante El Pesquerito**, serves inexpensive breakfasts and lunches. Lots of local atmosphere and ideal for budget travelers. It's open daily from 7 AM–4:30 PM.

Set next to the PO, the **Culebra Deli** has sandwiches, hamburgers and other greasy fare, as well as ice cream. Sandwiches and seafood dishes are available for lunch.

In the Villa Naniqui just to the N of town, **Barbara Rosa's** is a good restaurant which serves homecooked food.

OUT OF TOWN: Near the baseball field on the road to Flamingo but not too far from the town center, **El Batey** (☎ 787-742-3828; open Tues. to Sun. from 8 AM–2 PM) serves sandwiches (around $3) and lunch. **El Patio Bakery** serves coffee, baked goods, and sandwiches for breakfast and lunch here.

If you wish to experience classic Puerto Rican greasy-spoon ambiance, **Tina's**, (☎ 787-742-3235) reached by making the first L after El Batey, serves traditional, fattening

Puerto Rican food platters. The absolutely unforgettable decor includes advertisements with girls in swimsuits, posters of jogging teddy bears, a photo of an egg-laying turtle, and plastic chairs — some of which have Good Housekeeping seals.

Near the airport, popular, and serving chiefly Puerto Rican food, the wonderfully named **Happy Landing** serves three meals daily.

Other restaurants the more deluxe **Club Seabourne,** which offers gourmet dishes.

Las Delicias Restaurant is on the L-hand side when you go up to Zoni.

FOOD SHOPPING: As everything is imported and no fare discounts are given to trucks bringing in food on the ferry, prices are quite high. The range of goods which may be obtained has expanded dramatically in recent years. There are a **food truck** which sell veggies, eggs, and the like near the dock. One usually sells Wed. AM (by the PO, 6 AM–noon and then moves later to a house in Bo. Villa Muñeco. Fishermen sell from the fishing dock at around 11 or so. You can try at the cooperative and see if they have any fish.

In town, you can shop at **Suprette Mayra** (right near Mamacitas), at **Milka**, and at **Colmado Esperanza**. The **Culebra Dive Shop** has a specialty and frozen food section, and they sell fresh fish in season.

A welcome new addition is **The Peppery Parrot Trading Company and Blue Moon Spice Company** sells a huge variety of hot sauces, including those made on island. Owner Laurie Knowlton also sells jams, chutneys, cookbooks, and other items. They're right next to the Dinghy Docks, and most Weds. from 4–6 PM they have a hot sauce tasting fair.

http://www.pepperyparrot.com

In Barricada Clark, the **Vietnam Grocery** has good prices. **Marco's Grocery** is here as well.

INFORMATION: A small **tourism office** (☎ 787-742-3521; 9 AM–noon and 1–3 PM weekdays) operates inside the Alcaldía (City Hall) which is up on a hill overlooking the piers. For additional information on the island (including details on temporary rentals) write them at Box 189, Culebra, PR 00775.

For information on visiting the **Culebra National Wildlife Refuge,** you can call 787-742-0115 or write in advance to Refuge Manager, Lower Camp, Fish and Wildlife Service, Box 190, Culebra, PR 00775-0190. Camping is currently prohibited on the island's beaches with the exception of the campground at Playa Flamenco.

SERVICES: The **Post Office** is just around to the L from the pier and pay phones are just past it. The *San Juan Star* is available at the **Paradise Gift Shop** which is across from the public school.

Sharing an office with the helpful and friendly **Four Seasons Travel, eXcétera** (☎ 787-742-0844, ☏ 787-742-0826) offers services such as fax, message service, package hold, prescription drug service, photocopying, and internet access. It also has a giftshop.

nadeen@hotmail.com

A **laundry** is near the ferry.

Gasoline stations are **Garaje Ricky** (near the ferry) and **Gasolinera Villa Pesquera,**

> **?!¢** The "biomass" of fish (the total weight of all individuals living in an area) doubles inside marine reserves within three to five years of their establishment.

Save the Culebrita Lighthouse!

The only Spanish building remaining in the Culebra area, Culebrita's lighthouse is in danger of collapse. Restoration costs are estimated at more than $3 million. It was registered as a US National Monument in 1981. The Coast Guard transferred control of the facility to the US General Services Administration in 1981. The Culebra Foundation is working to have the site transferred to them and to raise the necessary funds. The **Culebra Foundation** (☎ 787-742-0240) or its president, Juan Romero (☎ 787-742-3832) welcome suggestions to save the lighthouse.

which is next to the fish market. **Joe's of Culebra** (☎ 787-742-1933) sells ice and car parts.

HEALTH: A **health clinic** (☎ 787-742-3511), the CDT de Culebra, operates behind the City Hall. It has two doctors and,visiting specialists, and it's emergency room is open 24 hrs. The clinic itself is open from 8 AM–4:30 PM daily. There is no pharmacy; orders are called into Walgreen's in Fajardo and sent over on the ferry.

MONEY: Banco Popular has the sole ATHs (instant teller machines) on the island. You can also draw a cash advance against your Mastercard or Visa at the Banco Popular; it's open 8:30 AM–3 PM from Mon. to Fri. Some small hotels accept credit cards (a 5% surcharge may apply); others do not.

CAR RENTALS: Unless you're staying in the boonies, it isn't really necessary to rent a car because of the island's small size. It's also expensive — around $50/day to rent a jeep.

Contact **Carlos Jeep** (☎ 787-742-3514), Coral Reef (☎ 787-742-0055) **Dick &**

Cathy (☎ 787-742-0062), **Jerry** (☎ 787-742-0587), Tamarindo Car Rental (☎ 787-742-3343), or **William Solis** (☎ 787-742-3537).

Gas (around $1.65/gallon) is sold at the **Fisherman's Cooperative's dock** and at **Garaje Ricky** (see "Services," above).

BICYCLES: Because cars are so few and the topography so flat, cycling is an excellent way to get out to Flamenco. However, it can be difficult to pedal out to Zoni, and you may face narrow roads and construction machinery. Culebra Contact **Dick & Cathy** (☎ 787-742-0062), who will deliver, and the **Culebra Bike Shop** (☎787-742-2209) in town

WATER SPORTS AND EXCURSIONS: Culebra Boat Rental (☎ 787-742-0278) rents motor boats and a sunfish sailboat. Boating experience is required. They're across from the library. **Charter Ocean Safari** (☎ 787-379-1973) offer snorkeling, kayaking, and pedal boats to location such as Culebrita and Luis Peña. Owner **Jim Peterson** rents kayaks for $25/half-day and $40/full day.

Tamaná (☎ 787-501-0011: cellular) offers snorkeling, water taxi trips, and glass bottom boat rides.

DIVING: The **Culebra Dive Shop** (☎ 787-742-0566, call 787-501-4656, ✆ 787-742-1953) is operated by Richard Cantwell who will take you out to the "Three Sisters" and other sites. Rates run around $45 for a one-tank dive and $85 for a two-tank dive.

http://www.culebradiveshop.com
divecul@coqui.net

At the Dinghy Dock, **Sea Ventures** (787-742-0581) is a respected dive shop.

Culebra Divers (☎ 787-742-0803) is across from the ferry terminal.

NIGHTLIFE: If this forms an important part of your vacation, you've come to the wrong place! Things are quiet at night, to say the least. The evangelical church hosts domino games on Thurs. nights, and you can watch the police drive around with their blue lights flashing as though to give thieves a chance to escape. Hoops are played at the court next to El Batey's at night. **Happy Landings** has dancing on Fri., and **El Batey** has the same on Sat. And, during the season, Mamacita's and Dinghy Dock do have a band sometimes.

SHOPPING: If you want to shop seriously, you should go to St. Thomas or do it in San Juan. There are a few local items (such as Treasure Candles). There are a few shops worth a visit. **Paradise Gift Shop**, **Mamacita's**, and **La Loma** are some of your shopping alternatives. Another is **Flamencos**, an eclectic and engaging gift shop next door to La Loma. **Culebra Dive Shop** and **Culebra Divers** also have a good variety. **Ramona's Fashions** is next to Chuck's Pizza. **Paul Franklin** (☎ 787-742-3136) makes furniture. **Erica** sells her jewelery daily on the plaza, and you can find the "**Barefoot Contessa**" selling by the bridge. A few other craftspeople and artists are listed in the *Tourist Times*.

Culebra National Wildlife Reserve

One of more than 400 wildlife refuges administered by the US Fish and Wildlife Service, the Culebra Refuge covers some 1,480 acres, which includes four tracts on Culebra itself as well as 23 islands and rocks. It was established by Teddy Roosevelt in 1909 and is one of the oldest refuges in the entire system. Although ornithologists had surveyed the archipelago's birds early in the US occupation, the wide variety of nesting seabirds in the area became known only in 1971. The offshore islands (with the exception of Cayo Norte) were added in 1975 upon the Navy's departure. An additional 776 acres were transferred from the Navy in 1982. For information on wildlife, see "flora and fauna" earlier in this chapter.

REGULATIONS: Stay on existing roads and trails. In the unlikely event that you should come upon any ordnance, do not approach or disturb it; remember that hands and feet can be useful appendages. Do not hunt or molest any animals nor collect any living or dead coral or plant material. Do not litter, bring in pets, firearms, a car, or start a fire.

Culebrita

This lovely cay can be reached only by water taxi, fishing boat, private yacht, or boat rental. Its century-old (1880) abandoned stone lighthouse overlooks a large bay and lagoon. Along with neighboring Luis Peña Cay (named after its second owner) to the W, it is a wildlife refuge site open to the public for daytime use. Other cays require special use permits. Contact: Fish and Wildlife Service, Box 510, Boquerón, PR 00622.

A 1980 plan, now discarded, would have transferred ownership to the Puerto Rican government so that the island could have been converted to recreational use, a move which would have been ecologically disastrous.

Luis Peña has a number of sandy beaches; a wonderful coral reef lies off its SW shore.

On Culebrita, be sure to hike up to the lighthouse (tremendous views but do not enter!) and visit the area known as the "baths," a collection of huge boulders that entrap small pools. This is off of the NE corner of Playa Tortuga, the most splendid of Culebrita's six beaches. If hiking along the E side, avoid the nesting tropicbirds and watch out for rat traps placed by Fish and Wildlife.

FLORA AND FAUNA: Heavily covered with vegetation including gumbo-limbo trees, frangipani, and bromeliads, the island provides haven for many rare and endangered species of animals and birds. Masked boobys, red-footed boobys, and brown boobys are found here. Red-billed tropic birds live in cliffs along the island's E shore, while mangrove swamps are home to birds and marinelife.

The Other Reserve Areas

An important nesting site for sooty terns, **Flamenco Peninsula** may be explored on foot. A special use permit is required to visit here.

Protecting one of Culebra's remaining tracts of dry subtropical forest, the **Mount Resaca Unit** includes boulder-covered areas that host cupey and jaguey trees. Orchids and bromeliads cover the boulders.

Providing a special habitat that fosters marine life (see "mangroves" in the Flora and Fauna section of the Introduction), the mangrove areas at **Ensenada Honda Unit**

and **Puerto Manglar Unit** form a vital link in the conservation chain. Puerto Manglar's mangroves provide a roosting area for the endangered brown pelican and protect the bay's phosphorescent qualities by filtering sediments from runoff.

Cayo Lobo is so named because its surveyor came from Tenerife in the Canary Islands where they have a similarly sized and shaped island.

FROM CULEBRA: Passenger ferries (☎ 787-742-3161 in Culebra and 787-863-0705 in Fajardo) depart from Mon. to Fri. at 6:30 AM and 11:30 AM, on Sat., Sun. and holidays at 6:30 AM, 11 AM, and 4:30 PM. The cargo ferry runs at 7 AM and 6:30 PM, and on Wed. and Fri. also at 1 PM.

BY AIR: **Isla Neña**(☎ 800-981-9355) flies to San Juan International, and **Vieques Air Link** (☎ 787-742-0254) flies to San Juan International. Both fly to Fajardo.

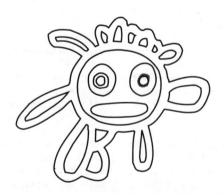

Southeastern Puerto Rico

Southeastern Puerto Rico has a lot to offer, including many relatively untouristed places. This an area where you can find the true rural Puerto Rico.

Roosevelt Roads

Located near the town of Ceiba and Playa Naguabo, Roosevelt Roads is the most important American base in the Caribbean, home of the Atlantic Fleet Weapons Range, the most advanced technical training area in the entire Atlantic. "Springboard," the full NATO fleet annual exercises, are conducted from here.

The nearest beach to here is **Playa Húcares** which has a boardwalk, shops, small restaurants, and good swimming (but no beach). It is outside Naguabo and is packed on weekends. It is a great place to hang out, eat inexpensive Puerto Rican dishes, and get a "feel" for the island.

On weekends, **Frank "Paquito" Lopez** (☎ 787-850-7881) takes visitors around **Cayo Santiago** on snorkeling trips for around $20. (You also should be able to rent a kayak and do this on your own).

Humacao

This small inland town is frequently visited by residents of Palmas del Mar; they put out a great map of the town, which you'll want to pick up if staying in the area. It has an attractive town plaza and architecture. The town's *fiestas patronales* take place around December 8. A *pana* (breadfruit) festival occurs early Sept. in Barrio Matina.

SIGHTS: Downtown near Carr. 3, **Casa Roig** (☎ 787-852-8380), C. López 66,was constructed in the 1920s by Antonín Nechodoma, a local architect much influenced by Frank Lloyd Wright. It is now a small museum devoted to Nechodoma and other local luminaries. Admission is free, and it is open from Wed. to Sun. from 10 AM–4 PM.

You can also view the **Panteón de la Familia Guzmán**, C. Padre Rivera at C. Casillas, which dates from 1864. Its architectural style is best described as ancient Greek. At the Plaza Pública on C. Ulises Martínez, the **Antiguo Ayuntamiento de Humacao** dates from 1848.

Now the City Hall, the **Antigua Corte de Distrito de Humacao** (1925) is on C. Dr. Vidal at C. Antonio López.

Dating from 1869, the **Iglesia Dulce Nombre de Jesús** is at the Plaza de Recreo.

You can see **folkloric houses** on Callejón Trujillo.

Palmas Botanical Gardens, 130 Candalero Abajo, has 208 acres (84 ha) of plants and trees plus a greenhouse. **Playa Humacao** is nearby.

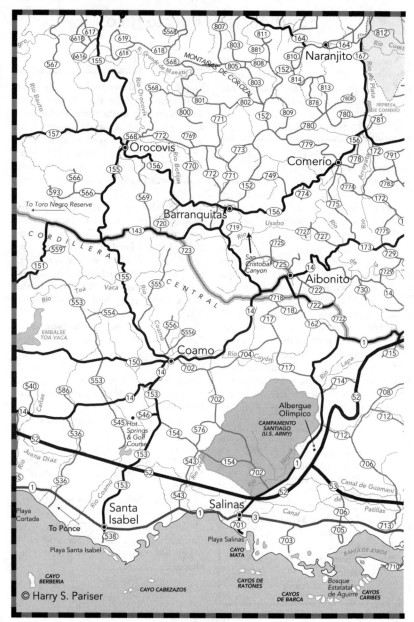

© Harry S. Pariser

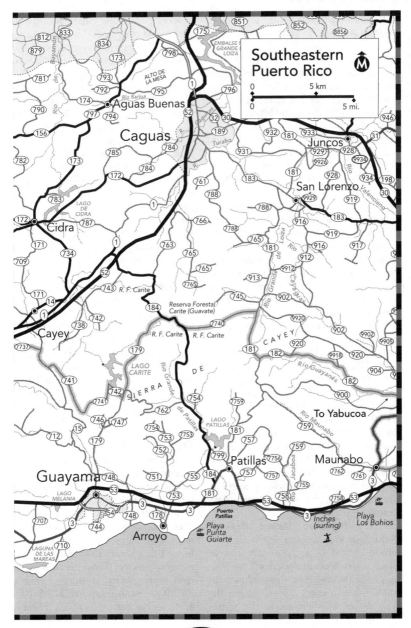

Southeastern Puerto Rico

0   5 km
0   5 mi.

OUTLYING SIGHTS: The abandoned **Antigua Aduana de Humacao** (1872) is at Punta Santiago near the NE.

In Barrio Quebrada Arenas in Las Piedras, the **Cueva del Indio** has petroglyphs. including the famous Sol Taíno.

In the old sugar town of **Yabucoa** to the S, you can find the **Antiguo Hospital de la Caridad** (circa 1880), C. Muñoz Rivera 29, and the **Casa de la Cultural**, a gallery, museum, and library which in past incarnations has been a city hall and library. The town is plagued by traffic jams at rush hour and on Sat.

Plagued by a strong undertow, attractive **Playa La Lucía** is near town.

The **Ruinas de la Hacienda Lucía**, the remains of an abandoned 19th-century sugarcane factory, is in Barrio Camino Nuevo off of Carr. 901. Off the same route, the 300-acre area surrounding **Punta Yeguas** has been titled the **Inés María Mendoza Natural Reserve** after the wife of a Governor who was a well-known conservationist.

The **Antigua Hacienda Mercedita/ Central Roig**, a still-operating sugar factory dating from 1870, is on Carr. 3 at Km 96.

Constructed in 1892, **Faro de Punta Tuna** is operated by the US Coast Guard. It's off Carr. 760 (and then Carr. 7760) to the S. A short path to the L of the front gate leads down to **Playa Larga**, the attractive yet usually deserted beach. For food, head from here to **Playa Los Bohíos.**

Beyond this point to the SW, the Sierra de Guarraya meets the sea at **Playa Mala Pascua** off Carr. 3.

The **Humacao Nature Reserve** (Refugio de Vida Silvestre de Humacao, ☎ 787-852-6088) is a 2,800-acre reserve which offers great birdwatching, particularly for waterfowl. You may see American and Caribbean coots, heron, egrets, the West Indies whistling duck, the white-cheeked pintail, the Puerto Rican woodpecker, and other birds. Don't miss Laguna Mandri with its peterocarpus forest. Sand dollars may be seen here, and sea turtles nest on the beaches. The entrance to this reserve is found just past the Balneario de Humacao in the Santa Theresa area on Hwy. 3. The **park office** (☎ 787-852-6088) is open from Mon. to Fri. from 7:30 AM–3:30 PM. You may rent kayaks here from **Proyecto Peces** (☎ 787-285-0696).

The refuge was originally a marshy forest which was drained during the 1930s and dedicated to sugarcane. Hurricane David and tropical storm Federico, which filled in the lagoons and attracted birds, has helped transform the area. The Puerto Rico Tourism Company is pouring in $300,000 to improve the reserve.

ACCOMMODATIONS: Hotel Palace (☎ 787-850-4180), Ave. Cruz Ortiz Stella, is right in town. Cabins are rented out at **Centro Vacacional Punta Santiago** by Fomento for $20 per night (see "Accommodations" under Introduction).

Palmas del Mar to the S (see following section) is the area's plushest accommodation.

Set amidst 45 acres on Carr. 3 at Km 112 near Patillas and the village of Guardarraya, the **Caribe Playa** (☎ 787-839-7719, 800-221-4483, ☏ 787-839-1817; HC764-Buzon 8590, Patillas, PR 00723) faces a beautiful beach and is surrounded by coconut palms. There are 32 beachfront studios with kitchenettes — a series of breezy, attractive concrete structures with balconies and porches. Accommodating up to four, they are supplemented by hammocks, a restaurant and honor bar, a library/TV/music lounge, and plenty of parking. Guests may use facilities (golf, tennis, scuba) at nearby Palmas del Mar. Rates run from around $75-$105 .; a $2.50 service gratuity is added. There is a

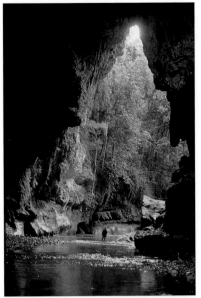
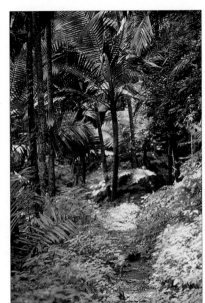

Top: Cave near Utuado (left); trail in Doña Juana (right)
Bottom: view along the Cordillera Central (left); Doña Juana waterfall in Toro Negro (right)

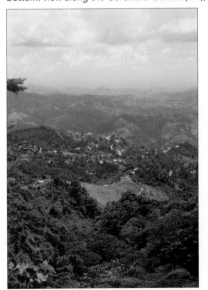
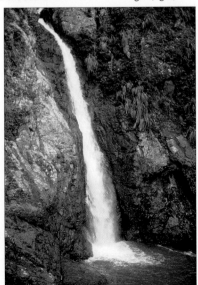

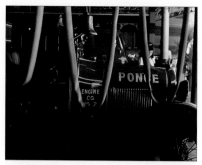
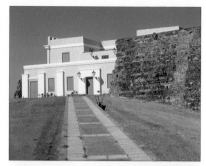
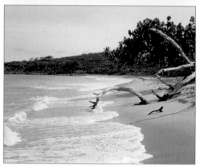
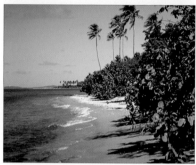

Clockwise from top left: Parque de Bombas, Ponce, Fort Conde Mirasol, Vieques, Zoni Beach, Culebra; Green Beach, Vieques. Bottom: The rainforest majesty of El Yunque.

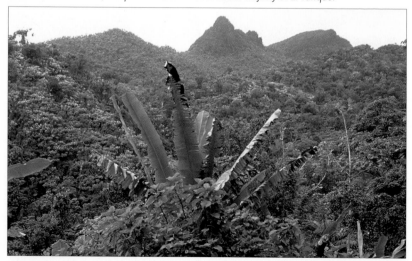

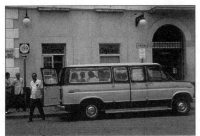

Público loads in Humacao.

minimum stay.
http://www.caribeplaya.com

On Hwy. 3 at Km 114.3, **Parador Caribbean Paradise** (☎ 787-839-5885, 787-839-7388, ✆ 787-271-0069) has 24 rms. with coffee makers and cable TVs. Convention facilities accommodate up to 150. The hotel has beach access and a restaurant. It charges from around $71-$89 d.
http://www.nbdigital.com/caribbean-paradise

At Km 113 on Carr. 3 near Patillas, the seven-unit **Villa del Carmen Resort** (☎ 787-839-7536/4711, ✆ 787-839-4711; Box 716, Arroyo, PR 00714) faces the beach and has two pools. A coral reef is offshore. It has an a/c furnished studio, as well as one-, two-, and three-bedroom apartments with a/c and cable TV. Rates start from around $50-$120 d.
http://wwwcottagelink.com/cottlink/o10/10-0010.html

At Maunabo and recommended by readers, **Playa Emajaguas Guest House** (☎ 787-861-6023; Box 834, Maunabo, PR 00717) has a/c rooms with sit-down full kitchen, pool table, playground, bar (BYOB), and tennis court. Rates run around $70 d. It's also right near the beach and the lighthouse.

Set on Playa Lucia to the E of Yabucoa and just off Hwy. 901 in Carr. 9911, the **Palmas de Lucia Hotel** (☎ 787-893-4423/0291, ✆ 787-893-0291; Apdo. 1746, Yabucoa, PR 00767) is right on the beach. Rooms include a/c, color TV, private baths, and balconies. Facilities include pool, restaurant, meeting room, game room, children's playground, and basketball court. There's not a lot to do in the immediate vicinity. Rates run from around $85–$105 d.
http://www.palmasdelucia.com
julopez@east-net.com

DINING AND FOOD: There are a large number of restaurants in town. **Nutrilife**, a vegetarian restaurant, is at Ave. Muñoz Marín and C. Miguel Casillas.
Alo (☎ 787-648-5647) serves vegetarian dishes for lunch.
A **Pizza Hut** is on Carr. 906 near Carr. 30.

OUTLYING DINING: Overlooking the ocean at C. Marina 7 in Punta Santiago, **Daniel's Seafood** (☎ 787-852-1784) offers a variety of seafood specialties, including *pescado al Daniel*.
Tulio's Seafood (☎ 787-850-1840), C. Isidro Andreu 5 in Punta Santiago, serves seafood dishes ranging from stuffed red snapper to grilled lobster and rice with crabmeat. Also in Punta Santiago on Carr. 3 at Km 70.3, **Marie's** (☎ 787-852-5471) serves gourmet seafood dishes.
Paradise Seafood (☎ 787-852-1180), Km 75 on Carr. 3, specializes in seafood.
At C. Emilia Príncipe 1 in Juncos, **Tenedor** (☎ 787-734-6573) is a steakhouse set in an old rum distillery.
Playa Lucía has basic eateries such as **Bar Ortiz** and **Coco Mar**. To the W at Km 9.8, **Nuevo Horizonte** (☎ 787-839-6173) has good views and food. Farther on is **El Mar de la Tranquilidad** which has an outdoor balcony.

SHOPPING: The **Humacao Plaza** is a shopping mall.

SKYDIVING: the **Puerto Rican Skydiving Center** (☎ 787-726-0326) operates from Humacao's airstrip.
http://www.skydive-rp.com

Cayo Santiago

The small island off Cayo Santiago, off the coast near Humacao, contains a large colony of rhesus monkeys being specially bred for scientific experiments by the US Public Health Service. The monkeys were trapped in India in 1938 by C. Ray Carpenter, a pioneer in primate field studies, who recognized the need for a "wild" rhesus population in a controlled environment. Victimized at first by tuberculosis, the monkeys almost starved during the war when grant money ceased. In addition to providing a model for behavioral studies, the monkeys have provided clues in the fight against diabetes and arthritis. Over 300 articles have come from research and field studies performed here since 1978 alone. One of the monkeys bred here gained notoriety in 1996 when it escaped from a Florida research facility after being exposed to the herpes B virus. At present there are 20 scientists on the island. Unfortunately, no visitors are permitted. Some kayaking trips, however, come near the island.
http://cprc.rcm.upr.edu/cayosant.html

Palmas del Mar

The island's largest resort (located just S of Humacao) and self-described "New American Riviera," the 2,750 acres of Palmas del Mar, a former sugarcane plantation, offers golf, riding, beaches, tennis, deep sea fishing and, of course, dining and dancing. It's a great place to escape the island — and everything else for that matter and is worth a visit, even if you aren't staying here. The resort has 275 a/c rooms, suites, and villas with cable TV. These are grouped into two hotels: the 27-suite **Palmas Inn & Casino** and the **Candelero Hotel** (☎ 787-852-6000, 📠 787-852--6295 800-725-6273) There are seven restaurants and six pools. Read the reviews on www.wheretostay.com before booking.
http://www.palmasresort.com

DINING: The resort's major restaurant is **Chez Daniel** (☎ 787-822-6000), which serves gourmet French and Spanish dishes. A second is **Hermes Creative Cuisine** (☎ 787-285-2277), which is a cousin of the one in Condado. Eat out on the terrace or indoors under candlelight.

Other alternatives in the area are more casual. Specializing in fried fish, **El Chinchorro** is on Carr. 906, near the spot where the local fishing boats berth.

On the same road and hard to spot, **La Pesqueria** is another choice. Watch for the parking lot and picnic tables outside.

DIVING: In Palmas del Mar, **Coral Head Divers** (☎ 787-850-7208, 800-635-4529; Box CUHF, Humacao, PR 00792) is one of the island's premier dive operations, according to no less an authority than Joyce Huber, co-author of *Best Dives Snorkeling Adventures*. The shop has rentals (Sunfish, Boogie Boards, kayaks, snorkeling equipment), NAUI instruction, and offers trips to over 20 dive sites. Dive packages and special group rates are available.

DIVE SITES: Owing to large waves and freshwater runoff from shore, the sites with the best visibility are more than a few mi. from shore.

Set three mi. (4.8 km) SE of Palmas del Mar, **The Cracks** is a novice-level dive set at a depth of between 50 and 70 ft. (15–21 m).

The visibility here is between 30–60 ft., but the ledges support amazing coral and fish.

Creole Canyon, a small wall with a drop from 45 to 80 ft. (14–24 m), hosts wrasse, butterflyfish, and lace and other coral. It is 3.5 mi. (5.6 km) from shore.

The Reserve, set 4.5 mi. (7.2 km) SE of the resort, is an intermediate-level dive which has a depth of between 60–90 ft. (18–27 m). Expect many schools of fish as well as a colorful potpourri of coral here.

Suited for novices, **Basslet Reef** is 3.5 mi. (5.6 km) E of the resort. Diving here is at a depth of 40–60 ft. (12–18 m) with compromised visibility. Crevices and boulders host exotic species such as sea cucumbers. Porcupinefish, porkfish, and peacock flounders are also present.

At 4.5mi. (7.2 km) NE of the resort, **The Drift** is a novice dive which centers around a line of coral ledges. Visibility is good (up to 100 ft.), and is it easy to find your way around. Expect to see Venus sea fans, squid, lobster, and colorful fish.

Named after the town in Dr. Seuss's *The Grinch Who Stole Christmas*, **Whoville** has a Seuss-like structure with magnificent coral formations as well as rays, barracuda, sea fans, and angelfish. Visibility is around 100 ft., and this is an intermediate dive with a depth of from 50–70 ft. (15–21 m).

FISHING: At the resort's Site 6, **Shiraz Charters** (☎ 787-285-5718) specialize in deep sea fishing charters.

GOLF: The **Doral Resort** (☎ 787-285-2256, ☉ 787-852-6273) has the **Palm** ($110) and **Flamboyán** ($100) courses. After 2 PM, the charge is $65 on either course. It's open daily from 7 AM–5 PM.

Cayey

Founded in 1773, Cayey (pop. 50,000) means "place of the waters" in the indigenous tongue. A former center of coffee and cigar production, the town now has a UPR campus as well as a variety of manufacturing operations. Although strip malls frame its periphery, the town's center still appeals. http://www.mcayey.com

EVENTS: Held on Aug. 15, the town's *fiestas patronales* are its major event. The traditional music group **La Tuna de Cayey** performs on the plaza or in the campus around Christmas.

SIGHTS: The 18th-century Catholic church **Nuestra Señora de la Asunción** is in the town square.

At the local campus, the **Museo Ramón Frade** exhibits works by this artist. The university has the **Sala Luisa Capetillo**, a library named after the famous Puerto Rican feminist who called for sexual freedom for women in 1911. Capetillo was a valiant union activist who lived openly with her lover, had children out of wedlock, and was arrested in Cuba for the crime of wearing a man's suit in public.

Off the Las Américas Expressway between Cayey and Salinas, the **Jíbaro Puertorriqueño** is a popular monument. The **sports complex** has a remote control racetrack.

DINING AND ACCOMMODATIONS: On Carr. 7737 at Km 2.1, **El Batey de Toñita** (☎ 787-738-1890) serves traditional Puerto Rican dishes.

On Carr. 1, **Jardín de Chiquitín** (☎ 787-263-2800) offers a variety of seafood. It has an indoor patio garden.

On Carr. 7737 at Km 2.8, the **Maramelinda** (☎ 787-738-9031/0715)

If you happen to go through the **Bosque Forestal Real de Patillas**, an excellent place to stop in the area for a taste of Puerto Rican atmosphere is **Vega's Place**, a small bar in an attractive location.

serves seafood and gourmet dishes.

Combining a Swiss chalet and medieval ambiance, **La Casona de Guavate** (☎ 787-747-5533), Carr. 184 at Km 28.5, offers a variety of gourmet items, including filet mignon stuffed with lobster. They also offer gourmet camping in large tents with queen-sized beds (for around $20 pn) at their **Posada El Castillo**. Statues of Jesus flirt with those of Greek gods, and flaming torches ward off the night.

In Barrio Jájome Alto on Carr. 15 at Km 18.6, **Jájome Terrace** (☎ 787-738-4016) has cheese soup and Puerto Rican specialties.

In Salinas, **La Barca** (☎ 787-824-2592) serves fresh seafood. Also here, **Ladi's** (☎ 787-824-2035) has Puerto Rican dishes, and **La Puerta de la Bahía** (☎ 787-787-824-7717), Principal 298 at la Playita, serves seafood prepared Puerto Rican style. It is spacious, a/c, and looks out over the water.

The Sand and the Sea (☎ 787-763-4004, 787-866-2991) is a moderately-priced four-room rustic lodge which is nowhere near either. Instead, it is on a ridge. Follow the signs to the restaurant next door, **Siempre Vida**, which is at Carr. 714, Km 5.2. Siempre Vida has great views from its open-air dining room and a unique menu which includes items such as Russian *tostones* (deep-fried plaintains topped with caviar and sour cream). Evenings are enhanced by piano music.

INFORMATION: For tourist information, call 787-738-3211, ext. 12.

Carite Forest Reserve (Guavate)

(Reserva Forestal Carite)

Reserva Forestal Carite ☎ 787-864-8903) is relatively small (6,000 acres, 2,428 ha) but refreshingly cool (average temperature: 72° F) and moist forest reserve contains sierra palms, teak, and mahogany. It borders **Charco Azul**, a 30-foot-wide cool blue pool and undeveloped **Lago Carite** (which features a partially abandoned housing project and has good fishing: bring your equipment).

A bit of dwarf forest surrounds the communication tower, an eyesore that mars the 3,000-ft. **Cerro La Santa** peak.

The reserve also includes **Nuestra Madre**, a Catholic retreat with lush gardens (the site of an Easter pilgrimage commemorating an alleged appearance of the Virgin Mary); **Campamento Guavate**, a minimum security penal facility; four picnic areas, and a camping spot.

Among the 50 species of birds found here are the Puerto Rican tanager and the Puerto Rican bullfinch (*como ñame*). **Lago Patillas**, in the area, is also worth a visit.

HIKING: From the Charco Azul picnic and camping site on Carr. 184 (the SE section of the park), a path leads to **Charco Azul**; from there an overgrown path ascends **Cerro La Santa** (2,730 ft, 832 m), the reserve's highest point.

The trailhead for the steep and strenuous three-mi. *Sendero El Seis* is in the Area Recreativa Real Patillas set at the SW end of the forest. Nice views. It terminates at a junction of Carr. 184. One car could be left at the start and end point if you wish to only hike one way.

Beginning at a junction with Carr. 184 and running along the Río de la Plata, the *Sendero Relámpago* is a challenging trail which runs around four miles.

The **Sendero Doña Jovita** starts near the NW entrance on Carr. 184 and takes a loop around the Río Guavate. Bring your binoculars for birdwatching.

The **Sendero El Radar** heads off the NW corner to the top of **Cerro Baliós** (3,000 ft. 1000 m) which, in typical Puerto Rican fashion, has a weather radar antenna facility at the top.

PRACTICALITIES: The town of Carite has *lechonerías* galore; there's live music and a roasted pig on every spit on weekends.

Permission to **camp** in the reserve ($4) must be obtained in advance from the **Recursos Naturales y Ambientales** (Department of Natural Resources and the Environment, ☎ 787-724-3724, 787-724-3647) in Puerto de Tierra, San Juan.

Carite Lake Village (☎ 787-763-4004/866-2991) provides lodging in moderately-priced villas. There's also a restaurant, pool, shop, and ball courts.

Las Casas de la Selva

This 1,000-acre, 2000-ft-high reserve is N of Patillas in the Sierra de Cayey next to the Carite reserve. The project is managed by Tropic Ventures. Site managers Cathy and Douglas Carasquillo welcome campers. You may either bring your own tent ($10 per tent) or rent one of the project's very spacious tents. Use of kitchen and bath is $5 pp, pd. You may rent a tent for $25 d. which includes bath and kitchen use. A double room with bath is also available. Meals can be provided if you arrange for this in advance and pay a deposit. There are two hiking trips offered here, subject to the availability of a guide, so you will need to book in advance. A three-hour visit ($30 pp, which includes lunch) offers a 1.5-hour walk on a loop trail with a possible stop at a small waterfall with a swimming hole. A

second trip ($100 pp) is to Hero Valley, one of three watersheds which intersect the reserve en route to Laguna Patillas and the Caribbean. Two hours from the homestead, you descend steeply to a river. Continuing downstream, you jump from rock to rock; a rope may be necessary. After a picnic at one of the swimming holes, you then continue downstream, where transport awaits; dinner is included.

Depending upon the route, you will need 5–8 hrs. for the trip, and you should leave no later than 9 AM. Good shoes and long pants are recommended for this trip. Overnight camping can also be arranged. A waterfall and bathing pool are near the main building. One of the premier forested tracts still remaining on the island, the reserve was once a coffee plantation that supported 30 families along with a coffee mill. Wild coffee trees and pineapples are still found. More than 40,000 trees have been planted on 220 acres — using a line planting method as opposed to monoculture — and the hope is eventually to maintain the reserve through sustainable tree farming. Research students (from as far afield as Yale) arrive on occasion, and for the last two years Earthwatch Foundation have sponsored the projects research and regularly send volunteers. At night blinking fireflies and *coquis* provide ambiance. For more information and camping rates call 787-839-7318. For more overall project information, contact Sally Silverstone at 505-424-8131. Be sure to call in advance as the front gate is generally locked.

GETTING HERE: To reach the reserve by road take Exit 33 (Carr. 184) from Carr. 52 and head through the Carite Forest Reserve towards Patillas. On the way you will pass a turnoff to the L, Carr. 179 to the R which heads to Guayama, and Carr. 7740 to the L which heads to San Lorenzo. From the latter, it's two miles to the woodyard at Km 16.1 on Carr. 184, which marks the turnoff to Las Casas.

www.ecotechnics.edu/lc.html

Patillas

The most famous structures in Patillas are the **Iglesia de San Benito Abad** (1930), on the main plaza, and the **Antiguo Hospital Municipal** (1906), C. Muñoz Rivera.

PRACTICALITIES: This small town has several small hotels. The **Caribbean Paradise Hotel** (☎ 787-839-5885, ✆ 787-271-0069), on Carr. 1, is locally owned and hospitable. Although it's near the beach, the water can be choppy at times. It has **Frenesí**, a gourmet restaurant a pool, and tennis courts. Horseback riding, scuba, and boat trips can be arranged. Rooms have a/c, TV, and coffee makers. Rates statt at around $90 d.

www.nbdigital.com/caribbeanparadise
caribbean@isla.net

Set on the shore, **El Mar de la Tranquilidad** (☎ 787-839-6469), Carr. 3, Km 118.9, serves a variety of seafood dishes. **Manatees** may be sighted here, off a concrete quay near the restaurant, but you need to be in place at dawn.

Guayama

Guayama, known as the "City of Witches," still retains a Spanish colonial aura. Founded in 1736, it was largely destroyed by fire in the 1800s. The city's many old buildings reflect its importance as a 19th C sugar port.

Over the opposition of the Association of Agronomists, the Environmental Quality Board gave its approval to the construction of a coal-fired energy plant in Guayama.

Expected to produce 9% of the island's energy needs, it will take five of the 6.1 million gallons needed from the water-treatment plant. In addition, some 75-100,000 tons of limestone are to be required on an annual basis. This will be mixed with the coal in order to neutralize the plant's sulfur emissions. It is not clear where the limestone will come from. The plant will open sometime in 2003 or so.

SIGHTS: Definitely don't miss the **Museo Casa Cautiño** (☎ 787-864-9083), C. Palmer at Vicente Palés on the central plaza, which is open Tues. to Sat. from 9 AM–4 PM and Sun. from 10 AM–5 PM; $2 admission.

Built in 1887 by Don Genaro Cautiño Vazquez, it is dedicated to his family who lived here and contains antique furnishings. This extremely white house, whose fancy grillwork and tall arched windows clearly set it apart, is set on a corner of the town's main plaza.

Designed by Manuel Texidor, it is part French and part Puerto Rican in its design. The living room and bedrooms contain art deco and Victorian pieces. Persian carpets abound, and the large bathroom has a sparkling white bidet, shower, and bathtub.

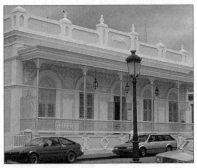

Casa Cautino in Guayama is not to be missed.

The Cautiño family made its fortune through exploiting sugarcane workers and dealing in tobacco and cattle. The home was forfeited to the government in lieu of back taxes in 1974 and was reopened as a museum in 1987.

The nearby church, the twin-turreted **San Antonio de Padua**, is the town's oldest standing structure, having been rebuilt in the 19th century.

The **Centro de Bellas Artes de Guayama** (☎ 787-864-7765), Carr. 3 (C. MacArthur.) exhibits historical artifacts and paintings in the rooms of a beautifully-restored classic structure. It's open Tues. to Sat. from 9 AM–4:30 PM, and on Sun. from 10 AM–4:30 PM.

A large **sugar plantation windmill** ruin stands on the outskirts of Guayama.

The **Mariposario Las Limas** (☎ 787-864-6037), Carr. 747, Km 0.7, is a wildlife reserve with trails, heliconia gardens, butterflies, museum and fish tanks. It's open from Thurs. to Sun. and on holidays from 10 AM–4 PM.

The **Guayama Trolley** (☎ 787-864-7765) offers a free guided tour to all local points of interest by reservation (Tues. to Sat.) and on Sun. from 10 AM–3:30 PM. It leaves from the Casa Cautiño.

From the Santa Isabel *malecón*, it's possible to hike several miles E past Punta Figuras (swimming not recommended) to Punta Guilarte.

PRACTICALITIES: The 20-room **Molino Inn** (☎ 787-866-1515, ✆ 787-866-1510), Carr. 3 at Km 138.5, is popular with business travelers and is relatively uncrowded on weekends. It has attractive carpeted a/c rooms with cable TV and desks and features a restaurant, pool, tennis court, and basketball court. Rooms run around $90 d. The restaurant offers both Caribbean and international dishes and has entertainment on weekends.

The **El Balcó Café** (☎ 787-864-7272), C. Hostos 47, is an attractive traditional house which serves breakfast and lunch weekdays, adding evening meals on the weekends. Grab a sandwich or coffee and sit out on the balcony and kick back. Locals head here on weekends and bring their guitars.

Set in another old house (1862), **El Suarito** (☎ 787-864-1820) is wildly popular with locals. It's open for three meals daily except Sun.

ENTERTAINMENT: The **Plaza Guayama Cinemas** (☎ 787-866-6666; Carr. 3, Km. 134.6) consists of a six-theater complex.

Arroyo

The small W coast town of Arroyo was founded in 1855. The main street, C. Morse, was named for the inventor Samuel Morse, who arrived in 1848 to oversee installation of telegraph lines. He ran a wire from his son-in-law's farm on the edge of town to the town center. His visit was undoubtedly the most thrilling event that has occurred here before or since the town's foundation. A monument to him stands in the town's main plaza. Several 19th-century houses, with captain's walks on the roofs, were built by New England sea captains who settled here.

On C. Morse near the Alcaldía, the **Antigua Casa de Aduanas** (Old Customs House, ☎ 787-839-8096) is now used as the *Centro Cultural*; it dates from 1937. Also see the nearby **old houses** (from 1850) at C. Morse 67 and (from 1890) at C. Morse 92.

El Tren del Sur, (☎ 787-271-1574) an old train, runs from Arroyo to Guayama. Afterwards, a trolley takes visitors on tours of the town of Arroyo for an hour. The train runs on the hour from 9:30 AM–4:30 PM on Sat., Sun., and holidays. It costs $3 for adults, $2 for children, and $1.50 for seniors.

Manatees are sometimes seen feeding offshore along the mangrove coast near Salinas. Good snorkeling is found off of Cayo Medio Luna.

The **Auberge Olimpico** (☎ 787-724-2290, off the Salinas toll booth on the Ponce Expressway, provides modern training facilities (including pool, track and field course, baseball and soccer fields, and a children's park) for Olympic athletes — facilities which visitors may use. The Central American Games were held here in 1993. It's open daily, 8 AM–10 PM.

In the town of Santa Isabel to the W of Salinas, the **Iglesia Nuestra Sra. de Las Mercedes**, C. Colón at Sanchez, dates from 1737; it was renovated in 1887.

EVENTS: The **Carnival Cristóbal L. Sánchez** takes place around mid-Feb. in July.

ACCOMMODATION: Cabins (and campsites) at **Punta Guilarte** are rented out by **Fomento** (☎ 722-1771/1551, 721-2800 ext. 225, 275) to bona fide family groups. For more information and a reservation form (apply 120 days in advance) write to Oficina de Reservaciones, Compania de Fomento Recreativo, Apdo. 9022089, San Juan PR 00904-2089.

Outside of town in Barrio Branderi, 22-room **Hotel Restaurant Brandemar** (☎ 787-864-5124) is off the road to Arroyo. It has a pool, popular seafood restaurant, and borders an attractive beach. Rooms rent for around $60 d. and have a/c and cable TV.

Located next to the boat slips at Playa de Salinas, 33-room **Posada Náutico** (☎ 787-752-8484, 787-824-3185, ⊕ 768-7676; 8 Chapin, Playa de Salinas, Salinas, PR 00751) at the **Marina de Salinas** caters to both yachties and landlubbers. Free trans-

port is offered to nearby islands. It has a seafood restaurant, the **Costa Marina** (☎ 787-824-6647) laundromat, and a miniplaza. Rates run from around $70 d on up.

The 23-rm. **Puerta La Bahía Hotel and Restaurant** (☎ 787-824-7117, ⊕ 787-824-7117), C. Principal, Sector Playita, is right on Bahía de Salinas. It charges from $75–150 d.

OTHER FOOD: The **Cafeteria Vegeteriano** in the town has a health food store.

La Llave del Mar (☎ 787-839-6395) is an expensive seafood restaurant on Paseo del Las Américas, which is across from the *malecón*.

Aguirre

This area was home to **Central Aguirre**, a large sugar mill which closed in April 1990. For an account of the mill's history and controversial closure, see *Kicking Off the Bootstraps* by Déborah Berman Santana.

The **Aguirre Visitor's Center** (☎ 787-853-3569/4617) is set in a former social club and bowling alley. It offers a photographic history of the town and information about the reserve. It's open weekdays but closes for lunch between noon–1 PM.

GOLF: The **Aguirre Golf Club** (☎/⊕ 787-853-4052) dates from 1925, when Bostonians built it for sugar mill executives. It's open daily from 7:30 AM–6 PM.

RESERVA FORESTAL AGUIRRE: Consisting of mangroves, salt flats, and estuaries, as well as a beach, the **Reserva Forestal Aguirre** (☎ 787-853-3569) is part of Bahía Jobos (and the Bahía Jobos Reserve) to the W. Manatees and sea turtles may be seen offshore here, and it is a great area for birding (from the boardwalk) as well as kayaking. Expect to see endangered brown pelicans and some 87 other species. Its **Mar Negro** consists of a number of dark colored lagoons. Enter from Carr. 3 at Km 144.7; it's open from 7:30 AM–4 PM daily.

TOURS AND KAYAKING: Hiking, kayaking, and eco-tours are available though the reserve. Call 787-853-3569 for information. **Marina de Salinas** (☎ 787-824-3185) rents out kayaks.

AGUIRRE DINING: In Aguirre, **Restaurant El Batey** (☎ 787-853-3386) doubles as something of a historical museum.

Aibonito

Aibonito (from *Artibonicu*, "River of the Night," the Taíno name for this region) is a small but colorful town set in a valley and surrounded by mountains. It has a Mennonite community, well-tended flower gardens, and boasts Puerto Rico's lowest recorded temperature (40° F in 1911). Once an important tobacco and coffee growing area, Aibonito is now known for its poultry farms and processing plants as well as its factories, which produce pharmaceuticals, clothing, electronic goods, and hospital equipment. The Seventh Day Adventists founded a high school here in 1920, the first of 19 academies all over the island that followed in its wake.

EVENTS: Generally taking place around the beginning of June, the town's best known celebration is its traditional **Flower Festival**, (☎787-735-4070) in which colorful flowers (including gardenias, anthuriums, and begonias), gardens, and exhibits occupy 10 acres. There's also music, food stalls, and shows. It all takes place on Carr. 722, next to City Hall Coliseum.

SIGHTS: Standing next to the town plaza, the beautiful white **San José Church** dates from 1825. The twin-towered structure was reconstructed in 1978. The plaza's trees are

trimmed in the shape of low-lying umbrellas.

Now notable only for its spectacular view, **Las Trincheras** ("the trenches") marks the spot where the last battle of the short-lived American 1898 invasion was fought — a skirmish that took place the day after the armistice had been signed!

Another famous panoramic landmark is **La Piedra Degetau**, a large boulder overlooking the town and on the site of the farm of Federico Degetau Gonzales, former Resident Commissioner in Washington, DC. It has a children's playground, where your brood can let off steam.

Signs marked "Casa Manresa" lead to the Catholic retreat center of the same name.

PRACTICALITIES: La Italiana, a pizzeria, and the **Tropical Surf Shop** are on a street running parallel to the plaza. There's also an attractive public library.

At Km 0.8 on Carr. 7718, **La Piedra** (☎ 787-735-1034) serves traditional local dishes using area vegetables and spices; they also have a helicopter tour service.

Offering disabled access, a small cafeteria and a/c, **El Coquí Posada Familiar** (☎ 787-735-3150, ☺ 787-735-2297), Carr 722, Km 7.3, is moderately priced at around $75 d. http://premium.caribe.net/~aibonito/coqui.htm

The **Swiss Inn Guest House** (☎ 787-735-8500), Carr. 14, is a moderately-priced hotel.

Barranquitas

At 1,800 ft., Barranquitas is not only one of the highest towns on the island, but also one of the most beautifully situated. Viewed from the massive volcanic rocks that cradle it, the town resembles a Spanish medieval print. The Catholic church towers above houses that seem to have been built right on top of each other.

> " "The most important living Puerto Rican is the President of the Senate and the leader of the Popular Democratic Party, the American-educated Luis Muñoz Marín. This man has striking qualities. Of all the political personages I met in Latin America, I would put him near the top. Powerful physically, contemptuous of formality, careless in appearance, with a vivid imagination and a brilliant critical mind, Muñoz Marín is destined to go far in the affairs of the Western Hemisphere." — John Gunther, *Inside Latin America*, 1941

Its chief claim to fame is as the birthplace of Puerto Rican statesman Luis Muñoz Rivera (see "History" in "Introduction"). At the **Museo Biblioteca**, in the wooden house where he was born in 1859, a small museum displays letters, pictures, newspaper clippings, a car used in his 1915 funeral procession, furniture and other items.

Down the road is the **Mausoleo de Don Luis Muñoz Rivera**, C. Muñoz Rivera, located next to the tomb where Don Luis (1859-1916) and his son Luis Muñoz (1898-1980) are buried. It documents his funeral vividly with objects and papers relevant to his demise. There are pictures of his life, his works, and bronze casts of his head and hands. Right in front of the entrance is the marble tomb. To the R are their wives. The pensive statue of Amistad, which gazes down at the tomb, is labeled "*hoy y siempre*," now and always.

The nearby **Casa Museo Joaquín de Roja y Martínez** (☎ 787-857-2065) houses the small tourist office. It's well worth a visit in order to look at the collection alone.

Ramón Luis and **Luis Angel Colón** (☎ 787-857-0117, 787-857-4394, 787-857-1513) carve cuatros in their Sector La Torre workshop.

The **Monumento al Jíbaro Puertorriqueño** is at Km 49 on the Expressway to the S of town. It depicts a rural family.

EVENTS: Barranquitas celebrates its *fiestas patronales*, that of San Antonio de Padua, around June 13.

The **National Crafts Fair** (☎ 787-857-2065) is held here in mid-July in the town plaza; over a hundred artisans participate.

ACCOMMODATION: The **Hacienda Margarita** (☎ 787-857-0414), Km. 1.7 on Carr. 152, has 27 comfortable rooms, perhaps the best in the area. Rooms have cable TV and balconies. A deluxe room with Jacuzzi is offered as is the original farmhouse which is suitable for a group. It charges from around $80 d.

FOOD: At Km 1.7 on Carr. 152 and commanding an impressive view, **Hacienda Margarita** (☎ 787-857-0414; see hotel mention above) serves steak and seafood dishes. It sometimes has live music on weekends.

On the same road, **El Coquí** (☎ 787-857-3828) is definitely not for vegetarians, let alone those shy of lard. Its *arroz con buruquena* features a crab that can only be captured in caves or on moonless nights. The shells are restuffed with a combination of meat, spices, and sticky rice. It must be ordered a few days ahead of time.

In the town, **Bar Plaza** (☎ 787-857-4909) offers reasonably priced local food.

Up on Carr. 152, **El Mofongo Criollo** (☎ 787-857-0480) specializes in mofongo and seafood dishes. It's very popular with locals. Another small local restaurant is on Carr. 156 to the N of town.

VICINITY OF BARRANQUITAS: Indian relics have been found in a number of caves near the town. Nearly inaccessible, the

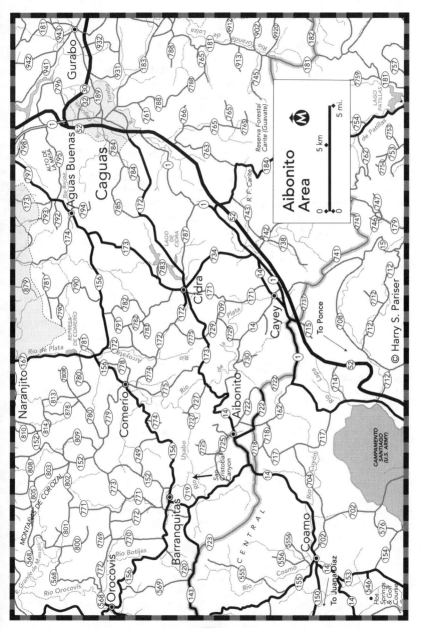

© Harry S. Pariser

Aibonito Area

deep gorge of **San Cristóbal Canyon**, located along the road to Aibonito, is the most spectacular and deepest on the island. Precipitous cliffs, densely covered with vegetation (guava, shortleaf fig, and climbing bamboo), plunge 500–750 ft. to a rocky valley where the Río Usabon races over boulders, dropping 100 ft. at one point. Catch a glimpse from Carr. 725 (and side road 7715), 156, and 162. Best of these is from the San Cristóbal Development on Carr. 156, Km 17.7. An unmarked trail leads into the gorge from here (see below). Some 1,200 acres of this six-mile volcanic rift have been purchased during the past two decades by the Conservation Trust. An old refurbished house here hosts visiting artists, researchers, and scientists, and a five-acre tree nursery produces some 45,000 trees each year.

HIKING: This area was a former dump before its acquisition by the Conservation Trust during the 1970s, and some overgrown debris is still in evidence. It remains undeveloped for hiking. Entrances can be difficult to find, and it can be dangerous, so a guide or organized trip is best.

One steep path branches off of Carr. 7725 between Aibonito and Barranquitas and leads to a 100-ft. (30-m) waterfall, the nation's highest. Allow about 1.5 hours RT. A second and yet steeper trail runs from Barrio San Cristóbal (Carr. 156, Km 17.7) down to the canyon floor (allow one hour), where you can explore the area by clambering over gigantic slippery boulders. Exercise caution while hiking here: in 1993, nine people were rescued from the canyon after being trapped by rising river waters.

In Aibonito, hikes through the canyon leave from the **Piedra Restaurant** (☎ 787-735-1034). You need to find your own guide. **Felix Rivera** (☎ 787-735-8721) is available to lead groups of five or more.

Miguel Angel de Jesús (☎ 787-875-3657) also leads tours. Be sure to bring food and water, good shoes, and rain gear.

ACCOMMODATION: The 13-rm. **El Coquí Familiar** (☎ 787-735-3150, 787-735-2225, ✆ 787-735-2297), Carr. 722, Km 7.3 is S of Rt 14 at the E end of Aibonito. It charges around $75 d.

The **Las Casitas** (☎ 787-735-0180), KM. 4.8 on Carr. 162, charges around $80 d.

Coamo

This small town has its old church set in a plaza enlivened by flowering bouganvillea. Once the site of two flourishing Taíno Indian villages, only a solitary Indian remained at the time of the town's founding in 1579. As the third oldest town on the island (after San Juan and San Germán), its name, San Blas de Illecas de Coamo, was derived from the patron saint of a major landowner — an expatriate from Illecas, Spain. Its *fiestas patronales* of San Blas/Nuestra Señora de la Candelaria take place in early Feb.

SIGHTS: The **Catholic church** is decorated with paintings by internationally renowned Puerto Rican artists José Campeche and Francisco Oller. The latter's Cuadro de las Animas features a blonde (rumored to be Oller's girlfriend) being tortured in purgatory. One of the church's three bells — said to have sounded so loudly that its vibrations killed fish off the coast and shattered lamps and glass in nearby homes — has been silenced by public pressure for over a century.

An elegant two-story masonry mansion built by Clotilde Santiago, the town's wealthiest and most powerful farmer and entrepreneur during Spanish rule, still stands at one corner of the plaza. Converted to a museum, the **Museo**

Histórico de Coamo (☎ 787-825-1150) it now houses historical memorabilia, gold-plated bathroom fixtures, and mahogany furniture. It is open weekdays from 8-noon and 1–4:30 PM. Admission is free.

The town's major landmark, however, is not a building but a group of **hotsprings**. First used by the island's indigenous inhabitants, the springs gained an international reputation by the end of the 19th century. Some assert that they are the Fountain of Youth Ponce de León had heard about from the Indians before taking off to search for it in Florida.

To reach them, take the road outside of town going toward the Baños de Coamo Parador, a government-run inn built on the site of the Coamo Springs Hotel, which once sheltered the likes of Franklin Delano Roosevelt. Proceeding past the *parador*, turn R to find the springs. There are two large concrete pools. One is hot and the other is warm. The overflow from the hotter one flows down into the warm one. The ideal time to visit is right at dusk, but many Puerto Ricans also have the same idea.

The 6,647-yard **Coamo Springs** (☎ 787-825-1370) is the only 18-hole, par-72 championship golf course in southern Puerto Rico.
http://www.coamosprings.com
coamogolf@coamosprings.com

WHERE TO STAY: The only choice is **Parador Baños de Coamo** (☎ 787-825-2186/2239, ☻ 787-825-4739; Box 540, Coamo, PR 00769) which is outside town on Carr. 546 at Km 1. One reader wrote "Our room was terrific and had a balcony with two rocking chairs. It was a beautiful place where we met a lot of interesting people." Its **Café Puertorriqueño** offers international and local fare. For reservations, call 800-443-0266 in the US; 787-721-2884 in San Juan.
http://www.banosdecoamo.com

Ponce

Often neglected by visitors, the S coastal city of Ponce has much to offer. An impressive fine art museum, a restored historical district, a colorful firehouse set on the main plaza, free tram buses to take you around, and nearby historical and ecological attractions number among its many attractions.

Though it's the second largest city in Puerto Rico, Ponce (pop. 191,000) has much more the feeling of a small town than bustling metropolitan San Juan. Set between the blue of the Caribbean and the green of the Cordillera Central mountain range, its central location makes it easy to visit other locales. Ponce is just big enough to be fun to walk around and still small enough to allow for an easy escape.

Ponce is a city of many names. It is known as "La Perla del Sur" (The Pearl of the South), "La Ciudad Senorial" (Manorial City), and "La Ciudad de las Quenepas" (City of the Honeyberries). Ponce has played host to many prominent islanders, including opera tenor Antonio Paoli, composer Juan Morel-Campos, and painter Miguel Pou. *Ponceños* exhibit noticeably more civic pride than do residents of other urban locales. For example, you'll actually see city residents putting garbage in garbage cans, an act of civic pride rarely seen elsewhere.

Ponce's official website is only in Spanish but has good info:
http://www.ponceweb.org

HISTORY: Established in 1692, Ponce was named after Juan Ponce de León y Loaiza, the great-grandson of Puerto Rico's first governor, Ponce de León. Originally, Ponce was a town with only two entrances: one would enter either via a mountain road passing by the Church of La Guadalupe or along the road that borders the S coast. Point of entrance was La Ceiba de Cuatro

The Renewal of Historic Ponce

The renewal of Ponce's historic district is a highly encouraging example of what a city can do when it listens to some of its more visionary citizens. Sadly, in these days of huge outlying strip malls and monotonous and tasteless chain architecture, Puerto Rico is losing much of the traditional charm which constitutes a large part of its appeal. In much of the world, a great deal of traditional architecture is not being maintained, and many historic structures have been demolished to make way for concrete and steel and plastic. Good global examples range from Singapore (which has destroyed much of its ambience) to Beirut (where a massive urban renewal project has destroyed nearly all old buildings in its downtown area). As in the Virgin Islands, Barbados, and other areas in the world, conservation-minded locals with a vision are working to preserve these sites, repositories of local history and keepers of the as yet unlearnt lessons of history.

Once a shining and bustling city of commerce, Ponce had nearly dipped during the mid-1980s down to the position of "historic ruin." Its historic zone was derisively referred to as the "hysteric zone." Ponceno-turned-governor Rafael Hernández Colón issued an executive order in 1985 which directed $600 million to be used in a program called "Ponce en Marcha," a massive urban development plan aimed at restoring Ponce's prominence.

Naturally, there was a lot of protest from other municipalities, but things moved right along anyway. Roads were constructed anew, water mains were replaced and power lines buried, and $200 million was spent to build a highway system on the city's circumference. Young architects were brought in to blueprint designs. The Institute of Puerto Rican culture assembled a 13-member group to research and survey what changes would need to be implemented, including zoning restrictions and restoration guidelines. Tax incentives were applied along with persuasion in order to get merchants to go along. Buildings were painted in pastels because architect Magda Bardina established that this was the area's original colors. Restoration of buildings on the main plaza — from the Fox Delicias (1847) to to the City Hall (1847) — was paid for by the Government of Spain.

Urban renewal has been halted in recent years owing to lack of funds. A few museums have closed, and the entertainment district faltered. The main new change in the past few years has been a concrete-and-tree park named after Rafael Hernández Colón's mama. The city still has major problems, ones shared almost universally with other cities in the States and worldwide, but the center of Ponce still shines. It's a shining example of urban preservation, one which will hopefully permeate and transmute to other locales.

Calles (Ceiba of the Four Streets) which led, as it still does today, to the main streets of Commercio, Cruz, Salud, and Mayor.

Plantation owners from S America, fleeing political unrest at home, arrived in Ponce in the early 1800s. These entrepreneurs founded coffee, tobacco, and agricultural plantations along the S coast. Plantations were worked by slaves who endured abominable conditions, but the town flourished.

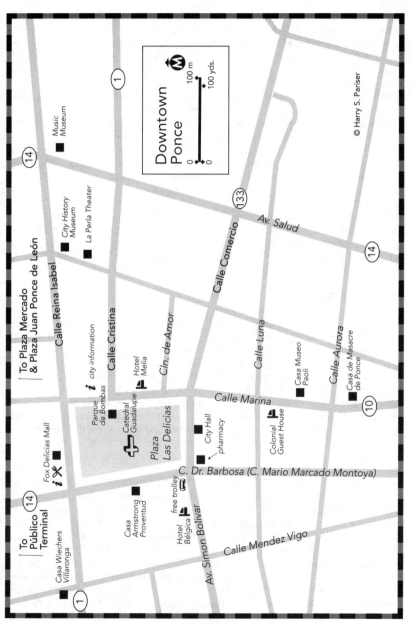

Downtown Ponce

© Harry S. Pariser

100 m
100 yds.

Music Museum

City History Museum

La Perla Theater

To Plaza Mercado & Plaza Juan Ponce de León

Av. Salud

Calle Comercio

Calle Reina Isabel

Calle Cristina

Cln. de Amor

Calle Luna

Calle Aurora

i city information

Hotel Melia

Casa Museo Paoli

Casa de Masacre de Ponce

Calle Marina

Parque de Bombas

Catedral Guadalupe

Plaza Las Delicias

City Hall

pharmacy

Colonial Guest House

Fox Delicias Mall

i ✗

C. Dr. Barbosa (C. Mario Marcado Montoya)

free trolley

Casa Armstrong Proventud

Hotel Bélgica

To Público Terminal

Av. Simon Bolivar

Calle Mendez Vigo

Casa Wiechers Villaronga

In 1877-78, when it was granted the title of Ciudad (city) by royal decree, Ponce was already the social, military, and commercial center of the S coast. The city stumbled on into the next century. Briefly revitalized by the oil industry from the mid-1970s to 1980s, Ponce collapsed towards the end of the 1980s.

Under the leadership of Ponce Mayor Rafael Cordero Santiago, downtown Ponce has been revitalized in recent decades under the "Ponce en Marche" program (see box titled "The Renewal of Historic Ponce"). Thousands of *Ponceños* participated in a protest in San Juan in 1993. That same year Ponce hosted the 27th Central American and Caribbean Games.

Those interested in learning in greater detail about the town's history should visit the Museum of the History of Ponce.

GETTING HERE: An expressway (Carr. 52) runs from San Juan to Ponce; every so often you must throw some change in the basket. You can also arrive via Guayama and Salinas (Carr. 1), Coamo and Juana Diaz (Carr. 14), Adjuntas (Carr. 10), and Mayagüez (Carr. 2). Ponce is approachable by bus from Utuado or Adjuntas, or by *público* from Río Piedras, Santurce, Mayagüez, or other neighboring towns. As you approach the town, you'll notice the urban sprawl beginning with Burger King, malls, and the like.

BY AIR: **American Eagle** flies from San Juan's Muñoz Marín International Airport.

GETTING AROUND: Ponce is small enough that any part of the main area may be reached on foot. Free trolley service, free train-cart, and free carriage rides (weekends only) start from Plaza Las Delicias. Running from 8 AM–9 PM, the trolleys are fun and allow you to get oriented, but they are slow. The nine trolleys have three routes; the train-cart takes around two hours and goes to the boardwalk. Trolley destinations may range as far afield as the ceiba tree and the cross. The best way to find out where it's going is to ask one of the friendly drivers.

Most **carros públicos** leave from the corner of C. Victoria and C. Unión, three blocks north of the plaza.

PARKING: A good multi-story **parking area** is on C. León between C. Sol and C. Isabel, on the E side of the street. Overnight parking is prohibited. Parking is also available under the new Parque Dora Colón on C. Marina.

TAXIS: Services include **Borinquen Taxi** (☎ 787-843-6000), C. Roosevelt; **Degetau Taxi** (☎ 787-840-7555), cor. C. Victoria and C. Molina; **Taxi Union** (☎ 787-840-9126), Centro Del Sur (shopping plaza); and **Ponce Taxi** (☎ 787-842-3370), cor. C. Méndez Vigo and C. Villa.

Ponce Sights

In recent years, an intensive $440 million revitalization project has increased the city's historic area from 260 to 1,046 buildings. Electrical and phone wires have been buried and streetlights in the shape of 19th-century gas lamps installed. More than 200 of its buildings have now been restored, and many of them are on streets radiating from the main square. The latest projects include a golf course for the Ponce Hilton, a Fine Arts and Convention Center, and a new business-class hotel for downtown.

THE PLAZA AREA: Ponce's beautiful **Plaza Las Delicias** (Plaza of Delights), with its fountains and gardens, is dominated by the **Cathedral of Our Lady of Guadalupe**. Built in 1670, it has been destroyed several times by earthquakes, and this version dates from 1931. Painted baby blue and with beautiful stained glass windows, the cathedral's entrances house wooden choir boys who solicit for alms.

Las Delicias is actually divided into two plazas. The first is **Plaza Muñoz Rivera**. In the plaza's center, the bronze statue of Luis Muñoz Marín, first elected governor of Puerto Rico and the son of Muñoz Rivera, gazes out over the banks, travel agencies, and stores that surround the plaza.

On the S side, the **Federico Degetau Plaza** (named after the island's first resident commissioner in Washington who was born in Ponce) constitutes the other half.

Ponce is renowned for its fountains and in the plaza's center stands the **Fountain of the Lions** (Fuente de los Leones), a monument dedicated to eight brave citizens who risked their lives in 1899 to extinguish a fire in the munitions depot that might have spelled disaster for the city. Purchased in 1939 at the New York World's Fair, it was restored in 1993 when its base was enlarged and a computerized lighting system installed. View it at night, when it becomes obvious why Ponce is famous for its fountains.

There's also the **Obelisco a los Héroes del Polvorín** (Obelisk to the Heroes of the Polvorín), which commemorates the seven firefighters and one local citizen who extinguished an 1899 fire that spread over the US Army powder magazine. It dates from 1958 and replaces the original, which was destroyed by the 1918 earthquake.

A monument to Juan Morel Campos, known as the father of the Puerto Rican *danza* (see "Music and Dance" in the Introduction) also stands here. Born in Ponce in 1857, his *danzas* are still played in Puerto Rico, and many of his symphonic works have received international recognition.

Situated just off the plaza is Ponce's gaudy landmark the **Parque de Bombas** or firehouse. Painted red, green, black, and yellow, it has become the symbol of the city. Sole survivor of several buildings constructed for the Industrial Agricultural Exhibition held here on the plaza in 1882, it was donated to the homeless firemen in 1885 and was in active use until 1990. Restored to its original design, it now is a small museum housing a shiny fire truck that would've done the Beatles' firehouse on Penny Lane proud. The reverential first- and second-floor exhibits chronicle firefighting in Ponce. It's almost a shrine to firefighting. Objects displayed inside include various types of axes, brass nozzles, and a collection of firefighters' hats. It's open Mon. to Fri. (except Tues.) from 9:30 AM–6 PM; admission is free.

Across from the cathedral stands Ponce's **Casa Armstrong Proventud**, a restored mansion housing a small museum. A two-story masonry building, it has stained-glass windows and parquet floors. It houses furniture and antiques that belonged to 19th-century statesman José de Diego, and is open Mon. to Fri. from 8 AM–4:30 PM.

Casa Wiechers Villaronga, (☎ 787-843-3363), C. Mendez Vigo at C. Reigns, is open Wed. to Sun. from 9:30 AM to 4:30 PM. This mansion was constructed in 1912 by architect Alfredo Wiechers as his residence. Partially destroyed by the 1918 earthquake, it has been restored and now serves as a museum.

Also just off of the plaza, the **Fox Delicias Mall** was originally built as a theater in 1931; it now houses shops and eateries.

Casa Alcaldía (City Hall) was built around 1840 and was first used as a prison. Its clock dates from 1877. Be sure to see the fantastic woodcuts representing popular songs, which hang in the main entranceway. Teddy and Franklin Roosevelt, Herbert Hoover, and even George Bush have paid their respects to local officials here.

Another beautifully restored area is **Paseo Atocha** along C. Isabel. It's chock-a-block with stores, and features a street fair every third Sunday of the month. Visit it at night when the walkway gleams from the streetlamps and a few romantic couples promenade.

NEARBY SIGHTS: After finishing with the plaza area, continue on to the surrounding area. As mentioned above, the area surrounding C. Cristina, C. Isabela, C. Mayor, and C. Salud have been transformed into a historical zone.

At C. Mayor 14, the **Casa Paoli** was the birthplace of legendary operatic tenor, Antonio E. Paoli y Marcano. Born in 1871, Paoli was known as the "King of Tenors and the Tenor of Kings." Here you'll find a small museum, the headquarters of the Society for Folkloric Investigation, and a souvenir shop. Admission is free, and it's open from 10 AM–noon and 2–4 PM from Mon. to Fri.

S OF THE PLAZA: Set at the corner of C. Marina and C. Luna, the **Antiguo Casino** (Old Casino) is a neoclassic structure that was designed and built in 1922 by a local architect. Its tapestries and other decorations were the creation of Miguel Pou, a local painter. Once the scene of some of the nation's most elegant parties, it now houses government offices on its first floor.

Commemorating the massacre of Ponce (see "History" in the Introduction) the **Casa de la Masacre de Ponce** (☎ 787-844-9722) is at the corner of C. Marina and C. Aurora. At the time of the 1937 massacre, it held the local Nationalist Party's Assembly. This small museum may or may not be open; hours are irregular. Generally however, it is open Wed. through Sun. from 8:30 AM–4:30 PM.

Also on the same street, the **Holy Trinity Parish** was consecrated in 1874 and became the first Episcopal church in Spanish America. Queen Victoria intervened personally with the Spanish Crown in order to allow it to function, but for nearly its first quarter-century of operation the church's bell remained mute. It first sounded with the 1898 American invasion.

Commemorating the abolition of slavery in 1873, the **Obelisco de la Abolición y Concha Acústica** (Abolition of Slavery Obelisk and Acoustic Shell) seats up to 2,000. It's on C. Hostos near Las Américas.

E OF THE PLAZA: Set in the first Puerto Rican House to receive telephone service and in the original home of the city's art museum, the **Museo de la Musica Puertorriqueña** (☎ 787-848-7016, Puerto Rican Music Museum) is at C. Cristina 70, just down the street from the Hotel Melia and across to the L. This museum is a must-see for those interested in Latin and Puerto Rican music. In addition to presenting an overview of the island's music, it includes displays on such local luminaries as popular singer Ruth Fernández and composer Rafael Hernández. Its one drawback is that everything is titled in Spanish. As you come in, the first thing you see is a display of traditional instruments, including a reproduction of a Precolumbian *tambor* or log drum.

A display on your L highlights instruments used to interpret indigenous music at the University of Cayey; they are based on a description by de Oviedo. There's also a woodblock print, various posters, pictures of musicians, and a collection of musical instruments such as the *tiple, cuatro, maracas,* and *güiro*. The *marímbola*, a large thumb piano that you sit upon and pluck, was used by the Blacks here during the 16th century.

Entering the next room to your R, you find musical instruments, including a cello inscribed with mother of pearl in the shape of a butterfly. Here, there are some more old posters, a piano stand, and a piano. There's also an old jukebox with various hits such as *Lamento Boriñcano* and a display of old record covers. Also on exhibit are conga drums and masks. There's a good gift shop out front that has T-shirts, cassettes, and CDs for sale. Concerts are held on some Fri. evenings. It's open Wed. to Sun. from 9 AM–4:30 PM.

The **Museo de la Historia de Ponce** (☎ 787-844-7071, Museum of the History of Ponce) was inaugurated on Dec. 12, 1992, the 300th anniversary of the city's foundation. Set at the corner of C. Mayor and C. Isabel, it occupies two old houses (Casa Zapater and Casa Candal Salazar) on C. Isabel adjacent to Teatro La Perla. The two homes are joined by a patio graced with a lime tree. The museum's 10 rooms illustrate important events in the city's history. The first shows the area's natural history. Another shows the roles played by the various cultural groups as well as the transformation undergone during the 19th and 20th centuries. Other rooms trace the evolution of daily life and the city's medical, educational, and political dimensions. The museum publishes its own journal, and the gift shop sells books and crafts. Admission is $3 for adults, $2 for senior citizens, and $1 for children, and it's open daily (except Tues.). It's open daily from 9 AM–5 PM.

Just next door, **Teatro La Perla**, a theater and cultural hub for over a century, is one of the area's highlights. It is a recreation of the original that was built in 1864. Check at the box office to see what's playing.

Commemorating famous baseball player Pancho Coimbre, the **Museo Pancho Coimbre** houses memorabilia relating to the star as well as Ponce's Sports Hall of Fame. While not of great interest to outsiders, special exhibits are held here on occasion. It's open Tues. to Sun. from 9:30 AM–4:30 PM; free admission.

Just up the street is the **Escuela de Bellas Artes** (Fine Arts School) which once functioned as the Spanish garrison headquarters as well as hosting the American Army, a court

of justice, and a prison. Built in 1849 as El Castillo, it was transformed into the school in 1992 after an $8 million restoration.

NORTH FROM THE PLAZA: Incorporating Byzantine and art nouveau styles, the **Iglesia Metodista Unida** (United Methodist Church) has remarkable stained glass windows; it was built in 1900 by a Czech architect and is located at C. Mendez Vigo and C. Villa.

The **Nueva Plaza del Mercado** is at C. Estrella and C. Salud. Even as early as 7 AM you'll find a Jehovah's Witness holding up a copy of *Watchtower* at the door. Many sandwich and other food shops are here. Upstairs and accessed by an escalator, a smaller third level has check cashing, tailor shops, and *botanicas*.

A narrow passageway originally used as a meat market, **Plaza Juan Ponce de León** was designed and constructed in 1926. It was informally known as **Plaza de los Perros** (Dog's Market) because of the hordes of dogs that once competed for scraps. Now housing a variety of stalls — which sell everything from drinking coconuts and magic tricks to crafts and musical instruments — it is one of the most pleasant places to visit. You will find it between C. Mayor and C. León near C. Estrella; the motorized trolley stops here for 15 minutes.

OTHER MONUMENTAL SIGHTS: Set in the town's NW at the intersection on C. Guadelupe and C. Torres, the **Panteón Nacional Baldorioty de Castro** (Baldorioty de Castro National Mausoleum) dates from 1843 and was converted into a park in 1991. A number of local notables rest here, and concerts and other activities are held regularly. Free guided tours are offered Tues. to Thurs. from 9-6, Fri. from 9 AM–7 PM, and on Sat. and Sun. from 9 AM–10 PM.

The three-plaza **Tricentennial Park** (Parque del Tricentenario) was completed in 1992 in time for the tricentennial celebrations. Its centerpiece is a fountain dedicated to the city's most illustrious citizens. Set on either side, two small sub-plazas honor Luis A. Ferré and Hernández Colón, two former governors who were born here. A second plaza honors the city's architecture and features a rotunda. The third honors Latin American statesmen.

Spanning the Río Portugués, the **Puente de los Leones** (Lion's Bridge) is the gateway to the historical area. Two brass lions guard the entrance. The older one represents wisdom and experience, while the younger stands for the glorious future.

PONCE MUSEUM OF ART: The city's best known attraction is the Ponce Museum of Art on Ave. Las Américas across from Universidad Catolica Santa Maria. Designed by architect Edward Durrell Stone and financed by conservative multimillionaire industrialist and former Governor Don Luis Ferré, this block-long building uses natural light to lend a spacious effect to its hexagonal galleries. It contains the best collection of European art in the entire Caribbean.

From an original 400 works, the collection has grown to include more than 1,000 paintings and 400 sculptures. Three sculpture gardens branch off the main floor. Two dynamic 18th-century polychromed wooden statues carved in Toledo, Spain — representing Europe and America — greet the visitor near the entrance.

Besides portraits and the representative works of Puerto Rican master painters like José Campeche and Francisco Oller, the first floor also contains a 15th-century Siamese Bodhisattva bust, intricate Incan pottery, and fine handblown decorated glass pieces.

The second floor holds many fine sculptures and old European thematic religious paintings: plenty of blood, breasts, and skulls. See St. Francis at prayer and Pero feeding Cimon with her breast.

The museum also houses works by masters such as Van Dyck, Reubens, Velazquez, and Gainsborough. There is a good gift shop. It's open daily 10 AM–5 PM; admission is $4 for adults, $2 children, $1 students.

A good place to eat that features both Italian food and seafood, **Pizza Heaven**, C. Concordia, is within walking distance of the art museum. From the entrance, turn L and then head L again.

http://www.museoarteponce.org

OTHER OUTLYING SIGHTS: La Ceiba de Ponce, an enormous 300-year-old silk cotton tree overhangs C. Comercio about a half-mile E of the plaza. Once a meeting place for the Taíno Indians, it was featured in one of Franciso Oller's paintings.

El Vigía Hill, on Carr. 1 near C. Bertoly, is a famous lookout point surrounded by homes of the wealthy upper class.

La Cruzette del Vigía, a gigantic 100-ft.-high concrete cross, has been erected here. From Tues. to Fri. 9:30 AM–6 PM and Sat. and Sun. from 10 AM–5 PM, it's possible to head for the top and check out the views; $1 admission is charged. In the distant past, a watchman, noting the arrival of a visiting merchant vessel, would raise a flag to indicate its nationality.

To your L is the Serralés Mansion, which has been transformed into the **Museo Castillo Serrallés** (Serrallés Castle Museum, ☎ 787-259-1774). Built in the Spanish Revival style popular during the 1930s for the family that produces Don Q Rum, it now offers tours. The mansion includes a library, formal dining room, and living room, all decorated with period furniture. There's also a gift shop and coffee shop. It's open Tues. and Thurs. from 9:30 AM–5 PM, and Fri., Sat., Sun. and holidays from 10 AM–5:30 PM. Admission is $3 for adults, $2 for senior citizens, $1.50 for children and students. To get to these two sights by car, take Carr. 1 to C. Isabel, then turn R on C. Salud, L on C. Guadalupe, and R on C. Bertoly.

ART EXHIBITS: The **Casa del Abogado** (☎ 787-841-2123), a house built by a German architect in 1913, is run by the Ponce Historical Society and has art exhibits. Open Wed. to Sun. 9 AM–5 PM. Art is also exhibited in the **Galerías** inside the **Alcaldía** (City Hall) off of Plaza las Delicias.

Ponce Practicalities

DOWNTOWN ACCOMMODATIONS: Many hotels are clustered around the main square. A new business-class hotel will open in 2003 or 2004. Right in town at C. Villa 122, **Hotel Bélgica** (☎ 787-844-3255, ☺ 787-844-6149; Ponce, PR 00731) has 20 a/c rooms with TV and balconies from around $60–75 d. Be sure to get a room away from the street.
http://www.hotelbelgica.somewhere.net

In front of the Old Casino at C. Marina 33, the **Colonial Guest House** (☎/☺ 787-843-7585) charges around $90 d.

The 75-room **Hotel Melía** (☎ 787-842-0260/0261/4276, 800-742-4276, ☺ 787-841-3602; Box 1431, Ponce, PR 00733) is at C. Cristina 2. Facilities include a/c, phone, and TV in rooms. There's also a bar and restaurant. Rooms start at around $85-$120 d including continental breakfast.
http://home.coqui.net/melia
melia@coqui.net

OUTLYING ACCOMMODATIONS: The **Ponce Hilton & Casino** (☎ 787-259-7676/7777, ☺ 787-259-7674, 800-HILTONS; Box 7419, Ponce, PR 00732)

has 156 a/c rooms and suites, two restaurants, three lounges, jogging track, pool, fitness center, spa and sauna, Jacuzzi, convention center (1,500 capacity), a golf course (in 2003), and nearby beach. It charges from $185-$220 d. For more information call 800-259-7676.
http://www.ponce.hilton.com
poncehil@coqui.net

The 120-room **Howard Johnson Ponce** (☎ 787-841-1000, ☺ 787-841-2560), on Carr. 2 at Km 221.2, offers 120 a/c rooms and suites with cable TV and balconies, two restaurants, disco, gym, and Olympic and children's pools. Rates run around $130 d.

Directly off of Carr. 52 across from the Interamerican University, the two-story **Holiday Inn Ponce** (☎ 787-844-1200 ☺ 787-841-2560; Mercedita, PR 00715) charges around $80-$90 d. It has 120 a/c rooms and suites with cable TV. Facilities include adult and children's pools, restaurant, nightclub, and nearby tennis.

IN JUANA DÍAZ: This small town on the way to Coamo has **Hotel Eden** (☎ 787-837-2075) on Carr. 149 at Km 4.6 in Barrio Guanabano. You can dine here at R (☎ 787-837-6638), Carr. 159, Km 5.7; it offers Italian, Spanish, and French dishes.

FOOD: Streets are literally packed with *cafeterias* and restaurants. Fast-food places are strewn along Ave. Las Américas and the plaza. During the season in Aug. and Sept. vendors sell *quenepas*, a fruit similar to lychee.

Right on the plaza, **Café Don Francisco**, C. Union 3, has inexpensive sandwiches, expresso, and cappuccino.

An old theater converted to an attractive mini-mall, **Fox Delicias Mall** contains a wide variety of inexpensive restaurants.

Practically opposite the firehouse, **King's Cream Helados** has natural fruit-flavored as well as chocolate ice cream from 75¢ for a cone on up.

Panaderia Reposteria Suizeria del Sur, across from the PO on C. Guadalupe, has sweets, a small cafeteria, and daily papers (behind the counter).

Open late, **Ginorio's Pizza** at Paseo Atocha 97 offers slices ($1) as well as whole pies.

Woa Kee is a cheap Chinese joint across from the *público* station.

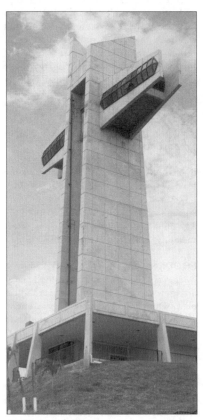

La Cruzette de Vigia

DOWNTOWN DINING: Set in a courtyard, **Lupita's** (☎ 787-848-8808), C. Isabel, offers Mexican dishes and has mariachi from 8 on Fri. and Sat. nights.

The Hotel Melía's **Mark at the Melía** (☎ 787-842-0260/0261), C. Cristina 2, serves seafood and international dishes.

At C. Ferrocarril 15, **El Mesón de René** (☎ 787-844-6110) offers a variety of international foods.

At C. Isabel 56, **El Café de Tomás** (☎ 787-840-1965) has international food and is an inexpensive lunch spot. as is **Olé Plena** (☎ 787-841-6162) down the street. Olé is open late.

NEAR LA GUANCHA: With gourmet seafood, **Restaurant El Ancla** (☎ 787-840-2450) is at Ave. Hostos 9 near the playa, as is **Restaurant El Naútico** (☎ 787-840-3044), which serves international fare.

Conda's (☎ 787-843-9223), C. Alfonso XII, serves local seafood. It has a very Puerto Rican atmosphere, including many carnival masks on the wall.

The **Ponce Hilton** (☎ 787-259-7676) has three restaurants: very expensive **La Terraza**, which has buffets (seafood on Fri.), and **La Hacienda** and **La Cava de la Hacienda**, which have international cuisine.

OTHER DINING: In the Urb. Santa María, **Pizza Heaven** (☎ 787-844-0448/3836) is an Italian steak house that features art exhibits by local artists. On Ave. Pámpanos, **El Señorial** (☎ 787-844-1785, 787-842-1320) specializes in filet mignon.

In Barrio Pámpanos, the **Tiara Seafood Restaurant** (☎ 787-843-5370; open daily) specializes in seafood, creole dishes, and sandwiches.

With grilled steaks, **La Casa del Chef** (☎ 787-843-1298) is at C. Jón Fagot 23 in Barrio Cuatro Calles.

Out at Las Caobas Shopping Center, **Lydia's Restaurant** (☎ 787-844-3933; open daily) has seafood (including creole lobster) and creole steaks.

In the Club Deportivo in Urb. La Alhambra, the **ND Restaurant** (☎ 787-259-8227) specializes in Puerto Rican and international fare.

At Ave. Las Américas 20, **Victor's** (☎ 787-841-8383) offers international and nouvelle cuisine.

Hotel Days Inn, Carr. 1, Km 123.5, has the **Taíno Restaurant** (☎ 787-841-1000, ext. 1002) with international food.

Off Carr. 2 in El Tuque at Km 255 in the Holiday Inn, the **Tamaná Restaurant** (☎ 787-844-1200) specializes in international cooking.

SEASIDE DINING: In the hotel of the same name out on Carr. 2, Km 218.1, **Las Cucharas Seafood Restaurant** (☎ 787-841-0620, 787-383-4073) serves a variety of tasty *mariscos*.

Offering gourmet dishes, **Pito's Seafood Café** (☎ 787-841-4977) is in the vicinity, as is **Yeyo's Seafood** (☎ 787-843-7629), which is open daily.

MARKET SHOPPING: Ponce's modern *mercado* is an air-conditioned showplace with fruits and vegetables, spices, bottles of pure honey, gigantic avocados, and drinking coconuts (65¢). *Botanicas* (shops selling spiritualist literature and goods), tailors, and other shops are upstairs. There are a number of supermarkets in and around town. **Grande** and **Pueblo Xtra** are on the bypass. Sample prices in Grande: Broccoli, 97¢/ea.; mangos 50¢/lb.; small apples, $1/lb.; onions, 75¢/lb., white onions, 99¢/lb.; bulk cheese, $2.59/lb.; eggs, $1.29/doz.; tomato juice, $1.49/16 oz.; and Grande pineapple juice, $1.53/46 oz.

ENTERTAINMENT: To find out what's happening locally, consult the local weekly, the *Periodico La Perla del Sur.*

At night the gleaming **Paseo Atocha** has a few couples strolling arm in arm, but is otherwise deserted. Inside the fire house, the engines shine. Illuminated by a constantly shifting array of colored lights, the fountain rises and then retreats. Its lions — seeming to spew out streams of water — appear at times to be escapees from a Stephen Spielberg movie. Cool dudes wearing sunglasses circle the plaza in their cars and blast hiphop.

In the main square area, **Cafeteria Tompy** is the place to go for late night munchies. Discos are at the **Day's Inn** and at **Holly's** in the Holiday Inn.

Completed at a cost of $2 million, the **Paseo Tablado La Guancha**, a long and wide wooden boardwalk, is one of the most pleasant places to visit, especially at night when it comes alive. An open-air stage at one end features live music on occasion; *salseros* as venerated as Tito Puente have performed here. To get here take Carr. 14 S from Carr. 163 or Carr. 2. Keep straight ahead and ignore the L turn toward the Hilton. The street makes a R turn toward some big warehouses. After that R turn, make a L toward the ocean; La Guancha is at the end on the R.

Park your car and walk in. You'll hear it before you arrive. Some toddlers receive their first dancing lessons here. At one end there's a video game center where you can play with the Teenage Mutant Ninja Turtles or test to see if you have *"la prueba cerebral de einstein."* At the other end, couples dance by the bandstand even when it is empty. In between, food stands sell everything from pastrami sandwiches to piña coladas. The choo-choo-train-style bus runs out here. Try the popular **Café de Puerto** here. Ponce's *fiestas patronales* are held here in Dec.

For **movies**, try **El Emperador** (☎ 787-844-2222) on the bypass, which has two theaters. The **Plaza del Caribe Cinemas** (☎ 787-841-6666) in the Plaza del Caribe has six theaters. The **Ponce** (☎ 787-843-7300), shows three films. Check *El Nuevo Día* for times and features.

GAY CLUBS: **The Cave** (☎ 787-840-5461), Barrio Tenerías, is one local gay hangout. **Michaelangelo's** (☎ 787-844-2914), Carr. 10) is more conservative.

CONCERTS: One activity not to be missed is the **Banda Municipal de Ponce** (Municipal Band), which presents free concerts in the Parque Urbano Dora Colón (at Calles Aurora, Concordia, Jobos, and Marina) at 8 PM on Sun. nights. The band was founded in 1883 as the Banda del Cuerpo de Bomberos de Ponce. Arrive

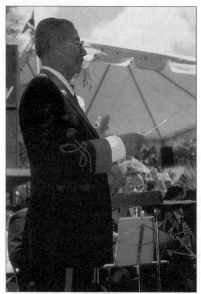

The Ponce band conductor

> **?!¢** The name *vejigantes* means "bladder," and the original vejigantes carried around a long stick with an air-filled cow's bladder *vejiga* on its end. The African-influenced colorful masks are made from coconuts. These devil-like creatures represent the Moors, the N Africans who conquered Spain. Legend has it that, during the time of slavery, landowners would dress their slaves up as *vejigantes* in order to frighten any prospective thieves.

early to get a seat. Selections include everything from *danzas* to *boleros* to the Boogie Woogie Bugle Boy.

Teatro La Perla (☎ 787-843-4399), near the plaza, presents plays in Spanish.

EVENTS: In Nov. an event entitled recreating indigenous island lifestyles, takes place at the ceremonial center in Tibes on the town's outskirts.

🎭 **Carnaval** is held the week before Ash Wednesday, marking the beginning of Lent. **Rey Momo** leads the parade, a Ponce tradition since 1951. Probably influenced by the Carnival of Niza in Barcelona and introduced by Catalans who settled in Ponce, the Rey Momo is the King of Carnival, a comic figure sporting a giant papier-mâché head. Similar figures are found throughout the Latin world, and he may be a remnant of Europe's pagan past. His identity remains secret until the final day, which is marked by the burial of the sardine. "*El entierro de la sardina*" is a Spanish tradition. It's not a real sardine, but rather a *papier-mache* version. Carnival's *vejigantes* sport colorful *papier-mâché* masks, which have an animal or devil design characterized by large, open fanged mouths and pointed horns. (One is on the cover of this book). Watch them parade on the festival's second day.

Held in May, the **Fiestas de Cruz** have a nine-step altar leading to a cross.

The **Fiesta Nacional de La Danza**, held in early May, sees finely clad couples swirling at a moonlit Plaza Las Delicias in celebration of the birthday of composer Juan Morel Campos. Campos was once the conductor of the municipal band.

The annual *fiestas patronales* of Nuestra Señora de Guadalupe, held from Dec. 6–16, centers on the main plaza. It includes a procession led by a mariachi band. *Salsa, merengue,* and jazz bands play, and *bomba y plena* dancing is supplemented by *aguinaldo* music. A variety of foods are served, and *artesanias* sell their wares. As part of the celebrations, Las Mañanitas, a religious procession, departs one morning at 4:30 AM to the cathedral. It is accompanied by *mariachis* who sing songs in honor of Guadalupe.

Feria Regional de Artesanias, a crafts fair, is held each Feb. or March, and the Festival de Bomba y Plena is held in the barrio of San Antón in June.

CRAFTS AND SHOPPING: Handicrafts — including crucifixes made from nails, weavings, and hammocks — are on sale during weekends in one corner of the plaza near the firehouse. All of the museums have good gift shops.

The Institute for Puerto Rican Culture runs the **Libreria y Tienda de Artesanias**, (☎ 787-843-2300), a fine craft store which is in the Edificio Sol de Boriñquen, on C. Villa at C. Torres.

Two shopping malls are the **Plaza del Caribe** and the smaller **Centro del Sur**. If you should be in Ponce during Feb. or March, an artisans' fair is held one weekend, offering music and a fine selection of crafts to choose from; prices are generally reasonable.

There're also a number of small shops around, including a dollar store, **Todo a $**, C. Union, and a couple of record stores nearby.

C. Atocha is also a great place to shop for bargains. **Toda a Mano** here has a good selection of crafts.

Mi Coqui, another craft shop (with a good selection of masks) is found on the second floor of Plaza Las Delicias, and **Isabel 30**, C. Isabel 30, also has a good selection of crafts and art.

SERVICES: The **Ponce Tourism Office** (☎ 787-843-0465), located on the second floor of the Plaza Las Delicias, is open Mon. to Fri. 8 AM–12 PM, 1 PM–4:30 PM. The friendly staff do what they can to help.

There's also a **City Government Tourist Office** (☎ 787-841-8044). It is cleverly hidden inside Citibank, across from the firehouse.You may be able to pry some information out of them, but they appear to be ill-equipped to deal with visitors.

Banks offer a number of ATH (instant teller) machines; Citibank's is the most entertaining. There are four **post offices**; the most convenient is on C. Atocha. **Pharmacies** include **Farmacias González** (☎ 787-844-1475) on C. Cristina at the plaza, **Walgreen's** (☎ 787-840-6093) at 35 Ave. Las Américas, and **Farmacias Moscoso** (☎ 787-842-1180) on Plaza Degetau. The best places to get a *San Juan Star* are at the **Farmacias González** on the square and (ask because it's behind the counter) at the **Panaderia Reposteria Suizeria del Sur**, across from the PO on C. Guadalupe.

NEWSPAPERS: The local rag is the Spanish-only *La Perla del Sur*.

INTERNET ACCESS: **Navacom** (☎ 787-984-2169), is at the cor. of C. Concordia and C. Luna and to the S of the Alcaldía (City Hall).

TOURS: Turisla (☎ 787-835-6788), C. Comerico 88, offers tours and excursions, as does **Arges Travel** (☎ 787-844-0740) in Galeria Poncena, C. Union.

Coches Exclusivos (☎ 787-648-0477, 787-396-0641, 787-380-4290) offers horse-drawn coach rentals.

DIVING AND WATER TRIPS: **Marine Sports & Dive Shop** (☎/⊖ 787-844-6175; Box 7711, Ponce, PR 00732) will take you to Caja de Muertos or other locations.

Island Venture (☎ 787-842-8546), will takes you diving and snorkeling. **http://www.islandventure.net**

CAR RENTAL: Payless (☎ 787-842-9393), Ave. Hostos 121, offers good value. Others include **Popular Ponce** (☎ 787-259-4848), **L & M Car Rental** (☎ 787-841-2482), **Avis** (☎ 787-284-4188), **Leaseway of Puerto Rico** (☎ 787-843-4330), **Popular Leasing & Rental** (☎ 787-841-7850), **Thrifty** (☎ 787-284-5229), or **Velco** (☎ 842-9292).

TAXIS: You can call **Boriñquen Taxi Cab** (☎ 787-843-6000), **Cooperativa de Taxis**, (☎ 787-848-8248, and **Ponce Taxi Association** (☎ 787-842-3370). **Oneida Star Line** (☎ 787-845-5883) provides charter transport for tours and excursions.

FROM PONCE: Numerous *públicos* and very occasional buses depart from the *Terminal Carros* for local destinations — Mayagüez, San José, Guayama, Yauco, Coamo, etc. Get an early start or you'll feel like a roast chicken while waiting for them to fill up. The terminal is right next to the United Evangelical Church. *Linea Atlas Trans Island* (☎ 787-842-1065/4375), with offices on C. Mendez Vigo, will take you to Río Piedras, Santurce, and directly to Isla Verde Airport. The first of nine *públicos* daily departs at 4 AM. Either reserve a seat or just hunt one up at the terminal when you're ready to leave.

BY AIR: *American Eagle* flies daily from Ponce's outlying Mercedita Airport to Luis Muñoz Marín International Airpor..

Vicinity of Ponce

Ponce is a good base for exploring the S coast as well as the mountains. You can head up into the mountains or along the coast in either direction. Watch out for vendors selling fruit along the highway as well as for the police, who are often out with their radar guns in search of a ticketing opportunity.

BEACHES: The nearest beaches are near Guánica. **Caña Gorda** is on Carr. 333 (down the road from the Copamarina at Guánica) and **Playa Santa** is at Ensenada. Farther on, are **Playita Rosada** in La Parguera and a beach at Boquerón. To the W is **El Tuque** on Carr. 2 off the Guayanilla exit road.

Caja de Muertos

On a clear day, it's possible to see this mile-long (1.6 km) island offshore. It may be named either for its coffin-like shape or from the legend of a young Portuguese named José Almeida, who fell in love with a married woman on Curaÿao. He returned to visit her after becoming a pirate, and her husband died of a stroke. They married, but she wa killed in an attack shortly afterwards. Almeida had her embalmed and placed in a cedar coffin with a glass door. He secreted her in a cave on this island and came to visit her. Later, he was caught and hanged, after which his crew revisited the site believing that booty was buried there. When they came upon the copper box, the two crewmen murdered the boatswain; then one crewman murdered the other. The remaining pirate jumped to his death in fright after viewing the contents of the coffin. When crew members came upon the corpse, they brought it to St. Thomas for burial. Some years later a Spanish engineer visited the island to survey it. When he found the copper planks that had been part

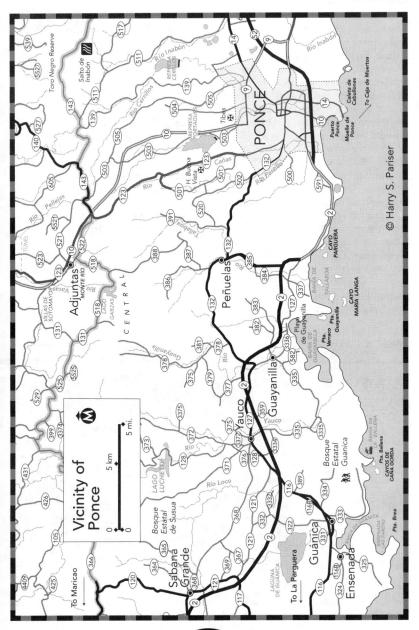

Vicinity of Ponce

© Harry S. Pariser

of the coffin, he was told about the legend and gave the island its present name.

These days, its name may be more apt because the island has been found to host four endangered plant species (extinct on the mainland) and several endangered lizards as well. Cacti and small thorny bushes predominate here. The island is surrounded by coral reefs teeming with life. Its nearby neighbors are Cayo Morillito and Cayo Berberia. Restored by the Department of Natural Resources, the lighthouse (built in 1880) has a lookout and museum. **practicalities:** Ferries used to run out to the island on weekends. Unfortunately, the Commonwealth government carted the ferry off to Fajardo for the Vieques run. For trips here, call Rafí Vega or his son at **Island Ventures** (☎ 787-842-8456). They offer trips from $20 as well as diving and snorkeling excursions. **iventure@caribe.net**

Tibes Indigenous Ceremonial Center

Marked by unlikely concrete buildings, this archaeological site (☎ 787-840-2255/4685) is located in a suburb of Ponce. Drive or take a *público* from the vicinity of the *mercado* to get there. It's open Tues. to Sun. from 9AM–4 PM; admission $2, $1 children. (If a holiday falls on a Mon., it is open Tues. and then closed on Tues.) There's a small cafeteria here. The accompanying gift shop has some unusual items, including T-shirts with Taíno sun petroglyphs. There is also a small museum (see below); bilingual guides are available, as are special natural history tours that can be prearranged by appointment.

EVENTS: *"Descubre tus raíces,"* a celebration depicting indigenous lifestyles, takes place here in Nov.

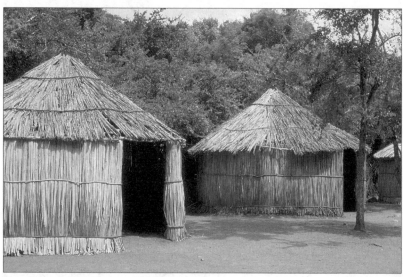

Tibes Ceremonial Center is to the north of Ponce.

HISTORY: Predating the Caguana site near Utuado, Tibes was discovered in 1974, after a hurricane and subsequent flooding, by Luiz Hernández, a local resident. The local government expropriated the 32 acres of land and Juan Gonzales, a local archaeologist, headed a dig. Tibes is the largest indigenous settlement and ceremonial center in the West Indies. Only some five acres have been uncovered; another 22 may be excavated in the future.

Archaeological evidence suggests two distinct periods of occupation: during the latter phase of the Igneri culture from AD 400-600 and in the pre-Taíno period from AD 600-1100. Both cultures were similar in terms of diet and lifestyle; cultural differences were due to an influx of new blood from outside or transitions in style over time. The older Igneri period is characterized by animal-shaped amulets, ceramic vessels, and axes.

The majority of the 182 graves excavated here, which were found to contain the remains of children along with ceremonial offerings, date from this period. Other ceramics and objects such as frog-shaped amulets, *cemi* figures, and adzes, are from the later pre-Taíno period. Moves are underway to declare the area a wildlife sanctuary, but political rivalries are holding up the process.

MUSEUM: If you have a wait before your tour, you can explore the museum, which compresses quite a bit of archaeology and ethnology into a small space. Ceramic reproductions are the first item to your R as you enter. *Dujos* (ceremonial seats), axes, *metates* (grinding stones), and stone collars are among the next exhibits.

Another exhibit is devoted to the ritual surrounding the hallucinogenic *cajoba* seeds (see below). Continuing on, you encounter a burial site under glass. Found under the main ball court, these human remains date back 1,200 years. Other exhibits are devoted to Arcaicos, Igneri, Pre-Taíno, and Taíno. Around the corner are *cemis* and other clay stamps.

The Igneri exhibit shows how their heads were purposely deformed. Taíno ceramics from E and W Puerto Rico are in two styles: *estilo capa* and *estilo esperanza*. While the former is near Utuado, the latter comes from Vieques. Another room contains temporary exhibitions.

Outside, ten ceremonial *bateyes* have been reconstructed. Petroglyphs, with animal and human faces, have been chiseled on some of the stones, which delineate the *bateyes*. The largest *batey*, measuring 111 by 118 ft., is bordered with walkways containing riverbed stones. The area of Tibes derives its name from these stones; *tibes* is the Taíno word for smooth riverbed stones.

While some of these *bateyes* were used for a game resembling soccer, others were used for *areytos*, ceremonial dances in which Indians, drinking beer made from fermented cassava and inhaling hallucinogenic *cajoba* seeds through a two-pronged pipe, would commune with the gods. There are no records as to what they talked about, but presumably they touched on politics, food, and sex. One elliptical *bateye* is surrounded by triangles, which suggests that it represents the sun.

One major archaeological find at Tibes, an adult male skeleton discovered within the foundations of a walkway bordering one of the *bateyes*, has been dated to A.D. 790, which pushes back the date of the earliest known indigenous stone constructions by 400 years.

The horseshoe *batey* here is three times as long as it is wide. The *cemi batey* is shaped like its namesake and is the longest such court discovered in Puerto Rico and the longest pre-Taíno court to have been discovered in the Caribbean. Excavating underneath, archaeologists unearthed 11 human remains. One was a man who had had his head cut off and his arms securely tied behind his back. Another woman also had her arms tied behind her back.

Dead were customarily buried in the fetal position, reflecting the belief that once a person passed on they returned to their mother's womb to face reincarnation. Wives would be buried alive with their husbands: such a fate was considered an honor and a privilege. Not just a sport, the games played on the *bateyes* were both a magic ceremony as well as a way of making important decisions. For example, a game might be played that would allow the winning team to decide whether prisoners of conflict should be set free or slaughtered.

Besides the *bateyes*, a small Taíno village nearby has been faithfully recreated.

THE TOUR: The entire area of your tour has been cleared and the site is immaculately manicured. Your informative guide gives you a complete rundown on everything that the Igneris did and where. He will point out indigenous trees such as quenapa, spiny ash, and calabash; fruit trees such as the soursop and tamarind; endangered plants like the moralon; batata, manioc and century plants; and medicinal herbs. You learn of the uses for each and what they meant to the inhabitants. On the tour, you stop at a set of reconstructed huts (actually outside of the site's limits), which you are free to explore; the rectangular chief's hut is the best one.

Hacienda Buena Vista

Restored by the Conservation Trust, this "Good View Estate," a former coffee plantation, contains slave quarters, a two-story estate house, and exceptional hydraulic machinery. Hacienda Buena Vista was founded in 1833 by Spaniard Salvador de Vives, who first emigrated to Venezuela. After Venezuela gained its independence, he, along with his wife, son and two slaves, migrated here in 1824. Purchasing 482 *cuerdas* of land, he named the estate Buena Vista because of its great natural beauty. Following in his footsteps, his son Carlos added hydraulic power to the estate along with a corn mill. His son Salvador, in turn, added the coffee depulping machine and a husking and polishing machine, which were placed in the corn mill's building and run off of the original water wheel.

After the San Ciriaco hurricane struck, 60% of the coffee crop was destroyed and the world coffee market collapsed by 1900. Coffee was replaced by oranges until the Government of Puerto Rico expropriated the property in the 1950s and redistributed the land to local farmers.

In 1984, the site was purchased because of its unique forest, river, and waterfall. Although the buildings had been largely consumed by termites and the machinery was covered with rust, it has been reconstructed through photos and other records. Carefully restored, it is truly one of the Caribbean's historical gems.

GETTING HERE: Set to the N of Ponce on the way to Adjuntas, the estate is located on Carr. 10 at Km 16.8; it's open to groups Wed. and Thurs.; general admission ($5 adults, $2 children) is on Fri. and Sat., with reservations required (☎ 787-722-5882, weekends 787-284-7020). Tours are at 8:30, 10:30 AM, 1:30 PM, and 3:30 PM; only the 1:30 PM tour is in English, and you must request this.

TOURING: Arriving at the entrance, you park your car and then pay. Inside the first structure, the former family home, there are exhibits on coffee processing as well as on the different varieties of wood used. Upstairs there is a recreation of how the plantation owners lived. Rooms have been restored in late 19th-century style using original construction techniques and traditional materials; several pieces of furniture were donated by the Vives family. There's a parlor with a Victrola poised to play *La Traviata*, a sewing machine, a rocking horse, tables and chairs; a study with wire-rim glasses still on top of the ledger; a bedroom with shoes tucked under the bed; and a kitchen with coffee beans in various stages of processing. In short, it appears as if the family has either just stepped out for a minute or has been kidnapped by aliens. In fact, the Vives family never lived here full time, with the exception of a brief period during the American occupation.

Outside, you continue on a path, along which the water is channeled, and pass entranceways into which small slave boys used to crawl to clean the canal (the water must be returned without contamination). Passing a secondary forest, you come to a 100-ft. waterfall at the path's end; this is the source for the hydraulic power. The next stop is at the hydraulic water wheel that separates the coffee beans from their chaff. This red water turbine is the only one of its kind still in existence: the water is fed in from the bottom rather than the top. The immense wooden wheels on top of the mechanism are what make it move.

Invented by Sir James Whitelaw of Scotland and cast by the West Point Foundry in 1854, the impressive hydraulic corn mill is the last stop on the tour. When operating, it sounds like a rainstorm. You are then escorted to where you began the tour, treated to a cup of freshly ground and brewed coffee, and offered the chance to try cleaning and grinding your own coffee beans; small packets are on sale for $1.

The Southwest portion of the nation has some of its most charming natural areas. Its mainstay is the city of Mayagüez. The area also includes the tropical dry forest reserve at Guánica, the historical town of San Germán, La Parguera with its phosphorescent lagoon, and the famous lighthouse at Cabo Rojo. There is spectacular diving off the coasts, and the offshore island of Mona is sometimes referred to as the "Galapagos" of the Caribbean because of its natural wonders.

Yauco

Built on a hillside W of Ponce, the small town of Yauco still has its step streets, old houses, great coffee, and a distinctly Spanish-American atmosphere. Its Plaza de Recreo Fernando de Pacheco was reconstructed in 1993.

FESTIVALS: Its **Festival del Café** (Coffee Festival) is held here in Feb. Activities include music, poetry, art, and desserts made from coffee as well as crafts.

The festival of patron saint **Nuestra Senora del Rosario** takes place around Oct. 7.

HISTORY: Originally known to the Indians as *Coayuco*, the surrounding area was settled by the Spanish, becoming an independent municipality in 1756. Haitian French, Corsicans, and other immigrants began arriving in the early 1800s. Sugarcane and cotton gave way to coffee cultivation. Low in caffeine but rich in taste, Yauco's coffee became famous in Europe for its exceptional quality and soon commanded a high market price. The loss of European markets after the Spanish-American War, combined with the devastation caused by a hurricane in 1899 and competition from mass-producing countries like Brazil and Columbia, led to the sad decay of the local coffee industry.

SIGHTS: Casa Fleming (☎ 787-267-0350) C. 25 de Julio, serves as the local museum of art and culture. It's in in a house built in 1907. Tours around Yauco and rural areas are offered in a trolley on Mon. to Fri from 8 AM–4:30 PM.

Hacienda La Salvación (☎ 787-856-3364), Carr. 128 at Carr. 428, is a nearby coffee plantation which may be visited by appointment.

PRACTICALITIES: Dating from 1959, **Restaurante La Guardarraya** (☎ 787-856-4222), on Carr. 127 en route to Guayanilla, caters to meat-eaters. Its *chuletas can-can* are pork chops that are "frilly," thus resembling a can-can dancer's skirt.

There's a movie theater in town. **Yauco Plaza** is a large shopping plaza just at the entrance to the town when coming from Mayagüez.

From Ponce, Yauco is just off the expressway, Sadly, you're welcomed by a Burger King sign. From here, *públicos* go to Ponce, Guánica, Guayanilla, and Sabana Grande.

CAMPING: The **Bosque Estatal Susúa**,(☎ 787-833-3700) to the NW of Yauco on Carr. 368 at Km 2.1, has two campsites ($4 pn) and a swimmable river.

Nearby **Embalse Luchetti**, Km 12.3 on Carr. 128, an artificial lake dating from 1952, also has a campground with seven campsites, an information center, fishing, and a friendly flock of ducks. It is now a wildlife refuge (☎ 787-844-4660). Both charge $4 per site, but a permit is necessary in advance from **Recursos Naturales y Ambientales** in San Juan (☎ 787-724-3724, 787-724-3647).

Guánica

Reserva Forestal Guánica, several beautiful beaches (Mangrillo, Grande and Playa Jaboncillo), and the place where the Americans landed during the 1898 invasion are all situated around this pleasant town of 9,000. The small town has a nice boardwalk. Guánica's ambiance is marred only by the chicken processing plant and the fertilizer factory. The reserve itself is one of the finest examples of cactus-scrub-subtropical dry forest in the world. It was designated by the United Nations as a Man and the Biosphere Reserve in 1975. Its dryness is assured by the Cordillera Central, which catches most of the rain before it reaches the coast.

Encompassing over 1,620 acres (4,000 ha), it has 36 mi (57 km) of old roads and trails. Over 700 species of trees and plants are protected here, and vegetation inside the reserve includes *aroma* (acacia) and *guayacan* (lignum vitae) trees.

Adjoining the forest is 164 acres fronting the **Bahía Ballena,** which was purchased by the Conservation Trust and the Department of Natural Resources for $1.7 million in 1992. It had originally been slated for a $12 million

Club Med resort. Local resident and park ranger Miguel Canales, leader of the fight, discovered that the *sapo concho*, a toad thought to have been extinct, lived in the area, and the planned resort would have restricted its movements and endangered its well-being. Plans are to develop tours and a variety of nature exhibits here.

The reserve currently gets around 300,000 visitors per year. However, 90% go to the beach; an estimated 36,000 visit the upland parts of the reserve.

http://www.guanicaturismo.com

GETTING HERE: Take *Carr. 335* to the end of the road in **Sector Jabonillo** where there's a ranger station with information and restrooms. *Carr. 334* leads NE from the town of Guánica to the reserve and ranger station. Several dirt roads (no vehicles allowed) are the best place to hike from there. (See the "Hiking Trails" chart).

Carr. 333 runs along the reserve's perimeter; an unmarked trail follows it to the ranger station. At the ranger station be sure to pick up literature, including the superb *A Guide to Trails of Guánica* by Beth Farnsworth.

FAUNA: Guánica is a birdwatcher's delight. Twelve of the 14 endemic birds are found here, including the sharpshinned hawk. The *guabairo* (Puerto Rican whippoorwill) survives on the island only in this reserve. Some of the other 40 species of birds found here include the troupial, the orange-cheeked waxbill (an introduced W African native), the Caribbean elaenia, the Puerto Rican bullfinch, the Puerto Rican nightjar (once thought to be extinct), and the Puerto Rican tody.

The endangered **sapo concho** (crested toad) is born in pools but lives in limestone crevices. Green and leatherback turtles still lay their eggs along the

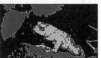

Sapo Concho

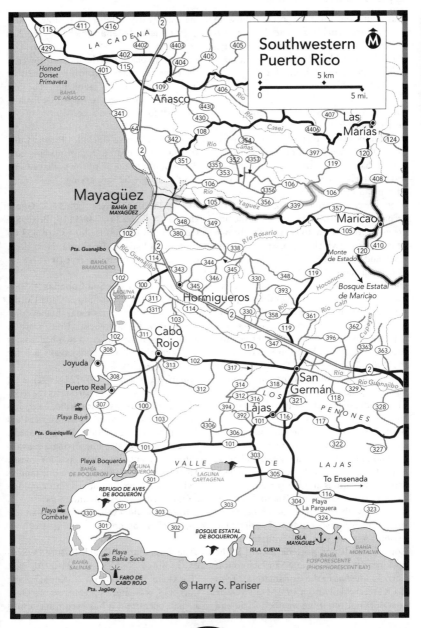

Southwestern
Puerto Rico

0   5 km

0   5 mi.

LA CADENA

Horned Dorset Primavera

BAHÍA DE AÑASCO

Añasco

Las Marías

Río Casei

Río Cañas

Mayagüez

BAHÍA DE MAYAGÜEZ

Río Yaguez

Maricao

Pta. Guanajibo

BAHÍA BRAMADERO

Río Guanajibo

Río Rosario

Monte de Estado

LAGUNA JOYUDA

Hormigueros

Bosque Estatal de Maricao

Hoconuco

Río Caín

Cabo Rojo

Joyuda

Río Guanajibo

Puerto Real

San Germán

Playa Buyé

LOS PEÑONES

Pta. Guaniquilla

Lajas

VALLE   DE   LAJAS

Playa Boquerón

BAHÍA DE BOQUERÓN

LAGUNA BOQUERÓN

LAGUNA CARTAGENA

To Ensenada

REFUGIO DE AVES DE BOQUERÓN

Playa La Parguera

Playa Combate

BOSQUE ESTATAL DE BOQUERÓN

ISLA MAYAGÜES

ISLA CUEVA

BAHÍA MONTALVA

BAHÍA SALINAS

Playa Bahía Sucia

FARO DE CABO ROJO

Pta. Jagüey

BAHÍA FOSFORESCENTE (PHOSPHORESCENT BAY)

© Harry S. Pariser

coast, but mongooses are posing a threat to the eggs and hatchlings. The *Ameiva wetmorei* is a black-bodied lizard with racing stripes on its back and a blue iridescent tail. Also be sure to watch out for the "crazy ants" which are common.

ARBOREAL ECOSYSTEMS: Comprising nearly two-thirds of the reserve's area, the **deciduous forest** contains mostly young trees. During the dry season (Dec. to April), almost half of the trees here shed their leaves, which release nutrients into the soil. At the end of the dry season, many of the trees flower and fruit. Check the trees for orchids and termite nests, as well as the tiny green Puerto Rican tody and the brown lizard cuckoo (which can be spotted by its black and white tail).

Covering about a fifth of the reserve's area and largely confined to moist ravines, valleys, and sinkholes, the **semi-evergreen forest** contains plants more commonly found at higher and damper altitudes. The dry scrub forest contains stunted trees and cacti. Many of its shrubs are members of the *Rubiaccae*, the coffee family; they may be recognized by their thorns, small opposing leaves, and tiny white tubular flowers.

The **coastal forest** endures low rainfall and salty wind spray. Its shrunken and twisted trees attest to the harshness of the environment. In this area you can spot buttonwood mangroves, sea grapes, and milkweed. Other parts of the reserve have been used as plantations and are in recovery.

The nearby **"Gilligan's Island,"** an offshore cay with mangroves and a beach., is very popular on weekends and during high season. A boat will pick you up at the Copamarina If not, you may board at the dock near the Restaurante San Jacinto (off Carr. 333 just after the Copamarina). Trips ($4 RT) leave daily from 10 AM–5 PM. The boat does not run if the weather is bad and

may stop early if business is slow. It also goes to **Isla Ballena** which may be less crowded.

Be sure to check out the lookout tower at the ruins of **Fuerte Cabrón** which may be hiked to from Playa Jaboncillo. The fort was built by US forces in 1898. (See the hiking chart for details on access).

BEACHES: These include **Playa Caña Gorda**, right near the Copamarina, and **Playa Santa** to the W of town. Playa Caña Gorda charges $2 for parking.

ACCOMMODATIONS: **Jack's Guest House** (☎ 787-821-2738/5117; Box 988, Guánica, PR 00653) is along Carr. 333 on the way to Playa Caña Gorda. Next door, there are apartments for rent (☎ 787-821-1168).

Mary Lee's By the Sea Cabañas (☎ 787-821-3600) is at San Jacinto in Caña Gorda. Mary Lee offers charming, homey digs which include hammocks. Units start at around $90 d for studios; a two-bedroom is also available. Boats and kayaks are for rent. No credit cards.

Gilligan's View (☎ 787-821-4901) is up the road. It has several apartments for rent.

The **Caribbean Vacation Villa**, Carr. 333 in San Jacinto, is hosted by windsurfer **Paul Julien** (☎ 787-821-5364). Boogie boards, windsurfing, kayaks, and diving are available on a complimentary basis for guests. The two expensive studios and one family-style unit are well equipped and comfortable. He will give lessons and tours. **http://www.view this.com/caribbean julienpr@yahoo.com**

The **Copamarina Beach Resort** (☎ 821-0505, 800-468-4553, ☻ 821-0070; Box 805, Guánica, PR 00653), at Km 6.5 along Carr. 333, is Guánica's premier resort. Once a small operation, it has been transformed

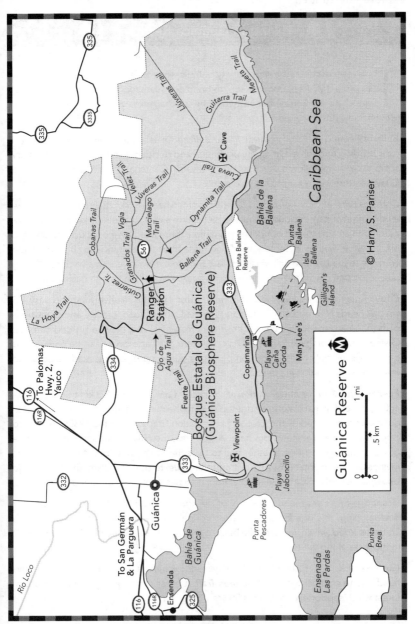

Guánica Reserve

© Harry S. Pariser

Caribbean Sea

Bahía de la Ballena

Punta Ballena

Isla Ballena

Gilligan's Island

Maseta Trail

Guitarra Trail

Lluveras Trail

Cueva Trail

Cave

Dynamita Trail

Velez Tre

Lúveras Trail

Murcielago Trail

Cobanas Trail

Vigia

Granados Trail

Ballena Trail

561

Gutierrez Tr.

La Hoya Trail

Ranger Station

Bosque Estatal de Guánica
(Guánica Biosphere Reserve)

Ojo de Agua Trail

Fuerte Trail

Punta Ballena Reserve

333

Copamarina

Playa Caña Gorda

Mary Lee's

334

To Palomas, Hwy. 2, Yauco

116

116R

Viewpoint

333

332

Guánica

To San Germán & La Parguera

Playa Jaboncillo

Punta Pescadores

Río Loco

To Palomas Hwy. 2, Yauco

116

116R

325

Ensenada

Bahía de Guánica

Ensenada Las Pardas

Punta Brea

1 mi

.5 km

0

0

🌲🌲 Hiking in Guánica Reserve 🌲🌲

This reserve contains a wide variety of trails—one for every level of hiker. Be sure to protect yourself from the sun, to bring adequate food and water, and to wear good shoes. Remember to avoid the *chicharron*, a poisonous shrub readily identifiable by its spiny reddish leaves.

Ballena *Entrance at Carr. 333 near Punta Ballena* An easy walk along a two km paved road heading through a mahogany plantation and deciduous forest which leads to dry scrub. After a km, follow a sign marked "Guayacán Centenario" to find a 700-year-old Guayacán tree with a trunk six ft. in diameter.

Cobanas *Enter at Carr. 334/Maniel Rd.* This old road heads 3.5 km E through a ridge covered with secondary deciduous forest to the reserve's end. At the three km point, it passes through an abandoned campeche plantation; these trees were once used to obtain a black dye as well as dysentery medicine. Just after the entrance to this trail is the entrance to the ***La Hoya*** trail which heads 2.5 km to the N. Traversing a verdant ravine, it passes through patchy thickets of evergreen forest which alternate with deciduous.

Cueva *Enter at the parking lot at the end of Carr. 333.* This relatively flat and easy 1.5 km trail heads N through a coastal forest to the Llúberas road; orange-and-black troupials (onomatopoetically named after their "troo-pial" call) may be sighted enroute. Owing to the ecological fragility of its ecosystem, the large cave near the path should only be visited only while in the company of a guide; permission should be obtained from the ranger station in advance.

Fuerte *Enter W of the ranger station at the end of Carr. 333.* This 5.5 km trail is of moderately difficult; it leads along a ridgetop road to the ruins of a fort where there's a lookout tower constructed by the Civilian Conservation Corps during the 1930s. Be sure to catch the spectacular view from here. A side trail, the ***Hoya Honda*** heads down to a grove of mahogany trees; another trail to try is the *El Ver*. Both pass through verdant ravines and old plantations. Also set off of the ***Fuerte trail*** at 1.2 km, the 1.5-km ***Ojo de Agua*** heads N to Carr. 334 (Maniel Rd.). It passes through a spring-fed forest.

Granados *Enter at around .25-km N of the ranger station off of Carr. 334.* Good for birdwatching, this one km trail passes through deciduous forest on the way to the ***Llúberas Road*** (which you can take back to the parking lot). Watch for fossilized corals in the rocks along the trail.

Gutiérrez *Enter at .5 km NW of the ranger station along Carr. 334.* The one-km road heads NE to connect with the ***Cóbanas Trail.*** It passes through regenerating tropical forest which supported plantations 50 yrs. ago.

Llúberas *Enter at the picnic area at the ranger station.* This eight-km road passes through the gamut of the reserve's vegetative zones. You'll pass by limestone and matorral scrub as well as evergreen and deciduous forests. The remains of a sugar plantation and mill (which give the road its name) are near the E end. The **Cueva** and **Guitarra** trails branch off of this road.

Meseta *Enter at the parking lot at the end of Carr. 333.* This easy 3.5 km trail follows the Guánica coastal dry forest. Expect to see soaring sea birds, cactus scrub, sea grapes, and cliffs covered with dwarf white mangroves. It ends at the reserve's E boundary. This is the author's favorite trail because of the magnificent scenery and the fields of cacti. Surf crashes against limestone bluffs, and the path ends near a grave marked with a cross made with PVC tubing. Be sure to wear a hat and bring adequate food and water as there are no facilities enroute. Weekdays are best.

Murciélago *Enter .2 km E of the ranger station behind the picnic area.* This 1.2 km trail heads off of the Llúberas Rd. and passes through a mahogany plantation, limestone bedrock (with nesting Puerto Rican todies), and deciduous forest before terminating in a moist ravine. The **Dinamita** trail, which heads off to your L near the Murciélago's beginning, leads to Carr. 333; it is not maintained, so going can be rough at times.

Velez/Vigía *Enter one km NE from the ranger station on the Llúberas Rd.* This one-km trail brings you up to Criollo II, the reserve's highest outlook. You can return via the **Grandados** to make a loop.

---

under the aegis of San Juan businessman Arnold Benus. The resort has undergone a $10 million renovation, expanding from 75 to 106 rooms, and added a marina and a set of spacious villas. To Mr. Benus's credit, the resort acts as a good corporate citizen: they have donated land to the forest reserve and paid for the printing of the reserve's trail guide.

Comfortable rooms have a/c, cable TV, and phone. Welcome pluses include hair dryer and coffee maker. Villas have amenities such as kitchens an dining areas. Its other facilities include tennis courts, swimming pools, and a small health spa and exercise room. The hotel's beach is not its highlight, but you can use the nearby beach at Caña Gorda or go off to Gilligan's Island for a small fee. It also has all of your water sports toys — kayaks, windsurfers, mini catamarans and the like.

An added feature is the full-service dive shop. Great sites are offshore. The Wall has a number of great dropoffs, and there are many other sites to choose from. This is the only operation which dives on this stretch of coast.

The resort's calling card is personalized service, and its staff are both helpful and friendly. It is definitely a Puerto Rican resort, so it is much more informal than a Westin.

The hotel will provide transport to San Juan ($60 pp) as well as to the airport in Ponce. Plans are to have a few rental cars on the property, so this will give guests the freedom to explore at their leisure.

There are two restaurants. One is open-air which serves breakfast and lunches at resort prices. They have a number of great Puerto Rican specialties. Gourmet chef Wilo plies his

trade in **Wilo's Coastal Cuisine**, his luxurious a/c restaurant. He specializes in unique Puerto Rican-style dishes such as a whole snapper deep fried. It is very popular with Poncenos as well as tourists. Sadly, there is no room service, so be sure to make a dinner reservation.
http://www.copamarina.com
info@copamarina.com

In **Guayanilla** to the E at Km 204 on Carr. 12, **Pichi's Hotel** (☎ 787-835-3335, ⊜ 787-835-3272; Box 115, Guayanilla, PR 00656) has 58 a/c motel-style rooms with satellite color TV, meeting rooms, game rooms, two restaurants, and a pool. Rates range around $85–130 d.
http://www.pichis.com

FOOD: You can buy inexpensive fish from Ameliana at the *pescaderia* just down the road from Jack's. **La Ballena** (☎ 787-821-0505) is a seaside seafood restaurant at Km 6.5 on Carr. 333.

At C. Principal C-4 in Playa Santa, **La Cocha** (☎ 787-821-5522) serves gourmet Puerto Rican food and seafood.

The upscale **Blue Marlin Restaurant** is at Ave. Esperanza 59. The **Brisas del Mar Bar and Restaurant** is on the same seaside boulevard, along with other eateries.

Café San Jacinto (☎ 787-821-4149 is at Playa San Jacinto, Km 66 on Carr. 333, which is the first R-hand turn after the Copamarina. At the Gilligan Island's ferry launching point, it serves reasonably-priced Puerto Rican dishes.

Finally, don't forget **Wilo's Coastal Cuisine** in the Copamarina (listed above).

SERVICES: Dive Copamarina (☎ 787-821-0505) is located in the Copamarina. (See "dive sites" under Boquerón). **Pino's Boat and Water Fun** (☎ 787-821-6864) is at Playa Santa to the W of town. They rent paddle boats and book boat tours.

KAYAKING: Paul Julien (☎ 787-821-5364) rents out kayaks as does Dive Copamarina.

WINDSURFING: Contact well-known windsurfer **Paul Julien** (☎ 787-821-5364) who runs a villa here.

FISHING: Guánica is one of the best places around to fish for tarpon, snook, and bonefish. The Copamarina and other hotels will help you make arrangements.

Sabana Grande

Founded by Spanish nobility and members of venerable Spanish families, Sabana Grande set up its own government during the Spanish-American War. It lasted only days. The *fiestas patronales* of San Isidoro Labrador take place around May 15.

This small, attractive community is chiefly noted for the miracle that took place here. One day in 1953, a group of schoolchildren chanced upon the Virgin Mary while pausing at a brook near the town. She was wearing a blue robe, white tunic, a neck brooch, a sash, and sandals. After chatting a few minutes with the children, the Virgin promised to return on May 25. When a group of 130,000 devotees arrived on that date at the spot, the Divine Lady failed to show up. However, many of the chronic ailments and diseases of those present were reportedly cured on the spot. Many eyewitness reports attest to serious diseases cured by the healing power of the brook where the Virgin was seen.

Numerous small shrines and a large chapel have been erected to commemorate the miracles that took place here, and the anniversary of the sighting was celebrated by a Mass each year until 1989 (when the island's cardinal ordered a halt to the services). Hundreds of thousands attended, and calls continue for official recognition of the sighting by the Catholic Church.

Plans once called for the establishment of a multimillion-dollar theme park on the site. To be called Monte Mistico de Maria. It would have included trams and a gigantic 25-story blue-robed statue of the Virgin Mary.

These days, a much quieter picture prevails. Dogs sleep out in the parking lot. A gift shop sells a holographic Jesus that bleeds, along with various chimes and rosaries. A sign reads "Please Don't Pick Our Ladies Flowers." There's one large statue under glass, a concrete grotto with stations of the cross, and a small room filled with clothing and other items left by devotees.

Another noteworthy attraction near the town, though of a completely different type, is **Langostinos Del Caribe**, a shrimp farm; (☎ 787-873-1026 for reservations).

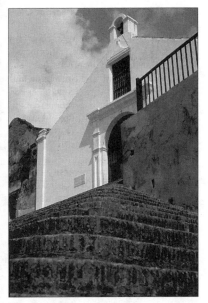

The church of Porta Coeli is now a museum.

San Germán & Vicinity

San Germán

Second oldest and certainly the most attractive town on the island, San Germán retains its quiet colonial charm and distinguished architecture. The atmosphere is distinctly Mediterranean. Local legend insists that the swallows of Capistrano winter here.

The town is named after King Ferdinand of Spain's second wife, Germaine de Foix, whom he married in 1503. Its nickname is Ciudad de las Lomas ("City of the Hills").

Today's residents are descendants of the pirates, Corsicans, smugglers, poets, priests, and politicians of days past. Although the pirates and sugar plantations may be gone forever, a feeling from that era still lingers in the town.

SIGHTS: Two rectangular plazas in the center of town face each other, separated only by the city hall, a former prison. Martin Quinones Plaza boasts **San Germán de Auxerre Church**.

Built in the 19th century, its wooden vault, painted in blue and grey, simulates a coffered ceiling.

The second plaza, **Parque de Santo Domingo**, now bordered with black iron and wooden park benches, was originally a marketplace.

The Church of **Porta Coeli** ("Gate of Heaven"), the town's main attraction, rises dramatically from the end of the plaza It is open from Wed. to Sun. from 8:30 AM–12:00 PM and from 1 PM–4:30 PM. Twenty-four brick steps lead up to the white walls of the entrance. Originally constructed by Dominican friars in 1606, it is believed to have been connected by tunnels to the main monastery, which no longer exists. It was used as a school in 1812, and almost became the district jail in 1842. In

1866 the monastery was razed and its beams and bricks were sold at public auction. In 1878, the chapel was restored and opened for services, which continued until 1949. Recognized as a historical monument in 1930, it was struck by lightning in 1948 and damaged.

The chapel was later sold by the Bishop to the commonwealth government for $1. Its most recent restoration was completed in 1982. Although the palm wood ceiling and tough, brown *ausobo* beams are original, the balcony is a reconstruction. The structure is set up to resemble a working chapel rather than a museum, though Mass is held here now only three times a year. Treasures gathered from all over have been placed along its sides. Exhibits include choral books from Santo Domingo and a surly 17th-century portrait of St. Nicholas de Bari, the French Santa Claus.

Others include a primitive carving of Jesus found in San Juan, several lovely 19th-C Señora de la Monserrate Black Madonna and Child statues, and a representation of San Cristóbal with a part from one of his bones inserted. To get here, keep to the R after you come into town.

Museo de Arte y Casa Ramírez de Arellano (open 10 AM-noon, 1-4 PM, Wed. to Sun.), C. Esperanza 7, has a number of prints — most of them silkscreens. It also displays computer graphics and mixed media works. Particularly notable is José Alicia's work *Niña con Granada*. It also has a cooling water fountain in back of the courtyard. Upstairs, you are taken back to earlier eras. The *Sala Ramírez Arellano* assembles a collection of 19th- and 20th-century furniture to resemble a living room. *Sala de Arte Indigena* holds a grinding stone, *cemi*, ax heads, and Taíno collars (which the chiefs used in a special ceremony). Across the hall is the *Sala de Arte Religiosa* with a crucified Christ and other ornaments and an old confession booth. Elaborate and placed on a pedestal, it dates from 1779.

OTHER ATTRACTIONS: At C. Santiago Veve 70, the **art nouveau residence** of Mrs. Delia Lopez de Acosta contains decorative murals inside. Built in 1911–12, it is a superb example of *criolla* architecture.

The **Perichi home**, C. Luna 94, is another classic. Constructed in 1920, it is a fine example of Puerto Rican ornamental architecture.

An interesting place to visit is **Botanica San Miguel**, C. Dr. Santiago Vevé, which has an unusual assortment of *Santeria* items

The lovely grounds of **Inter American University** are on the edge of town just off the road to Cabo Rojo. Founded in 1912 as the Instituto Politécnico, its name was changed in 1956.

ACCOMMODATIONS: The **Parador Oasis** (☎ 787-892-1175, 800-942-8086; Box 114, San Germán, PR 00683) is a classically styled hotel at C. Luna 4. Its facilities include 52 small a/c rooms with private bath and color TV, a restaurant, and convention hall. Rates are around $75 d year round. For current prices and to make reservations, contact Paradores Puertorriqueños, Box 4435, Old San Juan, PR 00905; ☎ 800-443-0266 in the US, 137-800-462-7575 in Puerto Rico.

The **Inter American University** (☎ 787-264-1912, ext. 7300, 7301), Carr. 102 outside of town, offers a/c accommodation in its attractive dorm rooms for around $22 pp, pn.
muriel@sg.inter.org

FOOD: Set on the main plaza, **Del Mar** (☎ 787-264-2715) is popular with locals. Entrees run around $15-$20.

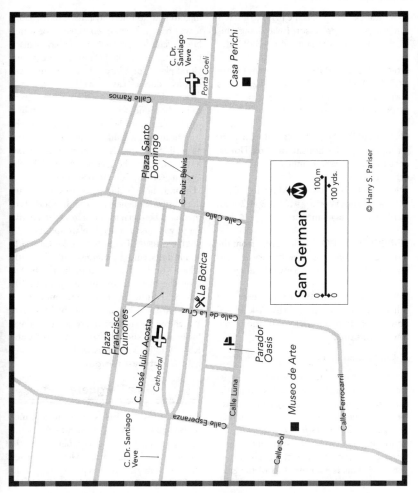

San German

100 m
100 yds.

© Harry S. Pariser

Casa Perichi

C. Dr. Santiago Veve

Porta Coeli

Calle Ramos

Plaza Santo Domingo

C. Ruiz Belvis

Calle Calle

La Botica

Plaza Francisco Quinones

C. José Julio Acosta

Cathedral

Calle de la Cruz

Parador Oasis

Museo de Arte

Calle Luna

Calle Esperanza

C. Dr. Santiago Veve

Calle Sol

Calle Ferrocarril

At Dr. Veve 33, **Bótica** (☎ 787-892-5790) is a converted drugstore (Farmacia Dominguez) which dates from 1877; it serves seafood and other dishes. It's open daily for lunch and dinner. Entrées range from $7 to $20.

Cilantro's (☎ 787-264-2735), is at C. Luna 85, a street which runs parallel to the main plaza. Set in an old home, it serves gourmet seafood and other dishes.

In the town center, **Antonino's Pizza** is a plush pizza joint.

The **Sol de Verano** has Chinese food.

The **Oasis** also has a gourmet restaurant.

For snack, light food including vegetarian dishes, and coffee, **Galería Lubben** (☎ 787-

892-7420), C. Luna 9, is the place to go. It is run by an art professor (who hangs his work), and it is open daily from 4:309 PM.

INTERNET ACCESS: **Password Internet Café** (☎ 787-892-4485, ✆ 787-892-4625) faces Porta Coeli on Plaza Santo Domingo. **http://www.password.com**

ENTERTAINMENT: The **Red Baron Pub**, set underneath La Botica, and **Los Tigres**, near the entrance to campus, attract a student crowd.

Norman's Bar, Barrio Maresúa, Carr. 318, and **The World** (☎ 787-264-2002), Carr. 360, are gay hangouts.

SERVICES: The **PO** is right across from the terminal for *públicos*. The **library** is right on one side of Parque de Santo Domingo.

FROM SAN GERMÁN: La Parguera and other coastal sights are nearby. Ask a local how to negotiate the tricky transition from town to this road.

Lajas

Named after the slate deposits found in its vicinity, this small town dates from the early 19th century. Originally a part of San Germán, it became an independent municipality in 1883. Lajas's *fiestas patronales* (in honor of patron saint Nuestra Señora de la Candelaria) take place in the beginning of February. This is also the start of the *zatra* or pineapple season, for which the area is famous. There's a great view to be had from atop Las Animas mountain to the W.

Laguna Cartagena

Laguna Cartagena is off of Carr. 303 to the SE of Lajas. Overgrown to the point where it resembles more of a swamp than a lagoon, Cartagena is one of the island's two freshwater lagoons, and is a crucial habitat for

migrating waterfowl and aquatic birds. Sadly, it was once a huge, open expanse of water, but agricultural practices in the have caused it to be largely choked off by aquatic plants. Good places for a birder to spot water fowl, herons, ducks, cave swallows, common ground-doves and the northern mockingbird can all be found here. The sora, a marsh bird rarely seen outside Puerto Rico, and the American purple gallinule can be found here as well. Some locals claim that spacecraft have landed in the lagoon. Amazingly, the lagoon gets only 300 visitors a year.

Uplands here include pastures and abandoned sugarcane fields. Set in the foothills of the Sierra Bermeja, its 263 acres host a native forest with many endemic plant species.

GETTING HERE: To get here, take Carr. 305 W until it seemingly merges with Carr. 303 where you head L. Then make the first R after the small yellow bridge (around 100 yds. S). Follow this road (once more Carr. 305) until you hit the village of Maguayo. Watch for the sign for the trail. (Weekdays, birdwatchers should also drive to the Cabo Rojo Wildlife Reserve as well). **http://southeast.fws.gov**

La Parguera

Located off Carr. 304 is the eastern branch of **Bosque Estatal De Boquerón**, commonly referred to as La Parguera, after the town of the same name. The name itself derives from *pargos*, a type of snapper. Its **Refugio de Aves** (☎ 787-851-4795) has great birdwatching, including yellow warblers and yellow-crowned night herons. To enter, head S from Boquerón along Carr. 301 and watch carefully for the sign. It is open from 7:30 AM–4 PM.

This area contains what is probably the most famous marine attraction in Puerto Rico. **La Bahía Fosforescente** (Phosphorescent Bay) contains millions of luminescent dinoflagellates, a microscopic plankton. Any disturbance causes them to light up the surrounding water. Pick a moonless night and take one of the twice-nightly boats (times vary) departing from Villa Parguera's pier. Dip a hand in the water and watch as sparks of liquid silver run through it. (Note: This bay's bioluminesence has been impacted and is no longer quite as bright as formerly).

Bahía Mondo José, nearby, also has a large population of dinoflagellates. In 1973 the Conservation Trust acquired some 400 acres in danger of development. This might have altered the drainage pattern, causing sedimentation, which would have played havoc with the bay's ecological balance. Also, the electric lights that go along with development would have competed with the bay's luminescence. The trust is seeking to acquire another 800 acres which will be used only for grazing cattle and for farming.

The small town of La Parguera lights up on weekends when there's live entertainment. Offshore are more than 30 mangrove cays. Check on transport out to **Mata de la Cay**, two miles offshore.

Visible from the outskirts of town is **Isla Cueva**. It's commonly known as "Monkey Island" because 400 monkeys reside there. Originally from India, they are allowed to pursue their favorite pastimes freely among the trees. Occasionally, a group of scientists arrives to check up on their habits. **Playa Rosada** Beach is E of town.

ACCOMMODATIONS: All of the guesthouses and hotels listed here are within the heart of town. **Andino's Chalet & Guest House** (☎ 899-0000; HC-01, Box 4691, Lajas, PR 00667), which has been strongly recommended by a reader, has one-and two–bedroom apartments for around $35–45 pn. According to the reader, Ernesto Andino is a "gracious" retired businessman who is "very knowledgeable"

and can arrange boat tours. It's at C. 8 #33, right near Parque de Pelota in town.

Parador Villa Parguera (☎ 787-899-3975/7777, 800-443-0266, ℮ 787-899-6040; Box 273, La Parguera, Lajas, PR 00667), Carr. 304, has 70 a/c rooms with private bath, cable TV, and phone. It has restaurant, swimming pool, children's playroom, sundeck, and gardens. Rates start at around $90 d.
http://www.elshop.com

The 24-unit **Posada Porlamar Parador** (☎ 899-4015, 800-443-0266, ℮ 899-5558; Box 405, La Parguera, Lajas, PR 00667), Carr. 304, is set in an old wooden building with balconies and a garden. Rates start from around $55 d.
http://netdial.caribe.net/~posada

The eight-unit **Guest House Viento y Vela** (☎ 787-899-4689/3030, ℮ 899-4698; Box 386, La Parguera, Lajas, PR 00667) is at Km 3.2 on Carr. 304. It's a wood-framed house with a/c and fan efficiencies. Rates start at around $60.

Up to the R, the **Hostal Casablanca** (☎ 787-899-4250), set near the docks, charges around $70 for its simple rooms. (Higher rates prevail on weekends). It has a pool. Germans love it.

The **Parguera Guest House** (☎ 787-899-1933/3993; Carr. las Colinas, La Parguera, Lajas, PR 00667) charges around $60 s or d.

The eight-room **Nautilus Guest House** (☎ 787-899-4565; Box 396, La Parguera, Lajas, PR 00667) has rooms with a/c and color TV from $55.

Gladys Guest House (☎ 787-899-4678) is down a sidestreet; it has a/c.

The **Parador Villa del Mar Hotel** (☎ 787-899-4265), 3 Ave. Albizu Campos, is set outside of town on top of a hill overlooking the phosphorescent bay Rates start at around $90.

In Bo. Boquerón, **Wildflowers** (☎ 787-851-1793) is a small inn with restaurant and bar. It has live music, and rooms have balconies.

The family-run **Papa Alberto Resort** (☎ 787-851-2900) has a set of wooden bungalows with kitchenettes which hold up to six. It has pool tables, TV room, children's play area, two pools, picnic area, and a store which sells musical instruments.

Sinda's Guest House (☎ 787-899-5540/4582), on C. 7 in the direction of Playa Rosada, is an inexpensive homey hotel with only 11 rooms and a few apartments. No credit cards are accepted.

La Jamaca Guesthouse and Restaurant (☎/❋ 787-899-6162), Colinas de la Parguera, Reparto Adolfo Laborde #5, charges around $75 d. A/c rooms have phones, and there is a restaurant, pool, and outdoor decks. One reader has recommended it.

FOOD: There are a large number of restaurants here. including the **Bahía** and **Restaurant Porto Parguera**, **Tony's Pizza**, **Café Vista al Mar**, **Mar y Tierra** (which features billiard tables), **Restaurant Reef Pop** (about the same price as the others but done up in fast food style), and the a/c **Shark Café**.

Los Balcones has seafood and steaks served in a pleasant atmosphere.

La Palmita Cocktail Lounge & Café (☎ 787-899-4320) has *sopa de pescado* and other seafood dishes; they charge $10-$15 for entrées. They're only open weekends.

Café Vista del Mar has a fantastic selection of *empanadillas*.

Pargo Mar has fish entrées for about $15. In the same building, **La Lucerna** offers inexpensive sandwiches and other baked goods.

In the Muelle shopping plaza, **Dave's Deli** sells sandwiches to go as well as stuffed baked potatoes.

Also in the same plaza, **Golden City** is a Chinese restaurant.

Zoé en el Naútico (☎ 787-899-5237), Playita Rosada, serves gourmet seafood dishes.

If you will be cooking your own food, there's also a *pescaderia* (fish market).

ENTERTAINMENT: La Playita offers live music on weekends.

La Tierra del Oz has shuffleboard, pool tables, and video games.

Parador Villa Parguera has a variety of live shows on Sat. nights.

Students frequent the **Blues Café**, which has live music on weekends, and the **Mar y Tierra** which also has live music on weekends.

BOATING: Cancel Boats (☎ 787-899-5891) rents 15-ft. motorboats. **Torres Boat Service** is nearby.

GLASS BOTTOM BOATS: *Fondo de Cristal II* (☎ 787-5899-5891; Box 427, Lajas, PR 00667) operates from the pier. It charges $5 but holds up to 150.

KAYAKING: Kayaks are available for rent. A one-person kayak is $10 ph; a two-person is $15 ph. Contact **Alelí Tours** (☎ 787-899-6086) which is in the dock area.

WINDSURFING: The area has winds which blow a steady 15-20 knots on most days. Contact **Ventolera** (☎ 787-808-0396) for info and rentals.

FISHING: Parguera Fishing Charters (☎ 787-899-4698, 787-382-4698; Apdo. 386, La Parguera, Lajas 00667) operates a 32-ft. twin-diesel Bertram Sportsfisherman which will take you snorkeling and fishing. It's to the W of town.
http://hometown.aol.com/mereja
mereja@aol.com

DIVING: Contact **La Parguera Divers** (☎/☻ 787-899-4171; Box 514, Lajas, PR 00667). They run a number of trips and are located in the Posada Porlamar Parguera. **divepr@caribe.net**

DIVING NEAR GUÁNICA AND LA PARGUERA:

This stretch of coast is renowned for its wall dives. A dropoff stretches over 20 mi. (32 km) to the E and W of Guánica.

While the top of the reef averages a depth of 65 ft. (20 m), it drops in places to as low as 600 ft. (180 m) and beyond. Visibility is generally 60-100 ft. (18-30 m).

The **Super Bowl** is set some five mi. (eight km) S of Punta Molino to the W of Boquerón. This is an intermediate-level 55–75 ft. (17-23 m) dive is an dive. Its numerous ledges create numerous swim-though cavities to explore. Sea cucumbers, creole wrasse, queen angelfish, the scrawled cowfish, and the peppermint bass are some species you may see here.

Set set some 6.5 mi. (ten km) S of Punta Molino, **The Chimney** is a N-facing ledge which is perforated with numerous holes. Beautifully colored algae, moray eels, trumpetfish, and creole wrasse are among the visual delights to be seen here. The site is 55–75 ft. down (17–23 m) and is an intermediate dive.

The Highlight, four mi. (6.4 km) S of Punta Molino, commands exceptional visibility: all the way down to 75–100 ft. The dive itself is from 65–100 ft. (20-30 m) and is intermediate. A variety of sponges, creole wrasse, and anemones are species to watch for here.

Set four mi. (6.4 km) to the SE of Punta Molino, the **Motor** is named after the sunken airplane propeller and motor found here. This 55–75-ft. (17–23-m) novice dive has numerous crevices where moray eels may be spotted as well as sponges, black bar soldierfish, and other species.

Barracuda City, set five mi. (eight km) to the SE of La Parguera, is a great place to see barracuda, sea fans, elkhorn coral, tilefish, and spiny lobsters. This is a 60–70 ft. (18–21 m) novice dive.

The Star is a novice dive at a depth of 45–65 ft. (14–20 m). It's set 6.5 mi. (ten km) SE of La Parguera and is a set of coral mounds atop a sand plateau which, taken together, resemble an irregular star. You may see barracuda, sponges, tilefish, and other fish here.

At nine mi. (14 km) from La Parguera, **Hole in the Wall** is an advanced-only dive which ranges from 50–125 ft. (15–38 m). It has a great swim through passage.

The Black Wall, eight mi. (13 km) S of La Parguera is named for its steep drop-off, one of the steepest, in fact, along the entire wall. This is a 60-130-ft. (18-40 m), intermediate dive with light to moderate current but with a surface that can be turbulent on occasion. Triggerfish, Spanish hogfish, dog snappers, and other species may be seen.

Set seven mi. (11 km) S of La Parguera, **The Buoy** is named for a long-vanished scientific buoy. Only its ceramic post remains. This 65–100 ft. (2030 m) intermediate dive is marked by less of a dropoff (an 80 ft. average) than other sites. There are numerous channels to be seen. Watch for the giant sponges.

Canyons, also seven mi. (11 km) S of La Parguera, is a novice dive with depths of 65–110 ft. (2034 m). The swimmable canyons here provide opportunities to see tube sponges, moray eels, and schools of Atlantic spadefish.

The unusually-named **1990** is a novice dive site set four mi. (6.4 km) S of La Parguera. You may spot stingray, angelfish, sea fans, chromis, and numerous varieties of wrasse here.

Set six mi. (9.7 km) S of La Parguera, **Efra's Wall** is a 55-120-ft. (17–37 m) intermediate dive named for a local dive shop operator. Whip corals proliferate here, gorgonians are numerous and spectacular, and lobsters and crabs may be spotted.

Two For You is an advanced dive site which is at a depth of 55–120 ft. (17–37 m). It is one of a number of deep dives in this area, 6.5 mi. (10 km) SW of Guánica. Currents along the wall are mild, and you may see butterfly fish, silver jacks, indigo hampets, and other fish around the magnificent sponges and coral.

An advanced dive set five mi. (eight km) SW of Guánica, **Fallen Rock** is named after a huge mass of tumbled rockface that has created a V-shaped notch in the wall. Corals have moved into the gap, and a wide variety of fish and coral may be seen on this 65–120-ft. (20–37 m) dive.

Cabo Rojo & Vicinity

Cabo Rojo

Founded in 1772, the small town of Cabo Rojo (not to be confused with the peninsula to its S) is a convenient jumping-off point for Mayagüez or destinations to the S. It reached its peak of prosperity in the 1800s when immigrants from Spain and other Mediterranean countries, fleeing revolutions in Europe, arrived to take up sugarcane cultivation. Today, the canefields have been displaced by pasture for cattle. Cabo Rojo's *fiestas patronales* take place around September 29.

SIGHTS: Erected in 1783, the **San Miguel Arcangel Church** stands next to the plaza. The **Museo del los Próceres** (Museum of Patriots, ☎ 787-255-1580) stands next to the police station at its SE end (Carr. 312 Km 0.4). Built in 1995, it contains archaeological remains, sculptures of local luminaries, local art, and a library with public-access internet. It is open Mon. to Sat, from around 8 AM–4 PM. Closed Sun.

The **Plaza de Recreo**, the town's main square , is also the resting place of national patriot, Dr. Ramón Emeterio Betances.

ACCOMMODATIONS: For accommodations in the area see San Germán, Boquerón, La Parguera, and Joyuda.

Camping is available around the Cabo Rojo area: **Villa Plaza** (☎ 787-851-1340) at **Denigno Obejo Plaza** is on Carr. 301 at Km 6.9; **Villa La Mela** at Carr. 307, Km 35, **Cabo Rojo** (☎ 787-851-1391/2067); and **Mojacascade Camp** (☎ 787-745-0305) at Carr. 301, Km 10.1, Playa Combate, Cabo Rojo.

Playa Joyuda/Punta Arenas

In an area also known as Punta Arenas, **Joyuda Beach**, with its numerous seafood restaurants, is off Carr. 102 to the NW. You can visit Isla de Ratones (see below) offshore.

The town has been built up for tourism, but the beach can disappoint. It's not been the same since dredging for a landfill for a Mayagüez tuna plant impacted the area.

ISLA DE RATONES: This "rat island" has a rather amazing recent history. Its owner sold it to MTV in May 1988, and Cyndi Lauper was booked to raffle it off as an "uninhabited, Caribbean fantasy island" to one of 225 viewers who had won cruises. Despite substantial protest, MTV announced in June that there was a winner: a young guy from Pontiac, MI. After a major demonstration followed, nothing further has been heard from MTV.

To get to the island, look for the sign "Pasa en Bote,:" and pay $33 pp RT. Note that it is flooded with visitors on weekends.

PRACTICALITIES: Tino's here is famous for its *mofongo* with seafood.

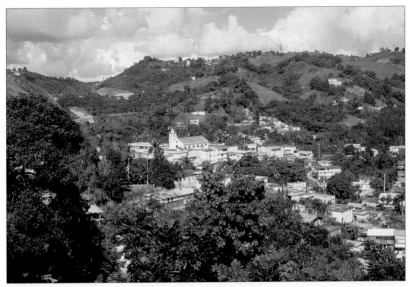

Top: The charming mountain town of Aibonito
Bottom: church at Hormigueros (left), Lago Dos Bocas (right)

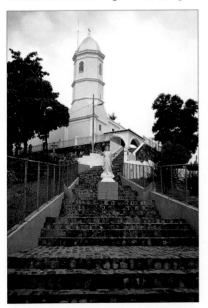

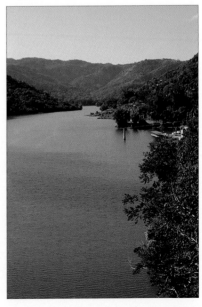

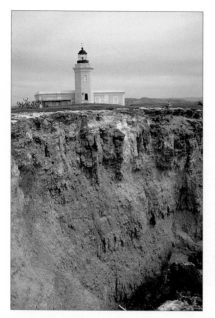

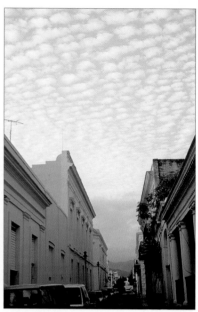

Above: Cabo Rojo lighthouse in the island's southwest (left) , Ponce (right)

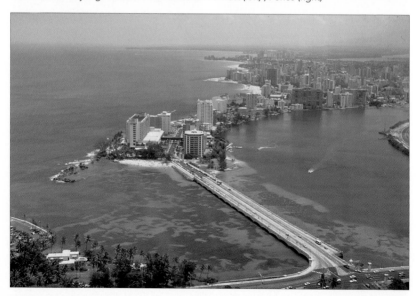

Other restaurants include Restaurante Raitos, Restaurant Island View, Restaurant Brisas de Joyuda, Restaurant Brisas del Mar, Restaurant Costa del Sol, Restaurant El Bohio, Restaurante Vista Bohio, and Restaurant El Pueblito.

At Km 11.7 on Carr. 102, **Hotel/Parador Joyuda Beach** (☎ 787-851-5650, ☻ 787-265-3750; Box 1660, Mayagüez, PR 00681), a *parador*, has 43 a/c rooms with TV, phone, and bath; some suites have sunset views. Facilities include restaurant and beach bar, beach volleyball, small children's playground, windsurfing, canoeing, and golfing (at the Club Deportivo); cabins with kitchens are also available. Rooms run from around $80–90 d.
http://www.joyudabeach.com

Set in Joyuda on Carr. 102 at Km 14.2, **Parador Perichi's**, (☎ 787-435-7197, ☻ 787-851-0560; Box 16310, Cabo Rojo, PR 00623) has 49 a/c rooms with balconies, color TV, and phone. There's a pool, restaurant, banquet hall, baseball and basketball courts, and game room. Rates run around $80–$90 d. For reservations for either of these two *paradores*, call 800-443-0266 in the US and 800-462-7575 in Puerto Rico.

Moreu's Inn (☎ 787-255-3861, ☻ 787-834-3670), Carr. 102, Km. 9.8, is along a relatively-secluded stretch of beach. It has a small pool for your offspring to use.

The 56-rm. **Joyuda Plaza** (☎ 787-851-8800, ☻ 787-851-8810), Km. 14.7 at Carr. 102, is set across from the beach. Rates start at around $50; studios are more expensive.

Also here are **Hotel Antibes** (☎ 787-851-8800), **Cabañas Tony** (☎ 787-851-2500), **Cabañas Don Carlos** (☎ 787-821-9264/0976), which has a swimming pool, and other hotels.

To the W, nearly half the island's fish are caught at **Puerto Real**. When it served as

Cabo Rojo's port (1760-1860), merchandise and slaves from St. Thomas and Curacao were off-loaded here.

Ostiones, a point of land protruding to the N of Puerto Real, is the location of an important indigenous archaeological site.

Of special interest to birdwatchers, **Laguna Joyuda** is 7.5 km NW of town. Its 300 acres (150 ha) contain a vast variety of birds, including pelicans, martins, and herons. It is luminescent on moonless nights.

Beachgoers will want to check out **Playa Buyé** and **Playa La Mela** to the SW on Carr. 307.

At attractive and relatively uncrowded Playa Buyé, you can stay at **Cabiñas Playa Buyé** (☎ 851-2923), Carr. 307 at Km 4.8.

Restaurante Caribe is at Km 4.3 on Carr. 307 here.

Puerto Real is a very small and attractive fishing village; the neighboring lagoon at **Punta Guaniquilla** harbors strangely-shaped boulders which protrude from and dominate the still waters of the sometimes dry lagoon. Birds squeal and cry overhead. Pirate Roberto Cofresi, who terrorized the coast during the early 19th century, hid out in a cave nearby. It's a good place to buy fish, if cooking on your own. Whale watching charters are sometimes available here from Jan. to April.

AREA DINING: At Km 13.9 on Carr. 102, **Bohío** (☎ 851-2755) serves seafood and meat.

Brisas de Joyuda (☎ 787-851-2488), at Km 14.2, offers a variety of reasonably priced seafood dishes.

By the beach on C. Principal in Puerto Real, **Brisas del Mar** (☎ 787-851-1264) serves similar fare.

At Km 9.7 on Carr. 102, **Casona de Serafín** (☎ 787-851-0066) serves lobster and other seafood dishes.

SOUTHWEST

Island View Restaurant (☎ 787-851-9264), Carr. 102 at Km 13.7, also offers steak and seafood. Right next door, **Tino's** (☎ 851-2976) specializes in *mofongo relleno de mariscos en salsa.*

INFORMATION: The **Cabo Rojo Tourism Office** (☎ 787-851-701) is by an off ramp on the southbound side of Carr. 100, about a mi. N of Carr. 101.

Cabo Rojo Tour Guides (☎ 787-255-1580), Carr. 312 at Km 0.1, offer free tour guides upon request.
http://www.mcr.org/mp

DIVE SITES: In addition to Mona Island, **Tourmaline Reef** or **Horseshoe** is an intermediate dive set 11 mi. (18 km) W of Punta Guanajibo. This 40-90 ft. (12-27 m) spot has a silty bottom with unusual formations. Giant orange sea fans, sea whips, black coral trees, and schools of goatfish and grunts may be spotted. It's around 20 min. offshore from Joyuda.

Set five mi. (eight km) W of Punta Arenas, **Los Caminos** is a novice dive which is a set of comparatively shallow canals, thus the name *caminos* (roads). Razorfish, blue tang, doctorfish, gobies, and other species may be spotted. It's a 35–40 ft. (9–12 m) dive.

GOLF: At Joyuda, the **Club Deportivo del Oeste** (☎ 787-851-8880) charges around $30 for the greens fee on its nine-hole course; cart is included. Although part of a private course, it is open to the public from 7 AM to 5 PM. It is renowned for its difficult opening hole, and it can be a challenging course.

FISHING: Tourmarine Adventures (☎ 787-851-9259), in Joyuda, offer charters for around $350 per half day, $500 per full day.

Refugio Nacional Cabo Rojo

This great birdwatching spot, **Cabo Rojo National Fish & Wildlife Refuge** (☎ 787-851-7297, 7258), is open from 7:30 AM–4 PM weekdays. It's on Carr. 301 at Km 5.1. near Combate There's an office, visitor's center, and some 12 mi. of trails, including a two-mi. interpretive trail . Birdwatchers can see the Puerto Rican tody, Adelaide's warbler, Caribbean elaenia, troupial, and the endangered yellow-shouldered blackbird. Note that Laguna Cartagena National Wildlife Refuge is just a short drive away.
http://www.fws.gov

Boquerón

Located S of Cabo Rojo and W of San Germán is the small town of Boquerón and the western branch of the **Bosque Estatal de Boquerón** (Boquerón Forest Reserve). Herons perch on mangroves in the bird sanctuary here. The town itself is well known for its *balneario* (public beach), as well as its raw oysters with lemon juice and other types of seafood. The protected bay here is excellent for windsurfing, boating, and swimming. Its harbor once sheltered pirates like Roberto Cofresi.

The US Border Patrol arrested 31 illegal immigrants here in March 1996. While 20 were from the Dominican Republic, 11 were Macedonian nationals who had paid $2,000 pp (plus airfare from Tirana, Albania) for the promised opportunity to enter the US.

ACCOMMODATIONS AND DINING: In Boquerón, **End of Rt. 100, Int Rt. 101.** off Carr. 307 and 103, **Parador Boquemar,** (☎ 787-851-2158, 888-634-4343, ☺ 787-851-7600; Box 133, Boquerón, Cabo Rojo, PR 00622) has 63 functional a/c rooms. It has a pool, and its **La Cascada Restaurant** is well known for gourmet dishes. It's within walking distance to Boquerón Beach and the village. For reservations, ☎ 800-443-0266 in the US and 800-462-7575 in Puerto Rico.Rates are around $70-90 d. http://www.boquemar.com

Set next to the Boquemar, **Adamari's Apartments** (☎ 787-851-6860) has a laundromat on the first level; it offers a set of efficiency apartments for around $70 pn.

The **Shamar Bar-Restaurant** (☎ 787-851-0542) rents rooms with balconies. It is less expensive than others but can be noisy.

Galloways is a nearby restaurant right on the water.

At Km 7.4 on Carr. 187, the three-story, 22-unit **Hotel Cuestamar** (☎ 787-851-2819, ☻ 787-254-2019; Box 187, Boquerón, PR 00622) has a pool and coffee shop; rates start from around $65 d. http://www.ihppr.com

The 31-unit **Lighthouse Inn** (☎ 787-255-3835, ☻ 787-255-3875) is set at the intersection of Carr. 102 and Carr. 100, which is around five mi. N near the town of Cabo Rojo. It has a pool and bar and restaurant. Rates run from around $70-$140 d. http://www.lighthouse.net

On Carr. 100 at Km 8.0, the 29-rm. **Parador Highway Inn** (☎ 787-851-1839, ☻ 787-851-1840), charges from around $55-75 d. They have a restaurant, bar and pool. http://www.paradorhighwayinn.com

Set at the town's entrance and the beach on Carr. 101, Km 18.1 is 93-rm. **Boquerón Beach** (☎ 787-851-7110, ☻ 787-851-7135; Boquerón, Cabo Rojo, PR 00622).They offer a pool, rec room with pool tables, and a children's arcade. Rates run from around. $70–125 d. http://www.boqueronbeachhotel.com

The three-story **Cofresí Beach Hotel** (☎ 787-254-3000/3100, ☻ 787-254-1048) rents one- to three-bedroom apartments which are fully-equipped and furnished with microwave, phone, and TV/VCR. Although it is not near a beach, it has a small pool. Rates run around $120–$200 d. It's set on Carr. 101 to the S of town at Muñoz Rivera 57. There are conflicting reports about this hotel. Some love it; others have problems with it. http://www.cofresibeach.com cbcsella@coqui.net

At the **Boquerón Centro Vacacional** (☎ 787-851-1900) the government agency Fomento rents out cabins here to "bona fide family groups" (i.e., parents and children). There is a two-night minimum stay, and reservations must be booked 120 days in advance. Payment must be with a credit card. For more information and a reservation form (apply 120 days in advance) write to Oficina de Reservaciones, Compania de Fomento Recreativo, (☎ 787-722-1771/1551, 787-721-2800 ext. 225, 275) to bona fide family groups. For more information and a reservation form (apply 120 days in advance) write to Oficina de Reservaciones, Compania de Fomento Recreativo, Apdo. 9022089, San Juan PR 00904-2089.

FOOD: The **Bahía** (☎ 787-851-0345, C. José de Diego 210, serves good seafood as does **Galloway's** (☎ 787-254-3302).

You can eat at the **Fish Net Restaurant**, the **Shamar Bar-Restaurant, Restaurant Villa Playera,** or at a number of others.

SNACKS: Small oysters are sold by the dozen near the marina. They are raised in a mix of fresh and saltwater. *Empanadillas* and *surullitos* (fried corn fritters) are sold by a vendor near the Parador Boquemar.

SERVICES: Punto Activa Internet Café (☎ 787-644-0787), Ave. Muñoz Rivera 62, has eight terminals which charge around $5 for 30 min. and $8 for an hour. They are open daily.

The **post office** is on the town's outskirts along Carr. 101.

SPORTS: Mona Aquatics (☎ 787-851-2185) offers diving, rents snorkeling equipment, and offers tours. They are on C. José de Diego, next to the Club Nautico to the W of town.

Kaipo Kayak Rentals (☎ 787-851-3413) is set on the main drag and rents kayaks by the hour.

SCOOTER RENTALS: Rent scooters at **Boquerón Skooter Rental** (☎ 787-254-0080, cell 787-640-5363). It's at the entrance to town on Muñoz Rivera and is open 11 AM-10 PM from Thurs. through Sun. Mopeds are around $20 for the first hr., $10 for each extra hour. Go-peds are around $15 for the first hr., $8 for each extra hour.

El Combate

This small fishing village to the N of the salt beds has an unmistakable 19th-century aura about it. It is famous for its long beach which is extremely popular with Puerto Ricans. The sea is plagued by jetskis, and weekends see tons of drunk teens and twenty-somethings.

ACCOMMODATION: The 31-rm. **Combate Beach Hotel** (☎ 787-254-2358, 787-254-7053, ⊖ 787-851-2134), is on Carr. 3301 at Km 2.7, right on the beach. Rates run from around $60-80 d. **http://www.combatebeachhotel.com**

There are also a number of other places to stay here. **El Combate Guest House** (☎ 787-747-0384) is near town. You can also try **Apartamentos Kenny** (☎ 787-851-0002), **Cabañas Marivan Playa Combate** (☎ 787-851-2433), **Cabinas Freddy** (☎ 787-851-7370), **Cabañas Miranda** (☎ 787-254-2992), **Cabañas Pou-Men** (☎ 787-254-2220), **Ranitt Cabinas** (☎ 787-833-2735), **Cabinas Cofresi, Cabañas & Restaurante Luichy's** (☎ 787-254-2358, "hospitable and warm female owner" — a reader), and **Cabañas Villa Ranil** (☎ 787-851-4297).

There are also some camping areas on the way out of town. **Annie's Seafood Restaurant** (☎ 787-851-0021) also has cabañas.

FOOD: Try **Santos Pizzeria, Restaurant El Combate,** or **Cafeteria Las Bohios. Willy's** (☎ 787-254-1111) rents jet skis and sells cooked chicken and pizza. You can buy basic items at **Colmado Chiquitin.**

Cabo Rojo Lighthouse

This structure is on Carr. 303, standing along a spit of land between Bahía Salinas and Bahía Sucia. It's a really beautiful trip to get here. You pass the turnoff to El Combate (where there's a campground). The road turns to clay, and you follow it along past the salt processing fields to your R; a lagoon is on the L. On the way you pass mangroves. Keep going and you find one parking place; follow the other road which branches off to the L, park right by the beach and climb up. Once inhabited by the lighthouse keepers and their families who occupied the two wings at its base, it has been electrified and is now automatic. This lighthouse was built in 1881 under Spanish rule in response to pressure from local planters.

Beneath the lighthouse, jagged limestone cliffs at **Punta Jagüey** drop sharply into the sea — an awesome sight to behold. The whole area has the feeling of being at the end of the world. There are large numbers of brown pelicans sitting on the rocks off the coast; it is a great place for birders. There's also a small but pretty beach at the base of the lighthouse.

Behind the lighthouse lies the Sierra Betmeja, low hills that date back 130 million years. The Salinas salt beds are nearby; salt harvested here is sent off to the Starkist plant in Mayagüez. The snowy plover can be seen in this vicinity.

The **Corozo Salt Flats** are found along Carr. 301. Be sure to stop and have a look.

ACCOMMODATION: Parador Bahía Salinas (☎ 787-254-1212, 800-981-7575, 877-205-7507, ✆ 787-254-1215) is a one-story 24-unit hotel. Rates run around $90-$125 d. Most rooms have balconies with views. Facilities include kayaking, TV, a/c, and a seafood restaurant. It is off of Carr. 301 at Km 11.5, near the lighthouse.
http://www.bahiasalinas.net
bahiasal@caribe.net

The **Punta Aguila Resort** (☎ 787-254-4454), next door, rents out efficiencies in a condo from around $100 pn.

Hormigueros

This town owes its name, meaning "ant hill," to the unique topography of the region. Originally a barrio of San Germán and later of Mayagüez, it became a distinct town in 1874.

Hormigueros is home to the **Shrine of Our Lady of Monserrate**, a majestic yellow church that towers above the town. According to a 17th-century legend, a peasant working in the field where the church now stands saw an enraged bull charging toward him. He pleaded with Our Lady of Monserrate to protect him, and the bull stumbled and fell; the man managed to escape and the church was erected in thanksgiving.

In commemoration of the miracle, the devout arrive for a religious pilgrimage and each Sept. 8, and climb the long bank of steps leading to the church on their hands and knees. See the oil painting by José Campeche, which portrays the miracle, on a wall inside the church. There's a great view from the top of the steps.

FOOD: If you need a bite after your visit to the church, **Cafeteria María** or the **El Palacio de las Sandwiches** are near the base of the steps and next door to each other.

Advertised by Bugs Bunny wearing a straw hat, **El Conejo Blanco** (☎ 787-849-1170/7744) is on Carr. 344 at Km 0. It specializes in Puerto Rican dishes such as *carne de conejo*.

Mayagüez

Despite its reputation as a center of industry, this western port, Mayagüez, the third largest city on the island, still retains much of the grace and charm suggested by its lovely name, taken from *majagua* — the indigenous name for a tree plentiful in the vicinity.

Although the city does have a fine collection of attractive homes and buildings, you have to look around for them. Many are in sadly deteriorating condition. Worth exploring is Barrio Paris, the student area which is N of Plaza Colón and along Ave. Méndez Vigo.

Mayagüez made world environmental news in 1993 after a grassroots movement triumphed and successfully rejected a 300-megawatt Cogentrix power plant. In addition to its zoo and agricultural research station, Mayagüez is a good place to base yourself for day trips to Maricao, San Germán, and the many beaches and small towns in the area.

GETTING HERE: Mayagüez is easily approached by *público* from San Germán, Ponce, San Juan, Arecibo, Aguadilla, or Rincón. Allow at least three to four hours from San Juan (around $20 pp). The station is located two blocks N of Plaza Colón in Barrio Paris. Major companies include *Blue Line* (☎ 787-765-7733) and *La Sultana* (☎ 787-767-5205).

BY AIR: American also flies daily from San Juan's Muñoz Marín International Airport, and there are flights to and from Santo Domingo as well

BY FERRY: A ferry also goes back and forth between the city and Santo Domingo, the Dominican Republic. See the intr

SIGHTS: Almost completely destroyed by an earthquake in 1917, one of the premier sights in this largely rebuilt city is the impressive **Plaza de Colón,** with its monstrous statue of Columbus, surrounded incongruously by statues of Greek maidens.

The old post office building is on C. McKinley nearby, as is the **Yaguez Theater.** In 1977 this theater was purchased by the federal government and declared a Historical Monument. Renovated, expanded, and modernized at a cost of $4.5 million, it presents all types of stage productions and is a center for artistic, cultural, and educational activities in the community.

Zoorico Park (☎ 787-834-8110), the Mayagüez Zoo, is home of innumerable reptiles, birds, and mammals, presented both in cages and in simulated natural habitats. See everything from Bengal tigers to capybara (the world's largest rodents). The spring of 2000 saw proud parents Coke and Sprite give birth to a baby camel (Odwalla?). However, although better than in the past, conditions for the animals here are still less than ideal. It's located on Carr. 108 at Barrio Miradero; open Wed. to Sun. 8:30 AM–5 PM, $6 admission; free for children under 11.

Much closer to town is the **Tropical Agricultural Research Station** (☎ 787-831-3435, 🖷 832-3435; Box 70, Mayagüez, PR 00681-0070) on Carr. 65, between C. Post and Carr. 108, next to the University of Puerto Rico at Mayagüez. It's open Mon. to Fri. from 7:30 AM–4 PM (free admission). Established at the beginning of this century on the site of a former plantation, its grounds present a dazzling array of exotic vegetation, ranging from a Sri Lankan cinnamon tree to pink torch ginger to the traveler's tree.

The station researches agricultural techniques and breeds hybrid plants that are more productive. Research has focused on plantains, sweet potatoes, sorghum, cassava, yams, bananas, beans, and tanier (taro root).

Improved varieties of these crops have been developed or introduced to Puerto Rico here. "Improvement" in this case means greater yields and higher resistance to disease.

Currently, research is ongoing with yam species imported from Southeast Asia; the hope is to develop a disease-resistant version that requires no fertilizer. Such a product would be a boon for the many people on this planet who are malnourished. Another attempt is to improve cassava, which is a problem-laden crop suffering from disease and poor crop management. Other projects involve tropical fruit trees. **http://www.ars-grin.gov/ars/SoAtlantic/ Mayaguez/mayaguez.html**

While you're in the station's vicinity be sure to check out the **Parque de los Proceres** (Park of the Patriots) across the street on C. Luna. The old pink **Aduana** (Customs House) has also been restored.

The **Planetarium** (☎ 787-832-4040, ext. 3073) Carr. 2 Ramal at C. Post at the UPR Mayagüez Campus, offers free admission on the second Tues. of each month at 8 PM. It's closed during June and July.

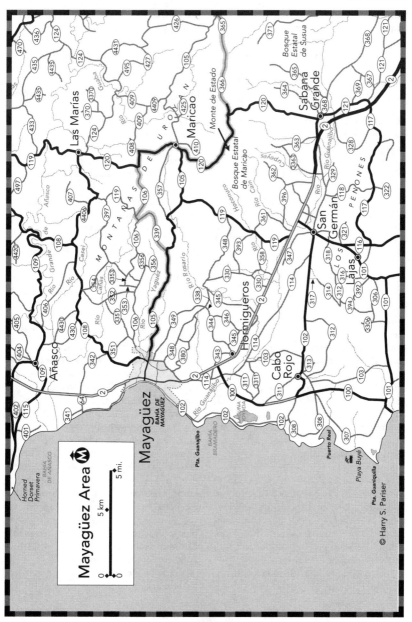

Mayagüez Area ⓜ

5 km

5 mi.

© Harry S. Pariser

EVENTS: Mayagüez's *fiestas patronales* honoring her patron saint, La Virgen de la Candelaria, held around Feb. 2 each year, is among the most spectacular of such events on the island.

The annual **crafts fair** is held in the beginning of Dec. at the coliseum.

ACCOMMODATIONS: On the campus of the University of Puerto Rico, **Hotel Colegial** (☎ 787-265-3891) provides "hostel-type" accommodation as well as a/c rooms with private bath. Rooms are disabled friendly.

The **Hotel El Embajador** (☎ 787-833-3340, ☏ 787-265-5030), 111-E Ramos Antonini (near C. McKinley and the main plaza), has 28 a/c rooms with cable TV and a restaurant. Rates run around $45–95 d.

The **Hotel Colonial** (☎ 787-833-2150, ☏ 787-833-2150) C. Iglesia 14 Sur, dates from the 1920s. The building was a convent until the 1960s. It charges from $32–100 d. Rooms have cable TV, and continental breakfast is included.
http://www.hotel-colonial.com
colonial@hotel-colonial.com

Hotel Mayagüez Plaza (☎ 787-891-9191, 888-300-8002), C. Méndez Vigo at Peral, has 47 a/c rooms (with TV and phone), restaurant, and bar. It charges around $75–$125 d. It has a great rooftop terrace.
http://www.ihppr.com

The **Parador El Sol** (☎ 787-834-0303, ☏ 265-7567), C. El Sol 9, has 52 a/c rooms, restaurant, bar, and pool. Its spacious rooms have cable color TV and phone; rates include continental breakfast. Rates run around $60–85 d. For reservations, call 800-443-0266 in the US or 800-981-7575 in Puerto Rico (787-721-2884 in San Juan).

OUTSIDE OF TOWN: The **Mayagüez Holiday Inn** (☎ 787-833-1100) on Carr. 2 has 154 a/c rooms with TV/VCR, am/fm clock radio, pool, bar, restaurant, cocktail lounge, and conference rooms. Rates run around $120–150 d.
http://www.holidayinn.com/mayaguezpri

The **Best Western Mayagüez Resort and Casino** (☎ 787-832-3030), is N on Hwy. 2 at Km 149.9 in Barrio Algarroba. It has has 150 a/c rooms, pool, restaurant, bar, conference rooms, disco, casino, and tennis courts. Set amidst 20 acres of gardens, it offers hilltop views. Rates run around $159–219 d.
http://www.mayaguezresort.com

OUTLYING ACCOMMODATIONS: Centro Turistico Rancho las Cuevas (☎ 831-0010), Carr. 352 at Km 2.8, offers cabins and a pool, and serves traditional Puerto Rican entrées as well as buffets.

FOOD: There are plenty of small, cheap lunchrooms, fast-food places, and restaurants. The expensive **Palma** is inside the hotel of the same name on Méndez Vigo, and **Perfect Nutrition Health Food** is next door.

Set in a red light district near the docks, **El Estoril** (☎ 787-834-2288), C. Méndez Vigo, is a Portuguese-owned gourmet restaurant. Entrees run from around $15 on up.

Across the street, the bakery **Brazo Gitano Franco**, was founded by the great uncle of Franco, the infamous Spanish dictator. It has great local atmosphere, and is the place to go for coffee and sweets. Its specialty is a jellyroll made with guava, pineapple, and other flavors. **Franco's Confectionary** is at C. Manuel Piradillo 3 in Barrio Marina Meridional.

Panaderia Ricomini is another good local bakery on C. Méndez Vigo.

The **Restaurant Parador El Sol** is at C. Riera Palmer 9.

The **Pong Wai** is in the Guanajibo Shopping Center at Carr. 102, Km 6.3.

Renowned for its sangría, **Fido's Beer and Wine Garden** is at C. Dulievre 90 in Barrio Balboa.

The Mayagüez Hilton has **La Rotisserie** (☎ 787-831-7575), which offers international cuisine.

Overlooking the sea at Km 5 on Carr. 102, **El Mesón Español** (☎ 787-833-5445) serves Spanish dishes.

The **Oyster Seafood Restaurant and Bar** (☎ 787-831-7575), C. Peral, stays open until 3 AM on weekends with live music.

ENTERTAINMENT: It's pretty dull here even on weekends. The only thing to do is walk around and watch the kids hanging out, trying to be cool just as they do everywhere else in the world. Check to see if **Teatro Yaguez** has a show on. The **Mayagüez Hilton** has live music nightly and dance music Tues. to Sat.

The **Mayagüez** (☎ 787-833-3335) shows three films daily.

SHOPPING: Mayagüez is a good place to shop for inexpensive bargains. Check the stores around the plaza.

SERVICES AND INFORMATION: The **Tourism Office** (☎ 787-831-5220, 787-833-9560, ☏ 787-831-3210) is inside the Citibank Bldg. at C. McKinley 53 on one side of Plaza Colón. They try their best to be helpful.

Conozcamos a Puerto Rico (☎ 787-831-0865) offers island tours.

Condado Travel (☎ 787-831-7790), is at Ste. 155, at Sam's Club in Western Plaza on Carr. 2. Open daily.

CAR RENTAL: Rent cars from **Hertz** (☎ 787-832-3314); **Leaseway** (☎ 787-833-1140), Carr, 2, Km 149.5; **Popular Mayagüez** (☎ 265-4848; **Payless Car Rental** (☎ 787-832-0101), C. 155 McKinley 155, **Popular Auto** (☎ 787-265-4848), 742 Ostos Ave.; **Thrifty** (☎ 787-834-1590).

FROM MAYAGÜEZ: *Públicos* leaving for surrounding towns depart from the area around the plaza. If heading for Maricao, get an early start.

BY BOAT: A ferry operated by **Feries Del Caribe** (☎787-832-4800) leaves for Santo Domingo in the Dominican Republic every other evening at around 8 PM for the 11-hr. trip. It holds 550 passengers 250 cars, and is equipped with restaurant, casino, disco, Jacuzzi, sauna, and other facilities. Rates start at around $40.

http://www.ferriesdelcaribe.com

Maricao-Monte del Estado

Maricao is a small coffee-trading center near Monte del Estado, a forest preserve which, confusingly, is also called Maricao. The town is tiny and traditional — right down to the guys galloping though town on horses. This is one of the best places on the island to experience Puerto Rican small town life.

The nearby preserve is one of the driest areas on the island and is a famous bird-watching area.

EVENTS: The *Festival del Café*, which marks the end of the coffee harvest festival, is held here in mid- to late Feb. The festival includes a parade, demonstrations of traditional coffee harvesting, live salsa, and booths with local dishes.

SIGHTS: At the **Maricao Fish Hatchery**, more than 25,000 fish (such as black bass and tilapia) are reared and schooled yearly in preparation for their journey to lakes and fishponds. It's open Mon. to Fri. from 7:30-noon and 1–4 PM and on Sat. and Sun. from 8:30 AM–4 PM; reservations are required (☎ 787-838-3710). A trail, which begins at Km 128 on Carr. 120, leads from Maricao ridge down to the hatchery.

Maricao or **Monte del Estado** also has picnic grounds, an observation tower, and a swimming pool. Climb the stone tower for a commanding view of SW Puerto Rico. On a clear day, you can even see the cliffs of Mona Island off in the distance.

Near the reserve's highest peak (2,625-ft., 800-m) **Las Tetas de Cerro Gordo** a stone observation tower affords views of Isla de Mona as well as three of the four coasts. The aged tower seems somehow medieval.

FLORA AND FAUNA: Of the 278 species of trees found here, there are 123 endemic species and 37 that are found only in the area. Its serpentine soil derives from once-submerged bluish-green rock of volcanic ancestry. Despite the heavy rainfall, the area resembles karst rather than rainforest. Among the 44 bird species are the Puerto Rican vireo, the Puerto Rican lizard-cuckoo, the Puerto Rican tody, the Puerto Rican tanager, the sharp-shinned hawk, and the rarely spotted elfin woods warbler.

ACCOMMODATIONS: Apply for permission to camp (follow the sign to Casa de Piedra) at **Recursos Naturales y Ambientales** (Department of Natural Resources and the Environment, ☎ 787-724-3724, 787-724-3647) in Puerto de Tierra, San Juan. **Cabins** at the *Centro Vacacionales* hold six.

More expensive is the **Hacienda Juanita** (☎ 787-838-2550, ☜ 787 838-2551), Carr. 105 at Km 23.5. Set in a still-operating coffee plantation, its facilities include swim-

ming pool, tennis and other ball courts, and hiking trails. Call 800-443-0266 in the US or 800-981-7575 in Puerto Rico (or 787-721-2884 in San Juan).Rates are around $100.25 s, $131 d, $164 t, and $197 quad. Children are extra, except for the quad. Rooms with TV run around $5 more pn. All rates include tax and breakfast and dinner.

Staying here is a real Puerto Rican experience. Puerto Ricans flock to the grounds on weekend. After dinner in the restaurant, the women sit outside and the men congregate in the lounge. Rooms are fairly spartan, reflecting their humble origins. A trail on the ground leads around to the old swimming pool (no longer in use) where the first coffee festival was held. It's a few min. by car from here to town. You'll need to turn R to head to the fish hatchery (preceded by a small Christian shrine). In the opposite direction is a small bakery which has great sandwiches. This is where the parador buys its bread. **http://www.haciendajuanita.com**

Añasco

Set on Carr. 109 off Hwy. 2, this attractive town is relatively untouristed. The town evolved after Spanish settlers and Taínos settled around the banks of the Río Grande de Añasco, which was named after settler Don Luis de Añasco. The town's plaza has a fountain as its centerpiece which depicts three Taínos drowning the Spanish conquistador Salcedo in 1511. (See "European Discovery" under the "History" section). A similar statue is found by the river near the town. The town's motto "*Donde Los Dioses Murieron*" ("Where the Gods Died") reflects this historical incident.

Be sure to try the town's *holjaldre*, a gingerbread-like cake for which it is renowned.

EVENTS: The Añasco *fiestas patronales*, is held around mid-Jan. The **Añasco**

Triathlon takes place in early Aug. The *Festival de la Juventud* takes place in early Aug.The *Festival del Chipe* generally takes place in early Oct. For information on these call 787-826-3100.

In Las Marías to the E, the **Festival de la China Dulce** (Orange Fair, ☎ 787-827-2280) generally takes place in the second week of March.

SIGHTS: 🏠 Set on Carr. 109 to the W of town, the **Parque el Sueño de los Niños** ("Park of the Dream of the Children," ☎ 787-826-6088) is an alternative for children. It features Disney classics in Spanish, a pool with wave machine, and a haunted house and amusement park. It's open Mar. to Oct. from Wed. to Sun., from 9:30 AM–4:30 PM. Admission is $10.

🏠 **El Mirador de la Bahía**, on Carr. 115, just south of Carr. 109 is a three-story lookout tower on a small cliff which overlooks the bay.

🏠 **El Salto de la Encantada**, Carr. 402 at Km 1.8, is a boardwalk with a waterfall and picnic area.

🏠 In Las Marías to the E, **Las Piscinas Públicas** (☎ 787-827-2325), Carr. 120, Matías Brudman Ave., is a recreational park with pool, picnic area, children's playground, showers, lockers and parking. Admission is free. Call for reservations. It's open Wed. to Sun from 10:30 AM–5:30 PM.

ACCOMMODATION: Set on Carr. 115 at Km 5.8 in Añasco, **Rincón Beach Resort** (☎ 866-589-0009, 787-589-9000, ☏ 787-589-9010) is an attractive "boutique" resort just S of Rincón. Facilities include two oceanview conference rooms, fitness room, wine bar, and the **Brasas Restaurant** which serves contemporary Caribbean cuisine. Rates run around $195-$625 d.
http://www.rinconbeach.com

The 13-rm. **Hotel Gutiérrez** (☎ 787-827-3100), Carr. 119, Km 26.1. in Las Marías to the E, is an attractive hilltop country villa which offers incredible views all around. It has great views, a pool, and bar. Rates are around $65 d.

FOOD: Owned by a former cook at the Horned Dorset, **Capriccio** (☎ 787-826-3387), C. Manuel Malave 12, offers gourmet fare. It's open Tues. to Sun., and reservations are required.

Mona Island

Least known and least accessible of all Puerto Rico's offshore islands, seven-mile-long (11.2-km) Mona lies in the southern center of the Mona Passage. Viewed from the air, this 20-square-mile island situated 50 miles W of Mayagüez appears as a perfectly flat oval surrounded by offshore coral reefs. The only ways to reach it are by fishing boat from Mayagüez (four hrs. OW), by private plane, or by yacht. Nine miles of rough trails lead from the S shore through the dense foliage to the northern, rock-littered mesa, which gives way on three sides to a sheer 200-ft. drop to the sea below.

FLORA AND FAUNA: The terrain, tropical desert and dry forest, contain some 500 plant species, some dozens of which are endemic. The plateau is covered with low-lying trees and orchids, and the indigenous Mona rock iguana (*cyclura*), an endangered species, scuttles furtively between rocks. Some grow as long as four feet. Mona also has the Mona coqui, a local variant. The only other land animals — wild boars, bulls, and goats — are descendants of livestock kept by the long-vanished pirates.

There are nearly a hundred species of birds. Land birds include the yellow-shouldered blackbird and the pearly-eyed thrasher.

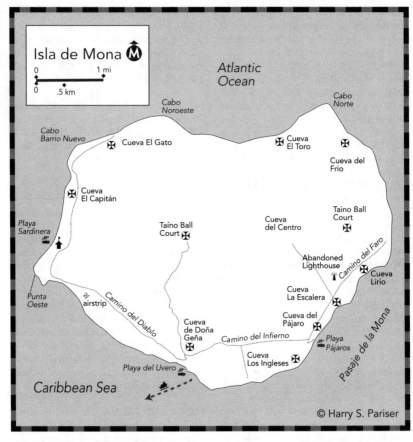

Isla de Mona

0   1 mi

0   .5 km

Atlantic Ocean

Cabo Noroeste

Cabo Norte

Cabo Barrio Nuevo

Cueva El Gato

Cueva El Toro

Cueva del Frio

Cueva El Capitán

Taino Ball Court

Playa Sardinera

Taíno Ball Court

Cueva del Centro

Abandoned Lighthouse

Camino del Faro

Cueva Lirio

Punta Oeste

airstrip

Camino del Diablo

Cueva La Escalera

Cueva de Doña Geña

Camino del Infierno

Cueva del Pájaro

Playa Pájaros

Pasaje de la Mona

Cueva Los Ingleses

Playa del Uvero

Caribbean Sea

© Harry S. Pariser

While red-footed boobies nest on the N side, magnificent frigatebirds, white-tailed tropicbirds and other birds nest on the neighboring Isla de Monito. The beautiful coral reefs offshore have superb visibility and are said to number among Puerto Rico's best.

Offshore, the waters host dolphins and, during winter and early spring, migrating humpback whales. Hawksbill and leatherback turtles are also found.

There's a website specializing in Mona

issues:
http://www.reefkeeper.org

HISTORY AND SIGHTS: Mona's history is steeped in romance, much of which carries over into the present. Discovered by Columbus during his second voyage in 1493, it later became a port of call for Spanish galleons. Ponce de León stopped here to secure a supply of cassava bread on the way to take up his command of Puerto Rico. By 1584, most of the natives had been exterminated. Today, their petroglyphs still survive as do the ruins of an ancient ball court.

A network of stalactite- and stalagmite-filled underground caves, containing pools of spring water used to supplement the average annual rainfall of 41 inches, served as a home for pirates over nearly three centuries. Fireplaces, cooking utensils, fragments of sabers, and chains have been found inside.

In **Cueva Liria**, where guano was mined until 1927, you'll find tram tracks and the rusting remains of equipment. This cave is part of the island's 18 cave systems.

The reefs offshore have proved forbidding. Eleven shipwrecks have been documented, including the *Alborada* whose steel hull still protrudes from the water.

The mid-1800s saw the island besieged by guano collectors, and Germans set up an operation which lasted until the Second World War. Ironically, the island was torpedoed by a Nazi sub, whose crew believed that the Allies had a secret base here.

On the W end of the plateau are the ruins of a lodge dating from the 1930s and '40s when Mona was a popular weekend getaway for sports fishermen. Legend has it that the remains of a Spanish galleon lie just off the lighthouse and radio beacon manned by the US Coast Guard on the E end of the island.

As the island became better known, its importance was understood, and it was protected in 1975. Its offshore depths, however, remain, unregulated.

The most recent chapter in the island's history came in 1993 when groups of Cuban refugees seeking asylum were dropped off on Playa Mujeres by boats coming from the Dominican Republic.

CAVES: Isla de Mona is one of the most cavern-packed islands on the planet, Mona is an uplifted carbonate platform which is bounded by 10-25 ft. (30 to 80 m) high vertical cliffs along three of its sides.

The cliffs have a number of caves (along the cliffs) and sinkholes (in the interior). The Taínos. The caves were later entered by Germans who collected guano (thus the name, Cueva Aleman, of one). Research by the U.S. Geological Survey, in the company of Dr John Mylroie of Mississippi State University, has found that Mona's caves formed via the intermingling of fresh and saltwater. (Continental caves, on the contrary, are formed by sinking streams.)

PRACTICALITIES: For information on renting available cabins and on obtaining the reservations mandatory for camping, call the **Recursos Naturales y Ambientales** (Department of Natural Resources and the Environment, ☎ 787-724-3724, 787-724-3647) in Puerto de Tierra, San Juan.

Visitors are permitted only during the dry season. Permits are $4 pp (adults) and $2 pp (children). Bring food and everything else you need, *and* take it out again. The only food you will find here is prickly pears. Water is in short supply so bring your own Fires are prohibited. During the hunting season (for goats and pigs) from early Dec. to the end of April, visitors are only allowed on the island on weekends. The total number of visitors is limited to 100 at any time. Sea turtle nesting areas are closed at night.

Boats are usually chartered from Puerto Real. Camp at **Playa Sardinera** or two other beaches for a small charge. The *Caminode Infierno* ("Hell Road") connects it with **Playa Pájaros** to the E; you may also camp here.

OTHERS: **Aero Borinquen** (☎ 787-890-5400) flies charters to Mona out of Aguadilla.

In Boquerón, **Mona Aquatics** (☎ 787-851-2185) offers weekend trips. **Encanto Ecotours** (☎ 800-272-7241) also offers trips **Oceans Unlimited** (☎ 787-823-2340, ☏ 787-823-2370; PO Box 666, Rincón,

00677-0666) offer one-day and multi-day trips as well as shuttle service. They can make it out there in two or three hrs. and in just two hrs. coming back.

Mona Aquatics (☎ 787-851-2185) offers diving, rents snorkeling equipment, and offers charters..

DIVING: Mona offers both great diving and snorkeling.

Mona Aquatics (☎ 787-851-2185) offers diving, rents snorkeling equipment, and offers tours, diving, and charters.. They are on C. José de Diego, next to the Club Nautico to the W of Boquerón.

Oceans Unlimited (☎ 787-823-2340, ☻ 787-823-2370; PO Box 666, Rincón, 00677-0666), offer trips (Mona, Desecheo, others), and courses. They're on Carr. 115 near Villa Antonio in Rincón.

http://www.oceans-unlimited.com
Oceans_Unlimited@hotmail.com

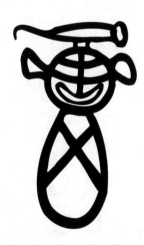

Northwestern Puerto Rico

This area is easily accessed from Mayagüez and the S and by heading W from San Juan. From the capital, the road is congested. After you pass Dorado, the traffic thins out. Housing projects with murals painted on their sides and shopping centers give way to trucks selling *lechon asado*, but there are still the ubiquitous McDonald's, Church's Chicken, and other such delightful health-food eateries. Just past Vega Alta you come to a string of roadside *chicharrones* stands.

Rincón

Although the name of this small town means "corner" (which suits its location perfectly), the town is actually named for Don Gonzalo Rincón, a 16th-century landowner. He granted a hill, known as *cerro do los pobres* ("hill of the poor") to local settlers. When the town was founded in 1772, they named it for their benefactor; its full name is Santa Rosa de Rincón.

Surfers began arriving during the 1960s, and, after the world surfing championships were held here in 1968, its popularity grew.

As a result a large number of mainlanders have settled here, opening a number of hotels and restaurants.

There are a half-dozen bathing beaches in this area, including **Punta Higuero**, where the World Surfing Championships were held in 1968. Charter boats are available to take divers over to the National Wildlife Refuge surrounding **Desecheo Island**. (See description in next section).

The town and surrounding area have an exceptionally nice feel to it. Shady roads are lined with mimosa trees and fruit stands, and resident expats seem to be laid back. You'll see signs such as a peace sign with "Save the Humans" next to it.

http://www.rincon.org
http://www.islandmon.com
http://rinconpr.com

GETTING HERE: *Públicos* run from various destinations. The station is on C. Nueva, just S of the town plaza.

SIGHTS: Dating from 1798, Rincón's **Catholic church**, facing the E end of the plaza, is built on the very site which Santa Rosa de Lima, the town's patron saint, recommended when she appeared in a vision. A small chapel dedicated to her — containing plastic flowers and a model boat — stands on a ridge just beyond the intersection of Carr. 414 and Ramal 414. Her **fiestas patronales** take place during the last week in Aug.

Pico Atalaya ("lookout peak"), easily recognizable because of its communication tower, commands a great view of the environs. A silver water tank, the sole reminder of a railroad that passed from San Juan to Ponce between 1907 and the early 1950s, stands on C. Cambija.

?!¢ The **Spanish Wall**, a series of rock embankments along many of Rincón's beaches, are a remnant of the now-defunct railway that once traveled these parts, hauling sugarcane as far S as Mayagüez and as far E as San Juan. The bakery and booze emporium, **L'Estacion** was once the station for the town, as the historical photos you'll see here attest.

The ruins of the storehouses and residences of the **Corcega Sugar Mill** (constructed 1885) remain behind trees where Playa Corcega meets Carr. 429.

Rincon's first **lighthouse**, rising 98 feet (30 m) above the sea at Punta Higuero, was built by the Spanish in the early 1890s. Today, the electric 26,000-candlepower beacon, a rebuilt version, is unmanned. Both the lighthouse and the reactor (see below) have surfing beaches right by them. Be sure to visit the **El Faro** gift shop right next to the lighthouse plaza.

The "lighthouse beach" is also known as **Maria's Beach**. You may be able to spot humpback whales (during the winter season; see the box in "Flora & Fauna" in the Introduction for information on the whales), as well as pilot and sperm whales, sharks, and sea turtles.

At the end of the road by the lighthouse are the rusting remains of the **BONUS Nuclear Superheater Plant**. "BONUS," as it was quaintly named, was the first nuclear energy plant built in Latin America. It ceased operation in April 1962. The $11-million, 16,300-kw facility was built with the intention of testing a new concept that would both reduce energy costs and train Latin American scientists and engineers (i.e., as a US government subsidy to the nuclear power industry).

In 1962, seven reactor employees were exposed to contamination via irradiated fuel elements. The reactor failed in 1964 because of problems with its superheater assembly. In 1968, the plant was closed due to "technical difficulties." In 1969, it was sealed off; the Atomic Energy Commission announced that they had decommissioned and decontaminated the reactor in 1972. Currently, there are plans to turn this reactor into a museum. It may be open by the time you visit.

ISLA DESECHEO: This small island is the coast's premier dive spot. *See the description in the next section.*

Rincón Practicalities

BUDGET ACCOMMODATION: Rincón Surf and Board (☎ 787-823-0610, ☎ 787-823-6440) offers dorm rooms for $20 pp, as well as standard rooms with a/c, cable TV, and balconies. They also have a surfing school.

http://www.home.coqui.net/surfsup
surfsup@coqui.net

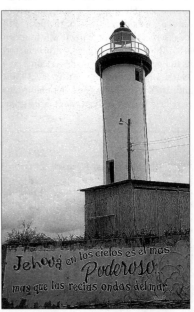

Rincón's lighthouse before its restoration.

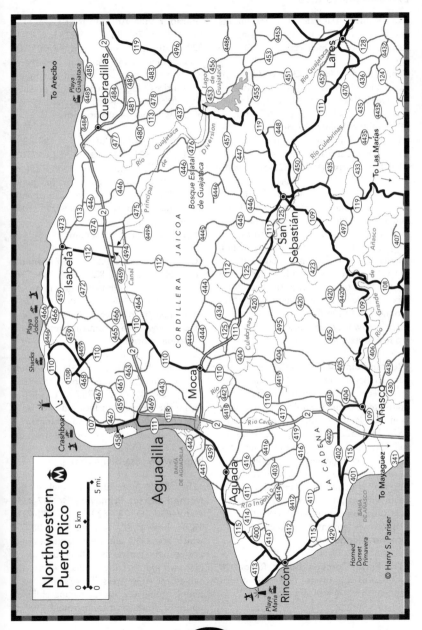

Northwestern
Puerto Rico

To Arecibo

Playa Guajataca

Quebradillas

Lago de Guajataca

Lares

Bosque Estatal de Guajataca

Río Guajataca

Principal de Guajataca Diversion

CORDILLERA JAICOA

Canal

Río Guajataca

Playa Jobos

Isabela

San Sebastián

Río Culebrinas

To Las Marías

Shacks

Crashboat

Aguadilla

BAHÍA DE AGUADILLA

Moca

Río Cano

Río Grande de Añasco

Añasco

Culebrinas

LA CADENA

Aguada

Río Ingenio

To Mayagüez

BAHÍA DE AÑASCO

Horned Dorset Primavera

Rincón

Playa María

© Harry S. Pariser

5 km

5 mi.

ACCOMMODATIONS: Many restaurants and guesthouses are open only during the surfing season, which runs from Oct. to April.

The **Parada Muñoz Guest House** (☎ 787-823-4725; HC-01 Box 5266, Rincón, PR 00677-9725), Carr. 115 at Km 15, has a swimming pool; kitchens are $5 extra.

Beside the Pointe Resort (☎ 787-823-0610/8550) is also outside of town on Carr. 413 at Km 4.5 in Barrio Puntas

The **Lazy Parrot** (☎ 787-823-5654, 800-294-1752, ☻ 787-823-0224) at Km 4 on Carr. 413. Its 11 individually-themed rooms are homey, attractive, and vibrant and feature cable TV. The honeymoon suite has a Jacuzzi. Its gourmet restaurant serves fish, eggplant parmesan, and other dishes. Guests have a buffet continental breakfast. Even if you aren't staying here, be sure to try the food or stop out in the back for a mixed drink by the small pool. Rates run around $100-$125 d.
http://www.lazyparrot.com
lzparrot@lazyparrot.com

Pelican Point (☎ /☻ 787-823-5683) is set next to Beside the Pointe. It offers four apartments in an attractive home. Three hold three to four, one holds up to eight.

On the island's S end, the **Lemontree** (☎ 787-823-6452, ☻ 787-823-5821) has six fully-equipped apartments of various sizes, each of which is named after a fruit and has its own individual, lively decorative theme. You may watch the pelicans fish from the chair on your porch. It's at Carr. 429, Km 4.1. Rates run around $110-$185 d.
http://www.lemontreepr.com
lemontre@coqui.net

The **Playa Corcega Beach Resort** (☎ 787-823-6140) offers tent and trailer camping areas as well as a cafeteria.

Parador Villa Antonio is at Carr. 115, Km 12.3 (☎ 787-823-2645/2285, ☻ 787-823-3380; Apdo. 68, Rincón, PR 00677). Facilities include 50 a/c rooms and apartments, two tennis courts, and swimming pool. Prices range from $90-$135 d. They also offer a honeymooner's special.
http://www.villa-antonio.com

The **Hotel Villa Cofresi** (☎ 787-823-2450, 787-823-1010, ☻ 787-823-1770), Carr. 115, Km 12.3. is next door. It offers basic but adequate rooms by the good beach. It has a souvenir shop, banquet hall, and offers water sports. Rates run from around $105-$155 d.
http://www. villacofresi.com

On Carr. 413 at Km 2.2, **Villa Ensenada** Guest House (☎ 787-823-5807, 888-779-3788) has four large two-bedroom apartments with a/c, TVs, and balconies. They have a pool, picnic area, and grill.
http://www.prwest.com/rincon
vencenada.html

On Punta Higüero at Carr. 413, Km 4.8, the nine-rm. **Casa Isleña Inn** (☎ 787-823-1525, 888-289-775, ☻ 787-823-1530) is set on the beach front location and has a pool. It has both privacy and personalized "island house"-style service. Rates run around $105-155 d.
http://www.casa-islena.com

The area's most elegant hotel is the **Horned Dorset Primavera** (☎ 787-823-4030/4050, ☻ 787-823-5580, 800-633-1857; Box 1132, Rincón, PR 00677), which offers 30 suites with antiques and poster mahogany beds. Billing itself as "a place without activities," this is where you can escape from stress. There's no TV, cell phones going off, or rampaging children under 12. Rates start from around $300 d;

weekly package rates are available. Their six course dinner costs $60 pp. The beach has rough surf, so relax by the pool.To get here, you must take Carr. 115 from Carr. 2 in the direction of Rincón for about four miles. Turn sharply L onto Carr. 429 after the "Kaplash" Restaurant. In another mile, you'll find the hotel on the L at Km 3.
http://www.horneddorset.com

The 13-rm. **Sandy Beach Inn** (☎ 787-823-1146, ☏ 787-823-1034) is another option and has a good restaurant and great views. It's on Carr. Linda Vista, off of Carr. 413 at Km 4.3 at Panaderia Puntas. Rates run from around $70-$85 d.
http://www.sandybeachinn.com

APARTMENTS: Tropicabañas (☎ 787-823-2967) offers a variety of rentals.
http://www.home.coqui.net/getwet
getwet@coqui.net

PRWest (☎ 787-823-4039, 888-779-3788) offers a variety of rentals in the area, as well as in other places on the island.
Another place to try is **Rob's Rentals** (☎ 787-823-0627).
Island West Properties (☎ 787-823-2323, ☏ 787-823-3254, Km 0.7 on Carr. 413, also have rentals.
http://www.rinconrealestateforsale.com
islawest@coqui.net

The six-unit **Coconut Palms Inn** (☎ 787-823-0147, ☏ 787-823-5431) is set in a neighborhood near the beach at C. 8 # 2734, Sector Estrella. Grounds have gardens, hammocks, and parasols. Each apartment-unit has a kitchen; some have balconies. Beach villas are available for weekly rental. Rates run around $75-150 d, depending whether you choose a studio or four-bedroom. They advise: "Leave your beepers, cell phones and laptops at home.

Pack one bag of shades, lotion, shorts, tank tops and flip-flops. For major holidays, call well in advance."
http://www.coconutpalmsinn.com

Pipon's Resort (☎ 787-823-5106), Carr. 413, is a set of six two-bedroom apartments with fans, full kitchen, and balconies and cable TV. Daily maid service is provided, and it is near the beach.
pipons@sprintmail.com

Casa Serena/Casa Tamara (☎ 787-823-5106) are two, two- to three-bedroom villas.
selmawaldman@aol.com

The **Vista Vacation Resort** (☎ 787-823-3673, 787-823-2769). C. Vista Nuclear in Barrio Puntas, has fully-equipped studios, and two- and three-bedroom apartments. It has a pool, Jacuzzi, and gardens.
http://www.vistapr.com

Pool's Beach Cabanas Verdes (☎ 787-823-8135) are one-, two-, and three-bedroom units with a/c, cable TV, and kitchens.
beach@coqui.net.

Amirage (☎ 787-823-6454, 877-677-9489), Km 4.0 at Carr. 429, is a "customized" beach house open Dec. 15 through July. It has suites which have a/c, cable TV, full kitchens, and balconies. Kayaks are available.
http://www.bedandbreakfastandbeyond.com
amiragerainbow@hotmail.com

Casa Vista del Mar (☎ 787-823-6437, 866-887-0175), Km 11.4 on Carr. 115, is a set of one-bedrooms with ocean views, a/c, full kitchens, cable TV, phone, and washers.
http://www.casavistadelmar.net
smithpr@caribe.net

CAMPING: The nearest spot is Añasco on Carr. 401 at Km 1.

Selected Rincón Surfing Spots

Little Malibu Speedy with tubes which break in the shallows. Fire coral is a concern.

Steps Named for the concrete stairs that remain from a train station. Speedable on the break but watch out for coral if you fall off.

Tres Palmas For the experienced when surf is up. Waves may reach 25-30 ft. (up to 10 m).

Dogmans Both L and R breaks.

Playa María Both L and R breaks. Resembles Hawaii's legendary "pipeline." Named after woman who once fed surfers in the 1960s. Good spot for spectators.

Indicators Famed for its R break. Dangerous rocks and coral-encrusted pipes.

Domes Mostly rights, with occasional lefts. Consistently good surf. Sometimes has a strong undercurrent. Long waves. Very popular.Good from 2–7-ft. faces. Most consistent spot in the Rincón area. Crowded most of the time. Puerto Rican surfers here regard it as their spot.

Spanish Wall Popular with locals.

Sandy Beach Waves favor L break. Sandy bottom. Good boogie boarding also.

Antonios Famed site of 1968 World Surfing Championships. Waves break on sandy beach. Rights superior to lefts. Average winter waves: 3–7 ft. (up to 2.5 m).

Wilderness Has one of the island's longest waves. A paddling channel is to the L of the parking lot. Be careful because waves may be larger than they appear from shore.

Jobos/Surfers Reliable for catching a long R break. Bottom is sandy. Packed on weekends.

Locals camp at **Black Eagle Marina** and at **Tres Hermanos**. However, it is insecure.

FOOD: Some of the best places to eat are in the **hotels**, especially in the Lazy Parrot and the Sandy Beach Inn (described above). More gourmet and expensive is the Horned Dorset Primavera,whose restaurant is one of the Caribbean's best.

Panadería la Estación and **Supermercado Econo** are on C. Luis Muñoz Rivera, and **Rincón Cash & Carry** is at the Plaza de Recreo across the street from the church.

The **Lighthouse Café** is right out at the lighthouse.

The **Kaplash Restaurant** (☎ 787-826-4582), Carr. 403, and **El Bambino** (☎ 787-823-3744), near the Parador Villa Antonio, offer seafood dishes. The latter offers a $5

weekday lunch special.

Trópico Jazz Restaurant (☎ 787-823-4922) is on Playa Córcega. It is a good place to dine or have a drink.

Set on Carr. 429 at Km 3.3, the **El Molino del Quijote** (☎ 787-823-4010) is a weekend-only destination for gourmetss. It serves seafood paella as well as dorado and snapper in a garden environment. They open on Fri. and Sat. from 4 PM and on Sun. from noon. They also rent out cabanas.

El Curvón (☎ 787-826-1465), Km 7.5 on Carr. 115, serves Puerto Rican dishes. It's open Wed. through Sun.

Red Pizza, a cheap pizza joint just up the road from the Lazy Parrot, also serves sandwiches.

ENTERTAINMENT: Tamboo Too! has live music, as does **El Nuevo Brisas** on Carr. 413.

Noted more for its entertainment than its grub, **The Landing** (☎ 787-823-3112, 823-4779) has live music (mainly rap). It sometimes goes to dawn on weekends. Machu Picchu (☎ 787-823-2787) is a popular gathering spot for partying surfers. It has a disco and is above the lighthouse on Carr. #413, Km 2.8, Barrio Puntas.

Café Con Leche is agay-friendly party bar, and **Calypso** at Maria's Beach is also popular.

INFORMATION AND SERVICES: Rincón Tours (☎ 787-823-0454) offers airline transfers, caters to groups, and offers other services.

The **Rincón Tourist Information Center** (☎ 787-823-5024) is helpful and has a map.

The **public library** is on C. Nueva.

The **Centro Cultural de Rincón** is open Tues., Thurs., and Sat. (9:30 AM–2:30 PM).

Paradise Watersports (☎ 787-823-4883, 787-598-4883) rents kayaks.

The **West Coast Surf Shop** (☎ 787-823-3935) is right in town. Rents boards and will hook you up with a guide.
http://www.westcoastsurf.com

You may **recycle** behind the sports center on Carr. 429 in Corsega.

SHOPPING: The town and surrounding area have some shops including **Out of the Blue,** a gift shop at the Lazy Parrot, Carr. 413 at Km 4.1, which sells seaglass jewelry and other items. **Ecologic** is a fine gift shop at the lighthouse.

 Although police monitor the beaches of Rincón, the best way to avoid theft is to leave all doors unlocked and leave nothing of value in your car.

Rincón Outdoor Activities

Even if you aren't a surfer, there's still plenty do do around here.

HIKING: A good beach hike might be from Black Eagle Marina to Playa Maria and on before doubling back.

MOUNTAIN BIKING: Moderately good routes are found behind the BONUS reactor shell. Park across the street from the lighthouse and head across a vacant lot until you see a track which leads into the trees.

HORSEBACK RIDING: Rancho del Mar (☎ 787-314-9820) offers great rides on the beach as do **Tropical Trails** (☎ 787-892-9256) in Isabela.

SWIMMING: To the N of town, **Sandy Beach** is a place that both nonsurfer and their surfing significant others can, depending upon wave conditions, find a happy medium.

Playa Córcega, to the S of town on Carr. 429, is unsuitable for surfing but great for swimming. It is near the Villa Cofresi hotel.

Set further to the S, on Carr. 401, **Tres Hermanos** has the added bonus of being next to a fish market. (However, you'll need to be an earlybird to get some fish).

FARTHER AWAY: Farther to the S, Boquerón's *balneario,* on Carr. 307, is one of the island's better beaches. Stay away on weekends.

Playa Buye, set off Carr. 307 between Puerto Real and Boquerón is a good, relatively shallow option.

Whales can be sighted offshore from Dec. to Feb.

Near the lighthouse to the far S, Bahía Salinas and **Bahía Sucia** ("Salty Beach" and "Dirty Beach") are surrounded by mangrove and dry forest.

DIVING AND SNORKELING: Dive shops are listed under Isla Desecheo in the following section. Most, if not all, should rent snorkeling gear.

OTHER DIVE SPOTS: In addition to those off of Isla Desecheo, there are two worthy of mention.

In Aguadilla, **Crash Boat Beach** is perhaps the most popular beach dive in the entire commonwealth. Visibility is around 50 ft., and you can see scorpionfish, soldierfish, frogfish, and pufferfish. Carry a knife because there are fishing boats in the area, and the fishing lines can be a nuisance.

Shacks, set to the N of Isabela's beach, has a depth of 5–30 ft. (1.5–9 m), and is best dived from May to Nov when the sea is calmer. Goatfish, anemones, blue tang, and other species may be seen.

SNORKELING SPOTS: **Steps Beach** has good snorkeling offshore. You might spot sea turtles, barracuda, and schools of angelfish and triggerfish. To get here head N along the beach from the Black Eagle Marina until you spy a set of weathered concrete steps by the water. Enter some 75 yds. (25 m) S of the steps and then snorkel around the point. *This beach is under the threat of development.*

http://www.surfrider.org/rincon/threats.htm

FISHING: Contact **Sheridan Charters** (☎ 787-787-823-5668) concerning trips.

Isla Desecheo Reserve

A large brown and green shrubby lump in the ocean, this federal reserve, set 14 mi. (23 km) W of Rincón, is off limits to landlubbers. What's the reason for this? The delightful US military has planted unexploded military ordnance on its 360 acres (145 ha). Brown boobies and monkeys live here, presumably gingerly.

The island has been occupied by Spain, Puerto Rico, and the U.S. The US military conducted bombing and survival training here. The NIH introduced rhesus monkeys for medical research.

At one time, Desecheo hosted the largest brown booby nesting colony in the world. Sadly no seabirds nest here today. The native forest, which includes the endangered higo chumbo cactus, has been severely degraded through the activities of introduced rats, cats, goats, and monkeys.

However, divers may explore its cornucopia of underwater delights. The deep water offshore provides amazing visibility right down to 80 ft. It's definitely one of the best islands to dive. An added bonus is that there is no chance of getting blown up while underwater! The reefs here are amazing, which is why plans are underway to establish a marine reserve. All but one are intermediate dives, and depths are generally from 60–90 ft.

http://southeast.fws.gov/Desecheo

DIVE SITES: The only site suitable for novice divers, **Candyland**, on the SE side, hosts healthy reefs with amazing coral formations. Sea fans rise as high as six ft., and schools of yellow-and-white goatfish travel through them. It has depth of 60–80 ft. (18–24 m).

Set on the leeward side, **K Wall** is actually a set of shelves which begin some 75 ft. from shore and plunge down to 100 ft. or so. When you visit, you might imagine that you are flying over a continent of some unexplored region. Watch for giant sea fans, elephant ear sponges, rope sponges, and giant sea turtles.

Near K Wall and just some 50 yds (45 m) w of the island, **Candlesticks** is a delightful patch of reef which has several channels. It gets its name from its boulder corals which resemble piles of melted candle wax. The yellow-orange icing sponges, which line their bases, help foster the illusion. It has a depth of 60 –90 ft. (18–27 m).

Set to the W but to the N of K Wall and Candlesticks, **Puerto de Botes and The Caves** is a magnificent site. From Puerto de Botes, where you find foothills of hard coral, you swim to the shallower area known as The Caves. The steep walls of its stone canyons are rendered a brilliant red by its coral, sponge, and algae dwellers. Keep an eye out for nurse sharks.

Also known as the **Middle Reef**, the **Middle Pinnacle**, a site to the NW and set less than a mi. offshore, this moderately-deep dive consists of a set of brilliantly-colored coral grottos, one of which is an exquisite canyon-spanning rock arch. Coneys proliferate. Watch for the rare yellow gold coney, a short life stage for this fish which changes color as it ages.

Marked by an underwater pinnacle — covered with orange, gold, and yellow sponges, **Yellow Reef** is off the NW site. It drops from 25–100 ft. and is an intermediate dive. Although one of Puerto Rico's best dives, it is sometimes affected by strong currents which make diving impossible.The Yellow Reef is a formation which has long tunnels and caverns which are covered with purple coral and orange ups as well as by innumerable blue chromis.

Set to the island's NW, **Lajas** is smaller but similar to Yellow Reef. It ranges from 30–70 ft. (9-21 m) and is an intermediate

dive. Barrel sponges happily coexist here with blue and brown chromis. There are plenty of places to explore.

The location of **East End Canyon** (or Los Pesones) is marked by giant boulders which are visible above water. On the island's less protected side, it can present a challenge, a situation which subsides once one is inside its steep canyons, which descent from 60–90 ft. (18–27 m). Queen Angelfish and barracuda reign over the colorful, multicolored coral-and-sponge carpet.

DIVE OPERATIONS: Generally speaking, dive trips run from 8 AM–4 PM. It takes around 40 min. each way.

Taíno Divers (☎ 787-823-6429, ☝ 787-823-7243), at Black Eagle Marina, offers courses, dives, and rentals.
http://www.tainodivers.com

Desecheo Dive Shop (☎ 787-823-0390) is on the road to the lighthouse in town. It offers courses, dives, and rentals.

Oceans Unlimited (☎ 787-823-2340, ☝ 787-823-2370; PO Box 666, Rincón, 00677-0666), offer trips (Mona, Desecheo, others), and courses including PADI instruction. They also offer whale watching in season. They're on Carr. 115 near Villa Antonio in Rincón.
http://www.oceans-unlimited.com
Oceans_Unlimited@hotmail.com

Aguada

Settled in 1510, Aguada is the island's second oldest settlement. Another Columbus monument and park is near this town, as is **Balneario Pico de Pidera**. Aguada made news headlines in Puerto Rico during Dec. 2000 when Alcalde "Yuyo" Román canceled the play "Sexo, p----, lágrimas" at Bellas Artes in Aguada, citing a ban on nudism.

SIGHTS: The **Ermita Espinar Ruins** (☎ 787-868-6400), on Carr. 442 in Barrio Espinar, Aguada, were built on behalf of the Lady of Immaculate Conception to convert the Taínos.

The **Museo de Aguada** (☎ 787-868-6300), C. Nativo Alers 7, is housed in a former train station. It features Taíno artifacts and *santos,* as well as a large collection of antique irons. It is open from Mon. to Fri., 8 AM–noon; *reservations are required for both of the above.*

PRACTICALITIES: On Carr. 416 and three minutes from Carr. 2, the **Hidden Village Parador** (☎ 787-868-8686/8687, ✆ 787-868-8701; Box 937, Aguada, PR 00602) has 25 a/c rooms with balcony and cable TV. Other facilities include pool, conference center (holds up to 300), and Las Colinas restaurant (seafood and other dishes). Built in 1990, its rooms start at around $70 d.

Aguada Seafood (☎ 787-868-2136), C. Jiménez 103, offers *mariscada* and other specialties.

El Jibarito Restaurant and Museum (☎ 787-868-3391, 787-868-0232), Carr. 416 in Barrio Piedras Blancas, serves local food.

The **Ann Wigmore Institute** (☎ 809-868-6307; Box 429, Rincón, PR 00677) is located in Aguada and set near the sea; this school specializes in raw foods. Developer of "Wheatgrass Therapy," the late Dr. Wigmore believed that "all disease is a result of toxicity and deficiency due to cooked and processed foods, drug, and negative mental attitudes." The curriculum includes internal cleansing, growing greens and wheatgrass, composting and soil management, indoor gardening, sprouting, food combining, energy soup, weight loss, and a 12-step program. Rates for a six-day program range from $660 for a day student to $1,335 for a private room with bath and meals. Rates extend up to 26 days. The school is located at Carr. 115, Km 20, Barrio Guayabo, Aguada, PR 00602. **http://www.annwigmore.org wigmore@coqui.net**

Aguadilla

Located on Carr 111 along the W coast, this small town boasts fine beaches, intricate lace, and historical sites. Christopher Columbus first stepped onto Puerto Rican soil somewhere between Aguadilla and Añasco on his second voyage in 1493.

Since then it's undergone numerous changes. For a while the population declined, owing to the economic depression caused by the phasing out of Ramey Air Force Base. However, recent census figures show a slight increase; the current population is about 67,000.

EVENTS: The **Rafael Hernández Festival** is held yearly from Oct. 22 to 24 in honor of this world-famous composer. His music is interpreted by soloists and orchestras during the two days. Festivities surrounding the town's *fiestas patronales* go on for two weeks around the main feast day of Nov. 4 on the main plaza. Music is performed and local specialties are cooked.

Another lively time is the **Velorio de Reyes** (Three Kings Celebration). Initiated 30 years ago by a wealthy local family, a religious ceremony with music, prayers, and chants takes place on the plaza the evening of January 6.

GETTING HERE: *Públicos* run from San Juan and other locales here. The station is in the town's main plaza.

BY AIR: *Continental Airlines* flies to Aguadilla's Rafael Hernández Airport nonstop from Newark. **North American Airlines** (☎ 718-656-2650).

?!¢ Crashboat Beach was so named because the US Air Force once kept rescue boats here which would pick up crews from the Strategic Air Command's heavy bombers which would fail to make the runway.

SIGHTS: Beaches (great snorkeling) extend from Crash Point to the N. Crash Point receives its name from the launches kept here to pick up crews in the event of a plane crash around Borínquen Point.

Bosque Estatal de Guajataca and **Lago de Guajataca** are located 30 km to the E of Aguadilla. The town is famous for its *mundillo* (finely embroidered lace), first introduced to the area by immigrants from Belgium, Holland, and Spain.

Ramey Air Force Base has been converted into **Punta Borínquen**, a tourist complex off Carr. 110 with complete sports facilities. To play at the 18-hole **golf course** here, call 787-890-2987. It costs around $20 for green fees and $30 for a cart. Great views. It's, naturally enough, on Golf St.

Playuelas Beach is divided by what was once the pier and docking facilities for submarines and fuel tankers.

Punta Borínquen Lighthouse, located W of town, has been designated a historic site worthy of preservation by the National Register of Historic Places. Severely damaged by the 1918 earthquake, this tower, built in 1870, was incorporated into Ramey Air Force Base as a picnic area.

Near the city's N entrance, between the foot of Cerro Cuesto Villa and the beach, lies the **Urban Cemetery**. This was established on what had once been a sugarcane hacienda. Although the 1918 earthquake destroyed many of the old tombs, those remaining are finely sculpted Italian marble.

Borínquen Archaeological site, the only significant indigenous site in the region, was excavated by Dr. K.G. Lathrop of Yale in the 1920s. Objects found include human skulls, shells, animal bones, and shards of broken pots.

Fort Concepción is the only remaining building from the Fuerte de la Concepción military complex, which was protected by a moat, walls, and guard and sentry houses. Extensively remodeled, it now houses schoolrooms.

A statue of Columbus, built in 1893, stands within the seaside **Parque Colón** (Columbus Park).

Parque El Parterre contains *ojo de agua*, a natural spring that once served as the water supply for arriving sailors.

Isabela, to the NE, has diving off of a beach called **The Shacks**, which is about a mi. W of Jobos on Carr. 4466. It is suitable for beginners, and the caverns here may be entered right off the beach. The reef is about 100 ft. off shore if you are snorkeling.

Parque Acuático Las Cascadas (☎ 787-882-3310, 787-891-1740, 787-635-4102) is an aquatic park on Carr. 2 at Km 126.5. Admission is around $13 for adults and $9 for children. Group rates are also available. The park has such sights as a magic fountain," a "lazy river," a "fantasy oasis," an "astroslide," and an "aquatic tunnel." It's generally open only from Mar. to the end of Sept. from Mon. to Fri, 10 AM–5 PM, and on Sat. to Sun. from 10 AM–6 PM.

Another place to go with children is **Parque Colón**, at the end of Carr. 4440 and on C. Yumet. It has a children's playground, recreational areas, and food stands.

ENTERTAINMENT: The **Twins I** and **II** (☎ 787-891-4421) show films. **Villa Ricomar** is a disco open on weekends in Isabela off of Carr. 459. **La Cabaña** (☎ 787-882-3070) ois a bar and dance hall which is open Thurs. through Sat. and has theme nights.

ACCOMMODATIONS: Most of the places here are located near Isabela as well as Aguadilla. Rent **cabins** at Punta Borínquen off Carr. 107 for $60 per night (☎ 787-890-6128/6330).

Camp freely but insecurely at Playa Crashboat, Carr. 2 Salida 458, Aguadilla.

The 50-room **Hotel/Parador El Faro** (☎ 787-882-8000, ☻ 787-891-3110; Box 5148, Aguadilla, PR 00605), Carr. 107 at Km 8.8 is a modern 32-room building dating from 1990. Set next to the former Ramey Air Force base (and its golf course), it has a restaurant (**El Caracol**), cocktail lounge, and pool. Rooms (from around $70 d) have a/c, cable TV, balconies, and phone.
http://www. www.ihppr.com

Also in Aguadilla, the 40-room **Cielo Mar Hotel** (☎ 787-882-5959/5960, ☻ 787-882-5577; Aguadilla, PR 00603) at Ave. Montemar No. 84, Carr. 111 in Urb. Villa Lydia, has 52 rooms with a/c, cable TV, and private balconies. Facilities include a restaurant/cocktail lounge (live music on weekends), 600-capacity convention hall, and a pool. Rates start from around $75 d. One reader praised the view but complained about the food here. It's on Carr. 111 at Ave. Montemar 84.
http://www.cielomar.com

The a/c **La Cima** (☎ 787-890-2016, ☻ 787-890-2017, Aguadilla, PR 00611) is set on Carr 110 at Km 9.2, in the relatively secluded area of Barrio Maleza Alta. The hotel is within driving range of six beaches. It has carpeted rooms and apartments with cable TVs and phones. Facilities and activities include sailing, surfing, golf, tennis, horseback riding, PO, pharmacy, and fitness center. It has a 200-person capacity conference room, and rates start at around $60 d and go up to $160.
http://www.lacimahotel.com
lacima@caribe.net

Hacienda El Pedregal (☎ 787-891-6068, 787-882-2865, ☻ 787-882-2875; Box 4719, Aguadilla, PR 00605) has 27 elegant rooms with a/c and cable TV. Facilities include restaurant, bar, billiard terrace, game room, and pool. Children under 10 (two to a room) are allowed to stay free, and it offers honeymoon packages. It's just five min. from Ramey, on Carr. 111, Km 0.1, C. Cuesta Nueva. Rates start at around $65 d.
http://www.hotelelpedregal.com

In Isabela, **Costa Dorada Beach Resort** (☎/☻ 787-872-7255; Isabela, PR 00662), Carr. 446 at Km 0.1, has 52 a/c units (rooms and suites), pool, restaurant, two tennis courts, basketball court, and meeting rooms which hold up to 600. Mixed reviews about staying here. Rates run around $112–140 d.
http://www.costadoradabeach.com

AT PLAYA JOBOS: Off of Carr. 466 around a mi. E of Playa Jobos, **Villas del Mar Hau** (☎ 787-872-2045, 787-872-2627, ☻ 787-872-0273) is a small resort with colorful wooden bungalows which house from 2–10. Some are a/c, some have hammocks, and all have kitchens. Grounds have pool, tennis, basketball, and volleyball courts. Activities include kayaking, horseback riding, biking and snorkeling. It is near Playas Montones, a beach with large boulders and a natural lagoon. Rates start from around $85 d.
http://www.villahau.com

Villa Montaña Resort (☎ 787-872-9554, ☻ 787-872-9554; 888-780-9195) is on Carr. 4466, several km after Hotel and Restaurante Ocean Front. Relatively secluded, the hotel has one-, two-, and three-bedroom suites with attractive Caribbean-style decor. It is right by Shacks Beach, and has more of a pruned resort atmosphere than other nearby hotels. Facilities include tennis courts, two pools, health center, and the **Eclipse**, its open-air bar and restaurant. Rates are around $245-$1000 d.

http://www.villamontana.com
Info@villamontana.com

Less expensive than both of the above are the 17-rm. **Sonia Rican Guest House and Restaurant** (☎ 787-872-1818), Carr. 4466, which charges around $75-108 d, and the **Hotel Restaurante Ocean Front** (☎ 787-872-0444), Carr. 4466. At the latter, #11 gives great ocean views of Playa Jobos. Expect to spend around $65-75 d.

http://www.oceanfrontpr.com

FOOD: Offering Puerto Rican and international cuisine, **Darío's Gourmet** (☎ 787-890-6143), Carr. 110, Km 8, serves dishes ranging from *bouillabaisse* to lobster thermidor. Look for a building which somewhat resembles a cottage one might find in the British countryside.

Down the same road at Km 9.2, **Golden Crown** (☎ 787-890-2016) serves Chinese food.

At C. Comercio 18-D, **Salud y Vida** (☎ 787-891-5755) has a veggie cafeteria as well as a store; it has another branch in the Aguadilla Mall.

Rosalinda's (☎ 787-890-5331) is a Tex-Mex restaurant next to Ramey Airforce Base.

Paradise Health Food (☎ 787-890-2043), Carr. 110, Km 108 (near Gate 5 at Ramey), sells vitamins and other health foods and serves meals.

The **Wine Garden and Cigar Shop** (☎ 787-890-0685), Carr. 110, Km 8.7, sells imported wine and cigars.

Local restaurants include **Manny's Restaurant** (☎ 787-895-2717), C. Ramón Saavedra 105; **Lantern on the Green**, Carr. 119 in Barrio Guajataca; **El Soberau**, Carr. 113, Km 1.3; **Restaurant Brisas de**

 Don't miss **Panaderia Los Cocos**, Carr 484 in Los Cocos near Aguadilla. It is known far and wide for its wood-oven baked bread and its *queso de hoja* ("leaf cheese).

Guajatacas (☎ 787-895-5366), 750 C. Estación at Los Merenderos; and the aforementioned *paradores.*

Olas y Arena (☎ 787-830-8315, 888-391-0666), at Villas del Mar Hau, serves seafood dishes (including paella) in a Casuarina-shaded bamboo gazebo. Expect to spend around $20 pp. (☎ 787-872-9554, 888-780-9195),

The Eclipse (☎ 787-872-9554, 888-780-9195), at Villa Montaña Resort, offers Asian-Caribbean fusion dishes.

Happy Belly's, Carr. 4466 after the turnoff to Carr. 466, is a restaurant set on stilts which serves seafood, pasta, and other dishes. It also has live music as does **Sunset Café** which is nearby.

Restaurant Ocean Front (☎ 787-872-3339), Carr. 4446 in Barrio Bajuras at Playa Jobos, serves seafood dishes such as *asopao* as well as meat.

Panadería Los Cocos has bread baked in traditional ovens (see tip above).

SERVICES: Agencia de Viajes Megar (☎ 787-890-2129) is a full-service travel agency. Another option is **Centro Viajes** (☎ 787-891-0260), Km 120, Carr. 2.

INFORMATION: The **Puerto Rico Tourism Company** has an office (☎ 787-890-3315) in the Rafael Hernández Airport. Aguadilla

http://www.gotopuertorico.com

The Aguadilla Mayor's Office (☎ 787-891-1005) is in town and open Mon. to.Fri

from 8 AM–noon and from 1–4 PM.
http://www.municipiodeaguadilla.itgo.com

CAR RENTAL: Savings Auto Rentals (☎ 787-890-3203) is 1.5 miles out of town outside Ramey's Gate 5.

Sánchez Aguadilla (☎ 787-891-7777) also rents cars.

L&M Car Rental (☎ 787-890-3010) is at the airport.

Payless Car Rental (☎ 787-787-882-0110) is at Parador El Faro.
http://www. www.paylesscarrental.com

Popular Auto (☎ 787-890-4848), is at C. Belt 245, Ramey.
http://www.popularautopr.com

Aguadilla Outdoor Adventures

TOURS AND DIVING: Tropical Beaches Tours (☎ 787-895-7736) offer complete packages.
http://www. home.coqui.net/tours

Aquatica Underwater Adventures (☎/℮ 787-890-6071) is at Carr. 110, Km 10, Gate 5, Ramey. It offers rentals, repairs, PADI and SSI certification, fishing, and wreck diving — including an excursion to the remains of a B-29 that crashed in 1953. (One way to benefit from your tax dollars squandered on the military). This is an advanced decompression dive.
http://www.aquatica.cjb.net
aquatica@caribe.net

Another operation is **La Cueva Submarina** (☎ 787-872-1094, ℮ 787-872-1447; Box 151, Isabela, PR 00662), which operates a full-service dive shop at at Playa Jobos, Km 6.3 on Carr. 466.They offer tours and dives to all of the area's sites, as well as rent equipment.

MOUNTAIN BIKING: Isabela Mountain Bike Tours (☎ 727-409-0842) organize rides for up to ten. Equipment and transport are included. Give them plenty of notice if possible.

HORSEBACK RIDING: Tropical Trail Rides (☎ 787-720-5454, at Carr. 4466, Km 1.8, enroute to Jobos on Carr. 110), takes you on a two-hr. trail ride along the beach. It costs $35 pp; two-person minimum.

Moca

Known as the "Literary City" because some noted Puerto Rican authors have been born here, Moca's name is believed to come from the Taíno word for the tree of the same name. It was founded in 1772.

EVENTS: The town's *mundillo* **festival** takes place each Nov. on Thanksgiving weekend. Its *fiestas patronales* run in early Sept. If you're in the area, be sure to check out the procession for the **Three Kings Festival**, which takes place each Jan. 6.

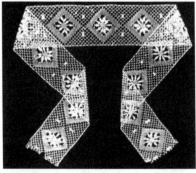

Mundillo was first woven by Catholic nuns who used proceeds to finance schools and orphanages.

SIGHTS: **Hacienda Enriqueta** is a small museum of colonial artifacts set at the town's entrance.

Los Castillos Meléndez, on Carr. 110 in Barrio Centro, resembles a medieval castle.

A French provincial-style mansion, **Palacete Los Moreau** or **La Casa Labadie** (☎ 787-830-2540; appointments required) contains the works of writer Enrique A. Laguerre, a local writer who was nominated for the Nobel Prize for Literature in 1999. His most famous novel was *La Llamorada,* which depicts the *jíbaro* lifestyle on sugarcane plantations near Moca. It was written here; the author had been befriended by the owner. Largely destroyed by fire in 1993, the current building is a restoration. To get here you must enter from a yellow gate (unmarked) off of eastbound Carr. 2 between Carr. 1110 and Carr. 464. It's only open on weekdays.

SHOPPING: **Moca** is famous for its *mundillo* lace. Shop at **María Lasalles' store** near the town plaza. **Artesania Leonides** is nearby at C. Ramos Antonini 114.

INFORMATION: Contact the **tourist office** (☎ 787-877-6015, 877-2270).

San Rafael de Quebradillas

This N coastal plain town (pop. 24,500) was originally founded by Spanish farmers and cattlemen. Popularly abbreviated to Quebradillas, its name derives from the *quebradas* (streams) that emerge when rain falls in this area.

EVENTS: The **Iglesia San Rafael Arcángel** attracts numerous visitors for its *fiestas patronales* on Oct. 24. A *carnaval* is held in Jan.

SIGHTS: Many *santos* makers live in the area.

The nearby **Playa Guajataca** (Balneario de Guajataca, Carr. 2, Km 104) is the area's scenic highlight. **Cueva Guajataca** is also in the vicinity and there's a statue of Mabodamaca, the Taíno chief who once controlled the area, at its entrance.

Another place to visit is the **El Arca de Noé** (Noah's Ark, ☎ 787-895-0377), an aviary, aquarium, and zoo. It's at Carr. 482, Km 1. and is open Wed. to Fri., 9 AM–4 PM, Sat 9 AM–5 PM, and on Sun., 9 AM–5:30 PM. Admission is $3 adults, $2 children.

Surprisingly, Puerto Rico's only **Barbie Museum** (☎ 787-895-1646) is here, at the intersection of Carr. 482 and Carr. 2. Watch for the signs. It's only open weekends. Admission is $3 adults, $2 children.

The **Parque de Dinosaurios** (Dinosaur Park, ☎ 787-895-3098), Carr. 113 at Carr. 480, is open Sun. through Tues. from 9:30 AM–5:30 PM. Admission is $1 pp. It offers concrete dinosaurs, slides, and the like.

Wenchis Mini-Golf (☎ 787-895-1782), Carr. 482 at Km 1.0, charges $2 pp. They also have an exhibit of Hot Wheels mini cars. It's open daily from 9 AM– 9 PM.

ACCOMMODATIONS: For local information, call 787-895-2840/3088.

On Carr. 2 at Km 103.8 near Quebradillas in Barrio Terranova, **Hotel Parador El Guajataca** ☎ 787-895-3070/3074/3091, 800-964-306, ☏ 787-895-2204; Box 1558, Quebradillas, PR 00678) offers 38 a/c small, simple rooms with cable TV, phones, and balconies facing the ocean. Facilities include a gourmet restaurant (**Casabi**), pool, conference room, live music on weekends, and two tennis courts.It's popular with Puerto Ricans. Rates run from around $75 d.
http://www.elguajataca.com
reservaciones@elguajataca.com

On Carr. 113 at Km 7.9, **Parador Vistamar** (☎ 787-895-2065, ☏ 787-895-2294, 888-391-0606; Quebradillas, PR 00678) has facilities including 55 a/c motel-style rooms with private bath, restaurant, swimming pool, game room, and tennis, volleyball, and basketball courts. It has a hilltop setting with great views, and a conference room which holds up to 250. Rates start at around $75 d. http://www.paradorvistamar.com

Camuy

This small town hosts its **fiestas patronales** on the last Fri. in May. It also hosts the **Carnaval del Río Camuy** in early Feb., the **Festival Playero Peñón Brusi** during the last weekend in June, the **Paso Fino-Peñón Brusi** in Aug., and the **Festival de la Cultura-Fería de Artesania** in September.

SIGHTS: In town, you can find the **Museo Histórico Cultural Camuyano** at C. Estrella Sur 6. Aside from the Camuy Caves (described below), the municipality contains the **Iglesia de Piedra**, a Methodist Church fashioned from stone and built in 1912, which is on Carr. 486 at Km 4.6 in Barrio Abra Honda de Camuy.

Another sight is the **Calavario la Milagrosa**, a replica of Mt. Calvary created by a local artist. It's on Carr. 483 at Km 4.1 in Barrio Piedra Gorda.

ACCOMMODATIONS: Posada El Palomar (☎ 787-898-1060, ☏ 787-820-1444), Carr. 119 at Km 7.5, offers 20 clean and quiet rooms which are disabled-accessible. It offers pool, Jacuzzi, library, music therapy. Its **Mesón Don Juan** restaurant is set in an old country home. A tennis court and golf range are planned. Rates run around $80–$125 d. http://www.xsn.net/palomarinn/1.html

Centro Vacacional Villa Brusi is on Carr. 485 at Km 1.8 in Barrio Puente and **Centro Vacacional Brusilandia** is also in Barrio Puente.

TOURS: IS Tours, Inc (☎ 866-207-0450), E Street in Bo. Campo Alegre in Camuy, offers cultural, historical, educational and adventure tours around the island and will plan customized group tours for four or more. http://www.istours-camuypr.com

River Camuy Cave Park
(Parque de las Cavernas del Río Camuy)

Located on Carr. 129 at Km 19.8, Río Camuy Cave Park taps the island's extensive network of underground caves — the result of carbonic acid dissolving limestone over the course of thousands of years. Spelunkers Russell and Jane Gurnee explored and mapped the subterranean caverns in the 1950s and were the driving force behind the park's creation. A totally blind and previously unknown species of fish, which was discovered in a subterranean pool, was named *Alaweckelia gurneei* in their honor.

TOURS FROM SAN JUAN: A number of operators offer tours here including **Caverns Express** (☎ 787-791-0666), which has pickups in Isla Verde and Condado.

TAKING A TOUR: Arriving, you purchase a parking ticket ($1) and make your way to the entrance where you buy a ticket for the next tour. Admission to the **Cueva Clara tour** (45 min.) is $10 for adults and $7 for children 2 to 12. Senior citizens are charged half the adult price. The last tour is at 3:45. An optional trip to the **Tres Pueblos Sinkhole** is included.

The **Cueva Catedral** ($30) has a collection of 42 petroglyphs. It is necessary to rappel down a rock wall to get to it, and it is only open to groups of eight or more. Reservations must be made a week in advance.

The **Mina del Río Camuy** allows you to mine for semiprecious gems.

A gift shop is set near the ticket window. While waiting you can walk around the grounds. Kodak, in a gesture of disinterested corporate beneficence, has donated signs indicating when you should take a picture. You may exercise your free will if you disagree with their choices. There are covered picnic tables and a children's playground.

After viewing a film in the theater building, you take a tram bus down into the entrance to Cueva Clara. You descend along a concrete roadway through 200 ft. of densely foliated tropical ravine and secondary forest, then proceed on foot down to the subterranean Río Camuy — one of the largest underground rivers in the world.

The tour guide is well informed and helpful. The upper cave, **Cueva Clara de Empalme**, is a dry chamber carved out by the river sometime during the past million years. The cave is oriented from S to N. The stalactites and stalagmites are beautiful. It takes from 200 to 1,000 years for them to grow an inch. Dripping water is everywhere and one has the feeling of being in another world, as if a Venusian mold might appear and gobble you up at any moment. The giant boulders on the cave's floor fell from the ceiling. You will pass by the pool filled with microscopic shrimp on your way to the opening, which leads to the **Sumidero Empalme** — a 400-ft.-deep, lushly vegetated pit open to the sky. The caves continue on from here for some 15 km but are inaccessible.

Returning up a side cavern, you can see the river flowing down some 150 ft., continuing inexorably to cut its channel. Bats are said to live down there. Similarly, the tour (optional, but included in your cost) of the **Tres**

Pueblos Sinkhole (so named because it is between Camuy, Hatillo, and Lares municipalities) offers views from a walkway and two observation platforms. One traverses the Lares side and faces the town of Camuy while the other overlooks the sinkhole and the Río Camuy. The sinkhole measures 650 ft. in diameter and is 400 ft. deep.

The caves are open Wed. to Sun. 8 AM–4 PM and holidays from 8 AM–5 PM. If Mon. is a holiday, the caves will be closed that Wed. Call 787-898-3100 or 787-756-5555 for more information and to confirm opening hours and tour times.

FOOD: There are two restaurants near the caves. The huge **Restaurante Las Cavernas** (☎ 787-897-6463) is on the L heading toward Lares (on Carr. 129 at Km 19.6) and the **Restaurante Vista Caverna** is across from the caves. The former is very plush and serves Puerto Rican dishes and seafood.

RAPPELLING: Participants in the **Cathedral Cave Wild Adventure** rappel 150 ft. down into a cave which has 40 pre-Columbian petroglyphs. You exit through a number of interlinked caves to the valley floor for the hike back to the canyon rim. Reservations are required, and bad weather cancels this trip.

La Cueva de Camuy

Not to be confused with the above caverns, this small cave (☎ 787-898-2723), under private ownership, has ponies, go-carts, and a pool with a slide as well as bridges. On Carr. 486 at Km 11.1, it's open Mon. to Sat. from 9 AM–5 PM and on Sun. from 9 AM–8 PM.

Hatillo

Meaning "grazing land," Hatillo was founded in 1823 and many of its early settlers came from the Canary Islands. It is noted for its dairy farms. Call 787-898-3835/3840 for tourist information.

EVENTS: The town's **Fiesta Las Máscaras (Festival of the Masks)**, held annually on Dec. 26, commemorates the Slaughter of the Innocents detailed in the New Testament. Costumes are abundant. The *fiestas patronales* are held in mid-July, and the entire town turns out for the procession.

ACCOMMODATIONS AND FOOD: Camping grounds are at Punta Maracallo. Dine and stay at the **Parador Buen Café** (☎ 787-898-3495, ✆ 787-898-7738) at Km 84 on Carr. 2. It has a meeting room and 20 comfortable rooms with cable TV, phone, and refrigerator. It features Puerto Rican dishes including *mofongo*. Rates run around $90 d. http://www.elbuencafe.com

Plaza del Norte, the island's fifth largest shopping mall, is just a few minutes drive from town.

Arecibo & Environs

This simple but refreshing town on the Atlantic is more of a transit point or base for exploring the rest of the area than a destination in itself. The town comes alive during the annual feast of San Felipe Apóstol on or around May 1. It is a good jumping-off point for the beaches to the E or the mountains to the S.

GETTING HERE: Take a *público* from San Juan or Bayamón. Another approach would be from Ponce via Utuado, but allow plenty of time.

SIGHTS: The town's name is derived from Aracibo, an Indian chief who had a settlement here, and a cave (**La Cueva del Indio**) four miles E of town that was used for Indian ceremonies before the arrival of the Spaniards. To get here by public transport, take a *público* marked "Isolte" four km, passing along a magnificent beach. Get off at the sign and the brown cement open-air igloo constructed with reinforced Coca Cola bottles. Turn L and it's a five-minute walk. Surf pounds on either side of the entrance. Descend the precipitous and makeshift staircase to view the petroglyphs adorning the walls. This area is spectacularly beautiful and well worth a visit.

NOTE: Park at the gas station nearby for safety. Readers have reported a case of attempted entry to their vehicle while parked near the entrance. It might be best to visit one at a time.

Set just to the E of town on Punta Morrillo along Carr. 681, the **Faro El Vigia** (Arecibo Lighthouse; ☎ 787-879-1625) has a small museum with rotating exhibits. Its new recreation facility features a deck well as a children's play area which contains reproductions of old sailing ships. It also has a restaurant, museum and sports facilities. It's open Mon. to Thurs. from 9 AM–6 PM, Fri. to Sun. from 9 AM–9 PM. http://www.arecibolighthouse.com

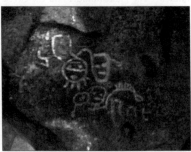

petroglyphs in La Cueva del Indio

The Church of Mita

Juanita Garcia Peraza experienced a series of mystical visions of the Holy Spirit in Arecibo in 1940. Juanita was given the name "Mita" and ordered to establish a church. Love, liberty, and unity are its precepts. Because Mita came from a wealthy family, she was able to found cooperative businesses which have supported parishioners. These have ranged from a bakery to a supermarket to a cement block factory. Remarkably, the church never asks for tithes. Membership peaked during the 1960s. Mita died in 1970, and the funeral was the largest every held in Puerto Rico . The wake lasted for three days. Today, the church is smaller, but its entrepreneurial principles still hold strong.

Puerto Rico's only theme park, **Fun Valley Park** (☎ 787-817-0415) is at Exit 75 on Carr. 22, Carr. 10 Km 83. It has rides, scenic train, bumper boats, go carts, bird museum, and cafeteria. It's open Wed. to Mon., 10 AM–10 PM.

Parque García, Ave. Victor Rojas Norte, has attractions for children. It's open daily from 6 AM-10 PM.

PESET or **Parque Educativo Para la Seguridad** (☎ 787-817-1715) provides free entrance to children ages 7 to 10. They learn how to drive correctly. It's in the Zeno Gandia Industrial Center, Carr. 129 and is open Mon. to Fri. from 8:30 AM–4 PM.

ACCOMMODATIONS AND FOOD: **Hotel Plaza** (☎ 787-878-2295), Ave. José de Diego 112, is inexpensive.

Hotel Villa Real (☎ 787-881-4134, ✆ 787-881-6490), Carr. 2, Km 67.2 in Barrio Santana, has 41 large and clean a/c rooms which attract both businessmen and families. Some have refrigerators; others have kitchens. Another building has 13 apart-ments.There are two pools and a restaurant serving Puerto Rican dishes.

Campsites are at San Isidro Village, Carr. 2 at Km 85, Hatillo or at **Punta Maracaya Camping Area** (☎ 787-878-7024/2157), Carr. 2 at Km 84.6.

At Ave. Rotarios 522, **La Parillada Restaurant Argentino** (☎ 787-878-7777) serves Argentinian meat and seafood special-ties. There are plenty of *cafeterias* around.

El Guardian del Salud (☎ 787-880-6464), set between Telefónica and the hos-pital at 563-C Ave. Rotario) is an intimate vegetarian restaurant with good prices and healthy food.

The Buen Café Hotel Parador (☎ 787-898-1000, ✆ 820-3013) is a nondescript parador near Arecibo (Carr. 2, Km 84) which have a restaurant. Rooms have cable TV and a/c; beaches are nearby.

Set at a truck stop at the junction of Carr. 2 and Hwy. 22 between Arecibo and Hatillo, **Café Restaurant La Nueva Union** (☎ 787-878-2353) serves traditional Puerto Rican food.

CAR RENTAL: Leaseway (☎ 787-878-1606), is on Carr. 2 at Ave. Miramar 1085. www.leasewaypr.com

Payless Car Rental (☎ 787-878-7600) is at Lloréns Torres 105.
http://www.paylesscarrental.com

Arecibo Outdoor Activities

DIVING: Arecibo Dive Shop (☎ 787-880-3483), Ave. Miramar 686, offers trips, instruction and certification, and rentals.
aredive@coqui.net

KAYAKING AND RAFTING: Locura Arecibeña/Río Grande de Arecibo Kayak Rentals (☎ 787-878-1809) offers trips (kayaking, birdwatching) in the Barceloneta, Arecibo, and Utuado area.

You might visit the Río Manatí near Ciales, the Río Grande S of Arecibo, or the Canal Caño Tiburones between Arecibo and Barceloneta. Rafting trips are offered on the Río Manatí during the winter. All trips are on weekends, and you must reserve three days in advance.

Arecibo Observatory

Don't miss visiting this amazing concrete, steel, and aluminum anachronism S of town. The 600-ton platform, largest of its kind in the world, is a 20-acre dish set into a gigantic natural depression.

The observatory, inaugurated in 1963, has a 1,000-ft. (305-m) spherical reflector which uses a natural depression for its bowl. Its collected radio waves are directed at a 900-ton triangular platform which hangs 450 ft. (135 m) above the dish, held aloft by cables suspended from three gigantic towers. The platform's underside has a six-story-high 90-ton dome which contains an 80-ft. Gregorian secondary reflector along with a smaller third-ranking reflector. These reflectors correct the spherical divergence of the primary reflector, establishing a wider, more focused radio image. The primary dish may send radar pulses from the Gregorian's transmitter to targets in our solar system; it then records echoes, which arrive back minutes to hours later. It is on the job 24-hrs.-per-day and is maintained by Cornell University in league with the National Science Foundation.

Using this telescope, Cornell University scientists monitor pulsars and quasars and probe the ionosphere, moon, and planets. Unlike other radio telescopes, which have a steerable dish or reflector, the dish at Arecibo is immobile, while the receiving and transmitting equipment, which hangs 50 stories in the air, can be steered and pointed by remote control equipment on the ground. Although it costs $3.5 million annually to operate this

Seti@Home

Initiated by David Anderson of the University of California at Berkeley, the Seti@Home Project aims to harness the under-employed resources of individual PCs throughout the world in the task of sifting through radio-telescope data in the hopes of discovering transmissions from space aliens.

The Arecibo Observatory provides the project with some 20 gigabytes of data per day. The plan is to parcel each day's content into chunks which represent a minute's worth of data and send each chunk to a PC which will each take around five days to process this information. Each packet will be scanned for two regularities: steady beacons of signal and patterns of pulses. The home PCs act as the first bastion of reception. Anything notable they find will be sent for further analysis. Some 80,000 PCs will be needed.

facility, it has been responsible for several major discoveries, including detection of signals from the first pulsar and proving the existence of the quasar.

The **Angel Ramos Foundation Visitor and Educational Facilit**y opened in March, 1997. Set at the base of one of the large towers which supports the platform, it commands a great view of the dish. A bilingual exhibit ("Exploring the Invisible Universe") compliment the views. A talking sun, meteorite collection, details on discoveries are presented. You learn about the daily life of the observatory in the 15-min. video presentation "A Day in the Life."

TOURS: Tours are given Wed. to Fri. from noon to 4 PM. Sat., Sun., and holidays, the observatory is open from 9 AM–4 PM. It is closed on Mon. and Tues. Admission is $3.50 adults and $1.50 children. For more in formation call 787-878-2612 or fax 787-878-1861.

?!¿ The August 2000 issue of *Science* announced the discovery of asteroid 216 Cleopatra by the Arecibo Observatory. This is the first asteroid found beyond Mars. It is shaped like a dog bone, the likely result of a collision between two asteroids.

GETTING HERE: Reach it via Carrs. 22, 651, 635, and 625 or via 22, 129, 134, 635, and 625; a special access road leads up to it. *Públicos* marked "Esperanza" also come here.
http://www.naic.edu

Forest Reserves Near Arecibo
In all of these reserves, camping is permitted with permission obtained from the **Recursos Naturales y Ambientales** (Department of Natural Resources and the Environment, ☎ 787-724-3724, 787-724-3647) in San Juan 15 days in advance.

CAMBALACHE FOREST RESERVE: Lying to the E of Arecibo near Carr. 682, **Cambalache Forest Reserve** (☎ 787-878-7279), offers camping by permit (around $10; reservations: ☎ 787-881-1004). One campsite holds eight sites, the other four. This 914-acre (370-ha) subtropical forest, has 45 different species of birds. There's also a plant nursery. It's great for hiking and picnicking.

ACTIVITIES: **Mountain biking** here requires a **permit** ($1) which you must obtain in advance from **Recursos Naturales y Ambientales** (Department of Natural Resources and the Environment, ☎ 787-724-3724, 787-724-3647) in San Juan. There are eight mi. of trails.

Tropical Paradise Horse Rides (☎ 787-720-5454) here offers beach rides. To find them, look for signs along Carr. 690.

GUAJATACA FOREST RESERVE: Guajataca Forest Reserve (☎ 787-890-4050, 787-890-2050) has limestone sink-

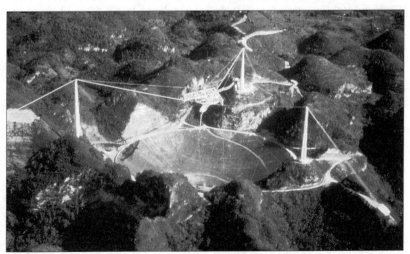

Arecibo Observatory is one of the island's most remarkable sights.

holes and haystack hills. (It has no camping.) Sandwiched between Quebradillas to the N and San Sebastián to the S, Carr. 446 slices it in half. *Cabralla*, one of the longer of the 25 miles (40 km) of hiking trails, ends at **Lago Guajataca** (which is great for fishing and boating if you bring your own boat and rod). Maps may be available at the ranger station where a trail leads to a lookout tower and other trails. Obtain permits for camping here from **Recursos Naturales y Ambientales** (Department of Natural Resources and the Environment, ☎ 787-724-3724, 787-724-3647) in San Juan.

To circumnavigate the lake, follow Carr. 119 S from Camuy or N from San Sebastián and circle the lake via Carr. 453 and Carr. 455. You can stop for a break along the way at one of the many small bars.

Kayaks may be rented from the moderately-priced **Hotel Lagovista** (☎ 787-896-5487) which also offers rooms, pool, and restaurant.

Next door to Lagovista, **Ninos Camping** (☎ 787-896-9016) offers cabins (around $200 for a weekend) and camping ($25 pn).

Campamento Guajataca here may be rented when available; for information contact the **Puerto Rico Council of Boy Scouts in San Juan** (☎ 787-790-0323). The setting is attractive.

La Vereda (☎ 787-724-3724) is the camping area within the reserve itself. Advance permits and reservations required.

RÍO ABAJO STATE FOREST: Río Abajo State Forest is S of Arecibo. This 5,080-acre forest was established in 1935. Here, the most rugged karst formations are found, and elevations reach 1,400 ft. Old lumber roads and paths lead to them. Indigenous West Indian mahogany, teak, and balsa coexist here with introduced blue Australian pines, bamboo, and the SE Asian teak that dominates the landscape. Birding

is good with turtle doves, nightingales, and thrushes present as well as the endangered broad-winged hawk. The Puerto Rican parrot is also bred here, and you may be able to set up a visit to the recovery project by calling 787-376-6625.

In any event, there is no problem with visiting the **aviary**. The **visitor's center** (☎ 787-878-7279) and picnic ground is open from 8 AM–6 PM. Tours are offered to groups of four or more. To camp here ($4), contact **Recursos Naturales y Ambientales** (Department of Natural Resources and the Environment, ☎ 787-724-3724, 787-724-3647).

Dos Bocas Lake

This is located at Km 68 on Carr. 10 at the junction of the roads to Jayuya and Utuado from Arecibo. Its name means "Two Mouths." This long, beautiful, and winding reservoir was created in 1942. Launches run scheduled two-hour trips around the lake at 6:30 and 8:30 AM and hourly from 10 AM–4 PM. Although these free trips are provided as a service for local residents, visitors are welcome to join. A one-hour trip to Barrio Don Alonso leaves daily at 12:40 PM.

PRACTICALITIES: There are a number of restaurants which serve Puerto Rican food, and have cabinas as well. These include **Meson Don Alonso** (☎ 787-894-0516), **El Fogón de Abuela** (☎ 787-894-0470), a local, atmospheric Puerto Rican restaurant only open on weekends, **Rancho Marina** (☎ 787-894-8034), and **Villa Atabeira** (☎ 787-767-4023). These restaurants have a dinner launch service which operates off of Carr. 123, near the entrance to Bosque Rió Abajo. The **Dos Bocas Quick Lounge** is set next to the main dock and serves snacks in the evenings.

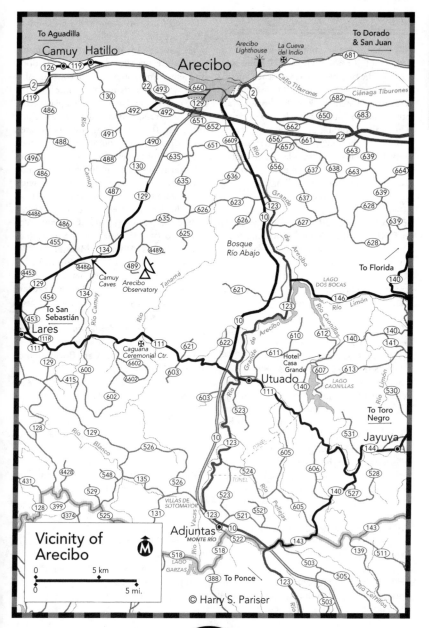

Vicinity of Arecibo

0   5 km
0   5 mi.

© Harry S. Pariser

Utuado

This small, sunny mountain town is a stronghold of traditional *jíbaro* culture and is one of the best places to experience Puerto Rican mountain life. You could see anything here: from a man braking his horse at an intersection to young *evangelistas* "singing in the rain," holding umbrellas over megaphones and shouting the praises of the Lord Jesus. Local buses run from Jayuya, Arecibo, and up from Ponce via Adjuntas. *Públicos* also ply these routes as well as connecting with other towns in the area.

FESTIVALS AND CRAFTS: The town holds its *fiestas patronales* on or around Sept. 29 every year, in honor of its patron saint, San Miguel Arcangel.

On the main road at night you can find tents with Haitian women selling handicrafts from all over the world.

ACCOMMODATIONS: Hands down, the best place to stay in the area is 20-room **Hotel La Casa Grande** (☎/✆ 787-894-3939, 888-343-2272, ✆ 787-894-3900), which is on Carr. 612 N of Lago Caonillas at the site of a former coffee plantation. This is a rustic yet comfortable getaway which is now owned by a former attorney who has left the fast lane for life as hotelier and yoga instructor. It has **Jungle Janes**, a terrace-side restaurant which serves hearty breakfasts and other meals, and a pool. The cozy cabins have two beds, fan, bath, and hammocks on the wooden decks. This is a good place to base yourself if you'd like to explore the area or just relax. Rates run around $80-90 d.
http://www.casagrande.com

Hotel Vivi having folded, the only low-budget accommodation is offered by **Motel El Lago**. Right at the intersection of Carr. 111 and Carr. 140, you drive up the hill to the L. At the top, you'll find the entrance. After paying $15, you drive your car into a shed, close the sliding panel garage door, and enter the room, which consists of a bath with pink flamingos painted on the shower doors and a bed (with a plastic covered mattress) surrounded on all sides, including the ceiling, by mirrors. There's also a poorly functioning air conditioner. The a/c works better in the $20 rooms. Obviously, it's better to be here if you have someone suitably nasty to share it with. Throughout the night, alarms are set off periodically whenever a car enters or leaves.

Other alternatives are **Cabañas Vall Rolando** (☎ 895-5648), Ave. San Miguel, and **Cabañas Albarran Manuel** (☎ 894-4834), Carr. 10, Km 59.4 in Río Abajo.
FOOD: There are many places to eat in town, including the **Taco Rico Restaurant** along Ave. Fernando L. Rivas, which serves Mexican food.

A bit plusher is the **Aquarium**, Ave. Esteres 29, which has entrées for around $11.

Another alternative is **Café Borínquen** on Carr. 111 at Km 2.2.

On Carr. 611 at Km 2.3, **Faro** (☎ 894-3206) serves Puerto Rican food such as *camarones al ajillo*.

Casa Grande specializes in Puerto Rican dishes such as *piniono* and *filete de pescado en mojo*.

FROM UTUADO: Yellow buses and *públicos* ply over steep hills to Jayuya and, via Lake Dos Bocas, to Arecibo. The road to Jayuya is beautiful, with bamboo groves and rolling hills.

FOR PONCE: A magnificent, steep and cool, lushly vegetated road leads through the mountain town of Adjuntas down to Ponce and the sea below.

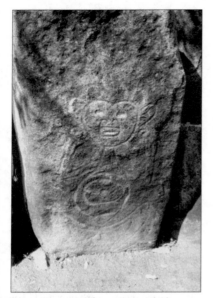

*Puerto Rico's most famous petroglyph:
La Mujer de Caguana*

Vicinity of Utuado

Near Utuado, the **Caguana Indian Ceremonial Park and Museum** or **Parque Indigena** (☎ 787-894-7325) is the most important archaeological site in the Caribbean (open daily 9 AM–5 PM; museum open Sat. and Sun., 10 AM–4 PM). To reach it, take a bus or *público* ($1) or drive 12 km W along Carr. 111 towards Lares. Originally excavated by the famous archaeologist J.A. Mason in 1915, the park has been restored and established under the auspices of the Institute of Puerto Rican Culture. Don't expect much; although a loyal band keep up the grounds, the funds needed for guides and markers have not been supplied.

The 10 *bateyes* (ball courts) are situated on a small spur of land surrounded by fairly deep ravines on three sides. Enter to find beautifully flowing arbors, roosters crowing, and mother hens tending their chicks. The largest rectangular *bateye* measures 60 by 120 ft. (20 by 37 m). Huge granite slabs along the W wall weigh up to a ton. A few are carved with faces (half-human, half-monkey) that are typical of Taíno-Chico culture. One has deep, cup-like, haunting eyes. *La Mujer de Caguana,* most famous of all the petroglyphs, is a woman with frog legs and elaborate headdress.

Originally, all of the slabs were decorated with reliefs, but most of these have been lost due to erosion. The *bateyes* are bordered by cobbled walkways. This site dates from AD 1200. Although the ball game played in these arenas was indigenous to the entire Caribbean, the game reached its highest degree of sophistication in Puerto Rico. Two teams of players, thick wooden

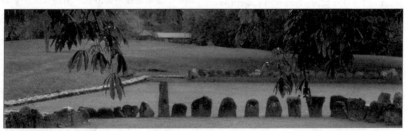

The ballfield at Caguana

313

belts lashed to their waists, would hit a heavy, resilient ball — keeping it in the air without the use of hands or feet. These balls still survive in the form of stone replicas. Other examples of petroglyphs are found in Barrio Paso Palma and Salto Arriba, Utuado.

There are a variety of **souvenir shops** near the ballpark and **La Familia**, a friendly and cheap pizzeria, is near the park at Carr. 111, Km 12. It's open daily.

HORSEBACK RIDING: 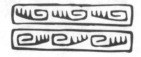 **Rancho de Caballos de Utuado** (☎ 787-894-9256), Carr. 612, Km 0.4 (across from Casa Grande), offers three-hour tours on Paso Fino horses.

ART AND CRAFTS: **Miguel Guzman** (☎ 787-894-8765) and wife **Olga Reyes** are among the area's finest artists. Olga is a fine painter, and Miguel is a talented muralist and painter. They also do craft work. Stop in and visit this friendly couple at Bo. Paso Palmas, Carr. 140, just outside Utuado.

Lago Caonillas

Lago Caonillas, an artificial lake near Utuado created by damming during the 1950s, came into the limelight some years back when droughts caused it to recede, exposing the bell tower of a reinforced concrete chapel. Dating from the mid-1930s, the chapel had been built by an American Capuchin priest. Superstitious Puerto Ricans flocked by the thousands on weekends to the site, much to the bemusement of enterprising locals who charged entry to their property or took them out in boats. Visitors saw the re-emergence as some type of miracle or message from God.

Expediciones Tamaná

One of the best tour guides in Puerto Rico, Roberto Bonilla runs **Expediciones Tamaná** (☎ 787-894-7685; Apdo. 167, Angeles, Puerto Rico 00611), one of the best grassroots tour operations on the island. Roberto has a great deal of enthusiasm for his work, and it shows. He or one of his guides will do a great job of showing you around. Even though he is not fluent in English, he can still communicate if your Spanish is nonexistent. His trips are for relatively fit people who wish to experience the natural wonders of Puerto Rico. He is adept at pointing out plant life and at introducing you to things you might otherwise miss. He charges around $60 pp. Allow a full day for the experience.

GETTING THERE: This is something of an adventure in itself. Head W on Carr. 111. After passing the ball park on your L, you will see the signs leading up a narrow road (Carr. 602) to his "office," an open-air part of a house which has a small display of artifacts he has collected. Be sure to wear good shoes, have water (although Roberto will bring juice), and a metal walking stick would be an asset as well.

TRIPS: Roberto offers one trip in two parts. The first is down a canyon via an overgrown trail which ends at Cueva del Arco, a large cave with lovely petroglyphs and great stalactites and stalagmites. From the cave, Roberto will take you down to the river where you will descend and wade through to a magnificent gigantic rock arch which has a river running through it along with a shelf with 150-million-year-old fossils embedded in it.

The second is through pasture and karstland. Roberto will show you the observatory off in the distance at one stop. Your destination is Cueva Urubú, a cave with 41 petroglyphs.

http://home.coqui.net/albite/albite/index.html

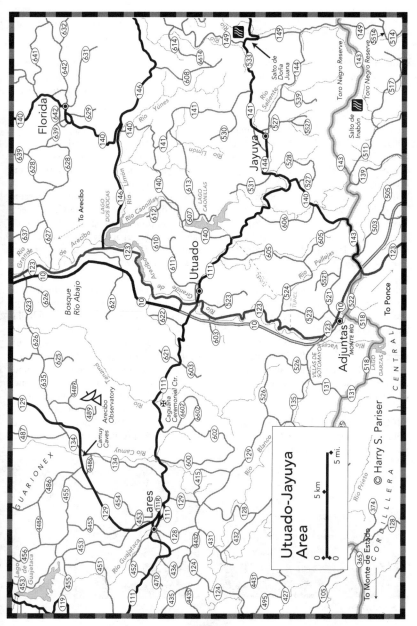

Utuado-Jayuya Area

© Harry S. Pariser

Jayuya

Jayuya is another small mountain town with strong Indian cultural influences. Its moment in history came with the one-day "Revolution of 1950," in which *independentistas* proclaimed the Republic of Puerto Rico, burned police headquarters and held the town for several hours before being dislodged by air assaults from the National Guard. The revolt, which was to have been coordinated with the assassination of President Truman, was quashed elsewhere before it could make much of an impact. The only industries here are the BASF and Baxter plants.

FESTIVALS: Jayuya's *fiestas patronales* (*Nuestra Señora de la Monserrate*) take place on and around September 3.

Held mid-Nov. in the public plaza since 1969, the **Festival Indigena Jayuya** (Jayuya Indigenous Festival) features parades, craft markets, presentation of Taíno sports and dance, plus a band that performs using indigenous musical instruments.

On Dec. 18, the **Fiestas Canalianas** commemorates the life of renowned local man of letters Nemesio Rosario Canales.

INFORMATION AND SIGHTS: Be sure to obtain the map from the Casa Cultural, which is open Mon. to Fri. from 8 AM–4:30 PM. From the Catholic church you head up the steps past the **Tumba del Indio de Boriquén**, a locked structure containing Taíno artifacts and replicas of petroglyphs from Caguana. The Taíno buried under glass here has had samples of earth from the island's 78 towns placed by his side. The statue is a representation of the Cacique Hayuya, the local chieftain. The Casa itself has an excellent collection of *santos* in the rear as well as a good gift shop with T-shirts, rocks painted with Taíno motifs, jewelery, and other memorabilia. You can sometimes see young girls taking dance lessons here.

To visit the **Museo Cemí**, a museum shaped like a large fish and modeled after a *cemi*, you proceed along Carr. 144. It contains a number of artifacts on loan from the Institute of Puerto Rican Culture. None of them originally came from the area. However, there are photos from area archaeological digs. It's open daily from 8-4:30, and you must ask in the main building for someone to let you in. The main building has an exhibit of local crafts including *santos*. There are *cuatros* for sale, a gift shop, and a restaurant. The **Casa Canales** here is a recreation of the house of a famous local writer. It was also the home of Blanca Doña Canales (1906-1996), a Puerto Rican nationalist who helped inspire and lead the "Revolution of 1950." She was arrested, sentenced to life imprisonment, and was

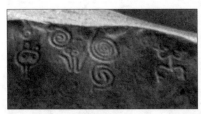

Petroglyphs on Piedra Escrita

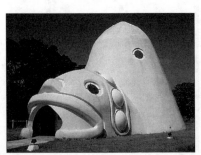

The unique Museo Cemi outside Jayuya

There are a number of fine crafts-people in the Jayuya area. Watch for signs that say "artesanas" or ask at the tourist board. **Elpidio Collazo** (☎ 787-828-1331) is a famous sculptor of wooden birds. You may view these remarkable creations at his home which is in Veguita Sama, across from the Centro Communal outside of Jayuya on the way to Hacienda Gripñas.

released after serving 16 years in prison. It is open for tours on Sat. and Sun.

From the *parador* climb to the top of **Cerro Punta** inside Toro Negro State Forest. Dwarf forest is found at the top. A shorter path is found along an unmarked paved road off of Carr. 143.

Small carvings of faces, frogs, and spirals are inscribed on the surface of a large boulder in the Saliente riverbed inside Barrio Coabey. It can be a bit hard to find (Carr. 144, between Carr. 539 and 527) but worth it. Head out of town and you'll find it along the side of the river; it's reached by a staircase. A peaceful and unforgettable spot.

Sol de Jayuya ("Sun of Jayuya"), found in Zama Province, is one of the most spectacular indigenous murals in Puerto Rico; it's essentially a sun equipped with eyes and mouth, which reflects surprise or fear. However, it's on private property and accordingly difficult to visit.

Los Tres Picachos (3,952 ft., 1201 m), near Jayuya, is the second highest mountain in Puerto Rico. You may see it from the museo. It is to the rear.

ACCOMMODATIONS: Hacienda Gripiñas (☎ 787-828-1717/1718, ✆ 828-1719), Carr. 527, Km 2.5, is a very attractive *parador* set on the site of a 19th-century coffee plantation. It is the birthplace of Ana Dolores

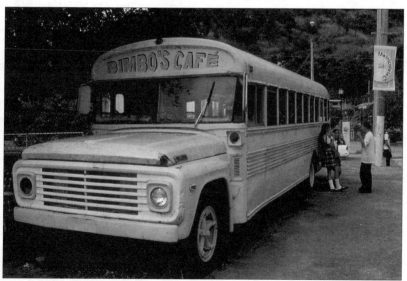

Bimbo's Café is parked at Jayuya

Pérez Marchand (1888-1983) who was Ponce's first female physician. Facilities here include 19 rooms with private bath (most with ceiling fans) in a 200-year-old restored coffee great house, pool, and restaurant. Guests offer mixed reports. For current prices and to book reservations, contact Paradores Puertorriqueños, Box 4435, Old San Juan, PR 00905; ☎ 800-443-0266 in the US; 800-981-7575 in Puerto Rico (or 721-2884 in San Juan).

Right in town at C. Guillermo Esteves 49, the **Parador Posada Jayuya** (☎ 787-828-7250, 787-828-1466), ☻ 787-828-1466) has 27 basic rooms with a/c, cable TV, and refrigerator. it has a pool and terrace, and its van is available for charters. Rooms run around $70 s or d. Extra beds are $10.

HOMESTAYS: *Hospederias* that provide simple lodging but a definite Puerto Rican experience include the **Hospedaje Viana** (☎ 787-828-0486) in Barrio Zamas off Carr. 528 near Carr. 144; **Casa Alfonso** (☎ 787-828-3742) in Barrio Coabey off Carr. 144 near Carr. 539; **El Cemí** (☎ 787-828-2164) also in Barrio Coabey off Carr. 144 near Carr. 539; and **Hospedaje Ché** which is in Barrio Coabey as well.

FOOD AND DINING: On the L hand side of the road coming into Jayuya, **Strubbe Delicatessen** has very friendly service. Other restaurants in and near town include **El Punto**, **Coré**, **Rivera's Café**, the **Naboria**, and **Rincón Familiar**.

Offering gourmet Puerto Rican dishes in a unique tent-like decor, **El Dujo** (☎ 787-828-1143) is just about a mile past the gas station on the R side of Carr. 140 (at Km 82) heading to Carr. 10.

Lares

This *independentista* town is in the heart of coffee country, where the famous Grito de Lares rebellion (see "History" in the Introduction) was raised in 1848. A white obelisk in the plaza lists the names of the revolt's heroes. Annual *independentista* rallies are still held here on September 24 in commemoration of the event. Locked amidst limestone hills, the town is cool and relaxed. There's a waterfall on Carr. 446 near San Sebastián.

EVENTS: Lares' *fiestas patronales* happens around March 19. In neighboring **San Sebastián**, the **hamaca (hammock) festival** is held each July. San Sebastián holds its *fiestas patronales* of San Sebastián on Jan. 20.

ACCOMMODATIONS: The nearest accommodation is in San Sebastián, where you can stay at the **Hotel El Castillo** (☎ 896-2365), Km 28.3 on Carr. 111, which is a kind of love hotel with mirrors, bidet, private drive-in entrances, and the works. It also has a pool.

FOOD: Don't miss the famous **Heladería de Lares** which serves ice cream in flavors such as bean, rice, and plantain. It's on the plaza.

SERVICES: **AdvenTours** (☎ 787-530-8311), San Sebastián, offers birdwatching, hiking, kayaking, biking, backpacking, private tours, coffee plantations, and other adventures.
http://www.angelfire.com/fl2/adventours

Tropical Beaches Tours (☎787-895-7736) is also in San Sebastián.
http://www.home.coqui.net/tours

Adjuntas

This small mountain town (pop. 20,000) lies on Carr. 10 between Arecibo and Ponce. *Fiestas Patronales* for San Joaquin and Santa Ana are held around August 21. Its name is short for *"las tierras adjuntas"* (attached lands). The town's main roads are frequently congested; you may find yourself passing through while attempting to follow the elusive Panoramic Hwy.

SIGHTS: The **Adjuntas Trolley** (☎ 787-829-3310) operates from Mon. to Fri. from 8 AM–4:30 PM and on weekends by request.

Casa Pueblo (☎ 787-829-4842), C. Rodolfo Gónzales 30, a cultural center in a historic home. It has exhibitions, library, crafts show, and **Mariposario** butterfly garden. It's open daily from 8 AM–4 PM.

The **Plaza de Recreo**, Arístides Mall in Boseana Square, has petroglyphs.

Cascada Las Garzas, at Bo. Garzas Centro Caneirro Muni, is a small waterfall in a clearing close to the town.

ACCOMMODATIONS AND FOOD: On H Street in Adjuntas just one block S from the town square, **Monte Río** (☎ 787829-3705, ☏ 829-3705) rents 23 rooms for around $45d and up. Rooms have a/c, TV, and views. There's also a bar/restaurant.

Citron

The area around Adjuntas has become the world's leading exporter of citron, a fruit which originated in Asia. Known since the Roman era, it may have been the first citrus fruit brought back from Asia. It is distinguished by its thick rind and small pulp, and its main use is as a candied ingredient in fruitcakes. After harvest, the fruits are fermented in brine-filled concrete troughs and covered by a wooden plank for up to 50 days. This process removes bitter oil, prevents spoilage, and softens the fruit, which enables it to absorb more sugar — one of the features that makes it attractive when candied.

After removal by workers, the fruits are split in half (by a circular saw) and the central cavity of rind and seeds is removed (by passing it through a pulper). After having been cut into pieces and packed in barrels, it is exported, and the importing firm cooks the fruit in salt water until tender, then sweetens it and drains off the excess syrup. Ironically, it is difficult to find the candied fruit pieces in Puerto Rico. The main importers are Holland and the US. Corsicans, who arrived around the turn of the century, began cultivating the fruit.

On Carr. 10 to the W of town and less than a half-hr. from Ponce, the 24-room **Villas de Sotomayor** (☎ 787-829-1774/1717, ☏ 787-829-5105; Box 661, Adjuntas, PR 00601) has 34 villas with color TV. On the premises are tennis courts, basketball and volleyball courts, putting green, swimming pools, and horseback riding as well as bicycles. Prices run from $50-$200. **Restaurant Las Garzas** (☎ 787-829-1717) serves international and Puerto Rican food including rabbit.
http://www.villassotomayor.com
roydelys@coqui.net

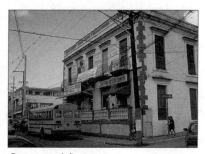

Downtown Adjuntas

An inexpensive Puerto Rican restaurant, **Monte Río** (☎ 787-829-3705) is in the center of town.

Set at the town's S end along Carr. 123, **Playita Café** is a bar where locals come to park their horse and socialize.

INFORMATION: The **Adjuntas Mayor's Office** (☎ 787-829-3310), Ríos Rivera y San Joaquín, is open Mon. to Fri. from 8-noon and, from 1–4 PM.

The **Adjuntas Tourism Office** (☎ 787-829-3310), Plaza Aristides, is open Mon. to Fri. from 8 AM–4:30 PM and on Sat. from 10 AM–2 PM. The **Casa Pueblo Forest** (☎ 787-787-829-4842), C. 30 Rodolfo González 30, may also be visited. Go to the town square and find the Casa Pueblo (an old mansion) where permits are issued. Tours are available daily from 9 AM–3:30 PM.

Bosaue Estatal de Guilarte (Guilarte Forest Reserve)

Divided among six areas of land and located along Carrs. 518 and 525 to the SW of Adjuntas, **Guilarte Forest Reserve** (☎ 787-852-4440) has Monte Guilarte, which is one of the few peaks on the island remaining unmarred by radio or TV towers. The steep, unmarked path (1.5 hrs RT) through rainforest extends to the top from the ranger station found at the intersection of Carr. 131 and Carr. 518. It also has a suspension bridge. To the NE and off of Carr. 525, **Charco Azul** is the local swimming hole.

Apply at **Recursos Naturales y Ambientales** (Department of Natural Resources and the Environment, ☎ 787-724-3724, 787-724-3647) for permission to stay in the cabins ($20 pn) here.

Bosque Estatal de Toro Negro (Toro Negro Forest Reserve)

Located to the E of Adjuntas en route to Barranquitas, the **Bosque Estatal de Toro Negro**, a 7,000-acre (2,833-ha) reserve (open 8 AM–5 PM), is also known as **Doña Juana Recreation Center** and encompasses the Cordillera Central's highest peaks, ones which frequently remain shrouded by clouds in a perpetually cool and damp environment. Information is available from the **Visitor's Center** (☎ 787-844-4660) on Carr. 143.

HISTORY AND ECOSYSTEM: Set in the cool yet humid Cordillera Central, the forest's lower elevations formerly hosted coffee plantations. Most of the forest is secondary; only the highest peaks have never been cleared. Over three million seedlings and some 19,000 lbs. of seeds were sown in the forest between 1934 and 1945. Most of the forest is sierra palm, which dominates at higher elevations. *Tabonuco* (subtropical wet) forest is also present and comprises some 31% of the area. The cloud forest higher up differs from El Yunque's in that it faces a more benign environment. The shrubs are more erect, and there is less moss.

HIKING: Trails here are wet and slippery and only for the truly adventurous. Facilities remain underdeveloped, to say the least. It's possible to climb **Cerro Doña Juana** (3,341 feet, 1016 m) and **Cerro de Punta**, which, at 4,390 ft. (1,338 m), is the tallest peak on the island. To get to the latter, drive or walk up a steep, short unmarked paved road on the N side of Carr. 143. Another approach is from near Parador Hacienda Gripiñas on Carr. 527 in Jayuya. Expect to spend about six hours or more RT.

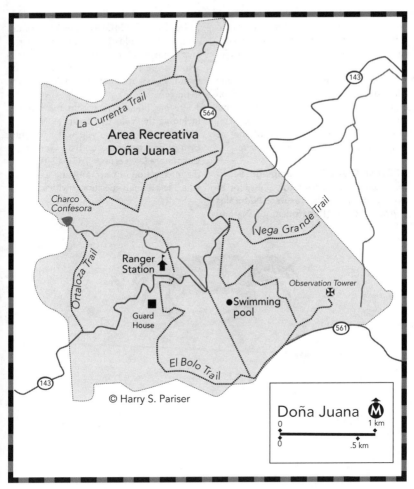

La Currenta Trail

**Area Recreativa
Doña Juana**

564

143

*Charco
Confesora*

Ortaloza Trail

Vega Grande Trail

**Ranger
Station**

■
**Guard
House**

●**Swimming
pool**

Observation Towner
✠

561

143

El Bolo Trail

© Harry S. Pariser

Doña Juana

0   1 km

0   .5 km

Cerro Maravilla here is the place where Puerto Rico's Watergate took place (see "recent political history" under "Government"). At the top, under the telecommunication towers, you'll find crosses commemorating Carlos Soto Arrivi and Arnaldo Dario Rosado, the two youths slain here in a COINTELPRO-like operation.

Although it's difficult to reach, hikers can also trek to **Inabón Falls** in the heart of the reserve. Inside the main part of the reserve (enter from Carr. 143 at Km 32.4) is an often-dry swimming pool (filled only from May 15-Sept.), barbecue pits, and an observation tower. There are plenty of birds and the bamboo creaks eerily in the breeze. From the entrance, the trail goes past the pool and on ahead over two bridges (reduced by the elements to concrete beams), then up to the road. Head L and you will see a sign marked Tower No. 3, which you can climb for a view.

Highest lake on the island, **Laguna Guineo** is set just off Divisoria, the junction of Carr. 143 and Carr. 149, which cuts through the forest E and W. A low temperature of 40°F (4.4°C) — a record for the entire island — has been recorded here.

ACCOMMODATION: Camping ($4) is permitted inside the reserve if applied for 15 days in advance at the **Recursos Naturales y Ambientales** (Department of Natural Resources and the Environment, ☎ 787-724-3724, 787-724-3647). Los Viveros, the camping area holds 14 tents, but part of the area is reserved for groups.

Rooms are rented on a daily, weekly, or monthly basis at **Quinta Doña Juana** within the reserve.

There are homestays within the vicinity, including the **Villa Eva Lourdes Mary** (☎ 787-847-0849) where you will have your own shrine to Jesus, and the **Terraza y Gasolinera Divisoria** (☎ 787-847-1073), at the intersection of Carr. 149 and Carr. 143 which has a small guesthouse with a pool.

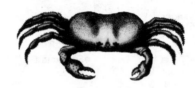

Glossary

agregado — refers to the sugarcane workers who, up until the late 1940s, labored under the feudal system wherein wages were paid partially in goods and services received.

aldea — village, hamlet

annatto — a small tree whose seeds, coated with orange-red dye, are used to color cooking oil commonly used in the preparation of Puerto Rican and other Caribbean cuisines.

Arcaicos — First known inhabitants of Puerto Rico.

areytos — epic songs danced to by the Taínos.

bacalao — dried salt cod, once served to slaves.

babalawo — Santería priest.

bahía — bay

balneario — a government-administered beach area.

bar típico — local bar

barrio — a city district.

batey— Taíno ball court

bohique — Taíno for "shaman"

bohío — Taíno Indian name for thatched houses; now applied to the houses of country dwellers in Puerto Rico.

bola, bolita —the numbers racket.

bomba — musical dialogue between dancer and drummer.

Boricua — Puerto Rican Spanish

Bosque Estatal — state forest

botanicas — stores on the Spanish-speaking islands that sell spiritualist literature and paraphernalia.

cacique — Taíno chief

calabaza (calabash) — small tree native to the Caribbean whose fruit, a gourd, has multiple uses when dried.

callejón — narrow side street; path through the cane fields.

campesino — peasant; lower-class rural dweller.

capilla — chapel

cañita — the "little cane," bootleg rum (also called pitorro).

carambola — see star apple.

caretas — masks worn at festivals.

Caribs — original people who colonized the islands of the Caribbean, giving the region its name.

casa — house or home

carretera — a road or highway (abbreviated Carr. in the text).

cassava — staple crop indigenous to the Americas. Bitter and sweet are the two varieties. Bitter must be washed, grated, and baked in order to remove the poisonous prussic acid. A spongy cake is made from the bitter variety as is *cassareep*, a preservative that is the foundation of West Indian pepperpot stew.

caserios — housing projects

caudillo — Spanish for military general.

cayos — Indian-originated name that refers to islets (cays) in the Caribbean.

cemies — Small figurines which represent Taíno deities.

centros vacacionales — Government-run rental accommodations geared towards local tourists

century plant — also known as karato, coratoe, and maypole. Flowers only once in its lifetime before it dies.

cerro — hill or mountain.

chorizo — Spanish sausage.

cocina — Criolla Traditional island cuisine.

compadrazgo — the system of "co-parentage" that is used to strengthen social bonds in Puerto Rico.

conch — large edible mollusk generally used in salads or chowders.

criollo — Island-born person of Spanish descent.

culebrenses —Culebra's residents

cuerda — unit of land measure, comprising ⁹⁄₁₀the of an acre.

curandero— traditional healer

danza — Spanish influenced Puerto Rican musical compositions.

dignidad — Dignity. The traditional Puerto Rican attitude towards others. Each individual is owed respect (*respeto*).

escabeche — Spanish and Portuguese method of preparing seafood.

espiritismo — spiritualism.

estadistas — Puerto Rican advocates of statehood.

Estado Libre Asociado — "Free Associated State." The Puerto Rican translation of the word commonwealth.

fiestas patronales — patron saint festivals that take place on Catholic islands.

fortaleza— fortress

garitas — Sentry towers seen in Old San Juan

guava — indigenous Caribbean fruit, extremely rich in vitamin C, which is eaten raw or used in making jelly.

guayacan — the tree *lignum vitae* and its wood.

guiro — rasp-like musical instrument of Taíno Indian origin, which is scratched with a stick to produce a sound.

iglesia — church

Igneris — Indian group which settled in Puerto Rico

independentistas — advocates of Puerto Rican independence.

Jíbaro — the now vanishing breed of impoverished but self-sufficient Puerto Rican peasant.

laguna— lake or lagoon

lechonería— local restaurant specializing in roasted pig

malecón —waterfront area, usually with a promenade

mascaras — masks

mercado — market

Mesones Gastronómicos — Gourmet restaurants as determined by the government.

mundillo — Spanish lacemaking found in Puerto Rico.

municipios — System of city and town governments which are ruled by mayors and assemblies.

museo— museum

naranja — sour orange; its leaves are used as medicine in rural areas.

Newyoricans — term used to describe Puerto Ricans who have left for NYC and returned.

padrinos — godparents.

Paso Fino — developed over the past five centuries, these horses have a characteristic gait. Competitions are a national sport, and there are over 7,000 registered Paso Fino horses on the island.

pegado — from the verb pegar (to stick together); used together with nouns in Puerto Rico as an adjective.

personalismo — describes the charisma of a Latin politician who appears and acts as a father figure.

playa — beach

plazuleta — small plaza

plebiscite — direct vote by the people on an issue.

plena — form of Puerto Rican dance.

ponceños —residents of Ponce

poinciana — beautiful tropical tree that blooms with clusters of red blossoms during the summer months. Originates in Madagascar.

público — shared taxi found on the Spanish-speaking islands.

puerta —door, entranceway, gate

reserva forestal —forest reserve

Ruta Panoramica —Network of scenic roads

sanjuaneros — residents of San Juan

Santeria — Afro-Caribbean folk religion

santos — carved representations of Catholic saints.

sea grape — West Indian tree, commonly found along beaches, which produces green, fleshy, edible grapes.

señorita — young, unmarried female, usually used in rural Puerto Rico to refer to virgins.

sensitive plant — also know as mimosa, shame lady, and other names. It will snap shut at the slightest touch.

sonda — sound

star apple — large tree producing segmented pods, brown in color and sour in taste, which are a popular fresh fruit.

trigueno — ("wheat colored.") Denotes a mulatto and differentiates brunettes from blondes.

urbanizaciones —planned residential neighborhoods

vejigantes —Traditional masks molded from papier-máché or coconut husks.

velorio — Catholic wake.

Viequenses — residents of Vieques

yautia — tuber also known as taro, dasheen, malanga, and elephant's ear.

zemi (cemi) — idol in which the personal spirit of each Arawak or Taíno lived. Usually carved from stone.

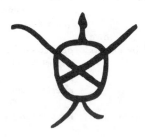

Booklist

Travel & Description

Babin, Theresa Maria. *The Puerto Rican's Spirit*. New York: Collier Books, 1971. Excellent information regarding Puerto Rican history, people, literature, and fine arts.

Caabro, J.A. Suarez. *El Mar de Puerto Rico*. Río Piedras: University of Puerto Rico Press, 1979.

Kurlansky, Mark. *A Continent of Islands*. New York: Addison-Wesley, 1992. This superb book by a veteran journalist is one of the best books about the Caribbean ever written, a must for visitors who wish to understand the area and its culture.

Lewis, Oscar. *La Vida*. New York: Irvington, 1982. The famous (1966) chronicle of Puerto Rican life.

Lopez, Adalberto and James Petras. *Puerto Rico and the Puerto Ricans*. Cambridge, MA: Schenkmann-Halstead Press, 1974.

Radcliffe, Virginia. *The Caribbean Heritage*. New York: Walker & Co., 1976.

Samoiloff, Louise C. *Portrait of Puerto Rico*. San Diego: A.S. Barnes, 1979. Descriptive and comprehensive profile.

Waggenheim, Kal. *Puerto Rico: A Profile*. New York: Praeger, 1970. A revealing if dated survey of Puerto Rico's economy, geography, and culture.

Flora & Fauna

Humann, Paul. *Reef Fish Identification*. Jacksonville: New World Publications, 1989. This superb guide is filled with beautiful color photos of 268 fish. Information is included on identifying details, habitat and behavior, and on reaction to divers.

Humann, Paul. *Reef Creature Identification*. Jacksonville: New World Publications, 1992. The second in the series, this guide covers 320 denizens of the deep. Information is included on abundance and distribution, habitat and behavior, and identifying characteristics.

Humann, Paul. *Reef Coral Identification*. Jacksonville: New World Publications, 1993. Last in this indispensable series (which is now available boxed as "The Reef Set"), this book identifies 240 varieties of coral and marine plants. The different groups are also described in detail.

Lee, Alfonso Silva *Natural Puerto Rico*. Pangaea Press, 2001. An illustrated introduction to the island's fauna.

Little, Elbert L., Jr., Frank J. Wadsworth, and José Marrero. *Arboles Comunes De Puerto Rico y las Islas Virgenes*. Río Piedras: University of Puerto Rico Press, 1967.

de Oviedo, Gonzalo Fernandez. (trans. and ed. S.A. Stroudemire.) *Natural History of the West Indies*. Chapel Hill: University of North Carolina Press, 1959.

If you have children or are a teacher, the book **The Incredible Coral Reef** is a superb educational tool. It is an "active learning book for kids." The companion volume, **The Incredible Rainforest**, is tremendous as well.
http://www.tricklecreekbooks.com

Riviera, Juan A. *The Amphibians of Puerto Rico*. Mayagüez: Universidad de Puerto Rico, 1978.

History

Bonnet, Benitez and Juan Amedee. *Vieques En La Historia de Puerto Rico*. Puerto Rico: F. Nortiz Nieves, 1976. Traces the history of Vieques over the centuries.

Cripps, L.L. *The Spanish Caribbean: From Columbus to Castro*. Cambridge, MA: Schenkman, 1979. Concise history of the Spanish Caribbean from the point of view of a radical historian.

Fernandez, Ronald. *Puerto Rico Past and Present: An Encyclopedia*. Westport, CT: Greenwood Press: 1998. Serves as a fine introduction to the island.

Fernandez, Ronald. *Prisoners of Colonialism: The Struggle for Justice in Puerto Rico*. Monroe, ME: Common Courage Press, 1994.

Golding, Morton J. *A Short History of Puerto Rico*. New York: New American Library, 1973.

Lewis, Gordon K. *Puerto Rico: Freedom and Power in the Caribbean*. New York: Monthly Review Press, 1963.

Loida, Figueroa Mercado. *History of Puerto Rico*. New York: Anaya Book Co., 1972. Comprehensive history of Puerto Rico from the Taíno to the late 19th C.

Maldonado-Denis *Puerto Rico: A Socio-Historic Interpretation*. New York: Vintage Books, 1972.

Mannix, Daniel P. and Malcolm Cooley. *Black Cargoes*. New York: Viking Press, 1982. Details the saga of the slave trade.

Mendez, Eugenio Fernandez. *Historia Cultural de Puerto Rico 1493-1968*. Río Piedras, Puerto Rico: University of Puerto Rico Press, 1980.

Silen, Juan Angel. *We, the Puerto Rican People*. New York: Monthly Review Press, 1971. Analysis of Puerto Rican history from the viewpoint of a militant Puerto Rican nationalist.

Wagenheim, Kal., ed. *Puerto Rico: A Documentary History*. New York: Praeger, 1973. History from the viewpoint of eye-witnesses.

Williams, Eric. *From Columbus to Castro: The History of the Caribbean*. New York: Random House, 1983. Definitive history of the Caribbean by the late Prime Minister of Trinidad and Tobago.

Politics & Economics

Anderson, Robert W. *Party Politics in Puerto Rico*. Stanford, CA: Stanford University Press, 1965.

Barry, Tom, Beth Wood, and Deb Freusch. *The Other Side of Paradise: Foreign Control in the Caribbean*. New York: Grove Press, 1984. A brilliantly and thoughtfully written analysis of Caribbean economics.

Bayo, Armando. *Puerto Rico*. Havana: Casa de las Americas, 1966.

Blanshard, Paul. *Democracy and Empire in the Caribbean*. New York: The Macmillan Co., 1947.

Cripps, L.L. *Human Rights in a United States Colony.* Cambridge, MA: Schenkmann Publishing Co., 1982. Once one gets past the ludicrous paeans to life in socialist countries, this contains valuable information concerning matters one never hears about stateside: Cerro Maravilla, the Vieques and Culebra takeovers, police brutality, etc.

Diffie, Bailey W. and Justine Whitfield. *Porto Rico: A Broken Pledge.* The Vanguard Press: New York, 1931. An early study of American exploitation in Puerto Rico.

Johnson, Roberta Ann. *Puerto Rico, Commonwealth or Colony?* New York: Praeger, 1980.

Langhorne, Elizabeth. *Worlds Collide On Vieques.* New York: Rivercross Publishing, 1992. An excellent book and a must read for any interested visitor to Vieques.

Lewis, Gordon K. *Notes on the Puerto Rican Revolution.* New York: Monthly Review Press, 1974. A Marxist analysis of the past, present, and future of Puerto Rico.

Matthews, Thomas G. and F.M. Andic, eds. *Politics and Economics in the Caribbean.* Río Piedras: Institute of Caribbean Studies, University of Puerto Rico, 1971.

Matthews, Thomas G. *Puerto Rican Politics and the New Deal.* Miami: University of Florida Press, 1960.

Roosevelt, Theodore. *Colonial Policies of the United States.* Garden City: Doubleday, Doran, and Co., 1937. The chapter on Puerto Rico by this ex-governor is particularly fascinating.

Tugwell, Rexford Guy. *The Stricken Land.* Garden City, New York: Doubleday & Co., 1947.

Vieques Conservation and Historical Trust. *Vieques: History of a Small Island.* Vieques, Puerto Rico: Vieques Conservation and Historical Trust, 1987.

Wells, Henry. *The Modernization of Puerto Rico: A Political Study of Changing Values and Institutions.* Cambridge, MA: Harvard University Press, 1969.

Sociology & Anthropology

Abrahams, Roger D. *After Africa.* New Haven: Yale University Press, 1983. Fascinating accounts of slaves and slave life in the West Indies.

Acosta-Belén, Edna and Elia Hidalgo Christensen, eds. *The Puerto Rican Woman.* New York: Praeger, 1979.

Berman Santana, Déborah *Kicking Off the Bootstraps.* Tuscon: U. of Arizona Press, 1996. Description of development and environment and community power in Puerto Rico.

Dávila, Arlene M. *Latinos, Inc.: The Marketing of a People.* Berkeley: University of CA Press, 2001. A great portrayal of how Latinos are marketed to by the major media.

Dávila, Arlene M. *Sponsored Identities: Cultural Politics in Puerto Rico.* Philadelphia, PA: Temple University, 1997. An excellent introduction to the marketing of Puerto Rican culture on the island.

Mintz, Sidney W. *Caribbean Transformation.* Chicago: Aldine Publishing Co., 1974. Includes an essay on Puerto Rico.

Mintz, Sidney W. *Worker in the Cane: A Puerto Rican Life History.* New Haven: Yale University Press, 1960.

Art, Architecture, & Archaeology

Buissert, David. *Historic Architecture of the Caribbean.* London: Heinemann Educational Books, 1980.

Fernandez, José A. *Architecture in Puerto Rico.* New York: Hastings House, 1965.

Rouse, Benjamin I. *Puerto Rican Prehistory.* New York: Academy of Sciences, 1952.

Willey, Gordon R. *An Introduction to American Archaeology, Vol. 2, South America.* Englewood Cliffs, New Jersey: Prentice-Hall, Inc., 1971.

Music

Boggs, Gordon. *Salsiology.* Westport, CT: Greenwood Publishing, 1992.

Gerard, Charlie. *Salsa: The Rhythm of Latin Music.* Reno, NV: White Cliffs Media Co, 1998.

Language

Rosario, Ruben del. *Vocabulario Puertorriqueño.* Sharon, MA: Troutman Press, 1965. Contains exclusively Puerto Rican vocabulary.

Literature

Babin, Maria Theresa. *Borinquen: An Anthology of Puerto Rican Literature.* New York: Vintage, 1974.

Baldwin, James. *If Beale Street Could Talk.* New York: Dial, 1974. Novel set in NYC and Puerto Rico.

Howes, Barbara, ed. *From the Green Antilles.* New York: Crowell, Collier & Macmillan, 1966. Includes four stories from Puerto Rico.

Levine, Barry. *Benjy Lopez: A Picaresque Tale of Emigration and Return.* New York: Basic Books, 1980.

Sanchez, Luiz R. *Macho Camacho's Beat.* New York: Pantheon, 1981. Novel set in Puerto Rico.

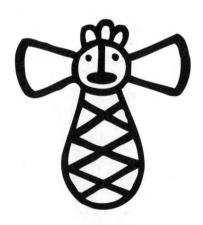

Spanish Vocabulary

Days of the Week

domingo	Sunday
lunes	Monday
martes	Tuesday
miercoles	Wednesday
jueves	Thursday
viernes	Friday
sabado	Saturday

Months of the Year

enero	January
febrero	February
marzo	March
abril	April
mayo	May
junio	June
julio	July
agosto	August
septiembre	September
octubre	October
noviembre	November
diciembre	December

Numbers

uno	one
dos	two
tres	three
cuatro	four
cinco	five
seis	six
siete	seven
ocho	eight
nueve	enine
diez	ten
once	eleven
doce	twelve
trece	thirteen
catorce	fourteen
quince	fifteen
dieciseis	sixteen
diecisiete	seventeen
dieciocho	eighteen
diecinueve	nineteen
veinte	twenty
veintiuno	twenty one
veintidos	twenty two
treinta	thirty
cuarenta	forty
cincuenta	fifty
sesenta	sixty
setenta	seventy
ochenta	eighty
noventa	ninety
cien	one hundred
cento uno	one hundred one
doscientos	two hundred
quinientos	five hundred
mil	one thousand
mil uno	one thous. one
dos mil	two thousand
un million	one million
mil milliones	one billion
primero	first
segundo	second
tercero	third
cuarto	fourth
quinto	fifth
sexto	sixth
septimo	seventh
octavo	eighth
noveno	ninth
decimo	tenth
undecimo	eleventh
duodecimo	twelfth
ultimo	last

Conversation

¿Como esta usted?	How are you?
Bien, gracias, y usted?	Well, thanks, and you?
Buenas días.	Good morning.
Buenas tardes.	Good afternoon.
Buenas noches.	Good evening/ night.

Hasta la vista.	See you again.
Hasta luego.	So long.
¡Buen suerte!	Good luck!
Adios.	Goodbye.
Mucho gusto	Glad to meet
de conocerle.	you.
Felicidades	Congratulations.
Muchas felicidades.	Happy birthday.
Feliz Navidad.	MerryChristmas.
Feliz Año Nuevo.	Happy New Year.
Gracias.	Thank you.
Por favor.	Please.
De nada/con	
mucho gusto.	You're welcome.
Perdoneme.	Pardon me.
Como se llama esto?	What do you
	call this?
Lo siento.	I'm sorry.
Permitame.	Permit me.
Quisiera...	I would like...
Adelante.	Come in.
Permitame	May I introduce...
presentarle...	
¿Como se llamo usted?	What is your
	name?
Me llamo...	My name is...
No se.	I don't know.
Tengo sed.	I am thirsty.
Tengo hambre.	I am hungry.
Soy norteamericano/a	I am an
	American.
¿Donde puedo	Where can I
encontrar...	find...?
¿Que es esto?	What is this?
¿Habla usted ingles?	Do you speak
	English?
Hablo/entiendo un poco	I speak/under-
español.	stand a little
	Spanish
¿Hay alguien aqui que	Is there anyone
hable ingles?	here who
	speaks English?
Le entiendo.	I understand you.
No entiendo.	I don't understand.

Hable mas despacio	Please speak
por favor.	more slowly.
Repita por favor.	Please repeat.

Telling Time

¿Que hora es?	What time is it?
Son las...	It's...
...cinco.	five o'clock.
...ocho y diez.	....ten past eight.
...seis y cuaro.	...quarter past six.
...cinco y média.	....half past five.
...siete y menos cinco.	....five of seven.
.antes de ayer	day before yest.
a noche.	yesterday eve.
esta mañana.	this morning.
a mediodía.	at noon.
en la noche.	in the evening.
de noche.	at night.
a medianoche.	at midnight.
mañana.	tomorrow.
en la mañana.	tomorrow AM.
en la noche.	tomorrow PM.
pasado mañana.	day after tomorrow

Directions

¿En que direccion	In which direction
queda...?	is...?
Llevemea...	Take me to...
por favor.	please.
Lleva me alla...	Take me there
por favor.	please..
¿Que lugar es este?	What place is
	this?
¿Donde queda	Where is
....el pueblo?	....the town?
¿Cual es el mejor ...	Which is the
	best
....camino?	road to...?
para...?	from?
De vuelta a la derecha.	Turn to the R.
De vuelta a la isquierda.	Turn to the L.
Sigaderecho.	Go this way.
En esta direccion.	In this direction.

¿A que distancia estamos de...?	How far is it to...?	**...bueno**	....good.
¿Es este el camino a...?	Is this the road to...?	**....barato**	....cheap.
		...cercano	....nearby.
¿Es....cerca?	Is it......near?	**...limpio**	....clean.
....lejos?	...far?	**¿Dónde hay**	Where is a
....norte?	...north?	**hotel, pensión,**	hotel, *pensión*,
....sur?	...south?	**hospedaje?**	*hospedaje*?
....este?	...east?	**Hay habitaciones**	Do you
....oeste?	...west?	**libres?**	have rooms available?
Indique me por favor.	Please point.	**¿Dónde están**	Where are the...
Hagame favor	Please direct	**...los baños?**	....bathrooms?
de decirme.	me to..	**...los servicios?**	.....toilets?
donde esta...	Where is	**Quisiera un...**	I would like a....
....el telephono?	...the telephone?	**....cuarto sencillo**	....single room.
...el excusado?	...the bathroom?	**....cuarto con baño**	....room with a bath.
...el correo?	...the post office?	**....cuarto doble**	....double room.
...el banco?	..the bank?	**¿Puedoverlo?**	May I see it?
...la comisaria?	..the police station?	**¿Cuanto cuesta?**	What's the cost?
		¡Es demasiado caro!	Too expensive!

Accommodations

Estoy buscando	I am looking for a
un hotel....	hotel that's...

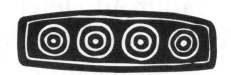

Payless Car Rental

◆ Convenient location

    ◆ Great service

        ◆ Puerto Rican hospitality

           ◆ Good prices

Payless Car Rental
112 Hostos Ave. Ponce
☎ 787-842-9393

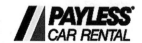

In Ponce: Pearl of the South

Index

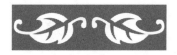

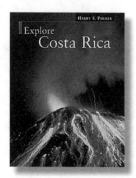
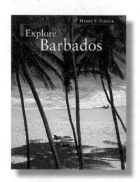

extraordinary places

Explore Puerto Rico
Harry S. Pariser

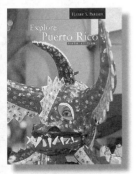

1-893643-52-2

$17.95 • 360 pages

"Hands down the best

   guidebook to the island!"

— Islands

Explore the Virgin Islands Pariser

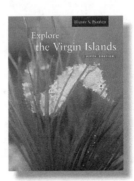

1-893643-53-0

$17.95 • 360 pages

"It's definitive —

   and very welcome in guidebook land"

      — Travel Weekly

out of **going there**

manatee
PRESS

the trade by SCB Distributors

Notes

Notes

The Lowdown

Single copies of Explore Puerto Rico signed by the author (upon request), may be ordered for the special cash or money order price of US$20 (which includes shipping and tax) from:

Manatee Press
P. O. Box 225001
San Francisco, CA 94122-5001
(415) 665-4829
fax 810-314-0685

➡ Single copies may be ordered with credit card at 800-729-6423. Price is US$17.95 plus shipping.

➡ Copies may be ordered on the Internet through Amazon. We encourage you to order through www.savethemanatee.com, so that the author and publisher may benefit from the referral fee. Or, much better, support your local bookstore!

➡ Contact the publisher for discount rates for quantity orders. Language schools, nonprofits, and Puerto Rico hotels and businesses are given special discount schedules.

➡ Chat room, mailing list, and free updates are available at www.savethemanatee.com

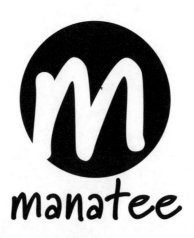

manatee